KU-628-139

# WIZARD OF THE CROW

Ngũgĩ wa Thiong'o is Distinguished Professor of English and Comparative Literature at the University of California, and is director of the university's International Center for Writing and Translation. His books include *Petals of Blood*, for which he was imprisoned by the Kenyan government in 1977. He lives in Irvine, California.

GREENWICH LIBRARIES

3 8028 01827671 4

## ALSO BY NGŪGĪ WA THIONG'O

### Fiction

*Petals of Blood*
*Weep Not Child*
*The River Between*
*A Grain of Wheat*
*Devil on the Cross*
*Matigari*

### Short Stories

*Secret Lives*

### Plays

*The Black Hermit*
*This Time Tomorrow*
*The Trial of Dedan Kimathi* (with Micere Mugo)
*I Will Marry When I Want* (with Ngũgĩ wa Mĩriĩ)

### Prison Memoir

*Detained: A Writer's Prison Diary*

### Essays

*Decolonising the Mind*
*Penpoints Gunpoints and Dreams*
*Moving the Centre*
*Writers in Politics*
*Homecoming*

NGŨGĨ WA THIONG'O

# Wizard of the Crow

A TRANSLATION FROM GĨKŨYŨ BY
the author

**VINTAGE BOOKS**
London

Published by Vintage 2007

2 4 6 8 10 9 7 5 3 1

Copyright © Ngũgĩ wa Thiong'o, 2006

Ngũgĩ wa Thiong'o has asserted his right under the Copyright,
Designs and Patents Act, 1988 to be identified as the author
of this work

This book is sold subject to the condition that it shall not
by way of trade or otherwise, be lent, resold, hired out, or
otherwise circulated without the publisher's prior consent in any
form of binding or cover other than that in which it is published
and without a similar condition including this condition being
imposed on the subsequent purchaser

First published in Great Britain in 2006 by
Harvill Secker
Random House, 20 Vauxhall Bridge Road,
London SW1V 2SA

www.vintage-books.co.uk

Addresses for companies within The Random House Group Limited
can be found at: www.randomhouse.co.uk/offices.htm

The Random House Group Limited Reg. No. 954009

A CIP catalogue record for this book
is available from the British Library

ISBN 9780099502685

The Random House Group Limited makes every effort to
ensure that the papers used in its books are made from trees that
have been legally sourced from well-managed and credibly certified
forests. Our paper procurement policy can be found at:
www.randomhouse.co.uk/paper.htm

Printed and bound in Great Britain by
Bookmarque Ltd, Croydon, Surrey

This book is dedicated to my late parents
Wanjikũ wa Thiong'o
Thiong'o wa Ndũcũ
&
to my wife,
Njeeri wa Ngũgĩ,
For your love, courage, strength, and support

| L B OF GREENWICH LIBRARIES | RE |
|---|---|
| 018276714 | |
| Bertrams | 16.11.07 |
| N | £8.99 |
| | |

In the spirit of the dead, the living, and the unborn,
Empty your ears of all impurities, o listener,
That you may hear my story

# CONTENTS

# BOOK ONE

## Power Daemons

# 1

There were many theories about the strange illness of the second Ruler of the Free Republic of Aburīria, but the most frequent on people's lips were five.

The illness, so claimed the first, was born of anger that once welled up inside him; and he was so conscious of the danger it posed to his well-being that he tried all he could to rid himself of it by belching after every meal, sometimes counting from one to ten, and other times chanting *ka ke ki ko ku* aloud. Why these particular syllables, nobody could tell. Still, they conceded that the Ruler had a point. Just as offensive gases of the constipated need to be expelled, thus easing the burden on the tummy, anger in a person also needs a way out to ease the burden on the heart. This Ruler's anger, however, would not go away, and it continued simmering inside till it consumed his heart. This is believed to be the source of the Aburīrian saying that ire is more corrosive than fire, for it once eroded the soul of a Ruler.

But when did this anger take root? When snakes first appeared on the national scene? When water in the bowels of the earth turned bitter? Or when he visited America and failed to land an interview with Global Network News on its famous program *Meet the Global Mighty*? It is said that when he was told that he could not be granted even a minute on the air, he could hardly believe his ears or even understand what they were talking about, knowing that in his country he was always on TV; his every moment—eating, shitting, sneezing, or blowing his nose—captured on camera. Even his yawns were news because, whether triggered by boredom, fatigue, hunger, or thirst,

3

they were often followed by some national drama: his enemies were lashed in the public square with a *sjambok,* whole villages were blown to bits or people were pierced to death by a bows-and-arrows squad, their carcasses left in the open as food for hyenas and vultures.

It is said that he was especially skillful in creating and nursing conflicts among Aburīrian families, for scenes of sorrow were what assuaged him and made him sleep soundly. But nothing, it seemed, would now temper his anger.

Could anger, however deeply felt, cause a mystery illness that defied all logic and medical expertise?

# 2

The second theory was that the illness was a curse from the cry of a wronged he-goat. It is said that some elders, deeply troubled by the sight of blood flooding the land, decided to treat this evil as they had epidemics that threatened the survival of the community in the olden days: but instead of burying the evil inside the belly of a beast by inserting flies, standing for the epidemic, into its anus, they would insert the Ruler's hair, standing for the evil, into the belly of a he-goat through its mouth. The evil-carrying goat, standing for the Ruler, would then become an outcast in the land, to be driven out of any region where its cry announced its evil presence.

Led by a medicine man, they mixed the hair, obtained secretly from the Ruler's barber, with grass, salt, and magic potions and gave it to the goat to swallow. Needle and thread in hand, the medicine man started sewing the seven orifices of the body beginning with the anus. The struggling he-goat gave out a bloodcurdling cry and, before the medicine man could seal its mouth, it escaped. It is said that it cried grief across the land, until the Ruler heard the cry and, learning about the curse, which he imagined to be a call for a coup, sent soldiers to hunt down the he-goat and all involved. Rumor has it that the goat, the barber, the medicine man, the elders, and even the soldiers were given over to the crocodiles of the Red River to ensure eternal silence about the curse. And it was to mark this day of his deliverance that the Ruler had the picture of the Red River added to Burī notes, the only picture besides his own to honor the Aburīrian currency.

Still, he worried about the fact that the goat had a beard, and he secretly consulted an oracle in a neighboring country, who assured him that only a bearded spirit could seriously threaten his rule. Though he read this as meaning that no human could overthrow him, for, since they had no bodily form, spirits could never grow beards, he became sensitive to beards and then decreed what came to be known as the Law of the Beard, that all goats and humans must have their beards shaved off.

There are some who dispute the story of the bearded he-goat and even argue that the Law of the Beard applied only to soldiers, policemen, civil servants, and politicians, and that the herdsmen shaved their he-goats out of their own volition, shaving goats' beards then being the fashion among Aburīrian herdsmen.

These skeptics wondered: what has the cry of a he-goat whose anus, ears, and nose being sealed, have to do with the strange illness that befell the Ruler?

# 3

Others now came up with a third theory, which said that since nothing lasts forever, the illness had something to do with the aging of his rule: he had sat on the throne so long that even he could not remember when his reign began. His rule had no beginning and no end; and judging from the facts one may well believe the claim. Children had been born and had given birth to others and those others to others and so on, and his rule had survived all the generations. So that when some people heard that before him there had been a first Ruler, preceded by a succession of governors and sultans all the way from the eras of the Arabs, the Turks, the Italians, to that of the British, they would simply shake their heads in disbelief saying, no, no, those are just the tales of a daydreamer: Aburīria had never had and could never have another ruler, because had not this man's reign begun before the world began and would end only after the world has ended? Although even that surmise was shot through with doubts, for how can the world come to an end?

# 4

The fourth theory asserted that his illness had its origins in all the tears, unshed, that Rachael, his legal wife, had locked up inside her soul after her fall from his grace.

The Ruler and his wife had fallen out one day when Rachael asked questions about the schoolgirls who, rumors claimed, were often invited to the State House to make his bed, where he, like the aging white man of the popular saying, fed on spring chicken. Of course, the Ruler would never admit to aging, but he had no problems with the "white man" comparison, and so he amended the proverb to say that a white man renews his youth with spring chicken. Imagine how he must have felt about Rachael's attempt to deny him his fountains of youth! How indiscreet and indecorous of her to ask the unaskable! Since when could a male, let alone a Ruler, be denied the right to feel his way around women's thighs, whether other men's wives or schoolgirls? What figure of a Ruler would he cut were he to renounce his right to husband all women in the land in the manner of the lords of Old Europe, whose *droits de seigneur* gave them the right to every bride-to-be?

Rachael thought she was being reasonable. I know you take the title Father of the Nation seriously, she told him. You know that I have not complained about all those women who make beds for you, no matter how many children you sire with them. But why schoolgirls? Are they not as young as the children you have fathered? Are they not really our children? You father them today and tomorrow you turn them into wives? Have you no tears of concern for our tomorrow?

They were dining in the State House, and to Rachael the evening was very special because it was the first time in a long while that they were alone together: the burdens of presiding over the nation hardly ever gave them time to share meals and engage in husband-and-wife talk. Rachael believed in the saying that clothes maketh a woman, and that night she had taken particular care with her appearance: a white cotton dress with a V-shaped collar, short sleeves pleated at the edges, a necklace highlighting her slender neck, rings on her fingers, and dangling from her elegant ears, diamonds sparkling all about her.

We can very well imagine the scene. Guiding his fork unerringly toward his lips, the Ruler was about to place a morsel of chicken into his mouth, when suddenly, at Rachael's words, the fork froze in midair; slowly, he lowered the fork to the plate, the piece of chicken still on it, took the napkin and wiped his lips with deliberation. Before replacing the napkin on the table, he turned to his wife and asked: Rachael, did I really hear you say that I have been forcing myself on schoolchildren? That I don't cry over our tomorrow? Have you ever heard of a Ruler who cries, except maybe, well, never mind him, and where did those daily tears of a grown man lead him? He lost his throne. Do you want me to end up as he did?

There is always a difference between a thought and its description: what the Ruler had been dwelling on when lowering the fork to the table and wiping his lips with a corner of the napkin was not the fate of a Ruler who wept and so lost his throne but rather what he would have to do to make Rachael understand that he, the Ruler, had power, real power over everything including . . . yes . . . Time. He shuddered at the thought. Even before the shuddering completed its course, he had made up his mind.

Speaking with studied calm, a faint smile on his face, he told Rachael that the unfinished meal would be their last supper together, that he would go away to give her time to think about the implications of her allegations, and since she would need space to think, he would bring to pass what had been written in the scriptures: In My Father's House Are Many Mansions. Even for sinners.

He built her a house on a seven-acre plot that he surrounded with a stone wall and an electric fence, and it was while contemplating the unbreachable walls that the idea of a building that reached . . . but we shall talk about that later, because the idea was given expression by one of his most faithful and adoring ministers. What was undisputedly the product of his own genius, in its conception and execution, was the construction of Rachael's mansion.

All the clocks in the house were frozen at the second, the minute, and the hour that she had raised the question of schoolgirls; the calendars pointed to the day and the year. The clocks tick-tocked but their hands did not move. The mechanical calendar always flipped to the same date. The food provided was the same as at the last supper, the clothes the same as she had worn that night. The bedding and curtains were identical to those where she had once lived. The television and radio kept repeating programs that were on during the last supper. Everything in the new mansion reproduced the exact same moment.

A record player was programmed to play only one hymn:

> Our Lord will come back one day
> He will take us to his home above
> I will then know how much he loves me
> Whenever he comes back
>
> And when he comes back
> You the wicked will be left behind
> Moaning your wicked deeds
> Whenever our Lord comes back

The idea of the endless repetition of this hymn pleased him so much that he had amplifiers placed at the four corners of the seven-acre plantation so that passersby and even others would benefit from the tune and the words.

Rachael would remain thus, awaiting his second coming, and on that day when he found that she had shed all the tears for all the tomorrows of all the children she had accused him of abusing, he would take her back to restart life exactly from where it had stopped, or rather Rachael would resume her life, which had been marking time, like a cinematic frame on pause. I am your beginning and your end.

What were you before I made you my wife? he asked, and answered himself, A primary school teacher. I am the past and the present you have been and *I am your tomorrow take it or leave it,* he added in English as he turned his back on her.

There was only one entrance to the seven-acre prison. An armed guard was stationed at the stone gate to make sure that she neither left or received visitors except officials who replenished supplies and doubled as spies, or else her children.

Her children? Apart from the numberless others he begot upon his bed-makers, the Ruler had four boys with Rachael. They were not the brightest in their class, and he had taken them out of school before they had obtained their high school diplomas. He enlisted them in the army—to learn on the job—where they quickly rose to the highest ranks. At the beginning of their mother's frozen present, the first-born, Rueben Kucera, was a three-star general in the army; the second, Samwel Moya, a two-star general in the air force; the third, Dickens Soi, a one-star general in the navy; and the fourth, Richard Runyenje, an army captain. But apart from their military duties they were all on the board of directors of several parastatals closely linked to foreign companies, particularly those involved in the exploration of oil and the mining of precious metals. They were also on several licensing boards. Their main task was to sniff out any anti-government plots in the three branches of the armed forces, as well as to receive bribes. The only problem was that the four were so partial to alcohol and drugs that it was difficult for them to keep up with whatever was happening in the armed forces or on the boards over which they sat. The Ruler was rather disappointed, for he had hoped that at least one of his sons with Rachael might inherit the throne, establishing a mighty family dynasty, and so he often scolded them for their lack of ambition and appetite for power. Yet on the days when they brought him their collections, there was the celebratory atmosphere of a family reunion.

They did not view their mother's life in a seven-acre cage as a dangerous confinement, and when they were not too drunk they would call her—Rachael could receive calls but she could not call out—to say how are you, and when they heard her say that she was fine, they took it that all was well with her and they would quickly return to what they knew best: alcohol, drugs, and bribes.

In calling her, albeit only now and then, the sons actually showed more humanity toward her than did their father, who never once visited the cage to say another word, good or bad. Despite this, Rachael was always in the Ruler's mind, for he received daily reports of her moods and activities; how she spent her day, how she slept, the words she muttered to herself, everything.

What he yearned to hear was any news of her tears, the one sign that would unerringly point to her breakdown and desire for redemption. But he didn't. It is said by those who hold the fourth theory that Rachael, aware of this insatiable desire for humiliating the already fallen, had sworn that she would never let him see her tears or hear about them, not even from her children or the numerous spies. And the more she held out, the more he needed her self-abnegation. Her tears had become the battlefield of their wills.

This obsession with her tears, claimed the creators of the fourth theory, led to the Ruler's strange illness.

The trouble with this theory was that it relied either on rumors or whatever could be deduced from the behavior of the Ruler's children.

It was also the least known of the five theories because it was whispered only among people who trusted one another: for who would be so foolish as to talk about this openly unless he courted death?

# 5

There were others who, to this day, are ready to swear that the illness had nothing to do with burning anger, the anguished cry of a wronged he-goat, the aging reign, or Rachael's tears, and theirs was the fifth theory: that the illness was the sole work of the daemons that the Ruler had housed in a special chamber in the State House, who had now turned their backs on him and withdrew their protective services.

It is said that the walls and ceiling of the chamber were made from the skeletons of the students, teachers, workers, and small farmers he had killed in all the regions of the country, for it was well known that he came into power with flaming swords, the bodies of his victims falling down to his left and right like banana trunks. The skulls of his most hated enemies hung on the walls and others from the ceiling, bone sculptures, white memories of victory and defeat.

The chamber was a cross between a museum and a temple, and every morning the Ruler, after first bathing in the preserved blood of his enemies, would enter, carrying a staff and a fly whisk, and then walk about quietly, looking at the various exhibits one by one; then, about to leave, he would suddenly stop at the door and glance one more time at the chamber and, with mocking gestures of triumphant contempt, at the dark holes and grinning teeth where once eyes and mouths had been.

What were you after? he would ask the skulls as if they could hear him. This fly whisk, this scepter, this crown? He would pause as if expecting an answer, and when the skulls failed to respond he would burst out in guffaws as if daring them to contradict what he was about to say: I plucked out your tongues and tore your lips to show you that a politician without a mouth is no politician at all. But there were times when it looked as if the skulls were grinning back in countermockery, and the laughter would stop abruptly. You fucking bastards, it is your own greed and boundless ambitions that led you here. Did you seriously think that you had a chance to overthrow me? Let me tell you. The person who would even dare has not been born, and if he has, he still will have to change himself into a spirit and grow a beard and human hair on his feet. You did not know that, did you? he would add, pointing at them with his staff menacingly, his mouth foaming with fury.

Let me say as the narrator that I cannot confirm the truth or falsity of the existence of the chamber; it may turn into a mere rumor or tale from the mouth of Askari Arigaigai Gathere: but if it exists, simple logic proves that it was the Ruler's morning rites in this chamber of skulls that long ago, before the Ruler's fatal visit to America and any talk of his illness, had given rise to a rumor that quickly spread throughout the country. Whenever two or three gathered together, the very first question was about the rumor: Can you believe it? Did you know that the Ruler is a devil worshipper, and that he worships his lord and master, Satan, in the name of a serpent?

The rumor about devil and snake worship took root in all Aburĩria following one of the most ambitious programs for birthday celebrations in honor of a Ruler ever undertaken in the country.

# 6

Now everybody in the country knew something or other about the Ruler's birthday because, before it was firmly set in the national calendar, the date of his birth and the manner of its celebration had been the subject of a heated debate in Parliament that went on for seven months, seven days, seven hours, and seven minutes, and even then the honorable members could not arrive at a consensus mainly because nobody knew for sure the actual date of the Ruler's birth, and when they failed to break the impasse, the honorable members sent a formal delegation to the very seat of power to seek wise guidance, after which they passed a motion of gratitude to the Ruler for helping the chamber find a solution to a problem that had completely defeated their combined knowledge and experience. The birthday celebrations would always start at the seventh hour of the seventh day of the seventh month, seven being the Ruler's sacred number, and precisely because in Aburīria the Ruler controlled how the months followed each other—January for instance trading places with July—he therefore had the power to declare any month in the year the seventh month, and any day within that seventh month the seventh day and therefore the Ruler's Birthday. The same applied to time, and any hour, depending on the wishes of the Ruler, could be the seventh hour.

The attendance at these annual assemblies always varied, but that particular year the stadium was almost full because the curiosity of the citizens had been aroused by a special announcement, repeated over and over in the media, that there would be a special birthday cake, which the entire country had made for the Ruler and which he might make multiply and feed the multitude the way Jesus Christ once did with just five loaves and two fishes. The prospect of cakes for the multitude may explain the more than usual presence of victims of kwashiorkor.

The celebration started at noon, and late in the afternoon it was still going strong. The sun dried people's throats. The Ruler, his ministers, and the leaders of the Ruler's Party, all under a shade, kept cooling their tongues with cold water. The citizens without shade or water distracted themselves from the hot darts of the sun by observing and commenting on what was happening on the platform: the clothes the dignitaries wore, the way they walked, or even where each sat relative to the seat of might.

Immediately behind the Ruler was a man who held a pen the width of an inch water pipe in his right hand and a huge leather-bound book in his left, and since he was always writing people assumed that he was a member of the press, although there were some who wondered why he was not at the press gallery. Beside him sat the four sons of the Ruler—Kucera, Moya, Soi, and Runyenje—studiously drinking from bottles labeled Diet.

Near the sons sat Dr. Wilfred Kaboca, the Ruler's personal physician, and next to him, the only woman on the platform, who was also conspicuous by her silence. Some assumed that she was one of the Ruler's daughters, but then, they wondered, why was she not speaking to her brothers? Others thought that she was Dr. Kaboca's wife, but then why this silence between them?

To the Ruler's right sat the Minister for Foreign Affairs in a dark striped suit and a red tie with a picture of the Ruler, the emblem of the Ruler's Party.

The story goes that Markus used to be an ordinary member of Parliament. Then one day he flew to England, where under the glare of publicity he entered a major London hospital not because he was ill but because he wanted to have his eyes enlarged, to make them ferociously sharp, or as he put it in Kiswahili, *Yawe Macho Kali*, so that they would be able to spot the enemies of the Ruler no matter how far their hiding places. Enlarged to the size of electric bulbs, his eyes were now the most prominent feature of his face, dwarfing his nose, cheeks, and forehead. The Ruler was so touched by his devotion and public expression of loyalty that even before the MP returned home from England the Ruler had given him the Ministry of Foreign Affairs, an important Cabinet post, so that Machokali would be his representative eye wherever, in whatever corner of the globe lay the Ruler's interests. And so Machokali he became, and later he even forgot the name given at his birth.

To the left of the Ruler sat another Cabinet minister, the Minister of State in the Ruler's office, dressed in a white silk suit, a red hand-kerchief in his breast pocket, and of course the Party tie. He too had started as a not particularly distinguished member of Parliament, and he probably would have remained thus, except that when he heard of the good fortune that had befallen Machokali he decided to follow suit. He did not have much money, so he secretly sold his father's plot and borrowed the rest to buy himself a flight to France and a hospital bed in Paris, where he had his ears enlarged so that, as he also put it in a press statement, he would be able to hear better and therefore be privy to the most private of conversations between husband and wife, children and their parents, students and teachers, priests and their flock, psychiatrists and their patients—all in the service of the Ruler. His ears were larger than a rabbit's and always primed to detect danger at any time and from any direction. His devotion did not go unnoticed, and he was made Minister of State in charge of spying on the citizenry. The secret police machine known as M5 was now under his direction. And so Silver Sikiokuu he became, jettisoning his earlier names.

The success of the two erstwhile members of Parliament was, ironically, the beginning of their rivalry: one considered himself the Ruler's Eye and the other his Ear. People at the stadium kept comparing their different expressions, particularly the movements of their eyes and ears, for it had long been known that the two were always in a mortal struggle to establish which organ was more powerful: the Eye or the Ear of the Ruler. Machokali always swore by his eyes: May these turn against me if I am not telling the truth. Sikiokuu invoked his ears: May these be my witness that what I am saying is true—and in mentioning them, he would tug at the earlobes. The gesture, rehearsed and perfected over time, gave him a slight edge in their rivalry for attention, because Machokali could never match it by tugging at his eyelids and he was reduced to doing the second best thing, pointing at his eyes for emphasis.

Other members of Parliament would have followed suit and had their bodies altered depending on what services they wanted to render the Ruler except for what befell Benjamin Mambo. As a young man Mambo had failed to get into the army because he was small, but the fire for a military life never died, and now, with the new avenues of power opened by Machokali and Sikiokuu, he thought this

his best chance to realize his dream, and he agonized over the best bodily change to land him the Defense Minister portfolio. He chose to have his tongue elongated so that in echoing the Ruler's command his words would reach every soldier in the country and his threats to his enemies before they could reach the Aburĩrian borders. He first emulated Sikiokuu and went to Paris, but there was some misunderstanding about the required size, and the tongue, like a dog's, now hung out way beyond his lips, rendering speech impossible. Machokali came to his aid by arranging for him to go to a clinic in Berlin, where the lips were pulled and elongated to cover the tongue, but even then not completely and the tongue protruded now just a little. But the Ruler misread the significance and gave him the Ministry of Information. This was not bad, and Mambo marked his elevation to a Cabinet post by changing his forenames and called himself Big Ben, inspired by the clock at the British Houses of Parliament. His full name was now Big Ben Mambo. He did not forget the help that Machokali had rendered him, and in the political struggle between Markus and Silver, he often took Machokali's side.

The idea of a special national gift had come from Machokali— though of course he had gotten strong hints from high above—and it was with the pride of the inventor that he signaled the military, the police, and the prison brass bands to get themselves ready to strike the birthday tune. The moment had come.

There was great curiosity among the crowd as Machokali, aided by members of the Birthday Committee and some police officers, dramatically unfolded and held aloft a huge cloth! Shoving one another aside, people tried to position themselves to see, and they were puzzled when they saw, on the cloth, a huge drawing of something that looked like a building. A drawing on a white cloth for the Ruler's birthday gift?

Taking full advantage of the curiosity and raised expectations, Machokali first appealed to the people to calm themselves because not only was he going to describe everything that was on that cloth, but he was going to make sure that copies of what the English call *an artist's impression* would be distributed to the entire country. He would in fact take that opportunity to thank the teacher who had volunteered his services to do the impression, but regretted that he could not reveal the teacher's name because the artist had forbidden him.

Teaching was a noble profession and its practitioners were modest, driven not by self-glory but selfless service, an ideal for all citizens.

At the far end of the congregation a man raised his hand and waved it frantically while shouting a contradiction, *It's okay, you can mention my name,* and even when told to shut up by those around him, he continued, *I am here—you can reveal my identity.* He was too far back to be heard on the platform but he was near some policemen, and one of them asked him, What is your name? Kaniũrũ, John Kaniũrũ, the man said, and I am the teacher the speaker is referring to. Turn your pockets inside out, the police officer ordered him. After he had made sure that Kaniũrũ was not carrying a weapon, the police officer, pointing at his own gun, asked him, Do you see this? If you continue disrupting the meeting, as sure as my name is Askari Arigaigai Gathere and my boss Inspector Wonderful Tumbo, I will relieve you of that nose. The man Kaniũrũ sat back. Not many people noticed this little commotion because all their eyes and ears were riveted on the bigger drama on the platform.

The whole country, the Minister for Foreign Affairs was saying, the entire Aburĩrian populace, had decided unanimously to erect a building such as had never been attempted in history except once by the children of Israel, and even they had failed miserably to complete the House of Babel. Aburĩria would now do what the Israelites could not do: raise a building to the very gates of Heaven so that the Ruler could call on God daily to say good morning or good evening or simply how was your day today, God? The Ruler would be the daily recipient of God's advice, resulting in a rapid growth of Aburĩria to heights never before dreamt by humans. The entire project, Heavenscrape or simply Marching to Heaven, would be run by a National Building Committee, the chair of which would be announced in good time.

As these wonderful ideas had come from the Birthday Gift Committee, Machokali went on to say, he would like to acknowledge their good work by introducing each of them to the Ruler. The committee members were mostly parliamentarians but there were two or three private citizens, one of whom, Titus Tajirika, almost fell to the ground as he jumped up when his name was called out. Tajirika had never shaken hands with the Ruler, and the thought that this was actually happening in front of thousands was so overwhelming that his whole body trembled in sheer wonderment at his good fortune. Even when he returned to his seat, Tajirika kept on looking at his hands in disbelief, wondering what he could do to avoid using his right hand to shake hands with others or to avoid washing it for some time. He detested gloves but now he wished he had some in his pockets. He would certainly rectify this, but in the meantime he would wrap the lucky hand with his handkerchief so that when he shook hands with his left, people would assume that it was because of an injury to the other. Tajirika was so absorbed in bandaging his right hand that he missed some of the story of Marching to Heaven, but now he tried to catch up with Machokali's narrative.

Minister Machokali was waxing ecstatic about how the benefits of the project could trickle down to all citizens. Once the project was completed, no historian would ever again talk about any other wonders in the world, for the fame of this Modern House of Babel would dwarf the Hanging Gardens of Babylon, the Egyptian pyramids, the Aztecan Tenochtitlan, or the Great Wall of China. And who would ever talk of the Taj Mahal? Our project will be the first and only superwonder in the history of the world. In short, Machokali declared, Marching to Heaven was the special birthday cake the citizens had decided to bake for their one and only leader, the eternal Ruler of the Free Republic of Aburĩria.

Here Machokali paused dramatically to allow time for an ovation.

Except for members of Parliament, Cabinet ministers, officials of the Ruler's Party, and representatives of the armed forces, nobody clapped, but nevertheless Machokali thanked the entire assembly for their overwhelming support and he invited any citizen eager to say a word in praise of Marching to Heaven to step forward. People stared at one another and at the platform in stony silence. The only hands raised were those of the ministers, members of Parliament, and officials of the Ruler's Party, but the minister ignored them and appealed to the citizenry. Are you so overwhelmed by happiness that you are lost for words? Is there no one able to express his joy in words?

A man raised his hand and Machokali quickly beckoned him to come over to the microphone. The man, clearly advanced in years, leaned on a walking stick as he pushed through the crowd. Two police officers ran to him and helped him toward the microphone near the platform. Age was still revered in Aburĩria, and the multitude waited for his words as if from an oracle. But when the old man began to speak it was clear that he had difficulty in pronouncing Swahili words for the Ruler, *Mtukufu Rais,* calling out instead, *Mtukutu Rahisi.* Horrified at the Ruler's being called a Cheap Excellency, one of the policemen quickly whispered in the old man's ear that the phrase was *Mtukufu Rais* or *Rais Mtukufu,* which confused him even more. Coughing and clearing his throat to still himself, he called out into the microphone, *Rahisi Mkundu.* Oh, no, it is not Cheap Arsehole, the other policeman whispered in the other ear, no, no, it is His Holy Mightiness, *Mtukufu Mtakatifu,* which did not help matters because the old man now said, with what the old man thought was confidence, *Mkundu Takatifu.* At the mention of "His Holy Arsehole," the multitude broke out in hilarious laughter, which made the old man forget what he had wanted to say, and he stuck religiously to the phrase *Rahisi Mkundu,* which made Machokali quickly signal that he be removed from the microphone. The old man did not understand why he was not being allowed to speak, and, as he was led back into the crowd, he let out a stream of *Rahisi Mkundu, Mtukutu Takatifu Mkundu, Mtukutu,* any combination of cheap and holy arseholes he thought might work, gesturing toward the Ruler as if begging for his divine intervention.

In order to distract people from the embarrassing scene, Machokali took the microphone and thanked the old man for saying that the entire enterprise was easy and cheap if only the people put their minds and pockets to it. But no matter what spin he put on it, the words *cheap* and *holy arsehole* remained in the air, an embarrassment that clearly left the minister lost in a quandary of inarticulateness.

Minister Sikiokuu seized the moment to deepen the confusion. Claiming that he was actually speaking on behalf of all the others who had raised their hands but had been ignored in favor of the old man, who Machokali was still showering with praise, Sikiokuu asked, Did "brother" Machokali and his committee not realize that the Ruler would get very tired climbing up the staircase to Heaven's gate on foot or riding in a modern elevator, no matter how swift?

He suggested that another committee under his chairmanship be set up to explore possibilities for the construction of a space luxury liner called the Ruler's Angel, and with it a land vehicle, something slightly bigger than the one the Americans had once launched to Mars, to be called Star Rover or simply Rock Rover in Heaven. Armed with the personal spaceship, the only leader in the whole world to possess one, the Ruler would make pleasure trips wherever and whenever he fancied, hopping from planet to planet, and once on the surface of each star he would simply use the Rock Rover in Heaven to move and pick up gold and diamonds in the sky. As Sikiokuu concluded, he dramatically tugged at his two earlobes as witness and sat down, shouting: A space luxury liner!

Having reclaimed the microphone, Machokali, after thanking his fellow minister for his support of the chosen gift and for his brilliant idea about the Ruler's travel needs in Heaven, quickly pointed out that if the minister had bothered to look at the drawing on the cloth he would have seen that the existing committee had already thought through the problem of heavenly travel. At the very top of Marching to Heaven was a spaceport where such a vehicle could land and take off on journeys to other stars. Machokali now swore a couple of times, pointing at his own eyes as a confirmation of his claim that the committee had been very farsighted.

But it was also obvious from the smile that hovered around the edges of his mouth as he countered Sikiokuu's challenge that he had something else up his sleeve, and when Machokali announced it, it took even the other ministers by surprise. The Global Bank would soon send a mission to the country to discuss Marching to Heaven and see if the bank could loan Aburĩria the money for its completion.

After a dramatic pause to let the news sink in properly, Machokali now called upon the Ruler to accept Marching to Heaven as the gift of a grateful nation to its Ruler.

The brass bands struck the tune:

> *Happy Birthday to You*
> *Happy Birthday to You*
> *Happy Birthday, Dear Ruler*
> *Happy Birthday to You*

The Ruler, a staff and a fly whisk in his left hand, stood up. His dark suit was almost identical to that worn by Machokali, but on careful examination one could see that the stripes were made of tiny letters that read MIGHT IS RIGHT. Rumor had it that all his clothes were made to measure in Europe, that his London, Paris, and Rome tailors did nothing else but make his clothes. What distinguished his clothes from all imitations by all political fawns were the patches on the shoulders and elbows of his jackets, because they were made from skins of the big cats, mainly leopards, tigers, and lions. In short, no politician was allowed to wear clothes with patches made from the skins of His Mighty Cats. This special feature had inspired the children to sing how their Lord:

> *Walks the earth like a leopard*
> *Lights the path with the eyes of a tiger*
> *And roars with a lion's fury*

With his height and his custom suits, the Ruler cut quite an imposing figure, and that is why the holders of the fifth theory keep going back to how he looked that day. He had been the very picture of good health as he cleared his throat and declaimed, "I am deeply moved by the tremendous love that you have shown me today . . ." adding that before speaking further, he would like to show his appreciation of their love with an act of mercy by announcing the release of hundreds of political prisoners, among them a few authors and journalists all held without trial including one historian who had been in prison for ten years for crimes that included writing a book called *People Make History, Then a Ruler Makes It His Story*. The alleged literary sins of the historian still consumed the Ruler, because even now he came back to the case of the historian. Professor Materu, he called him, sarcastically referring to the fact that on his arrival in prison the professor's long beard had been the first thing to go under a blunt knife. This terrorist of the intellect has spent ten years in jail, said the Ruler, but because of this historic occasion, I have let him out early. But Professor Materu would not be allowed to grow his beard a length more than half an inch, and if he transgressed, he would be reimprisoned. He was to report once a month to a police station to have the length of his beard measured. All the other dissidents had to swear that never again would they collect and pass on rumors as history, literature, or journalism. If they mended their ways, they would know him as Lord Generosity who rewarded the truly repentant, he said, before turning to the sole woman on the platform.

"Dr. Yunice Immaculate Mgenzi," he called out.

Slowly and deliberately, the silent woman stood up; she was truly striking in poise and general appearance.

"Do you see this woman?" he continued. "In the days of the cold war this one you now see was a revolutionary. Very radical. Her name said it all. Dr. Yunity Mgeuzi-Bila-Shaka. You see? A revolutionary without a doubt. Maoist. *Alikuwa mtu ya* Beijing. But in the final days of the cold war, she gave up this revolutionary foolishness, repented, and pledged faithful service to me. Did I jail her? No. I even asked Big Ben Mambo to give her a job as an information officer, and now I am happy to announce that I have appointed Dr. Yunice Immaculate Mgenzi as the next deputy to my ambassador in Washington. The first woman in the history of Aburīria to hold such a post."

Dr. Mgenzi acknowledged the thunderous applause from the crowd with a bow and a wave of the hand, and then sat down.

"And now," continued the Ruler when the applause subsided, "I want to talk about another radical who used to breathe fire and brimstone at imperialism, capitalism, colonialism, neocolonialism, the whole lot. He used to go by the name of Dr. Luminous Karamu-Mbuya-Ituĩka. You see, calling on luminous pens to scrawl revolution? An agitator. A Moscow man. Educated in East Germany's Institute of Marxist Revolutionary Journalism. There was even a time when some of our neighbors, drunk with the foolishness of African socialism, had hired his services to write radical articles calling for class struggle in Africa. As soon as it was clear that communism was a spent force, he too wisely repented and hastened to remove the word *revolution* from his name. What did I do? Jail him? No. I forgave him. And he has proven himself worthy of my forgiveness with his work. In the *Eternal Patriot,* the underground leaflet he used to edit, he used to denounce me as a creator of a nation of sheep. Now in the *Daily Parrot* he helps me shepherd the sheep with his literary lashes."

To protect the country against malicious rumormongers, so-called historians, and novelists, and to counter their lies and distortions, the Ruler appointed him to be his official biographer, and as everyone knows his biography was really the story of the country, and the true history. "My Devoted and Trusted Historian," roared the Ruler, "I want you to stand up that they may behold you and learn."

The biographer obliged, and it was then that everybody realized that the man with the leather-bound notebook and a pen the size of a water pipe was the Ruler's official biographer. My beloved children, the Ruler now called out, turning to the multitude, I want to say, may you all be blessed for your superwonder gift to me. Not least of what made it so endearing, he said, was that it came as a complete surprise: not in his wildest dreams had he thought that Aburīria would show its gratitude by attempting something that had never been done in the history of the world. He had never expected any rewards; doing what he had done had been its own reward, and he would continue to do so out of a fatherly love. He stopped, for suddenly near the center of the multitude issued a bloodcurdling scream. A snake! A snake! came the cry taken up by others. Soon there was pandemonium. People shoved and shouted in every direction to escape a snake unseen by many. It was enough that others had; the cry was now not about one but several snakes. Unable to believe what was happening and with none wanting to be first to show fear, the Cabinet ministers cast surreptitious glances at one another, waiting for someone to make the first move.

Part of the crowd started pushing its way toward the platform, shouting, Snake! Snake! Some police officers and soldiers were about to run away but when they saw the Ruler's guard ready their guns to shoot into the crowd, they stood their ground. The chaos continued unabated.

To calm things down, the police chief shot his gun into the air, but this only made matters worse and the melee turned into a riot of self-preservation as people took to their heels in every direction; after a few minutes, only the Ruler and his entourage of ministers, soldiers, and policemen were left in the park. The head of the secret police woke up from a stupor and whispered to the Ruler, This might be the beginning of a coup d'état, and within seconds the Ruler was on his way to the State House.

# 7

The media never mentioned the pandemonium at the park. The headlines of the following days were all about the special birthday gift and the impending arrival of the Global Bank mission. MARCHING TO HEAVEN IN SPACE, intoned the front page of the *Eldares Times*. Said the newspaper: *America, take notice that we will not let you monopolize Space. We are right behind. We might be several years behind you in science and technology, but we shall surely win the race like the Tortoise in the story, who defeated the Hare.*

So if it had been left to the media, the story about snakes would have remained only a rumor. Ironically, what subsequently gave life to the rumor was the strangeness emanating from the State House.

# 8

For a number of days the Ruler did not utter a word about what had happened. Those who claimed to be in the know asserted that he was furious and that much of his fury was directed at Sikiokuu. Sikiokuu's calls for a personal spaceship and a Rock Rover in Heaven came back to haunt him. So intrigued had the Ruler been by Sikiokuu's suggestion that even in his anger he asked for a video on the exploration of Mars, but when he saw the size of the spacecrafts, especially the early one, *Sojournertruth*—all the vehicles, to him, seemed smaller than toys made by boys—he seethed and kept muttering to himself, This Sikiokuu has no shame—how dare he, my Minister of State, suggest that my Might be associated with so tiny a thing? His agitation knew no bounds when he later learned that Sojourner had been a slave, a woman, and a freedom fighter, a terrorist, as he called her.

For some days, the Ruler would not receive Sikiokuu, who became so worried that he took steps to stave off the impending explosion. He began by sending his first wife by night to plead for him. The Ruler ignored her. Sikiokuu then sent the second wife. The Ruler ignored her. Sikiokuu sent his much younger third wife. The Ruler ignored her. Finally, he sent his two daughters. It was only then that the Ruler softened and he started to see Sikiokuu again, but then only to vent his anger on the hapless minister.

It was not simply the size of the star surface cruisers or that one bore the name of a slave woman that made the Ruler angry with Sikiokuu. The disruption of the birthday gathering, the memory of the multitude melting away and leaving him and his retinue alone on the field made him boil inside: What message had this sent to the world? Where had all the M5 gone? The intelligence services were under Sikiokuu; hence the Ruler's fury at him. Why had these services not heard anything about those snake people? he kept asking Sikiokuu.

To save their skins, the head of M5 and Sikiokuu explained that the snake people were members of an underground party, the Movement for the Voice of the People, and that the intelligence agents had known all along about them but had kept the knowledge to themselves to buy time to sort out the truth from rumors to get at the roots of the entire movement. It was not a good idea, they explained, to give the group unnecessary publicity before the fullness of its perfidy was known. One does not rush to hit a snake before it has fully come out of its hole.

This made the Ruler even angrier. And so you gave it time to come out of its hole? How dare anybody say that I cannot strike a snake before it has fully revealed itself? Who says that I don't have the power to strike at that which is most hidden from view? Sikiokuu's attempt to diffuse the Ruler's wrath by explaining that his statement was only a proverb made matters even worse. Was Sikiokuu suggesting that there were proverbs that superseded the Ruler's mighty sayings? The Ruler had power over all proverbs, all riddles in Aburĩria, and no proverb could bar him from hitting the hidden, even in the most inaccessible of holes.

To remind people of this point the Ruler decided to address the nation.

The performance, carried live on all the airwaves, was visually compelling, and people talk about it to this day. His government knew, he told the nation, that certain malcontents, the self-styled Movement for the Voice of the People, had duped university students into scattering plastic snakes at gatherings. He wanted to remind the nation that, in direct response to their wishes, the government had long ago banned all political parties. In Aburĩria there was only one party, and the Ruler was its leader. Let it be known to the entire world, he declaimed, that from this minute the Movement for the Voice of the People ceases to exist aboveground or underground. The Ruler was the sole voice of the people, and they loved it so.

To fight the lies of these terrorists he ordered the formation of a new squad, His Mighty Youth, and he asked all school and college students to join and become the Ruler's youthwings. Their main responsibility was to tell all the land that his might was the might and the light of the nation. The wingers would teach the catechism: Aburĩrians can never have a party except the Ruler's Party or worship political idols imitating the Ruler. On His Mighty Service would be their motto, and this would be inscribed on all their badges, stationery, clothes, and vehicles. OHMS.

The Ruler paused to allow that to sink in within the minds of his televiewers. And then came what has become the talk of all Aburĩria and probably the basis for the rumors of snakes, devil worship, and supernatural powers. Emphasizing the warning he was about to issue, he pointed at the cameras with his club-shaped staff as if at the terrorists of the Movement for the Voice of the People. He, the Ruler, would outsnake all their plastic terrorist snakes with real ones. In biblical times, it was the Mosaic snakes that swallowed the Pharaonic ones. Today in Aburĩria, it is the Pharaonic snakes that will swallow all of you who think that you are the new Moses.

And suddenly he raised the club higher in the air as if ready to throw it at any and all self-styled Moseses. The cameramen ducked behind their cameras, and all at once, as if hit by the same object simultaneously, every television screen in the country split into seven pieces. The viewers did not know whether the Ruler had actually thrown the club or simply had the power of mind to disintegrate their screens; disagreements remain to this day. Whatever the truth, the television performance did inspire a new snake dance, which became all the rage so that wherever and whenever two or three young people met, they would move their bodies—heads, torso, and hands—in serpentine motions as they sang:

> *The pot I made is broken*
> *Little did I know that freedom*
> *Would bear a viper and a devil*

# 9

At first the Ruler did not mind the rumors about devils and snakes because he hoped that these would only deepen the fear among his enemies and strengthen his hold on Aburĩria. But when his M5 told him that far from creating fear the rumors were actually making people have a low opinion of his reign, verging on contempt, and that this might lessen people's support for Marching to Heaven, the Ruler saw the need to take steps to deny these rumors their power. But which action would bring about the biggest impact?

As a schoolboy in a colonial classroom long ago, he had come across stories of an ancient king of Babylon who used to appear among the populace disguised as one of them, and when later the citizens found out who he was they were amazed and flattered. A king had walked among them. The image had faded in time, but it sprang back to life, and when he tried the idea on his handlers, they said, Yes, perfect. A well-publicized spontaneous Sunday visit to a church to draw attention to his religiosity would surely counter the basis of the malice toward him.

The church chosen was All Saints Cathedral, Eldares, and what a clever choice! Located between two of the most populous districts in Eldares, Santalucia and Santamaria, the cathedral stood on a hill, and this would make a dramatic scenic background for television pictures.

The cathedral was headed by the slightly eccentric Bishop Tireless Kanogori. His followers had given him those names because long before he became a bishop he used to say that Jesus Christ was the eternal tireless remover of the burden of all the sins weighing heavily on tired souls. Soon his followers started talking about him as the priest who never tired of talking about the tireless redeemer. When promoted to the bishopric he legalized his name out of respect for his followers.

On the chosen Sunday, surrounded by newspaper reporters, television cameras, and handheld microphones, the Ruler and his motorcade arrived at the Santamaria marketplace, where the historic journey to the church would start. He got out of his Rolls-Royce and surveyed the market before the startled faces of the many fruit sellers who did not know whether or not they should rush forward to lure sales by singing praises for their wares. The contrast between the motorcade of sleek Mercedes-Benzes and the line of donkey-pulled and hand-pushed carts loaded with goods of various kinds was stunning. But another scene was even more so. The Ruler saw a lone donkey and, seemingly impulsively as choreographed by his image builders, decided to ride a donkey in imitation of Christ. Some of his secret service agents, dressed as ordinary citizens, grabbed some palm leaves from the sellers and lay them on the ground. At the foot of the hill, he got off the donkey and walked the rest of the way. The long camera shots showing the Ruler at the foot of the hill and the church on the hill made him look as if he was leading a pilgrimage to the City of God.

With slow and thoughtful strides, his entourage allowed the principal actor a foot or so; the performance was almost flawless, and the inner circle even started imagining a social celebration of the victory of guile over rumor.

As it turned out, those following the performance on TV, at home or in community halls, had sensed that something was amiss when, as soon as the Ruler set his foot at the doors of the cathedral they lost the pictures, reminding them of that other time when their TV screens broke into seven pieces. The glitch denied them a view of what happened next, and they had to glean bits and pieces from those who were there and saw the Ruler enter the building.

Though details conflict, all agree that as soon as the Ruler set foot inside the cathedral, the walls shook as if moved by an earth tremor. Crosses on the walls, people's clothes, or pieces of paper danced strangely, as if struggling to flee. And when Bishop Tireless Kanogori placed on the altar a small Bible he had been holding in his hands, the altar shook and the Bible fell to the ground. He did not pick it up but instead disappeared into an anteroom, and before all had finished wondering what had made him abandon the holy book and the congregation, he reemerged holding a very big Bible in his right hand and a huge cross in his left, both hands outstretched toward the Ruler. The bishop's lips were moving as if making an incantation, but nobody could catch his words and so were unable to repeat them afterward.

Then the whole congregation heard the sound of something crashing through a window, breaking the glass into seven pieces, and then, just as suddenly, all the shaking walls and dancing crosses became still and the whole cathedral was embraced in silence and peace; the sound of Bishop Tireless Kanogori's voice as he continued his ceremony as if nothing untoward had happened only served to underscore the silence.

At home, all television sets that had a break in proceedings returned to normal. Those already sitting in front of their sets and those who happened to turn on their TVs at that moment found Bishop Kanogori at the beginning of his sermon. Among the latter group, a few voices ridiculed the tales that went beyond the donkey ride, the palm leaves, the hoarse hosannas, and the long walk to the hill.

But the tellers of the uncanny event did not give up and went as far as to insist that the All Saints Cathedral was not the only shrine of worship where the drama had occurred. It is said that the Ruler did thereafter attend a few other services in other churches with similar results: in all cases at least one glass window was shattered into seven pieces by whatever force the cross-and-Bible-wielding priests had driven out. That is why, so they say, the Ruler of Aburīria suddenly announced, without clarification, that to demonstrate his belief in the equality of all faiths he would now also connect with Islam, and out of modesty and deference to the Islamic hatred of images no cameras would be allowed to follow him.

The idea was to stage this at Islamic mosques, Sunni, Shiite, or Wahabi; then at Indian temples, Hindu, Buddhist, or Jain; and Sikh gurdwaras; and end up in Jewish synagogues, with the hope that these spontaneous appearances would wipe out images of what had happened at All Saints and other churches.

For his first visit to an Islamic shrine, he ordered his handlers to look for a mosque without glass windows. After scouting around Eldares, they managed to find a mosque with a beautiful dome and minarets but, more important, with windows of wood and iron bars.

An even bigger drama ensued, but since it was not captured on film once more we have to rely on hearsay that when the imam in charge of the day's ceremony realized, on the Ruler's entry, that something was not right, he quickly raised the Quran in midair and called out in Arabic:

28

*Allahu Akbar Allahu Akbar*
*Ash-hadu an la-Ilaha ill-Llah*
*Ash-hadu anna Muhammadar-r-*
*Rasuwlu-Llah*
*Hayya ala-swalaah*
*Hayya alal Fataah*
*Allahu Akbar*
*La-Ilaha illa-Llah . . .*

Those in attendance say they felt something like wind whirl through the air and the next minute they heard the iron bars of one of the windows creak and then saw some of them bend outward as if someone were pushing the bars to set himself free. Brandishing the Quran and the rosary at the window, the imam shouted something like *Satan*, and lo and behold the creaking stopped abruptly and the only sound was the imam calling out, *Allahu Akbar*. There are some who, like the biblical Thomas, doubt everything about this tale, but even they are unable to explain how the iron bars came to be so bent; for it is said that the mosque's ruling council, after much internal debate, decided that they would not repair the window but let it stay like that, a witness to the victory of the Holy Quran over the wiles of Satan, even when disguised in the modern fineries of earthly glory.

The entire program of spontaneous appearances at places of worship was scrapped quietly, and a devilless normal order of worship was restored to these religious shrines. Some city dwellers put up posters: ELDARES IS A DEVIL-FREE ZONE.

# 10

It was not, for soon they found that the Satanic daemons had escaped the churches and the mosques to roam the land, for how else were people to explain two amazing reports that soon began to circulate in Eldares? The first was comic, claiming that Satan visited Maritha and Mariko in their home at Santalucia just to pick a fight.

The scarier second, beyond the realm of religion, told of Satan going about the towns and villages plucking out people's hearts, leaving their bodies as empty shells on roadsides and dumpsites.

But there were a few people who argued that the two, Satan's picking a fight with Maritha and Mariko and Satan's plucking out people's hearts, were connected, a clear case of Satan's showing that though he had lost some battles he had not lost the war. But why pick a fight with an elderly couple?

# 11

Maritha and Mariko, wife and husband, were well known in Santalucia because they were always in each other's company, going to market and shops or attending wakes, funerals, and weddings. If one or the other was spotted alone, people knew—and they were hardly ever proven wrong—that the other one was not far away.

Their cat, black except for a white patch on its forehead, sometimes followed them, and when once it came to church children adapted a familiar song:

> Mari had a little cat,
> Little cat, little cat
> Mari had a little cat
> With a skin as black as soot
>
> And wherever Mari went,
> Mari went, Mari went
> And wherever Mari went
> The cat was sure to go
>
> It followed Mari to church one day . . .

Maritha and Mariko were faithful members of the All Saints. They dusted pews and windows and arranged flowers. When the cathedral started a program of feeding the homeless and sheltering them in the basement on Fridays, Saturdays, and Sundays, Maritha and Mariko volunteered to minister to the needy wayfarers. They even fed doves and other birds nesting on the roof of the cathedral.

Maritha and Mariko were as twins. Many were the times when one would complete a sentence begun by the other. They were in their sixties, their bodies had held remarkably well, and their children, now young men and women, were secure in their different jobs. All in all, Maritha and Mariko were without a blemish, and they seemed a model for a wholesome marriage and family life.

That may explain why the entire church community was so shocked when one Sunday, not many months after the event involving the Ruler and the broken glass at All Saints, Maritha and Mariko stood before the congregation and confessed that they were tormented by an irresistible lust for other people's flesh. In keeping with how they always did things, they told their story as if reading from the same book.

"Even walking in the streets is becoming a torture," Mariko said.

"There is not a single night we have not prayed that this burden be lifted, but our prayers have not yet been answered," added Maritha.

"Our own bodies no longer call out to each other, but other people's make ours burn with desire."

"As if Satan is beckoning us to leave the path of righteousness to break some of the Ten Commandments . . ."

". . . which say," they intoned together as in a chorus, "'Thou shall not commit adultery and Thou shall not lust after another person's property.'"

"So far, the lust has remained in our eyes only," Maritha explained.

"But even that is a sin," Mariko hastened to add, as if to quell any doubts the audience might harbor about how seriously he and Maritha took these temptations.

The congregation prayed that the couple be made strong and the Satan of Lust be crushed. After the service was over, Bishop Tireless Kanogori, a fellow brother in Christ, had a heart-to-heart talk with them and told them to remain steadfast, that they should remember that when Christ was once alone in the wilderness, hungry, thirsty, tired, Satan chose that very moment to tempt him for forty days and nights, and Jesus wrestled with numerous desires but remained steadfast in his courage and righteousness and in the end defeated Satan; and it was this great struggle with the Temptor that prepared Christ to assume his role as the redeemer of all the sinful. Consider, then, he went on, how lucky you are that you are not alone with Satan for forty nights and days in a wilderness full of howling winds and wild animals, that you are still there for each other in your own home in Santalucia, and we are all around you, shouting at the Temptor: *Shame on you, Satan!* And the trio broke into a hymn:

> *His evil Angels will come*
> *And Satan himself will come*
> *But my soul is armed with faith*
>
> *I will knock him down*
> *I will strike and tell him*
> *Get behind me, Satan,*
> *I will never become your follower*

But even then Satan would not leave them alone, and every Sunday Maritha and Mariko would tell scarier and scarier stories of how Satan had dogged their paths for seven nights and days in different guises, and wily as ever, trying to stoke their lust for other people's flesh. The only place where they felt safe from him was within the cathedral. Elsewhere, especially when one or the other was asleep, at home, or walking the streets alone, Satan was back. Theirs was now a war on a grand scale; testifying about his tactics was their one way of fighting back so that if Satan struck a pound's worth they would hit back with their two cents' worth. It was because they feared most the possibility of Satan catching one of them alone in a dark alley that they were now inseparable. Their saga was very moving, and every Sunday more and more people would congregate at the All Saints to listen to the latest episode in the daily battles between Maritha and Mariko and Satan.

The cathedral became a popular spot packed every Sunday with people eager for titillating details about the couple's lust and engagement with Satan. There was not even standing room left inside, and many would simply gather outside the doors and windows the better to catch glimpses of the heroic couple as they told their story.

It was bound to happen that this story would reach the desks of news editors, and one newspaper, the *Daily Gossip,* increased sales severalfold when it started carrying versions of Maritha and Mariko's serial confessions; and the war against Satan became the subject of talk at crossroads, marketplaces, shopping centers, and bars. Whenever and wherever young men and women met, they would say half in jest: Oh, my dear, you have afflicted me with a severe case of Maritha and Mariko, or I feel a Mariko and a Maritha for you—what do you say to that?

To the dwellers of Eldares, particularly those living in Santalucia, the story of Maritha and Mariko and their epic battle against the Satan of Lust became bigger than even the arrival of the Global Bank mission to study the feasibility of funding the proposed Marching to Heaven. The story of an ordinary man and woman standing up to the mighty Satan gripped their imagination, curious as they were as to how it would all end.

# 12

On the fortieth day of Maritha and Mariko's first confession to visitation by the Devil, people flocked to All Saints as never before. Forty was significant. It was after the same number of days that Jesus Christ had returned home from the desert victorious over Satan. But when Maritha and Mariko gave witness to the Lord and confessed that Satan was still after them, people, and especially the young, were confused, some clearly upset. Why hadn't Satan taken on his equals in Hell instead of relentlessly pursuing Maritha and Mariko? What particularly annoyed them were Satan's cowardly tactics: preying on old Maritha and Mariko when alone or just about to close their eyes. Satan is a big bully, they said. He dare not come here.

But others cautioned the congregation not to become complacent; the only reason Satan had not dared to come back to soil the holy grounds was because the ignominious exit forced on him by Bishop Tireless Kanogori only a few months before was still fresh in his memory.

The youth, especially the recently saved, took up the challenge and after the service remained behind to put their heads together, quickly vowing to do for Santalucia what the bishop had done for All Saints. They would comb every nook and creek in Santalucia to ferret Satan out, and if they failed to catch him they would at least scare the shit out of him.

So, they took on the name Soldiers of Christ and vowed to fight till the Devil let Maritha and Mariko live their lives in peace. They would arm themselves with the Bible for a shield, a hymnbook for a diet, and the cross doubling as a walking stick and a cane with which to chase out Satan. The Evil One must move or be made to move. They broke into a call-and-response battle hymn.

> *Where are you going,*
> *Carrying food and armed with a staff?*
> *We are pilgrims on a warpath*
> *To battle Satan and his worshippers*

They strode with hope and confidence that other young men and women would answer their clarion call to war and join them in their hunt for Satan.

# 13

The Soldiers of Christ did not at first know exactly where or how to begin their hunt for Satan.

Tourists, beggars, and prostitutes dogged one another in the streets during the day and met again in the evenings outside seven-star hotels, as if these shrines of luxury belonged equally to the rich, the tourist, and the prostitute, the major difference being that at night the rich, the tourist, and prostitute stayed in while the beggar found himself out in the open, enduring rain or cold. But as soon as dawn broke they all reconnected.

Every beggar knew one or two words of English, German, Japanese, Italian, and French, though Kiswahili dominated their speech.

Help the poor. *Saidia Maskini. Baksheesh.* There were a few who played music on homemade guitars and drums, while others performed comic sketches that now and then lured a coin or two from an amused tourist. They tried to station themselves on streets most frequented by tourists, resulting in a lot of pushing and shoving for advantage.

Sometimes the police raided the beggars, but just for show, for Aburīria's prisons were already full. Most beggars would have been quite happy to be jailed for the meal and a bed. The government also had to be mindful not to upset tourism by sweeping too many beggars off the streets. Pictures of beggars or wild animals were what many tourists sent back home as proof of having been in Africa. In Aburīria, wild animals were becoming rare because of dwindling forests and poaching, and tourist pictures of beggars or children with kwashiorkor and flies massing around their runny noses and sore eyes were prized for their authenticity. If there were no beggars in the streets, tourists might start doubting whether Aburīria was an authentic African country.

The Soldiers of Christ took stock of the situation. What kind of places was Satan likely to haunt? In what guise? He is full of tricks, for, as they would remind themselves, was he, Lucifer, not born before even the world came to be? If he could turn himself into a snake and crawl through the walls of the Garden of Eden under God's surveillance, what was to prevent him now from assuming the form of a human, another animal, or even a stone? Why were Maritha and Mariko unable to name the objects of their desire? Because it was Satan himself who appeared to them in different guises. Maybe Satan had now disguised himself as a tourist, a prostitute, a beggar, or any of the hundreds milling the streets, or . . .

"Look," one of the soldiers shouted, pointing a finger at something across the street, a sculpture of the Ruler on horseback. The Soldiers of Christ quickly read his mind, for the bronze sculpture reminded them of the not so distant spectacle of the Devil worshipper riding a donkey in imitation of Christ, an act of sacrilege for sure. But why did the vision appear to them at this moment? In their hour of need? They recalled that God had forbidden the Children of Israel to make graven images. Why? Because Satan could easily hide in a sculpted image. Inspecting the sculptures of the Ruler was no easy task, as they soon found out. The Ruler's monuments were all over every street in Eldares.

There he is on a horse in full flight and on others cantering. Here he is standing on a pedestal with hands raised in a gesture of benediction over passersby. There the commander in chief in military garb, a sword raised as if inspecting a guard of honor, and on another as if leading a charge. Here he is, the great teacher in a university cap and gown. There the thoughtful ruler in a moody pose.

They did not find Satan among the sculptures. They looked inside high-rise and low-rise buildings, side by side with shacks made of discarded cardboard and sheets of plastic. Italian, Chinese, Indian, and Greek restaurants faced kiosks serving soul food of collard greens and *ugali*. From the big restaurants issued the smell of sizzling steaks; from the sidewalks came the smell of cracking corn and hazelnuts on charcoal.

Results were not good. Like the wise men from the East who encountered numerous difficulties on their way to see the infant in the manger, the Soldiers of Christ endured many hardships in their search for Satan inside the many buildings of Eldares. In some bars they were met with derisive laughter, and once some drunks threw orange peels at their faces. In the seven-star hotels they were often thrown out and eventually banned as nauseating to guests. And outside, in the streets, where sleek Mercedes-Benzes, donkey carts, and hand-pulled carriages competed for space and the right of way in potholed roads, the sun and dust were not anymore merciful; not to speak of the police who sometimes chased them, suspecting them of being beggars, and tourists who ran after them with cameras, taking them to be holy beggars. They were often hungry and thirsty and tired, and the stench in the streets of Eldares did not improve matters.

Those were the days when instead of being lined with trees the streets of Eldares were lined on either side with mountains of garbage. Some shop owners paid private garbage collectors to clear access to their premises, so that here and there, particularly in the central business zone, there were some clean patches. In many other streets there was nothing but flies, worms, and the stench of rot.

Was this stench part of Satan's arsenal with which to drive us away? they wondered. For all we know he could be hiding in the garbage hills, laughing at us even as we look for him among people, buildings, and the sculptures of the Ruler? No, he is not going to stink us out of our search, they said defiantly.

But no matter how brave they felt, the more they talked about the wiles of Satan, the more they came to realize that fighting with someone they could not actually see with their own eyes was not easy. In these low moments, they would remind themselves that they were Soldiers of Christ, and as the Bible says, they had to fight the good fight. Happy are they who suffer for my sake. Revived by such thoughts, they would hold their crosses aloft with renewed vigor and sing themselves hoarse.

> *This place amazes me*
> *At the cross*
> *Because there is joy after sorrow*
> *At the cross*

One Friday afternoon in the outskirts of Santamaria as they were feeling good about themselves, three men ran toward them shouting in pure terror, Satan! Satan! They hid behind the banner of the Soldiers of Christ. Please help us . . . Satan is after us . . .

The soldiers, who had been singing and speaking in tongues, were struck by the irony of the situation. When they were thinking only of Satan, they did not find him. But now, at the height of joy and consciousness of Grace Abounding, when they were thinking only of Jesus, they heard news of Satan.

"What are you talking about?" they asked in unison.

"Satan . . . he is giving us hell! Help us!"

"Where is he?" asked the Soldiers of Christ excitedly, though still baffled and a little frightened by this dramatic turn of events.

Perhaps battling Satan in the spirit was less daunting than facing him in the flesh . . . but this was their moment and they were not about to shun the call.

# 14

He was tired, hungry, and thirsty and felt beaten down by the sun. He wanted to climb to the top, when suddenly he felt very weak in the knees and collapsed at the foot of the mountain of garbage. He could not tell whether he was in a temporary coma or a deep sleep, but when a slight breeze blew it lifted him out of himself to the sky, where he now floated. He could still see his own body lying on the ground and the mountain of garbage, where children and dogs fought over signs of meat on white bones. The body needs a rest from you and you need a rest from the body, he heard himself saying to himself. He decided to let his body lie there in the sun, and, free of the body, he wandered Aburĩria—why leave the exploration and enjoyment of our country to tourists? he said with a chuckle to himself—comparing the conditions in the different towns and regions of the country.

This is really funny, he said to himself when he saw that he looked like a bird and floated like a bird; he enjoyed the rush of cold air against his wings. He now recalled a Christian song he had once heard:

> I will fly and leave this earth
> I will float in the sky and witness
> Wonders never seen before
> Being done with the earth below

He started to sing but because he could not open his beak as wide as his mouth what came out was a whistling reminiscent of the song of the birds he had listened to in the mornings in the wilderness.

From his vantage point, he had a bird's-eye view of the northern, southern, eastern, western, and central regions of Aburĩria. The landscape ranged from the coastal plains to the region of the great lakes; to the arid bushlands in the east; to the central highlands and northern mountains. People differed as much in the languages they spoke as in the clothes they wore and how they eked out a living. Some fished, others herded cattle and goats, and others worked on the land, but everywhere, particularly in towns, the contours of life were the same as those of Eldares. Everywhere people were hungry, thirsty, and in rags. In most towns, shelters made out of cardboard, scrap metal, old tires, and plastic were home to hundreds of children and adults. He found it ironic that, as in Eldares, these shacks stood side by side with mansions of tile, stone, glass, and concrete. Similarly, in the environs of cities and towns huge plantations of coffee, tea, cocoa, cotton, sisal, and rubber shared borders with exhausted strips of land cultivated by peasants. Cows with udders full with milk grazed on lush lands as scrawny others ambled on thorny and stony grounds.

So I am not alone, he heard himself say to his bird self. Maybe he should abandon his human form and remain a bird, floating effortlessly in the sky, bathing in the fresh air of Skyland, but then he started sneezing as a whiff of gases from the factories below reached him. Is there no place on earth or in the sky where a person might escape this poison? A bit confused, he thought that before making any decision about the form in which he would lead the rest of his life he should return to his body lying in the sun to recover and review the shocks of the day. But what if his body had been completely scorched by the sun? At the thought he flapped his wings and hurried back to Eldares.

He arrived not a minute too early. A rotation truck full of garbage had just pulled up at the foot of the trash mountain. He was about to reenter his body but he held himself in check and floated a bit longer to see what they would do with his shell.

The driver and two men got out and looked at the body for a few seconds. Then one of them bent, put his ear to the chest, and proclaimed the body dead, provoking an exchange as to what they should do with the corpse. They did not want to call the police; it would take the cops a whole day to come, and they had work to do. In any case they did not want to get caught up in endless court proceedings. There was always the possibility that they might be accused of murder and end up in prison or have their heads chopped off or lose a lot of money to bribe their way out. But to leave the body there might result in as much.

The corpse was in a somewhat threadbare suit. Was there money in the pocket? At the thought, all fears about touching the body disappeared and the three searched frantically but found nothing. No money. They noticed that the corpse still clutched a bag on which it partially lay. It had to contain something important for its owner to cling to it so tenaciously through his death throes. The three read one another's minds and unceremoniously they quickly turned the body over and searched the bag. They were so sure that the bag was full of money that they became very angry at the corpse when they found it held nothing but rags; one of them started cursing the corpse as if it were alive. You stupid liar. I am sure these rags are your real clothes and the suit you have on is stolen property. Have you no shame, stealing other people's clothes? And you did not even have the good sense to steal a suit less worn out; at least we could have taken that.

They were about to go when they suddenly realized that their fingerprints were all over the body. They could not leave the corpse there and decided to bury the evidence of their involvement. Dead men do not speak, especially if they and their bags are buried in a rubbish dump. So many were dying of hunger or illness, not to mention the ones in despair who took their own lives, that the police would have no reason to search for yet another corpse amid the stench.

Maybe I should let them bury my body, he told himself, or rather his bird self: What use am I in Aburĩria? The body is a prison for the soul. Why shouldn't I cut off the chains that now tie me to it, let the body and the soul say good-bye to each other? That way my soul shall be free to roam across land and all over this sky. Yes, to go wherever it wishes without the endless restraining demands of the body: I am thirsty, I want water to drink; I am hungry, I want food to eat; I am naked, I need some clothes; I am out in the rain, I need some shelter; I am ill, I must find a doctor. I must catch a bus but I have no money. I must pay school fees, taxes . . . isn't it simpler to let everything go?

But when he saw the men actually lift him, or rather his body, and throw it onto the pile of rubbish in the back of the lorry headed for the dump, he heard a voice from within cry out that the body was the temple of God and the soul had no right to cut loose its connection to the world before it had completed its sojourn on earth. I am human, I am a human being, a soul, and not a piece of garbage, no matter how poor and ragged I look, and I deserve respect, he heard himself say time and again as he descended to and repossessed his body.

The stench, which hit his nostrils, was so strong that it made him sneeze even as he tried to sit up. He started removing garbage from his face. About to get into the passenger side of the lorry, two of the men heard the sneeze. They each stood fixed to the ground. The driver also froze, his hands on the door, one leg on the rung and the other still on the ground. What was that? he asked. But his men did not answer. Having gone to peer at the body risen from the dead, they just ran away. The driver also fled the lorry after his friends, beseeching them not to leave him to the mercy of the Devil. But the word *Devil* only served to spur them on; the three were now screaming out Satan! in different pitches. Not until they saw a group of young men and women with crosses and a banner on which was written the words SOLDIERS OF CHRIST did they stop to compose themselves and ask for help . . .

# 15

The three garbage collectors were trembling as they told their tale of how they had found a dead body and were about to bury it in the dumpsite when it came to life, or rather rose from the dead, and started chasing them around the vehicle, trying to ensnare them, all the while threatening to put them into the huge bag he carried and take them home to his evil angels in Devil Land. And was that not the site of the everlasting fire, the garbage collectors asked, and the Soldiers of Christ said yes. The collectors could not recall how they managed to escape from the Devil's grasp, but when they saw their chance, they seized it and fled.

It was a story of sadness and terror and relief—oh, what a narrow escape—and even before they were done with the tale one of them was saying that there would be no more garbage collection for him; all three agreed that they would never again touch a body, no matter how dead it appeared to be. The dead were truly deadly.

"Don't worry," the Soldiers of Christ told them, nodding their heads knowingly to show that they were well aware of all the wiles of Satan. "It was Jesus calling on you to leave these earthly brooms behind and become cleaners of the hearts of men," they assured them as they now broke into a hymn.

> *The Lord told the fishermen to follow him*
> *And leave their fishing nets behind*
> *He told them he would take them to Heaven . . .*

The hymn and the singing made the Soldiers of Christ feel courage course through their veins, and a couple started weeping with bravery, eager to go to war immediately.

The garbage collectors said thank you and they allowed that they now felt safe being, as they were, in the company of believers; but when asked to take the soldiers to the scene of their recent woe and narrow escape, they at first refused and agreed to do so only when they were told that they could hide behind the banner and that the soldiers would guard them with crosses on every side. The Devil lives in terror of the cross, the soldiers assured them. Didn't he stop chasing them the moment he saw them heading toward the cross? And they sang, *At the cross, at the cross where I found the Lord . . .*

And so behind the safety of the banner and the cross, the three men were able to point to a lone figure walking toward the center of the city. They were able to confirm that it was the Devil himself because they recognized the bag he carried. And now they said very firmly that they would not take another step in the direction of the Devil. They hurried to get back into their truck before Satan changed his mind and came back to collect them.

With their crosses and Bibles held out in front the way Bishop Tireless had done at All Saints, the Soldiers of Christ followed the figure from a safe distance, for as they said they must not be fools who tread even where angels fear to tread. They must keep in mind that Satan had been a leading angel before he was banished from Heaven for plotting a rebellion against God. A being who had almost pulled off a palace coup against God was not to be taken lightly. But they kept their eyes on him, for with Jesus leading them they were bound to succeed in containing the Devil. As one of them pointed out, Satan had succeeded in misleading so many angels to join him in his coup attempt because Jesus Christ was then not born.

What happened next, however, only went to confirm their fears about the devilish wiles of the figure before them. Even today the Soldiers of Christ swear that they never once took their eyes off him, but still they cannot explain how the figure disappeared right in front of their watchful eyes. All they know is that when they reached the street they, too, had seen the figure enter, they met so many people with similar bags that they could not tell who was whom among the hundreds pushing and shoving one another for the right of way. The Devil had vanished.

And then they remembered the tribulations of Maritha and Mariko and the same thought chilled their hearts: what if Satan had played his devilish tricks on them to pin them down in the central streets of the city while he went to Santalucia to snare Maritha and Mariko and pluck out their souls, leaving their bodies empty shells on the roadside or by some dumpsite?

They decided to go back to Santalucia. But before they had gone too far, they heard steps behind them. It was one of the garbage collectors.

"I have decided to leave the earthly brooms behind to become a cleaner of the hearts of men. I too want to become a Soldier of Christ," he told them.

The Soldiers of Christ were amazed at what had just unfolded before them. God works in mysterious ways his wonders to perform. After days of trying without success, now, when they least expected it, in the most unlikely of places, they had just gotten their first convert. They accepted him as their new brother in Christ and they baptized him Sweeper-of-Souls.

And suddenly they saw the light of their next act and within seconds, accompanied by their new convert, they were on their way back to Santalucia, where they set up what would become a nightly candlelight vigil for the Satan who had appeared before the garbage collectors in the wilderness and later disappeared in the central business zone of Eldares. With Sweeper-of-Souls now among them, they would no longer have difficulties in identifying and then catching the Devil.

# BOOK TWO

# Queuing Daemons

# SECTION I

## 1

A little dazed, his belly aching with hunger, Kamĩtĩ stood on a sidewalk to collect himself. He did not want to lie down because he feared a recurrence of what had happened to him earlier at the dumpsite. This was not the first time that he had felt himself ease out of his own body; he had had this sensation at night in the wilderness. There, in the open, lying on his back, looking at the stars and the moon, he would see himself abandoning his body for the sky as if pulled by a force intent on impressing him on the grandeur and mystery of a universe with no beginning or end. He would think of the prophets of old, Confucius, Gautama Buddha, Moses, John the Baptist, Mũgo wa Kĩbirũ, who had all retreated into the wilderness to commune, in total silence, with the law that held the universe together. Were their lives not enhanced by what they had picked up during their pilgrimage? He would roam free in the universe the whole night, endlessly fascinated by the being of things, and when he returned to his body in the morning he would feel his spirit imbued with fresh energy, ready to face another day of walking about the streets of Eldares, knocking at every door, hoping for something that would improve his life. Thus he retained hope and even looked forward to his free flights into the universe as relief from the wounds of fruitless quests. But he had never experienced in the sunlight, at a dumpsite or anywhere else for that matter, what he just underwent in the noon of day; he took it as a warning to keep away from dumpsites and take a different path. Surely the Universal Sharer, who looks after creatures that fly and those that crawl, can't do any less for the ones made in his own image?

He saw a piece of chapati carried in the air by the breeze and followed it with his eyes. Now the bread was floating just above his head. Instinctually, with whatever energy he still had, he retrieved it and put it in his mouth. Oh, no—it was only a piece of paper. He felt sick. He took the paper out of his mouth hastily but instead of throwing it away he looked at it as if he had intended to read it all along. It was a bit of newspaper.

On one side was a picture of the Ruler. His head was torn off so only a headless torso with hands holding a club and a fly whisk remained. It was a little grotesque and he felt like laughing, but that required energy.

On the other side was a four-man Global Bank mission that had come to Aburĩria to discuss the proposed national project of a palace aspiring to Heaven's gate. Machokali, the Minister for Foreign Affairs, was going to host a reception and a dinner at . . .

Dinner? Food? Apparently there were people in this world who still had food to eat. Where was this dinner? He looked at the fragment again but the words were missing. He threw it away but it did not fall to the ground; it was picked by the breeze and continued floating in the air, mockingly, conjuring images of food so near yet so far away, making him a Tantalus in Eldares. He felt dizzy again. He leaned against a post at the nearest shop, his eyes taking in the human masses in the streets as he held his nose at the stench in the air.

Kamĩtĩ had always had a strong sense of smell, and even as a child he could scent things in distant places. His power of smell was so strong, animal-like, that he often knew the identity of a person before he appeared. He could follow, if he concentrated hard enough, the trail of a person. He was sensitive to the different smells in a crowd.

But the smell he had recently begun to detect was very different from any he had come in contact with before. At first it was only a whiff among many others, but it intensified to a point at which it assaulted him from all around. He could not tell whether it was coming from the mountains of uncollected garbage, the factories in the industrial area, or simply from human sweat: it did not smell quite like rotting leaves; it was more like the stink of rotting flesh—not of dead flesh but of a human body at once alive and decomposing and yet . . . not quite; it was intensely familiar and unfamiliar. The rot was stronger in some people than in others. When he first became aware of it he used to wonder if it emanated from his own belly because of hunger or fatigue, but then, in the wilderness, deep in the forests away from Eldares, the smell was absent no matter how hungry, thirsty, and tired he was. Walking among people in towns and cities, Kamĩtĩ often tried to suppress his sense of smell and pretend that the nausea he felt was an illusion; that way he could get on with looking for jobs without constantly thinking about odor. Now leaning against the post he tried reading the names and the ads on storefronts to suppress his hyperactive sense. They were mostly in Hindi, Kiswahili, and English. NAMASTE. KARIBU. WELCOME. SHAH DRAPERIES, SHA KA HŨRĨ KHANA.

The Indian shop owner came out and threw orange peels into the street, and as he went back inside he cast an evil eye at Kamĩtĩ, as if warning him that if he did not move from that post quickly the owner would call the police. Kamĩtĩ's eyes fixed on the peelings that seemed to beckon him to pick them up and see if when squeezed hard enough they might yield drops of sweetness. A voice within cautioned him: What did you say to yourself this very morning about picking things from the rubbish? Have you already forgotten the fate you were about to suffer at the dumpsite when you broke the law of your own words?

The earlier debate in his mind between the voice in defense of picking up garbage and a voice defending begging from strangers now resumed with fury. Which was less contemptible? The latter eventually overpowered the former by numerous references to the scriptures. Prayer after all is a form of begging and it was the cornerstone of all religions. Ask and it shall be given. Everyday followers of the different faiths, whether named after Jesus or Muhammad or Buddha, get on their knees and beg God for this or that. They pray that their Lord and Master will hear their cry. Yes, prayers are blessed. Begging is blessed. Among the followers of Buddha, the holiest are known by their vows of poverty, and they are sustained in the path of holiness by begging. Didn't Buddha himself renounce the trappings of wealth for a life of begging and purity? At the center of the Sangha, the monastic community he founded after his Nirvana that followed forty-nine days of struggle with the Tempting Mara, was Bhikkhus, the order of the begging monks. Alms, give me alms. Surely what

Kamĩtĩ had experienced earlier at the city dumpsite, almost being buried alive in rot, was a clear signal that it is better to beg. He thought of entering the very next shop with hands outstretched, and then he quickly realized that the gray suit he was wearing on his job hunt was not the proper attire for seeking alms. He felt like laughing but held himself back when it occurred to him that even asking for a job is a form of begging. Begging, like everything else in this world, had its time, place, and clothes. The evening begging was some time away; there were still a few hours left for job hunting. Who knows— maybe things would start turning his way and he would not have to act like a Buddhist monk.

And then he could not believe his eyes. Right across the street was a signboard, ELDARES MODERN CONSTRUCTION AND REAL ESTATE, and beside it a billboard. A job! The word blotted out all the others around it. Rising from the dead, he was now delirious with hope.

# 2

It was about five, and fearing that the office might close for the day before he had taken advantage of this godsend, Kamĩtĩ dispensed with knocking at the door and barged right in.

The secretary, who was reading a book as she waited for the close of business, did not see him enter but, sensing his presence, raised her head. Their eyes met. Kamĩtĩ felt something he had never experienced in all the offices he had visited. The stench that had oppressed him in the streets of Eldares had suddenly been replaced by a more powerful smell, a fresh one, like the scent of flowers, but there were no flowers in the room.

"What do you want?" the secretary asked, keeping her place in the book.

"I would like to see the boss. The employer."

"Tajirika? Titus Tajirika?"

"Whatever the name."

"Do you have an appointment?"

"No."

"Then you cannot see him."

"But I must, please!"

"Young man, do you want me to lose my job?" she chortled. "I was hired only a few months ago," she added as she closed the book and placed it on the table.

The eye goes wherever it wants, so the saying goes, and Kamĩtĩ's eyes wandered to the title of the book: *Shetani Msalabani*. What kind of secretary was this who was not busy trimming her nails or immersing herself in cheap romantic novels? Her voice was gentle to boot.

For years Kamĩtĩ had searched for work up and down the streets of Eldares. He had met with company bosses, African, Asian, and European, who all tended to regard black Aburĩrians as potential thieves. He had frequently been insulted. Once security guards had even set dogs on him. He had also met all kinds of secretaries; a few had spoken kindly to him but many had barked at him as if asking for a job were a crime. The secretary he now faced seemed to carry herself altogether differently, but he could not pin down the difference.

"Madam, if I told you my story you would know why I have to see your boss. Right now I don't mind even cleaning toilets."

"Are there any toilets left in Eldares?" she asked, a little bemused.

"Well, there are pails."

"Emptying them of shit? Then washing them clean?" she shot back.

"Any job will do."

The secretary glanced at Kamĩtĩ with a curious eye. He was dark, tall, and slim, and in his hand he held a bag. His gray suit must have been nice when it was new, probably quite expensive, but now it was worn, the elbows patched.

"I see. In that case, I suggest that you come back tomorrow. It is now five. My boss is about to leave. I would have left already but he asked me to stick around for a while. So you are in luck. Let me check his schedule of appointments tomorrow."

"Let me see him now, please—he will understand when I tell him my story."

"You know . . ." She paused, leaned forward slightly, and lowered her voice as if imparting a secret. "My boss is a very important member of Marching to Heaven, and he is attending a dinner reception in honor of the mission from the GB."

"GB? Great Britain?" Kamĩtĩ asked, a little puzzled. What was she talking about and what did it have to do with her setting up an appointment?

"Not Great Britain! Global Bank!"

At that very moment Tajirika emerged from an adjoining room, ostentatiously putting a handgun into the inside pocket of his jacket, making it clear to this argumentative intruder that he was armed.

Kamĩtĩ was overcome by a stench blast to his nose and for a few seconds found it difficult to breathe. But he held himself upright, trying hard not to react to the foul smell as he sized up the boss. Tajirika's belly was a bit too impressive and his dark suit a bit too tight. His snugly gloved right hand matched his skin and held a small staff, an imitation of the Ruler's, which he pounded in his left for emphasis while he spoke.

Tajirika looked from Kamĩtĩ to the secretary as if to ask, From what dunghill did you pick this one out?

"He wants to see you," the secretary said in response.

Tajirika gave Kamĩtĩ another look. Kamĩtĩ tried to speak but Tajirika interrupted him.

"Didn't you hear what my secretary said? I am about to go welcome the delegation from the GB. Do you get it? The Global Bank, the bank for the whole world. I have *a personal invitation* from the minister himself, a great friend of mine, and . . ."

"A job. All I am looking for is a job," Kamĩtĩ sputtered.

"At this hour?" Tajirika said, slightly irritated that Kamĩtĩ had interrupted him when he was just beginning to warm up about himself.

"I have been to several other offices," Kamĩtĩ explained.

"So you assumed that the owner of these premises has all the time in the world?"

"What I am trying to say is that I have been on my feet all day," Kamĩtĩ said, trying to mollify him.

"So on other days you rode from office to office in a Mercedes?"

Kamĩtĩ let the insult pass, hoping helplessly that the boss would show pity and give him an interview.

"An interview. I just want an interview."

An idea suddenly struck Tajirika. His cheeks puffed up a little as if he were stifling laughter, but he did not laugh. He sat on the edge of the table, his right foot grounded, his left hanging a few inches above the floor. He now held the staff with both hands.

The secretary was captivated by what was unfolding before her eyes. This man, whoever he is, must possess some secret power, she thought. How else could one explain his softening of the boss's heart so quickly?

"What type of job are you looking for?"

"Whatever is available," Kamĩtĩ hastily answered, clutching his bag more tightly. Maybe a bird of good omen had greeted him this morning. That was one of the most rewarding things about spending nights in the open. Birds were bound to wake you up, and whether they carried good or bad luck, at least they woke you up with music.

"What is your educational background?"

"BA, economics. Master of business management, MBA." He stuck his hand into his coat pocket as if dipping for something. "Sorry, I have no visiting cards."

Tajirika and the secretary looked up at Kamĩtĩ with enlivened interest and curiosity. But their trains of thoughts diverged. The secretary thought she could see herself reflected in the man's pain and problems and anxiety to please. Tajirika thought that the man was lying about university degrees and business cards. Sensing this skepticism, Kamĩtĩ hastened to pull out his certificate, handing it over before the boss could change his mind. Tajirika held his staff under his left armpit to receive the paper with his gloved right hand. He scanned it and nodded as if satisfied.

"India?"

"Oh, yes. In fact, today India is producing some of the world's top computer scientists. The Silicon Valleys of northern California in America are full of whiz kids from India and Pakistan."

"How did you cope with their masala curry and hot pepper?"

"It's the same with food everywhere," said Kamĩtĩ. "It is a matter of getting used to it. Our cooking here in Aburĩria is influenced by Indian cuisine."

"Oh, I almost forgot, of course—we have Indians here and some of our streets smell of nothing but garlic and curry," said Tajirika as if to himself.

At the thought of food, Kamĩtĩ became a tad dizzy. He could have done with a morsel of anything right now, even of the hottest pepper. But he stilled himself and added, "Let's not forget that India is not all curry and garlic. Or that India and Pakistan are nuclear powers. They have both successfully tested nuclear bombs to the surprise of the West. Many computer chips are produced in India. And there are not many universities in the world without professors from India—that is, originally educated in Indian schools and colleges. An Indian is not all dukawallah and nothing else, just as an African is not all shoeshine and nothing else."

"But did you learn how to make good curry?" Tajirika asked, unaware of how he was torturing Kamĩtĩ with this talk about food. "Here they don't let us into their houses."

"Well, survival skills," Kamĩtĩ said vaguely, trying to veer away from the subject.

"Mhh! So you are highly educated?" Tajirika muttered, scrutinizing the certificate.

"Just trying to give myself a chance," Kamĩtĩ replied with a hint of modesty, but not displeased with hearing an appreciation of his achievements.

"You must have read the Karma Sutra cover to cover?"

"What is that?" Kamĩtĩ asked, genuinely puzzled, because he had never read this ancient manual of lovemaking.

"And gave yourself a chance to put it into practice?" Tajirika said, taking his eyes off the papers.

He glanced at his secretary in an unconvincing attempt at an apology, as if he had just realized that he had said something he should not have said in front of her; but the glance also seemed to say that he had much more he would have liked to ask had she not been present.

Tajirika glanced at the secretary again and laughed rather uneasily. He had not yet figured her out, and he felt her judgment even in her silence. He dropped the subject of the Karma Sutra and went back to the certificates.

"India? Madras?" Tajirika continued as if genuinely interested in the man's educational achievements. "Tamil Nadu! And what is this? Another Indian curry?"

"No," Kamĩtĩ answered, not knowing whether or not he should laugh, and began to patiently explain. "India is divided into many regions just like Aburĩria is divided into several provinces. Tamil Nadu is the name of a state in southeastern India. Kerala is another southern state, but on the western side. So both have a common border. Tamil Nadu also neighbors two other states on its northern side: Karnataka and Andhra Pradesh. *Pradesh* means the same thing as *province*. But really, Indian provinces are like countries. Madras—but I think they now call it something else . . . Chennai, yes, something like that—Madras was . . ."

"I asked you to tell me about your education, young man, and you give me a whole lecture on Indian geography?"

"I am sorry," Kamītī said. "India is rich in geography and history."

"Like that of the Black Hole of Calcutta?" Tajirika remarked with a self-satisfied grin. "That is the only history of India that I know, and I don't really want to know more. If my advice were sought as to what should be done with the Indians of Aburīria, I would say that they should all be cast into the Modern Black Hole of Calcutta. Whenever a black man in Aburīria tries to raise himself up, there is an Indian in his way. And when he deals with a black man, it is nothing but insults. They have no respect for the people on whose soil they have prospered. And where do they take their money? To India, Pakistan, and now Bangladesh. No loyalty to Aburīria. Some have even refused to take up our citizenship. They prefer to remain British, actually English. And the others, with dual citizenship, are always ready to take flight should things ever go wrong in Aburīria. The Indian should *count his blessings one by one* that we have a ruler like the Ruler."

"But don't some black Aburīrians also spirit their money to Swiss bank accounts?" Kamītī asked. "What is the difference?"

"Why are you defending the Indian?"

"I am only saying that *obviously* in India, as in Aburīria and throughout Africa, there are greedy people. But there are also others who care and who struggle against whatever harms human life. My opinion is that there are many things we could learn from India and other Asian countries, just as they have much to learn from us. We in Aburīria, more than others, should strengthen our ties with India because some of our citizens are of Indian origin . . ."

"You dare call Indians here citizens? Aburīrian citizens?"

"Why not?" Kamītī thought his prospective boss was trying to see if he could stand his ground with customers. He added, as if revealing a secret to the boss, while appealing to his Pan-Africanist sentiments, "You know, it is thought by some that some Indians are of African descent—the Siddis, for instance. The Dravidians, who speak Telugu, they look like they came from Ethiopia or Egypt. Historians talk of an African general named Malik Ambar, who . . ."

"Ruled India?" Tajirika completed the sentence mockingly.

"Yes," said Kamĩtĩ enthusiastically, "but not all India. You see, in the sixteenth century or thereabouts, India was not one . . ."

"So you also studied the art of telling lies?" Tajirika interrupted with a burst of laughter, winking at the secretary as if to say, You have heard him for yourself. "Or are you merely adding a little salt and pepper to your tales?"

"I am not lying; it is just a hypothesis," Kamĩtĩ said as he tried to steer the conversation away from the African presence in India. "Even if we put aside questions of origins and citizenship, India and Indians did play a role in the struggle for African independence. Quite a few joined with Africans to oust colonialism. And Mahatma Gandhi—wasn't it only after fifteen years of anticolonial struggles in South Africa that he went back to India to organize Satyagraha and ahimsa against British rule in India? There is beauty in the man clad in calico and sandals, armed with nothing but a walking stick and his creed of nonviolence, taking on the might of the British Empire, don't you think?"

"There, now you see my point?" Tajirika said. "He lights a fire in South Africa and what does he do? Runs away when the going gets rough and leaves others to put it out or burn in it. Young man, you have learned quite a lot of propaganda in India. So what else apart from Gandhi's propaganda and the Nehrus' monopoly of power did you learn?"

"Let's say I learned that there is not much difference between the political character of the Indian and the African. There are some who love their history and their skin color and there are others who hate their history and their skin color . . ."

"There you go again! I asked you what else you learned in India and you answer by telling me about skin color?" Tajirika said sternly, angrily.

Even the secretary was surprised by what she saw as an overreaction, almost as if he had taken the reference to skin color as a personal affront.

Kamĩtĩ, who had been trying to impress a prospective boss with his depth and breadth of knowledge, was now not sure where all this talk was leading or what Tajirika really wanted, for each time he tried to demonstrate his education, he heard only barely veiled mockery and now anger from him. What was the difference between Tajirika's abuse and what rich Indians were alleged to dole out to black Aburīrians? Kamītī realized that he needed to be brief and precise in answers without worrying about implications. At the same time he did not want to leave the premises jobless and so felt driven to display his learning so as not to give any impression of shortcomings in his education. People in Aburīria said bad things about Indian education, some even claiming that Indian degrees can be bought in the marketplace, and he did not want to leave the impression that he himself had one day walked the length of Mount Road into George Town, Chennai, bargaining for the cheapest set of certificates.

"Well," Kamītī continued, with forced enthusiasm, "as I was saying, in India one can learn a lot. I even took an extra elective, herbology, the study of the medicinal properties of plants. I can assure you, sir, that there is no aspect of plants, roots, leaves, or barks that I have not looked into; and if I had the money I would undertake more research into the varieties of plants in Aburīria with a view to discovering and documenting their medicinal properties, but even without formal research . . ."

"Is that why you were baptized, Kamītī Mr. Woods?" Tajirika said, laughing.

"My mother tells me that even when I was a child I showed a great interest in plants and in all living things."

"By the way," asked Tajirika, "in which language did you study this herbology of yours? Hindi?"

"No, no," Kamītī hastened to answer. "To be honest with you, I did really want to know Hindi—it is the most widely spoken language in the country—but I didn't get to know it very well because all our classes were in English. Just as here, a result of British rule. Besides Hindi, India has many languages: Gujarati, Bengali, Telugu, Urdu, Malayalam, and countless others. In Madras, where I went to college, the language is Tamil. I know a few mutterings of Tamil, such as 'Please show me the way to' or 'Please give me some water' . . ."

"Begging for water! There, for the first time you have spoken an undeniable truth. I understand that in India beggars fill up the streets; some even have PhDs in the art of begging. It is understandable that you would pick up words to do with begging . . ."

"Ah . . . well . . . beggars . . . there are . . . in Aburīria," Kamītī stuttered, a little confused.

"There are beggars in our streets, that's true, but not as many as in India," Tajirika said with a tone that suggested the conversation was coming to an end. "Now, young man. What did you say your name was? It looks to me as if you know more about history than about woods. Whatever I ask you, you give me a history lesson."

Kamĩtĩ did not know whether to take this as compliment or mockery.

"One can only try," he responded vaguely.

"Good," Tajirika said as he rose from the table. "You have tried your best in this interview. I like that. I wanted to make sure you are proficient in the English language before administering the *real* test. Follow me. I will conduct the test myself, to make sure you have understood everything."

Kamĩtĩ felt joy leap within. I could tell that this man would not have asked me so many questions without his wanting to give me a chance. And that was all he ever asked for: a chance to show just what he was capable of doing with his hands and his mind. Now he clutched his bag even more firmly. This was truly his day. During all his years of job hunting, he had never had an interview that lasted more than a few minutes. How different this boss was from all those others who would not allow him to express his needs! This one had invested time in carefully probing Kamĩtĩ's educational background. This was going to be his first real interview, and he was determined to do well by answering all the questions clearly, firmly, and completely. Even though it is said that one should not count one's chickens before they are hatched, Kamĩtĩ could not help but count a few as he looked to the future. If I get this job . . . when I start my new job . . . and all at once he stopped counting. For instead of leading him into the inner office, Tajirika was walking out through the front door.

Even the secretary was baffled: where was Tajirika taking the young man? Being newly employed, she wondered whether he was taking the young man to an affiliated office of which she was unaware. Kamĩtĩ had a similar thought, keeping hope alive again: maybe Tajirika had already hired him and he was taking him elsewhere to start right away. Kamĩtĩ patted himself on the back. It was good that I gave him all those details about my education. It is good that I kept my cool and was detailed in my responses. Truly, patience is the gateway not only to knowledge but also to riches, or at least a job.

The secretary stood at the door to see what transpired. Her heart skipped a beat when she saw the two standing by the signboard at the road. Unfortunately, from where she stood she could not hear their conversation and so she focused on their gestures.

"You said you knew how to read and write in English," Tajirika now said to Kamĩtĩ.

"Yes. *Yes! One of my best subjects!*" Kamĩtĩ replied in English. "Even today Madras University has maintained many English traditions. Officers of the British East India Company founded the town itself in 1639. One of the early governors of the region, Elihu Yale, or a name like that, is the one who later gave his fortune to found Yale University, one of the Ivy League schools in the States. So you see that . . ."

"We are not on the premises of the British East India Company; we are on those of Eldares Modern Construction and Real Estate, and your Elihu Yale is not the governor. Here I am the boss, and my only interest in Yale is in Yale locks and keys. And another thing, young man: we are now at the beginning of a new millennium, the third millennium since Christ was born, and not in the middle of the last one. Or do you really mean to tell me that at Madras University they were teaching you seventeenth-century English?"

"*Oh, no no!*" Kamĩtĩ replied in English, thinking the man was still testing him with snares. "*Modern English. The King and Queen's English.*"

"That's good, because I will test you in modern English!"

"I am ready," Kamĩtĩ said, prepared to use every bit of English that he learned in Aburĩria and India and from books.

"It is simple. I want you to read loudly what is written on this signboard."

Even before uttering the words on the board, Kamĩtĩ knew that Tajirika was toying with him. But the words came out of his mouth and he heard himself read loudly: *No Vacancy: For Jobs Come Tomorrow.*

"There! You have read it correctly!" Tajirika said triumphantly. "What is it that you don't understand? Or do you need a Hindi interpreter? On these premises, there is no use for your herbology. Here are your Indian papers. Over there is the main avenue. And now you'll excuse me, for I have an important engagement in Paradise."

# 3

Even as he took back his papers, Kamītī could not believe what his eyes had seen and his ears heard. His tongue was lifeless in his mouth and his feet stuck to the ground. So he stood there, dumbfounded, not knowing whether to walk away, sit down, or continue standing. Only when Tajirika had moved several yards away did it dawn on Kamītī that everything he had seen and heard had indeed taken place. He did not know whether to run after the man and kick him in the butt or to beg the earth to swallow he himself. He felt like weeping but no tears came. Why had Tajirika set him up for this coup de grâce?

He sat on the raised ground by the roadside. He felt that even the buildings facing him had witnessed his shame and, in their stony silence, pitied him. In the streets, motorcars and people on foot hurried past one another as if they all knew what they were doing and where they were going, while he did not know what to do with himself. He did not have a cent of fare for a *matatu*, a *mkokoteni, mbondambonda,* or any other human-drawn carriage. But even if he had money, where would he tell them to take him?

Has someone cast an evil spell on me, or am I under a family curse? The question startled him. He did not believe in curses and evil charms; he believed in science. But what had just passed for a job interview defied the logic of science. And just at that moment, as if to add an exclamation point to the exercise, Tajirika passed by in a chauffeur-driven car.

How far up the ladder of education had Tajirika climbed, Kamītī wondered? Or was it business that had educated him to be a heartless interviewer of needy job seekers? Kamītī had often given serious thought to starting a business. With his BA and MBA, he surely had the necessary educational background, but starting a business required capital and land. Even with abundant fishes in the sea, one still needed a net or a line and hook, at least.

He felt, as he often did many a day, that he had wronged his parents terribly. They were peasants, really, at least his mother was; they had sold their parcel of land to see him through schools and colleges. Ever since he left home for Eldares, Kamĩtĩ had not been back to Kĩambugi, his village, not even once, and had even stopped writing to his parents. Write to them and tell them stories of the number of times he had been thrown out of offices like a stray dog? Tell them that all those degrees for which they had paid with years of toil and frugal living could not secure him even bus fare? Oh, why did he not allow the garbage collectors to bury his body? Were he to say good-bye to this earth, his parents would hardly miss him, for surely to them he must be as good as dead by now. A solution, simple and attractive, suddenly presented itself, but just when he was about to carry it out he smelled the scent of flowers behind him. He raised his head briefly. It was the secretary. Was she coming to add her own insults to her boss's?

Kamĩtĩ did not want to look at her in the face or even talk to her: he did not want her to become the object of his vengeful thoughts. So he turned his head away and looked down. The woman ignored this and tried to strike up a conversation.

"May I sit down?" she asked.

Kamĩtĩ did not respond. The woman sat down beside him anyway; for a few seconds there was nothing but silence between them. Then Kamĩtĩ heard the sound of sobbing, a whimper, coming from the woman. He did not want to shoulder anyone else's burden—he had enough of his own—but he was sensitive to suffering.

"What is the matter?" Kamĩtĩ asked.

"Why could he not tell you there were no vacancies and leave it at that? Why the calculated insult?" she said.

"It is all right," Kamĩtĩ said, struck by the way her words echoed his own.

"These are really the ogres said to have two mouths, in front and at the back," she said.

"In stories?" Kamĩtĩ said in a tired, almost indifferent tone.

He was unaccustomed to making connections between his woes and those of the community at large.

"Yes," the woman said. "But those in stories are more human by comparison."

"Why?" he asked in the same tone.

"Because those in stories sometimes get tired of human flesh and swallow fried flies for a change. But the modern ones live on people all the time and they never stop."

"It's all right," said Kamĩtĩ.

"What do you mean, 'it's all right'?"

"It is the way of the world," Kamĩtĩ said in the same indifferent tone, wishing that the talk would end and she would go away.

"I don't understand."

"The world has no soul."

"Then change the world. Give it a soul."

He said nothing for a while. Is she one of those who talk of revolution? To Kamĩtĩ, damaged souls produced damaged policies, not the other way around. Some people have a sickness of the heart. Cure them of the sickness and good will follow. For him the human soul inherited badness or goodness and there was nothing anybody could do about that. Yet it was clear that he had not given his position much thought; he was just mouthing it.

"Listen to me. The world will always be what it has always been. Luck rules our lives."

"The way luck has lately been ruling my life?" she said, suddenly laughing. He raised his head and looked at her. Hers was not forced laughter; it seemed to come right from the belly. The laughter of a contented person, Kamĩtĩ thought. Who would not laugh as well, knowing he or she had a secure job!

"Why are you laughing?"

"Please, just ignore it. I laugh quite often. In all the days and months I spent on the road looking for jobs I used to seek relief in laughter. Even when I got *We regret that we have no vacancy*, I would sometimes laugh about it. Laughter is my secret weapon against adversity. The job I now hold is, well, not quite a job—it's temporary, so to speak," she added and paused, then she lowered her voice as if talking to herself. "There came a time when I asked myself: what is the point of the BA that I struggled to get? It's as useless as dog shit, I would say in frustration. Even holders of PhDs are unemployed. They walk the streets till their soles wear out, looking for work. Quite often, these PhDs have to bribe their way into a job. And others are told to get a delegation of elders from their village to take them to the State House so that the elders can plead with the

Ruler on their behalf—just to get a job. Whom to blame? Degree certificates? This made me laugh. The certificates are not to blame. What did you just say? The world is the way it is and will always be so? The world is upside down, and it should be put to right by those who on earth do dwell, to borrow a phrase from the hymn."

Still absorbed with his recent humiliation, Kamĩtĩ was at first oblivious to what the woman was saying. But when it registered, he was startled from his engagement with his injured self.

"You are a university graduate? I would never have guessed . . ."

"Why? I don't have a mark on my forehead?" the woman said rather sharply before laughing and extending her hand. "My name is Nyawĩra. Grace Nyawĩra, but I prefer Nyawĩra by itself."

"I am Kamĩtĩ wa Karĩmĩri. But there was a time I used to be called Comet Kamĩtĩ."

"Comet? That is a new one."

"When I was a kid I read somewhere about stars and something about comets streaking across the sky, and I said: That is my Christian name."

"Comet? A Christian name?"

"Why not? It is as European as your Grace."

"When I was in Brilliant Girls High School I was in charge of saying grace before meals. We thank you Jesus for the food we are about to eat, etcetera. The other students started calling me Grace, and soon after I adopted it as my own, replacing Engenethi."

"Engenethi? A version of Ingrid?"

"I believe it's derived from Agnes."

"Engenethi? Ingrid or Agnes? A Christian name?" It was his turn to wonder aloud.

"Well, it sounded European," she said. "All European names are Christian, African ones are satanic," she added with a wry smile.

"Is that what you got from that novel you were reading, *Shetani Msalabani, Satan on the Cross*—or is it *Devil on the Cross*?"

"When did your eyes steal away to what I was reading?" Nyawĩra asked as she touched her handbag to indicate that the book was still in there.

They both laughed and for the first time in a while Kamĩtĩ felt the heaviness inside him lighten, and he was now attentive to her story.

Grace Nyawĩra had gone to Eldares University, graduating with a degree in English, history, and theater arts. She could not find a job for a long time. She sustained herself with all manner of temporary ones. Even so, what helped her to get these tempas, as they are called, was not her degree but a computer course she took at the Ruler's Polytechnic in Eldares.

"You and I could be called Twins in Trouble," Kamĩtĩ said with a light tone.

"Twins on the Beat," they said in unison, and stared at each other, laughing again.

"All the same, you have crossed the river of tribulations, haven't you, for you now have a job!" Kamĩtĩ said.

"It's hardly that. I'm simply passing time in this tempa, waiting for good luck."

"When did you start working?"

"Not long ago. Let me see. Soon after the nation presented the Ruler with the special birthday cake. When was that?"

"I don't remember," said Kamĩtĩ. "I don't keep up with politics."

"You mean to tell me you were not there when the plans for Marching to Heaven were first announced?" Nyawĩra asked.

Kamĩtĩ thought of telling her about his odd sense of smell. He did not like being in crowds, foul smells galore assailing his nostrils. But he did not talk about his curious sensitivity. He had not attended the ceremony because he had gone into the forest to pick wild berries.

"I wasn't there, but I heard rumors about it," he said.

"About Marching to Heaven? Or about the snakes?" But as soon as she had uttered the questions she looked at her watch and jumped to her feet. She did not notice Kamĩtĩ wince at the mention of the word *snake*. "It's getting late. I must get going," she said.

"Where do you live?" Kamĩtĩ asked.

Nyawĩra paused, dwelling on the question and its answer.

"In Santalucia, two rooms and a kitchen. What about you?"

"Bahati," he said and did not give details.

While they were clearly reluctant to talk more about themselves, they seemed as reluctant to leave each other's company.

"I have to get home before dark," Nyawĩra said again. "Now that you know my place of work, if you ever find yourself with time to spare, you can come over for lunch. I know many nice fish and chips places around here," she said, and left.

Kamītī followed her with his eyes until her figure was lost in the massing crowd.

Her presence and their talk had taken him away from his troubles, but now they came back with a vengeful fury. He indulged in self-pity edged with self-contempt. Why did I lie to her about Bahati? I wish I had told her straight out that I did not have shelter for the night. I should have asked her to let me stay in her place tonight or asked her for dinner tonight instead of lunch in the future.

He rose and walked toward the city center. Many shops were now under lock and key. Elsewhere armed security guards reported for night watch. It was as if the city were at war. His parents used to tell him that in the olden days in the villages and the countryside, they never even bothered to lock their doors, pulling them shut only to prevent stray animals from entering. He jumped to one side to avoid colliding with two men who were pushing empty *mkokoteni* carts, racing toward Santamaria Market.

Soon he reached the market, where hand- and donkey-pulled carts were competing for customers and the right of way, as were a motley assortment of rickshaws pulled by bicycles, scooters, and mules. The scene reminded him of a street in Old Delhi where ox-pulled carriages competed for the right of way with cows, tricycles, decrepit motor vehicles, and of course the latest models. He thought, Why don't I look for a cart and start bearing loads for a fee like all these others? But even a *mkokoteni* costs money. Besides, unlike picking through garbage or begging, this trade could not be done surreptitiously; it would be embarrassing for a Masters of Business Administration to be running about with a *mkokoteni* hand-pulled cart, shouting for customers.

Embarrassing? No, it would be humiliating . . .

The humiliation he had suffered on the premises of Eldares Modern Construction and Real Estate came rushing back with such a force that for a few seconds he felt dizzy and had to still himself against the wall of the nearest building to keep from falling down. His heartbeats became drumbeats. His mind jumped from place to place, image to image, turning over and at times mixing up the different things that had happened to him in the last two days. He had tried to suppress his memory of some of the events, but there was no denying the return of the repressed. His mind was flooded with happenings, big and small, in the near and distant past, and he had to yield to them.

Like the case of Margaret Wariara.

# 4

Kamītī met Wariara on a bus soon after his return from India. They talked; they were attracted to each other; they became friends. Their friendship deepened, especially when it came out that they were from the same village, Kīambugi, a few miles from Eldares, and they had attended the same primary school. But they had not known each other then because Wariara was in her first year and he in his last, about to go to a secondary school. And after his secondary education, he had gone to India. Wariara completed her primary education and she went on to Harambī Community High School and ended up with an Aburīria school certificate.

Years after leaving school she still had not landed a job despite her high school diploma now boosted by a secretarial course—typing, shorthand, and computer literacy. So at the time they met, Wariara was still looking for a job. The newly arrived Kamītī was bubbling with hope and told her not to worry. He thought that with two university degrees in his pocket, he would get a job in no time; he and Wariara would marry and start a family, and even if that failed to work he would still help her build her own life. But instead of any of that coming to be, they found themselves beating the streets together. Although each would try a separate turf, they would often take the same matatu from Kīambugi to Eldares in the morning, and in the evening they would take separate transport back to Kīambugi because there was no way of timing their different searches. In the evening they would meet to compare notes, and it was always the same story: No Vacancy. At first they met every evening to enjoy each other's company and share their day's experiences, often, in those early days, narrating some of their encounters in the city. They would burst into hilarious laughter over the twists and turns of their day's quest, almost as if hunting for a job in the city jungle was an adventure. But as days and months elapsed and the ending of their stories never changed, they found themselves feeling embarrassed and even guilty about their own failures. They began meeting less and less. They could not explain it to themselves, but their failures were putting a strain on their relationship and they were drifting apart. Wrapped up in their own guilt and sorrows, they did not want to live the same pains thrice over: first in experiencing it directly, second in retelling it, and third in having to carry the burden of the other's identical pain.

Early one morning as the sun was rising, Wariara told him: Look. Two blind men cannot show each other the way. Go your way and I'll go my way and we should not try to find out where each is going. I want to go wherever fate calls.

They sat under a tree on a hill overlooking Kīambugi village, and they were like any man and woman wooing under the shades while the cocks of the village were crowing and the dogs barking. It had been her call that they meet there before the break of day so that they could talk and still have time to catch their early rides to the city. It was also her call that he should take her under the dew of the morning. At first Kamītī was taken aback by this, because they had so far refrained from lovemaking in the hope that it would be a special gift to themselves on the dreamt day to come, a way of initiating themselves into their married life and sealing their union. He felt cheated out of a dream, a hope, a promise, and more so when the act turned out not to be so great, as if it had been forced on them. He felt as if he had swallowed dregs where he was expecting cool water. Her final call for a separation did not therefore come as a surprise, but still Kamītī kept quiet, he himself lost for words that could answer hers. What was he to tell her? Stay with me awhile longer and I will land you a job and right the wrongs of yesterday? He searched his heart and found that it was not in him to judge her in praise or blame. It was the way of the world, their world, and he did not even have the strength to weigh her words and try to suggest a way out. The sun was slightly higher up in the sky and the dew on the grass was beginning to fall. Kamītī stared at two grasshoppers and for a few seconds he remained absorbed in their hopping play. Far, far away came the sounds of two donkeys braying, as if in competition. Kamītī did not take his eyes away from the dance of the grasshoppers, even when he heard Wariara sing what would later turn out to be a song of farewell.

> Happy were they
> That gave up fishing in the lakes
> And they became fishers of men

The tune was not happy—it was actually sad, at least in the singing of it. Even when it was over the tone remained in the air, and it made Kamĩtĩ feel tears at the edges. He raised his head to tell her that he loved her and that he would not bear any ill will toward her or presume to judge her choice of what she would do, but Wariara was no longer there. He wanted to say, Please don't go, but he had nothing to call her back to, not even a sense of hope that things would be better tomorrow. So he sat there under the tree, the shade and morning dew of which they had shared, watching her go down the hill until he could no longer make out her form against the distant landscape. She never once looked back, and now Kamĩtĩ let his tears flow down his cheeks and did not make any effort to wipe them away.

He decided not to go to the city. But what was he to do with his time? Kamĩtĩ never took alcohol. Now he turned his pockets inside out and found enough to take to the nearest bar. Instead of walking about the streets of the city, he would stay indoors, a lone fixture at the counter. Maybe if he tossed down two or three beers he would feel good, and even if he failed to feel good, he would at least forget the turn his life had taken. He closed his eyes and gulped down the first bottle. He did the same with the second and the third. He stopped counting and he did not know how many he tossed down. He continued drinking thus for a week or so, as if he did not really want to wake up to reality, and as he did not have much money, he resorted to cheaper brews. There was a night when he drank so much of the brew that he could not tell how and when he eventually staggered out of the bar to the backyard and fell asleep, seduced by the warmth of his own vomit. When in the morning he woke up and found himself covered with his own spew, he decided that alcohol was not the cure for his problems, be they of the body or the spirit. But how could he have succumbed to the seduction, he often wondered, afraid of his weakness, and he thereafter avoided bars like the plague.

Kamītī never saw Wariara in Kīambugi again. He continued staying in the village, but without Wariara life was no longer the same. Although in the last days of their friendship their review of their encounters in the city had become rarer and rarer, he still missed their occasional review of the day's hunt for jobs. It was increasingly difficult and hollow to live in the village where everything, even matatu rides in the morning, reminded him of her. Besides, he feared that everybody was aware of his alcoholic spell. He too decided to leave Kīambugi for Eldares for, as he reasoned to himself, a fisherperson does not cast the net in the same spot or a farmer continue planting seeds in the same hole.

He continued looking for a lucky break in Eldares but without ever getting it and without even seeing any glimpses of light at the end of the tunnel of his life up to that point. In the first few months Kamītī thought about Wariara, often wondering where she was, what she was doing, how she was surviving, or even whether she was alive. But months and months of daily problems eventually removed any lingering images of Wariara from his mind. He had enough problems of his own without having to add to them by worrying about another free agent.

Yes, there were countless disappointments in his three-year search for a job, some heart-wrenching, but none had plunged him into such depths of humiliation as the fake job interview. Was it because it was the culmination of what had happened to him the entire day since morning? Indeed, were he a believer in witchcraft, curses, and evil spells, Kamītī would have taken what had happened to him in the morning as a sure sign that, right at the break of day, somebody had cast evil his way.

On waking up to start what he now called his day of humiliation, Kamītī had made an important decision about the way he would support himself in this cruel city. He would follow what he called Buddha's footsteps, or at least those of his followers. The best hours for this would be in the evening when it was a little dark: he did not want any of his friends or former classmates to meet him in his new occupation, however holy. He therefore set himself two tasks for daytime: continue knocking at offices for a job and also look around for the most promising premises of his new occupation of begging. Market survey, he called it.

He started his scouting mission at the Ruler's Plaza, situated in the city center. Around the plaza were some of the leading hotels, the haunts of foreign clients, particularly tourists from Europe, America, and Japan. He passed by Angel's Hotel and when he saw how crowded it was with tourists, even at that hour of the morning, he stopped, and the thought crossed his mind, Why don't I take the first step in the imitation of Buddha here and now instead of waiting for the evening hour? His eyes moved along the crowded veranda all the way to Angel's Corner, famous for its acacia bush around which were chairs and tables graced by waiters in white flowing dresses, red bandanas, and of course marching red fezzes.

It was then that his eyes fell on . . . who? Margaret Wariara? He had not seen her for more than two years, and now this! She was dressed in a miniskirt, high heels, and a brown wig. She stood holding hands with a white tourist whose hanging belly was held in place by two suspenders, waiting for the waiter to finish clearing and tidying up their table. And then Wariara turned her head and for a split second hers and Kamĩtĩ's eyes met before she resumed her previous posture by her man. Both Wariara and Kamĩtĩ knew that they had seen and recognized each other, but they acted as if their eyes had not actually met. They never exchanged a word, a look, not even an embarrassed gesture of recognition. Kamĩtĩ moved away quickly as if safari ants had suddenly bitten his legs.

He tried to make himself feel angry with her, but no matter how he tried he did not feel anger, for he could not see the difference between what he had decided to do, the Buddha way as he called it, and what she was doing at Angel's Corner—the way of the fishers of men, as she had called it in the song of farewell. But the encounter with Wariara at Angel's Corner did temper his earlier embrace of the Buddha's way, and he decided to knock at more office doors and see if one of them would open for him to enter. One lucky break after more than three years of searching was all he needed.

And indeed, moving from office to office asking the same question, is there any vacancy, was what he did the rest of the morning, until the middle of the day when hunger drove him to the foot of the garbage mountain to see if he could find some cast-off tomatoes or the remains of any other edibles. What he liked about tomatoes, pineapples, and bananas was that no matter the dirt on them he could always peel off the skin and reach the clean content. As it turned out, he did not pick up anything because that was the time he collapsed and felt himself, or rather his soul-self, disconnect from the hungry body.

The two incidents, the encounters with Wariara and then with death, were what made him desperate to get a job before he had taken a step in Buddha's way. He did not want his and Wariara's paths to ever cross again in any angel's corners in Aburĩria or anywhere else. And it was this desperation that had made him ingratiate himself with Tajirika, ending up with his drinking dregs from the cup of humiliation.

# 5

Standing by the side of the road, pressing hard against the wall, he felt all his afflictions coalesce into one, and an intense pain suddenly jolted him away from the wall and onto the road again to beg. The first step in any enterprise is the most difficult, but procrastination was not an option. The only place he had to skirt was the Ruler's Plaza, where he had seen Wariara and her new lover; otherwise it did not matter to him where to begin.

Absorbed by what had to be done, he forgot his thirst, hunger, and fatigue. He walked on determinedly, ignoring his surroundings, and paused only when he found himself near the Ruler's Square. The square was as good a starting place as any, he told himself, and headed toward a public toilet not far from a seven-star hotel. The septic system had collapsed; all the pails were overflowing with human waste. Even the floors were full of shit. Still, the public toilet would be his changing room. In one corner he found space relatively free of shit and piss and went about disguising himself. He opened his bag, took out some rags, and quickly changed. With a felt pen, he drew lines of misery on his face. In no time he had transformed himself from a respectable-looking job hunter to a dire seeker of alms.

Somewhere, bells for the evening Angelus rang, and as if by coincidence the muezzin also started calling the faithful to prayer. For a moment it was as if the two were in competition, the bells intoning *Angelus Domini* and the muezzin calling out:

> *Allahu Akba! Allahu Akbar*
> *Ash-hadu an la-llaha illa-Llah*
> *Ash-hadu anna Muhammada-r-Rasuwlu-Llah*
> *Hayya ala Swalaah*
> *Hayya alal Falaah . . .*

A good omen, he thought, perhaps the beginning of a reversal of fortune.

It was a good thing that praying and begging were not yet crimes against the state.

# 6

Paradise, where Machokali was hosting a welcome dinner for the visiting mission from the Global Bank, was one of the biggest hotels on the Ruler's Square, famous for the seven statues of the Ruler all in watchful silence, as seven fountains from the mouths of seven cherubs performed a kind of water dance in obeisance to the sculptures. Four statues stood at the corners of the square and showed the Ruler on horseback in different postures, while three at the center depicted him riding a lion, a leopard, and a tiger. The cherubs spouted jets of water into the air in turns night and day. Spots lighted the statues and fountains in the hours of mist and darkness.

One could always tell the origins of the guests at the various seven-star hotels by their different reactions to the statues and fountains: foreign guests would often stop for a minute or two to admire the dance of the fountains and comment; native dignitaries, so used to the scene, would march right through the square without so much as a glance, except when they were in the company of foreigners, in which case they would pause here and there to explain what was unique to Aburīria in the design of the statues, the placement of the fountains, and the choreography of the fountains, not forgetting the significance of the number seven. It's the Ruler's sacred number, they would say, as if imparting a secret. And the big cats? a visitor might ask. The Ruler's totems, they would say solemnly.

It was not much different tonight as guests streamed into Paradise; a few foreigners stopped and made perfunctory remarks as the native majority went straight to the reception area as if afraid of missing out on what had brought them there.

The rumor circulating in the country was that the delegates might actually be bringing a lot of cash to give to the poor; after all, it was not called the Global Bank for nothing. So in addition to invited guests who arrived in chauffeur-driven Mercedes-Benzes and others answering the call of duty, scores of others, barefooted but armed with expectations, waited outside the gates of Paradise for a share of largesse. The crowd camped outside the gates fell into three distinct groups.

The police were there to protect the visitors from any intrusion by hoodlum beggars, but they were under strict orders not to use excessive force. Visiting dignitaries should not be given the impression that Aburĩria was awash in conflicts. The image of a country at peace was crucial for wooing finance for Marching to Heaven.

The media were there in great numbers because no matter how one looked at it the entire business was news. No one had ever heard or read, even in the Global Book of Records, of a country asking for a loan for such a project, at least not in recent memory; the only comparable scheme had been in biblical times, but even then the children of Israel had been unable to complete the Tower of Babel. The media had two overriding questions: What did the delegates from the bank think about this revival of a scheme that had proved too much even for God's own chosen? Would the Global Bank come up with the money?

The third group was actually not alien to these premises. There were always beggars loitering around those kinds of hotels at all hours of day and night. But that night they were there in unusually large numbers, looking for all the world to see like wretchedness itself. The blind seemed blinder than usual, the hunchbacked hunched lower, and those missing legs or hands acted as if deprived of other limbs. The way they carried themselves was as if they thought the

Global Bank had come to appreciate and even honor their plight. So they sang, *You are the way; we are the world! Help the poor! Help the poor!* in different languages because the delegates were assumed to have come from all the corners of the globe. The beggars would occasionally push one another out of the way, but as long as they did not try to break through the cordon around Paradise the police did not interfere. Even when goaded by some, the police remained calm, at least for a while.

But when all the guests entered with "no comments," the media in the yard became visibly and increasingly restive about the state of equilibrium. News was generated by storms, not doldrums. Some started training their cameras on the beggars with their crutches and deformities. The foreign journalists were particularly interested in the scene, for they believed that a news story from Africa without pictures of people dying from wretched poverty, famine, or ethnic warfare could not possibly be interesting to their audience back home.

Almost as if in answer to the prayers of the media, a group of beggars started shouting slogans beyond the decorum of begging. Marching to Heaven Is Marching to Hell. Your Strings of Loans Are Chains of Slavery. Your Loans Are the Cause of Begging. We Beggars Beg the End of Begging. The March to Heaven Is Led by Dangerous Snakes. This last slogan was chanted over and over.

Many observers agree that the slogans would have elicited nothing more than gentle rebuke from the police but for the mention of the word *snakes,* all too reminiscent of those snakes that had disrupted the Ruler's birthday celebration. The M5 relayed the hostility of the beggars to Sikiokuu, stressing that the hoodlums had said "snakes" not once but repeatedly.

Sikiokuu had been in his office working late yet keeping his ear to the ground, hoping that something would go wrong at Paradise so he could make it look even worse. The news from M5 was not unwelcome. He recalled how the Ruler had taken him to task for not acting quickly enough to prevent the disruption of his birthday party. He was determined not to make the same mistake again. He did not even consult the Ruler. He gave the orders.

Although they had tried to be stoic and some even aspired to good humor, the police had been chafing under their order of restraint. So they were now jubilant about the business at hand. With their riot gear—clubs, shields, and guns—the police attacked the crowd.

Birds of a feather may flock together in times of peace, but when there is danger each flies alone. A miracle appeared as the beggars dispersed. Those with humps fled upright; the blind could see once again; the legless and armless recovered their limbs as they scurried from the gates of Paradise.

# 7

Two unfortunate beggars found themselves being chased by three police officers. Covered in rags from head to toe, both carried bags clutched tightly, which was their undoing, for the police had convinced themselves that the bags were full of Burĩ notes the two had been collecting all day and night; their six eyes more on the bags than on the beggars themselves. The beggars found wings.

The scent of money made the three police officers deaf to all calls to return to their ranks. One police officer shouted a promise to let them go free if they would only let loose their bags, but pointlessly. Discouraged, he gave up. But like dogs on a hot trail, the other two police officers kept up the chase as if bewitched and could not say no to their feet. They did not even realize that they had now left the well-lit streets of the city for the dimly lit Santalucia.

Santalucia was a sprawling village of tiny houses of every shape and material. Tiled roofs with walls of well-cut stone shared narrow streets with tin roofs and walls of red clay and cardboard. The sewage pipes were always clogged and there was a permanent stench in the air that was particularly nauseating on a hot day. But when the moon shone, as it did tonight, the village looked peaceful and quite attractive.

The beggar in the lead seemed to know his way around the narrow streets. The other followed closely. As for the police officers, they hoped that sooner or later the beggars would tire, enter a house, or come to a cul-de-sac. But the beggars did not oblige; they ran right through the village to the outskirts of Santalucia, the vast prairie surrounding all of Eldares.

One of the police officers was so deflated by this turn of events that he started reasoning with his crony to give up the chase. It was stupid to continue; what if they were being led to an armed den of thieves? Why risk their lives for money? But his fellow officer would have none of it, so he, too, decided to go back.

The remaining police officer seemed possessed because by now he had forgotten why he was running even as he increased his pace in a pointless pursuit of shadows of rags in the prairie.

They came to a bush and, though it was darker inside, the leading beggar, followed by the second, dashed in. The police officer did not hesitate and ran after them, only to fall down, trapped by something hard, like a stone. Soon he was up and running again through the bush, now guided only by the sound of the beggar's footsteps. Emerging from the bush he saw the outskirts of Santalucia. Were they running him in circles? Between the bush and the outskirts was an open space. The police officer could see only one beggar crossing it and reentering Santalucia. Where has the other one gone? he wondered, as the beggar he had in sight disappeared behind some houses.

The police officer ran to the corner of the street. He looked to his right and left and back, but he could not see a shadow or hear any sound. He had no way of telling where the beggar had gone. The streets of Santalucia are narrow and badly lit, and although there was moonlight, to the police officer, a stranger, the streets and the houses all looked alike. Not knowing whether he was looking for one or two beggars, the police officer wondered what to do, and for the first time since the chase began he was indecisive, but only for a moment, because a more insistent inner voice was urging him not to quit. He continued with the hunt. He would force whichever beggar he caught first to lead him to wherever the other was hiding.

By now the two beggars were ensconced in a house, crouched near a window, straining to hear the slightest sound outside. They heard the police officer's footsteps clearly but could not see him and were uncertain as to where he was.

One beggar peered through another window, and, yes, he could now see the police officer and what he was doing: his gun drawn, the policeman was going from door to door, interrogating residents. The officer stopped in front of a house where what looked like a bundle was hanging. He hesitated and moved on, and an idea came to this beggar.

"Have you got a piece of paper?" he whispered to his fellow beggar. These were the first words they had exchanged since their flight from Paradise. The beggar addressed said nothing but looked through his bag and took out a piece of paper. "No, not so small, bigger. And see if there are any bones, dry cobs of corn, rags, and a piece of string in there."

If he was surprised by the request he did not show it; he simply groped in the dark and came back and produced a cardboard, a bone, some rags, and a string, silently handing them over and continuing his watch at the window.

The other beggar tied the bones and the rags together. He then took a felt pen from his bag and wrote on the cardboard in big letters: WARNING! THIS PROPERTY BELONGS TO A WIZARD WHOSE POWER BRINGS DOWN HAWKS AND CROWS FROM THE SKY. TOUCH THIS HOUSE AT YOUR PERIL. SGD. WIZARD OF THE CROW. With great care not to make any noise, he slowly opened the door and saw something even better, a dead lizard and a frog. He added them to the bundle of bone and rags and hung the omen just above the door before quickly retreating to join the other beggar at the window.

Crouched together, the two beggars could just about make out the area around the doorway. Soon they saw the police officer walk near, anxiously wondering what he would do. Would he break the door down? But when the officer saw the bundle of rags and bones, he took a step back. He gathered courage and approached the bundle. He was about to touch it when he saw the leg of a frog and the tail of a lizard, and he was petrified. On reading what was written on the cardboard, he found his voice and let out an anguished cry: Oh, the Wizard of the Crow! He took to his heels, muttering to himself all the while: I knew they were not thieves; they were devils, djinns of the prairie, sent by the Wizard of the Crow to trick me to death. Woe unto me! I am now bewitched. Woe unto me! I am going to die! Actually, I am a dead man walking!

The two beggars were now beside themselves with laughter. One voice sounded male and the other female, but neither beggar registered the difference. The one who seemed to know his way about the house now put on the lights. The laughter stopped. The two stared at each other, not daring to trust the evidence of their eyes. When finally they spoke, their simultaneous questions collided in the air.

"Nyawĩra?"

"Kamĩtĩ?"

# 8

At Brilliant Girls High School, Nyawĩra went through a period when she really struggled with her names. There was a time when she called herself Engenethi Nyawĩra Charles Matthew Mũgwanja Wangahũ, often writing it as E.N.C.M.M. Wangahũ. She was not very keen on Engenethi and became Grace Mũgwanja. Grace Mũgwanja stuck, mostly in the village community, and she held on to it for a while. Her father liked Grace more than Engenethi, and Roithi, her mother, liked Engenethi more than Grace, and both hated Mũgwanja with equal intensity, and so to her parents she would always be either Engenethi or Grace. She herself continued struggling with these markers of identity, and after going to college she eventually settled for Nyawĩra wa Wangahũ, though there were some who could not bring themselves to call her anything but Grace Mũgwanja.

For his part, her father liked initialing his two African names, Mũgwanja and Wangahũ, to form Matthew M. W. Charles, and sometimes, leaving them out altogether, he was Matthew Charles or simply Mr. Charles. He was angry with those who called him Carũthi, the African-language version of Charles, even if prefixed with a title. He would not of course have raised any objections if they had called him Sir Charles, but in their ignorance the village folk insisted on calling him Bwana Carũthi.

Wangahũ's wealth came from timber, coffee, and tea. He had three children, two boys and the girl Nyawĩra. The boys did not do particularly well in Aburĩrian schools, and Wangahũ sent them off to America, where they enrolled in colleges to study accounting and computer science, or so they claimed. They wandered from college to college without graduating, but every year Wangahũ sent them money for tuition and room and board. Although as a parent he was concerned about their lack of progress, as a man of means he had something that would boost his already considerable standing among his peers: to pay full tuition and room and board for two in America was no easy task, and he was showing that he was indeed a man of some financial clout. He did not send Nyawĩra to America, for he did not want his daughter to marry white, though he had no such reservations for the boys. Even so, he wanted her to have a lifestyle commensurate with his class. The rich bought their sons and daughters cars jokingly referred to as toys, Japanese in contrast to all German makes, which were of course for grown men and women. Nyawĩra's was a brand-new Toyota Corolla, and early on she bought into the lifestyle. Parties, keeping up with the latest fashion, speeding on the highways, these were the chief joys of her life, and she had not stopped to look under the surface of things. In those days, the likes of Yunity Mgeuzi-Bila-Shaka and Luminous Karamu-Mbu-ya-Ituĩka were often in the news, being denounced by the Ruler for preaching revolution. She hated the very mention of these rebels: Why were they so critical of the government? And why were they in exile?

Then there was this accident. She was driving on a highway, fascinated with speed, pushing her car to its limit when it skidded and crashed on the roadside. Though she suffered minor injuries, she knew that she had narrowly escaped. What surprised her then and later when she recalled her near fatality was the number of cars that simply passed her by; no one had stopped to see if anyone was hurt or needed help. The people who hurried to her rescue were the barefooted, mostly. One unloaded his donkey cart to rush her to the nearest medical center many miles away, the donkey announcing their arrival at the emergency room by braying loudly and shitting.

During the period of recovery she learned how to play guitar. At first it was hard pressing the strings and putting the chords together, but when she started strumming and producing music, it was strangely soothing. The music contributed to her healing. It was then that she started thinking seriously about her life. If she had died, what would she have left behind as her legacy to the living? There had to be more to life than fast cars, parties, and beauty parlors. She was in her first year at Eldares University, and from then on she started taking an interest in social issues. She became active in theater and student politics and acquainted herself with the activities in exile of Yunity Mgeuzi-Bila-Shaka and Luminous Karamu-Mbu-ya-Ituĩka, who inspired her teenage imagination. She also loved the stage, and nothing made her happier than playing this or that tragic or comic role, eliciting tears or laughter from an audience. She was a brilliant actress. She could change herself into any character, sometimes so realistically that even those who thought they knew her well because of seeing her on the platforms in many student political events were often unable to say whether it was really Nyawĩra on the stage. As for history, it excited her curiosity the way a crime scene focuses a detective. History, particularly African history, was the scene of many crimes with many conflicting witnesses. Historians were detectives of time, and she loved the challenge of putting the different pieces of the puzzle together to make out the hidden shapes of things past. So, the pursuit of beau monde had given way to a search for a model society. This change in how she looked at the world is what caused a rupture in her relationship with her father.

Matthew Charles Wangahũ wanted his daughter to marry into a wealthy family so that wealth would produce more wealth, power, and social standing. Before the accident, she had seen this as natural and inevitable. But now Nyawĩra wanted to marry somebody with whom she could build a new tomorrow. At college, she met a young man of her new dreams of self-reliance.

Kaniũrũ was an artist very much involved in his art. Even if he was indifferent to student politics, he did not seem to mind her involvement. He was not one of those who forbid their girlfriends or wives to get involved in public issues or those who believed that politics and civic matters were a man's domain. What convinced her that she had found her life's mate was that Kaniũrũ did not come from a wealthy family. He told her that he was an orphan; his parents had died when he was a child, and he was brought up by a grandmother who died when he was at college. She felt for him and fell in love with her image of a self-made man.

What Grace Nyawĩra did not know was that Kaniũrũ did not share her notion of a pure and blissful union. When his eyes rested on her, they saw beyond her looks to the even more alluring looks of Wangahũ's wealth and property. Through Nyawĩra, he would rise from the depths of poverty and misery to the heaven of leisure and well-being. He kept on dreaming and looking forward to the day when he and Nyawīra would walk down the aisle; Nyawīra in white satin and he dressed to kill in a dark suit with a boutonniere. There would be ten bridesmaids and ten best men, a huge wedding ceremony with a hundred Mercedes-Benzes, bumper to bumper, shuttling dignitaries to the reception. Holding hands, he and Nyawīra would be the center of everybody's attention, gladly having to endure speech after speech from all those dignitaries, this endless prelude to that moment when he and Nyawīra would slice through a ten-layer wedding cake. Whenever Nyawīra saw the glint in his eyes, she assumed it reflected the light of desire and love, and she felt humbled by the intensity of his devotion. Nyawīra's dreams were for a simple wedding ceremony, not a display of affluence. She wanted a celebration of life, not a performance of its denial.

As for Wangahū, her father, he would have been surprised to know how close his own vision was to Kaniūrū's. But Wangahū's contempt for anybody who had not made it was so deep that even this shared vision would have struck him as presumptuousness of the poor. The thought that his own daughter would marry a man who did not even have a family was too painful to contemplate. What kind of a man is an artist? To Wangahū, drawing pictures was the work of cripples, children, and feeble women or men afraid to use their muscles; he would never see his own blood connected to such misery.

So Nyawīra and Kaniūrū put wedding rings on each other's fingers without the blessings of a grateful father, and not before a multitude but at the district commissioner's, their witnesses being a man and a woman whom they had met only a few minutes before the civil ceremony. The split between father and daughter was now complete. Wangahū kept on insisting, She has disrobed me in public, why? She has left me naked before my entire church community, why? She has turned me into a laughing stock, why? Why elope with a man so poor that he does not even have a family? How will he support her, by hawking wood carvings of giraffes and rhinos to tourists?

The estrangement between father and daughter caused tension between the newlyweds. Kaniūrū felt that the lifeline that was supposed to pull him out of his sea of troubles had been severed and Nyawīra was now the only person who had the power and the means to put things to right. No sooner had the two returned from their honeymoon than Kaniūrū started urging Nyawīra to fall on her knees and beg her father's forgiveness. Nyawīra, for her part, needed to break with her past; she yearned to make it on their own and earn respect through hard work, the simple dignity of their home, and a happy family life. Every day the newlyweds clashed. Kaniūrū continued nagging her, even after he got a job at the Ruler's Polytechnic at Eldares. He would often accuse her of ruining their lives by refusing to reconcile with her father, until one day Nyawīra exploded: Was it me you wanted to marry, or my father's money?

In the heat of the moment they rushed to the district commissioner's and filed for divorce, parting company in less than a year of failed married bliss.

Nyawīra now found herself on a new road to freedom. Kaniūrū felt he had lost his way to riches and never tired of trying to win her back.

Nyawīra started laughing as she recounted his pathetic attempts to Kamĩtĩ.

By now the two beggars were at table, enjoying a meal of *ugali* and collard greens Nyawīra had quickly prepared in the kitchen. Kamĩtĩ was inwardly grateful. He could not remember the last time he had eaten good home cooking, and it was with tremendous self-restraint that he did not gulp it all down.

The little house comprised a bedroom with a guitar hanging prominently on the wall, a sitting room, a kitchen, and a bathroom with a toilet and shower. The beggars had already washed themselves and changed, Kamĩtĩ into his job-seeking shirt and trousers and Nyawīra into a simple homely dress.

"And what does Kaniūrū do now?" he asked her.

"I believe he is still a teacher at the Ruler's Polytechnic. But you won't believe this. I hear he recently became a member of the Ruler's glorious youthwing that the Ruler talked about in his famous television address to the nation, following the incident of the snakes at the park, in an effort to attract the youth away from the propaganda of the Movement for the Voice of the People."

"A new Aburĩria, indeed," Kamĩtĩ commented. "Even a college teacher a youthwinger!"

They were silent for a while.

"And how did you end up in the streets, begging?" Kamītī asked, wondering whether she shared his desperation. Or did the divorce from Kaniūrū and the separation from her father have anything to do with it? "I would never have imagined meeting a university woman begging in the streets!"

"Weren't you just talking about a new Aburīria? If fifty-year-old university professors are becoming the Ruler's youthwingers, why can't university graduates become beggars?"

"I didn't mean university graduates in general, but women graduates. Like you, for instance."

"Does rough weather choose men over women? Does the sun beat on men, leaving women nice and cool?" Nyawīra asked rather sharply. "Women bear the brunt of poverty. What choices does a woman have in life, especially in times of misery? She can marry or live with a man. She can bear children and bring them up, and be abused by her man. Have you read Buchi Emecheta of Nigeria, *Joys of Motherhood*? Tsitsi Dangarembga of Zimbabwe, say, *Nervous Conditions*? Mariam Ba of Senegal, *So Long a Letter*? Three women from different parts of Africa, giving words to similar thoughts about the condition of women in Africa."

"I am not much of a reader of fiction," Kamītī said. "Especially novels by African women. In India such books are hard to find."

"Surely even in India there are women writers? Indian women writers?" Nyawīra pressed. "Arundhati Roy, for instance, *The God of Small Things*? Meena Alexander, *Fault Lines*? Susie Tharu. Read *Women Writing in India*. Or her other book, *We Were Making History*, about women in the struggle!"

"I have sampled the epics of Indian literature," Kamītī said, trying to redeem himself. "Mahabharata, Ramayana, and mostly Bhagavad Gita. There are a few others, what they call Purana, Rig-Veda, Upanishads . . . Not that I read everything, but . . ."

"I am sure that those epics and Puranas, even the Gita, were all written by men," Nyawīra said. "The same men who invented the caste system. When will you learn to listen to the voices of women?"

"To be very frank," Kamītī said, trying to steer the talk away from the subject of women writers, "the books that most fascinate me are those about Egypt and Ethiopia, the entire area of the Nile, the Red Sea, and the coastline. I have a theory that the coastline of the Indian

Ocean was once a cultural highway with constant migrations and exchange. There are hardly any women who write about that. I will start reading books by women writers. Perhaps you can recommend some. But you did not answer my question. What were you doing in beggars' clothes at the Ruler's Square?"

"What about you?" Nyawīra asked. "What were you doing there?"

Before Kamītī could answer, she was laughing again, as if a new thought had seized her.

"What is it?" Kamītī asked. Was her laughter at the expense of his ignorance about women writers?

"It occurred to me as you were talking about Egypt and Ethiopia . . . how did you become so knowledgeable about witchcraft and magic potions?" she managed to say in between bouts of laughter.

At the mention of his foray into magic, and remembering the look on the police officer's face, Kamītī, too, broke into hysterics.

# 9

"When we were children we used to play witchcraft. We would stick a wooden spike through a bundle of leaves, a dead frog or lizard, and one or two Sodom apples and then plant the spike in a path. From a safe distance we kept an eye on it, and what excited us most was to see adults, grown men and women, avoiding any contact with the bundle. Some would even take a step or two back, then give it a wide berth. Nobody dared touch it; there were times when the bundle remained in place, Lord knows, for days.

"Just outside the village was a big orchard of plums, pears, mangoes, oranges, tangerines, and lemons, and whenever we passed anywhere near this garden of Eden, the landowner would set his dogs on us children so that we would not steal his fruit. Some of the children did actually find a way of climbing over the fence; they would come back with their pockets bulging with fruit. Still, we did not like his chasing us with dogs on a public path, and we hated even more that he took us all to be thieves deserving of punishment whether we had stolen anything or not. One day we decided to test our witch power on our tormenter. We prepared the magic bundle in the same way but made it more potent. To the dead frogs and Sodom apples and leaves we added dead chameleons and planted the wood spike in a corner of the orchard where passersby could see it.

"Well, it did work, a bit too well for our comfort. The farmer was so terrified that he hired the services of a witch doctor to undo the power of the evil no doubt planted in his land by envious rivals. His countermeasure did not help, for people were now afraid of getting caught between two contending magics. Word spread so that whole-sale buyers and retailers from other areas refused to touch the man's fruit.

"He was saved from ruin by an Indian buyer who said that African magic was no match for Indian magic and bought the fruits at the price of damaged goods. He claimed that he was going to spend more money getting the fruits cleansed with potent potions imported directly from India.

"At first we the magic workers were happy about our success and thought that we were cleverer than the adults and all the professional witch doctors because we had fooled them all. But, thinking that our parents, who also hated the landlord, would be happy, we let them in on our triumphs. The thrashing we got removed all thoughts of our ever dabbling in witchcraft again, until tonight."

"Why did they beat you, for indulging in witchcraft or for using it to ruin the landlord?"

"Probably both; how dare children do that to an adult and a neighbor at that, but I think more for playing at witchcraft. Who knows? Even innocent deeds by babes might excite dangerous spirits from the netherworld to come and haunt the living. Whatever the case, we should have known that our parents were unlikely to say to us, Thank you for your ambition to become witch doctors."

"But thank you for your magic tonight. It saved us," Nyawĩra said. "Now tell me this," she added in a slightly more serious vein. "When did you join the band of beggars? I had not seen you in the group before."

Kamĩtĩ gobbled another mouthful of *ugali*.

"Where shall I begin?" he asked as a means of clearing the way for his story. "I come from Kĩambugi. My parents were not rich, so paying for my schooling was a burden. They had to sell off their chickens, goats, and eventually their land, thus leaving us with nothing for a rainy day. When I finished college, I thought my time had come to show my gratitude. Aburĩria thought otherwise. I have been a pest to my friends—this one for a place to spend the night, another for something to put in my belly. Borrowing here and there for bus fare."

"And Bahati? You told me you lived in Bahati!" she asked.

"I am sorry—I lied, or rather I misled you. I was playing with the word's dual meaning, suggesting a place to you, which it is. But it was really that I live wherever luck and chance guide me. Then one day I told myself, I must no longer burden my friends. I will follow in the footsteps of John the Baptist and make my bed in the wilderness. And like the homeless I would seek my sustenance in the garbage dump. At first it felt good that I no longer humiliated myself before my friends; but still, even my self-debasement was hard on the soul. If you lose self-esteem, what are you left with?

"The question nagged me, and then one day I decided that my life must take another direction, a different direction, the way of a Buddhist monk. So it was that I decided on two uniforms: that of the job seeker by day and that of the beggar by night. Tonight was my first night as a beggar, and see where it got me . . ."

Kamĩtĩ stopped abruptly. He felt that Nyawĩra was not really listening to him, and he was right. He looked at her and her eyes said it all, even as she voiced her disbelief.

"You mean you were there to beg for real?" she asked.

"Why, weren't you?" Kamĩtĩ responded, puzzled.

"You mean . . . you are not . . . not one of us?"

"How do you mean, one of you? What were you doing outside Paradise in the rags of a beggar?"

"Nothing. Nothing, really. We oppose the Ruler's birthday cake and the Global Bank mission of putting us in a permanent debt trap. We must all oppose this business of Marching to Heaven."

"By pretending to be poor and beggars?" Kamĩtĩ asked, a tinge of bitterness in his voice. "What is the connection between doing politics and donning rags? Do you think that begging is theater?"

"A theater of politics," she shot back. "The water I drink, the food I eat, the clothes I wear, the bed I sleep on, are all determined by politics, good or bad. Politics is about power and how it is used. Politics involves choosing sides in the struggle for power. So on which side are you?"

"Must one always be on this or that side? I believe in humanity, divine, indivisible. We all need to look deeply in our hearts and the humanity in us will be revealed in all its glory. Then greed and the drive to humiliate others will come to a halt."

"And this glorious humanity you wax so poetic about, what turns it against itself? Original sin?"

"Listen. I am not a priest. I am not a politician. The tribulations of this world are too much for me and my will."

"So why did you choose to stand outside the gates of Paradise when there were so many other seven-star hotels around?"

He did not respond immediately. Images of what had happened all day flashed across his mind. Tell it all to her, a stranger? No, not everything.

"I did not choose to be there," he now told her. "I just found my-self there. I was blinded with anger and hunger. I went where they led me. What happens in life is fate. Fate falls like rain from Heaven above, and like rain it does not fall on all equally. Fortune, good and bad, comes from God."

Nyawĩra interrupted him with a hymn:

> *In the Christian Heaven we shall meet*
> *We shall meet in the Christian Heaven*

She laughed a little. Kamĩtĩ looked at her: this woman was chameleon-like. One moment she was a faithful secretary, then a player in the politics of poverty, and even a singing religious fanatic.

"Are you religious?" she asked him.

"Why?"

"Because you said that the good and the bad come to us ready-made from Heaven above. Did you, when in India, convert to some religion that believes that the poor and the wealthy are born so? That their fate is predetermined? Then what would be the point of one looking into one's heart for humanity revealed in all its glory? What if what one sees is tainted? What if the taint is fated?"

"I don't know," Kamĩtĩ said vaguely.

"What do you mean, you don't know?" Nyawĩra pressed him. "How can you be religious and not know, or not know what religion you subscribe to?"

"Because . . . because . . . I don't know. Sometimes I feel overcome by unanswerable questions. Who created the universe? The lives in the bodies that die—where do they go? Or is life an illusion? *Maya,* as the Indian Shankara would teach. Sometimes at night, alone in the wilderness, lying on my back, looking at the stars and the vast universe, I feel lifted out . . . I mean, I hear voices telling me, Kamĩtĩ, why do you burden yourself with so much worry? See how big the universe is? What are you in the face of its immensity and eternity? No, I would not say that I am religious, but I believe in something greater than us. And you?"

"Have you ever heard of the Animal of the Earth?" Nyawĩra asked him suddenly. "Surely you've heard the rumor that the Ruler of Aburĩria is a Devil worshipper and that he does so in the name of the Animal of the Earth?"

Kamĩtĩ sensed rather than knew clearly what she was talking about, but it was enough to raise in him new suspicions. Could this woman be a member of the dreaded Ruler's M5? And would that not explain why she had impersonated a beggar? Was he the victim of a new plot? Had she been trying to compromise him? If so, she was good at it. Her talk and kindness had already softened him. For although they did not see eye to eye on all the issues, their disagreements had so far not degenerated into anger or hatred. They talked as if they had grown up together, knowing each other in times of sorrow and happiness. Kamĩtĩ was so at ease in her presence that he felt as if he could reveal his innermost thoughts and experiences. But weren't the agents of the State renowned for seducing their victims into lowering their guards, and then pouncing on them? Kamĩtĩ became wary of Nyawĩra and withdrew into himself.

"What do you mean by Animal of the Earth?"

"That which crawls on its belly?"

"I don't know what you are talking about."

"The one that deceived Adam and Eve?" Nyawĩra continued as she rose and went to her own beggar's bag and bent over it. Kamĩtĩ was quite sure that he saw her take something out, which she now held behind her as she stood facing him.

"Close your eyes," she said, smiling.

Kamĩtĩ pretended to cover his eyes with the palms of his hands while peeking through the gaps between his fingers.

"Look now!" Nyawĩra told him, dangling what she had been holding a few inches from his face. Kamĩtĩ jumped from his seat.

"A snake!" he cried, bolting for the door.

But Nyawĩra beat him to it.

"No, I will not let you go," she said, brandishing the fork-tongued snake at him. "It is a viper. Very dangerous," she whispered menacingly.

# 10

When growing up Kamĩtĩ used to hear stories of women who lived in the big waters who would sometimes appear alongside unsuspecting male swimmers and accompany them to the edges of the sea. Their faces were very beautiful, their swimming tops hung delicately over the tips of their pointed breasts, and their narrow waists seemed to be inviting the onlooker to embrace them.

Standing on the shore, one could often spot them in the middle of the sea, astride the crests of the waves, splashing water on every side, racing one another to an unknown destination. Sometimes they would whistle the softest of tunes in the ears of male swimmers, and not many such men, especially when alone, could resist the power of the wordless songs. There were frightening stories of some who had followed these water-women all the way to their lairs under the sea, only to discover that the women had no feet, or rather that their lower body comprised a fishtail with scales big enough to cut a person into a thousand pieces. A few were lucky and escaped, but there were many others who were lost forever, victims of the alluring power of the female riders of the sea.

There were other stories of other women who had the power to change themselves into whatever form they chose, gazelles, antelopes, but mostly cats. Many a young man had gone for a walk at twilight holding hands with the woman of his dreams, waiting for darkness to fall to satisfy his desire, only to find himself staring at the glowing eyes of a cat.

Was Nyawīra one of these women of his childhood fears? Different images of her flashed across his mind. In the office, she is a secretary, on the roadside, a comforter. In the evening, she is a beggar among beggars. Later, in the prairie, she effortlessly outruns him and three police officers. Now she was blocking his escape, dangling a fork-tongued snake in front of him? Come to think of it, when telling stories, she had constantly been changing her voice in her mimicking of various characters. The number of times she had changed her name hinted at something! Had she not walked away from a car accident unscathed? And the bit about the donkey braying at the clinic . . . there was something about her that did not add up.

A mixture of fear, frustration, and curiosity rooted him. He had always been terrified of snakes; the mention of them made his body quiver. She had said this one was poisonous. A bite on the nose or the eye would surely mean his end. What a day! What a night! The day had seen him narrowly escape burial in a dumpsite, but the night would see his life end with a snakebite! He feared what would transpire next. Would she change into an antelope, a gazelle of the prairie, or a cat? Or the mermaid that she was? She seemed indeed human, but with these women one could not be sure. What was a water-woman doing on land, anyway? He looked at her eyes and light danced in them. No, she was trying to hypnotize him, to distract his eyes from the snake.

His eyes focused on the snake, he started moving backward, slowly, the water-woman following him step by step and in rhythm as in a choreographed dance. Even when he entered her bedroom, Kamītī did not see the bed in the middle, riveted as he was by the impending danger. Her mission, his death by snakebite, accomplished, she would turn into a bird and fly away to trap some other unsuspecting male or return to the sea to tell her water-sisters about her wicked triumph.

Kamītī felt defiant. Even a bull in a slaughterhouse resists to the last; he refused to be a helpless victim. He pounced on Nyawīra.

They wrestled on the floor as Kamītī reached for the hand that held the snake to pin it down. Nyawĩra was too quick for him; she slipped his grip and grabbed his shirt as he tugged at her dress. Soon they were both half naked, pausing to stare at each other with mutual fascination. Kamĩtĩ had never seen a neck so long, so beautiful. Her eyes still shone brightly, like those of a cat at night. He looked for the snake on the ground, only to see it lying inert.

"Oh, that! It is a plastic snake," she said chuckling.

Kamĩtĩ did not grasp the import of her words; he was transfixed on Nyawĩra, her long gazelle neck, her shapely breasts so full, her nipples, the color of blackberry, so erect, the light in her eyes animating her. It was only after a second or two that the meaning of what she had said dawned on him.

"A plastic snake?" he asked, relief embedded in disbelief.

"Yes," she said, and laughed again.

His relief was superseded by anger. Nyawĩra sensed this and tried to slink away from his rage. He strode after her as if intent on strangling her or something. In silence, they circled each other, Kamĩtĩ trying to catch her, she just managing to slip away. Then suddenly he flew toward her and they fell on the bed. They were tremulous amid the rustling of clothes. Their lips met.

Kamĩtĩ had not been with a woman since that disastrous morning with Wariara. The act had left distaste in him, diminishing his desire. He had not felt deprived during his time of abstinence. But now he knew that something important had been missing in his life. Nyawĩra was in a similar position. Her relationship with Kaniũrũ had soured her on love, and she had not taken up with any other man. Now they felt themselves drawn to each other by a power they could not resist.

"Slowly and gently, young man," Nyawĩra told him. "Some men rush as if they are late for an appointment. A woman is not a service station."

She guided his hands to her nipples, down to her thighs, his touch forcing her to sigh and groan. They were now ready to move to the next step.

"Put it on now," Nyawĩra told him.

"What?" he said in a daze.

"Don't you have a condom?"

"Condom? Oh, no!" he said.

It was as if some red ants had bitten Nyawĩra, for she suddenly threw him off, jumped up, and sat on the bed.

"What have I done wrong?" Kamĩtĩ asked, baffled.

"Wrong? Did I hear you right?" Nyawĩra asked, full of fury. "You would enter me without protection?"

"I have not carried condoms with me for a while. I assumed that you were on the pill or something . . ."

"Do you think that pregnancy is the worst that can happen to a woman? Pregnancy is not a malignance. It is only a problem when people are not prepared to shoulder the responsibility of bringing a child into the world. Don't you know about the virus? Pregnancy is life. The virus means death."

"I don't have the virus!"

"How do you know? And even if you know about yourself, how do you know that I am not carrying AIDS, syphilis, gonorrhea, or any other STD?"

Discomfort had now replaced desire. Kamĩtĩ went to take a cold shower to cool his body. Nyawĩra waited for him to finish and followed suit. Both clothed once again, Kamĩtĩ, in a shirt without buttons, went back to the sitting room, and Nyawĩra, in a fresh dress, went to the kitchen.

Kamĩtĩ's mind drifted to life with Wariara. They had never talked about their sex lives before meeting each other; he was surprised by how little he knew about that aspect of her. Recalling their encounter at the Angel's Corner earlier in the day, he felt uncomfortable in his own body. What if he had caught a virus from their sole intimate encounter and had been about to pass it on to . . . no, he did not want to think about his possible carelessness. He was grateful to Nyawĩra for having put a halt to things, even more so now that she interrupted his thoughts by offering him some tea.

"I'm sorry," he told Nyawĩra. "I should not have lost it that way. I have never been so drawn to anyone. Usually I prefer to get to know someone better before this kind of thing happens. But something about you makes me feel that we have always known each other. Maybe it has something to do with our shared experiences today. But I want you to know that I am not trying to excuse my behavior."

"I am sorry, too. In college I always kept a couple of condoms in my handbag, because even then I believed that people who do not know each other well should protect themselves; because you can never tell who is carrying death into the act of love. When I got married, I stopped; and even after the marriage ended, I continued with the bad habit of not arming myself. But now I should have known better, for nobody knows when she or he might be in a situation where the body overpowers the will. If a person refuses to wear a condom in these days of the deadly virus and he still wants to go the distance, he is my enemy, not my lovemate, and I should not let him touch me. That is why I threw you off, because I thought you were one of those men who think it unmanly to wear condoms."

"I can hardly criticize you."

They were now relaxed with each other.

"What was the plastic snake all about?" Kamĩtĩ asked in a new key.

"You really thought that it was alive?"

"It seemed lifelike, its eyes roving, its tongue flexing. I am terrified of snakes. I hate practical jokes involving snakes."

Nyawĩra looked hard at his face. No, she and Kamĩtĩ were not of the same mind; they had arrived at the gates of Paradise by different routes. All they shared were the beggar's rags they wore. Nothing more. And yet to her he had a good heart. He had grown up poor; he could be one of her party. Then she recalled that Kaniũrũ, in spite of his humble background, was now a member of the Ruler's Youth, protecting the rich against the poor. She checked herself. Kamĩtĩ might turn out to be another Kaniũrũ. Besides, he seemed a loner, the type only drawn by the desires of the spirit.

"These days, no woman is safe walking the streets alone. I carry the snake to help me get out of dangerous situations."

"No, Nyawĩra, you are holding something back," he said.

"Do you really want to know?" she asked with a bit more passion.

Kamĩtĩ felt pulled in opposite directions: he wanted to know, and he did not; he did not feel that he had the will to endure the weight of knowing and the agony of choice. Was certain indeterminacy not better?

Nyawĩra saw the hesitation in his face and said to herself: This one is scared. She looked at her watch.

"It is almost dawn. You won't have to go to the wilderness. Sleep on the couch. I'll give you a blanket."

As she headed toward the bedroom, Kamĩtĩ persisted despite his fears.

"But you did not really answer my question."

Nyawĩra stopped and turned her head.

"You know the Movement for the Voice of the People?"

By instinct, Kamĩtĩ quickly looked over his shoulder before answering.

"I don't, but you mentioned it. Didn't the Ruler declare it illegal?"

"Yes," she said, not sure what to make of his skittishness.

"What is the story?" Kamĩtĩ asked, not too enthusiastically.

"There are two kinds of saviors: those who want to soothe the souls of the suffering and those who want to heal the sores on the flesh of the suffering. Sometimes I wonder which is right. Sleep well. The couch may not be as comfortable as your leaves of grass, but there is a roof over it," she said lightly.

"But what does the movement stand for? Who are its members? Its leaders?"

"Someday I'll tell you more," she said, wondering about his sudden desire for details. She went to the bedroom, from where she now threw him a blanket.

The guitar from the wall had been disturbed by their play earlier. She adjusted it before climbing into bed.

Kamĩtĩ sighed with relief, but relief from what? He was unable to fall asleep; he kept turning over in his mind the events of the last twenty-four hours. As in a dream, he didn't know where he was headed, he thought, yawning from fatigue.

There was banging at the door. Kamĩtĩ, who had fallen asleep, was tied to his bed of dreams by a thousand strands of rainbow colors. Who was waking him in his flower garden? Ah, yes, Paradise. A million-star hotel, with a boundless sky as its roof. Oh yes, he thought, a hailstorm must be kissing the gates of Paradise. How soothing. But the knocking at the door persisted, and Kamĩtĩ woke up.

He tiptoed to Nyawĩra's bed and woke her up. They both listened, hoping that the intermittent knocking would cease. It didn't, and Nyawĩra put on a shawl and went to the door.

She hesitated as she opened it.

"Don't be afraid, mother," the man said, quickly taking something from his pocket and showing it to her. "I have not come to rob you. I am just a plainclothes police officer."

"What do you want?" Nyawīra asked gruffly, trying to hide her panic.

"I beg you, please don't be angry. I am the police officer who was here last night. Well not here, exactly—I mean, I happened to be in Santalucia last night, and in passing I saw something hanging from the wall. When I went home, well, I thought about it. True, *Haki ya Mungu.* I tell you, I hardly slept trying to figure things out. So I came to the conclusion, perhaps, then the doubt, how shall I know the house? But I gathered my courage and came here before dawn, and imagine my relief when I found the thing still there. And I said to myself, you are in the right place."

Chagrined, Nyawīra remembered the bundle of make-believe witchcraft hanging from the roof outside. How careless of them not to have taken it down! The magic that had sent the police officer away had led him back to the house, though now he seemed unarmed. She became a little defiant within: So what if he has found us? What could he arrest us for? What crime have we committed? Then she recalled that the dictator of Aburīria had decreed that the Movement for the Voice of the People was illegal. She resolved to remain calm and scrutinize the words of the police officer for anything that might be useful.

"What do you want?" she asked imperiously.

The police officer winced at her tone. He kept looking over his shoulder as if ready to bolt at the first hint of danger. Yet he seemed determined, almost desperate, to unburden himself of something.

"My name is Constable Arigaigai Gathere. I have many matters that weigh heavily on me. Please, mother, I want—please—I would like to see you."

"Me? You want to see me?" she asked, quite puzzled by all this.

"Yes, you. No, yes, true! *Haki ya Mungu*, Wizard. I would like to see you. Sorry, I mean, I need to see the Wizard of the Crow."

# 11

Later, after his own life had taken twists and turns defying all rational explanation even for him, a trained police officer, Constable Arigaigai Gathere always found himself surrounded by crowds wanting to hear story after story about the Wizard of the Crow. It was then that people started calling him fondly by his initials, A.G., some listeners allowing that they stood for "attorney general of storytelling." If his storytelling took place in a bar, it was fueled to new heights of imagination by an endless supply of liquor. When the setting was a village, a market-place, or the crossroads, Constable Arigaigai Gathere felt charged with energy on seeing the rapt faces of the men, women, and children waiting to catch his every word. But whatever the setting, his listen-ers came away with food of the spirit: resilient hope that no matter how intolerable things seemed, a change for the better was always possible. For if a mere mortal like the Wizard of the Crow could change himself into any form of being, nothing could resist the human will to change.

"And when I talk of him changing himself into anything," he would stress, "I am not passing on hearsay. True, *Haki ya Mungu*. I talk of what I saw with my own eyes."

The story they came to hear over and over again was about the night A.G. chased two beggars from the gates of Paradise. At first A.G. used to say that he was with two other police officers, but in the course of the telling and retelling of the story, they disappeared from his narrative.

"Yes, it all began outside Paradise, where we had been sent to make sure that the visitors from the Global Bank would not be harassed by the crowd of beggars. Early on, the beggars were orderly, but when they started shouting words I would never let pass my mouth, we received orders from on high to silence and disperse them. It was in the evening, I remember. I saw a man in rags look at me with eyes burning brighter than those of a tiger in the dark. I felt his eyes forcing me to follow him as he moved away. I tried to tell him to stop but was dumbstruck. What was even more amazing was that he was not running. True, *Haki ya Mungu.* The man just strolled swinging a big bag he was carrying; yet no matter how hard I ran after him, the distance between us remained the same.

"It seemed to me that the man was not alone; there was another walking beside him, guiding him through the dark. How do I explain? Now I see one. Now I see two.

"When I tried to stop and take stock of the situation, I found that I could not slow down. True, *Haki ya Mungu,* and eventually I found myself in the prairie. Don't ask me how I got there—to this day I don't know. There was moonlight, all right, but clouds would get in the way; it was as if the heavens were conspiring with him to play games of light and shadows with me. He made me run around in circles the whole time. Then I saw him go through some bush and I followed him. It was dark in the thick growth. I tripped over something and fell. It was a rock cleft in two. I got back up and resumed running. Only when I reached the other side of the bush did I realize that I was near Santalucia. Between the edge of the bush and where the houses begin was an empty space, and as the man crossed it I saw that what I had taken to be two was actually one. And yet I could have sworn that I had seen two persons! No sooner had I blinked than the man was gone. As there was no gap in the hedge, I could not tell how he got through."

"You mean to tell us that you did not even see him jump over the hedge?" some would ask him.

"No. I didn't. True, *Haki ya Mungu.*"

"Maybe he turned himself into a hedge," another would suggest.

"Yes. You have said it."

"And what did you do, quit?"

"Me, quit? Oh, no. I decided to look for him everywhere."

"A.G. You are brave, man! Me? Had I had ten guns in each hand, I still would not have taken another step."

"I confess that I don't lack courage. I looked for a way into Santalucia. Now, you know that Santalucia houses are dense and they all look alike. The streets are narrow. The lighting is poor. Now imagine me. I am holding my gun firmly in my hand. I try this house. I try another. Police. Open the door. People looked at me with fright and dry mouths. Then I said to myself, This isn't working. I should go from door to door, eavesdrop and peer through cracks in the walls, demand that the owners open up only if I see or hear something suspicious. I put my new plan into action. And then, how shall I tell it? Suddenly I felt a force take ahold of me, turn me around, and compel me to look at it. One glance at the thing hanging from the roof and I knew that I was facing powerful magic. Approaching it, I saw some letters jump from the wall toward me: WARNING! THIS PROPERTY BELONGS TO THE WIZARD WHOSE POWERS CAN BRING DOWN EVEN CROWS FROM THE SKY. TOUCH THIS DOOR AT YOUR PERIL. SGD. WIZARD OF THE CROW. Then the letters retreated into the wall. Foolish me. I was about to touch the thing when I felt hands I could not see lifting me up. They swung me in the air and dropped me to the ground, again and again. Seven times. When I was released, I fled and did not once look back . . ."

"And your gun?" somebody would ask. "How come it did not fall?"

"That, in fact, was an issue that would not let me sleep, for, true! *Haki ya Mungu*, I lay awake, turning the matter over and over in my mind. I was lifted up and felled seven times, but why did I not sustain even a scratch? A little pain in the butt, maybe, but nothing worse. And how did my gun stay in my hand? Yes, I talked to myself: Constable Arigaigai Gathere, why do you think the man chose you and forced you to follow him to the magic? What was he trying to tell you? For a long time, I had had many problems weighing on me, even more so in the weeks before this fateful encounter. All at once I saw the light. A sign. The whole thing was a sign that pointed to he who could solve my problems.

"That was why early in the morning I went back to the house of magic. Fortunately the bundle and the writing on the wall were still there. He opened the door for me. And do you know? Listen to this. The man appeared to me in the form of a very beautiful woman. At first he/she asked me questions in a soft voice, then all of a sudden a voice boomed from the back of his/her head.

"'I am the Wizard of the Crow. Who is that standing in the shadow of my magic? How dare you break my circle of magic? Go, clean those feet first before . . .'

"I did not wait to hear more. For a second time I fled for my life."

# 12

Even Nyawīra at first was surprised by the booming voice. But when she saw the police officer wince, stand at attention, salute, and then take to his heels, she recalled what the same police officer had done earlier that night, and doubled with laughter.

"Has he gone?" Kamītī asked.

"He sped away like an arrow. How did you think that up so quickly?"

"I don't really know. I was buying time for us to work out a common story. But I blundered a little!"

"How?"

"I gave him the choice to return or not. I should have told him never to come back, or else, or words to that effect."

"The way he took off does not support a person eager to return here anytime soon."

Nyawīra went to the kitchen and made tea and scrambled eggs with bread. She put hers to the side to cool while she got ready to go to work. She was eager to hear what Tajirika had to say about the Global Bank dinner party and the gathering of beggars outside the gates of Paradise.

Nyawīra's preparations jolted Kamītī out of his fear of the police. His jaws cupped in his hands, he ignored breakfast and brooded about his personal woes. It was as if he had dreamt that he had eaten a homemade meal, slept on a comfortable couch, and woken up to a bountiful breakfast in the company of laughter and warmth, and suddenly the dream had ended. He was engulfed in a simple if brutal reality. It was very early in the morning and he had no clue as to what to do or where to begin his daily search for a job.

Now ready, Nyawīra went back to the kitchen for her breakfast. Between the kitchen and the living room was a small window through which plates, pans, or cups could be passed from one room to the other. She opened the window and spoke to Kamītī through the opening.

"Your breakfast is getting cold," she said. "Shall I warm it up for you?"

"No, thank you. I will take it as is," he said, glancing quickly at her.

From where she stood, Nyawĩra could see him sitting, his head bowed.

"I am going to the office to hear all about the goings-on in Paradise," she said, trying to disrupt his dejection. "What about you?"

"I have no plans. May I stay here a few more hours before setting out? It's too early for me to cope with another Tajirika-type interview. I might be tempted to wring his neck," he said, trying to match her lighthearted tone.

"And end up strung up for murder? I will not allow that," she said in the same tone. "If staying here for a few more hours might save your life, imagine what a whole day here can do for you! Seriously, why don't you take a day off? You're welcome to the couch for one more night."

"No, a few hours will do. But thank you for the offer. I shall never forget your kindness," he said with a slightly teary voice.

"It's not much," she said. "Didn't you say that luck, bad or good, comes from God? Thank God, not me," she said, trying to steer him from self-pity.

"God works in mysterious ways, His wonders to perform," Kamĩtĩ said, again trying to match her lightness of tone. "He used you as His vehicle to help me. So I am grateful to you for being a willing vehicle of His will. Who knows, I might one day turn up in the offices of Eldares Modern Construction and Real Estate."

"For another interview?" she shot back, with an amused look.

"No! No! To take you up on your lunch offer. I love fish and chips. Or chicken and chips."

"You will be most welcome. I sincerely hope you land a job," Nyawĩra said, turning serious as she picked up her handbag.

At the door, she turned to look back at him.

"Don't forget to take down your bundle of magic, unless you want to continue advertising that here dwelt, for one night, the mighty wizard whose power brought down all birds, even crows, from the sky!"

# 13

By the time Nyawĩra reached the premises of Eldares Modern Construction and Real Estate, her boss, Titus Tajirika, was already there. Her office, which also served as reception, adjoined his, and before taking her place she went to announce her arrival to him. Tajirika was engrossed in the *Eldares Times,* so she stood awkwardly at the doorway, wondering if she should clear her throat to attract his attention. She could tell that he was angry, obviously not with her but with what he was reading. Tajirika was in fact aware of her presence and soon began to unburden himself.

"These beggars are just too much," he started telling Nyawĩra, who was relieved that he did not ask her why she was late. "I don't know what should be done with them. How dare they stretch out their hands at the very same place where their own government was . . ." He was going to say "stretching out its hands" but he did not like the sound of it, and checked himself. ". . . busy entertaining very important guests?"

"I have not seen the papers," Nyawĩra said. "What happened?"

"Well, we the hosts and guests were inside Paradise, so we did not actually hear the commotion outside. In fact, if it were not for these newspapers—why for goodness' sake did this paper feel it necessary to mention anything about those rioting beggars, giving them publicity for nothing?" He held the paper in his left hand and pointed at the offending column with his right, his face twisted in disgust and contemptuous incomprehension.

Nyawĩra craned her neck and saw the banner headlines: BEGGARS IN PARADISE. She also caught a glimpse of the picture of beggars running away just a few yards ahead of baton-wielding police officers but did not want to show an undue interest by moving closer to the table. As Tajirika was talking, she did not want to interrupt him.

"That is why I have always said that the government should ban all newspapers. We can do without them. Before the colonials came to this land, didn't our ancestors live to a ripe old age without ever reading a newspaper? They are a curse, these newspapers, but if I was asked what was at the root of last night's fracas, I would answer with one word: envy. Those beggars must have been sent there by our political enemies to blemish the reception. Do you know that there are ministers who are very envious of my friend Machokali simply because he is a man who can see far? Let me tell you what is wrong with us black people. Unlike Indians and Europeans, we lack group solidarity. We hate to see one of us succeed."

Nyawīra thought that this was the perfect moment to milk information.

"Did the Bank agree to bankroll Marching to Heaven?" she asked.

Her sympathetic curiosity touched him, and he responded with an alacrity that surprised her.

"Why are you standing? Pull up a chair and sit down."

Tajirika sat up, ready to pour out everything about the reception in detail, especially his own role in it. Their interest in his narrative was mutual, and the telephone, which rang at that very moment, irritated both. Nyawīra made as if to go and take the call in her office, but Tajirika, not wanting to lose his audience for a second, told her to answer the phone from his desk.

"Eldares Modern Construction and Real Estate. May I help you? . . . Yes . . . But may I please know who is calling? . . . Your name? . . . Hold, please . . . Let me see if he is in." She covered the mouthpiece. "It's for you."

"Who is it?"

"He is not saying. He wants to speak to you personally, and he says it's urgent."

Tajirika grumpily snatched the handset, annoyed by the interference. "Congratulations? For what? . . . *Today?*" he asked, his sourness gone as he stood up and walked away from the chair while holding the phone to his ear. "On the radio? . . . The morning news? . . . Are you sure? . . . I think we'd better not talk about that on the telephone . . . Yes . . . Yes . . . Why don't you come to the office? . . . Yes . . . We shall talk."

As soon as he put the phone down it rang again; this time he himself quickly picked it up.

"Yes . . . Thank you . . . Come to the office."

It rang a third, a fourth, and a fifth time, and he gave the same response: Come to the office. He glanced at the window and walked toward it, whistling and beckoning Nyawīra to join him there.

She staggered at what she saw. The road leading to their place of business was jammed with cars, the latest models of all makes, but mostly Mercedes-Benzes.

"What is this all about?" Nyawīra exclaimed, looking directly at Tajirika.

Rapt in thought, Tajirika paced the office, then stopped, looked at Nyawīra, and, in a somewhat tremulous voice, said, "This is one of the greatest days of my life, if not the greatest ever. You might think of it as the day I was born again. This morning Minister Machokali announced that he has recommended and the Ruler himself has agreed that I should become the first chairman of the Marching to Heaven Building Committee. Do you know what that means? You don't, I can see it in your face, but those people you see in those cars all know the meaning and financial implications of that position. Every one of them wants to introduce himself to me—*make my acquaintance* is the phrase they will all use. But, as you can see, most of them did not even bother to call—they came immediately. I am sharing this with you because since you joined my firm you have brought me nothing but luck. Oh, no, not another call of congratulations! No. Just let the phone ring. I want you to go to your office, receive the visitors, and show them to my office one by one. Keep answering the telephone and making appointments *in the usual way. This is manna from Heaven,*" he said in English, as if loudly talking to himself.

Nyawīra hurried back to her office as Tajirika, sitting at his desk, struck the pose of an executive immersed in paperwork. Soon the reception area was packed, with an even bigger crowd outside trying to get in. And the telephone kept ringing. Nearly overwhelmed, she quickly worked out a solution. She wrote on two pieces of paper MAKE A QUEUE: NO SERVICE FOR THOSE NOT IN THE QUEUE. She pasted one on the wall inside and the other on the outside.

The people pushed and shoved, hurling insults at one another as each tried to move up the queue, like children, Nyawīra thought, and all this for the sake of an introduction to the chairman? The dignitaries, all from Eldares itself, were of different communities, nationalities, races, and each wanted to meet with Tajirika face-to-face, and alone. Nyawīra let them into Tajirika's office, one at a time.

The first dignitary stayed for only a few minutes, but he must have had his needs met, because when he came out he was beaming. It was the same with the second, third, fourth, fifth, and so on. A few minutes with the chairman, and they all seemed in possession of a little happiness as they returned to their Mercedes-Benzes. Tajirika the sharer of happiness with all who came to see him! How was that possible, Nyawīra wondered.

Nyawīra, who had been ushering visitors into Tajirika's office, taking down names, arranging files, and answering calls, was soon able to figure out what was happening. Each one was pitching business as a subcontractor for Marching to Heaven and hoped to be looked upon favorably. Whether they offered to supply cement, wood, nails, toilet paper, food, or drinks, they talked and behaved as if they knew for sure that the Global Bank had released the money for the project.

Tajirika was frank, impressing upon them that the matter of the loans had not yet been discussed with the Global Bank; that the reception at Paradise was purely social; and that, in any case, no contracts would be given until far into the future. But they would hear none of it. For them it was a matter of simple logic: why would Minister Machokali appoint and release the name of the chairman of the Building Committee unless he was reasonably sure that the Global Bank would release the money? Some of them had read of the billions upon billions that the Bank had loaned Russia as a bribe to abandon socialism for good. How much more was to be had by a country whose leadership had neither dreamt of democracy nor experimented with socialist nonsense? No wonder they left their visiting cards.

Each card was handed over with thousands of Burīs. A few dignitaries had tried to write checks, but Tajirika would not hear of it. Cash or nothing, Tajirika told them, and they were quick to say that they completely understood. A few insisted on a business luncheon appointment, adding even more Burīs with their cards. None so much as whispered about the money left behind. All they would say, even to their closest friends, was that they had been to see the chairman and had left their visiting cards. The money had piled up so quickly that, with his desk drawers stuffed, Tajirika was forced to send Nyawīra to buy sacks and cartons for the rest of his abundance.

By four o'clock the queue had diminished but the telephone was still ringing with calls from dignitaries mainly living outside Eldares who also wanted appointments to see the chairman. Nyawĩra knew, by the volume of appointments, that in the coming days she surely would not be able to handle all the work by herself. At the close of business, when the last man in the queue had left, Nyawĩra acquainted her boss with her problem.

"Don't worry," Tajirika told her, happy at the news, for it meant more visiting cards and attendant money. "Remove the No Vacancy sign at the road and put up another one announcing that we are hiring temporary help. Something like 'Tempa Jobs Available.' Or just 'Tempa Jobs.' That's what we do when the volume of work increases, but it has never been like this. And Nyawĩra, after you put up the sign, call it a day. Go home and I will see you tomorrow. Try not to be late," he added, to let her know that nothing escaped his notice. "Tomorrow every minute will count!"

Nyawĩra spotted, in one corner of the room, three sacks full of Burĩs. The boss had been right, this was truly manna from Heaven, she told herself as she left. She went into a small storage room adjoining the reception area and took out a big piece of plywood to serve as a billboard, but it was quite big and heavy. She thought it better to leave her handbag on her desk and come back for it after she had posted the advertisement.

It was about five. She walked down the main entrance by the road. Looking upon the old board announcing NO VACANCY: FOR JOBS COME TOMORROW, she recalled what had happened to Kamĩtĩ, the deliberate humiliation. She was so angry that her hands shook and the new board fell to the ground. Anger gave way to a spurt of energy. She pulled the old board out and tossed it aside. With a sense of triumph, she replaced it with the new. As Nyawĩra stood back to survey her work, she felt a presence behind her.

"John!" Nyawĩra cried out, startled.

Kaniũrũ stood a few feet from the new board, almost on the same spot Kamĩtĩ had stood the day before, pondering his humiliation. Kaniũrũ read the new ad aloud: TEMPA JOBS: APPLY IN PERSON!

"What are you doing here?" she asked him.

"Let's go for coffee at Mars Café," he said.

"I don't like coffee," she said.

"Have tea, a milk shake, soda. Anything. I have some news for you."

"I can read newspapers for myself. I listen to the radio."

"This is no ordinary news. It's something you ought to know."

Nyawīra turned the matter over in her mind, though she tried her best to seem uninterested in whatever Kaniūrū had to tell her. She yawned and sighed as if reluctantly giving in to his pestering.

"Okay. I'll be right back," she said. "In fact, I'll meet you at Mars."

She headed back to the office, carrying the old signboard to put it back in storage.

The door was locked. She dug into one of her pockets and fetched the keys. She opened the door and froze in terror. She was dumbstruck as she stood staring at a gun pointed at her. She closed her eyes, awaiting the worst.

"Oh, it's you?" Tajirika said, moving the gun away from her. "I thought someone was trying to break in. I thought I told you to go home?"

"My handbag," she said in a trembling voice. "I have just finished putting up the new sign," she added in a daze, pointing at the old signboard. "I was returning for my handbag."

"Good. Help me carry some sisal bags to my car."

The bags, packed tight with Burī banknotes, were heavy. Tajirika dragged two and Nyawīra one to the boot of his cream-colored Mercedes-Benz.

She watched the car merge with others along the road before disappearing altogether. Then the reality of what might have been struck her with full force. She sat down, weak at the knees, to recover her composure before going to meet Kaniūrū at the Mars Café.

# 14

The Mars Café was well known in Eldares for its low-priced but quality offerings of tea, coffee, cocoa, milk shakes, ice cream, breads, cakes, sandwiches, and soft drinks. Many people used it as a rendezvous because its owner, who went by the name Gautama, did not seem to mind customers sitting and talking for long stretches after consuming what they had ordered. But the café was probably better known for its celebration of space exploration through the decorations on the walls and Gautama's dedicated vivacity.

Over the years, the café's name had changed to reflect landmark moments. It had variously been called Sputnik, Vostok, and Moonapollo. Gautama especially liked Moonapollo because it not only alluded to a Greek deity but also rhymed with Marco Polo, who had sojourned to the Orient, where space voyages were first imagined in folklore. He often cited, as proof of the Asian origin of the space race, ancient Chinese astronomers who were among the first to focus on supernova. But he moved on to Mir Café and the International Space Station Café before settling on Mars Café, which he vowed to keep until humans landed on Mars, for he believed that the Red Planet held the secrets of the origins of life and the universe. He wanted the name of the café to reflect the eternal human quest for truth, freedom, and knowledge. So its walls were papered with newspaper and magazine cuttings featuring not only rockets and other spacecraft and stations but also space travelers. So Yuri Gagarin and Aleksei Leonov could be found side by side with Neil Armstrong and John Glenn and so on.

But though he always looked dreamy when talking about space, Gautama was very down to earth in his café and was attentive to his customers. He now watched Kaniũrũ enter alone, and he hoped to engage him in small talk about the universe. But when Kaniũrũ told him that he would wait to place his order until his guest arrived, Gautama retreated to the counter and his mental wanderings. Kaniũrũ kept looking at his watch, wondering if once again Nyawĩra had given him the slip. He planned to wait a few more minutes before leaving and would most likely go to her office the next day to ask her why she had stood him up. He felt calmer about having an excuse to visit Nyawĩra's workplace and inspect Tajirika's properties.

Just then somebody touched him on the shoulder, and, thinking that it was Nyawĩra, Kaniũrũ turned around quickly. His beaming face turned ugly when he saw that it was yet another beggar. He became even more irritated when he saw that the man was crippled. Upon hearing his chant, *Help the poor, these legs were broken during the war of independence,* Kaniũrũ lost his patience altogether. He pushed the cripple away and screamed at him, Go away! How dare you touch me with your filthy fingers! He yelled at the poor beggar so incessantly that Gautama, forced out of his spaciness by the commotion, interceded on behalf of the intruder. Gautama gave him a few coins, asked him not to disturb his customers, and guided him to the door.

"I just want a cup of tea and a piece of cake," Nyawīra shouted to Gautama as she walked in and sat at the table. "Why did you want us to meet?" she asked brusquely.

"I was passing by and I thought I would drop in on you," Kaniŭrŭ told her, and by the look on her face he knew that she knew that he was not telling the truth. "So that's where you work?"

"Didn't I tell you to leave me alone?"

"Yes, but we need not be enemies."

"I don't want your friendship."

"I wasn't insisting that we be friends."

"Listen. I have no time to waste, quibbling over words."

"Nor I. I was simply saying that even if people part ways, they need not pass one another without so much as a wave of the hand."

"What do you want?"

"I just want you to know that I still love you."

"You are wasting your time and mine trying to pick up spilled water. If you start that up again, I am leaving."

"What else do you want me to talk about?"

"I didn't ask you out. Why not sing about how great it feels to be a youthwing of His Royal Mightiness?" Nyawīra said, barely hiding her sarcasm.

"Look, you are quite right to be critical of some of the pillars of the Party, pretenders who are out to ruin and discredit our country, such as those in favor of Marching to Heaven! The verdict was in long ago when the children of Israel first attempted the Tower of Babel."

"Rumor has it that you drew up the plan, or rather the artist's impression. Why this about-face against your baby?"

He tried not to wince, recalling the humiliation he had suffered at the birthday celebrations, revived by the woman he most wanted to impress with his new connections to power and privilege. He kept quiet, dwelling on the origins of the whole fiasco.

It all began when Machokali gave a talk at the polytechnic where Kaniŭrŭ taught. On learning that there was an art department, the minister wondered aloud whether its students could be trusted to breathe life into the lifeless drawing of an architect? If you can, then call on me in my office, he said, just that, an invitation so vague that many people correctly took it for the usual rhetorical challenges by politicians. The minister himself had forgotten all about it when Kaniũrũ went to his office a few days later, abruptly allowing that, yes, it could be done, and he was there to volunteer his services. It took Machokali a while to grasp what the man was talking about until Kaniũrũ reminded him of his visit to the polytechnic. Oh, that, the minister said. You mean you can look at a two-dimensional plan and give a visual impression in three dimensions? You know, with the color of life and all that? "It is not easy, but it can be done." Not of course by every Tom, Dick, and Harry, but he, John Kaniũrũ, had a degree in art and art history from the University of Eldares and had even studied a little architecture. An artistic rendering was no big deal.

Kaniũrũ was melting inside at the prospect of working with so famous a minister when the first obstacle to happiness presented itself. After describing in general what he wanted from an artist, Machokali instructed one of his trusted aides to show Kaniũrũ the drawing. "Look at it only once," he had said. "The rest I leave to your imagination." Kaniũrũ did not then know the significance of the drawing that would serve as inspiration for his art, but when he found himself working under lock and key, being body searched every time he left the room, he figured it was something important. And when he learned that it was somehow connected with the Ruler's birthday celebration, he gave the aide a note begging the minister to acknowledge his contribution to the national effort. The aide was reassuring; not only would his name be mentioned but he might even be introduced to the Ruler himself, or at least be asked to come forward so the people could see him. These words made Kaniũrũ thank the minister's aide profusely, calling him "my friend," while ignoring all the hints about greasing the palm of the messenger. The aide was compelled to wonder, What kind of person is this who does not seem to know that the carrier of a message must eat? Peeved by the meanness of art teachers, the aide later told the minister that the teacher had said that his name should not be mentioned anywhere, so selfless was he. Unaware of this treachery, Kaniũrũ for several days considered how best to grandstand in public. He would sit far back so that when his name was called he would have to walk through the throng all the way to the platform. And even if asked simply to stand up, he would be looked at by a thousand heads turning toward him. But instead of being the object of everybody's grateful attention, he attracted only angry gestures from those who sat near him, and a warning about keeping the peace from a cop who added injury to insult by threatening to blow off his nose with a gun. How could he ever forgive Machokali for treating him like dirt?

Even as the bitterness of the moment came back to him, he controlled himself so as not to show weakness before the woman he was trying to woo back.

He was a little relieved to learn that Nyawīra had not been present at the ceremony, and, as truth is in the eyes of the interpreter, he tried to make her see things through his eyes.

"Believe me, I painted that madness at Machokali's insistence. He gave me, or rather his aides gave me a copy of the architectural design and they wanted an artistic rendition of Marching to Heaven. To be very frank, I thought that the whole project was stupid and that's why I insisted on the minister's not mentioning my name."

"I admire your modesty," Nyawīra said. "Humility is certainly more becoming than humiliation."

"Spare me your mockery. Let me tell you something. There are still many pillars of the Ruler's Party that are as solid as a rock. For instance, Minister Silver Sikiokuu. He, too, can see through this nonsense, and that's why he came up with the brilliant idea of a personal spaceship modeled on some of those we see on these walls. What has been done is doable. Imagine the Ruler ruling space. Sikiokuu is a political genius, a genuine visionary."

"This is getting interesting. Who owns you, Minister Sikiokuu or His Royal Mightiness? Whose youthwinger are you after all?"

"I'm not ashamed to say that I belong to the Ruler's Party. Total loyalty. One hundred percent. Were it not for his wise leadership, where would we all be? Imagine the disaster if the likes of Machokali led this country! To be one of the youthwings of the Ruler is not a partisan act; it is a patriotic duty. Even university professors and PhDs are enlisting. Girls like you are now needed. The Girl-Youth."

"I am a woman, a divorcée."

"I just wanted to make sure that you knew that in the Ruler's Youth there is no discrimination based on gender or age. Some of our most vocal members are women. A few professors are more than fifty years old. Sikiokuu himself is head of the youthwing movement; he is a genuine man of the people. He aims to make his youth happy. He wants women like you to join . . ."

"Go back to your Sikiokuu with his rabbit ears and tell him that Nyawĩra does not bow to political bosses."

"What is the difference? You now work for Tajirika, a loyal follower of Machokali."

"Yes, but I am not employed as a political activist. I am an ordinary employee with an everyday job."

"What is so ordinary about the ever-present queue outside your offices these days?"

"Didn't you tell me just now that you happened to be passing by? So you have been here the whole day? And by the way, when are you going to London to get a bigger nose?" Nyawĩra asked, and laughed as she tried to imagine how his nose would look if even larger. "Machokali has had his eyes enlarged, Sikiokuu his ears, and Big Ben Mambo his mouth, or rather his tongue. Who better than you to sniff out enemies of His Royal Mightiness?"

"Nyawĩra, listen to me: You are right. I do pass by here from time to time. But not because of Tajirika. Neither Tajirika nor his business brought me here today. It is the prompting of my heart—please don't go. Stay and hear me out; you don't even know what I am about to say. I want you. I find it difficult, almost impossible, to stay away from you. But I won't intrude on your privacy, even if I knew where you lived. But I am free to be out and about in public. Yesterday I was walking by this road and I saw you with another man, engaged in a deep conversation."

"Am I not allowed to speak to whomever I wish?"

"But that is my point. The man you were talking to is no ordinary man."

"How terribly interesting."

"Please hear me out and judge for yourself. Both of you were sitting not very far from where I found you replacing the signboard. After you parted company, I had an urge to follow you just to say hello, but there was something about the man that made me want to stay and observe him further. He sat there for a long time as if waiting for somebody or as if he had nowhere else to go. Eventually he did walk down this street, and I followed him. At Santamaria or somewhere there he stopped and stood against a wall as if he had lost his way. He was soon on the road again until he reached the Ruler's Square near Paradise. And do you know what he did? He walked into a public toilet . . ."

Nyawīra could not help laughing aloud. His tone was dead serious. What was so strange about people going to public toilets? But she recalled how horribly filthy they were and was almost ready to concede his concern.

"Laugh all you want, but I assure you that this is no laughing matter. I saw him with my own eyes go into the toilet; I stood guard at the entrance, and only a beggar dressed in rags came out. He didn't. I am not holding anything back; I am telling you the whole truth. After a long while, I thought to relieve myself and went in to see what was happening. There was nobody there, not a soul. The man had vanished into thin air."

"An alien. Back to Mars," she said, trying to make light of the whole thing.

"This is no joke. Do you know the man well?"

"No," she said, yawning as if she was bored with Kaniŭrŭ. "Or, I should say, if the person you are talking about and the one I have in mind are the same, I can tell you truthfully that I don't know much about him beyond the fact that he wandered into our office looking for work."

She would have failed a lie detector test, because even as she said that her anxiety was mounting. How was Kamītī? Had something happened to him? Was Kaniŭrŭ holding back something?

"Whether you want to hear it or not, I care about you and would not want you to come to an evil end because of bad company. I am not superstitious, but that man is no human. He might be a djinn or an ogre."

"An ogre, and not in the government?" Nyawīra asked with forced laughter. "I can defend myself."

She grabbed her handbag and stood up to go. She thought of Kamītī, wondering where and how he had spent his day. In addition to his travails, now he had to put up with an ex-husband on his trail.

She felt weary, but at the thought of harm coming to Kamĩtĩ something flashed across her heart, and she did not know whether to be sad or happy.

"Look," she told Kaniũrũ. "Even if you come across someone plotting to kill me, keep it to yourself. I want nothing from you. Don't pretend that you are acting on my behalf."

He watched her walk to the counter to pay for the tea and cake. She left without once looking back. He sat there gloomy at not having been taken seriously, yet he was so sure of what he had seen. Could his eyes have deceived him?

"No. The man is human, yet more than human," he murmured to himself, still puzzled by the mystery he had witnessed outside the gates of Paradise.

# 15

Constable Arigaigai Gathere had used the same words when he told the story of what had happened to him the day the Wizard of the Crow had ordered him to leave the haunted house. Strange. First he talks to me with the soft voice of a woman. Then out of the same mouth comes a bellowing masculine sound ordering me to go away and wash my feet, which had defiled the playground of his magic powers. That man? I swear, true! *Haki ya Mungu,* that man, he is human yet more than human. For A.G. the words conveyed not malice but awe, respect, and admiration, for he told his listeners, "All that I am, all that I have now, I owe to the craft of the Wizard of the Crow.

"How could I not obey his first words of command to me? Without any hesitation, I ran all the way to my place, where I washed my feet and hands over and over again, and within the hour I was back in Santalucia. Now I was careful not to touch the door or stand too close to it. The door opened all by itself as if to invite me in, and I entered the sacred grounds of his living space. Then I heard another command: stand in front of the small window. The window looked like that of a confessional in a Catholic church, except it had no lattice and one could clearly see his face and eyes. But what eyes? They were more like balls of fire.

"'Your heart is a little weary,' the voice said.

"'Yes! Yes!' I said quickly.

"'Weighed down by many burdens?'

"'Yes! Yes!'

"'A particular burden that brings you to the Wizard of the Crow?'

"His voice was round, soft, and soothing, so different from before that I could not tell whether he was making a statement or asking a question.

"'You have spoken my thoughts exactly,' I told him. 'You see, I have been in the police force for many years, and no matter how hard I work I have never been promoted. Wizard of the Crow, I am sure I have enemies who are hindering me through magic.'

"'Is your heart telling you that?'

"'Yes!'

"'Why? What makes you so sure it's the truth?'

"'Because the heart never lies. You see, I am a workaholic. When I am on traffic duty, for instance, I hand out more tickets than any other cop. I am particularly hard on *matatus*. I ask myself, Why is it that I have not been promoted? And I always hear the same whisper: There is a person whose shadow crosses yours.'

"'The person whose shadow crosses yours, do you know him?'

"'Oh, no. Such people work in the dark. He could be anybody, my neighbor or one of my workmates. Or, for that matter, any of the *matatu* drivers to whom I have issued tickets.'

"'What do you want from me?'

"My heart was beating loudly. I had not realized how bitter I had been toward my enemy, whoever he is. But that aside, he will now know that I am none other than Constable Arigaigai Gathere. Never again will he harm my career or anybody else's as he has all these years. 'Look for him everywhere. Ferret him out. Remove him from the face of the earth,' I said with gleeful expectation.

"'To kill a man—you know that is a hard thing to do?'

"'Not for us, the Ruler's police officers,' I told him. 'Any life that threatens the Ruler's power is nothing to us, nothing at all.'

"He paused.

"'You know, it may be easy for the Ruler's police officers to kill the body, but not the spirit.' His voice was still enriched with softness to soothe even the most turbulent of souls.

"'You have spoken the truth,' I told the Wizard of the Crow, 'because if I knew who my enemy was it would be easy for me to blow him to pieces, but as I don't know who he is, he torments me whether I am awake or asleep. So I ask myself: How is it that somebody can always be on my mind and in my heart and yet I cannot say who he is? Now you have made me understand. It is because he comes in the form of an evil spirit. Yes, it is not easy to kill spirits. Believe me, Wizard of the Crow, I have been to every witch doctor in and around these towns and villages, and to each I have given the same riddle. *I have enemies I don't have—who are they?* And none has been able to ease my torment within so that I can sleep soundly.'

"'What makes you believe that I am capable of what others have failed to do?'

"'I know your power,' I told him bluntly. 'Last night, when I set eyes on the bundle of magic hanging from the roof, I felt my legs rooted to the ground. I said to myself, Here is the wizard for me. You have already proven me right in thinking so. You are the only one to solve the riddle of the enemies I know I have and don't have. For the first time, I know who my enemies are. They masquerade as evil spirits. Not that I needed proof. You who can make birds lose the power of their wings, yes, you who can bring down even crows and hawks from the sky, how can a mere mortal resist your power, as a spirit or not? Wizard of the Crow, your very name is proof of the powers you possess.'

"'Do you have a mirror?' he asked me.

"'No.'

"'You don't carry a mirror?'

"'No.'

"'How do you look at yourself?'

"'I am clean in my ways. I never look in the mirror too often.'

"'How do you know if you hardly ever look at yourself?'

"'I just know.'

"'You told me that sometimes you are on traffic duty?'

"'Yes.'

"'Have you ever stopped a driver in a vehicle with no mirrors?'

"'No mirrors? How can he drive without mirrors? A driver of a vehicle without mirrors is a menace to his own life and that of others. Even a broken mirror poses danger.'

"'You said that there are shadows crossing yours.'

"'Yes.'

"'We need mirrors to see our shadows. We need mirrors to see other people's shadows crossing ours. You can rent mine for two thousand, two hundred and fifty Burīs,' he told me.

"I didn't have much money on me then, so I told him that I would come back in the afternoon.

"Back at home, I put on my uniform and reported for duty. I was late. My boss, Wonderful Tumbo, was very angry with me. I saluted and called him Effendi, and I told him—you who are listening to my tale, when I say that I have no idea how the next words came into my mouth, believe me—I said straightaway that I had spent the entire night chasing some people who had gone to Paradise to ruin the Global Bank mission. I told him that I was sure those creatures were not ordinary mortals but djinns. I knew this to be so because even when I tried to stop myself I could not. They forced me all the way to the prairie surrounding Eldares, where they hoped I would lose my way. And let me tell you, Effendi, they were not running and yet I could not catch up with them. I tried to shoot them but my gun would not fire. And I said to myself: I will wrestle with them until daybreak. I knew from the bottom of my heart that the two djinns meant no good to the health of the Ruler and it was my loyal duty to thwart their plans even at the risk of my own life. As my story of the night before unfolded I saw the face of my boss change from anger to concern and alarm, and then to fear. But it was respectful fear, as if, having heard how I had locked horns with dangerous djinns in the dark, he saw me in a new light or maybe thought that some of their powers had rubbed off on me. He did not ask any more questions, and instead of rebuking me he told me to run along and that he would report my extraordinary ordeal to his superiors.

"I got on my motorcycle and went to the road. I targeted big carriers because most of them carried contraband and would rather pay bribes in thousands rather than have their goods inspected. To a police officer they were a blessing, unless bad luck crossed your path and you harassed a carrier belonging to the big men including the biggest of all: even if they were packed to the max with illegal goods, by stopping such a carrier you might end up losing your job. One had to be careful soliciting grease for one's palms until one was sure of the carrier's real owner. But I was good at sensing when to be zealous and when not to be. By one o'clock I had more than two thousand, two hundred and fifty Burîs in my pocket. Cash. True! *Haki ya Mungu!* By one o'clock my pockets were bulging with banknotes.

"For the third time, I was back at the premises of the Wizard of the Crow. The door again opened by itself. But as I was about to enter I heard the voice say that I must not defile the sacred grounds with my uniform, badge, and gun.

"Again I returned home. Do you hear that? The Wizard of the Crow made me return to my place four times that day; this was what finally convinced me of his powers. Have you ever heard of a witch doctor with an eye for that kind of detail? I put on my civilian clothes and in no time I was back. What do we say? Deeds define needs, and the promptness with which I executed his commands and wishes must have convinced him of my desperate need for a cure against the ill designs of my invisible enemies.

"He told me to put the money on the table, which I did promptly.

"'Listen very carefully,' he told me in the same soothing voice. 'Close your eyes and then empty your head of all thoughts: in the shadows of your mind, a picture will form, and when it forms I will capture it in the mirror the way fax machines and computers copy images and transmit them invisibly. Once the image is a captive in my mirror, I will take a sharp knife and scratch it, and from that moment on your enemy will vanish forever.'

"I covered my face with my hands, shut my eyes tight, and waited. And indeed, after a few seconds, somewhere in the darkness of my mind an outline of an image was forming, but I could not tell whose it was because it kept changing shape and location. Still I shouted, 'Yes! I can see an image, but it is slippery.'

"'Your enemies are very cunning, very slippery, but there! Hold it there!' he ordered me. 'Whatever it is, try with all the power of your mind to hold it still! And don't let it go. There. Like that.'

"The sound of his knife scratching the mirror made my teeth hurt, as if they were being scratched. All at once I saw the vague image in my mind explode into a thousand stars disappearing into the edge of the darkness in my mind.

"'His image, is it still there?' he asked.

"'No,' I answered. 'It's gone. Stars disappearing in the dark.'

"'That's it,' he said.

"I opened my eyes and felt a strange sensation. True, *Haki ya Mungu*! This person who is now telling you the story, this person you now see in front of you, this person who answers to the name Constable Arigaigai Gathere, this man felt tears, but they were not tears of sorrow but of joy at having the burden of many years lifted from my heart and from my life abruptly.

"'Go home now,' he told me in a gentle voice, 'and all you have to do is find out if there has been a road accident involving *matatus*. If not today then tomorrow, if not tomorrow then the next day. Your enemy is most likely one of the fatally injured. From today on, never molest a beggar, a diviner, a healer, a wizard, or a witch. If you ever do any harm to the helpless, this magic will turn against you. Everything that you have, including peace of mind, will be taken away. Go now. Your actions will be the mirror of your soul. Look into the mirror, always.'

"I hesitated. He asked me if I had anything else on my mind. Yes, there was something else pressing. Although I had seen a mental outline of an image, I still could not tell who my enemy was even if I were to meet him in the street. I asked the wizard: 'Can you tell me the name of my enemy, the one whose image you scratched?'

"'No,' he said. 'I don't want you to go sleepless at night obsessing about his disappearance. Your own actions are a better mirror of your life than the actions of all your enemies put together. That is why I told you to watch what you do to others instead of always thinking about what others do to you.'

"So you see? That's why I have said that the man is human yet more than human. He removes all burdens from the heart. I say that because I used to trust my actions completely—I have told you that I am a workaholic—and yet he was asking me to look at my own actions. Maybe the enemy was hidden within my actions. Had I known that, I would have discovered my enemies much earlier and I could have spared myself a lot of torment. I again returned to my place of work having changed into a police uniform. I now had no worries in the world. I was whistling and walking jauntily and I had a 'how are you' ready on my lips for whomever I met, including my boss, Wonderful Tumbo.

"Instead of going back to the road again, I went straight to police headquarters. Why lie to you? Even though I now had no fear in the world, I wanted to know if the first prediction had occurred. Were there any reports of accidents involving *matatus*? Given the state of our roads—even the few that used to have tarmac at independence were nothing but potholes—I would have been surprised if there had been no accidents, but one could not be sure, fate being so tricky."

At that point, A.G. would pause as if to consider the murderous roads. His listeners would call out, A.G., go on with your story. My throat is dry, he would say, but once his listeners replenished his glass he felt a resurgence of energy and resumed his narrative.

He would then tell how he got to police HQ and asked for the DOB—daily occurrence book. His heart raced: What if the potholes had not claimed their daily sacrifice? What if no *matatu* was involved in an accident? But he was anxious for nothing; when he saw what he saw he let out an involuntary squeal. In only the previous hour, no fewer than ten *matatus* had been involved in accidents all over Aburĩria, three in Eldares alone. One of these accidents was a head-on collision with a police vehicle, killing fifteen people including three policemen.

His initial shock was quickly replaced by an irresistible desire to know whether his enemy had been among the fatally wounded: he started flipping through the pages of the DOB like one possessed. His fellow policemen looked askance at him. But A.G. did not notice the looks on their faces. He was entirely absorbed in the DOB.

He needed the names of the fatally wounded, but the information was scant. Then he remembered that he knew neither the name nor physical characteristics of his enemy. What was important, as the Wizard of the Crow had said, was that his enemy, whoever he was, had been scratched out of existence and must be among the fifteen corpses.

So the divine prediction had come true. His enemy was no more. He now waited to see whether his life would take a different course. Forward, of course, never backward, his heart sang . . .

# 16

What struck Nyawīra when she got home was the tidiness of the house. Kamītī had dusted away all the cobwebs, washed the floor and the walls, cleaned the entire kitchen, and made up the bed with fresh sheets. He had also washed, dried, and ironed the old ones. She was ecstatic after her ordeal at work and at the Mars Café. Now she felt embraced by warmth and neatness.

Kamītī had even made a broth of tomatoes and spinach, and all that remained to complete the supper was *ugali*. In all the months she had lived with Kaniūrū, he had never done as much. Even when both had arrived home at the same time after working all day, Kaniūrū would always sit down and expect Nyawīra to cook, serve him, and wash the dishes.

"I will give you a new name," Nyawīra told Kamītī as she put her handbag on the table and pulled up a chair. "Henceforth you are the Sorcerer of Cleanliness."

"Just call me Kamītī son of Karīmīri. Tea?"

"I will not say no," Nyawīra chirped happily.

Kamītī went to the kitchen and put a pot of water on the gas grill. Nyawīra stood up and leaned against the door frame leading to the kitchen and watched him go about his work.

"I will now be the talk of the whole region," she said.

"Why?"

"Letting a guest cook for the host?"

"What did Mwalimu Nyerere of Tanzania say? 'A guest for two days . . .'" Kamītī started.

"'. . . On the third you pick up a hoe,'" Nyawīra completed it. "It is not Nyerere's saying. It is a common Swahili proverb."

The water in the pot reached a boil. Kamītī went to the cupboard to look for tea leaves, but Nyawīra beat him to it.

"I am being lazy. Let me do this," she said, taking out a packet.

"No, I will make the tea," Kamītī said, and grabbed the packet from her hands. He scooped some tea leaves with a spoon, but as he was about to put them in the water he paused and asked, "How do you like your tea? The English or Aburīrian way?"

"The Aburīrian tea, brewed in milk, please."

Kamītī put the tea leaves into the boiling water and then added milk, boiling the brew some more. Minding the pot, he said: "Did you know that our way of making tea is not original to us but comes from India?"

"I thought they had borrowed the method from black Aburīrians."

"No, it's the other way around. Tea, anyway, originally comes from India, China, and Japan. The English were initiated into tea drinking by India, probably in Madras, the first capital in colonial India. But tea making differs from country to country. In Japan they have very elaborate tea ceremonies."

"Been to China and Japan also?"

"No, my knowledge is secondhand. Letters, mainly, from a friend in Japan at Kyoto University. Went there the same time that I went to Madras. He now lives in Shikoku, the island of eighty-eight temples. So, really only in India can I say I saw some practices firsthand, especially in Madras. Some friends once drove me from Hyderabad to Warangal. We stopped at several roadside tea shops, and I can tell you that the similarities . . ."

"Hey! Watch out, the tea will boil over," Nyawīra shouted, stepping toward the grill, but Kamītī beat her to it and switched off the gas.

"I cannot fully trust a man in the kitchen," Nyawīra said as they sat by the table to drink their tea. "This tastes good."

She complimented him on his talent for housekeeping, and they laughed about it. Then Kamītī grew serious.

"Do you want to know the truth? I was really trying to clear the stench left in the house by that police officer."

"Constable Arigaigai Gathere? He came back?" she asked, and she now sat back, all ears to the tale. "Was he so in need of witchcraft?"

"To tell you the truth, even I did not expect him to come back," Kamītī said. "He returned just as I was about to leave the house to look for work. I saw him from a distance and went back inside, leaving the door open. I quickly decided that this kitchen would be my shrine and the living room his waiting room. We would talk through the small window between the shrine and the waiting room."

Kamītī narrated the whole saga including the warning to Constable Arigaigai Gathere never to molest beggars and diviners.

"What if his situation does not change?"

"His situation started changing even before he left here."

"How?"

"His self-imposed burden of endless suspicion had been lifted."

"What if he does not get a promotion?"

"Then he will come back here."

"For his money?"

"No, to bring more money to find out why the initial divinations did not work. The question is whether I myself can go on with this business."

"Why not? All you need are a few seashells, dry bones, Sodom apples, a sackcloth, and a stool and you are all set. Or better still, why not form your own NGO?"

"NGO? Of witchcraft?"

"Yes. And soothsaying. Magic healing. You'll become a consultant for everything to do with magic," Nyawīra went on, laughing at her own suggestions.

"A consulting wizard? Maybe I could even have a visiting card: 'Wizard of the Crow. Divining powers. Specialist in soothsaying, healing, and magic cleansing,'" Kamītī said in the same mood. "Yes, everything and anything to do with magic. I cannot think of a business as profitable with so little investment. But the smell!" he added with a discernible change of tone in his voice.

"Smell? What smell are you talking about? Oh, yes, you said you had tidied up to remove the smell of the police officer. Surely it could not have been worse than the stench of uncollected garbage in our streets," Nyawīra said.

"I don't know what it is," he began quietly, as if talking to himself. "I can't quite explain it, but the smell was stronger than that of rotting garbage, a rancid belch, or a ripe fart. Sometimes when I am walking the streets I can detect it from among all other scents in the air and often I come across people and buildings that have it about them more often and more strongly than others. But by the same token I also come across people whose fresh smell seems to drive the foulness away. There are times when the foul and the fresh appear to struggle for the right of passage into my nostrils, like evil and good spirits fighting for the domination of the soul. Today it somehow had to do with your going away and the police officer coming here. How shall I put it?

"You have seen open fields when the sun is shining after the rains. You have seen dewdrops hanging delicately on leaves and petals, like silver beads, before flowing down. Sometimes smoke rises from the ground to the sky, as if sending out an offering to a deity? Watching it, you feel like bathing in the warmth that hints of imminent birth. Nyawīra, when you are around I feel immersed in the freshness of the fields when flowers are in bloom and bees and butterflies flit about gathering nectar to make the honey of life. That was the atmosphere that you had left behind in the house this morning.

"But then Constable Arigaigai Gathere arrives. The whole house stunk during his entire stay. And even after he left, the heavy stench remained. That is what propelled me into a cleansing frenzy."

Still, no matter what he did, the stench would not go away. Maybe a dead rat was rotting somewhere in the house, so he searched under the bed, the chairs, everywhere, turning things over, but to no avail. Tired and frustrated, he sat by the table in the living room. Suddenly he knew the source of the foulness: the police officer's money. Kamītī immediately put all the notes in a plastic bag, put the bag into an empty cocoa can, and closed the lid. He dug a hole outside and buried the can.

"The smell grew faint but was still in the air," he told Nyawīra. "But when you entered the house it disappeared altogether, replaced by the fresh scent of flowers."

Nyawīra felt like laughing and saying something lighthearted but, seeing how serious Kamītī was, she restrained herself.

"Just now I don't feel like I smell of any flower," Nyawīra said, "let alone a fresh one after the rains. But thank you. I love flowers."

"The same kind of thing happened yesterday when I entered your office. I inhaled a sweet scent of flowers from where you sat, but when Tajirika emerged from the inner office I scented the stench of . . ."

". . . a corpse?" Nyawīra suggested.

". . . a rotting heart, soul, but how can one smell a soul? Besides, I sometimes scent the same from buildings, and now the money left here by that police officer. But money and buildings have no souls."

"You know," said Nyawĩra, "if you had talked only about Tajirika I would have said, Yes, I see what you mean. For everything about him rots. Did you see his right hand? It is always in a glove. Why? Because that is the hand that once shook the hand of the Ruler and he wants to retain the touch of power. The hand and the glove are never washed. So whatever he touches stinks. I sometimes wonder what his wife, Vinjinia, thinks about the gloved hand. But the rot goes beyond the hand. Money has corrupted his soul completely. You can't even begin to guess how much he collected today, and all because he was made the chairman of the committee for Marching to Heaven."

"What? How?" Kamĩtĩ asked. "What is the connection between being appointed a chair of Marching to Heaven and collecting money?"

Now it was her turn to tell Kamĩtĩ the story of her day. She told him everything except her encounter with Kaniũrũ at the Mars Café. She did not want to burden him with worries about being followed. But she did talk, almost triumphantly, about the signboards.

"We removed the old signboard. If you came tomorrow you could get a job as my assistant."

"Work a job at that man's place? I would rather set up a shop as a witch doctor," he said flippantly.

"So what are your plans for tomorrow?" Nyawĩra asked.

"I don't know. I just want to go back to the wilderness tonight. I stayed because I thought you should know that the police officer came back, and about what happened in your house today."

"And the money?"

"I will bury it in the prairie. The earth shall be my bank."

"Or are you planting it?" Nyawĩra added; the idea of burying the money seemed absurd to her. "Are you planting it like a farmer plants seeds to secure abundance? Well, all I can say is that when your money tree grows, please come for me at harvest time." She stood up and said: "But let us first eat something before you begin your journey into the wilderness."

Nyawĩra cooked *ugali*. Dipping *ugali* balls in the broth that Kamĩtĩ had made earlier in the day, they ate their last dinner together in near silence, each self-absorbed. They had mixed feelings about their encounter and imminent parting. They felt they had always known each other; at the same time they were complete strangers. Their shared experience of the previous night now appeared as events involving other people in another country far away and long ago. Even though they now teased each other into laughter, they felt a little awkward and slightly embarrassed.

"And when you leave this place," Nyawīra asked, breaking the silence between them, "how will your patients know where or how to find you?"

"Who tells you that I intend to go on with this business of witchcraft?" Kamītī said, almost irritated by the question. He was not a witch doctor. He was a make-believe Wizard of the Crow.

About to respond, Nyawīra looked at her watch, and she suddenly let out a cry as if she had just remembered an important appointment. She stood, grabbed her handbag, and hurriedly addressed Kamītī:

"I have to be somewhere. Don't go to the wilderness tonight. Be my guest one more day. I will be away for a few hours only, but don't wait up for me. Sleep on the sofa, like last night. Please don't open the door for anybody. I have no friends or family who visit me here, even in the daytime."

She did not wait for him to respond. She just left.

Who is this woman? Kamītī walked over to the couch, befuddled. Where is she going? Who is she going to meet? But soon he was lost in thoughts and worries about himself.

He was glad that Nyawīra had offered her couch once more. But what was happening to him? Yesterday morning I was a job hunter. Midday I was a corpse, a piece of garbage about to be buried among other garbage. In the afternoon I was an object of Tajirika's self-amusement. In the evening I was a beggar among beggars outside the gates of Paradise. Last night I was on the run, pursued by His Mighty's police force. This morning I was the Wizard of the Crow, divining for one of His Mighty's police officers. And tonight I am a watchman in the house of a mysterious woman whom I met only yesterday.

Brooding on all of this, he fell asleep. Nyawīra shook him out of his stupor the following morning and offered him tea and bread for breakfast.

"You don't want to tell me that it is already the morning of another day?"

"Yes, dawn is breaking and bright is the light of a new day," she sang.

"When did you come back?" he asked. "I did not hear you open the door."

"Early this morning," she said, and he noted her silence about where she had been and what she had been doing. He chose not to probe further.

Before they finished breakfast, there was a knock at the door. Nyawira opened it to reveal Constable Arigaigai Gathere. Kamiti quickly hid. Nyawira's face showed fright, which turned to wonder as Constable Arigaigai Gathere fell to his knees and bowed his head.

"My Lord Wizard of the Crow. I told myself you had to be the first to know. I am so happy and I don't know how to thank you."

"What happened?" Nyawira inquired, as if she herself was indeed the Wizard of the Crow.

# 17

What happened? These were the words his listeners said whenever A.G. came to this point in his story. But A.G. was not to be hurried: it was his narrative and he would tell it his own way, letting events unfold instead of abridging them into a phrase. Stories, like food, lose their flavor if cooked in a hurry.

"How could you kneel down before another human being like you and me?" someone would ask him.

"Human? The Wizard of the Crow is more than human: had you been in my position, you would have done the same."

"Why?"

"Because he changed my life," A.G. would say, and then paused.

Seeing how attentive they were, A.G. would tell his listeners how on the day after the fulfillment of the oracle foretelling the *matatu* accident, he reported for duty. He had wanted to reach his place of work before anybody else, certainly before his boss, so as to make up for his lateness the day before. To his surprise he found his superior, Inspector Wonderful Tumbo, anxiously awaiting him. Let's walk together to my office, Tumbo said, and for a moment A.G. thought he was going to be reprimanded. Did someone yesterday see him going to the witch doctor's? But his boss's gait and tone of voice showed no anger. In the office his boss fetched him a chair. Do you know what happened last night? No, A.G. said, thinking that maybe there had been more fatalities.

As if imparting a secret to an equal, his boss then told him about the protest against the Global Bank mission and the anti–Marching to Heaven leaflets distributed to every door of every home and every office in Eldares and the country. Even inside the Parliament and outside the gates of the State House. Can you believe it? Outside the gates of the State House, under the very noses of the police and the soldiers guarding the palace! The question is, how did the pamphleteers get inside these heavily guarded locations without detection? We have the best trained force in Africa, if not the world. There was not a single report from any of the hundreds of police stations about the elusive intruders. Who were they? Djinns, of course! Do you hear that? Djinns.

And then, inexplicably, Tumbo bent forward and said in English: Congratulations, my son. Never may you forget your friends. A.G. was perplexed by his tone and manner. Was Inspector Wonderful Tumbo toying with him, or what? A.G. was not kept in the dark for long. Tumbo reminded A.G. that he was the one who had written and faxed the comprehensive report of the night that A.G. chased djinns across Eldares and the prairie. As a result of it, the powers above had become interested in A.G.: he appeared the only human in all Aburĩria who had the most recent experience with djinns.

"In short," A.G. would tell his listeners, "the report of my extraordinary courage in challenging djinns to a nighttime wrestling match in the prairie had reached the ears of the office of the Ruler. An important decision was made and faxed back to my boss that very morning. I was to be transferred to the office of the Ruler immediately to work under Minister Silver Sikiokuu. Even Tumbo was given a raise in recognition of his training of police officers willing to risk their lives for the Ruler.

"What caused this big and sudden change in my career?" A.G. would ask his listeners, only to answer the question himself. "The Wizard of the Crow."

These were words he uttered to Nyawĩra when, taking her for the

Wizard of the Crow, he knelt before her, his head slightly bowed in humility, and said repeatedly, Thank you. He was so mystifying that Nyawīra was forced to ask, "What more do you want?"

"Nothing. You see, I am being transferred to the Ruler's office, but I decided to steal away to let you know how effective your magic has been. They want me to help them catch the dissidents who distributed anti-government leaflets all over the country last night. Believe me, O Wizard of the Crow, I will never forget what you have done for me. Now I must go."

A.G. stood up. After a step or two he stopped as if he had suddenly remembered something he should not have forgotten. He looked back at Nyawīra and a hint of a conspiratorial smile lit up his face momentarily.

"Wizard of the Crow, those dissidents are very cunning. They go about their work in the dark, disguised as djinns, but they will come to know that nobody can fool Arigaigai Gathere. You see, with each leaflet they also left a plastic snake. They must be the same people who ruined the Ruler's birthday celebration. But if it should happen that they are really djinns disguised as dissidents, then I shall come back to you for a little help in capturing them. I should not have said 'nothing' when you asked me what else I wanted. I know that not even djinns can match the power of the Wizard of the Crow. But we shall talk." A.G. then left to start his new life as a security agent in the office of the Ruler.

Trembling, Nyawīra leaned against the door frame for support, then went inside, where she stared dumbstruck at Kamītī. Was this all a coincidence?

"Who are you, really?" she asked him.

"I should be asking you the same question," Kamītī responded. "Why are you so frightened? Please, I don't mean to get into your business, but where were you last night?"

"I hear you. And you're right; you deserve an answer. So please don't go away today," Nyawīra told Kamītī. "I have to be in the office on time, but when I come back in the evening we'll talk at length and sort a few things out. As I told you the other night, I am a member of the Movement for the Voice of the People. I was unnerved when the police officer mentioned the leaflets and plastic snakes we distributed last night. At first I didn't know what he was up to. If you want to rise to the top, you can turn me in to His Royal Mightiness. You will stay, won't you? It seems you have magical powers," she added wryly, before dressing and leaving.

# 18

Kamĩtĩ was troubled by Arigaigai Gathere's promotion to work in the Ruler's office, for it happened so soon after Kamĩtĩ's dabbling in the make-believe. What if his playing at magic had had something to do with it? Did he possess occult powers without knowing? He found himself in a bind.

He had played at childhood games to elude the police officer. But Constable Arigaigai Gathere, having been promoted, would now be hunting down enemies of the state. Nyawĩra had just admitted to being a member of the Movement for the Voice of the People. What would prevent A.G. from persisting in his investigations under the guise of seeking more divinations? Kamĩtĩ felt more vulnerable than ever.

Kamĩtĩ wanted to lead a decent life apart from politics. His aversion to political engagement, especially mass movements, was shaped by the experience of his family. His father, once a primary school teacher, had lost his job because of his attempts to unionize teachers in his area. And his grandfather had died in the Aburĩrian war of independence. Political struggles had brought his family only misery, and he wanted nothing to do with them. Was it not ironic, then, that the very politics he had so pointedly tried to avoid were now being forced on him by the actions of others? What if A.G. came back, as he had intimated he might, to ask the Wizard of the Crow to use his powers to reveal the secrets of the anti-government movement and its followers? Would he be able to wriggle out of this predicament through another fiction? If only Nyawĩra had not told him of her involvement! He feared that his wildest imaginings might contain truth, as in the turns the life of the police officer had taken. Would he find himself unwittingly revealing truths about this woman who had been kind to him? No, Nyawĩra and Constable Arigaigai Gathere might later place on him an intolerable burden of choice. He would not sit around waiting for the return of either—he needed to get away from both, and having so decided, he felt better almost immediately.

In his mind he started singing, *I am going . . .* but out of nowhere he heard the combined voices of Nyawĩra and Constable Arigaigai Gathere singing different lyrics to the same melody: *No, you are not.* Their voices seemed so real that he heard himself shouting back, *No! You cannot stop me,* even as he felt that by shouting back he was being rude to his benefactors. He was no longer the penniless beggar that he was when he first ventured into Nyawĩra's house; he had the money from the police officer. But Kamĩtĩ would never have gotten it had Nyawĩra not offered him a place to stay.

He went outside and unearthed the container of his loot. Its stench was that of a rotting corpse. He rushed back inside the house, put the plastic container with the money into his big beggar's bag, put his jacket on, threw the bag over his shoulder, and strode to the door, intending to vanish in the streets of Eldares.

There was a man standing outside the door.

The stranger looked frail, ill, and tired.

This must be the shrine of the Wizard of the Crow, the man said, and without waiting for confirmation proceeded to unburden himself of his problems. He was suffering, he said, from a big stomachache.

"I do not want to claim that I am bewitched. I have no money and therefore I cannot go to the hospital. All I want from you are a few roots and leaves to chew to make the pain go away."

Kamĩtĩ tried to deny that he was the Wizard of the Crow, but the words stuck to his tongue. The unexpected twists and turns of his life were becoming ominous. The old man was forcing him down a path he did not want to go.

"Wait for me here," he found himself telling the man, after a few cursory questions about his illness.

He lied; his intent was to run away. Kamĩtĩ strode across the prairie not daring to look back for fear of losing his resolve. But once in the heart of the prairie, doubts troubled his peace of mind. What will Nyawĩra think when she comes home from work and finds a stranger, a sickly old man, waiting outside her door? Was he like the ass in the proverb who showed gratitude by kicking his benefactor?

Nyawīra had given him food and shelter; had in effect saved him from arrest the night at the gates of Paradise. She had guided him out of the crowded streets into the prairie and had shared warmth and hospitality. Now all she would have to show for it was his disappearance without explanation, his way of saying thank you. Then he wondered: How did she know her way so well in the prairie? He tried to find the bush that had saved them during the police chase. He retraced his steps, and after an hour of searching he came upon the place. On the night of their escape, he had failed to notice that the bush was some distance from Santalucia. In the middle of the bush was a ridge divided by a path. Kamītī sat on the rock to sort out the things swirling in his mind.

It always refreshed him to be among plants and trees, and now the stench trapped in his bag seemed to have vanished. His eyes roamed, and before he knew it his curiosity had been aroused by the abundant multiplicity of plants. He soon found himself among them, searching out those he thought had medicinal properties. Whatever he picked he put into his bag, oblivious of how much time was passing. By now he knew that he was not looking for medicinal roots and leaves for their own sake but because there was a patient outside Nyawīra's house waiting for a cure. Maybe the old man has left by now, he told himself as he returned to Santalucia. But the old man was still waiting at the door patiently.

Kamītī let him in, gave him the leaves and the roots, and instructed him to boil them and drink the liquid at regular intervals.

"And make sure to drink the extraction with food," Kamītī told him.

"Food? Did you say food? You think I have eaten anything for days? If the medicine depends on food, then it is no good to me."

Kamītī went into the kitchen and quickly scrambled some eggs with tomatoes and gave the food to the old man, adding a glass of milk. He was sure that Nyawīra would not mind his being so generous with her provisions. He handed him a leaf and a piece of bark to chew. Then suddenly an idea struck him: to renounce his role as the Wizard of the Crow, he had to dispense with the income derived from it. And what better way to achieve this than an act of kindness? So he dug into his bag and took out the entire bundle of notes and gave it to the old man as part of the medicinal treatment.

"What is the matter?" Kamĩtĩ asked anxiously. The old man had screamed at the sight of the money. At first Kamĩtĩ thought the old man's scream resulted from the stench, which reassured him that he was not alone in smelling it. But the old man was screaming for joy, gratitude, and disbelief.

"Already I feel better, almost cured," the old man said. "You are a true wizard and a guardian of justice; may God above bless you always."

"How did you know about this place?" Kamĩtĩ asked.

"Everybody in Santalucia is talking about you. It's obvious why. Witch doctors never advertise themselves. They do their nefarious work in the dark. But you actually put up a notice outside your house. What does it mean? That you work openly in the light of day. A deity held me by the hand and guided my steps right to your household. I say again: may the same deity pour blessings on you so that your art may blossom to bewitch the evil and charm the good!"

Instead of being cheered up by the news, Kamĩtĩ felt gloom descend on him. But he no longer had any doubts about fleeing the scene, and he knew he must do so before news of the wizard spread any further. He had treated the old man. He had gotten rid of the money. How stupid of him to have left his calling card hanging on the veranda for so long! Even as he led the old man out, he once again took up his bag. This time there would be no turning back.

Now it was Kamĩtĩ's turn to let out a cry of surprise, even dismay. He stood rooted to the ground. He feared he would fall but just stared in disbelief: standing outside were ten more patients. The old man winked at him as if to say there was nowhere for him to hide, that he had better accept his role as healer. Why here? Kamĩtĩ thought to himself. A trick of fate. Every time I try to escape, fate stands in my way.

He went back into the kitchen to patiently attend his clients, one at a time.

But another surprise awaited him: according to the first, all ten were police officers in civilian clothes. Had they come to get him?

"We want you to do exactly the same magic you did to our police mate, Constable Arigaigai Gathere, formerly a traffic nobody, now a big chief in the Ruler's office. Sir Wizard, we want you to use the mirror to scratch out all enemies that stand in the way of our raises and promotions."

The ten men spoke, each stressing the importance of the magic of the mirror and sprinkling every sentence with what they assumed to be his name, till he himself began to see it, a sign in neon lights flashing before him: THIS IS THE SHRINE OF THE WIZARD OF THE CROW.

# SECTION II

# 1

When news that some beggars had been clobbered outside the gates of Paradise reached the State House, the Ruler was furious, egged on, so rumors say, by Machokali, who had gone there the following day and reported how smooth the dinner would have been had the riot police restrained themselves. At least the Global Bank mission would never have known of the protest. Now he, Machokali, did not know how the missionaries would respond to the news. But he would use all of his diplomatic skills to contain the damage done by the otherwise able security team.

What later brought the Ruler to a boiling point were anti–Global Bank mission leaflets distributed throughout Aburīria, even at the gates of the State House and inside the Parliament grounds. The Ruler immediately summoned Sikiokuu to the State House and read him the riot act: "Bring me the leaders of the Movement for the Voice of the People dead or alive. Failing that, you . . ." and the Ruler trailed off so as to compel the minister's mind to concentrate on what might happen to him.

Sikiokuu, however, was good at turning the worst situation to his advantage. Now he fell to his knees and lowered his head, his ears actually touching the Ruler's shoes.

"I beg Your Mighty Excellency please to give me more powers to smoke out those who are behind the latest plot to dishonor your person and government. I want to increase the number of state ears, eyes, and noses so that not a school, a marketplace, or any public place however small shall go undetected. I want to present you with all the enemies of you, Our Ruler, and of the country."

"You little cunt of a man!" the Ruler shouted angrily. "Why do you go on and on about *my* enemies and those of the Country? Is there a distinction between me and the Country?"

"Forgive me, My Lord and Master. I wished only to intone your name twice. As with God above! We know Him by many names. O My Lord, you don't know how sweet your name sounds in the ears of those who truly believe in you and who know that you and the Country are one and the same."

"That will do; I don't like people comparing me with God," the Ruler said, a little mollified. "But why do you need special powers to crush enemies of the State?" the Ruler now scolded him. "I say, what more power do you need than my order to use all means, necessary and unnecessary, to bring my enemies dead or alive to me? I don't want to hear ever again of leaflets and plastic snakes being scattered anywhere in this land by visible or invisible men. Employ as many men as you need and any means you deem necessary. I want your men to work as courageously as the police officer who I understand wrestled a whole night and all alone in the prairie with beings from another world. I would feel safer if I knew that I had such dedicated security men in my office. Do you hear?" the Ruler said now, emphasizing every point by knocking the minister's skull with his club-shaped staff.

Sikiokuu remained on his knees, enduring his knocks as if they were blessings; with every knock he tugged at his earlobes to indicate that he was taking in every word. Once again he seized this moment of humiliation to gain elevation.

"I swear by my two ears and before you, My Lord on Earth and Heaven, that I shall do everything within the powers you have now given me to crush the members and leaders of this so-called Movement for the Voice of the People. Even if they are djinns, I will get djinns that can outdjinn them. O My Lord, their cries for mercy will be heard in all corners of the globe."

This assurance of crying with a global reach alarmed the Ruler, reminding him that he and Machokali had earlier talked about putting the country's best foot forward while the Bank missionaries were around. He did not want to risk a repeat of what happened outside the gates of Paradise. So he told Sikiokuu that although he had given him special powers, Sikiokuu had to restrain himself for the duration of the Global Bank's visit. The nation must be shown to be at peace and wholly united behind its Ruler and his vision of Marching to Heaven. "What I need," he said, "are brave men like that policeman."

Sikiokuu was not happy with this check, because he had hoped to use his new powers to stir things up a bit and somehow mar the visit of the bankers and so prevent Machokali's frequent appearances on national television and his daily visits to the State House. But he was too smart to let his face express any dissatisfaction; he nodded vigorously to show his agreement with both the Ruler's sentiments and the order to ensure peace and calm. And he did not forget about the police officer.

On leaving the State House, Sikiokuu ordered the immediate transfer of Constable Arigaigai Gathere to the Ruler's office. He did not want to ignore the djinn angle. Then he created a special three-man squad consisting of A.G., Elijah Njoya, and Peter Kahiga to deal specifically with the Movement for the Voice of the People. Their first task was to monitor Machokali's goings, comings, doings, and contacts. They were also to make a list of suspects. The actual torture of the listed would await the departure of the Global Bank mission.

This may explain the curious fact noted in many of the accounts that during the Global Bank mission Aburĩria enjoyed the most peaceful days in recent memory: for weeks no one heard the cry of families whose loved ones had been shot dead by the regime's murderous Angels. It was as if, so said those inclined to grand images, the whole country was under a spell of magic more amazing than any performed by Moses in the land of the Pharaohs thousands of years before Christ was born!

In fact, apart from the usual gossips here and there about the never-ending squabbles between Machokali and Sikiokuu, the biggest cause of anxiety during that period arose from the sudden invasion of Eldares by queuing daemons . . .

# 2

The invasion started outside the headquarters of Eldares Modern Construction and Real Estate.

"And all because of a billboard," Nyawīra observed when she and Kamītī talked about the daemons later.

How? asked Kamītī, and even Nyawīra could not tell how the daemons came to be or how they had fanned out to all corners of Eldares. What she recalled quite clearly was setting out for the office, hoping to get there before Tajirika. The only other thought that had crossed her mind as she went to work was A.G.'s early-morning visit and more so his scary last-minute wink and reference to leaflets. She did not like the way A.G. smiled as if he knew more than he was letting on. He seemed to believe in the Wizard of the Crow, but was he thus setting them up to be killed? She was so absorbed in this worry that she did not note as peculiar that all parking areas in the streets around the offices were taken up by Mercedes-Benzes of all sizes and hues. Imagine her surprise when she raised her eyes and found two long lines of people in the yard outside her office!

One was made up of people in custom suits, standing stiffly and solemnly as if at a fashion parade; it reached all the way to the door. She had dealt with people of their ilk the previous day, and so it was not a big surprise.

The second line started at the billboard TEMPA JOBS: APPLY IN PERSON. It was composed of people in patched-up clothes and worn-out suits in all colors of the rainbow, a stunning contrast to the array of black and gray in the queue of the rich.

Whereas the occupants of the first queue toted briefcases and stood silent and solemn, those in the second, with the exception of the few who read newspapers, held nothing and so could gesture freely as they talked, exchanging anecdotes of the wows and woes of life. Those in the first queue who smoked put out their cigarettes after only a few puffs, crushing the butts under the soles of their shoes, but those in the second smoked the cheapest brands, even unprocessed leaves, and were given to sharing. In the first queue there were a few pipe smokers, in the second, none at all. And while the first had been set in motion due to the appointment of a chairman of Marching to Heaven, encouraging the belief that the Global Bank had green-lighted the project, the second was triggered by the billboard, which, as Nyawīra later learned, had sparked a rumor that the chairman was hiring thousands of workers for Marching to Heaven.

As she walked across the yard to open the office, Nyawīra had no inkling about this rumor. She was just glad that she had arrived before the boss: with so many customers queuing outside, he would almost certainly have scolded her had she gotten there after him.

Even before she could tidy up her desk those at the head of the first queue had begun pushing their way into the reception area as the telephone was ringing off the hook. But for Tajirika's absence, it all reminded her of the day before. Could you please call back later? she would ask those on the phone. She said as much to those who had barged in to the office and even gave them the option of leaving their visiting cards, which they quickly declined, wanting only to meet the boss face-to-face. Please wait outside, she told them, and this almost caused a riot, for everyone feared that he would lose his place in the queue, but after a little discussion all decided to walk backward, pushing back those behind them in domino fashion.

Nyawīra shared their hopes that the boss would arrive shortly, for she was desperate for him to hire the extra help she needed. There were more than enough applicants in the second queue, she mused, wondering at the same time how or even whether the boss would interview them all.

After an hour or so of answering the same question many times over, Nyawīra started getting restless and anxious: Why was he so late? She had expected him quite early. Had he been involved in a car accident? Had he been robbed on the way home?

Tajirika's wife, Vinjinia, who came to the office, was the one who finally resolved matters, but her news was not good: Tajirika was unwell and would not be coming to work today, she said tersely, without elaborating. What illness could have prevented Tajirika from coming to collect more bags of money? He had seemed in excellent health when they parted last night, but Nyawīra did not dwell much on that because she was now preoccupied with what to do about the two queues.

"Was there no message for me?" she asked Vinjinia, who just shook her head.

"Is this place always like this?" Vinjinia asked, as if steering the conversation from her husband to the subject of queues, but she was genuinely curious.

Vinjinia was a homebody, basically Tajirika's housekeeper. They had three boys and two girls. The eldest son, who had a degree in mechanical engineering, worked for a German firm that sold tractors and agricultural implements. He was married and lived on the coast. The second son and the eldest girl were both residential students at the University of Eldares, the girl majoring in education and the boy in business administration. The youngest, Gacirū and Gacīgua, a girl and a boy, were in a day primary school and lived at home with their parents. Tajirika wanted to send them to a boarding school but Vinjinia resisted—she wanted to look after them a bit longer. Tending the farms and the children kept Vinjinia busy at home in Golden Heights, and she had rarely visited her husband's office. She was so cut off from his business and political circuit that she had not even attended the famous birthday rally when her husband had shaken hands with the Ruler. She found out about it only after Tajirika returned home, one hand wrapped in a handkerchief, and she had wondered whether something terrible had happened to him. Sensing her concern, he had laughed and explained the sweet mystery, promising to buy a glove for his hand to keep the memory of the handshake from the Ruler alive. She did not understand what he was talking about, but she trusted her husband to deal with outside matters while she worried about life at home.

Only church on Sunday could lure her into Santalucia and Santamaria. She was a member of All Saints Cathedral, and on Sundays she would mingle with other parishioners—not to catch up with the latest news in the political and business worlds but to ascertain the latest state of her fellow churchgoers' souls. She was among those who never wanted to miss a single episode in the epic battle of Maritha and Mariko with Satan.

"I have never seen anything like this," Nyawīra told her, referring to the queues.

"What shall we do about it?" they asked each other.

Why not tell them the truth? they said, looking through the window. The queues were now so long that the women could not even see the rear.

The two women marched to the front of each queue and put up a notice: TAJIRIKA IS NOT IN TODAY: COME BACK TOMORROW. They went back inside to await the outcome.

And now a sight even more amazing unfolded. When those at the head of the queue read the notice and broke the news, those immediately behind them refused to believe their ears and insisted on seeing the notice for themselves. In the end those who read it did not even bother informing those behind them and simply went away in silence, the others imagining that they had simply met with bad luck or did not want to show elation for fear of exciting envy. Those at the back of the queue thought the lines were moving and were joined by others. Even those who had already left, on seeing this apparent movement, would rejoin the queues at the rear. This game of attrition at the front and replacement at the rear continued. Queues without an end, Nyawīra said to Vinjinia as they sought a way out of this dilemma.

They decided to seek help from the Santamaria police station. It was the nearest, and its head, Wonderful Tumbo, was a friend. He promised to dispatch traffic police to deal with the situation.

But it was not until the afternoon that the promised police officers arrived, two in a Land Rover and the other two on motorcycles, wielding bullhorns. They conferred with Nyawīra and Vinjinia. From what they had seen upon driving up to the office, it was obvious to them that their shouted instructions, no matter how amplified, would not carry to the end of the queues. Do something, the women appealed.

After animated discussions among themselves, the police officers decided on a course of action: the two on motorcycles would ride along the queues and shout their instructions through the bullhorns. The others would hang around the premises to spot and quell trouble.

The two riders took to the road, repeating the same message over and over again: Tajirika is not in the office, people should go home and come back another day. But nobody believed them; the queues showed no sign of thinning out, the game of attrition, replacement, and apparent movement in full swing, serving only to confirm that the police officers were lying.

In the office, Nyawīra remembered that an answering machine had recently been installed, and she quickly programmed it to respond, *This is Eldares Modern Construction and Real Estate. Mr. Tajirika is away from the phone at the moment.* She toyed with the idea of inserting the sentence *Your call is important to us,* but then she changed her mind and continued. *But if you leave your name, telephone number, and the time you called, we shall get back to you as soon as possible. Please begin recording your message after the tone.* Nyawīra felt relief and rejoined Vinjinia, who had been at the window, monitoring the goings-on outside.

They had thought that the two police officers on motorcycles would come back within a few minutes, but they were still missing even after one hour. The first to return after two hours was the one who had shadowed the queue of the rich, and he had been able to do so because, in his own words, "my line was not as long as the other one," adding that in all his life as a police officer he had never encountered such long queues. Even so, his message had had no effect: the queue of the rich remained as it had been all day.

But shortly after five o'clock, something strange happened. The queue of the hunters of contracts vanished. Just like that. Starting apparently at the back of the queue, they had stolen away one by one, and within a few minutes their stealthy retreat had turned into a stampede toward their Mercedes-Benzes; in a short time all parking places were empty. Curious that they should refuse to heed a law enforcement officer but then flee within seconds of one another for no apparent reason! Very strange, the women told each other. Perhaps the same thing would happen to the other queue, they hoped, but no such luck: the queue remained intact with no indication that it would vanish like the other. The police rider attending it was nowhere in sight. As much as the two women strained their eyes and ears, they saw no police officer, no motorcycle.

If you had been there when Nyawīra was telling Kamītī all this, you would have wondered, just as he did, whether to cry or laugh, for, as she told him, there came a time when she and Vinjinia felt that the office had become their jail. The sun was calling it a day, but not the queuers. And the women hesitated to go home without a report from the missing police rider.

Vinjinia would now and then call to see if her husband was feeling any better, but there was no comfort from the homefront, and as the afternoon wore on Vinjinia became depressed, which did not help the atmosphere in the room.

All day long the two women had been on their feet, but now Nyawïra pulled up a chair, and, as she continued looking through the window, found herself wondering what could be ailing her boss so much as to force him to stay away from easy money, but not serious enough to make him see a doctor. Maybe it was a bad case of flu. But why would Vinjinia have been so reticent about that? And if Tajirika did not feel better soon, what was she to do about the queue? As if reading Nyawïra's thoughts, Vinjinia herself pulled up a chair next to Nyawïra. When she spoke, her voice sounded teary.

"I know what you are asking yourself," she started. "Believe me, I am as much in the dark as you. Where shall I begin? He came back last night with three sacks full of Burï notes. Throughout the evening he kept muttering things to himself, calculating I don't know what. Even when he eventually heeded my call to come to bed, he did not fall asleep but continued working things out in his mind. From the few words that I could make out, he seemed to be calculating the impact of Marching to Heaven on our lives. I fell asleep and left him wide awake.

"The illness itself seized him this morning. It started when he went to the bathroom: suddenly it was as if he stood frozen in front of the mirror. And every time he looked at the mirror, he could say nothing save *If! If only.* He would remain there, gazing hard at the mirror as if trying to talk to his shadow. Now tell me, how would I report these symptoms to a hospital or doctor? What could I tell them without sounding ridiculous? That my husband, the chairman of Marching to Heaven . . . ? But if he does not get better tonight, what shall we do tomorrow when we wake up to this or another queue?" Vinjinia asked, echoing Nyawïra's concern.

Nyawïra recalled how at the close of the previous business day Tajirika had pulled a gun on her, fearing that she might be a robber. Maybe he was terrified of being robbed.

"It was unusual for someone to have so much money in his house," Nyawïra said. "Maybe he was paralyzed by the prospect of robbers. His train of thought must have been something like this: If they find me with all this money, they will kill me. If! If only I had left the money in the office or put it in a bank?"

The sudden entrance of one of the three police officers now

guarding the grounds interrupted their conversation. He wanted to know what to do next: it was getting late, the queue was still there, and the police motorcycle rider had not yet returned.

Vinjinia paid him and his cohorts off to guard the premises for the night and to wait for the return of the missing rider.

The two women then closed up the office and left through the back door. The queue of job seekers was still intact. Maybe the darkness would drive them away. Maybe tomorrow would be another day. Vinjinia left in her black Mercedes-Benz without offering Nyawĩra a lift. "See you tomorrow" were her last words.

What a day! Nyawĩra thought as she walked down the road to the bus stop. She suspected that there was a lot more to her boss's illness than Vinjinia was letting on. If the police officer had not interrupted their tête-à-tête, maybe . . .

She had just crossed the road when she felt a hand on her right shoulder. She turned around quickly, clutching her handbag firmly. There were so many stories of daylight robbery in the streets that it had now become second nature to hold one's bag tighter at the slightest friction with another person.

She did not know whether to laugh in relief or shout in anger.

It was the ubiquitous Kaniũrũ.

Nyawĩra thought of pretending that she had not seen him, but a voice within told her, Let's hear what he has to say, we might glean a thing or two about what's going on in the higher reaches of government.

# 3

At the Mars Café, they again sat across from each other in barely veiled hostility. Kaniũrũ ordered coffee, Nyawĩra a chicken and vegetable sandwich, which she proceeded to eat with gusto, as if it had been the best meal she had ever had.

From where they sat, they could see a section of the endless queue.

"What's this all about?" Kaniūrū asked.

"Is that what brings you to this side of the city?"

"No, you!"

"Stop stalking me!"

"It is not me. My heart!"

"I didn't know that you had a heart."

"Stop that sarcasm. I just wanted to tell you that since we last met I have now done a little arithmetic, and some of the answers might interest you."

"You have now taken up math? What happened to the painter's easel and brush?"

"You know what? I have come to agree with your father. Were I in his shoes, I would not let my daughter marry an artist. Art is for women and children. There is something *effeminate* about it. That's why you dumped me, right?"

"Dumped you? On which heap?"

"Let's be serious. Now, about the man we discussed the other night . . . When I went home I thought a great deal about him. I concluded that the man in the suit who went into the public toilets was the one who left in rags. Nyawĩra, I must tell you this: he was one of the beggars outside Paradise, and we now know that the real force behind the beggars' gathering is the so-called Movement for the Voice of the People. He must be a member, as are all these people in the queue outside your office. How do I know that? The queue begins where I first saw the man standing, which could mean that while he was talking to you he was actually casing the joint. These people all want to smear the Ruler's good name by exaggerating the severity of unemployment, by dramatizing the plight of the unemployed. That man, your friend, is a threat to the stability and security of the country."

"You're out of your mind. You seem to have acquired the art of spinning tales! Yesterday he was a djinn; today he is provocateur, inciting anti-government activity!"

"There is no reason he cannot be both. You wait and see. The government has engaged an expert in djinns and djinn warfare. My own view is that those djinns are fake, mortals pretending to be djinns. And the policeman—what is his name? Gathere, Ariga, or something—is just a storyteller."

"And you, of course, are not."

"A human or a djinn, the man is a member of the Movement for the Voice of the People. He and you were together. Therefore you too could be a member. QED."

He knows nothing, she said to herself. Still, she was not amused by his logic, however warped. She sought to distract and confuse him.

"So Grace is talking to John. John is a youthwinger. Therefore Grace is a youthwinger. QED. Your logic is impeccable, worthy of Aristotle."

"It's not only white people who know logic. We too have logic, black logic found in our proverbs. You know the saying that he who keeps the company of lepers becomes a leper?"

"Well said," Nyawīra responded, laughing. "Preacherman, whose company do you keep? Crooks and looters. Therefore . . ."

"Listen to me. I am now the only one who can save you. Surely you've heard or read that the Ruler has banned the Movement for the Voice of the People?"

"An old song. Why don't you sing a new one through His Master's voice? Since when are you a spokes-youth for His Mightiness? Yet I have not seen you driving a Mercedes-Benz, the hallmark of arrival."

"That's only a matter of time. Nyawīra, you don't seem to understand what I am trying to tell you. Let me be more blunt. Do you know what the dissidents have been doing lately? Scattering plastic snakes and anti-government leaflets all over the country. The Ruler has given Sikiokuu special powers to crush this movement: its entire leadership, membership, supporters, and misguided fellow travelers. The minister intends to mobilize the entire secret security system, including us, the youthwings of the Ruler's Party. You see where I am coming from? I am giving you one last friendly warning. Come back to me or else . . ."

"That sounds more like a threat than a friendly warning; either way, you are wasting your breath," Nyawīra said as she stood up to go.

"Nyawīra, please listen to the logic of your heart. Since you and I parted, you have not taken up with another, and neither have I. What does that tell you?"

"Exactly what you've just said and nothing more," Nyawīra said, and left chuckling to herself.

"You woman. You! One day you will come back to me crawling on hands and knees!" Kaniūrū mumbled to himself in frustration.

# 4

Nyawīra had put on a brave face in order not to show worry in Kaniūrū's presence, but her heart was racing. She was sure that Kaniūrū and Sikiokuu knew very little about the movement. However, caution would not be cowardice if she could find a way to stop Kaniūrū from finding her again. Quitting her job was one option. But how would the movement be able to gather inside information about Marching to Heaven and the activities of the Global Bank mission? Changing her workplace was another. But would she always have to be on the run because of one man, Kaniūrū?

She thought about Kaniūrū and the years they had known each other. Their beginnings had looked so promising, at least to her, and she used to conjure up beautiful images of a future together: how they would always wake up at dawn, and with their youthful eyes raised to the azure they would hold hands and boldly step out into the world to build a home, the foundation of their new tomorrow! How differently this had turned out! Both came to look at the failed dreams differently: whereas she became convinced, with each passing day, that she could never change his ways to fit her ways, Kaniūrū always believed, even after they divorced, that he could convert her to his own way of looking at the world. He was the man to lead and she a woman to follow.

So absorbed was she in her thoughts that Nyawīra hardly noticed anything about the bus and *matatu* ride. Not that it mattered. She had taken the route so many times that she knew almost by instinct where to get off and her way home.

And that was why, suddenly, Nyawīra halted a few yards from her house, her mouth agape. Moonlight supplemented poor street lighting. She was baffled: in front of her house stood a queue.

At first she thought that she had lost her way. Perhaps she had taken the wrong bus. She should not have wasted so much time at the Mars Café, leading her to miss her regular bus and *matatu*. Or maybe she had gotten off at the wrong stop or taken a wrong turn! Maybe the job seekers had seen her leave the office and had followed her home. But she could have sworn that at the time she left the Mars Café, the queue that began at the billboard outside her office was still there. Looking more carefully at the men lined up before her, she saw that they were all dressed in suits, a far cry from the patched-up, worn-out vestments of the job seekers. But she could not make out their faces; the men wore hoods and wide-rimmed hats.

Nyawīra thought of approaching one to ask what this was all about. She took a step and stopped. What if they were the newly activated eyes and ears and noses of the Ruler? Suddenly she thought about Kamītī. What had happened to him? Her fear deepened as she recalled how Kaniūrū had told her that Sikiokuu had been given special powers to crush opponents of the regime. Kaniūrū was obsessed with Kamītī, and he may have directed the state security forces to her home. Or had A.G. returned with a police squad? A.G. had hinted that he would do as much, and now that he seemed to have been entrusted with the task of capturing djinns, he might be intent on bagging the Wizard of the Crow.

She walked briskly to the house of one of her neighbors to find out what was going on. But on her way, she saw a man come out of his house and go to the back, where he pissed against the wall. She approached him just before he reentered his house.

"What is all this about?" she asked nonchalantly, gesturing toward the queue without revealing that she was the occupant of the house under siege.

"Those? Leave them alone!" the man said. "It is all because of the witch doctor—what does he call himself?—the Wizard of the Crow. The ways of witch doctors are strange. Two days have come and gone since he put up the notice outside his door announcing his nefarious business, and at first no more than ten clients came to consult him. Now look at this. All of a sudden, today, well, this evening. I've no idea what this is all about. Lady, go your way and I'll go mine; it's never good to ask too many questions in the dark."

Nyawīra had seen many wonders in Santalucia, but this topped them all; she did not know whether to laugh or cry. She went to the back of her house and knocked at the window. There was no immediate response. She waited for a little while and knocked again. At the third attempt the curtains parted. She saw a human silhouette. At the sight of Kamītī, Nyawīra felt relief. He helped her climb through the bedroom window and he gestured to her to be quiet and not budge, and then he went back to his business.

# 5

From the bedroom where she sat, Nyawīra could not see the actors, but she heard every word between Kamītī and his clients. The whole thing seemed like ritual theater.

"What ails you?" she heard Kamītī ask the man on the other side of the kitchen pass-through.

"My enemies."

"Your enemies?"

"Yes, my fellow businessmen. You might see us dining and wining each other, and laughing and slapping one another on the back, but this is all a lie. Now it looks as if the Global Bank is about to release funds for Marching to Heaven. Do you know what that means? A contract to supply even tea, butter, cigarettes, or the smallest necessities could make one wealthy for the rest of one's life. You see my point? If we are always scheming against one another even when the stakes are low, imagine what's going on now. I own many quarries. All I want is to become the chief supplier of cement, stone, and sand for Marching to Heaven. But believe me, Sir Wizard, my enemies are many, they are everywhere, they are ruthless, and they want what I want."

"So what are you after at the shrine of the Wizard of the Crow?"

"I want you to add firmness to my hands, smoothness to my tongue, and power to my eyes, so that when I meet Chairman Titus he and I will bond immediately. I want to mesmerize his eyes with mine, soften his heart with my tongue, and seal the deal of friendship with a warm handshake. At the same time, I want you to take away all powers of persuasion from my competitors. Make their hands limp and wet with sweat so that when they shake those of Chairman Titus, they will only piss him off; roughen their tongues so that when they roll them out to sing his praises, they will produce rasping noises worse than the screeching of metal on metal; cause their eyes to run with filth so that when they try to make him captive to their wishes they will only disgust and repel him. Do you know the story of the great battle between the Sun and Wind over who could make Man take off his coat? Wind made Man only cling more to his possession. Sun made him surrender it willingly. Wizard of the Crow, make my enemies the Wind. Make me the Sun. Put me at the head of my class, first among equals in guile and venom."

"Do you know your enemies? Who they are?"

"Not that well. And that is why I have come to you. We have heard of your amazing powers, that you can tell one's enemies long before one even knows that one has enemies; and that you can capture the shadows of these in a mirror and scratch them out of this world. Now I am not asking you to kill them—I am a good Christian and I believe in forgiveness—but I want you to do that which only you can do."

"And who told you all this about me?"

"It's a long story, but I shall make it short. I was in another queue outside the office of Chairman Titus. He was unable to come to the office, but we stuck to our guns, waiting in line the whole day. Then a friend who heard it from a friend who heard it from a friend who had been told about it by a police officer who supplies him with useful information in exchange for a fee—you know how it is in Aburĩria today, nothing is for free and information is power—anyway this police officer told him what you had done for one of his police mates: sent all his enemies packing to the other world and had him promoted to a rank that he could never have dreamt of. Later, rumor has it, you received ten other policemen, the original informant being among them. So I thought, let me sneak out of this queue in front of Titus's office and secure more powers before I meet with Chairman Titus tomorrow."

Nyawĩra now understood why at about six the queue of the rich and the powerful had mysteriously ceased to be, leaving her and Vinjinia wondering.

"Sir Wizard of the Crow," the patient was now saying, "I want you to use only your mirror, and whatever you want will be yours. How much do you charge for divining with a mirror?"

"I don't put a price on divining. But the mirror demands some effort and decision on the part of he who seeks its power to reveal the hidden. The mirror sees and sends back only what is placed in front of it. You place more, it sees more, you place less, it sees less. So the matter is entirely in the hands of they who seek its powers of divination."

"Money is nothing to me," Nyawīra heard the man shout. "I want you to use the most powerful mirror possible. Maximum power. I will place an offering of the biggest envelope possible before the oracle, and I am sure it will please the mirror."

"I grant you your wishes," said Kamītī, and he now outlined the same steps he had earlier worked out with Constable A.G. and the ten policemen. "Close your eyes tight. Look for the image that forms in the night of your mind. The moment you see it, you must alert the Wizard of the Crow. Once I capture the image in your mind in my mirror, I will then scratch its hands, mouth, and eyes to weaken them. Weakening the organs of your enemy is the same thing as strengthening yours. It is like any scale. There are two ways of changing the balance between two opposing forces. You either add weight to one side or you remove weight from the opposite side. Divining is a science."

"It is not the love of science that brought me to your shrine," the man said with passion. "I want something that occurs without discernible rhyme or reason. I want the pure play of occult powers. I want magic, not science."

Nyawīra could hardly believe her ears. If she had heard an account of what she herself had heard, she would almost certainly have dismissed it as a lie: the rich and the powerful denouncing scientific reason in favor of illogical mumbo jumbo. And to know that these men belong to the same class as the leaders of new nations? What did the future of the country hold with these men at the helm?

Her ruminations were suddenly interrupted by a rapturous scream from the divinee.

"I can see an image! I see it!" the man was saying in the tone of a child who has discovered a new ability.

"Can you tell whose image it is?" asked the Wizard of the Crow.

"No! No! But it does not matter—let this image stand for all my enemies."

"Hold it! Hold it right there! Don't let it slip away," Kamītī told him, and he started scratching the mirror.

"The image is now no more. Instead I see numerous starlets falling in the dark," the man said. "Maybe it is my enemies shattered like broken glass! This is wonderful! Starlets falling about me, leaving me the lone star in the firmament!"

"Then the deed is done. You saw what you wanted to see. You can now open your eyes. Your luck lies before you."

"Thank you! Thank you, Sir Wizard," the man said. "New powers course through me. I can now march in step with Marching to Heaven."

He left and instantly another took his place. To Nyawīra the procession was like one cinematic frame dissolving into another. The frames may have had different characters, but the story was the same. In the end Nyawīra grew tired of hearing it and fell asleep.

Water splashing woke her up. Kamītī was showering, and she waited for him to finish. He was scrubbing himself with grim determination.

"You almost used up all the water," she said when they were together in the sitting room.

"It is the stench they left behind," Kamītī said. "I still feel that I never got rid of it. Look through the window; see if they're all gone."

Nyawīra peered outside. The queue of hooded human silhouettes did not appear to be diminishing. She closed the window and looked at Kamītī askance.

"When midnight came," Kamītī explained, "I wrote a notice, CLOSED FOR THE NIGHT: COME BACK TOMORROW, and I asked the one I saw last to hang it outside."

"They are doing exactly what they did in the day when I posted the notice about Tajirika's absence," Nyawīra said.

"What are you talking about?" Kamītī asked, puzzled.

She told Kamītī about her day at the office and about the grant of special powers to Sikiokuu to crush the Movement for the Voice of the People. Kamītī in turn recounted his adventures as the Wizard of the Crow.

"A never-ending dream," Kamītī concluded.

"More like a never-ending nightmare," Nyawīra said, looking at her watch and suddenly standing up. "It is very late. Tomorrow we shall need all the strength we can muster to face the queuing daemons."

"When we wake up," Kamītī said, "we shall find them gone."

# 6

But the queues did not go away. For a while all the news of the Global Bank mission, the battles of Mariko and Maritha with Satan, and the saga of flying souls and pamphleteering djinns was supplanted by the drama of the invasion of Eldares by queuing daemons.

Nyawīra and Vinjinia arrived at the office at about the same time every day. They talked of how curious it was that the queue of hunters for future contracts had dwindled to zero, Nyawīra neglecting to tell Vinjinia that it had simply changed location. Pressed by Vinjinia to do something about the remaining queue, the Santamaria police said there was not much they could do without the report from the police motorcycle rider who had still not returned. So the two women waited patiently for the return of the rider to signal the end of the queue.

Their monotony was broken only when Vinjinia brought her two children, Gacirū and Gacīgua, to the office during midterm break. The children said that they did not want to stay home with their father because he kept on barking a single phrase over and over, and they were a little afraid that he might be turning into a dog.

Gacirū and Gacīgua were so excited by the sight of the queue that they quickly forgot about their father's illness. They stood by the window, looking out and asking endless questions. Were they students? For only in school had they seen people queue. They soon grew bored with the whole thing, as there was little out there by way of shoving, hide-and-seek, or frantic chases eliciting admonition.

Gacīgua was the first to ask their mother to tell them a story, and Vinjinia pointed at their new auntie.

Nyawīra sang them work songs and recited poems about weaver-birds and elephants. But the children wanted stories. Nyawīra told them that stories were for evenings only, at home by the fireside and not daytime in the office by the phoneside. *Hakuna matata*. Gacirū and Gacīgua would pretend that it was evening and the office was home and all the people in the queue were listeners. Eventually

Nyawĩra yielded and said she would tell them a story about a black-smith, an ogre, and a pregnant woman.

What are ogres? they now wanted to know, and Nyawĩra explained that the *marimũ* were humanlike creatures who sometimes fed on humans, including little children. The creatures had two mouths, one in front and the other at the back of their heads, and they ate flies through the mouth at the back. Otherwise the mouth at the back was well concealed by the creature's long hair, which fell over its shoulders.

"Like my mother's hair?" Gacirũ asked.

"Gacirũ, are you saying that your mother is an ogre?" interjected Vinjinia, laughing.

"My mother is not an ogre," said Gacĩgua. "She does not eat other humans."

"Tell us the story," they said in unison.

A certain blacksmith went to an iron smithery far away. In his absence, his pregnant woman gave birth to two children.

"Like us two," Gacirũ said in a tone between a question and a statement.

"Yes, like you two, a boy and a girl, but in their case they were twins."

"What were their names?" Gacĩgua asked.

Nyawĩra was caught off-guard, for in the version she had received the children had no names.

"At the time of the events of the story, the woman had not given them names," she said.

"Why?" Gacirũ asked.

"Because it was an ogre who helped her deliver and who now nursed her, and she did not want the ogre to know their names," Nyawĩra improvised again.

"Why did the ogre do all that?" Gacirũ asked.

"Silly. Because the husband was not there," Gacĩgua chimed in.

"Mummy! Mummy, Gacĩgua is calling me silly!"

"Stop it, you two," Vinjinia shouted from where she was, "or I shall ask Nyawĩra not to tell you stories anymore."

The ogre was really a very bad nurse. After cooking food, he would dish it out and put the plate in front of the woman, but as soon as she stretched her hand to pick it up the ogre would quickly take the dish away and say: "I see you don't want to eat my food, but it is all right, I will eat it for you." The ogre did the same with water: "You don't want it? I shall drink it for you."

"Gacīgua teases me in the same way," Gacirū complained.

"You do the same to me," Gacīgua shot back.

They argued back and forth, each accusing the other of the same mean crime, and they would have gone on except for Nyawīra's warning them that if they did not stop the story would disappear.

"Tell us what happened next," they pleaded.

All four grew big tummies: of kwashiorkor for mother and children and of fat for the ogre.

One day the woman saw a weaverbird in the yard.

"Is that the same weaverbird that you sang about?" Gacirū asked.

"Which one?" Nyawīra asked, for she had forgotten about the earlier song.

"How can she tell the story if you two keep on interrupting her with endless questions?" Vinjinia interjected.

"We shall not ask anymore," Gacirū and Gacīgua said together, "until the end."

In exchange for castor oil seeds, the bird agreed to take a message to the blacksmith far away. Nyawīra described how the bird flew and flew and flew until it finally reached the smelting yard and landed on the branches of a tree. It was very tired, but it sang.

> *Blacksmith smelting iron*
> *Make haste, make haste*
> *Your wife has given birth*
> *With the ogre as the midwife*
> *With the ogre as the nurse*
> *Make haste, make haste*
> *Before it is too late*

Nyawīra asked Gacīgua and Gacirū to join in the singing so that they would help in defeating the ogre. The weaverbird jumped from tree to tree, trying to attract the smith's attention. Now, the blacksmith was with others, and at first they simply chased it away as a nuisance, but seeing the bird's persistence they took the time to listen to it more carefully. It was then that the blacksmith remembered that he had left a pregnant wife behind and realized that the bird was telling him of the danger facing his wife and children. He gathered his spear and shield and ran as fast as his legs could carry him, soon reaching home, where he joined his wife and children, and with their combined strength they were able to defeat the evil creature.

"Did you say 'their combined strength'?" Gacirū asked. "I thought that babies cannot fight?"

"Or women?" added Gacīgua.

"Who told you that women cannot fight?" asked Gacirū. "Me, I cannot let a boy, any boy, beat me without fighting back," Gacirū said, glaring at Gacīgua.

"I talked about their strengths, big and small, being combined," Nyawīra told them, explaining how the babies cooperated by not crying too much and how the woman, though weak, gave the husband all the details she had learned about the ogre and even suggested the best way of defeating the big ogre, for by now she knew all about the evil creature. She would taunt him to distract him while the husband came out of his hiding place to attack. And that was exactly what happened.

They spent the day spinning tales, songs, and riddles, and the scene was the same the next day. To Gacirū and Gacīgua, this was the perfect midterm break, and they hoped all of life would be like that: an endless festival of storytelling with Nyawīra as the sole narrator, for she could change her voice to sound like a bird, a lion, an old woman, a man, a child, anything. They liked stories of the trickster hare the best, though they were fascinated by the scary ones of the ogre.

Indeed, a couple of days later, Gacirū revisited the issue of ogres and the second mouth concealed under a thick mass of long hair. This time Gacirū had Nyawīra all to herself and sat on her lap. Vinjinia and Gacīgua were looking through the window at the never-ending queue outside.

"You know, I have been thinking about the story of the ogre, and I don't think that it was their hair alone that hid the mouth at the back. Both the mouth and the hair were hidden under the hats the ogres wore. Don't you think so? Hats can also hide the mouth, can't they? Like those worn by those policemen outside? Tell me, are policemen ogres?"

"Sssh!" Vinjinia said from where she sat by the window.

"That's clever," Nyawĩra said. "I mean about the hats. How did you work it out?"

"It is simple. My mother has long hair but she does not wear a hat. Therefore, Mummy," she now called out, "you are not an ogre."

"Thank you," Vinjinia said. "Is that what has been waking you up at night, making you turn my hair over?"

"You see, Mummy, ogres are bad and cunning and they can make themselves look like somebody else. In school the teacher read to us the story of Red Riding Hood and how she went to see her sick grandmother, and you know what, Mummy? The girl found a big bad wolf hiding in the bed, pretending to be the grandmother. And you know what? The wolf had already eaten the grandmother . . ."

Gacĩgua, who had seemed not to be following the conversation, now shouted a question.

"Do ogres ride motorcycles?"

"Why?" asked Nyawĩra.

"A stranger on a motorbike is riding this way . . ."

# 7

The rider returned after seven days and, to some, he sounded like a madman. There was continuity to his narrative, all right, but he kept rolling his eyes as if to show that even he found it difficult to believe the story he was telling his debriefers.

Those privy to his report tell of his amazing claim that for seven days, he, the rider, one hand holding a bullhorn, the other steering the motorcycle, had done nothing but follow the queue; he did not even get off his vehicle but actually slept on it while still in motion, for, aware of his duty as a loyal police officer, he wanted to reach the end of the queue as soon as possible so as to give a report both prompt and thorough. But whenever he thought that he was nearing the end, he found that more job seekers had already gotten in line.

During the first two days he had raced along the queue, only to discover on the third day that others were feeding it. He was uncertain as to which direction to go, not wanting to be like the hyena who once tried to travel more than one path at the same time, with tragic results. So he decided to stick to the main branch, or what he assumed was the main queue.

At the beginning of his mission he had proudly announced the message to the people standing in line: *Chairman Titus Tajirika is not in the office today. Please go home and come back tomorrow.* But he soon found it cumbersome, speaking as he was on his motorcycle, a bullhorn in one hand. He would start proclaiming it to some, only to pass them by without completing his remarks. As a result, people were getting bits of information. So the rider figured that it would make more sense to shorten the sentence. First he cut out all unnecessary words like *Chairman Titus Tajirika.* Next, all the explanations about the boss not being in the office. Then he stopped telling people that they'd better go home and abbreviated it to *Come back tomorrow,* which he subsequently shortened to one word: *Tomorrow.* But even so, some people heard only syllables, some catching *to,* others *mor,* and yet others *row.*

He became the subject of heated discussions among the queuers, who concluded that he must be possessed of the daemons that usually force politicians to spew out words for the sake of hearing themselves talk, whether or not they made any sense. They nicknamed him Motorized Madman, soon the name of choice for all traffic police officers.

After roaming for seven days through towns near and around Eldares in pursuit of the end of the queue, he eventually found himself back in Santamaria. The tail of the queue had somehow joined the head to make a huge circle, and that, in the view of analysts, was the real problem that faced the rider. He had been moving in circles, and only when he spotted the Mars Café did he realize that he had traveled back to the beginning. How many times he had circled the city without his knowing will forever remain a mystery, even to him. All the rider could now say was that had it not been for the Mars Café, he might have spent the rest of his life searching for the end of the queue.

Actually, this rider could talk only about the one queue that he had attended to; countless others appeared in every corner of

Eldares. For a time it was as if everybody in Eldares was possessed. If a person happened to be window shopping, he would suddenly find that a queue had formed behind him. People did not even bother to ask what the queue was about; they simply assumed that there was good reason for it and wanted their share of whatever was being dispersed. Rumors that Marching to Heaven was already underway and that the financial missionaries from the Global Bank were doling out cash served only to intensify the fever. Sometimes a person would start a queue without being aware that he had done so, go home, and on the following day join the same queue, still ignorant that he had been its innocent first cause. Lines simply assumed lives of their own.

At the conclusion of his oral report, the police officer fell asleep from utter exhaustion at police headquarters. For seven days and nights, he tossed and turned in his own filth, as one gripped by a nightmare. When, after seven days of sleep, he awoke screaming for his Yamaha to continue with the unfinished task of following all the queues to their origins, he was committed to a psychiatric ward for observation and later given indefinite leave without pay to recuperate.

When his report reached the ears of the Ruler, he immediately summoned his ministers to an emergency cabinet meeting to figure out ways of preventing the daemonic queues from spreading to the other cities.

# 8

It became obvious, at the emergency session at the State House, that what most concerned the Ruler was the crazed rider's observation that the queues seemed to have no beginning and no end. That sounds dangerous, doesn't it? he asked the cabinet, without a trace of humor.

Sikiokuu, the first to respond, said that since it was illegal, in all Aburĩria, for more than five people to gather without a police permit, the unlicensed queuing was a clear violation of the law and suggested to the whole world not only that unemployment had reached a crisis but that there were shortages of goods in shops. This was terrible for the image of the country. But why was all this happening now, during the Global Bank mission? To frighten investors? Were there some in their midst who were subtly inciting citizens to queue as the first step of a revolt of the masses? Perhaps those who had arranged the Bank's visit had something else up their political sleeves. Ban the queues. Yes, let them go the way of the Movement for the Voice of the People, Sikiokuu added, tugging at his earlobes for emphasis.

Machokali, the Minister for Foreign Affairs, who spoke next, started by pointing at his eyes to show that he was watchful at all times and, most important, that he was not about to let Sikiokuu get away with damaging innuendos.

"What does Minister Sikiokuu mean by saying that queues should go the way of the Movement for the Voice of the People?" he asked. "Does he not know that the movement to which he refers dwells underground like a mole, its members frightened of the Ruling light? Is the minister intimating that these queues should be forced underground, where they will be harder to detect and ferret out? I am sure that the minister will soon clarify his intentions."

As long as the Global Bank mission was in the country, Machokali advised, the Ruler should stay the course, carefully weighing his words and actions, and not allow himself to be provoked into recklessness by people with their own agendas.

"Your Mighty Excellency, we should not do anything that can be used against us by those in the world who infer from the fact that we have only one Party and one Ruler that fear rules Aburĩria. If anything, the queues should help to undermine their unfounded allegations. The sight of people lining up for whatever the reason, wherever, whenever, and however, should create a very good impression of the State in the Global Bank missionaries."

"Is the minister implying that our country takes orders from the Global Bank?" Sikiokuu interjected, stung by Machokali's words.

With that one question, Sikiokuu had slipped. He did not realize this immediately, but the others had seen the Ruler frown and had grown tense.

"Mr. Sikiokuu, are you saying that I take orders from the Global Bank?"

"No, no, Your Mighty Excellency, I was not talking about you," Sikiokuu tried to explain. "I was talking about the Country."

He had slipped again.

"There is a difference between me and the Country?" the Ruler growled. "Have we not visited this already?"

Machokali seized the moment to further isolate his rival. He was on his feet, chanting: *His Mighty Ruler is the Mighty Country and the Mighty Country is the Ruler.* Led by Big Ben Mambo, the other ministers also stood up and chanted, *The Ruler and the Country are one and the same,* and soon it became a call-and-response ceremony led by Machokali.

The moment that he saw Machokali jump up with unalloyed alacrity, Sikiokuu had realized that he had slipped again, very badly, and for a second or so he did not know whether or not to stand up and join the others. How could he sing a song initiated by his enemy, moreover a song meant to isolate and humiliate him? So instead of joining the chorus he fell to his knees and bowed his head so low that his ears touched the ground, as if to demonstrate that action spoke louder than words.

The jubilant Machokali intensified his orchestration, and the calling and responding would have gone on for quite a while had the Ruler not gestured to them to sit down and let him hear what the man on his knees had to say for himself.

"There is nobody in the whole world," Sikiokuu pleaded tremulously, "who does not know that the Ruler is this Country and this Country is His Mighty Country. It is also well known that many other leaders are jealous of that irrevocable identity. All I was saying is that unlicensed queuing should be banned so as not to be exploited by your enemies within and without to question that identity. Otherwise, I am a firm believer that You are the Country and the Country is You, and I propose that this fact be stated in the constitution. I swear before Your Mighty Presence that I shall myself make a motion in Parliament to amend the constitution accordingly."

The Ruler signaled Machokali to carry on, and it was not lost on anybody that the leader had not only ignored Sikiokuu's words but had not even asked him to return to his seat. Sikiokuu remained on his knees for the entire meeting.

A triumphant Machokali could not help but beat his rival into the ground. There was no point, he said, in changing the constitution to include something as obvious as the fact that the sun is the source of heat and light. "But I don't want to get embroiled in this foolishness," he said. "I want to go back to the report of the police rider. It is obvious that the queuing is connected with Marching to Heaven. Employers and workers knew the project meant economic growth and jobs galore; that was why even before the project had been launched employer and employee stood shoulder to shoulder in the streets of Eldares in support of Marching to Heaven! Has anything like this ever happened in the history of the world? The lion and the lamb lying together? Fear not those who queue in hope but those who fear those who queue in hope. Take a cue from me: use the queue, don't abuse it. Instead of banning queuing, we should present it to the world as the very picture of a nation lining up behind its leader's vision."

The Ruler was pleased with the idea. Ever since the people abandoned him in the park for fear of snakes, he had tried to hatch a scheme that would prove how much they still loved him, how much they desired nothing more than to follow in his footsteps. Here now was an opportunity.

As soon as the other ministers realized that the Ruler was excited by Machokali's motion, their tongues loosened, each claiming, one after another, that queuing was most intense in his respective region with his constituents singing nothing but songs in praise of Marching to Heaven. A few regions where the mania had yet to break out said they would send word to the grass roots to immediately get busy. Others suggested that the Bank missionaries should tour the city and other parts of the country to see for themselves the extent of popular support for Marching to Heaven.

Even the humbled Sikiokuu tried to swim with the current, claiming that the Ruler was the founding father of all queuing and others were merely following his example. In his capacity as the Minister of State in the Ruler's office entrusted with security, he, Sikiokuu, would add hundreds of M5s to the queues to ensure that no one would abuse the queuing mania as a referendum on anarchy.

"A queuing referendum for Marching to Heaven," Big Ben Mambo burst out, resenting Sikiokuu's continuing attempts to deflate Machokali's ideas. This triggered a round of political discussion, especially after Big Ben Mambo suggested that the queuing referendum could produce a new theory of politics, a point strongly supported by the Minister of Education. The latter insisted that such a theory, bearing the Ruler's name, could be taught in all Aburīrian schools and colleges, supplanting the outmoded theories of Plato, Aristotle, Hobbes, and Pope. Another minister said that the political theories of ancient Greece belonged to the dead and should be thrown out the window. "We cannot allow the sepulchral mud of the dead to besmirch the spectacular mind of the living," he said, and they all laughed. Even the Ruler graced the remark with a smile and a humble opinion.

"Some people think that it is only white people who can come up with new theories, and they are wrong!" he said, and all the ministers chorused back: *Yeees!*

They had gotten the hint and unanimously selected Machokali to head a committee to write down the Ruler's Theory of Politics and Government.

Fearing that all the blessings would pass him by, Sikiokuu, speaking from his kneeling position, said that by queuing people were already putting theory to practice and only the Ruler could claim credit from it. What they needed to do was find a way to thank the people for queuing with such boundless enthusiasm. He himself volunteered to announce the Ruler's gratitude over prime-time radio and TV and to tour the country thanking the people in the name of the Ruler for supporting the vision of Marching to Heaven.

Machokali glared at him. He would not give the cunning fellow an opportunity to put a foot in the door of Marching to Heaven. The idea of ensuring that every queue was infiltrated by M5 was excellent, Machokali said, and it showed that Minister Sikiokuu, even on his knees, could be quick on his feet when it mattered. But it was best to leave media to the Minister of Information, Big Ben Mambo, for were the announcement to come from the Ruler's office it would create the impression, totally false, that the people had been coerced into queuing, and this would definitely take away from the positive impression of a spontaneous grassroots anticipation of Marching to Heaven. And even then, a simple statement would suffice.

Years later a few of those present would look back on this moment and wonder, Had Machokali foreseen it all, or in trying to crush his kneeling rival had he stumbled onto something with a significance that could be seen only in hindsight? All they could recall was Machokali whispering almost to himself, "They were four, but we can send five." Some even claimed that the words were preceded by a light from his eyes so intense that it momentarily lit the room.

"What are you talking about?" the Ruler asked, puzzled.

"The four horsemen in the Book of Revelations," he said without any hesitation.

"And what has that got to do with us?"

There was absolute silence as Machokali revealed his plan: they should send a rider to each of the five regions—northern, southern, western, eastern, and central—to assess firsthand the heat of the queuing fever and its effect on the general populace. The first thing he would impress upon the five riders selected by him was that they should make haste and not spend a whole week going in circles. He would tell them to roam all Aburĩria and take a census of existing queues while conveying the Ruler's gratitude and pleasure at the queuing and urging even more spontaneous eruptions in support of Marching to Heaven.

Sikiokuu felt outmaneuvered and wished that he could answer with something from the Quran or another holy text. But, mindful of the saying that if you can't beat them, join them, he argued that the duty of sending out more riders rested entirely with his department, as security matters were involved.

Those ministers who normally monitored the war between the two rivals, always leaning toward the winner, named the struggle that just ended the Battle of the Five Riders, but they were not quite sure which side had won.

As he left the State House, Sikiokuu fumed, and some even say that, like a hippo's under water, his heavy breathing produced bubbles of air from his mouth and nostrils and that the bubbles surrounded him and his car all the way to the office. The minister was seething with rage. He had to be obedient, but in so being he did not want to further enhance his rival's standing in the eyes of the Ruler. How could he at once obey the Ruler and avenge himself? He would use the written word to account for the letter of the law, and the spoken to subvert its spirit.

On five sheets of paper bearing the letterhead THE OFFICE OF THE

RULER, Sikiokuu typed the title *Riders of the Ruler*. To each he specified precise instructions: *Know ye by this letter that I am sending ye to
said direction* . . . ; the duty of each being to observe and assess; convey the Ruler's satisfaction with the queuing; and spread the gospel
where it had not reached. Sikiokuu would have signed the letters on
behalf of the Ruler but thought better of it; he took them to the
leader who, berating Sikiokuu—Why did you waste my time with
such petty matters? Why did you not sign them yourself?—affixed his
signature with relish and even stamped the letters with the seal of the
State House.

Armed with the authorization, Sikiokuu summoned the chosen
five to his office and handed each a letter, the most precious document they had ever come across. They were particularly delighted
with the Ruler's signature, for it made them see themselves truly as
his envoys to the country and the world. But Sikiokuu took pains with
his instructions.

He told the Riders of the Ruler that while there was some urgency
to the matter, what was most important was absolute diligence: he
would have no mercy for any who returned without having visited
every nook and cranny of the country wherever there were queues,
rumors of queues, or possibilities of queues. They could even go
beyond the country, the Ruler's envoys to the world, if necessary, he
added, hoping in a light touch, but it did not come out that way. In
short, there was really no hurry and they could take their time and
space performing their duty, he told them, before sending them off to
the world on brand new motorcycles.

At the time that Sikiokuu was tweaking his own instructions, his
rival, Machokali, was recalling, not without a sense of wonder, his
inspired "riders of the apocalypse" moment. What most pleased him
was that Sikiokuu would be sending riders to all the five regions of
Aburĩria to spread the very gospel of queuing, upon which he had at
first tried to heap scorn. Furthermore, queuing as mass support for
Marching to Heaven now had the Ruler's blessings. Machokali was
certain that the five riders' reports would redound to his credit. What
foresight on his part to have put forward the name of Tajirika as
chairman of Marching to Heaven, for from all accounts, including
that of the crazed rider, the queuing had started outside the offices of
Eldares Modern Construction and Real Estate.

Following the emergency Cabinet session, Machokali placed a call to Tajirika's house to congratulate him on the fact that the daemons of queuing had started outside his offices. But he was disappointed to hear that Tajirika was still indisposed. What a time for his friend to get the flu! With whom would he share the joy of victory?

That night he dreamt that he beheld four messengers, four riders on white cycles . . . He woke up in a sweat. Why four and not five?

He called Tajirika's house again. Would Tajirika please call him back as soon as he felt better?

# 9

Tajirika, chairman of Marching to Heaven, CEO of Eldares Modern Construction and Real Estate, and friend of the Minister for Foreign Affairs, was not in a position to return any calls. He sat in front of the bathroom mirror all day long, his chin in cupped hands, staring vacuously into space. Sometimes his sight would stray into the mirror, slightly, ever so slightly, and he would mutter the word *if* and then resume looking nowhere. But when his eyes rested on the mirror a bit longer, he would bark the word continuously, his body shaking uncontrollably, until he moved his eyes away from the mirror and achieved an uneasy calm.

In the early days of the affliction, Vinjinia believed that the mirror was somehow responsible for her husband's condition, so one evening she lured him into bed, and when he fell asleep she relocated the mirror elsewhere, hoping to put an end to Tajirika's violent *if*s.

The following morning Tajirika's face was cheerfulness itself, as if the illness had vanished along with his having missed work the previous day. He set about his morning rituals with gusto, indications that he intended to go to the office as usual, and, seeing this, Vinjinia felt no need to bring up his erstwhile malady. There was one more hurdle to jump and all will be well, she thought as she watched him go to the bathroom. A second later, Tajirika was shouting, demanding to know who had removed the mirror from the wall. How was he supposed to shave without a mirror? He accused the children of being the culprits and threatened to beat them, forcing Vinjinia to own up to what she had done. I forgot to put it back when I mopped the wall clean, she said. Her stratagem had failed. For no sooner was the mirror in place when the *if*s came back with debilitating force. It was Vinjinia who once again went to the office while Tajirika remained at home, in the bathroom, same as the day before.

Things got worse. Vinjinia helplessly watched as Tajirika scratched his face between his *if*s and *if only*s. He then removed his clothes and jumped into the bathtub, where he scratched himself all over, not uttering a word. He had lost all speech, save two words. Again she removed the mirror from the wall, but this time nothing would make her put it back.

Emerging from the bathtub, Tajirika seemed shocked and confused when he did not find the mirror on the wall. But, having lost the ability to speak beyond "if" and "if only," he just gesticulated frantically in frustration. Finally, he rifled through Vinjinia's handbag and found a small mirror. He spent the whole day holding the mirror in one hand, scratching himself with the other, and now and then jumping into the bathtub. Even when he went to bed that night he held on to the mirror the way a child clings to a beloved toy. When she came home from the office, Vinjinia once again waited until he fell asleep, took the mirror from his hands, and hid it. In the morning she instructed the workers to make sure that there was not a single mirror lying about in the house or anywhere else on the compound. Mirrorless, Tajirika became increasingly depressed.

Vinjinia started phoning up doctors she knew to be discreet, telling them only that her husband was low in spirit and occasionally scratched his face, omitting even the slightest reference to the mirror and Tajirika's loss of speech. When some suggested that she bring him to their clinics she would quickly downplay the seriousness of his malady. Others said flat out that they could not prescribe a cure over the phone; a few suggested over-the-counter drugs to relieve the itching and depression. The drugs did not work.

What was she to do? As the days passed without her husband getting any better, Vinjinia felt a need to share her secret with others.

"I think he has been bewitched," Vinjinia one day told Nyawīra.

They were now into the second week as coworkers. The rider had come back all right, but for Vinjinia and Nyawīra the news of endless queues and motorized madness was depressing. Gacirū and Gacīgua had gone back to school, and Nyawīra missed the storytelling sessions.

"You see, a lot of people are envious of his success," Vinjinia went on, "and particularly his appointment to head Marching to Heaven. Now he is not even eating well. If you saw him you would not recognize him, he has lost so much weight."

"Who would want to cast an evil spell on him?" Nyawīra asked, curious as to whom Vinjinia considered an enemy.

"I don't know; maybe any of those so-called businessmen who came here to make his acquaintance. They don't come around anymore. Why? Perhaps as soon as they knew their evil had worked, they stopped."

"But how do you know he is bewitched?" Nyawīra asked, recalling that Vinjinia was a devout Christian. "Did he do, eat, or wear anything unusual before or during his illness?"

Vinjinia remembered the glove he wore on one hand, which was very strange because even when he ate or went to bed he never took it off.

"Yes," Vinjinia said, after wondering to what extent she should confide in Nyawīra. "Since the Marching to Heaven craze began, my husband has taken to wearing a glove on his right hand. He never takes it off, and so he never washes the hand."

"Remove the glove," Nyawīra suggested.

That night, after making sure that he was asleep, Vinjinia removed the glove from Tajirika's hand, and it stank so badly that she threw it to the floor. Was the stench attributable to the bewitchment? What if she herself became a victim of the same dark powers? she suddenly thought in fright. She was determined to avoid further contact with the glove or with the hand that wore it. But how could she allow these powers to dictate what she should or should not touch in her own house, including her husband's hand? She brought her Bible, kept it near, and felt more courageous. She examined the hand. There were small crusts of dirt under the long fingernails. She thought of trimming the nails, washing the hand, and throwing the glove into the garbage bag, but this would have been tantamount to discarding evidence. She picked up the glove from the floor and put it in a drawer.

The following day she told Nyawīra that she was now sure that her husband had been bewitched by the evil placed inside the glove.

"Why in the glove?" Nyawīra asked. "And why did the evil not strike when he first wore it?"

"You have a point there," Vinjinia said. "The bewitchment must have happened as they shook hands in this very office or slipped in the envelopes with the money. He became ill soon after counting, well, touching the money with the glove."

"Money? Was there a lot?" Nyawīra asked, not only to keep the conversation alive but also to learn the actual figure.

"You should see how much!" Vinjinia said with pride and fear, looking around to make sure that the police officers guarding the yard were not within hearing distance. "Each of three sacks was full of notes, and no note was worth less than a hundred Burĩs."

"Three sacks bulging tight with notes?" Nyawīra asked histrionically.

"So you can see why not everybody might be happy for him," Vinjinia said. "The evildoers could have been any of those who brought the sacks of money."

"Yes, I see," Nyawīra said, a little tired of the talk of sorcery. "What you now need is a good witch doctor," Nyawīra added, in part to shock the good Christian, but it was she, Nyawīra, who was shocked by Vinjinia's impassivity.

"The only problem," said Vinjinia in a matter-of-fact tone, "is that I have no idea where to find a witch doctor."

It was clear that she imagined that Nyawīra would be as clueless as she was, but she was wrong.

An idea struck Nyawīra. Why had she not thought of it earlier? There was, after all, the Wizard of the Crow! She was amused by the thought of Tajirika seeking a cure from the very person he had humiliated.

"As for witch doctors," Nyawīra said, "I hear there is a new one in town. The Wizard of the Crow!"

"Where is he to be found? I mean, where is his shrine?"

"Santalucia. Southern."

"Southern Santalucia?" Vinjinia screamed with genuine horror. "You mean the southern slums where the poo . . . poo . . . people . . ." she stammered, a little confused, remembering that Nyawīra lived somewhere in Santalucia.

Vinjinia seemed sincerely appalled by the prospect of visiting a slumyard. But the more she recalled the stench of the glove and Tajirika's elongated nails encrusted with dirt, the more she realized that she had to control her squeamishness about such places. Her husband's illness was getting worse. She didn't see that she had any alternative but to pay the Wizard of the Crow a visit.

"I am a faithful member of All Saints Cathedral, and I know what they would think of me if they suspected or found out that I have had dealings with witch doctors," she said. "I don't want to be excommunicated or become like Maritha and Mariko, the subject of weekly tales. But just now there is no place I would not go in search of a cure. Where does one find this Wizard of the Crow? And please, Nyawīra, not a word of this to anybody," Vinjinia pleaded.

# 10

What? Tajirika is to come to me to be cured? No, no, I can't deal with that, Kamītī responded instinctively. The humiliation he had suffered at the hands of this man had scarred him badly, and he feared that the sight of his tormentor would inflame him further.

"I take the trouble to bring my boss to you so you can take his money," Nyawīra reasoned with him, "and all you can say is no? Why else would I lure him here, knowing that the malady is hopeless? All you need do is look at him, shower him with saliva, sputter some mumbo jumbo, send him home, and pocket his money."

He wanted no part of this, Kamītī insisted.

"I will bring him in the dark; there is no danger of his shadow crossing yours," Nyawīra said, and with that the tension between them broke as they burst out laughing.

It was while laughing that Kamītī suddenly felt possessed of an emotion so powerful that it almost made him tremble. Revenge. Good luck was bringing his enemy to his door for him to exact the sweetest vengeance. Strange that the prospect of evil had excited him more than the thought of doing good.

Kamĩtĩ told Nyawĩra nothing of this, for he did not want her to dissuade him from his course of action. Besides, he wanted to enjoy the unfolding of his scheme by himself. He imagined possible encounters with Tajirika, wondering how best to set his plan in motion. Before Tajirika's arrival, Kamĩtĩ would make a billboard, NO CURE TODAY: FOR CURE COME TOMORROW, and plant it nearby. He would then take Tajirika down memory lane by testing him on his English literacy.

An eye for an eye, a tooth for a tooth: the words from the Bible had never rung truer for Kamĩtĩ.

"All right, let him come," Kamĩtĩ told Nyawĩra enigmatically.

# 11

Vinjinia drove her black Mercedes-Benz to the Santalucia shopping center where Nyawĩra was waiting. They had agreed to meet very early in the morning so as to get to the shrine of the Wizard of the Crow before the arrival of other clients. Although Nyawĩra herself had suggested the shopping center, she acted as if she were unfamiliar with this section of Santalucia.

Nyawĩra sat in the passenger seat and looked around at Tajirika. She was expecting a sickly-looking person, but the Tajirika she saw did not seem ill at all. His belly had shrunk a little so his dark suit fit him better. He sat in the backseat of the car, its windows shuttered. Sometimes he would cast an eye in her direction, but when Nyawĩra tried to meet his gaze it was clear that he was in a world of his own and did not recognize her. So she concentrated on directing Vinjinia to the shrine.

It was then that she noticed that Vinjinia was driving without the aid of rearview and side-view mirrors. When Vinjinia needed to turn, she stuck her neck out her window or sought Nyawĩra's assistance to see if the coast was clear. Nyawĩra was about to tell her that the mirrors were not properly adjusted, but the evil glance that Vinjinia cast in her direction froze the words on her lips.

Though she understood, it did not lessen the terror at being in a car in a part of the town the driver hardly knew. Fortunately, the traffic at that hour of the morning was light, though Nyawīra was relieved when they got to her street. She showed Vinjinia where to park, a few houses from her own, and they walked the rest of the way.

On entering the house, they heard the voice of a man they could not see order them to seat the patient in a chair facing a small window in the wall between the waiting room and the inner chamber. Nyawīra and Vinjinia sat close by. For Nyawīra, this business of pretending to be a stranger in her own house tested all her patience and acting skills.

While Kamītī could see the entire body of the person before him, the patient could see only the face of the Wizard of the Crow, but Tajirika did not seem to care whether or not there was a face; in fact, he did not seem to take in any of his surroundings. He just stared into space, completely silent, his hands cupping his chin. His stillness was now and then interrupted by a seizure of *ifs*.

The man must be living in terror of his own silence, Kamītī thought, and witnessing this misery Kamītī felt sorry for him: all thought of vengeance vanished. Kamītī was now preoccupied with the challenge posed by the malady: What was this that had made voluble Tajirika a prisoner of silence? And why *if* and *if only*?

# 12

Of all the cases he had faced, Kamītī would say afterward, Tajirika's would rank among the most difficult. As a diviner, Kamītī worked out the nature of a problem by how a client answered questions. But Tajirika could not and did not answer any questions. It was as if he were deaf, his mind in another world and distrustful of the one he now inhabited. It was frustrating, but Kamītī kept on whispering to himself, To save one's patients, one must keep one's patience.

The Wizard of the Crow asked Vinjinia to sit next to her husband. This took her aback, for she thought a sorcerer divined without questions. She was hesitant about revealing the more embarrassing details of Tajirika's story. A few omissions will do, she told herself. But she heard the Wizard of the Crow echoing her unspoken words. No omissions, the Wizard of the Crow told her, looking her straight in the eye. If she needed help, she had to tell him the whole truth, he told her firmly but gently. How quickly this wizard has read my mind, Vinjinia thought to herself, a little scared; she was largely forthright in her retelling.

She recounted how Tajirika had come home one night with three sacks full of Burī notes, how he had sat at a table in the living room and counted the money, bill by bill, jotting down subtotals, every now and then jumping up for joy. He had called on her to keep him company as he did his figures. He had told her that this was just the beginning of better days to come. She recalled very clearly Tajirika stretching his legs on the table, leaning against the armchair, and talking as if in a dream, repeating the words *this is only a beginning of things to come* over and over.

My dear Vinjinia, you have no idea, he had said. My appointment as the chair of Marching to Heaven was announced this morning, and by the evening I had come into possession of all this. The morrow would bring even more money, for there were many more people coming to see him. If in just one day I have harvested this much and Marching to Heaven has not even begun, when the Global Bank releases its loans and the construction actually begins, my money will go through the roof. By the time all is said and done, I will be the richest man in Aburīria, the richest man in Africa, probably the richest man in the whole world, and I will be in a position to have anything I want, except . . . except . . . and it was then that he started coughing uncontrollably, not finishing the thought. He rushed to the bathroom in that state and stayed for a long time. Vinjinia told of how worried she was and how she had gone to the bathroom to check on him. Well, she found him staring at himself in the mirror, repeating the word *if*. This continued day after day, and she had decided to remove all mirrors from the house. As the days went by, Tajirika's seizures became increasingly worse, and now he sat staring into space as the wizard saw him now . . . That is all, she said, rather abruptly.

Nyawīra compared this version of the story to what Vinjinia had told her in the office and found some telling discrepancies. In the first version, Vinjinia had not mentioned anything about Tajirika's obsession with being the richest man in Aburĩria, Africa, and the whole world. She had not mentioned that Tajirika had started his *ifs* on the same night he took the money home and counted it. She had told her that the *ifs* had seized him the morning after.

Vinjinia waited, her heart pounding, for a response from the Wizard of the Crow. She had wanted to tell him everything, but she could not bring herself to talk about how Tajirika had scratched his face, the real reason for the removal of the mirrors.

"Have you told me the whole truth?" the Wizard of the Crow asked.

"Yes," Vinjinia replied. He might be able to bring down even crows from the sky, but there was no way he would know what she had left untold, she reasoned.

"It is all the same," said the Wizard of the Crow. "My divining mirror will reveal to me whatever you may have left unsaid. Now turn his face this way and make him look directly at this opening."

Again Vinjinia felt her heart racing. How did he know that she had not told all? Maybe I should confess . . . but before she had completed her thought, a mirror had already replaced the face of the Wizard of the Crow at the aperture.

The effect of the mirror on Tajirika was immediate. He woke up as from a dream, stared at the mirror, and started scratching his face. Vinjinia let out a frightened cry. She lurched forward, grabbed him by the waist, and began pulling him away from the mirror. Tears flowed down her cheeks in a mixture of fear for him and embarrassment at not having been straight with the Wizard of the Crow. Tajirika planted his feet firmly to the ground, his hands reaching out for the mirror. Vinjinia struggled with her husband to no avail: his hands remained outstretched toward the mirror and he groaned time and again. *If! If only!*

If something were not clearly the matter with Tajirika, Nyawĩra would have burst out laughing, for the scene reminded her of cartoons she had seen on television. When the Wizard of the Crow withdrew the mirror, both husband and wife fell to the floor, as if Tajirika had been released from his bewitchment. After struggling to free herself from the entanglement, Vinjinia managed to put him back into the chair. She was panting from the effort, even as Tajirika was weeping freely, like a child whose favorite candy had been snatched away. As he heaved, he kept on saying, *If! If! If!*

"I am sorry I forgot to tell you the bit about his scratching himself," she said to the wizard without much conviction, "but this weeping is something new," she added.

"Let that not trouble your heart."

She was relieved that the Wizard of the Crow had shown understanding and did not dwell on the sin of omission; this drew her closer to him and she made a sincere effort to catch every word from his lips.

The Wizard of the Crow started talking as if thinking aloud in their presence. His voice was round and soft, and it soothed and carried the listener along. Nyawira felt her heart drawn to the voice almost as if she had never heard it before. To Vinjinia the voice felt particularly powerful because it was disembodied. Even Tajirika responded to its soothing tone, gradually quieting down, and, for the first time in a long while, he seemed to be listening to someone. Vinjinia noticed this change in him and was even more grateful to the mysterious voice.

". . . that is where we diviners come in," the Wizard of the Crow went on, as if continuing talking to Vinjinia. "Words are the food, body, mirror, and sound of thought. Do you now see the danger of words that want to come out but are unable to do so? You want to vomit and the mess gets stuck in your throat—you might even choke to death. Your husband's illness is not yet fatal because its cure is not beyond the reach of our powers. Woman, identifying a sickness is the first step on the road to recovery and I think the problem with your husband can be seen in the difference between his *ifs*. They describe negative and positive wishes. Woman, your husband's thoughts are stuck in his head so that his wishes cannot be denied or fulfilled. His wishes are shards of words stuck in his throat. His enemies lie within him, and they want him to choke over his unvoiced wishes . . ."

Vinjinia felt a mixture of dread and amazement.

"So what are we going to do about it?" she asked the wizard.

"I do not charge for divining ills, but the cure may require one to dig deep in one's pockets."

"How much will it cost to get these thoughts unstuck?"

"How much is his life worth?" asked the Wizard of the Crow, who, as Kamītī, had decided that though he would not seek vengeance he would certainly relieve Tajirika of the three bags of bribe money.

"There is nothing I would not give to free him from what is killing him inside. Wizard of the Crow! Smoke out his enemies! Pursue them to the very gates of Hell."

"Well, it is up to you to decide what you want to do. The bewitching is in the very money he has received. Bring the three bags of Burī notes here so that we can find out where the evil is hidden. Go home and think about it. Come back tomorrow or any day you want. Then we can talk about my fee for releasing your husband's wishes."

The authenticity of the wizard convinced Vinjinia, but his putting into words what she herself had been thinking, that the evil resided in the bags of money, made her believe in his powers even more.

She wanted Tajirika healed that very morning, she told him. She promised to return with the three money bags and more to cover whatever fee he might charge for rooting out the evil.

The Wizard of the Crow told her to take her patient with her and hurry back before other clients arrived. Or, better still, they should leave the young maiden behind to keep their places warm. He was a first come, first served wizard.

# 13

"Where were we?"

Vinjinia suddenly applied brakes and the car skidded to the side of the road. Fortunately, no other cars were near them. She could not believe her ears. Was this her husband talking? She dared not turn her face.

"What did you say?" Vinjinia asked, just to make sure that she had heard right.

"I am asking you—where were we?" Tajirika asked again, like a person coming out of a deep sleep.

When she glanced at him over her shoulder, his face did not tell her much. The voice was decidedly his before the *ifs*.

"So you are well again? Praise the Lord," she said, not trying to hide her joy. "We have been to the shrine of the Wizard of the Crow!" she added, as if they had visited a family doctor.

"What? The shrine of a sorcerer?" he asked in a sleepy voice.

Vinjinia decided not to hide anything from him and told him that he had been seriously ill since the night he brought home three bags of Burĩs. The illness had perplexed ordinary physicians and she, Vinjinia, was now glad that she had brought him to the healer's shrine because even before the Wizard of the Crow had done his business, Tajirika was already on the mend, talking for the first time in a long while.

"Who has been spreading rumors that I am ill?" Tajirika said, interrupting her. "If I have been ill, then know that now I am quite well, thank you."

"But we have to go back," Vinjinia said.

"For what?" he asked with mounting irritation.

"To bring him the three bags of money. The evil is in the bags."

Tajirika felt like climbing over the front seat and giving Vinjinia a few slaps to the face.

"This is why I have always said that African women are gullible. You would actually let a sorcerer ensnare you with his tales? I cannot believe that you, a grown-up, the mother of my children, a churchgoer, were about to take three big bags of my money to a sorcerer!"

"You decide what you want to do. All I wanted was for you to get well, even if it meant my visiting places that I would not ordinarily go. All I wanted was for you to be well enough to go back to work as before. Think of the thousands of Burĩs you have lost since becoming ill!"

"So you thought you would add to the loss by giving my money to a witch doctor?"

"I don't deserve your insults. If you feel fine, then let's not go back to the shrine. We don't owe him anything. He has not administered his cure."

As soon as they got home, Tajirika insisted on being shown where Vinjinia had kept the three bags of money. She pointed to the strong room and left feeling wearied by his lack of interest in what had happened to him and chafed by his lack of gratitude.

He opened the bags one by one just to make sure that all the bills were there. After sewing the sacks shut, he lifted them in turn, as if weighing them, before placing them side by side. He then kneeled before the one in the middle and stretched out his arms as if gathering them to himself, forming a cross with his body. Then he tried to close his eyes as if in prayer, but they would not close. He tried to say something. Nothing would come out. He tried to force words out. Then suddenly the coughing came back, and the *ifs* and *if onlys*.

Vinjinia rushed to where he was kneeling. That did it. The Wizard of the Crow was the only person who could exorcise the evil, and after the exorcism no force on earth could make her bring the bewitched bags of money back into her house.

# 14

Kamĩtĩ did as he had done earlier, placed a mirror at the window, and once again Tajirika was drawn to it as a moth to light and started scratching himself. This time Vinjinia, who kept mum about what had occurred at home, the temporary recovery and sudden relapse, did not try to hold him back. Kamĩtĩ then removed the mirror, and Tajirika's eyes and his own were locked in a stare. Tajirika's seemed to beg for the return of the mirror.

"I will let you see the mirror," the Wizard of the Crow told him gently, softly, and clearly, as if dangling the prospect of candy, "but you and I must first have a talk. If I put the mirror back, do you promise to try to force out the words stuck within you? Will you let me help you complete your thoughts?"

Tajirika nodded impatiently as if he was ready to do anything just to see the mirror once more. When the Wizard of the Crow put the mirror back, Tajirika resumed scratching himself while muttering *ifs*.

The voice of the Wizard of the Crow now seemed to issue from inside the mirror:

"Vomit the words, the good and the bad!"

"If . . ." Tajirika said, and paused.

"Now," urged the Wizard of the Crow.

"My . . ." Tajirika added, and then got stuck.

"More."

"Skin . . ."

"Keep going."

"Were not . . ."

"Good, good . . ."

"Black."

Tajirika paused as if to take breath before climbing another mountain. From inside the mirror came the same commanding voice.

"Complete the thought. The good and the bad. Complete the thought!"

"If only . . ."

"Yes!"

"My skin . . ."

"Don't stop now!"

"Were . . . white . . . like a . . . white man's . . . skin . . ." Tajirika said, enunciating each word like one learning how to read.

"There! You have voiced the treacherous thought!" the Wizard of the Crow said in congratulation, removing the mirror from the window.

Tajirika no longer lusted for the mirror. His face shone as it had not done for weeks. He looked at the Wizard of the Crow with awe.

"Now I want you to voice your thoughts without the aid of the mirror," the Wizard of the Crow told him.

"If . . . my . . . skin . . . were . . . not . . . black! Oh, if only my skin were white!" Tajirika said in the triumphant tone of a child who for the first time has read a complete sentence without stumbling. A burden had been lifted from his heart, and as he finished voicing his secret desire he turned his head away from the window and, with a sigh of relief, glanced at his wife, his face beaming with an all-embracing gratitude, like that of a person who has just confessed his sins and given himself over to Jesus as his personal savior.

"You have heard for yourselves," the Wizard of the Crow now said to Vinjinia. "Daemons of whiteness took possession of your husband the night he brought home these three bags of money. You remember how you told me that it was after he counted the money that he rested his legs on the table and closed his eyes? That was the evil hour! As he looked into the future, he suddenly realized that at the rate the money was coming in he would end up being the richest man in Africa, and the only thing missing to distinguish him from all the other black rich was white skin. He saw his skin as standing between him and the heaven of his desire. When he scratched his face, daemons within were urging him to break ranks with blackness and enter into union with whiteness. In short, he suffers from a severe case of white-ache."

Tajirika kept nodding to signal agreement with every word of the diagnosis. He was happy and relieved, because even before he came into that kind of money he had always borne the burden of self-hatred but had managed to suppress it. Now, thanks to the affliction and to Vinjinia, who'd brought him here, this sorcerer had managed to make him own up to it. Before today he had not had anybody with whom to share his secret, but now he felt as if those present were witnesses to his coming pact with his white destiny.

But soon he fell into a deep depression. People did not become white or black; they were born so. His was an unattainable desire, and to yearn for the unattainable to the point of paralysis was indeed an illness that might plague him for the rest of his life.

"And what is the cure for white-ache?" Vinjinia asked, happy that her husband had given voice to his desires, and fearful that the malady might return.

Tajirika awaited the answer, and, thinking the Wizard of the Crow too slow in his response, added to his wife's plea: "What is the cure?" he asked.

"Tajirika, you know about smallpox."

"A terrible disease, that one, a scourge. Almost wiped out black people at the end of the nineteenth century. In some ways it was worse than the current virus of death. Quite infectious, and there was no way of avoiding it. Except through good luck. Thank God it is no more."

"How was it conquered?"

"Through mass vaccination."

"Exactly. Inoculating people with the germs of smallpox. The same with tuberculosis. Tajirika, have you ever fried bacon?"

"Eggs, sausages, and bacon are my morning favorites for breaking my nightly fasts," Tajirika said. "But of course it is my wife who cooks them."

"What oil does she use for frying the bacon?"

"Mr. Wizard of the Crow, don't make me laugh. Have you not heard the saying that a pig is fried with its own fat? But tell me, what has smallpox, tuberculosis, and pig's meat got to do with white-ache?"

"Use the disease against itself! Become white!"

Tajirika could not believe his ears. Here he was, depressed by the realization that he could never become white no matter how wealthy he became, and here was this sorcerer, saying that there was actually a way to whiteness. That the impossible could be made possible!

"How?" he asked doubtfully after recovering from the pleasant shock. "I hope you are not thinking of a skin transplant?"

"Oh, no, it's far simpler and less painful than that," said the Wizard of the Crow. "Becoming white is actually quite simple, but it calls for work, hard work."

"Say no more—the shoe fits," Tajirika said now, abandoning himself to his joy at this unexpected turn in the tide of his earthly fortune, for he would kill two birds with one stone: cure his white-ache and become white. "Mr. Wizard of the Crow, tell me how to become white. I am ready to do what is needed. And when the deed is done, whatever you may want from me is yours to command."

"First, help me solve a riddle!" said the Wizard of the Crow.

"Go ahead!"

"What is the first thing that tells who a person is?"

"The color of one's skin."

"No, Tajirika. Let's go back to history. When African people were taken as slaves across the Atlantic Ocean in the sixteenth, seventeenth, and eighteenth centuries, what was the very first thing that the whites took away from the New World Africans?"

"I don't know," said Tajirika, wondering what slavery in centuries past had to do with what they had been talking about.

"Okay. Let me ask you another question. When children are born, what do their fathers and mothers give them to distinguish them from others?"

"Names?"

"Exactly. So what did the white slavers do to their black slaves? Took away their original names to make them over into what they wanted them to be. Are you with me?"

"Yes, Mr. Wizard of the Crow."

"So to become white you must first give up your name. And, unlike those Africans who were forced to do so, you must give yours up willingly. Become a willing slave."

"That is not such a big deal. Tajirika is out!" Tajirika wondered why the Wizard of the Crow had said that becoming white required work. "And then?"

"Slaves were forced to take on the names of their owners. But you are lucky, Tajirika, because you have the freedom to choose from among thousands of European names."

"That is even easier. I have already got one. Titus," he said proudly, as if he had been on the right path all along.

"Titus? Mmm, let's see. Do you know where it comes from? I mean, to whom it points?"

"No."

"What's come over you, Titus, forgetting your religion?" Vinjinia interjected suddenly. "Don't you know that Titus was a convert and helper of St. Paul? Paul even wrote him a letter, Epistle to Titus?"

"Oh, is that where the name comes from?" Tajirika said.

"There was also another Titus," said the Wizard of the Crow. "Titus Flavius Vespasianus. Roman emperor. In the construction business, like you. Completed the Colosseum in Rome. Emperor and saint. Not bad, a name that carries both."

"But this emperor and this saint, were they white?" Tajirika asked in a tone tinged with doubt.

"Yes," said the Wizard of the Crow.

"So Titus is white!" said Tajirika, now happy again.

"But it has been tarnished by its years of contact with your African Tajirika," said Vinjinia.

"Yes. Go for a name that you think best points to the whiteness of your dreams. Freedom of choice. Choose what you want to be. Do you follow me?"

"Yes, Mr. Wizard of the Crow."

"Now, Titus," the Wizard of the Crow suddenly called out in a commanding tone, "what is your name? What is your new name in full?"

"Clement Clarence Whitehead," said Tajirika, as proud as a peacock. "What next?" he asked, rubbing his hands together.

"A slave first loses his name, then his language. So, Mr. Clement

Clarence Whitehead, you now know what to do next. Your language. Give it up."

"Gone!"

"Then start speaking English like a white man."

"That I have already started doing," Tajirika assured the Wizard of the Crow, and he started drawling out a couple of sentences: *Hi! Give me fi! I am Clement Clarence Whitehead* . . .

"No, no, not American, Mr. Whitehead. The so-called American English has been completely contaminated by Black English, or what they now call Ebonics."

"Blame it on the cheap American TV we watch. They are ruining our tongue. I don't want Ebonics—I want the real thing. I swear that from now on I will keep on trying to perfect my English tongue. It is not easy and it will need much practice."

"You have spoken well," said the Wizard of the Crow. "Nothing comes from nothing."

"I have what it takes. Next?" Tajirika asked a trifle impatiently, ready to leap over the remaining steps to whiteness.

"I want you to know, Mr. Whitehead, that we are now coming to the most difficult part of the matter, so I want you to listen very carefully. What does the Holy Bible say about matrimony, holy matrimony?"

"That women should obey their husbands."

"But that is after they are married. What about the marriage itself? What does the Bible say?"

"Mr. Wizard of the Crow, aren't you digressing a bit?" Tajirika said, treading lightly so as not to offend his benefactor.

"You see, when two people are joined in holy matrimony, they become one flesh, or something like that."

"What has that got to do with becoming white?"

"Logic, Mr. Clement Clarence Whitehead, simple white logic. A certain African sage says that whites are driven by logic and blacks by emotion. Think with white logic, not with black emotion. If it is true that when a man and woman are joined in holy matrimony they become one flesh, then the quickest and surest way to change the color of one's skin is to marry into the color one wants to become. That means, Mr. Whitehead, that you must marry white so as to take on the whiteness of your spouse."

"I hear you, and what I have heard so far is good," Tajirika said.

"But how do I know that my wife will not take on my blackness, leaving me in the same black hole? Or does she become black and I white?"

"Why should you care? This is all about your becoming white. Look for a white woman who wants to be black, one of those forever frying herself under the sun, and you simply exchange colors. A kind of barter trading in color, don't you think?"

Up to that point Vinjinia had not seen anything wrong with the steps the Wizard of the Crow proposed to cure Tajirika's white-ache. But when now the talk turned to possibilities of Tajirika's marrying white, she became wary: visions of a broken marriage, a broken home, seized her, and she could no longer hold her tongue.

"What are you saying, Mr. Wizard of the Crow? You are telling my husband to divorce me and marry a white woman? And you, Titus, how dare you even think of it? You would divorce me just like that after all the years we have been together? And with God blessing us with children?" She said all of this hastily, for she did not know to whom to direct her pain.

"Keep out of this and let the Wizard of the Crow finish what he was saying," Tajirika shouted at Vinjinia with piercing, angry eyes. I have always said that black women have no manners, he said to himself as he turned back to the Wizard of the Crow, ignoring his wife completely. "After I marry white, what next?"

Nyawīra could hardly believe what she was hearing or what she saw unfolding before her. She felt like laughing but the laughter stuck in her throat as she witnessed another crisis erupt.

Vinjinia had started trembling and shaking like one possessed. At first Nyawīra thought it was from anger. Then she saw her fall off the chair onto the floor, where she started rolling. Tajirika rushed to Vinjinia and tried to lift her up but failed. Nyawīra was about to help him but then thought better of it. Let them settle their differences on their own. But Tajirika did not seem to be in a mood to settle anything, resentful as he was that the wizard's rituals of magic transplant were now at the mercy of female daemons. After struggling to get his wife back on her feet, Tajirika managed to make Vinjinia sit up on the floor. Her eyes were wild and it seemed as if she was not even aware who Tajirika was. In a world to herself, she now took out a mirror from her bag and looked at her face. And then, to

Nyawira's utter amazement, Vinjinia started coughing and muttering, "If! If only!"

To Tajirika, this seemed like the proverbial nail in the coffin of his dreams.

"Oh, Vinjinia, why have you done this to me?" he groaned, as he now turned helplessly to the Wizard of the Crow.

"She has caught your illness," the Wizard of the Crow told Tajirika. "The disease is contagious, you know."

He asked that Vinjinia and Tajirika trade places so that Vinjinia now faced the window directly, Tajirika silently observing.

The Wizard of the Crow took her through the same paces as Tajirika earlier on.

"Even wisdom locked in the heart never won a lawsuit," the Wizard of the Crow now said, trying to massage her soul. "So vomit every word and let your thoughts come out without fear."

Vinjinia did not need much coaxing.

"If my skin were not black would my husband have thought of leaving me? If only I could become white!" she said.

As soon as she uttered the last word, Vinjinia felt a big load off her mind; she, too, experienced the joy and relief of one who had just confessed her sins. She went through the steps already taken by her husband, even changing her name to Virgin Beatrice Whitehead, finally turning to her husband as if to say: I am a black sinner like you, and together let us seek salvation in whiteness.

"What shall we do to become white?" husband and wife asked in unison.

"Whites come in various tribes: Germans, French, Russian, Italians, Portuguese, Spanish, and even Japanese . . ."

"We want to be English," they said, interrupting him.

"The English? *Hakuna matata*," the Wizard of the Crow assured them. "But one small hurdle and we shall be on our way. The English, just like other whites, are of different varieties. And today there are also those black Britons who come from Bangladesh, Pakistan, India, Hong Kong, the Caribbean, and even from Africa . . ."

"We want a pure English skin," they said promptly.

As Nyawira sat in constant amazement at the drama unfolding before her eyes, the Wizard of the Crow told husband and wife to close their eyes and picture the kind of English person each wanted to become. He would capture these images in his mirror, the better to realize their dreams. Both shut their eyes.

He began with Tajirika, who quickly said that he could see an image in his head. Not very clearly, though, he added.

"Hold it there and don't let it go," the Wizard of the Crow told Tajirika. "There, I see him . . . yes, the man is as white as can be, in rags for trousers, and a leather jacket with brass buttons. His hair is blue and green and yellow, and is porcupine-style . . . a punk, no doubt about it, a punk . . ."

Tajirika interrupted him in horror: "No, not that kind of Englishman for me. I told you, I want to be a real Englishman."

The Wizard of the Crow told him to open his eyes to let the image of the punk vanish.

Now it was Vinjinia's turn. At first she was excited when the Wizard of the Crow spoke of a woman dressed in fur walking about in the streets of London. Oxford Street. Dean Street. A side street. But the woman was a Soho Square prostitute. Vinjinia screamed in protest, being the Christian that she was. The Wizard of the Crow then told her to open her eyes to allow the undesirable image to go.

A heated quarrel erupted between husband and wife, each berating the other for their respective choice of image: punk and whore.

The quarrel would have gotten worse, but the Wizard of the Crow intervened, warning them that if they continued fighting like that they would end up a cantankerous English couple. And it would certainly interfere with the emergence of other images that might present far more desirable choices.

The Wizard of the Crow ordered them to close their eyes again. They should try their best to imagine a more harmonious joint image of a ripe old age together.

"The colonial type, like the ones who used to lord over us here in Aburĩria," Tajirika clarified.

"They looked pure white, with their special clubs and attack dogs," added Vinjinia.

"Lords. Aristocrats. Blue blood," they agreed.

They shut their eyes and soon were joyful when they heard the wizard say that he had managed to capture their joint image in the mirror.

"It is a video, a moving picture," the Wizard of the Crow said excitedly. "I see a silver-haired couple, Sir Clement Clarence Whitehead and Lady Virgin Beatrice Whitehead, holding hands, crossing a road near palace gardens in London, talking about their life in the old colonial days. A pair of authentic colonial aristocracy. They talk of how he was nearly made the governor of Aburĩria . . ."

"Governor, did you say?" Tajirika and Vinjinia asked in unison.

"Sshh! Now you have made the image vanish," the Wizard of the Crow admonished them.

"Not another word from us," Vinjinia said.

"Please search it out. Get that image back, especially the bit about being the governor of Aburĩria," Tajirika pleaded.

"All right, it is back, the image is back," said the Wizard of the Crow, "and, yes, they are still talking about how he almost became the governor of Aburĩria and she the first lady of the colony. They recall their palatial house on a hill overlooking the city and their holiday digs at the seaside. Yes, ten servants at the palace and five at the estate by the sea. They recall the expensive lawns, green hedges, the swimming pool, the fleet of cars, so many that they now do not remember all the models, except that they were partial to the Jaguar and Rolls-Royce.

"Two horsemen, actually two policemen, come galloping by, and Sir Clarence and Lady Clarence look at the horses long and critically and shake their heads, thinking of their own thoroughbreds in the colonial stables, and the talk and envy of other settlers. They cross another road. Where are they going? Oh, yes, they are stopping at Harrods, where they used to fly for annual shopping sprees. Now they are window-shopping. I want that silk scarf for Christmas. I want that handbag. They argue a little about this and that and the prices, accusing each other of being extravagant. Their arguments suddenly cease when they remind each other that they have no money with which to pay for the flashy luxury items in the windows of Harrods.

"There! They cross the road again, oblivious to cars that screech to a halt to avoid hitting them. They are now standing beside some garbage cans. What? A homeless couple? No, no, they continue on, still deep in conversation. But would anyone really call this a conversation? They are actually lamenting, crying and cursing all the dirty politics of the sixties, which ended the good old colonial days. They don't know whether to blame it on the Americans or the Russians or both, but they are definitely cursing all the forces that supplanted the British Empire. Wait. I have lost them. Where have they gone?

"Oh, yes, they are back. I see them now kneeling down before the altar in a church, and they are praying to God for the recolonization of Africa and Asia now that communism had been defeated. They cross another road—how many times must these two keep on crossing and recrossing these London roads? And now, oh my God, Sir Clement Clarence Whitehead and Lady Virgin Beatrice Whitehead are definitely heading for an old people's home, still dreaming about the possible return of their good old days of power and glory in Africa.

"In short," said the Wizard of the Crow, staring straight at Tajirika and Vinjinia, "your white English destiny is as a homeless ex-colonial couple living solely on the memories of what used to be. Now, how soon would you like to achieve your white destiny?"

"No! No!" Tajirika and Vinjinia shouted, opening their eyes in fright. "Black is beautiful. Give us back our blackness," they moaned, as if the Wizard of the Crow had already shorn them of it.

# 15

When his clients left, the Wizard of the Crow felt relief, only to sink into depression at being all alone. He went to the living room, hoping that Nyawĩra was there so that he could unburden himself of his amazement at what had just transpired. Suddenly a stench blasted his nostrils as if to bring him back to reality.

The putrid smell was most intense where the bags of money stood like three guardians of evil stopping him in his tracks. He felt weak, faint, and he held on to a wall. I need fresh air, he said to himself. I have to go outside. And with that resolution he propelled himself forward, struggling for air as if in an asthmatic seizure.

He collapsed just outside the door. Were the three bags of money really possessed of evil? he wondered.

# 16

They had taken a few steps in silence toward their Mercedes-Benz when, as if to acquaint himself with his surroundings, Tajirika glanced back and froze, startled. Following close behind them was the woman of the shrine: it was his secretary.

"Nyawīra! What on earth are you doing in these parts? Do you live around here?"

"Don't tell me that you're only now making out who she is," Vinjinia said. "She has been with us all along."

"Surely, I'm truly bewitched. I had taken her to be an assistant wizard," he muttered, trying to laugh off his embarrassment.

"You may laugh all you want," Vinjinia said as they resumed walking toward the car, "but had it not been for Nyawīra you would still be locked in the house, barking *IF*! How else would I have known my way around these slums? Count your blessings; God has been generous in granting you a secretary like her. One in a million."

"Thank you, Nyawīra. I will never forget this," Tajirika told her. "And even if I did, you can see that you will always have a strong advocate in my house."

"Count your children, Gacirū and Gacīgua, as her advocates, too," Vinjinia said. "Now they talk of nothing without mentioning their aunt, the teller of tales of two-mouthed ogres."

Tajirika felt no need to know what his wife was talking about. He had just gotten to the car and noticed how the side and rearview mirrors had been turned away from the driver's vision.

"What's the matter with the mirrors?"

He felt like laughing at the explanation, which only served to confirm that he had been very ill, for he could not remember any of these oddities.

"You're no doubt an excellent driver," Tajirika said, as if congratulating Vinjinia. "But now I will take the wheel," he added, adjusting the mirrors.

Vinjinia sat in the passenger seat, next to him.

Nyawĩra tried to make herself as invisible as possible in the back-seat. She did not want to get involved in their conversation in case questions arose for which she did not have credible answers. But she need not have worried. Man and wife were absorbed with themselves, talking about what they had just gone through as if they were alone in the car.

"The Waswahili were right," Tajirika was saying. "*Kikulacho kimo nguoni mwako*. My enemies wanted me to become a poor white so that they would take over Marching to Heaven and reap the benefits."

"But they did not reckon on your being a step or two ahead of them," said Vinjinia.

"Yes, yes," agreed Tajirika, now very happy with what had taken place at the shrine, especially his remembering, just before they left, to ask the Wizard of the Crow to thwart the ill intentions of his enemies. It was strange, on looking back, how he had felt, when first seeing the Wizard of the Crow, that he had met him before, in a previous life perhaps? It did not matter.

He and his wife were now agreed that the evil was hidden inside the three bags of money; they felt good about leaving them behind at the sorcerer's shrine. Even Nyawĩra, recalling that Tajirika had nearly shot her dead because of the three bags, was inclined to agree.

"How about some breakfast? Shall we try Mars Café?" Tajirika asked as they approached his office in Santamaria. "Or do you know of a nicer place around here?" he added, turning to Nyawĩra.

"Mars Café will do," Nyawĩra said, though it reminded her of Kaniũrũ.

"We are already there," Vinjinia was about to say when Tajirika suddenly stomped on the brakes; the car swerved to the side of the road, nearly hitting a passerby. Vinjinia screamed. Nyawĩra thought that Tajirika must have been trying to avoid a collision, but there were no cars approaching.

"What is that?" Tajirika asked, in shock.

"What?" Vinjinia asked, puzzled.

"Look! Look over there," he said, pointing to the entrance of Eldares Modern Construction and Real Estate.

"Oh, the queue!" Vinjinia and Nyawĩra said in unison.

# 17

"They are waiting for you," Vinjinia said, her matter-of-fact tone surprising Tajirika even more.

"Me? For what? Some kind of protest or demonstration?"

"They are looking for work," said Vinjinia, gesturing toward Nyawĩra for support.

"It is the billboard you asked me to put up outside the office," Nyawĩra said. "Don't you remember? Tempa?"

"*Temporary jobs?* All these people?"

"Daemons of the queue," Nyawĩra said.

She recounted the mania that had spread to all the corners of Eldares, starting at the foot of the billboard.

"This is too much. And what is the government doing about it?" he asked angrily, regretting his absence from the scene. "The army should be called to teach this mob a lesson. Listen, you two. No breakfast for me. Please, go along, eat, and come back to the office afterward. This is surely the work of the enemies who first charmed me with the money bags, but now I will show them that I still have power and influence. I will let my good friend Machokali, Minister for Foreign Affairs, know about this riotous mob. I tell you, after only a few minutes the army and the police will surround the place and this mob will be running for their miserable lives in all directions."

With those words he parked the Mercedes-Benz properly and strode toward his workplace, though careful to take a detour to the back door.

Vinjinia and Nyawĩra went to the Mars Café, and at the entrance Nyawĩra instinctively surveyed the interior. She had good reason to be apprehensive. Kaniũrũ was seated in a corner, his face buried in a newspaper. He pretended not to have seen her, and Nyawĩra decided to act likewise. Does this man spend all his nights and days in this café? What is he doing here so early?

Even as they were finishing placing their orders, Tajirika joined them. They could see self-satisfaction in his gait.

Tajirika was very much aware of their curiosity about why he was back there so soon after he had given up on breakfast, but he was not in a hurry to enlighten them. He kept them anxious for his revelation. He ordered six eggs, three sausages, and a pile of bacon.

"You will make people think that I don't feed you," joked Vinjinia.

"I want both of you to eat properly, all on me," he said, pausing for effect before adding: "And rejoice."

"Why?" the women asked. Had he been assured that the army and the police were already on their way?

"We are celebrating the daemons of the queue," he told them as soon as their orders had arrived.

Nyawīra and Vinjinia put down their forks and looked at him with befuddlement.

"What did you tell me about the queues?" he asked after swallowing one or two mouthfuls. "That they started outside our office and now are all over Eldares, even spilling into neighboring towns. I have just spoken to Machokali, and he cast a different light on all this. It is quite simple. The fact that all these people are coming for jobs at the office of the chairman of Marching to Heaven shows that all the people in Eldares support the project, and you know that when Eldares calls, the entire country answers sooner or later. You could say, taking the contract hunters and then these job hunters into account, that there is not a single Aburīrian who does not want to have a piece of the project. The Ruler and his most beloved minister, who is also my friend Machokali, are very pleased with this development and have even sent five motorcycle riders to all corners of the country to spread the gospel of queuing and gather even more grass-roots support. And we started it. Nyawīra, you and I started it. Next week the Global Bank mission will tour Eldares and the surrounding towns, wherever there are queues, to see for themselves how happy the people are with the prospect of Marching to Heaven.

"It will all culminate in a mass rally at the Ruler's Park, at which the Ruler will formally dedicate the site. They used to say that all roads lead to Rome, but on that day all queues will lead to the park. Imagine all the cameras capturing the drama of lines and lines of people making their pilgrimage to a new Mecca? *See the point?* Get the picture? And now comes the sweetest part.

"Minister Machokali is very pleased with my illness. He did not even want to know what kind of illness it was—he was just glad that I had been ill and therefore absent from the office. In fact, he sounded very alarmed when I told him that I was now well and ready to resume work. Of course he was happy to hear that the illness was not fatal—he is a very good friend of mine, you know—but he does not want me to get well quickly, at least not well enough to return to the office. The crowd will keep waiting for my return. So he wants me to resurface from my illness only after the Bank missionaries have visited all the queues and witnessed the mass support. I am to reappear only on the day of the dedication. Thus the government will have made effective use of the queues in its bid for money from the Bank."

He paused to study and enjoy the effect of his words on their faces. Tajirika was speaking as if he had originated the idea of queues. He turned toward Nyawīra with eyes lit up with pride.

"So Nyawīra, the billboard that you planted is now bearing fruit that even the Ruler is glad to gather. In short, a simple billboard is about to change the history of Aburīria, the history of Africa, the history of the world. And everyone gains a little from this mania, including you two."

Nyawīra and Vinjinia looked askance at each other, wondering how they were going to benefit from a billboard that simply announced that the company was now hiring temporary staff.

Tajirika felt good inside. "So congratulations," he told them, laughing, his half-shaved chin moving up and down rhythmically.

"For what?" asked Vinjinia.

"Who do you think will be running the firm in my purposeful, patriotic absence? You, my faithful duo. You, Vinjinia, are now the acting general manager of Eldares Modern Construction and Real Estate, and you, Nyawīra, the assistant general manager."

He paused to take in the gratitude from their eyes at the promotions he had just announced.

"And no coup d'état against the absent boss!" he joked. "You must not remove the billboard: as far as the public is concerned I am still indisposed and therefore unable to come to the office. When answering the phone or talking to people, I want you to remember at all times that I am still ill. If these people want any business that might come this way, they are to make themselves known to the acting general manager, Mrs. Vinjinia Tajirika, and leave their envelopes with

her. But should there be some who insist on speaking to me personally, then, Vinjinia, call me at home and connect me to the person,
but only after the person has added a considerable sum to the envelope as an inducement for the sick to leave his bed to pick up the
phone. These promotions are my way of saying thank you to both of
you for conspiring to take me to the Wizard of the Crow. His powers
have already changed my life."

Nyawīra quickly glanced at the corner where Kaniūrū was sitting
and saw that he was still there, absorbed in his paper. He is just pretending to read, Nyawīra said to herself, for she was sure that his eyes
and ears and nose were taking everything in. Despite this, Nyawīra
decided to squeeze more information out of Tajirika about the coming dedication of the proposed site for Marching to Heaven.

"What day is the Ruler going to bless the site?" she asked as if
making talk without the slightest interest in the actual date.

"I don't have all the details," Tajirika told her. "But don't worry. As
soon as I know them I will let you know. I would like you both to be
present. What did I tell you, Nyawīra? I will never forget you. Since
you started working for me my affairs have been running smoothly,
and I would like to express my gratitude and appreciation. On the
blessed day I shall ask my friend Minister Machokali to have you
stand on the platform in front of the Ruler so that he and the whole
world will know that it was you and me who set the lines of people in
motion. The Ruler might even shake your hand as he once shook
mine . . ."

He looked at his right hand, and for a second or two there was disbelief and dismay on his face.

"What happened to my glove?" he asked, looking at Vinjinia.

Vinjinia sensed an impending explosion and quickly moved in to
contain it: she explained that she had taken it off thinking that his
enemies may have tampered with the glove out of envy of the hand
that smelled of the Ruler's. But to the utter relief of Vinjinia, he was
not angry.

"Then my enemies will die of envy, because on the day of the dedication of the site this very hand will shake that of the Ruler, and this
time I will thwart them by not wearing a glove that would indicate the
spot blessed by his touch. Nyawīra, take note of that. After the Ruler
touches your hand, no glove!"

He stopped himself and collapsed in hysterics.

"Yes, you and I must have released these daemons in support of Marching to Heaven. We removed the other billboard, NO VACANCY: FOR JOBS COME TOMORROW, just in the nick of time. And see the results! These university boys who claim to be the Movement for the Voice of the People opposed to Marching to Heaven are now in a dark hole, completely isolated. Their propaganda against the project has come to naught: everywhere people are now voting with their feet, thanks to you and me. Up with the billboard! Those boys will die with envy when they see you, their age-mate, shake the Ruler's hand. But remember, no glove . . . Leave that to me," he added, attempting self-deprecating humor.

He continued laughing, amusing himself.

Kaniũrũ could no longer contain himself; his head rose from his newspaper to look at the center of this hilarity.

# 18

At the close of business, Nyawĩra took the unusual step of asking Vinjinia for a lift to the bus stop. She wanted to avoid any possible encounter with Kaniũrũ, but she also wanted to get home early.

On the bus ride home, all her thoughts were on Kamĩtĩ. She recalled how they had first met in Tajirika's office; how she had empathized when he told about his more than three years of fruitless job searching; how she had felt his humiliation at the hands of heartless Tajirika; how later that same night they had been chased by A.G. across the prairie; and how they talked through the night, on the verge of carnal intimacy.

Now they hardly ever talked about that moment, even in jest, and neither had they come close to repeating it. Otherwise, she was at peace with Kamĩtĩ and surprised herself by opening her heart to him. Yet she was careful about revealing details of the movement: its members, leadership, and plans. In all personal matters, she felt that she could talk to him without embarrassment. He was unlike most men she had encountered; he had no set views of a woman's place in the world. She felt close to him, yet she was haunted by a question: who was Kamĩtĩ, really?

Nyawĩra did not believe in divination, prophecy, or the power of magic potions to change hearts and minds. She did not believe in the material existence of good and bad spirits. People built their own heaven or hell through their deeds on earth. If they abuse themselves and others, they are merely stoking the fire of a hell of their own making, a terrible legacy for those to come. Good deeds, on the other hand, are worthy of inheritance by future generations. Her guiding principle was simply Do Unto Others as You Would Have Them Do Unto You. Yet her skepticism about rites of magic was being shaken by Kamĩtĩ. How was he able to see into the souls of people? What was it that A.G., the old man, and now Tajirika saw in Kamĩtĩ? How, for instance, was it possible for Tajirika to leave three bags of money behind without so much as a hint of regret or a whimper of protest, she wondered, knowing as she did how much he loved and worshipped money?

As for herself, she had to admit that Kamĩtĩ had also touched her life. She could not tell what it was, but since meeting him she did not see life quite the same way; it was as if just his being there gave her something to smile about, even in the face of the scandals and cruelties of the state. The way he had dealt with Vinjinia and Tajirika made her feel proud of him. There was no rancor in his manner, no lust for revenge against a fallen enemy, unless relieving the Tajirikas of three bags of money could be termed revenge. As Kamĩtĩ had questioned Tajirika about his malady, a picture of the nature of the illness had also formed in her mind, and she felt as if Kamĩtĩ understood it as pervasive among the rich and educated of Aburĩria. Perhaps this explained in part what was wrong with the leadership of the land and the incredible turns the country had taken since independence.

She noticed without quite acknowledging it that whenever she thought of Kamĩtĩ she felt indefinable warmth suffusing her being, making her heart race with anticipation. But anticipation of what? She was unsure; all she knew as she got off the bus and crossed the road was that she missed him. They had parted only that morning, but for her it was as if they had not seen each other in years.

At the Santalucia shopping center she decided on how to celebrate being with him this evening. She would do the cooking. She bought some rice, tender mutton, lasciviously ripe tomatoes, fragrance of parsley, and two candles. She imagined the course of the evening over and over. She would cook, they would sit at the table facing each other, playing footsie; they would sit by the fireside and chat, enjoying the play of shadows on the walls. Her vision of this togetherness made her feel giddy. She felt like singing, but no particular tune came to mind.

In recent days she had tried to get home early to avoid the formation of the evening's queue for the wizard's services, these men who stood waiting to be empowered with evil. She and Kamĩtĩ, as a result of them, hardly ever had the time to talk, except after midnight. In recent days the line had become progressively thinner and shorter, but even so, the few who would be there tonight were bound to interfere with her arrangement for a candlelight dinner for two. She grew defiant; she would not let them ruin her evening.

She knocked at the door four times, their secret signal. She waited for him to open the door, a smile forming. She tried the doorknob, a trifle impatient. The door was shut tight. Maybe he was having a bath, she told herself. She took out her key and opened the door. She stood and waited for a sign of life in the house. She checked all over and noticed that even Kamĩtĩ's bag was gone. She sat down on the bed, drained. Where was Kamĩtĩ? Where had he gone?

# 19

*It is now past midnight, the fourth night since you went away without a trace,* Nyawĩra scribbled in a notebook, *and I find myself unable to fall asleep. The hours of the day and the hours of the night seem all the same to me. I have been going to the office but I feel like a sleepwalker in the streets of Eldares. I have nobody with whom I can talk about you, and even if I had, I don't think that there are many who can see you as I do. I write to myself to still my heart, but no matter how I try I cannot find words to say how I felt when I came home that night and found that you were gone.*

*I think about you day and night. Each day has had its pains, memo-*

*ries, and worries. I do not know whether you are alive, in the hands of the police, or dead, killed by thieves, though it is hard to distinguish between the police and thieves in our country. But what would a thief want with your bag, containing as it does only a beggar's suit of rags? On the other hand, why would the police arrest you? What would they want from you?*

*They say that desperate times call for desperate measures; the other night I even found myself wishing that I might bump into A.G., hoping that he would blab something about you. Then I remembered that A.G. thinks that you and I are one; in his eyes, there is only one Wizard of the Crow, who can manifest himself in male or female form. No, A.G. cannot help me.*

During Kamĩtĩ's disappearance, it seemed to Nyawĩra that her house was encased in unrelieved sepulchral silence. As she sat on the bed the first night, staring at nothing, she remembered that the nighttime queue outside her house would be starting up soon. What was she to tell these people? How would she send them away? The last thing she needed was a reminder of his absence. She decided to do what she thought Kamĩtĩ would have done were he in a similar predicament: use their fear of witchcraft to send them away. She wrote on cardboard: YOUR ENEMIES HAVE PLACED EVIL ON THESE GROUNDS TO ENSNARE YOU: I HAVE GONE TO GET CLEANSING POTIONS; DON'T BOTHER COMING BACK LOOKING FOR ME: I WILL PUT UP AN ADVERTISEMENT IN THE NEWSPAPER TO ANNOUNCE MY RETURN.—WIZARD OF THE CROW. She hung the board on the wall outside, shut the door, and put out the lights, preferring to move about the house in the darkness. She felt as if there were hundreds of eyes staring at her in the dark, and she felt safe only in bed.

Since parting with her husband, Nyawĩra had gotten used to living alone. She hardly ever entertained in her house. Even her girlfriends from her days in school and college used to visit her more at her job than at home. Her two cousins were the only ones who came to see her at the house, but that was mostly on weekends. At first it was hard living in a house alone. But over time she came to enjoy and appreciate her freedom. She did not have to explain to anybody where she had been, how she had spent the day, or why she was late coming home. She had been answerable only to herself. Why, then, this sudden loneliness after the disappearance of someone she hardly knew?

Her makeshift sign had had the desired effect; later when she peered through the window she saw no shadows of men lingering in the streets. Over the next few days and nights, the unwanted visitors had dwindled to none. By the fourth day she took down the sign.

Completely preoccupied with Kamĩtĩ, Nyawĩra would comb the papers for news of accidents or legal proceedings, at once hoping and fearing to find Kamĩtĩ's name.

A thought crept into her mind. What if Kamĩtĩ was not what he had pretended to be but was actually a police agent sent to entrap her? Might this not explain Tajirika's cryptic comments about movement members being her age-mates and finding themselves in trouble? Was Tajirika being sincere when he promised to introduce her to the Ruler? Her mind also raced with suspicions about Kaniũrũ's presence at the Mars Café so early in the morning. But when she recalled Kamĩtĩ's voice, face, and laughter, as well as his concern for others' well-being, she calmed down.

Her second and third nights alone were made easier by having attended scheduled meetings of the movement. She had reported everything she knew about the plans for Marching to Heaven. She'd told them that the Ruler and his Minister for Foreign Affairs intended to take the Global Bank missionaries to where the queues were thickest and longest to prove that people were voting with their feet in support of Marching to Heaven. Most important, the government would soon select a day for the Ruler to dedicate the site for Marching to Heaven. At great length, they debated how to respond. Some suggested distributing more leaflets to expose the Ruler's cynical plans and urge people to dismantle the queues as a means of thwarting the plans to exploit them. Others argued that since the queues were the result of high unemployment, there was no way the people would abandon them. Another course of action was debated: how to make use of the queues so as to steal the Ruler's thunder.

Until now, the only free spaces in Aburĩria were the churches and mosques and other authorized places of worship; liquor stores, bars, and other authorized alcohol consumption centers; and prison yards and police cells—wherever authority brandished its fearsome might, fearless of the words of unarmed inmates. The unemployment queues constituted such a site of democracy where gatherings did not require police permits. The movement decided that whenever they wanted to have a meeting, they would form a queue. They would use the queues for purposes of political mobilization.

Members decided that, come what may, they would disrupt the Ruler's dedication as they had his birthday. On top of what she was already doing, gathering information on Marching to Heaven, Nyawīra had been further charged with gathering anything and everything about the government's plans for the day of dedication.

Nyawīra welcomed these sessions and tasks, for they distracted her from her inner turmoil, her doubts regarding Kamītī. But as soon as she left the meetings, his many faces would invade her peace of mind with an intensity verging on vengeance. Yet she concluded that he was a man of wisdom and integrity whom the movement could usefully have recruited. But still, how could he have left without saying good-bye? How could she have trusted him?

Whenever she'd felt low in the past, Nyawīra had played her guitar. The sound of music from a guitar had acted as therapy after her car accident and after her divorce. Now she took it from the wall and tried picking the strings. But she felt as if the sounds were deepening instead of alleviating her sorrow. She hung it back on the wall.

Then suddenly anger seized her. What was it that had blinded her into believing that Kamītī was any different from any other male? I received him in my house and even gave him space for his witchcraft nonsense, and what does he do in gratitude? The anger gave her new energy. She must come to grips with herself.

On the fifth day she woke up, made some tea, and sat at the table. She did not even want to look at the couch, Kamītī's bed. Nothing, no memory of laughter, was going to distract her from her resolve. She took out the letter she had written to him, and after reading it she calmly tore it into small pieces, some of which fell down to the floor by the legs of the table. Then she thought it better to burn all those pieces of paper so that the words would vanish forever, as if they had never been written or thought.

As she bent down to retrieve them, she noticed a note not in her handwriting. It was Kamītī's hand. He had written her a letter and must have put it on the table. It had fallen, and she had failed to see it until now.

# 20

There was a time when the vast prairie surrounding Eldares was the domain of wild animals: rhinos, elephants, and hippos. In those days a traveler was likely to find leopards and lions lying in the grass, waiting for their prey among the grazing herds of zebras, dik-diks, duickers, bushbucks, gazelles, impalas, kudus, elands, warthogs, hartebeests, and buffalo. A most common sight was that of giraffes loping along or simply towering over the thorn-trees of the prairie. Occasionally an ostrich would scuttle across the prairie, and if a traveler was lucky he might find a newly laid ostrich egg inside a sand nest. But things had now changed. The wild animals had abandoned the prairie, leaving it to the emaciated cows and goats whose ribs protruded in times of drought when the grass completely dried up.

The prairie ended abruptly at the foot of ridges forming a gigantic semicircle. The ridges were often covered in mist so that from a distance they looked like a continuous one, and it was only after reaching the foot that one could marvel at their natural formation of ascending steps to the misty sky. Each ridge was a series of hilltops, which against the light of the setting sun, looked like undulating silhouettes of cow humps. But there were a few times when the wind swept the mist away and the ridges, hills, and mountains would reveal their breathtaking beauty, sun rays dappling the forest trees with their mellowing leaves of green, yellow, and orange. Sometimes when the sun is rising or sinking one can glimpse a rainbow arched over the hills.

This forest was now threatened by charcoal, paper, and timber merchants who cut down trees hundreds of years old. When it came to forests, indeed to any natural resource, the Aburīrian State and big American, European, and Japanese companies, in alliance with the local African, Indian, and European rich, were all united by one slogan: *A loot-a continua*. They knew how to take but not how to give back to the soil. The unregulated clearing of forests affected the rhythm of the rains, and a semidesert was beginning to creep from the prairie to the hills.

Crossing the prairie on foot was a whole day's journey. Nyawīra had started early, but her crossing took longer because she kept looking from side to side to see if she could catch sight of Kamītī. She also carried a basket full of things she knew Kamītī might need, and the weight slowed her. As tired as she was, Nyawīra did not really mind. She had decided to seek out Kamītī wherever he might be, for she felt she owed him an apology for the hard feelings she had harbored against him before she read his letter. The letter talked vaguely about his return to the wilderness but mentioned no specific location. She recalled that he had often talked to her about one of his favorite retreats among some rocks between the end of the prairie and the foothills. This was now her destination. But what if she did not find him there, or anywhere else, for that matter? She would have to go back, crossing the prairie alone in the dark; she did not even want to think about it.

She walked along the foot of the ridge, scared to venture into the forest. Hope was beginning to fade, and soon she started blaming herself for what she now saw as a fiasco. Am I also bewitched? Why would I follow a stranger into places I don't even know, like the girl in the story who saw a handsome man at market and followed him to his dwelling in the forest, only to find out that he was a man-eating ogre? Appearances could be deceiving. Had she been deceived by Kamītī's looks and deeds? Was he deliberately misleading her in his letter? Who after all was Kamītī wa Karīmīri? She recalled the gentleman of the jungle in Amos Tutuola's book *The Palm-Wine Drinkard,* who had returned borrowed body parts to their owners and now dwelled in the forest, a skull among other skulls. What if . . . ? She suddenly felt her knees drained of strength.

She saw a tree stump at the side of the hill and sat on it to rest and take stock of her situation. She had to make up her mind whether to go on with what seemed like a fruitless search or return to the city. She looked at the wide-open prairie before her, and it appeared to have no beginning or end, though in the horizon the skyline of Eldares was barely discernible in the mix of encroaching darkness and smoke from the factories.

"Nyawīra," a voice called out behind her. Her heart raced, suffusing her with warmth. She had recognized the voice but dared not believe her ears despite the echo. Slowly, she turned her head to where she thought the voice came from. Kamĩtĩ was standing there, somewhat hidden by the bush.

She stood up and walked toward him and Kamĩtĩ held her hand. At the touch, Nyawĩra felt her body tremble from head to foot while Kamĩtĩ felt blood rush to his fingertips, his entire body awash in a sensation he had not felt for a long time. Nyawĩra let him lead her farther up into the bush to a grassy moor surrounded by piles of gray stone, almost like a courtyard. He led her into a rocky cave. "Welcome," Kamĩtĩ said in a shaking voice.

Nyawĩra was surprised at herself. Everything she had wanted to say to Kamĩtĩ as she walked across the prairie had vanished; she felt incapable of speech. If she spoke now she would frighten away the goodness she felt in the air. So, amid the darkness of the evening and a deep silence, they just stood there holding hands, as if neither could believe the reality of the moment.

"I have come for the honey of life—isn't that what you called it?" Nyawĩra said just to break the silence, setting her basket of provisions against the rock wall.

"You have spoken," Kamĩtĩ replied.

Both thought that their words were a prelude to their usual lighthearted banter, but instead they found themselves stripping each other, wild-eyed, breathing heavily, their bodies taut with anticipation. He was about to remove her chemise when he stopped.

"I am sorry that I don't have any condoms," he said.

"No, no, don't stop," Nyawĩra told him. "I brought some," she added as she unbuttoned his trousers.

On the ground, in the cave, now wrapped in darkness, they found themselves airborne over hills and valleys, floating through blue clouds to the mountaintop of pure ecstasy, from where, suspended in space, they felt the world go round and round, before they descended, sliding down a rainbow, toward the earth, their earth, where the grass, plants, and animals seemed to be singing a lullaby of silence as Nyawĩra and Kamĩtĩ, now locked in each other's arms, slept the sleep of babies, the dawn of a new day awaiting.

# 21

They woke up as the sun was rising, their bodies cold. Beads of dew on their clothes shone like diamonds, and neither could recall when or how they had interrupted their sleep to put on clothes, for even now they felt as if in a dream. They shook off the dew.

"Show me where I can wash my face," Nyawīra asked him.

He led her to a stream, where they bent down and washed themselves. The water was clear and cold, almost numbing. Then they returned to their hiding place among the rocks.

Nyawīra had brought a few boiled eggs, some sugar, some cocoa, matches, a kettle, a small cooking pot. Having gathered goods from the earth still in abundance around them, they prepared a simple meal and conversed like in old times, cheerful talk that massaged their souls and kept them laughing. Kamītī thanked Nyawīra and an abundant nature for the meal.

"Nature may be abundant," said Nyawīra in response, "but it is also good to build a granary for when nature has the flu. I understand that long ago there was no home that could answer to the name of home without a granary being part of the architecture. Look at our Aburīria today. How many households have a granary? None, because they have nothing to store. Am I straying from my point? I suppose what is bothering me is the image of a hermit competing with animals for honey and wild berries."

"You are still lawyering?" Kamītī said. "You should have taken a degree in law and become an advocate."

"Even now I am an advocate. An advocate of the people . . ."

"And me? A self-appointed advocate for the rights of animals and plants," Kamītī said, laughing. "But you will agree with me that my lawyering is more selfless, because animals and plants have no tongues with which to lawyer for themselves."

"What are you trying to say?"

"That I am going to take you on a tour to meet my friends, all the natives of the forest."

"Tree and animal friends?"

"Yes, and the birds and the plants and the mountains and the valleys."

"I am looking forward to the guided tour. But don't lawyer for the natives—let them lie for themselves," Nyawīra said.

"Let's make a plan for the first day: what would you like to see?"

"Wherever you take me I shall follow and say it is good," she said.

Throughout the day they never talked about the Tajirikas, or the Wizard of the Crow, or even Kamītī's abrupt departure from Santalucia and his adoption of the wild. It was as if they had made a secret pact not to let recent events in Eldares intrude on their communion with each other and nature. They felt good and at peace amid nature's bounty.

They were like-minded about so many things. They often punctuated their talk with songs, stories, and friendly banter, such as when they came across a zebra rat and then a field mouse. They stopped and in unison sang about the animals.

> *Zebra rat*
> *And field mouse*
> *Once went to*
> *A granary*
> *Of an in-law*
> *To feed*
> *And out came*
> *Nine goats*
> *Of youth*
> *To turn ten*

It was a song that helped them count up to ten, but the logic was in the rhythm instead of the meaning of the words. Once again they laughed together, and as they looked in each other's eyes they were suddenly without words. They resumed their walk in silence, taken up by the light they saw in each other's eyes.

Love was everywhere: in the tree branches where the nests of weaverbirds hung; in the fern where the widowbird had left two long black tail feathers; in the murmurings of the Eldares River as it flowed eastward before turning into a roaring waterfall; in the sun's rays, which pierced through the waterfall, splitting into the seven colors of the rainbow; in the still waters of a small lake made by the river where Kamĩtĩ and Nyawĩra now swam and bathed and chased each other, splashing water on each other; in the blackjacks, the goosegrass and other plants, the flowers and seeds of which stuck to their wet clothes; in the movement of porcupines and hedgehogs; in the wings of the helmeted and crested guinea fowls, francolins that scampered away after stealing glances at the couple; in the honeybees and butterflies hopping from flower to flower; in the cooing of the doves; in the mating calls of the river frogs from among the reeds and water lilies. Love was there among the creeping plants that twined around the tree trunks; yes, in the blackberries, some of which they plucked and fed to each other. Love was there in the breeze that made the leaves sway ever so gently. Love was everywhere in this forest, but neither Nyawĩra nor Kamĩtĩ mentioned the word.

Later, seated on the ground, leaning against the trunk of a sycamore tree, they sipped cocoa, sometimes in silence, each lost in a world of his or her making, thinking the same thoughts and now and then indulging in small talk. Love had followed them here as moonlight illuminated the leaves to form patterns of light and shadow on the ground and their bodies. Yet still they could not pronounce love to each other or even silently to themselves.

But they felt enveloped in peace beyond understanding, peace emanating from the forest even though the crickets were calling and hyenas were howling from afar, and when Kamĩtĩ and Nyawĩra looked at each other, their eye beams pulled them together, Kamĩtĩ's fingers straying to Nyawĩra's nipples, the color of blackberries.

They slid into wordless wonder, and even on waking up in the morning they were still firmly locked in each other's arms as if they would never ever part.

# 22

However, by the late afternoon a chill had grown between them, not because their disposition toward each other had changed but because they had put many issues on hold, issues that could no longer be ignored.

Kamĩtĩ tried to answer questions that must have been bothering Nyawĩra; the letter he had left behind for her had been cryptic.

"Not that I knew what prompted me to turn my back on healing, divination, and the money, to embrace the life of a hermit in the wilderness," Kamĩtĩ struggled to explain.

He spoke in an even tone, neither high nor low, neither sad nor joyful, a little introspective, perhaps, as if in addressing Nyawĩra he was holding a dialogue with himself.

"Maybe there were many reasons; maybe there was only one; the truth is that nothing is very clear in my mind. I did not choose to play at being the Wizard of the Crow. I was thrust into it. You know how this whole business began. What was his name—I mean the police officer who chased us across the prairie that night? Arigaigai Gathere. A.G. What a name! Arigaigai! Had you ever come across such a name before? It was A.G. who set me on the road to sorcery. My own troubles made me all too willing. At first I thought that I was merely playing a role, briefly. I was proud that I never once dispensed magic that could harm anyone; and I never really lied to my clients. I never employed conjuring tricks to mesmerize. I worked with thoughts and images already in their own minds. But still I pretended to be what I was not. Did I not heal under falsehood? Imagine going to a doctor only to learn afterward that he has no training in his craft, no license to practice? I was a quack of a wizard. But that is beside the point. My divinations were an appetite for evil. Take Tajirika and his ilk; did I not breathe new life into him, increasing his self-confidence in doing evil? Protected by magic as he now imagines himself to be, is he not now free to rob with impunity? Did my divination not facilitate his thievery? I was an accessory to the very evil that revolted me.

"Maybe at the very beginning I harbored the illusion that there might come to me one or two who would be bold enough to see the error of their ways and say, I have a blemish, help me remove it. This might have given my role some worth. But no, they were all driven by greed and hatred.

"They were interested in only two things: to be empowered and to cripple their rivals. Yes, when it came to greed, they were clones of one another. Their greed stank. Even as I asked them questions about their afflictions, the smell of evil and greed oozed out of their every pore and made it difficult for me to breathe. For a time I was able to endure the ooze by sniffing the scent of flowers that you always left behind. But Tajirika's rot proved more terrible than any that I had experienced before: a black man celebrating the negation of himself. This final blast of foul air was unbearable.

"I don't know where I got the strength to do it, but I eventually did find myself outside the door, and still the foulness pursued me. I panicked. Whenever I had gone out into the open I had been able to rid myself of their stench and breathe fresh air. This was now not the case. I collapsed. When later I came to my senses I felt that I did not want to go back to the shrine, but I managed to force myself into the house to write you the letter. By then I had already made up my mind."

"To do what?" Nyawīra asked.

"Flee Eldares. Abandon human community for the wilderness."

"In your letter, what did you mean by the words 'I am going to find myself'?" Nyawīra quizzed him.

"I don't want to say that at the time of writing the letter I was in a position to convey all my thoughts in words. Say I just wanted to escape the stink. I told you that when I went outside the house I felt that the rot had followed me and as if it were now oozing through my clothes, my body, me, and I had never felt like that before. I asked myself: If I start stinking like them, what will be the difference between them and me?"

"And the rot that you talk about so movingly—what do you suppose will bring it to an end?"

"The affairs of the people are too heavy a burden for me to carry."

"Did you yourself not say that the needs of the many call for more than the hands of a single person? Is that not why they say that many hands make work light?"

"I just want to stay in the wilderness to find myself. I want to know what I really want from my life. Maybe the blood of the hunters in me is calling."

"You mean it is telling you to run away from the people? To heal yourself?"

"One must find oneself before one can try to help others."

"Physicians do not heal themselves. And our people say that even the most skilled barber needs another to cut his hair. To strike a fire you need tinder and a stick. The problems of the country are ours. Nobody can bear them alone. We cannot run away and leave the affairs of the land to ogres and scorpions. This land is mine. This land is yours. This land is ours. Besides, in Aburĩria, there is nowhere to run. As you've said, even these forests are threatened by the greed of those in power."

"What am I to do? Return to divination?" he said, as if repeating questions he had already posed to himself.

"The power to divine is a gift. No matter how hard I may try, I don't think I can settle cases with the wisdom I have seen you display. It is as if you can see into the hearts of people as well as read the very thoughts in their minds. Like the way you dealt with Tajirika and Vinjinia. Who would ever have thought that wishes could so afflict the body and mind? What an affliction it was! A white-ache so deep-seated that it almost made him lose his business!"

Kamĩtĩ looked away to the hills far in the distance.

"What is it?" Nyawĩra asked anxiously.

Kamĩtĩ did not answer immediately. He slowly turned to face Nyawĩra again.

"Nothing," he said. "Nothing, really, but I hope that a day will come when we can talk about everything . . ."

"Let's talk now," Nyawĩra said encouragingly, "even about that which you call nothing. Didn't you ask me a minute ago what a person can do? Let me ask you. If you found a grown man taking food from a child by force, would you just stand there and watch the drama?"

"No. What do you want?" Kamĩtĩ asked her. "You didn't come here just to be with me."

"Marching to Heaven will swallow our land. Where shall we take shelter from the sun and rain? It will snatch water from the mouth of the thirsty and food from the mouth of the hungry. Skeletons will people our country. How shall we get back the body, the mind, and the soul of the nation?"

Nyawĩra now told him about the secret plans of the Ruler: that they had chosen a day in which to dedicate a site to the project of Marching to Heaven. She told him of the State's sinister intentions to use the queues in Eldares to convince the Global Bank mission that the people were fully in support of the project.

"For a time we in the movement thought of campaigning against the queuing, but given the level of unemployment in this country, there was no way we were going to stop the mania. So instead we are going to make our own procession of protest. All of us men and women of Aburīria must join hands in opposing this madness of Marching to Heaven. We oppose the right of might with the might of right. We want you to be one of us. Use your God-given powers of divination for the benefit of the people, the movement."

Kamītī stood up and once again stared beyond the hills. When he turned to her, his eyes shone with a light Nyawīra had not seen, a light more of sorrow than joy, the light of one burdened with a knowledge he would rather not possess. He sat next to Nyawīra and put his arm around her shoulder, and Nyawīra felt a tremor in her body as she awaited his response.

"In truth, something other than the stench of corruption drove me from Eldares," Kamītī started. "A combination of events forced me to look within myself, and I saw no clear purpose in my life. My only goal had been to educate myself so as to earn plenty of money to make good my parents' sacrifice. As you know, this dictated my choice of business studies as my main subject. The irony was that although I was doing well in my studies, I did not feel that I really wanted a life in business.

"In India, by studying the art of healing through plants, I suppose I had also a hazy notion of becoming a physician of wounded souls. But as to who my patients-to-be were, I hadn't a clue.

"I was drawn to the religions of the East. I wanted to learn more about the prophets and the teachers from the East like Buddha, Jain's Mahavira, Guru Nanak of the Sikhs, and even Confucius of China. Some of their beliefs, like the doctrine of karma, are close to what I have heard you say about human deeds and actions as determinants of life on earth. The Buddhist karma is a deed, physical, oral, or mental, containing within it a potential power. Each of our actions results in the good or bad effect and influences our future. A good deed repeated accumulates the good, and its potential power will affect the future as a beneficial influence. Each person has his own karma, his own potentiality for good or evil. Like the chi among the Ibo.

"Our ancestors tell us that a builder can only build you a house with the building blocks you bring him. You bring him stones? You get a house made of stone. You bring him wood? You get a house made of wood. You bring defective stone, wood, iron, or steel, you get a defective house. The chief difference between your position and the religions I've studied concerns belief in the transmigration of souls. If you do beastly deeds in this life, then in your next life you will be born a greedy hyena or an ugly warthog or simply a beast. A person should lead a life of good works to ensure that in his next cycle of being he or she is reborn as a superior being.

"The Buddhist attitude to property attracted me. A person who chases after fame and wealth and love is like a child who licks honey from the blade of a knife. While tasting the sweetness of honey he risks damaging his tongue. But what fascinated me most was the notion of nirvana. I understand that the word literally means 'to blow off.' It is a state of perfect light, a state in which all human defilement and passion have been completely extinguished through practices and meditations based on the right wisdom. Buddha means the 'enlightened, the one who has found the light.' And it was not lost on me that Gautama Buddha himself reached this state in his old age, lying between two large trees in a forest.

"When I returned to Aburĩria my spiritual preoccupations yielded to necessity: I had to find a job. There was a time when I thought that maybe a person could do business in a righteous way—you know, without greasing palms—and so remain incorruptible. As it turned out I did not even have the opportunity to find out if that was possible. The rest you know.

"I've come to believe that there is a power outside of us that drives human affairs. It is the power hinted at by the religious when they say that God works in mysterious ways, His wonders to perform. You and I had not chosen to meet when we did. The same power has brought you here. There is a purpose to all this.

"Nyawĩra, please don't go back to Eldares, back to the corruption. Let's build a shelter here; listen to what the trees and the animals have to tell us. Long ago, my ancestors, the hunters, believed that the sun was our god because it was the source of fire and light. When we were children and we captured its heat in pieces of glass, we believed we'd captured a bit of its power. Let's stay here and find out the secrets of the heat of the sun and the light of millions of stars."

Nyawĩra could not quite believe her ears. She had not expected this response. He was asking her to turn her back on Eldares, Aburĩria, the people, so as to become a hermit, one of the children of the new-millennium Buddha in the Abūrīrian forest, searching for the meaning of life. Without thinking of what she was doing, she removed Kamītī's hand from her shoulders.

"Maybe we are different. You are drawn to the ministry of wounded souls, I to the ministry of wounded bodies. I may not know which is the better ministry. But this I know: human beings are free to choose how they use the gifts given to them by God, nature, sun, fate, call it what you like, I mean that transcendent power that you say governs our lives, whether to use it to seek personal salvation or a collective deliverance."

It was not a question, but again Kamītī squirmed under its implication.

"When I look into the distance of time I see only a kind of darkness, a mist, smoke, nothing clear. Nyawīra, I smell tears and blood . . ."

"Whose tears and blood?"

"I don't really know. I will not ask you and your friends to give up the plans you have for disrupting the rites at the site of Marching to Heaven. However, on my part I don't feel ready for the task. I still want to hear what the animals, plants, and hills have to tell me. I need to find myself."

"For us," she now said as she stood up, "we see Marching to Heaven as means of turning our earth into hell, and we have chosen to do something about it."

She started collecting her things, ready to leave. She did not pack the boxes of matches, the kettle, or the pot.

Then she suddenly remembered something at the back of her mind that she had not yet voiced.

"Tell me," she said, "what happened to the three bags of money? What did you do with them, or rather with the money?"

"I buried it," Kamītī said, exhausted.

"You buried the money?" Nyawīra asked, as if she had not heard the words clearly. "You should have given it to us!" she said. "The movement would have made good use of the money against these criminals."

"I will tell you where it is. It is all yours. But be forewarned: that money is cursed."

"There is no money that is blessed or cursed," Nyawīra said. "It depends on the uses to which it is put," she added, and then suddenly paused.

She recalled that the three bags of money almost took her life the day she returned to the office to collect her handbag and ran into Tajirika's gun. The three bags had provoked white-ache in Tajirika.

"Forget the whole thing," she said. "I don't even want to know where it is buried. Our movement believes more in the actions that people do than in the money that people give. So let us leave the money bags to red ants and termites. It is time I returned to my lair in the city."

"The sun is about to set. Why don't you stay for the night and leave in the morning so you can cross the prairie by the clear light of day?"

"No, I will start right away. I have to report to work tomorrow."

"I will see you across the prairie," Kamĩtĩ offered.

"No, no. Let me do the prairie alone. That way I will get to know it better. The wild beasts of the prairie are less cruel than the beastly humans embarking on Marching to Heaven."

"But don't burn your bridges. What is the saying? One may find oneself back to places one had thought that one had left for good. I am now a dweller in the forest. If ever you come back, please leave a piece of your cloth here in the cave or on any rock in the forest and I am confident that I shall find you."

"Thank you, but I have no intention of returning to these parts anytime soon. Eldares calls me."

They walked in silence to the foot of the hills where the prairie begins. Kamĩtĩ watched Nyawĩra cross the expanse of the land until she became indistinguishable from the acacia in the distance.

# SECTION III

# I

Weeks later when Nyawīra was on the most wanted list and the police, under the Ruler's orders to take her dead or alive, were looking for her all over the country, what most helped was her knowledge of the prairie, and Kamĩtĩ's admonishment not to burn bridges was very much in her mind as she crossed the plains in the dark alone with nothing more than the dress she had worn to work and a handbag.

She recalled how firmly she had resolved not return to these parts anytime soon and was struck by Kamĩtĩ's prophetic insight. She felt fearful of the darkness but also grateful for the protection it offered against pursuers. The stars above were her best companions, and it was now that she most appreciated the talks she and Kamĩtĩ had had about the sun, the moon, and the stars.

She went to the cave where she had last seen him. There were no signs of human presence. She stood there; she grew teary-eyed. Not that she regretted what she and the other women had done, although she grudgingly admitted to herself that it was no less provocative than if they had pelted a police station with rocks.

The moon appeared in the horizon, and though it did not shine as brightly as it had that other time with Kamĩtĩ, still its light enabled her to make out her surroundings. She did not want to stay in the cave because it was near the foothills, so she decided to try her luck farther in and wander among the places where she and Kamĩtĩ had earlier stayed to see if she might find him.

The forest seemed transformed, though not many weeks had passed since she had last been there. Then the entire place was enveloped in a magic of love and wild beauty. Now it seemed unbearably perilous. She dreaded encountering a lion, a leopard, or any of the cats she had earlier wished to see. How would she escape from them? She imagined cobras, puff adders, and pythons lurking somewhere in the dark, and with every step she pictured herself being ensnared by a snake or a three-horned chameleon. She did not fail to note the irony of her having carried plastic snakes in her handbag in the past. Now she was in a bush where real snakes resided, and she was terrified. What if I should escape human fangs only to end up in the belly of a puff adder? She imagined her body slowly decomposing in the belly of a viper and she shivered, but when she pictured herself inside the Ruler's torture machine, she thought the belly of a beast less terrifying.

There was a crack of a dry bush behind her. She froze. She thought of dashing farther into the bush, but she could not move her feet. She glanced to the left, now to the right, to see if there was a tree nearby to which she could run and climb.

She heard the sound again and in a split second took flight, unaware that she had screamed. And then she tripped over something. It must be a snake. She tried to crawl away, whimpering, and then collapsed.

She did not know how long she stayed unconscious. All she now felt was the sudden flooding of her eyes when she came to and found herself in Kamĩtĩ's arms. As the tears of joy streamed down her cheeks, Nyawĩra felt rather than saw the question etched in the folds on his forehead.

"It is all because of the women's demonstration against Marching to Heaven," she told him, heaving and crying without restraint.

# 2

How had she slipped through their fingers? people in Eldares were asking, entertaining many versions of what had happened. One rumor had it that more than a thousand policemen had been deployed to seal off the office where she worked, that some were in armored cars with rapid-fire submachine guns trained on all exits, and helicopters like hawks hovered to swoop on the fugitive.

Some of these gossipmongers even swore that they were there, had seen her with their very eyes, that she was dressed to kill, that those policemen who laid their eyes on her were seized by a desire the likes of which they had never experienced, so powerful that it turned them into drooling fools struggling to stifle their erections.

Yet according to another rumor, Nyawīra had disguised herself as a man: some said as an old man wrapped in a tattered blanket, and others saw her as a handsome young man, clean-shaven but with a handlebar mustache bushier than the tail of a horse.

All the rumors, however, agreed that some police had been dispatched to Nyawīra's workplace with a warrant for her arrest.

# 3

Two of the policemen, with Kaniūrū as their informant, sat at separate tables in the Mars Café, waiting to pounce on Nyawīra on her way to the offices of Eldares Modern Construction and Real Estate. Three in plainclothes were deployed at strategic points around the area. Perched in his accustomed corner, reading or trying to read a newspaper, Kaniūrū was so conscious of the weight of the task entrusted to him that it took him a while to realize that he was holding the newspaper upside down.

The recent drama at the dedication of the site for Marching to Heaven had given Kaniūrū the opening he had sought all these years to ingratiate himself properly with the powers that be, and he seized it with alacrity. He placed a direct call to Sikiokuu in the Ruler's office.

The minister could not believe the good fortune coming from the other end of the line. He felt a guardian angel had come to his rescue even as he was drowning. He recalled vividly how as they left the scene of the drama the Ruler had called him aside and in an icy tone had asked rhetorically, How could so shameful a scandal have taken place without the ears, eyes, and noses of the State having even an inkling? I shall need a convincing explanation at the next cabinet meeting, the Ruler had warned him in English, and Sikiokuu had been in Aburīrian politics long enough to know that this amounted to a death sentence.

Days later, Sikiokuu had locked himself in his office, desperately trying to figure things out but all in vain. Unless fate intervened, his days were numbered. And then came the telephone call from Kaniūrū. In all the time he had dealt with his numerous informers, none had ever given him information that made him so tremble with relief and anticipation. Sikiokuu could hear the words clearly but kept on asking Kaniūrū to repeat them: Am I hearing right? You know some of the women? Oh, you don't know if she is the leader? Ah, a follower of the movement? Boy, if we catch her, the latest Mercedes is yours. Oh, we'll put such a squeeze on her that she will shit out everything she knows, he told Kaniūrū as he summoned him to his office.

Sikiokuu would have wanted to be present at the moment of Nyawīra's arrest, but he feared to be absent should the Ruler call an emergency cabinet meeting concerning the affair. In any event, it would be a little undignified for a cabinet minister to participate in the arrest of a common secretary deluded into anarchy, no doubt, by a cunning lover. After his face-to-face with Kaniūrū, Sikiokuu decided that he did not trust the local police of Santamaria with the task of arresting Nyawīra. He would dispatch a special squad from his own office to do the deed, he told Kaniūrū.

He had already formed a standing squad of Superintendent Peter Kahiga, Superintendent Elijah Njoya, and Superintendent Arigaigai Gathere as his eyes on the movement, and he now enlisted three constables to assist them. A.G. was to coordinate the operation not only because he had worked in Santamaria and knew the area well but also because of his legendary chase of djinns across the prairie, resulting in a reputation of relentlessness. A.G. was also to liaise with the informer Kaniūrū, whose main task was to point out the criminal.

A.G. and Kaniūrū agreed that the Mars Café would be the focal point. Kaniūrū was to make sure to be there before the main squad and order a cup of tea. He would be wearing a white shirt and reading a newspaper as identifying markers for the squad.

The squad was to arrest the woman in secrecy, throw her into a van with a fake license plate, and take the prisoner directly to Sikiokuu. No one else, be he a police officer or cabinet minister, was to know. Sikiokuu did not want to share even the slightest credit with his political enemies like Machokali; he licked his lips at the thought of the dramatic arrest, his first crack at the women who had brought shame to the state in the eyes of the world. The state would now strike back, and he, Sikiokuu, was thankful that fate had chosen him to be the instrument of the Ruler's revenge.

# 4

Nyawīra would always recall the morning of that Tuesday with trepidation. The Monday and the Friday before had been declared public holidays in honor of the dedication on a Saturday. Tuesday was her first day of work after the drama at Eldares. Later, describing the events of the fateful morning, she talked about how she had woken up at her usual hour in a state of bliss, quickly showered, and set out for the bus stop. The bus to Santamaria had been on time. In the bus Nyawīra was in a zone all her own—she felt like singing to celebrate being a woman. The victorious drama at Eldares was still fresh in her mind. She knew that security forces would be on the lookout for the members of the movement, but she did not feel unduly concerned about her own personal safety. She believed that nobody could possibly connect her with what the women had done. In Aburīria, politics was strictly a masculine affair; men would never think that women could plan and execute anything like what had happened. Ever since she started working for Tajirika she had covered her tracks well, acting the perfect secretary—a bit priggish, perhaps, which had earned her Tajirika's respect and that of his circle of friends, who kept their lustful thoughts to themselves. She got off at her usual stop a few blocks after the Santamaria market. She crossed the Ruler's Avenue and Parrot's Way and went down Main Street to the offices of Eldares Modern Construction and Real Estate. She was very keen on getting to the office to glean gossip from Vinjinia. Vinjinia had not been at the scene on Saturday, but she surely would have picked up a few tidbits from Tajirika.

Nyawīra knew that he had been at the meeting because a few days before the dedication, Tajirika, according to Vinjinia, had suddenly recovered from his so-called illness, saying that the queues had already served their purpose and swearing that no illness, real or fake, would keep him, the chairman of Marching to Heaven, away from participating in so historic a day.

She thought of stopping at the Mars Café for a cup of coffee before going to the office. Giddy with bliss, Nyawīra never entertained the possibility of encountering Kaniūrū. At the thought of the aroma of fresh hot coffee, she did, however, think of Kamītī all alone in the forest, but she quickly shooed the image away. After all, Kamītī had freely chosen to dwell among the fauna and flora, and if he was happy with that, who was she to tell him that he was missing good coffee at the Mars Café on a glorious Tuesday morning? She did not envy him, and she most certainly did not miss the frosty morning air of the mountains.

She was a few blocks from Mars Café when she felt somebody touch her right shoulder. She ignored the brush, casually shifting her handbag to her left shoulder and moving on. It happened again and she turned around quickly. It was A.G. Nyawīra started ever so slightly. She had never seen him in daylight other than at her place, and not since the morning that he had come to tell of his promotion. What is he doing in plainclothes in Santamaria so early in the morning? Trying hard not to show surprise, she at first acted as if she could not tell who he was.

But A.G. was already murmuring gratitudes. What is the man talking about? she asked herself, but she had no way of getting a word in edgewise.

"I recognized you in the distance but I just wanted to make sure," A.G. bubbled, lowering his voice as if he did not want anybody else to hear what he was saying. "Me? There is no way I would not recognize you even if you were to turn yourself into a bird or a turtle. True! *Haki ya Mungu.* And don't think that I don't know that you can change yourself into anything. Where did you go? I sent some other friends to you and they found the shrine closed with a notice that you had gone away . . ."

Now Nyawira realized why he was thanking her so effusively, and it was with some effort that she managed to hold back her laughter. She recalled that ever since the flight from Paradise, A.G. had taken it into his head that Nyawira and Kamītī were two manifestations of the same identity: the Wizard of the Crow. Nyawira did not attempt to dissuade him, and she was sure that even if she had A.G. would not have believed her. In any case, she did not want to prolong the conversation. He was keeping her from coffee at the Mars Café and work. It would be easier to get rid of him by just going along with his madness. So she half nodded in agreement and played at the role of the Wizard of the Crow:

"Don't you dare tell anybody that you saw me in the streets. If you do . . ." she said, and then paused as if the consequences of so doing were simply too awful to contemplate. "I don't want anyone to know who I am," she added, deepening her voice.

"Oh, trust me, Sir Madam Wizard of the Crow. Your every wish is my command. True! *Haki ya Mungu!* How can I ever forget what you did for me? Have you been away on safari, or what?"

Nyawira confirmed that she had indeed been away, to collect herbs in addition to legs and tails of frogs and lizards, skins of hedgehogs and porcupines, and horns of chameleons, not to mention skins of grass snakes to make more potent magic, and, oh yes, she had also gone to get mirrors that could capture a person's shadow no matter how far he was and a person's thoughts even before that person himself had thought the thoughts. She would be returning to the shrine soon, she told him, and if ever he was in trouble he should not hesitate to come back. A.G., whose eyes grew larger with awe and admiration, was visibly delighted at the invitation. But Nyawira realized she had made a mistake: what if he should come tomorrow? So she was quick to add:

"Mark you, it will take a while before I return. The new powers must mature. But what are you doing this early in Santamaria? I know that all is well with your new job."

"You truly amaze me with the way you read my mind," A.G. said. "My affairs are going smoothly," he added boastfully, "and all this thanks to you. Let me tell you . . ."—he lowered his voice even more—"I am here on a special mission. I have been sent to these parts by no other than Sikiokuu himself, and not as just anybody but as the director of a very special operation. True! *Haki ya Mungu!* And imagine this: in all the years I had worked in the force before you empowered me, I had never been given any task with the word 'special' attached to it. But now look at me. I am coordinating the entire operation, and that's why you see me in the streets. Three of my men are waiting at the Mars Café and two others at street corners covering the way in and out of the office. There is no escape route. As you can see we are in plainclothes. I myself cannot go inside the Mars Café, because as you know I used to work in these parts, and the criminal, who I understand goes there for coffee sometimes, might recognize me and suspect something is afoot."

"But who is this criminal? A murderer, a bank robber?" she asked, now bored, a little impatient even. She was anxious to get to the office. She might even have to give up on coffee—no, she wouldn't give up, she told herself; she would dash in and order it to go.

"Worse than a bank robber or murderer," A.G. whispered, presuming a bond she found irritating. His next words shattered her composure. She felt goose bumps all over her as she became fully alert.

"Between me and you, Sir Wizard, what those women did at the site of Marching to Heaven is very bad, really shameful. True! *Haki ya Mungu*. But we now have a suspect. Minister Sikiokuu has ordered us to capture her and take her to him directly. I personally don't know who she is or what she looks like, but that's not a problem. We have a very cooperative young man who will identify her for us. Sikiokuu likes him very much. To tell you the truth, and speaking like a professional and a well-trained police officer, I don't much care for these youthwingers who think they know everything. Still, we the police depend on tips from informers, and this Kaniūrū seems to have used his nose quite well in sniffing out this woman."

Nyawīra felt drained of energy. She feared her knees would buckle, but she summoned inner strength not to let her face or voice betray her. She asked him a few more questions to determine how much they knew about her. She was very grateful for being mistaken as the Wizard of the Crow and would assume the role no matter what happened.

"This John Nose, where is he now?" Nyawīra asked.

A.G. burst out laughing, making Nyawīra apprehensive. She had not intended to be funny: was he playing a game of cat and mouse with her?

"Sir Madam Wizard of the Crow," A.G. said to Nyawīra's relief, "we the police have nicknamed him the same, Johnny the Nose, and when one of us mentions the nickname we break into laughter. But we don't underestimate him—oh no, not me. He is quite smart. After all, he is the one who offered up this Nyawīra. He is now in the Mars Café with two of my officers, Kahiga and Njoya. I must go now. Let me not delay you," A.G. said apologetically. "I'm sure you have a lot to do, but when you return I will certainly take you up on your invitation and come for the more potent stuff," A.G. said, and went away still laughing and muttering the name "John Nose."

Nyawīra made as if she were entering the nearest shop, but only the better to sneak a peek at the direction A.G. had taken. For a second she toyed with going past the Mars Café just to make sure that Kaniūrū was indeed there, but this would have been like putting a finger in a hornets' nest. She left the shop front and walked as if continuing in her original direction, but at the end of the block she quickly turned the corner.

"I had never felt so grateful at the presence of so many people in the streets of Eldares," Nyawīra told Kamītī.

# 5

If Nyawīra had gone past the Mars Café she might have detected a trace of irritation in the way Kaniūrū turned the pages of his newspaper. His eyes were mostly fixed on the road and on the pavement to Tajirika's offices, and he was annoyed at how long this was taking.

He was preoccupied with the changes in his lifestyle that were about to take place once he pulled off this feat. He kept glancing at his watch, becoming increasingly upset with Nyawīra, as if she had betrayed him. She has always gone to work on time. Why not today? How can she do this to me? If only I knew where she lives! I would burn her house down to dust and ashes.

Kahiga and Njoya, A.G.'s lookouts, just sat there waiting, hoping for a signal from Kaniūrū that would simply not come. Was this informer sure of his facts? They had drunk so much coffee that they felt like throwing up; they, too, were growing impatient.

By early afternoon it had become clear that there was something amiss, and it was decided that one of the police officers, new to the area, would go to Tajirika's office, but treading carefully so as not to arouse any suspicion. He returned almost immediately, panting with excitement. There was a woman in the office. Ignoring Kaniũrũ completely, A.G. gave the orders and Njoya and Kahiga acted swiftly, arresting the only woman in the office.

It was said that when Sikiokuu learned that the captive was Vinjinia, he surprised even himself by not becoming despondent. Instead, he fell to his knees and tugged at his earlobes in gratitude at the unexpected turn of events. Thank you, Lord of the Universe, for giving me something to save my skin and skin my enemies.

# 6

There was nothing contradictory in his behavior. For what Sikiokuu saw in this case of mistaken identity was a win-win situation. If Vinjinia was connected with the women of the movement in any way, her actions would implicate Tajirika, who in turn would drag Machokali under the umbrella of suspicion. And if it turned out that Vinjinia was innocent, Sikiokuu would blame it on Kaniũrũ and the squad for following the woman's trail to her employer's offices. Tajirika, Machokali's friend, would still have to explain how he came to employ a rebel. But he did not want to think of any unforeseen complications. He would cross that bridge when he came to it—just now he wanted to savor the triumph of the moment at the detention of Vinjinia, Tajirika's wife.

# 7

Tajirika, along with other members of the Marching to Heaven Building Committee, spent all day closeted in a hotel room, trying to figure out how to recover the image of the State: what steps could they immediately take to remove the shame brought on the nation by female renegades? They competed over who could most denigrate womankind. Women had always been the thorn in the flesh of the human race; hardly surprising, most of the men concluded, given their descent from Eve. One member of the committee pretended dissent. With a knowing smile and a wicked glint in his eye, he asked, Who hides the sly snake between their legs? They all laughed and on that hilarious note ended the all-day meeting.

As Tajirika returned to his Golden Heights residence, his head was stuffed full of thoughts about the treachery of women throughout history, and when he found that his wife was not yet home, he was left to wonder: Has Vinjinia become yet another wife of the rich and powerful, taken up to spreading her legs to just about anybody in the name of women's lib?

By midnight, when Vinjinia had still not appeared, Tajirika's anger and jealousy turned to worry and concern. Had she been in an accident? Had she been stricken ill? Was she in a hospital?

He hardly slept, and the following morning he set out for the office early: he was sure that Nyawĩra would know what had happened to his wife. When he saw his wife's Mercedes-Benz outside the office, he felt rage. So she had decided to stay out all night? But why? Imagine his surprise when he found the doors of the office locked. There was no sign of Vinjinia anywhere. All his hopes now reverted to Nyawĩra; but when she failed to turn up on time he became agitated. He, too, did not know where Nyawĩra lived. His knowledge of southern Santalucia did not go beyond what he had seen on his last visit to the shrine of the Wizard of the Crow. How could both women be unaccountable on the same day? He went down to the Mars Café to see if Nyawĩra was loitering there.

He tried to engage the proprietor, but as usual Gautama was far more interested in talking about the latest exploration for water and life on Mars than in small talk about happenings in Eldares. Through persistence Tajirika did manage to get Gautama to tell him about the three men who looked like government agents; he knew they were up to something by the quantity of coffee they consumed and the way one of them was holding his newspaper upside down, pretending to read it. At one point Gautama claimed he saw or thought he saw some of the men go to the offices of Eldares Modern Construction and Real Estate. Are you sure? Tajirika asked, fear creeping in. Tajirika's spirits were not lifted when Gautama whispered that even now, as they were talking, the whole town was full of uniformed and undercover police officers looking for a woman: You know the woman—what's her name? Nyawīra. I think she is the lady who works for you, and she comes here often for coffee, but yesterday and today I have not seen her. Tajirika's fear became terror. What was the connection between Vinjinia and Nyawīra? And why would the police be looking for one or both?

He went back to his office and tried to call his friend Machokali, but he could not reach him and left a message for the minister to call him back. He stayed put, waiting for a call that did not come. In the evening, back at home in the Golden Heights, Tajirika again tried to reach the minister, dialing all the numbers at his disposal, including one for a mobile phone, but to no avail.

On the third day he decided to call Inspector Wonderful Tumbo, the head of the Santamaria police station. Tajirika considered Officer Tumbo a good friend. The friendship was rooted in deeds of mutual benefit. Every now and then Tajirika would make sure that he extended to the officer what he called best wishes wrapped up in Burī notes and stuffed in an envelope. Sometimes the envelope bore wishes for a Happy Christmas and a Prosperous New Year for the officer and the entire station. He also used Tumbo for contact with low-level military: not for anything in particular, but just to support our men in uniform, as he would say. It was of course understood that in exchange the police would see to Tajirika's interests, even passing on information useful to a businessman who needed to conform to the prevailing political wind. As for the military, well, with Africa one never knows. The moment the officer recognized Tajirika's voice at the other end of the line he kept him on hold for so long that Tajirika put the receiver down. When he called back he was told that the officer was busy.

Later that evening Officer Tumbo passed by Tajirika's residence, but in a borrowed car and in civilian clothes and a false mustache, his head covered by an egg-shaped hat. The officer did not attempt to explain his disguise but went straight to the point. Tumbo told Tajirika that Nyawīra, his trusted secretary, was a wanted person in connection with the drama at Eldares. What about my wife? What about Vinjinia? Tajirika asked when he saw the officer ready to leave without so much as mentioning her name. Officer Wonderful Tumbo seemed genuinely surprised by this, as if her disappearance was also news to him. After Tajirika described the mystery of his wife's vanishing, how his office had been locked up, and how her Mercedes was parked outside, the officer said that everybody who had been in touch with Nyawīra was under suspicion and his guess, but it was only a guess, was that Vinjinia might be in the hands of the political police in the Ruler's office. A new squad had been created recently to crack down on members of the Movement for the Voice of the People, and everything Tajirika had said showed their hand, but he could not be sure. Tumbo now seemed to want to fly out of the house. He was already at the door when he turned and asked Tajirika not to call him at the station again, promising that if he came across any more information he would be sure to pass it on.

Tajirika was more shaken than he was before Tumbo's visit. How did I come to employ an enemy of the State? He started reviewing Nyawīra's working for him. She had started soon after he was appointed to the committee that eventually came up with Marching to Heaven. How could a woman so beautiful, so polite, so well mannered, so hardworking, so meticulous, become involved in subversive movements? Or had she been taking him for a ride? Yes, that must be it.

How had he failed to detect Nyawīra's hypocrisy? There were signs, but he had been too blind to see. For one thing, how was it possible that a woman so beautiful never put her good looks to work, as others, even at the university, were doing these days?

Nyawīra's eyes never shone with a flirtatious glint. Not by word, gesture, or look did she give an opening for those lurid jokes and comments that often opened floodgates of easy passion. It was rare in Aburĩria for a woman to have such strong morals, and it clearly indicated something not quite right about her, and he, Tajirika, who prided himself on his ability to read character, especially that of women, should have paid more attention to this.

But what about his wife? What was the connection between Nyawĩra and his wife? Had she, too, been deceiving him, pretending to be a good wife, a woman who never raised questions even though she knew that Tajirika slept with other women? A woman who was so uninterested in politics and world affairs that she would rather switch off the television and the radio rather than watch or listen to a news program? Was she faking a lack of interest? Had she become involved in radical politics when he was incapacitated? It is said that two women together are a pot of poison and one is influenced by the company one keeps.

He recalled that when he was suffering from white-ache, it was these two women who had taken him to the shrine of the Wizard of the Crow. That in itself was strange, and it should have alerted him. Vinjinia had always proclaimed herself a Christian. She never missed church on Sunday and had remained a faithful member of All Saints Cathedral. Why had she not turned to her Christian congregation for support instead of opting for the services of a sorcerer? Inwardly he was grateful to her for not exposing his illness to her fellow church members, but still, how did she arrive at witchcraft? Maybe she and Nyawĩra had been in collusion all along and he, Tajirika, had been sharing his office with an enemy of the State by day and his bed with an enemy at night. What madness made him employ Nyawĩra as a worker and Vinjinia as a wife?

His conversation with his mates came back to haunt him. Daughters of Eve. Black Daughters of Black Eve. They are going to know that I am the man, Tajirika swore to himself. They would forever rue the day they started playing radical politics in his office.

During these bouts of self-bolstering bravado, he would feel a sudden resurgence of hope quickly followed by deep despair at the thought of the absent Vinjinia and the renegade Nyawĩra.

That Machokali had not responded to any of his many telephone messages increased his worry. Even when he dialed Machokali's cell phone, it was the chauffeur who picked up only to tell him that he would pass on the message to the minister. To make matters worse, officer Wonderful Tumbo had not shown his face again.

He tried to figure out how he could extricate himself from the mess he found himself in. He wanted to save his skin and those of his children from disaster. He even thought of calling a press conference to publicly disassociate himself and his family from the activities of Vinjinia and Nyawīra, reaffirming his loyalty to the Ruler, his government, and the plans for Marching to Heaven. But how could he do a thing like that without first alerting his friend Machokali? After turning this idea over in his mind, he decided to put it off. He would wait a few days, but if after the third day he still failed to connect with his friend the minister or get fresh information from his friend Officer Tumbo, he would go ahead and denounce his wife and Nyawīra in public. He had to save his investments by any means necessary, and after this resolution he felt slightly better.

He started drafting the press statement. He stumbled over words and phrases, but he persevered and for a time the task kept his mind busy. *Dear Gentlemen of the Press. I have called you here today to tell you and, in telling you, tell the world that I would give up my life for the Ruler. As I am so loyal, how could anyone imagine that I could possibly have anything to do with a worker,* a simple secretary, *or a simple housewife, subverting the Mightiest of Governments . . . etc.*

Three days passed and still there was no call from the minister or visit from Officer Tumbo. Tajirika stared at his unfinished press statement and felt he had arrived at a cul-de-sac: how could he denounce women accountable to him whose whereabouts he did not know? What if his statement was turned against him, claims made that he had probably murdered them and buried their bodies in the backyard and was only pretending that they had disappeared?

Dispirited, weighed down by having no clear way out, he simply clung to his glass of whiskey for support and comfort.

It was then that he heard the screech of a car coming to a stop outside. He stood up, and as he was about to peer through the window the telephone rang. For a second he was torn between the car and the phone. He went for the phone. He was glad: it was Machokali, and he was certain that a conversation with his friend the minister would clear things up or clear the way for his press conference.

It was obvious that Machokali did not want to talk on the phone, and within seconds they had agreed on a time and a place to meet.

As he put the phone down, he heard the sound of the car leaving. He rushed to the door.

Vinjinia entered.

"Where in heavens have you been?" Tajirika asked.

"In the secret grip of the State," Vinjinia said lifelessly.

"What are you talking about?" Tajirika asked, unnerved more by the confirmation than by his previous uncertainty.

# 8

*State* and *secret* often go together. The secrets are known to only a few called secretaries in some countries and ministers in others, but both names reflect their roles as servants of state secrets. The Great Dictator of Aburĩria alias the Ruler of the Free Republic of Aburĩria did not trust anybody to keep his secrets. Even those ministers reputed to be close to him because they were the last to see him at night and first to see him in the morning were never sure about their fate, or whether by sunset or sunrise they would still be holding their jobs.

There was chilling precedence for this.

How many times had the dictator lifted a few, singing their praises, taking them with him everywhere for every ceremony, and just when they started believing that they were indeed "the beloved of the father" the dictator would suddenly pull the magic carpet from under them. Having fallen, the ex-beloved, bruised and broken, would crawl on all fours, crying out for mercy and forgiveness, this for a day, a week, a month, a year, or several years. Then suddenly, out of the blue, the dictator would hear the man's cry and send political fixers to assuage his misery. Arise, you may walk again, the dictator would say to the saved, and the man, so grateful, would forever wax lyrical about the dictator's boundless generosity, especially when blessed with a directorship of this or that marketing board, chairmanship of this or that wildlife society, or even another ministerial post.

The dictator's reputation for making minister plot against minister, region rise against region, and community fight against community was now a matter of legend. He would side with one warring faction, which would rejoice at its alliance with power only to wake up one morning to find that the dictator had sided with its adversary, for a time, at least, before changing sides again or even goading altogether another faction into the fray. The dictator, seemingly above it all, looking good as he appealed for peace and understanding, would be embraced by all the feuding parties as a Solomonic prince of peace.

Though aware of this, the well-to-do, the self-appointed leaders of communities, members of Parliament, and especially cabinet ministers never ceased competing to sit on the right side of the father. Yet the winner always lived in terror of being displaced by a rival wilier in the ways of sycophancy. The problem was that the Ruler never let anyone know what was expected of him to retain his place of honor. Even humility and self-abnegation, however abject, were not enough to prevent one's downfall. For in his long ascendance to ultimate authority, the Ruler had himself been the nonpareil master of humility and self-abnegation.

As to how he rose to the mountaintop of power, many stories are told. According to one version, he emerges in history as a champion of an unquestioning humility before power. He was first widely known during the colonial times for seeming meek and mild-mannered to every white man with whom he came into contact. All the white settlers' and missionary reports about him concurred that he was a good African, and later, "our man." Whether in school, the government bureaucracy, or the army, his servile bearing facilitated his climb up the ladder of success. He had failed to attain his high school diploma, but nonetheless he ended up an assistant headmaster of an African school on a settler's farm in western Aburĩria. Seeing that full headmastership was the most that he could ever attain in education, he quit the profession and went into the colonial army, becoming a self-proclaimed Military Officer of Information. His main job was helping to produce leaflets in praise of the heroic deeds of the colonial army against the nationalist insurgents. He rose to the rank of corporal, and there he would probably have remained had the nationalist insurgents not forced the colonialist mother country to rethink her strategy. When it was clear to the white settlers that independence for

Aburĩria was inevitable, the Ruler-to-be was once again appointed their man in the coming rearrangement of things. He was a natural choice, and it took careful planning that spanned several years. First they shrouded him in a mantle of nationalism. Even though the future Excellency was then just a journalist, he found himself climbing the military ranks from corporal to sergeant to sergeant-major all in a matter of weeks. It was then that the future Excellency produced a carefully worded statement completely unlike any of the leaflets he had hitherto produced. For now he called for improvements in the working conditions of the black people in the army; he vowed that otherwise he would quit his military post and forfeit promised honors to struggle for the rights of his people. A week later, he resigned and announced his intention to form his own nationalist political party.

The party not only would fight for improved working conditions for black Aburĩrians in the army and for the promotion of blacks to higher ranks, but would also champion the causes of all the smaller pastoral communities and fight for their right to wear traditional clothes and carry cultural weapons like bows and arrows, spears, and knock-berry clubs. They would sooner do without schools or even adequate grazing grounds than give up these cultural symbols so crucial to the defense of their traditions now threatened by larger ethnic communities, mostly supported by so-called progressive parties who had joined hands with terrorists to demand freedom now. Freedom now? All that these progressives wanted was for the whites to leave so that they would appropriate the grazing fields and watering holes of small communities and abolish their culture. Whereas those other parties wanted land and freedom, the Ruler-to-be's party wanted freedom with honor and scoffed at the idea of a timetable for freedom. The mother of the colonial state was happy. The white settlers were happy. The blacks in the colonial army were jubilant: they now had a champion and need not fear about their place in the new black order.

When independence was negotiated, the white settlers rallied behind the man and his party with secret money and diplomacy, and urged him to demand that as the representative of smaller communities he must be the second only to the first president, who was from the bigger communities. Failing that, the smaller communities should demand self-rule and secede if necessary. Most important, he and his party would have nothing to do with the armed insurgents.

The former colonial army, now renamed the national army even before negotiations had begun, also made its preferences known. The nationalist insurgents were shut out of direct negotiations in Europe. All else followed a preordained logic. Why not talks between the "main" parties to avoid future ethnic strife? The result was predictable. The agreement to merge all the nationalist parties into a United Party to ensure harmony between the major and minor ethnic groups, with the future Ruler now as number two to the First Ruler, a man advanced in years, was hailed as a triumph of moderation by all sides, and mostly by the mother of the erstwhile colonial state.

That is one version among many, but all agree on one thing: the Ruler's rise to power had something to do with his alliance with the colonial state and the white forces behind it. They also agree that he had come to value self-abnegation as the way of dealing with anybody with authority above him.

In his dealings with the First Ruler of the Free Republic of Aburīria, he humbled himself in every possible way, taking all shit from his new boss, marking time as Vice Ruler but biding his time. His capacity for absorbing every kind of abuse became legendary, and nobody who saw him kneel, crawl, or cringe before the boss could see the future greatness of the man.

But the more he humbled himself to his superiors, the more he expected the same from his underlings to assuage a deep-seated self-doubt. This need for assurance often resulted in acts of implacable brutality against the weak. No sooner was he fully in charge after the mysterious death of the First Ruler than he asked for the list of all condemned prisoners awaiting clemency and signed the warrant for their immediate execution. When he saw that his signature on paper or a word from his mouth could bring about the immediate cessation of a life, he there and then truly believed in his omnipotence. He was now sovereign.

What even those closest to him did not then realize was that the worst had yet to come. His lust for blood revealed itself when a breakaway group from the United Party formed the Aburīrian Socialist Party, attracting in no time a grassroots following across the ethnic divide. At the time, the cold war was starting. His friends in the West demanded that he do something about this. He immediately declared Aburīria a one-party state. The United Party changed its name to the

Ruler's Party and became the only legal political authority. The leaders of the socialist splinter group, having announced that they would take up arms and seek assistance from Cuba and Russia, went underground. Some say that the socialists were careless and irresponsible in what they did, ill prepared for consequences. Others have since claimed with documentation that the call to arms was the Ruler's fabrication. Whatever the case, his friends in the West needed him to assume the mantle of the leader of Africa and the Third World, for Aburīria was of strategic importance to the West's containment of Soviet global domination. The Ruler accused the Socialist party of forming one link in the chain of the Soviet ambitions. Aburīria did not fight Western colonialism in order to end up under Eastern Communist colonialism, he declaimed, the first time he had used the phrase "fight Western colonialism" in a positive context.

It is said that in only a month he mowed down a million Aburīrian Communists, rendering the Ruler the African leader most respected by the West and landing him numerous state visits with kings, queens, and presidents receiving him in their palaces at lavish dinner parties. The Western media was bountiful in its praises: *a bulwark against world communism,* some called him. *A leader not afraid to lead,* others said. At long last, AN AFRICAN STATESMAN OF WORLD STATURE, screamed headlines. Countless were the many pictures of him shaking hands with the most powerful of European and American statesmen.

The Ruler broke the back of organized resistance, and it took some years for opposition to regroup and retrieve fragments of memory and piece them together into a whole. Even then this opposition largely existed underground or in exile, as was the case of Luminous Karamu-Mbu-ya-Ituĩka and Yunity Immaculate Mgeuzi-Bila-Shaka in the days when they used to toy with revolutionary ideas. Aboveground, the Ruler proved adept at stifling all other nascent opposition through the carrot and the stick. He gave the carrot to the elite of the various ethnic communities and the stick to all signs of defiance. But sweetness was reserved for the armed forces, who never forgot his dramatic resignation as Military Information Officer from the army they had served under during colonialism. Our man in the State House, some of the generals called him, and the Ruler returned the favor by frequently reminding the nation that the only votes that mattered were those cast for him by the armed forces.

He was baffled by anyone not motivated by greed. He could never understand the type who talked of collective salvation instead of personal survival. How was one supposed to deal with these recalcitrants? A fisherman puts a worm at the end of the line, but if the fish ignores it, how is the fisherman to catch the fish?

That is why he could not understand what drove the women to do what they had done. If they had come to him for money, he would gladly have given them thousands of Burīs. If they had come to him to beg for a piece of land, he would have heard their entreaty. If they had come to him to complain about their men spending money and time in bars, he would have given them sympathetic hearing and addressed the nation on the matter; but they had asked for no favors. He had not denied them anything. Why then their need to shame the nation?

Before the event, the Ruler would have sworn that he thoroughly understood women through and through. How many men, particularly his ministers, had he humiliated by ordering them to send him their wives, daughters, or girlfriends? At first he assumed that the women would offer at least some token of resistance to his advances, and he was always surprised by how quickly they yielded to his amorous gropings as an act of personal honor and recognition! Some would become indignant at having to make the bed of the Ruler, but as soon as their husbands turned their backs, they would be coquettish and genuinely flattered to be of service to power!

Why were these other women acting out of character? How could they be so oblivious to his might? Wasn't Rachael a shining example of what he could do to them?

Vengeance is mine, sayeth the Lord, and was he not the Lord of all Aburīrian women? Yet no matter how hard he considered the matter, he remained unsure as to what to do or where or with whom to start the vengeance like that which he had shown Rachael. Unable to act, his torturous thoughts always returned to the treacherous drama at Eldares in which the women shamed the nation before the eyes of foreign dignitaries and, worse still, in front of the Global Bank missionaries.

For days on end, after the drama at Eldares, the Ruler kept to himself, trapped in secrecy. Terrified by what his silence might mean for his future, every minister preoccupied himself with working out strategies for salvation. Some tried calling the State House under one pretext or another, but the Ruler refused to take their calls. Sikiokuu and Machokali were the most affected, and their troubled souls were reflected in Sikiokuu's drooping ears and in Machokali's lifeless eyes.

Machokali's woes worsened when one day the Global Bank mission announced that they would be returning to New York. Aware that his reputation had seriously suffered as a result of the recent drama at Eldares and that his hope for redemption lay in their continued presence, Machokali begged the missionaries not to go until they had taken formal leave of the Ruler. They agreed to postpone their departure for a few days, but still Machokali was unable to arrange a get-together at the State House and was too embarrassed to ask them for a further postponement. He blamed a general indisposition for the Ruler's unavailability. They understood the minister's predicament, and, to ease his mind, they said he should not worry, that if he or the Ruler ever happened to be in New York they were most welcome to drop by the Bank for further talks. As politic as they thought they were being, they were taken aback when Machokali begged them to put the invitation in writing, which they did, also confirming their flight to New York a few days later.

Machokali clung to the letter as if it were a talisman and looked forward to the day that he would present it to the Ruler. Unlike his archrival, at least he had something in hand, he consoled himself.

But he was mistaken about his archrival. In the wake of Kaniũrũ's good intelligence, Sikiokuu had started feeling confident that he could weather the storm. Nyawĩra might still be at large, but Sikiokuu was no longer completely in the dark about the Movement for the Voice of the People. His morale was high. Vinjinia was Tajirika's wife. Nyawĩra was Tajirika's employee. Tajirika got the powerful position of chairman of Marching to Heaven through Machokali. Vinjinia's guilt would connect Machokali to the Movement for the Voice of the People and probably to the women who had shamed the nation.

The Ruler's continued taciturnity worked in Sikiokuu's favor, for it gave him time to work out his next move in the game that he and Machokali had been playing to see which was stronger, the Ears or the Eyes of the State.

It is said that the Ruler stayed closeted in the State House for seven days, seven hours, seven minutes, and seven seconds before calling an emergency session of his cabinet. He had yet to come up with a satisfactory course of action in dealing with the women, whoever they were; meantime, he just wanted a chance to vent his anger at a less elusive target: his ministers.

# 9

The cabinet ministers jumped to attention like terrified cadets at the entrance of their commanding officer. The Ruler sat down and gestured for them to do the same. He then let his eyes wander from one side of the table to the other, resting briefly on each face before finally dwelling on Sikiokuu. The Ruler did not have to utter a word for Sikiokuu to know that he was being asked a question.

"Your Mightiness, you are father to us all, and I, as a dutiful son, know that you are asking me to say something about the whole women thing. In my humble opinion, the people who are best placed to explain the fiasco are those who persuaded us that the queues should be interpreted as a mania in support of Marching to Heaven. In light of what happened, they might want to enlighten us as to what they really intended."

The Ruler glanced at Machokali. Big Ben Mambo, Minister of Information, quickly followed suit. He was like that: always alert to see who, Machokali or Sikiokuu, would eventually come out on top in order to side with the victor. Machokali seized the challenge.

"Ruler who art our father here on earth, the English who gave us civilization, freedom, and parliamentary democracy taught us the doctrine that *cabinet decisions are collectively binding*. If a given minister does not agree with a collective decision, then he should resign his post. At our last cabinet meeting I did not hear Sikiokuu say that he was going to resign his post on account of his principled opposition to the mania of the queues. Instead he offered to dispatch motorcycle riders to the *north, south, east, west, and center* to advance the cause. They left weeks ago. By the way, where are their reports?"

Sikiokuu hardly wanted his five riders and their mission to be-

come the dominant subject of discussion, and he considered distracting attention from it by accusing Machokali of talking as if the British
still ruled Aburĩria but thought the better of it, recalling how the
Ruler had reacted when Sikiokuu said something similar in relations
to the Global Bank. He was confident about what he had up his
sleeve and was waiting for the right moment to pounce, so he just sat
quietly like a cat awaiting its prey, allowing Machokali to continue
without interruption.

"If truth be told, without adding or subtracting A or B," Machokali
pressed on, "we must admit that except for the one unfortunate
occurrence, Eldares has never had so well attended a gathering. All
Eldares was practically there."

Sikiokuu saw his opening:

"Yes, but what was the outcome? How do we know that the amassing of the crowd was not part of their plan? Who was the mastermind
of this woman thing?"

One of the consequences of the event was the effect of the words
*woman* and *women* on the Ruler; at their mention the Ruler's heart
beat faster; he became visibly agitated. Now everybody noticed the
look he gave Sikiokuu, as if demanding to know what pleasure the
speaker was getting out of constantly repeating the accursed word.

"He is evading responsibility for the five riders," Machokali complained. "As to who is behind the event, he should ask himself. Everyone knows that it is the so-called Movement for the Voice of the
People. Toy snakes were again scattered all over the field. What I
want to know is this: what has Sikiokuu done to ensure the arrest of
these criminals?"

With melodramatic slowness, Sikiokuu rose and intoned: "Your
Holy Fatherness, to eradicate an underground movement is not as
easy as some people might think. These renegades are cowards,
meeting under the cover of darkness. They dare not into the light
because they are not men at all. They are women, cowards. I am very
happy to report that we have identified someone high up in the movement. Her name is Nyawĩra."

"Is she in custody?" the Ruler blurted.

"No, not quite—she slipped through our fingers."

"Oooh," other cabinet ministers sighed, disappointed by the
anticlimax.

"But we know where she works," Sikiokuu hastened to add, firing their curiosity. "We are keeping round-the-clock surveillance of the premises to make sure that her employers are not hiding her."

"Why don't you arrest the whole lot? Employees, employers, whatever?" the Ruler asked.

"One is now in custody," Sikiokuu said, looking around triumphantly. "And this person is cooperating."

Wanting to share in the imminent triumph, some ministers started singing: Sikiokuu *singe* the enemy! Siki *singe* them all.

"And who might that be?" the Ruler inquired, waving the singing ministers to silence.

Sikiokuu cast a victorious glance at Machokali as if to say, You want a piece of this? I am not finished with you yet. Machokali tried his best not to panic, but his crestfallen look belied his attempts at indifference.

"It is with deep regret that I announce that the person in question is none other than Vinjinia, Tajirika's wife, Tajirika the chairman of Marching to Heaven, and as everyone knows a great pal of our friend here," he said, nodding toward Machokali, expressing more sorrow than anger at this treachery and ingratitude.

"The wife of the chairman of Marching to Heaven?" Big Ben Mambo, heretofore a staunch Machokali ally, asked, preparing to jump ship.

"Yes, one and the same," Sikiokuu said, and sat down, lowering his head in sorrow yet again, confirming the awful truth.

Silence filled the room; Machokali felt it creep under his skin. His first inclination was to fall to the ground and ask for mercy, but he knew that by doing so he would be stepping into the trap that Sikiokuu had laid for him. His second impulse was to jump up and be the first to denounce Tajirika: demand his immediate arrest and summary execution. He realized the problem with this. Machokali cursed himself for his own negligence. Tajirika had tried to reach him, had left countless messages at his office and with the chauffeur, but Machokali, busy as he was trying to delay the departure of the Global Bank missionaries, had put them off as social calls. Had he returned them, he would now have the facts of the situation instead of being at the mercy of his enemy.

He rose, not knowing what he was going to do or say. But when the Ruler icily told him that he need not bother to stand up, that he could say whatever he wanted to say seated, Machokali knew without a doubt that he was in big trouble. But he would at least go down defending himself, like a wounded animal.

"Our Holy Father, who art . . ."

"Skip the preliminaries and go to the point," the Ruler snapped.

"Any person who threatens the peace and stability of this nation should be done away with, even if that person is the wife of who is who in Aburĩria. I know for sure that Tajirika was at the big ceremony. I remember him telling me that he had left his wife at home. Answer me this: Was Vinjinia at the meeting or not? Has she admitted to being a member of the movement or not? Or is the issue that she and her husband employed the madwoman Nyawĩra? Anybody can inadvertently employ a thief or a murderer; criminals don't go about announcing their crimes. But even if it turns out that she was at the meeting or is a member of the movement, it does not follow that Tajirika has anything to do with this. A wife can well turn against her husband, for as the Waswahili say, there is no man who is a hero to his wife."

With his Swahili proverb and statement about the treachery of trusted wives, Machokali stumbled into scoring an important point with the Ruler, who was reminded of the recalcitrant Rachael.

"I don't understand why Machokali is defending his friends with such vigor," Sikiokuu said, sensing this shift and a little taken aback that his rival had put up such a gutsy defense of Tajirika and Vinjinia. "I have not claimed that Vinjinia is actually a member of the movement or that she was at the meeting. We arrested her because we believe that she has important information that will lead to the arrest of the criminals. Even she has not denied that in Tajirika's absence from the office she and Nyawĩra worked closely."

Machokali sensed that even the other ministers were becoming exasperated with Sikiokuu, and he smelled advantage.

"We have been told that Vinjinia is still helping in the investigation. But this is what I don't understand. How long has she been in custody?" he asked with mock interest.

"Oh, not long at all, about seven days," Sikiokuu answered quickly.

"And in those seven days, what has she coughed up that might lead to Nyawĩra's arrest?"

"This is not the proper forum to disclose that," Sikiokuu said, angry at being compelled to answer Machokali's questions. "I mentioned only a few details to show how much we who truly love Our Lord and Master have already done."

The Ruler cleared his throat and twice knocked the table with his club. Already he was feeling a little better, for there was nothing more likely to put him in a good mood than an acrimonious exchange between his ministers. He was able to compare what they said to what he had gleaned from his own sources. That he already knew about the arrest of Vinjinia was more than a distinct possibility.

"Have you questioned Tajirika?" he asked.

"No. Not yet."

"Does Tajirika know that his wife is in police custody?"

"I don't know, but I am sure we have not yet told him of her arrest."

"And why have *I myself* been kept in the dark about these developments? Or are you, Sikiokuu, the one governing Aburĩria today?"

"Oh, Jesus Christ no, no, my Holy Almighty. I tried to contact you but, I mean, I don't know why my calls were not being passed on to you. I wanted you to hear it from my own lips because of the delicate nature of the matter."

"Is there anybody else who has something to say?" asked the Ruler, addressing them all. "Or have you all decided to be keepers of secrets from me? Yes, for seven days, and then claim you could not reach me? It seems to me that you have all joined Sikiokuu in governing Aburĩria."

The pendulum of power was swinging unpredictably, and, sensing that his rival was in trouble, Machokali once again took advantage of the moment.

"Almighty Esteemed Father, it would have been much better if Sikiokuu had arrested Nyawĩra first and forced her to give up names. Then further arrests could have been made. But Sikiokuu, despite his big ears, seems deaf to the din of the obvious. He arrested the wife of the chairman of Marching to Heaven in the vain hope that she would reveal where Nyawĩra is hiding. I have only two more points to make. First I would like some guidance on what to do about Tajirika. Shall I dismiss him from the chairmanship of Marching to Heaven? And how would that be perceived by the Global Bank?"

There was nothing more likely to command the Ruler's attention than an obstruction to the flow of money for Marching to Heaven.

"Sikiokuu," the Ruler called out, "if you have ears, listen. Did it not cross your mind that the arrest of the wife of the chairman might make it appear as if the people around me are not to be trusted?"

"She hasn't really been arrested, just in custody," Sikiokuu back-tracked. "She is helping us out, that's all."

The Ruler ignored Sikiokuu's blabber and turned to Machokali.

"How is the Global Bank mission taking the whole matter?" he asked without rancor or sarcasm but with anxiety.

"Your Holiest and Mightiest Excellency, Beloved of the Whole World," Machokali quickly responded, his eyes a little brighter, "well, about the shameful acts in Eldares, I told them, just as you had then tried to explain, that what they *saw* was a sacred Aburĩrian dance per-formed only before most honored guests. They seemed quite satisfied and, to tell you the truth, the Bank is not particularly concerned with our traditional customs. Their main concern is only those forces, remnants of a bygone socialist age, that threaten stability and pose danger to the free flow of capital. If Nyawĩra herself had been arrested, it would have made them happy. And since Sikiokuu has gathered sufficient information to effect an arrest, it would be good for him to do so before the Bankers leave for New York."

"What, are they leaving?" asked the Ruler.

"Yes," Machokali said.

"When?"

"Tomorrow!"

"Without seeing me?"

"My Lord of Excellency, I tried everything possible to delay their departure so they could have the honor of being received by you. They did delay out of respect, but in the end said they simply had to return to New York."

"What of their report?"

"They are going to work on it in New York and come up with appropriate recommendations."

"How do things look?"

"Not bad. Not bad at all. In fact, they have invited you or me to visit New York should we need to bolster our case before they make a final decision. I told them to put it in writing, *in black and white,* as the English say."

Slowly he pulled out an envelope from his pocket and handed it to the Ruler, who, try as he did to restrain himself, could not contain his curiosity and ripped open the envelope immediately. He perused the letter and a smile lit up his face.

"The invitation is a bit general, though," remarked the Ruler. "It says if I happen to be in New York . . . what do they mean, Markus?"

With the Ruler's comment about the invitation being open and vague, Sikiokuu saw a chance to talk himself into favor and deflect the focus from the issue of Nyawīra and Vinjinia.

"Congratulations to you, Our Savior," he chimed in confidently. "The invitation is timely indeed; and the new American president might even be behind its issuance. The Global Bankers are cunning. They may have made the invitation open only to see if Aburīria is serious about securing the loan. To send one minister might make the bank think that the project is not very high on our list of priorities, but if Your Mighty Excellency went there in person, accompanied by some of us who know how to listen"—and here he touched his earlobes for emphasis—"it would make the directors know that we mean business and that we are all united behind Marching to Heaven."

"Yes," another minister commented. "Let's leave the messengers aside and go straight to the man at the top for a face-to-face."

"Time for a state visit," another minister offered.

"And it would be good for His Royal Excellency to appear on TV, especially on GNN's *Meet the Global Mighty,*" Big Ben Mambo suggested. "All the greats of the twentieth- and even twenty-first-century Western civilization have appeared on it."

The discussion had become a free-for-all.

"I have heard it said that there has not been a single leader from Africa on that program, is that true?" another one asked.

"Except Nelson Mandela," another one said.

"You see how these people discriminate against Africa?" another said with a touch of anger. "From the West they choose statesmen but from Africa, jailbirds. Unbridled racism."

"That means," observed yet another, "that if and when the Ruler agrees to appear on the program, he will be the first real leader from Africa to join the Global Mighty."

The chance to go to New York to be wined and dined while lobbying for support for Marching to Heaven was medicine to the Ruler's wounded soul.

"It is time for all of you to listen," he barked, instantly creating a hush. "It is said that there is no smoke without fire. Dark clouds precede a storm. I was not very happy to hear that Tajirika, my chairman for Marching to Heaven, employs people without first checking their background and history thoroughly. Do you hear me, Machokali? At the same time I was not pleased to hear of the arrest of his wife, what is her name, Vinjinia, and I don't want the story to spread beyond these walls to the press. I want Vinjinia released immediately. I don't want even a whisper of this botched affair to reach the Bank people. But I want Tajirika investigated, though subtly. Do you hear me, Sikiokuu?"

"Yes, sir. And will Tajirika continue as chairman of Marching to Heaven?" Sikiokuu asked, emboldened by the Ruler's judgment. "I suggest that he be relieved of his post immediately so that he cannot interfere with the investigation."

"Shut your mouth," the Ruler warned Sikiokuu, "or I will do so for you. We do not change horses in midstream. Tajirika remains in his post."

It was Machokali's turn to feel victorious; he even managed a smile that vanished as quickly as it had come.

"I will appoint a deputy chairman; I charge Minister Sikiokuu to give me recommendations. And Sikiokuu, I want you to set up a commission to investigate this matter of queues and the ensuing mania. The commission of inquiry must find out where, when, and how the queues began and how the enemy came to exploit it as cover for her shameful acts. While the other ministers are welcome to suggest members of the commission, I leave its composition, including the election of chairperson, to Sikiokuu."

Sikiokuu was elated by the developments. He had triumphed over his archrival, or so he thought. His euphoria was dashed when the Ruler announced: "I want full reports on my desk when I return from New York!

"And as for you, Machokali," the Ruler said, turning toward him. "Busy yourself with arranging my forthcoming trip to New York. Fit in as many state visits as you can. I don't want these Global Bank people to think that I am making the trip for the sole purpose of negotiating with them."

As disappointed as Sikiokuu was about not going to New York, Machokali on his part was displeased to leave his archenemy conducting a possibly damaging investigation. He tried to figure out ways to tie Sikiokuu's hands.

"What is to be done about Nyawīra?" he asked. "If the back of the Movement for the Voice of the People is not broken, the Global Bank might feel reluctant to release money to a country threatened by insurgency."

These words pierced the soothing dreams of state visits, reviving memories of the scandal of Eldares. The anger at the women and the lust for vengeance came back with a force that almost choked the Ruler. *Why did they do that to me in front of all the eyes of the world?*

# 10

How does one separate fact from fiction in telling the story of what the women did on that day? All who told it, and there were many versions, insisted they had witnessed it with their own eyes. Not in dispute was this: there had never been so large a public gathering than at the site of the dedication for Marching to Heaven.

What accounted for the crowd? Party stalwarts? The radio station that kept on urging people to go to the site? The answer may very well lie in the statement that Big Ben Mambo, in his capacity as the Minister of Information, disclosed that the Global Bank missionaries would be the major guests of honor. This revived and intensified the rumors that the delegates had come to dole money out to the people, a radical departure from their normal practice of giving it all to the State.

NGOs sprang up to advise the grass roots on how to use the money. Yet others on the rights of the grass roots vis-à-vis free gifts from banks. Some feminist groups, noting that the members of the Global Mission and the ministers who took them from queue to queue were all men, saw male intrigue and formed a Just for Women movement for a share of the Global Bank. Rival NGOs initiated their own queues with their own slogans.

When the day of promise came, all the queues that had mushroomed in Eldares for different needs now zigzagged their way to the park. People, some of whom came from far away, began camping out at the site days before the event.

# 11

"We, too, were there," Nyawīra told Kamītī. "Some of our people, mostly women, mixed with others at the site days earlier. In the glow of overwhelming attendance, we planned to champion democracy and denounce dictatorship in broad daylight, and the promised presence of the Global Bank made things easier for us. How ironic! Democratic space guaranteed by the bank we opposed!"

It was the morning after her night flight into the mountains. Nyawīra had not slept well in Kamītī's rudimentary shelter under a sycamore tree. Nightmares of impending captivity had recurred. The makeshift bed of dry fern and reeds she had slept on had not helped. She had woken several times and was glad when dawn came.

The terror of the night had subsided, although occasionally she would feel her heart race at the thought of how narrowly she had escaped being caught. The peace surrounding her and Kamītī was a far cry from the occurrences during the previous weeks when she and her companions had waged their struggle. Some of their planning sessions had lasted a whole night. Weekends, they held meetings in the queues, better to study what people were up to. As the day of dedication approached, they had made sure to the smallest details of the State's plans, intentions, and mood.

The Ruler and his advisers were elated, especially when they saw that people started arriving at the site a week early. Radio commentaries enthused about the pilgrimage to the site and the people's love and support for Marching to Heaven. Machokali was tireless in his praises of the wisdom and vision of the Ruler and as the queuing intensified he kept the Bank Mission appraised.

Naturally Sikiokuu was not happy about the whole thing, but he swallowed his hurt and envy, hoping that something would go wrong.

To bring this about, the minister was lax in demanding effective vigilance on the part of the M5.

Nyawīra and her companions had gone to the site on Thursday night to join the others in the movement; they wanted to use Friday to put the finishing touches on their own plans.

"I have never seen such a large gathering," Nyawīra told Kamītī. "The crowd at the unveiling of Marching to Heaven paled in comparison. Now the government provided free buses and lorries plastered with posters of the Ruler. People, some carrying green twigs, banged the sides of the vehicles, beating out the rhythm of their songs. Others on foot waved green branches as they sang. Each queue had its own song, and the songs reflected as many interests as there were queues. There was no unifying theme except a general feeling that the Global Bank was on a mission that had to do with money and jobs."

In the wake of the big turnout, the state functionaries concentrated on the important business at hand: the seating of the dignitaries, reflecting the order of importance of the guests, at least in the eyes of the State. To the right of the Ruler sat the Bank missionaries. Next to them were foreign ambassadors, with the American having pride of place. Religious leaders were in abundance—Catholic cardinals, Protestant bishops, Muslim sheikhs, rabbis, and priests of various Indian sects. The Ruler and his advisers were keen to refute rumors that the religious community had rejected him as an incarnation of the Prince of Darkness. To the Ruler's left were his ministers, members of Parliament, and leaders of the various branches of the armed forces. Directly behind the Ruler sat his official biographer, Luminous Karamu-Mbu, who as usual held a book and a pen so huge that both items could be seen from afar.

When the Ruler arrived surrounded by his guard, he shook hands with all the members of the Global Bank mission, all the ambassadors, and leaders of the various religious communities.

In his opening remarks, Machokali once again stressed the colossal magnitude of Marching to Heaven. He asked the people to imagine Mount Kilimanjaro multiplied by a thousand! Imagine, he went on, a shadow across Eldares, Aburīria, the African continent, extending to the other end of the Indian Ocean on the eastern side and to the other end of the Atlantic Ocean on the western side: even that could not begin to describe the shadow that, on completion, Marching to Heaven would cast across the globe.

"Aside from the Tower of Babel, it will be the only other human attempt to reach Heaven's gate," he continued, "and once completed it will be the *one and only superwonder of the world!* That is why we in Aburĩria are so happy and feel extremely honored that the Global Bank mission has joined this assembly of ordinary citizens. The mission, which also represents the Global Ministry of Finance, has not yet issued its report, but we are confident that when they do so they will not forget what they have seen with their eyes: this project enjoys massive grassroots support. The mission has seen for itself the queues cropping up all over the city. And what are the queues and this assembly telling the Global Bank and the world? It is all quite simple. The Aburĩrian masses are ready to forgo clothes, houses, education, medicine, and even food in order to meet any and every condition the Bank may impose on the funds it releases for Marching to Heaven. Upward Ever, Downward Never. That is our new slogan. We will not rest until we get to Heaven's gate. We swear by the children of the children of the children of the children of our children to the end of the world—yes, we swear even by the generations that may be born after the end of the world—that we shall pay back every cent of the principle along with interest on interests ad infinitum. The Ruler is not like some of those Third World leaders who are always whining about their commitments, going so far as to ask that their debt be forgiven."

Those who had thought that the Global Bank was on a mission of doling out dollars directly instead of to the State were a little disappointed; some even groaned in protest, but they assumed that Machokali was only dampening expectations, that the real thing would be announced by the Ruler or by the leader of the Global Mission.

Machokali, who did not want a repeat of the public display of interministerial tensions that had surfaced at the birthday ceremony, did not give any other minister an opportunity to speak. After his opening remarks he quickly announced that various performing troupes would now entertain the Ruler and his guests, preparing people for words of wisdom from the great leader himself.

First were schoolchildren from Eldares and its environs, singing mostly in praise of the leader's well-known trips abroad in search of food for the people, particularly in times of drought and famine. His cry on behalf of the people had reached even the ears of the Global Bank, who had now sent a mission to Aburĩria to give money for Marching to Heaven. They sang of their hope that the project would be completed as soon as possible. Then the Ruler would be at one with God.

Machokali was ecstatic: the songs had succinctly summarized the major themes of the project. He asked the crowd to give the children a round of applause. Didn't you hear what they said? he asked the crowd rhetorically. He who is close to God will always be the first to close in on His blessings.

Most of the other groups, including adults, ended their songs and dances with the same praise for the leader and his efforts on behalf of Aburĩria in the capitals of the Western world. Holding his customary club and fly whisk, the Ruler received these praises with a broad smile, leaning now toward his guests on the right or left to remark on the detail of the performance. At other times he would simply raise his fly whisk as if conferring a blessing.

And now the turn of the women. The expectation was that their songs and dances would climax in prolonged ululation, a prelude to the main item, the Ruler's speech. Women's performances, particularly by those advanced in years, always produced a stir in audiences, as if those present identified with the women's celebration of youth in age. A similar air of predictable anticipation was now pervasive.

Sikiokuu, who resented not sharing the limelight, now found, in the women, an opening to ingratiate himself. He walked up to the leader to tell him that at some appropriate moment it would be nice and an excellent photo opportunity for the Ruler to mingle with the dancing women and even attempt a step or two himself. He should then invite some of the diplomats to join him, for that way the whole world would see that the Ruler was truly a man of the people. Machokali could not oppose an idea that seemed to please the leader so enormously, but he modified it by proposing that it would be better for the Ruler to do so after his speech, during the grand finale with all the singers and dancers grouped together. The Ruler was pleased with the phrase *grand finale* and agreed.

And now, boomed the voice of Minister Machokali, here are the women.

The women, Nyawĩra now among them, walked in pairs into the

arena from every direction, dressed no different from the crowd. Nothing in fact stood out except their disciplined formations and dignified entrance. They were silent, somber, as if in a funeral procession. In response, the crowd, too, grew silent, watching the seemingly endless queues of women with awe. When those at the head of the separate formations reached the part of the arena nearest the platform, they crossed, turned around, and moved toward the seated crowd, where they sat seemingly only to rise and continue their procession. It was difficult, after a few seconds, to tell whether those who were now marching were the same as before. From the platform it appeared as if the formations had no beginning and no end, or rather it was one movement with the end and the beginning being the multitude. Their continuous movement remained extremely disciplined. The Ruler was touched by this display of support expressed with such solemnity; he raised his fly whisk and waved it as a sign of respect for and appreciation of their devotion to Marching to Heaven.

And then the fly whisk fell and his heart sunk; he became agitated, as did everybody else on the platform. The women had suddenly stopped moving. They stood absolutely still, facing the platform, their fingers pointing at the Ruler, and with one voice they shouted: Set Rachael free! Set Rachael free! Their chant was deafening, and those on the platform seemed dazed by their audacity.

"And then, just as planned," Nyawĩra told Kamĩtĩ, "all of us in the arena suddenly faced the people, our backs turned to the platform. All together we lifted our skirts and exposed our butts to those on the platform, and squatted as if about to shit en masse in the arena. Those of us in the crowd started swearing: MARCHING TO HEAVEN IS A PILE OF SHIT! MARCHING TO HEAVEN IS A MOUNTAIN OF SHIT! And the crowd took this up. There were two or three women who forgot that this was only a simulation of what our female ancestors used to do as a last resort when they had reached a point where they could no longer take shit from a despot; they urinated and farted loudly. Maybe need or fear overcame them, or both."

Some foreign diplomats laughed out loud, thinking that this was a humorous native dance, but when they saw that state officials and ministers were not laughing, they restrained themselves and assumed that, pornographic as the act might have seemed, it was actually a solemn native dance.

The Ruler was of course solemn because he did not know what to do: walk away or stay. The police raised their guns, waiting for the order to fire, but even they were not sure at whom or where they should start shooting.

Machokali felt like crying. Why oh why had he asked the women to perform? Why had he not stopped it at schoolchildren and official youth? He knew as well as anybody that no entertainment of state dignitaries such as these would be deemed authentic without a performance by women. Still, in hindsight, a sin of omission on his part would have been preferable to this heinous and disgusting scandal enacted under his very nose.

Although he was not so foolish as to openly show it, Sikiokuu was one of the very few on the State's side who felt genuine mirth. Anything that brought ruin to his rival's schemes was always a joy to him. The only thing that nagged him was his having suggested that the Ruler mingle with the women, but he quickly dismissed this concern because fortunately the Ruler had not acted on his initial recommendation, thanks to his rival's interference. Still, he hated to think of his fate had the women squatted to shit with the Ruler and foreign diplomats mingling among them.

The police chief ran to the Ruler to ask for permission to fire in the air. Bloody fool, the Ruler said, that will make this crowd riot, and what will you then do? Kill them before these cameras? The microphone was live and their remarks were heard, but people who did not know what was really happening assumed that they were talking about the twenty-one-gun salutes planned for guests from the Global Bank.

Soon the parading women had disappeared from the arena and were indistinguishable amid the seated multitude. For a few seconds those on the platform thought they had witnessed an elaborate conjuring trick.

# 12

Even the Ruler thought his own eyes had deceived him. Where had all the dancers of shame gone? He stood up to explain away the illusion and calm any nerves that may have been rattled by the women and the police chief. He tried to be glib, reminding people that they were after all in black Africa, and what they had seen and heard or thought they had seen and heard was *black humor* from an ancient Aburĩrian ritual. But before elaborating on the ritual and its significance, he glanced at his guests to see how they were taking his attempt at humor only to see them all staring at something. He was back in his seat through an involuntary act of sheer amazement. Would this nightmare never end?

The platform on which he and the guests sat had begun to sink slowly, as if a power from within the bowels of the earth were pulling it down. A liquid oozed from the platform, slowly forming a muddy pool. Had the platform been erected on a bog?

The foreign diplomats and Bankers were among the first to flee. The Ruler and his ministers stood up, trying to maintain dignity. Machokali, in response to a gesture from the Ruler, grabbed the microphone to announce that the ceremony was officially over. When Machokali next looked around the Ruler and the other ministers were nowhere to be seen. The muddy pool had grown bigger, and his shoes were now half sunk in the darkish mess. The smell was that of a mixture of urine and shit, but he could not tell for sure what the substance was. He ran toward his car, no longer caring what was happening around him, and he spotted the Ruler and other ministers beating a hasty retreat in their own cars.

Some tellers of the story claim that they did see the Ruler and the ministers sink in the bog and police officers pull them out to safety. Others dispute this, insisting that the platform sank after the dignitaries had fled. This they had seen with their own eyes, so they asserted. But all versions agreed that there was indeed a mysterious foul-smelling pool.

"I myself did not see the pool, but something must have happened to make His Mightiness run away like that," Nyawĩra told Kamĩtĩ. "I can only assume that the sewage system installed by the colonial administration and never since maintained or repaired had run amok.

"But at the moment of our triumph our thoughts were not on whether or not there had been a pool or even its implications; we simply basked in the afterglow of having made it clear that not every Aburĩrian was happy with incurring more debt to finance Marching to Heaven or being ruled by a heartless despot. You do not have to look too deeply into it to know that a man who could so imprison his own wife in her home is a beast in human form! Rachael's fate speaks volumes: if a woman who had been at the mountaintop of power and visibility could be made to disappear, be silenced forever while alive, what about the ordinary woman worker and peasant? The condition of women in a nation is the real measure of its progress. *You imprison a woman and you have imprisoned a nation,* we sang in a song of celebration.

"When I went home that night I felt as if I had sprouted wings. All the sleepless nights, all the days spent running here and there, had been worth it. Driven away by Women Power, we had said," Nyawīra told Kamĩtĩ, her eyes still flashing with pride at the memory of the women's courage and their well-earned victory. "And that night I kept on repeating the words. Women Power did it."

The Ruler shut himself inside the State House for seven days, seven hours, seven minutes, and seven seconds, completely inaccessible to all, before calling the cabinet meeting that decided that he would seek refuge in state visits to the West.

An immediate ban was imposed on queues involving more than five persons. No matter the time or place or business, it was illegal for more than five people to stand in line, whether entering a church or mosque or riding a bus or meeting in an office. If there were more than five people at a bus stop they could form several lines each of five people but not one continuous line. Queues were a Marxist invention, according to the Ruler, having nothing to do with African culture, which is characterized by the spirit of spontaneity. Mass disorganization—pushing and shoving—was to be the order of the day.

But the ban only served to fuel the many stories about the day already circulating in the country, and it created many jokes about the fiasco. The site had been dedicated and blessed with piss, some argued back. The regime was almost swallowed whole by a bog, others would add, laughing so hard their ribs hurt, noting that all subsequent attempts to fill it with sand and stones came to naught. They said that the liquid would rise and reform above the sand and the stones. The City Council went into damage control: they hired a company to plant flowers all around the pool and another to pour perfume into the pool, but no matter what the companies did, the flowers would not grow and the perfume could not drive the stench away, and the City Council was finally forced to hire the same two companies, owned by Soi, Runyenje, Moya, and Kucera, to plant and maintain plastic flowers and trees all around while also regularly pouring perfume into the pool.

*Who were these women?* was the question most frequent on people's lips. The question, whether asked by those who had been absent or by those who claimed to have been present, was only the rhetorical commencement to more storytelling. Those absent would recycle what they had heard from others. Those who were present talked with the authority of eyewitnesses. They said that as they themselves left the field they saw that among the litter, empty cans and bottles, were many plastic snakes, and by now everybody knew that those plastic reptiles were the signature of the Movement for the Voice of the People. You mean the women were part of the movement? some would ask. What do you think, the others would say, and continue to narrate how disciplined the women had seemed and how they had miraculously melted into the crowd after they had asked the Ruler to lick their shitholes. It was their day; it was their triumph. Women? They may be silent, but, like silent streams, you can never tell their depth.

"In the first two or three nights I could hardly sleep," Nyawĩra told Kamĩtĩ. "My mind was crowded with all that had happened. I was walking on clouds: what had been accomplished by the movement, against so many odds, excited me. Even when I was about to report for duty at the Eldares Modern Construction and Real Estate, I was still in bliss. But imagine my shock at finding A.G. and his group of M5, including Kaniũrũ, waiting for me at the gates!" Nyawĩra told Kamĩtĩ for a moment, reliving the terror she felt after Arigaigai Gathere stopped her in the streets and by chance dropped the news of the ambush. "Fortunately, or should I say through the magic of being mistaken for the Wizard of the Crow, my captors went home empty-handed."

Nyawĩra had not known then about the arrest of Vinjinia and, like many others not in the know, she learned about it only long after Vinjinia had been released in accordance with the decision of the Ruler at the same cabinet session that came up with the idea of a series of state visits to Europe and America.

# 13

Machokali left the cabinet session haunted by a desire to know what Sikiokuu's men had asked Vinjinia, and a get-together with his friend Tajirika was the best way to satisfy his curiosity without attracting much attention from his enemies. Unfortunately he and Tajirika were unable to meet when they were supposed to because Machokali soon became preoccupied with soliciting state visits. As the real purpose for such visits was a meeting with the directors of the Global Bank to finalize details for loans for Marching to Heaven, the USA visit was the most important, but additional visits to England, Germany, France, and Scandinavia would add glamour and dignity to the business at hand. But Machokali was having difficulty in securing invitations from those countries.

All the ambassadors had more or less the same response. A state visit had to be mutually acceptable; even then it would take time to work out all the details. Machokali knew that a successful state visit was not something to be conjured up out of thin air, but he had trouble convincing the Ruler, who kept reminding him that earlier state visits, despite the cold war, had taken no time to arrange—why not now when the war was over? Sikiokuu seized every opportunity to incite the leader in his presumptions.

There was for instance the time when Sikiokuu went to see the Ruler to give him a report on the status of the hunt for Nyawīra and what he had learned from Vinjinia and, because he did not have much to report, he adroitly drifted to the subject of state visits, intimating that if it had been he who was in charge he would long ago have secured the requisite invitations. Despite the Ruler's telling him to mind his own business and effect the arrest of enemies of the State like that Nyawīra woman, Sikiokuu was resolute and through persistence managed to persuade the Ruler to pounce on the Global Bank open invitation, or better still, make a private visit, and while in the country turn it into a state or an official visit.

When Machokali next conferred with the Ruler, he was startled to find himself confronted with this firmly held position. He knew its source and managed a concession of sorts: the Ruler would go to the USA as a tourist and while there his Minister for Foreign Affairs would try to convert his stay into a state or official visit, and if that failed to materialize Machokali would try to secure a meeting between the Ruler of Aburĩria and the American president to take place before the one with the chiefs of the Global Bank. Even an hour or two with the president of the United States would send a positive message to the Bank.

Machokali was, however, able to arrange from Aburĩria for the Ruler to address the United Nations General Assembly in Manhattan, New York; Machokali presented this as a big triumph of diplomacy. New York being also the headquarters of the Global Bank, the Ruler would kill two birds with one stone. He would have face-to-face talks with the directors of the Bank and then have a platform to tell the whole world about Marching to Heaven, the One and Only Superwonder in the Universe.

Still, the task of arranging the private visit fell on Machokali's shoulders, and it was only after he completed the necessary arrangements and set the date for the leader's departure that Machokali decided to go to Santamaria to meet with Tajirika to talk about Vinjinia. Machokali also had important information that he wanted to share with Tajirika in person before it came out in the press. Suspecting that Sikiokuu was spying on him, Machokali decided to forgo riding in his official Mercedes-Benz and hailed a taxi instead.

They met at the Mars Café for quieter privacy, the M5 having the run of five-star hotels. As it turned out, it was Tajirika who was most desperate to meet; no sooner had Machokali sat down than Tajirika began unburdening himself.

"My friend, I am glad you have come. I am sure that it is me they were after and not Vinjinia. What should I do? I did not know that Nyawĩra was a member of this movement. I took her for an ordinary girl in search of work and I hired her. What should I do now to prove that I am still loyal to the Ruler? Here, I brought along something for you to see and edit as necessary. It is a press statement to announce that I am divorcing Vinjinia for consorting with dissidents . . ."

"Ssshh! Not so fast," Machokali said, waving the statement away. "Tell me this: was Vinjinia at the ceremony or not?"

"How do I know? She might have been there in disguise."

"But at the meeting you told me that you spoke to her on the phone?"

"That is true."

"So how could she have been both at home and at the ceremony?"

"Markus, women are very complicated. Besides, these mobile phones are deceptive," he added conveniently, forgetting that Vinjinia had refused to own one despite her husband's entreaty to do so as a mark of being in tune with the times.

"Have you asked the workers or any of your children if she was at home?"

"Yes, and they all say that she was in all day. But how do I know if they are telling the truth? She may have bribed them to cover for her. *Never trust a woman! I trusted Nyawīra to my sorrow!*"

"As to Nyawīra, later. Does Vinjinia know where the police took her?"

"She says no. She says that after they arrested her they blind-folded her, and after driving her in circles put her in a dark cell with dim light, and it was in this dark chamber that she was interrogated by people she could not see."

"What did they ask her? I mean, what did they want to know?"

"They demanded that she tell them everything she knew about the Movement for the Voice of the People. There were questions about Nyawīra. How long had she known Nyawīra? How had they met? When did Nyawīra start working for Eldares Modern Construction and Real Estate? Who actually offered her the job? They also wanted to know if there was a personal relationship between either Nyawīra and me or Nyawīra and you. Had you and Nyawīra ever met in or out-side my office? Was she your girlfriend? Questions like that. Vinjinia says that she told them all she knew, which was very little, for she herself had not been a regular at the office, that she started working there only after I was stricken ill . . . You see now what I told you about women? Was it really necessary for her to bring up my illness?"

"Stop trembling and listen to me. *Hold yourself together like a man.* Everybody in the government knows that you were down with the flu. Everybody in Aburīria gets the flu. So that's nothing to worry about. As for employing Nyawīra, anybody can make a similar mis-take. A person may employ a thief, but it does not follow that he is himself a thief. Besides, a thief does not go about the streets shouting: I am a thief. The sins of the employed cannot be visited on the employer. Mark you, Nyawīra is an enemy of the State and if there is anything that you know that can lead to her arrest, tell me. Do you understand? To me first. When I am in the USA, I shall be calling you from time to time to find out what you have uncovered. But if I am nowhere to be found and you do have information on Nyawīra, then I suggest that you take it to the nearest police station, to that friend of yours—what was his name, Wonderful Tumbo? Yes, that would be wonderful. As for your wife, why do you want to divorce her when it appears she has done you no wrong?"

"*Oh, thank you.* So I am not *in danger?* You are not angry with me? The Ruler is not angry with me?"

"Why would the Ruler or I be angry with you?"

"*Thank you! Thank you, my Minister!*" Tajirika said as if the minister and the Ruler were now one and the same.

Machokali was about to tell him to shut up, that he was a minister of the Ruler only, but he held back. The more he talked with Tajirika, the more he felt depressed. He had never seen this side of him. No backbone, he thought, and wondered if it was worth telling him all he had wanted to tell him, like suggesting that Tajirika be his watchdog while he was away. He also considered withholding information about impending changes in the structure of the Marching to Heaven Building Committee. Then he thought that it was only fair that he should impart the news himself instead of Tajirika's reading about it in the papers.

"I want you to listen very carefully. Even among us state ministers there is a fierce struggle for power and influence. Not every other minister loves me. Our birthday cake did not please everybody, not because they hated the idea of Marching to Heaven but because it did not originate with them. Some, and I think you know whom I mean—I don't want to mention their names—resent the project so intensely that they would do anything to scuttle it. Failing that, they will do anything to put their stamp on the project. Now, I don't want to beat about the bush. I want to tell you straight out that at long last they have managed to do so. Of course they wanted to push out all my allies, like you, from the Building Committee, but fortunately the Ruler in his unfathomable wisdom refused their demands. Neverthe-

less, there will be a few changes that you should know about. For instance, you will now have a deputy."

"What? He will take over my job?" Tajirika asked, alarmed.

"No, no. You will remain the chairman of Marching to Heaven.
Your deputy will only assist you."

Tajirika looked relieved, as if he had expected news much worse.

"That is not a bad idea, you know," Tajirika said. "I hold the chair
and my deputy holds the pen. My clerk."

"It will not be exactly like that," Machokali, who had expected
Tajirika to grow furious, tried to explain with a touch of annoyance.
"Your deputy will not work for me but for my enemies. He will be the
eyes of my enemies in my camp. So I want you to be very careful in
what you do or say in his presence. I want you to note down what he
does or says and on my return from the USA you will brief me. Of
course just now the committee has very little work to do, and so in
practice having a deputy means very little. Work will begin only after
the Global Bank has released the funds. But if he tells you to do anything with him, or if he asks you to sign any document, don't do it
until I return from the USA, certainly not before you and I have at
least talked on the phone."

From the moment Tajirika realized that he was not on the Ruler's
hit list and that he still retained his position as the chairman of
Marching to Heaven, all his worries vanished. He wondered why
Machokali was getting all worked up about this matter of a deputy.
Isn't a deputy a kind of glorified clerk, doing whatever the chairman
wants him to do?

"It would have been better if I had been allowed to choose my
clerk, give him a proper job interview, but I suppose it does not matter. Who is my deputy, anyway?" Tajirika asked.

"His name will be announced sometime this week in the official
gazette, but I thought I should let you know so it does not come as a
surprise. His name is John Kaniūrū. Previously he was a senior
youthwinger."

"What, a youthwinger as my deputy?" Tajirika asked, now insulted. "What do these youthwingers know except . . . except . . . I
don't even know what they do. But on second thought, even this is
okay. He will be my boy, running errands for me . . ."

"That is not all," Machokali added, somewhat embarrassed by

how naive his ally was proving to be. "There will also be a Commission of Inquiry into the Queuing Mania. The commission will try to find out who started it and where, and how it came to be used against the State."

"That's easy—they don't need a whole commission for that," Tajirika said, standing up and pointing toward his office. "It all started over there, outside my building. Unfortunately," he said, sitting down again, "it was when I was ill. But my secretary can tell them everything, for she was there the whole time." Then he remembered who his secretary was and quickly sidestepped the issue.

"My wife, Vinjinia, was also there, and she can truly testify that the queuing started outside my offices. Why? Are people trying to claim credit?"

"It is not that," Machokali tried to explain, and then suddenly he felt overwhelmed by the futility of his attempts to convey the gravity of the situation to Tajirika. How did I become involved with a fellow so thick that he has not the slightest sense of the traps in the way? "There is nothing to fear about this Commission of Inquiry. The most important thing is that you speak the truth as you know it. If you just speak the truth, all will end well."

Tajirika agreed, but in his heart he knew that no commission on earth would make him talk about the money that came his way from those seeking lucrative contracts in the future. Even if it turned out that Vinjinia had spilled the beans, he would strenuously deny it, no matter the consequences.

"And who is the chairman of this Commission of Inquiry?"

"John Kaniũrũ."

"The youthwinger?"

"Yes."

Again, instead of being alarmed by this development, Tajirika quickly lost interest in the commission, his mind racing to the impending visit to the USA. An idea had just struck him. If he, Tajirika, were to join the delegation bound for the USA, he surely would have time and opportunity to talk directly with the Ruler. At the very least, he would be nearer to the source of power instead of wasting his time here with useless commissions and deputies, without work to do. He cleared his throat.

"Let me ask you, Mr. Minister, as the chairman of Marching to

Heaven, should I not be part of this delegation to the USA? And now that I have a deputy, it is not as if the chair will be left empty or become cold. My deputy Kaniūrū will keep it warm till we come back from America."

"Oh, no! I want you to stay behind as my eyes and my ears." Machokali said quickly and emphatically what he had been trying to hint at all along, but he did not want to dwell on it because doubts had crept in about the character of his friend. "I have to go back to my office. The Ruler might call at any time, and I do not want to see any newspaper headlines reporting that the Minister for Foreign Affairs is missing," he said, trying to end their conversation on a light note.

Months later, in a torture chamber, swearing his innocence in the name of his ancestors, his children, God, anything that might give him temporary respite from needles in his fingers and cigarette burns on his body, Tajirika kept telling the police interrogators the same thing over and over again: "That was my last conversation with Machokali. I swear to God."

Tajirika would break into tears and plead with his torturers: "I beg you to leave me alone. We said farewell to each other at the Mars Café, and I never saw him or talked to him again on the phone before they left for the USA. To speak the truth, I resented the fact that I was not included in the delegation and so I did not even bother to know the day and the hour they were going to leave."

# 14

It is said that time heals, but for the Ruler time seemed to deepen the pain. Even with his imminent departure for the USA, he still squirmed with horror at the thought of what the women had done to him. He could not understand why they had taken up Rachael's cause and, although he would never whisper it to anybody, that was what really hurt. They had intruded in his private business, something that no one had ever done before. Male authority at home was absolute, and this was the one belief shared by despots and democrats alike, colonialists and anticolonialists, men and women and leaders of all established faiths. How dare these women question that which was so clearly ordained in Heaven and on Earth? The most miserable beggar in Aburĩria was now more secure as the king of his home than he as the husband of his home and country. How and when did they get to Rachael? he would ask himself time and again. His nerves tingled at a suspicion that kept on haunting him: had one of his beloved sons acted as the go-between for Rachael and the women? But which of the four sons would dare so heinous an act of filial disobedience and male betrayal? He recalled their faces and contemplated each in turn: now that of Rueben Kucera, now that of Samwel Moya, now that of Dickens Soi, now that of Richard Runyenje. But these faces only teased him into greater doubt.

His suspicion became so intolerable that he sought to still it by summoning his sons under the pretext that he wanted to see them before leaving for America. He opened the family council by telling them that in his absence they must keep their ears open for any intrigues among the armed forces. They should also keep an eye on the ministers who would be left behind, particularly Sikiokuu. He cautioned them against too much drinking, and, as a warning, he disclosed the reports that had reached him that one of them, the two-star general, once left part of his army uniform in a bar while pursuing a whore. The son so accused jumped to his feet in his own defense and told his father that those were tales of envy and malice from some sections of the M5. The Ruler seized on that denial to steer the conversation to the subject of Rachael, their protected mother. He asked them about their last visit to her; what subjects they and she had touched on; whether she had ever asked them to bear greetings to any of her friends and relatives. And had anybody ever approached them with messages, innocent greetings, even, for their mother? They seemed completely at a loss as to what he was talking about, since as it turned out none of them had recently talked to her in person or on the phone. Looking at their puzzled faces, noting the confusion in their voices, and comparing their reactions to what he had gleaned about his sons from M5 reports, the Ruler could tell that none of them would have done anything to jeopardize the privileges they now enjoyed. To prove that he was not singling out their mother for his fatherly concerns, he asked them about their wives and urged those not yet married to get on with the job of starting a family, while advising them to be careful with women because all women, be they mothers, wives, sisters, or daughters, were an enigma and not to be trusted. Never trust a woman, he told them bluntly, for woman is the source of all evil.

He was deep in his lecture when he was struck by an idea: how to strike back at Rachael and the women. For the first time since the day of shame, he felt jubilant—such is sweet vengeance. He told his sons about it immediately so that they would not inadvertently undermine his plan while he was away in America. For security reasons, he said, he would order that the electricity in Rachael's home be disconnected in his absence. He warned them against visiting the area while he was away, that were they to do so and disaster befell them they would have nobody but themselves to blame. What he did not of course tell them was that he intended for Rachael to rely on wood and dry leaves for energy. The deprivation would teach her a lesson and force her to cut off all ties to the evil and shameless women. And even if no communication had yet taken place between Rachael and them, the Ruler wanted to make that impossible during his absence from the land.

Following the family conference, electricity to her farm prison was disconnected. Tongues started wagging. People who lived on hills adjoining Rachael's prison farm and who had always been able to catch glimpses of the house at night despite the high walls started seeing a light moving about in absolute darkness, sometimes outside Rachael's mansion, at other times inside, and because they could not see who carried it, they concluded that it was really Rachael's ghost prowling, uttering curses, and the only reason they could not hear the exact words was because of the never-ending song amplified by loudspeakers at the four corners of the woman's farm for all the world to hear.

> *I will become more diligent*
> *In removing all evil from my heart*
> *I will repent all my sins*
> *Before my Lord comes back*

The light that walked at night and the relentless song made them conclude that Rachael had long been dead and, as revenge, her ghost walked the night, cursing the Ruler and his plans for America . . .

# 15

"What will you do?" Kamĩtĩ asked Nyawĩra after she had finished talking about the drama at Eldares.

"I want to live in the bush with you, at least for a few days."

"But what if they should follow you here?"

"I fled in the dark. Nobody saw me slip out of Eldares. They don't even know what I look like."

"Kaniũrũ does. You and Kaniũrũ used to share the same bed, and you might have talked about the hills and forests as political hideouts."

"When he and I were students at the University of Eldares," Nyawĩra explained, "my friends and I played guitar and talked a lot about neocolonialist politics in Aburĩria and Africa. How many times did we go without sleep, analyzing the class structure of our society and the politics and history of Aburĩria? Those were the days when the exploits of Yunity Mgeuzi-Bila-Shaka and Luminous Pen-Scream-Revolution, as we sometimes called his name in English, were the topics of the day among us students and youth. Although we did not know them personally, for they were then in exile, we read and talked about whatever they had said or written on revolution. Even the books they said they read, like Gorky's *Mother,* became our reading list. Kaniũrũ was not outspoken on these matters, but he was always around and now and then he would put in a few dissenting words. When he failed in his arguments he would dub us *starry-eyed idealists.* More often than not he was simply there, a silent listener, a man without opinions. But I don't remember us talking about forests and mountains and hideouts."

"A person does not recall everything he or she talked about with a lover or spouse when their hearts were in sync, their eyes set on a shared future. Kaniūrū might not even have known that you are a member of the movement, but adding two and two he stumbles on the truth and even if he does not get all the details right he comes close enough to do effective damage."

"What do *you* think I should do?"

"Go back to Eldares," Kamītī said without hesitation.

"What?" Nyawīra asked, a little surprised.

"Yes. Back to Eldares."

"You don't want me to be here? Not even for a few days?" Nyawīra asked, suspicious of his words and motives.

"It is not a matter of what I want or don't want. I have a hunch that if they fail to find you in the towns, they will try to search for you in these hills, even if only as a deterrent to others who might think of fleeing to the mountains."

"Why can't you just say that you don't want them to interfere with you?"

He winced at her tone, hurt by the accusation.

"It is not like that," he said. "I care about your safety."

"So what do you want me to do? Go and parade myself in the streets of Eldares?"

"The best hiding place is under the nose of the enemy," Kamītī said.

"Are you saying that I go and hide in a police post? *No way!*"

"I am not suggesting that we surrender. I am saying that we hide under their very noses."

Had she heard him say "we," or were her ears deceiving her?

" 'We'? Are you coming, too?"

"Yes, Nyawīra, this time you will not leave me behind. I will be at your side wherever you decide to go."

"I am sorry for my tone and suspicions," Nyawīra said, "and I am truly moved by what you have just said. But you also know that I would not want you to do something in which you do not believe for my sake."

"There is nothing for you to be sorry about," Kamītī said. "Since we parted I have been turning over what you and I talked about. You were right. There is a foulness inundating our society, and if we do not do something about it we shall all drown in it. I confess that I may not be able to deal with the demands and the discipline of your movement. I am not even sure whether I want to become a member. But a fellow traveler in the journey against the evil you are fighting? Yes. I am a seer of the spirit only. I am concerned about the welfare of the heart. But I also know what the scriptures say: The body is the temple of the spirit, or something like that. A healthy spirit needs a healthy body. Many hands, it is said, make heavy work feel light. You and I can work together, you with matters of the body and I with those of the spirit. You women of Eldares have shown the way."

"What are you talking about?" Nyawĩra asked, now laughing. "Which way?"

Kamĩtĩ was silent for a while as if pondering the question. Then he responded with something that sounded like lines from a poem:

> The way that can be told of is not the eternal way
> The name that can be named is not the eternal name
> The nameless is the origin of Heaven and Earth

"Excuse me, what's that?" Nyawĩra asked.

"The lines are taken from *The Lao-Tzu or Tao-te Chung*, a small book written by a Chinese seer more than five hundred years before Christ was born. Tao. The Way. May you walk in the middle of the way—don't we have a saying like that?"

"Okay, show me the way to go home. When do we set out? Now? Today? Tomorrow or the day after?" Nyawĩra said quickly, still attempting to be lighthearted as she exorcised the remnants of the heaviness in her heart.

"Not today. Not tomorrow. Not the day after. We must prepare ourselves."

"We must do what?"

"*Tulia! Tulia kidogo mama!* What did you tell me when we last talked in this very place? That I should become a people's seer. I will start with you, and I want you to trust yourself in my hands. Before I disclose what I think we should do and where we shall hide, I want you to learn what nature and solitude can teach us. Simplicity and balance, the Way. Call it the Forest School of Medicine and Herbology. I shall offer you such medicine that will make your eyes see what I see. Only then will you be able to say, I used to see as in a mirror darkly but now I see clearly."

"Did you learn all this in India?" Nyawīra asked a couple of days later, after realizing how much medicine even a tiny bush contained, what he described as nature's pharmacy.

"Nature is the source of all cures. But we have to be humble and willing to learn from it. I supplemented what I already knew with what I gleaned from my contact with Indian healers of the Western Ghat hills, places like Kottakkal, Ernakulam—siddhar healers especially. A siddhar is a poet, a seer, a soother of souls, and an expert in herbs. It is said that he has the power to come out of his body and enter those of other beings, even animals, and stay there for some time before returning to his own."

"Imagine what I could do with such power," Nyawīra said with a laugh. "Just when the agents of the State are about to pounce on me, I just change into a cat with all its nine lives, or a bird, and just float away."

"This is not a laughing matter," Kamītī said in a solemn tone, which made her look at him, puzzled.

One night, after making love, they lay on their backs in the yard and communed in silence. Kamītī thought of telling her how when alone he sometimes went out of his body and floated in the sky above but stopped when he recalled her tone of voice when they had talked about the power of siddhar healers.

"The skyscape is another field of knowledge," Kamītī said. "The stars guided shepherds across deserts and prairies."

"Not just the shepherds," Nyawīra said. "The same stars led me across the prairie."

"Did you know that our people believed that the sun is God?" Kamītī said, still gazing at the stars.

"Deities are never far from your thoughts," Nyawīra commented.

"Shall I show you something?" Kamītī suddenly said. "You promise not to make fun of me?"

"Why should I make fun of you for showing me one more herb?" Nyawīra said, curious about the excitement in Kamītī's voice.

Holding her hand, he took her to a cluster of sycamore trees and stopped in front of one with branches so low that they were indistinguishable from the thicket around it.

Kamītī let go of her hand, bent down, picked something up, and handed it to her. It was a wooden figure, but one with such an intense expression on the face that for a moment Nyawīra thought it alive. Then she saw that there were more, half covered by the bush.

"So you are also an artist and you never once mentioned this side of you to me?" Nyawīra asked. Did I escape from the arms of one artist only to fall into those of another? she wondered as she now picked up one sculpted figure after another.

"I started here," Kamītī said. "When one is alone in the forest, one is forced to contemplate the universe and creation. My thoughts were mostly on African deities. I caught myself thinking: Why don't I carve a Pan-African pantheon of the sacred? They will keep me company. My heart and body trembled, and when I set out to work it was as if an invisible hand were guiding my hands."

"They are all truly powerful and beautiful, and they feel very much alive," Nyawīra said. "You should be renamed Wangai. But what we now need is a little applied art. It is time I returned to confront the real and the concrete in the struggles against the dictatorship."

"Okay, tomorrow we apply applied art to you," he said.

They stretched dried animal skins and softened them for wear, and made necklaces of sharpened wood, animal teeth, and dried berries. They made a leather skirt and matching top for Nyawīra, and really it became her so well that Kamītī himself swore he would never have recognized her in it.

"With this," Kamītī pronounced, "Mr. and Ms. Wizard of the Crow are ready to open a business in witchcraft in Eldares."

# 16

The name Wizard of the Crow kept cropping up during Tajirika's ordeal in captivity: his torturers kept on asking the same question over and over again, which irritated Tajirika so much that once, despite the pain and the fear of more lashes, he shouted back at his then nameless and invisible torturers.

"What more do you want to know about the Wizard of the Crow that I have not already told you? Should I tell you that he is maker of Heaven and Earth?"

"Just tell us everything. When, where, and how you first met; what he wore that day; the exact words he uttered on the day you met, and most important, whether you ever met with him again . . ."

"Who? Machokali or the Wizard of the Crow?" Tajirika asked, now confused, for he had met the Wizard of the Crow only once.

Their interrogation regarding the Wizard of the Crow and even Machokali was just pretext. The torturers were after bigger fish: they wanted a word, a gesture, that would lead them to Nyawĩra, the woman who had awakened women's daemons, which in turn had awakened Rachael's daemon, now prowling her prison plantation at night, an illumination for all who lived around to see.

Nyawĩra, a woman who could raise female and male daemons at once, was dangerous, a menace to Aburĩria. It was necessary to hunt her down by any means so as to comply with orders repeated by the Ruler with ever-increasing urgency and desperation and last uttered just a few minutes before he boarded the plane for the USA, a large entourage, including his official biographer with his giant pen and book, and his security team, now including Arigaigai Gathere, accompanying him: Give me Nyawĩra; look for her here on earth or in the land of the spirits.

"True! *Haki ya Mungu!*" A.G. would pause in his narrative to swear. "I was one of the security specially chosen to accompany the Ruler to America, and I was standing close by, at the airport, and I heard him tell Sikiokuu: By the time I come back from America, I want that woman, Nyawĩra, in my arms . . ."

# BOOK THREE

# Female Daemons

# SECTION I

# 1

Come, all you who were there, and help us tell the story of what followed the Ruler's visit to the USA. This tale needs many tongues to
lighten the sense, for none of us was at once in Aburīria and America.

As to what happened in America, there are many sources from
which to weave a narrative. There is, for instance, a paper written by
Professor Furyk of Harvard about the Ruler's strange illness. The
paper is rich with information, but even richer is the diary the professor kept about his struggles to find a cure for the malady. Bits of truth
may also be gleaned from the archives of responsible newspapers and
even the fanciful tabloids. Libraries the world over, including the
Library of Congress in Washington, may also prove useful for documentation. Alternatively or in addition, we may turn to the invisible
global community of Internet users for postings from their local
media.

Our own media, needless to say, was very thrilled with the American angle, though they may have gone overboard in describing how
well the visit was going and how Americans, dying to hear about
Marching to Heaven, mobbed the Ruler and his entourage. Even the
delegates to the UN were quoted as eagerly awaiting the Ruler's
promised address. AMERICA IS A SUPERPOWER, BUT ABURĪRIA HAS THE
SUPERWONDER, declared the headlines of some of the Aburīrian
newspapers. TV and radio followed suit. The Aburīrian media, however, was hesitant in predicting the outcome of the journey because
the Global Bank, like fate, would have the last word, which the Ruler
was waiting to hear.

So it is only events within Aburīria where we may find it difficult to get a full picture, and for that part of the story we must rely on countless rumormongers, who at the time were abuzz with the return of the Wizard of the Crow to Santalucia and his wondrous powers of healing and divination.

# 2

There was not a single bodily ill he could not heal. Some, swearing by whatever was most sacred to them that they had witnessed with their own eyes the drama, claimed that the Wizard of the Crow could ferret any disease out no matter where it hid, all the while murmuring mockingly, "So you thought you were more cunning than the Wizard of the Crow!" The illness, sensing ignominious defeat, would flee the body of the victim, it was said. He knew so much about the healing properties of herbs, the tellers claimed, because he could turn himself into a plant and would return to human form armed with the secrets of plant life.

Kamĩtĩ may have sparked the rumors with his advice to his clients: All life is one and it flows like a river or the waters of the sea. Plants, humans, animals down to the creatures that crawl, all draw their share from the one indivisible river of life, just as they all draw breath from the air.

They had started at Nyawĩra's place, but because of the influx of so many new clients they built a much bigger shrine in the prairie a short distance from the outskirts of Santalucia. The House of Modern Witchcraft and Sorcery: this was the name they gave it. Divination was at the center of all activities at the House. Most clients believed that all diseases were rooted in sorcery and could not imagine a proper diagnosis or relief not requiring some kind of divination ritual. They wanted the magic of pure performance. Kamĩtĩ and Nyawĩra adjusted their role as Wizard of the Crow to the imperatives of the occasion. Their fee was the same for the rich and the poor, set according to what Kamĩtĩ and Nyawĩra thought an average working person could afford. But they were mindful never to turn people with no money away. These invariably would promise to pay when they could and always kept their word. Nyawīra never knew whether they did so out of honesty, gratitude, or simply fear of the wizard and his sorcery.

Though they performed divination, Kamītī and Nyawīra based their practice on the philosophy that illnesses of the mind, soul, and body were bred by social life. They even wrote down seven suggestions of healthy living:

> *Take care of the body, for it is the temple of the soul*
> *Watch ye what you eat and drink all the time*
> *Greed makes death greedy for life*
> *Cigarettes arrest life; alcohol holds the mind prisoner*
> *Life is a common stream from which plant, animal, and*
> *humans draw*
> *The good comes from balance*
> *Don't abandon yours for a mirage*

"Let's give them a fitting name," Kamītī suggested excitedly when Nyawīra first came up with the idea during an evening meal at Chou Chinese Gourmet.

"What shall we call them?" Nyawīra asked. "Seven Commandments of Healthy Living?"

"Or Seven Principles of Grace," Kamītī suggested. "You used to say grace at Brilliant Girls High School, remember? These commandments will grace life. We give them your names of Grace and Mūgwanja because you came up with the idea."

"You know I no longer use the name Grace?"

"That is why we should use it. That means that only you and I shall know its origins."

"Okay, then let's call them the Seven Herbs of Grace. But only on the condition that you and I pledge to be bound by the same commandments. We don't want to be those who preach: Do as I say, not as I do."

"Accepted," Kamītī said. "I swear never to abandon these rules!"

They gave their patients copies of the Seven Herbs of Grace. They even identified a holy day when people were to think of the mind and body as a wholeness that made up a person. To the destitute, they offered a bowl of soup, beans, and rice or *ugali*. And to all who came there for the holy day, they talked about healthy living, elaborating on the Seven Herbs of Grace. They baptized the occasion the Day of the Way.

This rite only strengthened the people's claim that there was no disease that could defeat the Wizard of the Crow, because even if it ran he would outrun it, and no matter where it went, even in the soul, it would find him waiting for it with potent potions.

The needy and the curious were drawn to the shrine.

# 3

Nobody knows for sure who first told Maritha and Mariko about the Wizard of the Crow, for in their Sunday confessions they never once mentioned the shrine, though a few times they were heard to say that God works in mysterious ways, His wonders to perform on Earth and in Heaven.

Despite their silence on the matter, rumors say that Maritha and Mariko originally went to the shrine as part of their campaign against Satan. They wanted to convert the Wizard of the Crow from belief in satanic rites to Christian faith. Some rumormongers even claimed to have seen the two near the shrine, carrying a big Bible and a big cross, and that as the couple approached the shrine the gate opened to admit them and closed by itself. Inside the compound, Maritha and Mariko were puzzled that their Bible and the cross did not take on a life of their own as they had when the Ruler had visited the All Saints, riding a donkey, or when the drama of Eldares had unfolded!

An assistant, or the person they took to be the assistant, received them politely and even offered them a cup of tea, which they quickly declined, saying that they just wanted to see the Wizard of the Crow himself. The assistant showed them where to sit and wait. In the middle of the wall facing them was a small latticed window, a one-way mirror through which Kamĩtĩ could scrutinize the clients without their knowing. This helped him not only to study their faces for purposes of divination but also to spot possible trouble, hostile elements hunting Nyawĩra.

Now the Wizard of the Crow took time to read the faces of his elderly visitors, slightly amused by the way they sat and looked about them, constantly clutching the cross and the Bible, their only veritable shields against evil.

"What brings you to my door? What troubles you?" the Wizard of the Crow said after opening the mirrored window.

Maritha and Mariko were startled because the voice they now heard did not sound satanic and it did not correspond to the one they argued with in their dreams and nightmares. Nevertheless, they decided to take the offensive to make clear that they were Christian witnesses and were not about to surrender to the great tempter of souls.

"First, we want you to know that we do not believe in magic and divination," Mariko said bluntly.

"What do you want from me?" the Wizard of the Crow asked, puzzled, though he took pains not to show it.

"To send you back to Satan," Maritha said.

"Satan?" the Wizard of the Crow asked. "Even if I knew how or where to find him, what would I tell him?"

"That we do not believe in adultery," Maritha added.

"That though he makes our bodies yearn for others . . ." Mariko said.

"And we are now advanced in age . . ." chimed in Maritha.

"And we have given birth to our last . . ." Mariko added.

"We shall never give in to temptation," they said in unison.

"What does the body, a progeny of Adam and Eve, really want?" Mariko said, almost as if he were now posing the questions to himself. "Is this not the work of the Devil, now, today, as it was in the beginning? When we look at other people our bodies are on fire with desire, but when we return home our bodies become as cold as ashes. It appears that the children were singing about us . . ."—and here, Maritha joined in the children's rhyme:

> *What belongs to another*
> *Whets your tongue*
> *What belongs to you*
> *Dries up your tongue*

For a few seconds they acted as if they were in a childhood world of their own, singing to each other; the Wizard of the Crow had to cough a little to remind them that he was still there, behind the lattice.

Maritha and Mariko were taken aback to find that they had been singing and actually enjoying songs they last sang when they were children, and they now looked at the face of the Wizard of the Crow, a little embarrassed that he had caught them in a foolish act. To cover their embarrassment they listened to him intently, and it took them time to realize that instead of doing the questioning they were now answering without defiance.

"Do you sleep in the same bed?"

"Oh, yes, we are not so rich as to afford the luxury of sleeping in two different beds," Maritha said.

"But we are not complaining," Mariko hastened to say.

"We sing to our Lord and Master in gratitude for being alive," Maritha said, and once again they both began to sing:

> Count your blessings one by one
> See what the Lord has done for you

The Wizard of the Crow made them stop with his second question.

"What is the last thing you do before you fall asleep?"

"We thank the Lord for looking after us and our children the whole day without harm coming our way. Is that not reason enough to make us say thank you to our maker?" Mariko said.

"And especially these days, when there are so many killings in the country," Maritha added.

"Nobody is safe, even inside their own houses," Mariko said.

"That's why our very last words are to ask the Lord to look after us in our sleep," Maritha said.

"And to protect us from the wiles of Satan!" they both said.

"So what do you want?" the Wizard of the Crow asked softly, out of curiosity as to what more they could possibly want out of life.

"We want that which heals the body," Mariko said.

"What heals the heart we leave to God," Maritha said.

The Wizard of the Crow looked at their faces and instead of feeling pity for the couple he felt something like envy. These two were so deeply in love that even their thoughts came out clothed in identical words and phrases. He felt like calling out to Nyawĩra to come and see this image of mature love, a model for them in the future. But quickly he dismissed the temptation and forced himself to resume the task at hand.

"Since you do not believe in magic and divination, old or modern, I don't really know how I can help you," the Wizard of the Crow said. "A person cannot get cured by word or deed unless he or she believes in the power of that word and deed. Now, our people say that good advice springs from frank words, and when it comes to curing an illness, taboos should not be in the way. So I am going to ask you one more question. When you go to bed, who unclothes the other?"

They became shy with each other, a little embarrassed by the question and thoughts of being naked in each other's presence.

"Doctor, can't you see that we are too old for that kind of foolishness?" they said in unison, not realizing that they had thought of him as a doctor rather than a sorcerer.

"So you have never carefully examined each other's bodies to see if there is any blemish, scar, growth, or anything?"

"No!" they said frankly, wondering why they had not done so, the better to account for the hot and cold behavior of their bodies.

"Now, I have no magic potions to give you," the Wizard of the Crow told them, unmistakably frank. "I have no magic incantations; just continue in the path you have been walking. But look to how you walk. Have you ever danced, because those who . . ."

"Oh, we used to dance all right when we were young," they both protested, as if the Wizard of the Crow had slighted them.

"We would swing each other around till all the others stopped to stare at us," said Mariko.

"So it is your generation who sang, 'Dancing is a matter of *two steps and a turn*'?" the Wizard of the Crow asked.

"Yes, but these days we dance only the dance of Christ, our Savior," Maritha said.

"Two steps and a turn to Jesus," added Mariko.

"Keep dancing to your faith," said the Wizard of the Crow, in his divination mode, "and if your faith allows you, you may want to try this. When you get back home, see if there is any oil in the house. Castor oil is the best. But first, tell me, in your home, who cooks?" he asked suddenly, as if the thought had just occurred to him.

"Are you truly a black man, doctor?" asked Mariko quickly, as if insulted by the question. "When we become Christian we don't give up each and every one of our traditions. Cooking has always been a woman's job," he said, but this time Maritha did not add a yes or a no to Mariko's words.

"Is there anything in the Bible that says a man must not cook?" the Wizard of the Crow asked.

"No, no," Maritha said.

"It is just a custom," Mariko explained.

"Then that is one custom that you may want to change, as it does not offend your faith." The Wizard of the Crow addressed Mariko. "One of these days, you should make her a delicious dish so that she may know how your cooking tastes. A little surprise. Then get a candle, light it, put it on the dining table, and dim all the other lights or even switch them off. Talk, tell stories, or eat in silence. The important thing is for you to eat together in soft light. Then warm some water. Undress each other. Wash each other. Then take turns rubbing oil onto each other; no spot, no scar, should be left untouched. Is it not you, Christians, who say that the body is the temple of the Lord? Take your time. The night will be yours. If you find blemishes on your bodies, go see a doctor or come back to the shrine for the right herbs."

They left clutching their Bible and cross, happy and relieved that the Wizard of the Crow had not engaged them in any magical rites involving dry bones, beads, and cowry shells, as they had heard that sorcerers and witch doctors were given to do. Perhaps their Bible and cross had warded off his intent. They were glad that they had brought their sacred icons with them. They went back to their home, engaging in small talk about what they had seen and heard for themselves at the shrine of the Wizard of the Crow, and still marveling at the power of their Redeemer, who had tamed the sorcerer, making him meek and mild.

"There was no evil in his eyes," Maritha said.

"There was no evil in his voice," Mariko added.

"What he told us is something that we ourselves should have thought about," Maritha said.

"Yes, he spoke the truth," Mariko said. "Our ancestors used to say that one cannot see the back of one's head."

Rumor has it that when they reached home they did not bother with the preliminaries, so consumed were they with curiosity about the scars they might find on each other's body. They locked the door from inside and went to their bedroom. Theirs was a gentle and tender search that produced endless sighs and hisses, and it seemed a miracle that at their age their bodies could grow such strong wings of glory yet so light.

From that day, Maritha and Mariko went everywhere hand in hand, their eyes full of light, their bodies exuding youth, their confident gait compelling passersby to stop dead in their tracks with unanswered questions.

# 4

So when it was announced that on a certain Sunday Maritha and Mariko would be making new revelations about their war with Satan, the regular and occasional worshippers now found their way to All Saints Cathedral. Among them were the Soldiers of Christ with their candles still lit, and Bishop Kanogori had to ask the sect to please stay outside in the yard and keep watch for Satan, who hates being exposed and might come to disrupt the proceedings, he explained to soften the obvious disappointment on their faces.

The place was jammed with the curious. What would their latest struggle with Satan entail? Would Maritha and Mariko finally reveal the identities of the people used by Satan to play havoc with their flesh?

As for those who had seen them recently in a new light, they joined the congregation in the hope of learning the secret of their rediscovered youth.

As it turned out, Maritha and Mariko did not offer any startling or scandalous news. Their bodies no longer yearned for those of others. They were now at peace with their union blessed by God though recently threatened by Satan. Life was hope, and they were very grateful to all the brothers and sisters in Christ who, through prayer and their presence at the Sunday confessions, had helped keep that hope alive, and how could they ever forget the Soldiers of Christ, who had kept their vigil every night so the light could overcome the darkness of Satan? You shared in our grief, now share in our victory:

> *I will knock Satan down*
> *I will knock Satan down*
> *I will tell him*
> *Leave me alone, Satan*
> *I don't belong to daemons*

Maritha and Mariko sang and danced with such joyous abandon that they infused the entire congregation with energy. Even those who at first felt cheated of a more titillating climax now joined in the celebration.

> *I will fly above the earth*
> *I will float in the sky*
> *As I behold our Lord do wonders*
> *Never seen on earth before*

But the group who gained most from the drama of victory was the sect of the Soldiers of Christ, whose fame started growing beyond the boundaries of Eldares. Their vigilance had driven Satan from Santalucia, and Maritha and Mariko's confessions of victory over Satan were both evidence and vindication of the sect's earliest claims that they had once encountered Satan face-to-face or, more accurately, face-to-back in the streets of Eldares. Satan had been driven away from Santalucia, but in case he thought of coming back, he should know that the Soldiers of Christ would stand their vigil with lighted lanterns.

Sweeper-of-Souls, one of the three garbage collectors to whom Satan had once revealed himself, now rose a few ranks in the sect of the brave.

# 5

As they had found no blemish on their God-given bodies, their scars having turned into stars, Maritha and Mariko did not return to the shrine of the Wizard of the Crow for a cure. Neither did they see the need to convert the Wizard of the Crow to Christianity. The whole experience had taught them that there were things on earth that defied understanding and it was better to let them be. God indeed works in mysterious ways to perform His wonders, and who were they to question God's mysteries?

Yes! Like the mystery of the young woman with a *kanga* wrap around her head and shoulders who one evening appeared at their doorstep unannounced to claim that she had come to convey the best wishes of the Wizard of the Crow and make sure that the couple was well. She followed this initial visit with others. Most times she seemed hurried and would not stay for long. But there were times she would hang around and engage them in conversation. Now she did not pretend that she was merely passing by as a well-wisher for any-one else; she did not even mention the Wizard of the Crow. She came, she said, to glean wisdom from their experience. She never pried into their private lives. They never asked her where she came from or where she went. For them her coming and going was an act of God.

They liked the *kanga* lady. They liked her words. They enjoyed the peace that followed their victory over Satan.

However, and despite the near unanimous agreement that theirs was a great victory, there were a few skeptics who scrutinized each and every thing, comparing and contrasting this and that, picking holes here and there, and they would shake their heads and say: Hmmm, isn't it rather strange that the victory of Maritha and Mariko over Satan came only a few months after the return of the Wizard of the Crow? Still, nobody had heard the couple say anything about the Wizard of the Crow, and nobody claimed any longer to have seen them anywhere near the shrine before or after the victory.

Except once. But that was several years later, and even then it was not Maritha and Mariko who were seen near the shrine but rather the Wizard of the Crow who was seen near their house, running for dear life, hounded by the Ruler's police, and it was on recalling this dastardly hunt for a human being that people would pause and say: Do you see? There are elements of truth in the rumors we used to hear. Why else would the Wizard of the Crow have chosen to bypass all the other homes to seek help from Maritha and Mariko when it was clear by then that all in Santalucia would have felt honored to help him escape the bloodhounds led by Kaniũrũ?

# 6

The name John Kaniũrũ started attracting attention in the country from the day a radio announcement said that he had been appointed deputy chairman of Marching to Heaven. Kaniũrũ, who? People asked. What a name, others commented. Kaniũrũ sent the press several pictures of himself, but controversy erupted when two people initially claimed the name. Both won. Both retained the name. Your works alone will tell who really owns the name, the judge told them. Unable to decide whose picture to carry, the newspapers ended up with a pictureless story.

A few weeks later people heard, again through the radio, that Kaniũrũ had been asked to serve as the chairman of the Commission of Inquiry into the Queuing Mania. The same Kaniũrũ? people would ask. Once again Kaniũrũ sent several photos of himself in different poses and sizes, but the newspapers once again carried the story without an accompanying picture. Kaniũrũ was so angry that he personally telephoned the various editors: why had they not used any of his pictures? They owed him no explanation, they told him. Kaniũrũ was bitter, he saw these editors as his enemies, and he felt frustrated because there was nothing he could do about what he then saw as a vast conspiracy of envy.

He quit his job as a teacher at Eldares Polytechnic, dismissing the teaching profession as pure misery. Then he bought a new Mercedes-

Benz, paid for it in cash, and engaged a uniformed chauffeur. The dramatic change in his lifestyle following the dual appointment confirmed people's suspicions of his role in the Nyawīra affair, especially after they learned that she had once been his wife.

To impress the university professors who had worked with him as youthwingers but denigrated him as merely a lecturer at the Polytechnic, Kaniūrū would spring on them at their homes or offices, telling them that he was only passing by, that he would not stay long, but as he left he made a point of asking if there was anybody who wanted a lift to town, assuring them that there was ample room in his Mercedes-Benz, one of the latest models. Knowing the power he now wielded, they would look at him with envious admiration, call him Big Man, and ask him where they might meet up with him again to renew their friendship and bring him a little token. We teachers should stick together, they would tell him. I am not a teacher, he corrected them, and they would quickly apologize for their gaff. He enjoyed these moments when those who used to think that they were more important than he groveled before him to buy favors.

An idea struck him. Why not take his enjoyment to a higher level? Why not pay a visit to Nyawīra's father, Matthew Wangahū, the man who thought he, Kaniūrū, was too poor for the hand of his daughter? Maybe Nyawīra was hiding there. Why not kill two birds with one stone?

"On to Wangahū's," he said, stroking his Mercedes, talking to it as if it were a horse.

# 7

When Wangahū saw a sleek automobile stop outside his house with what he took to be a cabinet minister inside, he rushed to meet him. The chauffeur came out and opened the back door and saluted. Wangahū almost collapsed when he saw Kaniūrū emerge, but, well schooled in decorum, he did not display undue surprise. He invited his visitor into the living room and called out for his wife, Roithi, to come and greet him. And remember that one does not ask a hungry person for news, he told her after she had rubbed her hands in her apron and shook the visitor's. She returned to the kitchen and ordered the house help to prepare a chicken dish.

"Congratulations on your recent appointments," Wangahũ told Kaniũrũ. "Our people say that hard work always pays. I was even thinking of coming to see you in your new role as the deputy chairman of Marching to Heaven, but you have beaten me to it, and I am glad. Just because you and Nyawĩra don't get on does not mean you and I shouldn't. You are an in-law, and in this house you will always be treated like an in-law. Now, what I was thinking is simple and straightforward. If and when the Global Bank releases funds for Marching to Heaven, you and I should put our heads together on a contract to supply timber. You and I can become partners. A kind of father and son partnership, eh? What do you think of that?"

Kaniũrũ, who had expected hostility, was surprised by this reception. The man who spoke so smoothly now was the same who had refused to let him marry his daughter, going so far as to disown her for defying him and associating with a beggar, as Wangahũ had called him then, but he did not let that get in the way of his appreciation of the moment. He enjoyed being in the living room from which he was once barred and hearing Wangahũ talk to him politely, even as an equal. Still, Kaniũrũ did not like Wangahũ saying that he was thinking of seeing Kaniũrũ only after the Global Bank money had arrived. Didn't the old man realize that many, some wealthier than he, had already started calling on Kaniũrũ in his capacity as the deputy chair to make themselves known? Each would be sure to leave a "calling envelope" behind. Did the old man have the slightest clue as to how he had acquired his Mercedes-Benz?

Kaniũrũ recalled the pain the old man had caused him, and, although he had now taken a step in the right direction by receiving him well, still Kaniũrũ thought to assuage past hurts. With the word *partnership* Wangahũ had given him an opening. He cleared his throat and tried to assume dignity, for despite his new elevation and Mercedes-Benz, Kaniũrũ felt slightly intimidated by the man's bearing.

"Actually, that is one of the things that brought me here, for, as the saying goes, the early bird catches the worm," Kaniũrũ said, throwing in a couple more proverbs for what he assumed to be greater profundity. "But you have already taken the words right out of my mouth, and I thank you for it. Let's start our partnership right here today. If you feel that you want to hand over to me one or two of your plots in town as a sign of goodwill, I will not say no. Or we could start by your giving me a few shares in your timber business. Again as goodwill. If you ask me, I would say that a plot or two or a couple of shares are nothing compared to what will flow to you from Marching to Heaven."

"My child," Wangahū hastened to say, alarmed by the direction the conversation was taking, "*Hurry and Hurry-it broke up the house of Harry and Harriet,* the English people say. It is not good to rush into decisions. We shall talk about everything and go into detail once the Global Bank has released the money. By the way, when is the Ruler expected back in the country?" Wangahū wanted to know, steering the conversation away from plots and shares.

Kaniūrū was not amused by the English proverb. He had never heard it before and did not realize that Wangahū had made it up on the spot. It sounded to him like a veiled reference to the breakup of his marriage with Nyawīra.

"Well," Kaniūrū said, somewhat disappointed, "as you like it, for as the saying goes, the one in need is the one who presses his needs. Let me remind you: don't be as slow as the tortoise in the story . . ."

Wangahū himself felt like reminding Kaniūrū that it was the slow tortoise who won the race, not the hasty hare, but he held back. I should have let the man say what brought him here before putting my cards on the table, Wangahū admonished himself, noting that Kaniūrū had sidestepped the question about the Ruler's return from America.

"I am not saying that we should walk with the pace of a tortoise," Wangahū explained. "But we should look for what the English call *via media.*"

"Actually, that is not English but Latin," Kaniūrū corrected him.

"Whatever you say. You are the teacher."

"Ex-teacher!"

"Well, you are the one with education, and if you say it is Latin, then it is Latin. If my Nyawīra had stayed at home, she would have been the one interpreting this Latin for me."

"That's the other thing that brought me here," Kaniũrũ said. "Now, about Nyawĩra . . ."

"What? Has she been found? Arrested? What could have corrupted such a dutiful daughter?" Wangahũ asked, hope and despair in his voice.

"No, she is still at large. Did you know that Nyawĩra is a member of the outlawed underground organization?"

"Why ask me? How would I know? We know only what we read in the newspapers or hear on the radio," Wangahũ said, again alarmed at this new turn in the conversation.

"Does Nyawĩra not visit you?" Kaniũrũ asked.

Roithi walked in at that moment with plates of food on a tray.

"Tell me, has she been found? Is she alive?" she asked with concern as she placed the plates on the table.

"Can you please give my driver some tea and a piece of bread?" Kaniũrũ said, ignoring her question.

"We have taken care of him. Not only tea and bread but also a chicken wing."

"Then you may sit down," Wangahũ told Roithi, pointing to a chair. "These days there is no separation between matters reserved for men and those reserved for women. Women are also elders. Our son here has words he wants to share with us, and you should hear them from his own mouth."

"Nyawĩra has not been found," Kaniũrũ said.

"Who or what put so much confusion in our daughter?" Roithi said, tears coming to her eyes. "So much for her education and book learning."

"There is a saying that out of the same womb comes a thief and a sorcerer," said Kaniũrũ, trying to be profound.

"What of yours has she stolen?" Roithi asked sharply. "And what sorcery has she ever practiced on you?"

"Listen to me," Kaniũrũ said, picking the last piece of meat from a chicken leg. "I came here to tell you that the government is determined to get Nyawĩra dead or alive. I want to help you, but you must help me to help you. I want you to tell me whether Nyawĩra calls here from time to time. Has she done so recently? Have you any idea where she might be hiding? I hold no grudge against her. I have always said that no matter what she does she will always be my wife."

"You know very well that I disowned Nyawĩra a long time ago

when she decided to defy me and . . ." Wangahū was about to refer to the time that Nyawīra defied him and married a beggar, but that beggar had been transformed into the man sitting before him, with his sword of death and seeds of great wealth. So he corrected himself and continued, ". . . refused to wait for me to give her away to you in a proper church wedding."

His self-correction came too late. Kaniūrū had already gotten the gist of what the old man had intended to say, and Kaniūrū felt a resurgence of the humiliation he had suffered.

"Nyawīra's father," Kaniūrū said, barely controlling his anger and pain, "let us not dance around each other like two bulls in a kraal. To the Point is my motto. Nyawīra is in trouble. I am the only person who can help her. You are in more trouble. Your wealth is in danger. Only you can decide what you want to do about it. There are two ways out. Give me some shares in your business. Through joint ownership, my name shall shield your wealth and property. Or hand over Nyawīra. I promise you that I shall use all my resources to ensure that no harm comes to her. I still care about her and hope that one day she and I will walk down the aisle in a proper wedding blessed by you and God."

"Young man, have you no ears?" Roithi said, barely disguising her own anger and contempt. "Didn't you hear that Nyawīra has not called here?" she added bluntly.

Like mother, like daughter, Kaniūrū was thinking, for Roithi with her sharp tongue reminded him of Nyawīra. Her blunt speech made him uneasy and a little afraid of her.

In contrast, Wangahū was quiet, very quiet. Kaniūrū's words that Wangahū's wealth was in danger had clearly shaken the old man, but once again he controlled himself so as not to give this scoundrel the upper hand. That he might have to be partners with Kaniūrū to protect his property made him feel sick. This scoundrel has always been after my property, he told himself, but I would rather give up Nyawīra than a single share to this shameless youth.

"What do you have to say?" Kaniūrū said, turning toward the seemingly less daunting figure of Wangahū.

"Concerning matters of property and partnership," Wangahū said, controlling himself with difficulty, "I told you clearly that we have to wait on the Global Bank. As for Nyawīra, the mother of my children has spoken for both of us. But shouldn't you, as the one close to the ears of the State, be advising us on what to do to show the government that we do not support Nyawīra's subversive deeds?"

Kaniūrū was desperate to leave Wangahū's house with something tangible, anything, with which to further endear himself to Sikiokuu. He knew that Sikiokuu's greatest wish was to be able to greet the Ruler at the airport with news of Nyawīra's capture, and he knew that he himself would benefit thereby.

He often lost sleep trying to figure out how she could have slipped his grasp on the day they had first gone after her. How had she fled without leaving a trace? he would ask himself bitterly, time and again.

Suddenly an idea came to him. What if Wangahū and his wife, Roithi, were to go to the offices of Silver Sikiokuu and before media reporters and television cameras make a teary appeal for their daughter to give herself up? And even threaten to disown her should she fail to heed their call?

"You have asked a good question," he said. "I can help you. Before the Ruler left for America, he appointed me not only as deputy chairman of the Committee for Marching to Heaven but chairman of the commission inquiring into the recent queuing mania in Eldares. The commission has the power to summon anybody to give evidence, and believe me, we have already done so with a number of people close to Nyawīra, and they are providing us with very useful information all pointing to your daughter as being part of the root of all the evil. As for you two, I don't want to drag you before the commission. As you said earlier, we are still in-laws, and thus we shall remain. I can see that you're not entirely comfortable with the idea of a business partnership. This is your only way out. Let me put it to you as clearly as I can. Cooperate with the State and save your property. Otherwise you will be staring ruin in the face."

As soon as Kaniūrū began to describe his plan, Roithi, Nyawīra's mother, stopped him in his tracks. She stood up and wagged a finger at him.

"You can forget about my denouncing my daughter. No power on earth can make me do that. Even if Nyawīra were dragged to the scaffold, I would still claim her as my daughter. I don't agree with her actions, but that does not mean that everybody else in Aburīria is clean. What kind of property is so precious that I would be willing to sacrifice my daughter to save it? If Nyawīra's father wants to appease

Sikiokuu, he will be doing so without me or my support. I leave you to your foolishness. I am going to church," she said with a tone of finality as she walked out of the room.

The silence she left behind was tense, almost palpable. Wangahũ's word was normally the law in his household. Roithi had faith in his judgment regarding many issues. But he also knew that when Roithi rejected a course of action, she would never change her mind.

"Well, you have heard for yourself," Wangahũ said to break the awkward silence.

"Women. They surely know how to bring disaster into homes," Kaniũrũ said. "You yourself heard her say that she does not care about property. Does she know the energy that goes into accumulating even the smallest amount? That's why our ancestors denied women the right to own property."

Matthew Mũgwanja Wangahũ could have strangled this scoundrel with bare hands and not regretted it. How dare he talk like that in his home! In earlier days, he would have thrown the bum out. But he was just as frustrated to know that part of him agreed with Kaniũrũ's assessment of women. They are all the same. Even the most educated. Look at the hole into which his own daughter, a woman with a university degree, had forced him! He faced ruin or more humiliation by this scoundrel. And look at how Roithi had dared to talk to the man who held their fate in his hands! What shall I do to save myself and my property? He silently counted the number of ministers he knew to whom he could appeal for help, but they were all in America with the Ruler. He had to try to buy time.

"I have to go to church," he told Kaniũrũ. "I will think about all you have counseled."

"What about a public call for Nyawĩra to surrender?" Kaniũrũ asked, thinking that Wangahũ had responded to questions of shares in his property.

"There is nothing more to add to what I told you," Wangahũ said.

# 8

In receipt of a steady income, Kamĩtĩ, with Nyawĩra's support, decided to take two weeks off to visit his parents. Don't worry, I can be the Wizard of the Crow by myself, Nyawĩra assured him.

The village where Kamĩtĩ's parents lived was called Kĩambugi, the Village of the Cowbells, because in the past its wealth had resulted from the raising of cows and goats. The herds used to be led by bulls with cowbells of different sizes and shapes, designating different owners. By the time Kamĩtĩ was born the wealth was gone, but he always remembered the song that the village children used to sing, prancing about, imitating both the movement and sound of cows.

> *Rain come down*
> *I'll offer you a sacrifice*
> *Of a bull and another*
> *With bells around the neck*
> *Making beautiful sounds*

Mwalimu Karĩmĩri, as his father was popularly known, and his mother, Nũngari, had grayed well. Kamĩtĩ was glad to find them in good health. They were happy to see him and jokingly chastised him for staying away so long without a word about how he was doing in Eldares. He told them of the many years he had spent on the road, looking for work: they laughed, observing that primary school education of their day must then be superior to even the higher learning of today, because, back then, with an elementary school certificate, one could get a job as teacher, nurse, agricultural instructor, or veterinary assistant and one did not have to walk the roads for three years to get it. He told them that he was going to buy them a piece of land and build a modern stone house for them to show his appreciation for their many sacrifices on his behalf. As pleased as they were to hear this, they reminded him that his happiness was paramount, that they were used to the village plot on which they lived and were accustomed to working on other people's farms for pay. Life was not hard, they assured him. What we earn is enough for the two of us, but we would not mind sleeping on a nice bed in a modern stone house and owning a plot of land with a cow or two for milk.

Later, one evening when Kamĩtĩ and his father were sitting at the veranda, Mwalimu Karĩmĩri inquired about his son's occupation. You talked to us about buying us a piece of land and putting up a modern house, his father said. Where would the money come from? And I did not hear you talk about a job. Or are you into some illegal venture? You know very well that I would not touch even a cent born of crooked ways.

Kamĩtĩ hesitated, wondering what and how to tell him about his new profession as the Wizard of the Crow. His father had eyes that pierced a person's heart; he could spot a lie a mile away.

He decided not to trim the truth and told him that he had set up a business venture under the name Wizard of the Crow. Kamĩtĩ, who expected his father's rebuke, was surprised to see him laugh. He laughed so hard, Kamĩtĩ later told Nyawĩra, that tears flowed down his cheeks.

"And what is it you do as Wizard of the Crow?" his father asked him between bouts of laughter. "Sorcery? You know that I cannot touch any money from sorcery. Before the whites came with their own forms of punishment, sorcerers, when caught, were burned alive. So what services does the Wizard of the Crow perform?" the old man asked again.

"I don't kill people, if that is what you are thinking. Let's just say that I punish evil itself, not the evil ones. I am a healer. I heal wounded bodies and troubled souls. I see things that are hidden from many. I did not choose divination; it chose me." He briefly explained to his father how the shrine came about.

As Kamĩtĩ recounted his story, his father became increasingly solemn. Then Kamĩtĩ saw him stand up abruptly and excuse himself, and after a while he came back, more serene.

"Listen to me, my son," his father began. "Human will cannot will away God's will. Maybe you are asking yourself why I became solemn after almost drowning myself in laughter. At first I thought that you were just joking, so I greeted your words with laughter. But the more you talked, the more I realized that you meant what you said, and I started looking at myself with a questioning eye. I remembered that you once asked me about our family's story. I don't quite recall why you wanted to know. At the time I only hinted at the strange past and fortunes of our clan. Let me tell you. The Mītī clan used to be mighty. But over the years it has been scattered by slave raids, colonial ventures, and world wars. In our house we have always desired peace, but what we have gotten are woes of war. What might we have been had we not been scattered to the four corners of the wind? But the water that has spilled cannot be scooped.

"We are descended in part from hunters who dwelled in the forest, mostly, and came to know it well. Nearly all were healers. There was not an illness against which nature did not provide the necessary juices of life. Not only were they healers, but some had the gift of seeing things hidden from ordinary eyes. Some could even fly like birds. Consider your grandfather, Kamītī wa Kīenjeku, from whom you take your name! He sometimes found himself atop a mountain impossible for humans to climb or floating in the middle of a lake though he did not know how to swim. I never fleshed out his story because I did not want you to follow in his footsteps. We sacrificed, sent you off to school, to prevent that from happening. But today you have taught me a great lesson. Or, you have reminded me of something no one should ever forget: that the will of God will always triumph over human willfulness."

How did my grandfather die? Kamītī wanted to know. In the past he had been put off with vague answers like he died of old age or in an accident or of an illness. Now his father was direct: his grandfather, Kamītī wa Kīenjeku, had been a holy seer, a spiritual leader working with forces fighting the British in the war of independence. "He lived with the fighters in the mountains, teaching them how to be at peace with one another, settling conflicts, leading units into battle, and cleansing them of evil after their engagement with the enemy. He knew every path, every plant, every living thing. No one knew the ways of the forest better than your grandfather. The British shot him dead one day, but his body was never found. Some maintain that he is still alive and that his spirit hovers over Aburīria, ensuring that the truth of our past endeavors shall never be forgotten. So you see, human will cannot change God's design," his father repeated.

How come his own father had not become a seer? Kamītī asked.

"My son," his father said, "a seer is chosen by powers beyond us."

"And how does one know that one is chosen?"

"With us, seers are born holding a seashell; and my son, you were born gripping a shell in your little fist."

This pronouncement was followed by silence between them, each lost in his own private thoughts about what had just been said. Kamĩtĩ then asked his father that if it was true that he was born a chosen one, why was he not told? Why was he not allowed to yield to his grandfather's calling?

"The blessing comes with a price; I did not want my only child to bear the burden unless he was ready and willing . . ."

"What is the price?"

"You cannot use the gift to acquire earthly riches beyond the clothes you wear, the food you eat, and the house in which you live. Clothes, food, shelter, that is all."

"And what if such a person should gather riches?"

"Anything could happen. A seer might wake up to find himself in a land unknown, far away from his possessions, relatives, and friends, wandering alone among strangers, a prophet in exile. Or he might wake up to find his home on fire. The true ones suffer that they may know what true suffering is. They go through want so they may know what true want is. A seer lives in self-denial in the service of others. I had hoped to remove this burden from your shoulders so that you could live your life like everybody else. But as you can see all my efforts came to naught. God's will triumphs."

"But what greater wealth could I possess than a healthy body and a soul cleansed of evil?" Kamĩtĩ gently remonstrated with his father.

It was then that Nũngari, his mother, walked in and just caught the last words, and chided Kamĩtĩ affectionately.

"There is no wealth greater than a home of one's own. A home is husband, wife, and children. Or am I to be a grandmother only when I'm buried?"

"Mother, must I remind you that my flame rejected me?" Kamĩtĩ jokingly responded.

"Who is this flame that you never brought home to light a mother's heart?"

"Margaret Wariara. Shall we make a deal? How about you go to Wariara's place and plead with her," Kamĩtĩ added, and laughed.

His parents grew eerily quiet.

"What's the matter?" he asked.

"Don't you know?"

"What?"

"Margaret Wariara came back home all dried up, drained of energy. She breathed her last, watched by the whole village."

That night Kamĩtĩ hardly slept, for different images of Wariara kept intruding into his mind. So when on the following day a young man he went to school with came over and asked him to join him for a walk through the village, Kamĩtĩ accepted immediately. A walk through the village, a walk through rural peace, a walk to evoke the happy images of his childhood, would wipe away those of pain and loss. They started reminiscing over old times, recalling the names of so-and-so, all their mates in primary and secondary schools. But the walk only deepened his sorrow. Whichever name he mentioned, his friend simply pointed to a grave. Men and women of his own age, simply gone. Just like that. In the end, he stopped asking about anybody, for the answers lay in the many old and fresh graves lined around the village, victims of the same deadly virus.

"It is no longer an urban thing," Kamĩtĩ told Nyawĩra after he came back to Eldares. "It's terrible when the old have to bury the young. But it is more terrible when neither the old nor the young are there to bury each other."

# 9

During the week that Kamĩtĩ spent in Kĩambugi, Nyawĩra found being the sole Wizard of the Crow at the shrine trying. There were so many clients with so many problems of body, mind, and heart that she hardly had time to read the newspaper. She swore that she would never again allow Kamĩtĩ to go off for as long as he had. A day, maybe, but a whole two weeks, no!

One day she noticed a client in the waiting room reading the *Eldares Times* and she could not resist glancing at the headlines. She stopped in her tracks; she felt as if her heart had stopped beating. She rubbed her eyes to see more clearly, but there was nothing wrong with her vision.

The picture that stared back at her was of her father standing next to Sikiokuu; the headline screamed A FATHER TO HIS DAUGHTER: COME BACK HOME OR ELSE . . . She thought of asking the client to let her borrow the paper but decided against it. Suppose it was a setup? She behaved as if she had noticed nothing but later sent a helper for a copy of her own.

The story, as she read it, was merely an elaboration of the headline, but it tore into her being nonetheless. Her father was appealing to her to come out of hiding, surrender, and thereby earn his gratitude and blessings.

"If you don't give yourself up within one week, I say publicly to the whole world, I will no longer call you my daughter, for I am loyal to God in Heaven and the Ruler here on earth."

Although Nyawĩra did not always see eye to eye with her father, she loved and revered him deeply, and this prospective public divorce was painful and humiliating. How many times would he deny her, she asked herself, recalling his response to her expression of love for Kaniũrũ. Yet his judgment of Kaniũrũ's character and intentions had proven correct. Might he not have a point now? she agonized. Would she end up regretting her involvement in the politics of change the way she regretted her liaison with Kaniũrũ? That her mother was nowhere in the picture or the story made her feel that there was more to this than it appeared.

Things became clearer as she read on. Sikiokuu was quoted as saying that the government would leave no stone unturned in its effort to capture Nyawĩra and the leadership of the Movement for the Voice of the People. He described them as reptilian, symbolized by their calling card, the plastic snake. They would be ground to dust.

When and how did her father come to join Sikiokuu? Nyawĩra began to wonder. She could not quite believe that her father would leave his businesses to come all the way to Sikiokuu's offices simply to denounce her. Matthew Wangahũ might believe in the status quo, but he, like the rest of his class, took pride in having made it on his own and not by availing himself of public funds—stealing from the people, as it were. He would never have stooped to deny his daughter in public unless he was under considerable pressure.

In another column she read, Sikiokuu was quoted as having an invitation from Mr. Kaniũrũ to officially open the offices of the deputy chairman of Marching to Heaven and those of the chairman of the Commission of Inquiry into the Queuing Mania. The dates and plans for the opening ceremonies would be announced later. Kaniũrũ's picture was not published, but even so he had been quoted in his dual capacity, appealing to all residents of Santamaria and Santalucia, especially singers and dancers, to be ready to welcome Minister Silver Sikiokuu. He, too, had called upon Nyawĩra to come forward and give peace of mind to her beloved, including her aged parents. He proclaimed that she would also be of use to the Commission of Inquiry.

Nyawĩra began to see things for what they were. Kaniũrũ's prosecutorial zeal was evident. From the moment she had heard of Kaniũrũ's appointment as the chairperson of the Commission of Inquiry, she knew that he was capable of using his new powers to terrorize families, but little did she suspect that her family would be an early casualty.

The irony of the situation struck her. Even as Kamĩtĩ, her new love, was away visiting his parents, Kaniũrũ, her old love, had dragged her own father to town to deny her. The only saving grace was that her mother had absented herself, and Nyawĩra felt tears of gratitude well up inside her.

Suddenly she became angry and defiant and she heard herself talking loudly to an invisible presence. No matter what you do, Kaniũrũ, I will never appear before your Commission of Inquiry.

# 10

When Tajirika received a summons to appear before the Commission of Inquiry into the Queuing Mania, he was furious upon seeing Kaniũrũ's signature on it. Wasn't he his deputy, actually his clerk, regardless of his being chairman of the Commission of Inquiry? Priorities had to be observed, after all. How would he show Kaniũrũ that he, Tajirika, was his boss and in the process teach him a lesson in humility and obeisance to his superiors? He thought of tearing the summons into pieces, putting them back into the same envelope, and writing on top *Return to Sender*.

Another idea intruded. Why not write his deputy a letter summoning him to Tajirika's office to discuss his role as deputy and impress upon him the importance of Marching to Heaven? He imagined the scene. As soon as Kaniũrũ entered the office he, Tajirika, would show him the summons or better still tear it to pieces and fling them at the clerk's face. Kaniũrũ would quake in terror; Tajirika would smile, walk up to him, and slap him on the shoulder in a friendly gesture of forgiveness: a joke between a deputy and his chief, he would assure the trembling fellow, and the matter would end there. Then he realized that he had no official letterhead or seal attesting to his new position. Only the Minister for Foreign Affairs or the Ruler himself had the power of issuance, and they were still in America. So who had approved Kaniũrũ's stationery? The upstart may have acted on his own. What should I do? See Sikiokuu and expose the fellow?

It was a day or two after this, before he had even settled on a course of action, that he read about Sikiokuu's plan to inaugurate the offices of the Commission of Inquiry and the deputy of Marching to Heaven. A little fear crept into his certainty. Sikiokuu was now in charge of the country, and as the Waswahili say, *Paka akienda panya hutawala*. Might he not be devoured by the rat that now ruled in the absence of the cat? But then he quickly dismissed those fears. There was nothing Sikiokuu could do to the chairman of Marching to Heaven, for that would be tantamount to interfering with a special envoy of the Ruler. Still, concerning Kaniũrũ, he decided on a different course of action.

He would visit the office of his deputy but not on the date specified by the summons, and then only to tell him that he had come for a quick get-to-know-you between boss and deputy.

So the day of the summons came and passed. Tajirika thought to put off his visit for another week. But on waking up the following morning he changed his mind and decided it was better to go there that very day and rein in his deputy right away.

Late in the afternoon Tajirika asked his chauffeur to take him to the street where Kaniũrũ's offices were located. In the car, Tajirika tried to form the words that would affirm his authority and silence his upstart employee, but his anxiety prevented him from doing so. Even after he told the chauffeur to park the car on Rais Avenue and wait, he had yet to formulate his reprimand. He strode across the road. The gate opened into a huge enclosed yard. At the end of the yard was a two-story building where there were two sets of offices with its own main entrance. Above one was the inscription OFFICES OF THE GOVERNMENT COMMISSION ON THE QUEUING MANIA and above the other, OFFICES OF THE DEPUTY CHAIRMAN OF MARCHING TO HEAVEN. Tajirika's eyes were transfixed on the second sign. The word *deputy* was written in such tiny letters that it was almost invisible, certainly difficult to make out unless a reader stood very close. By contrast the word *chairman* was in big letters and in color so as to be easily read from afar.

Tajirika's first reaction was to blame himself: why had he not thought of setting up a separate office for the chairman of Marching to Heaven? He was consumed by envy, anger, and frustration: why had Kaniūrū minimized the word *deputy* except to dupe readers into thinking that the occupant was the real chairman?

He then took in the people waiting in the yard. They stood in groups of five to conform to the new decrees regarding the length of queues in public places. His anger deepened. Some of them were those who used to come to his office bearing envelopes of introduction. So the traffic of favor buyers had been redirected from his place to the offices of his deputy? So that was why he, Tajirika, no longer received calls seeking his acquaintance? So that's why the flow of envelopes into his offices at Eldares Modern Construction and Real Estate had dried up? So it was Kaniūrū who had diverted his river of fortune?

Tajirika would have liked nothing better at that moment than to strangle Kaniūrū. There was no point in his going inside. Might Kaniūrū not be impertinent enough to imagine Tajirika as another envelope-bearing supplicant? No, he could not afford the possible humiliation of having to explain himself. Returning to the car, he was beside himself; he could not even speak to his driver and simply gestured him to drive back to the office.

If only he could get in touch with his friend Machokali! Why had the minister not called him from America? When they last met at the Mars Café, the minister had said that he would be calling from time to time to get reports about the activities of his political enemies. Was this not an activity that Machokali ought to know of and even talk to the Ruler about with a view toward stopping Sikiokuu and Kaniũrũ from taking over other people's jobs? He feared that the pair's success in sidelining the boss of Marching to Heaven might embolden them into setting their sights on higher jobs . . . No, he did not want to think about the possibility of a Sikiokuu coup d'état; he might go crazy.

Tajirika decided that as long as his friend Machokali and the Ruler were in the USA he would not appear before the commission as summoned, and with that bold resolution he felt at peace. He redirected the chauffeur to take him not back to the office but to his Golden Heights residence.

They came for him at midnight, men in plainclothes. They threw him into the back of a Land Rover like a log of wood, ignoring the entreaties of Vinjinia. They said not a word, did not identify themselves. They drove into the night, leaving Vinjinia standing at the door in darkness and silence.

# 11

Vinjinia lay awake, not knowing what to do or even think about the whole thing. Were Tajirika's abductors police or common thugs pretending to be plainclothes police? What had Tajirika done to deserve this? She had not been pleased with her husband since her own return from police custody. Coldness had settled between them. They hardly talked, and when they did Tajirika simply wanted Vinjinia to go over the questions she had been asked while under interrogation, and only those relating to him and his businesses.

How Vinjinia had felt when the police arrested her, what she thought while in their custody, how she dealt with the ordeal: these were clearly not priorities for Tajirika. What most pained her was her suspicion that deep down Tajirika believed her to be guilty of secretly associating with the women who had brought shame on the Ruler and Marching to Heaven. Unlike her husband, however, she was not indifferent to her spouse's newfound woes.

She began her inquiry at the Santamaria police station because the boss, Wonderful Tumbo, was a family friend. She did not know that when Tumbo saw her coming from afar he left through the back door. The men Vinjinia found in the office acted as if they did not believe her story: who would be so crazy as to arrest Tajirika, owner of Eldares Modern Construction and Real Estate, friend of the Minister for Foreign Affairs and chairman of Marching to Heaven? Wait a few days, they advised, her husband would almost certainly turn up. She moved from station to station, receiving virtually the same answer to her entreaties. At one, they were so callous as to advise her to look for her husband in the city morgue. She had no success there, either.

At first Vinjinia went about her search quietly, trying to avoid unnecessary publicity, but soon she turned to the newspapers. One editor told her that the disappearance of an adult was not news he could use. Another pitied her and explained to her why.

Political disappearances had become commonplace as the powers that be proclaimed ignorance and innocence even though relatives and friends swore that they had seen their loved ones hauled off in police cars. Besides, he added with a smile, Aburīrian men were notorious for having multiple homes, some official, others on the side.

Next she tried Tajirika's friends, but none wanted to have anything to do with the case. At first they would listen to her sympathetically, but as soon as it dawned on them that the government might be involved they would become alarmed, some going so far as to ask her not to call again.

She was advised to get a lawyer to file a habeas corpus, but no one would take her case, citing one excuse or another. "You are wasting your money for nothing," one lawyer was honest enough to tell her. "In Aburīria we are governed by personal whims." With the Ruler in America, who was making new laws under which people were being abducted at night? she wondered.

She turned to the church and to her Christian friends for help and moral support but they offered only their prayers; some made it clear by their body language that Vinjinia was not welcome in their homes and at their social gatherings.

One day she stopped her Mercedes-Benz by the roadside, got out, and sat on some raised ground and began to weep: everything—the government, her friends, and her fellow Christians—seemed to have conspired against her. She started questioning the truths she had taken for granted, like the fairness of government and solidarity of the religious. To whom would she now turn for an answer to her troubles?

In the midst of tears and numerous questions, Vinjinia suddenly thought of the Wizard of the Crow.

# 12

Early one day Vinjinia set out and, as on the first visit, parked her Mercedes-Benz in the street and walked to the old shrine, where she got directions to the new complex of wood and stone walls and iron roofs, far tidier than many of the state-owned clinics and hospitals she had recently visited. She was led by an assistant into an inner chamber, where, after being left alone for what seemed an eternity, she suddenly heard the sound of a latticed window opening to reveal a face.

"I'm here to see the Wizard of the Crow," Vinjinia said.

"Your wish has been granted," a voice said, and Vinjinia was surprised to hear that it was that of a woman.

"When I was last here, he spoke in a male voice."

"I wear many faces. I talk in many voices. What brings you to me today?"

Vinjinia hesitated. Then suddenly the floodgates of woes within opened and she told of her tribulations as she searched for her lost husband. By the time she came to the end of her story she was feeling much better, as if by merely listening the Wizard of the Crow had lifted the load she had been carrying all by herself.

"Might he not be in hands similar to those in which you found yourself not so long ago?" Nyawīra asked, having suddenly recalled her disbelief when news of Vinjinia's capture reached her secretly in the forest.

Vinjinia almost fell off her seat: How did the wizard know that I, too, had been plunged into a similar darkness?

"The Wizard of the Crow knows what he knows," the voice said, answering her unspoken thought, which surprised and impressed her even more.

"They have refused to confirm his arrest," Vinjinia said. "Actually, they have denied it."

"So even if I use my mirror to find him, they will not admit to holding him?"

"Yes, but it would ease my heart to know."

"Or burden it even more."

"Not knowing is worse."

"But you yourself saw them take him away?"

"Yes."

"So what you want to know is not whether they have got him. What you want is for them to say that they have got him."

"You have read my heart completely," Vinjinia said.

What would Vinjinia do were she to uncover my identity? Nyawīra wondered. Would Vinjinia rush to report her to the very forces that had made her life miserable? While incarcerated, had Vinjinia said anything about Nyawīra to her captors? Was Vinjinia worn down not just by Tajirika's abduction but also by questions she was asking herself and for which she had no ready answers? She saw herself in Vinjinia: after her car accident, she, too, had started by asking herself questions she had not asked herself before the trauma. Nyawīra felt very strong sympathy for the woman, and her own political stance against the regime in power only strengthened the bond. No matter how she despised the likes of Tajirika, she acknowledged that he had rights, too, like any other Aburīrian. But how could she help Vinjinia? She wished that Kamītī were around so they could put their heads together to find a way to make the government publicly declare that they were holding Tajirika. But Kamītī had not yet returned from Kīambugi.

Her mind drifted to the contrast between Vinjinia's public devotion to her husband and her own father's public denial of her, and Nyawīra felt a creeping sadness. Kaniūrū had ruptured her ties to her father. Her recollection of Kaniūrū's words in the media revived and intensified the pain and bitterness she still felt. Kaniūrū thinks he can build success on the ruins of other people's lives. Contemplating the man's arrogance and mean spirit, Nyawīra found herself forming an idea.

"Listen carefully," she told Vinjinia. "Friday is the Day of the Way at the shrine. I want you to come back dressed like any ordinary working person, and on foot like most clients. Bring some traditional women's clothing with you: twelve leather skirts with front aprons and twelve red-ochered tops."

# 13

By evening the following Friday, Vinjinia was back at the shrine, seated among the other seekers of the Way, waiting her turn patiently.

"Here is the bundle," she told the Wizard of the Crow.

"Are you ready to know the fate of your husband?"

"Yes."

"Even if it means your coming face-to-face with those who took him away?"

"If only I could, I would let them know that I will not be silenced."

"Everything you need is at Kaniūrū's place."

"What! The deputy to my husband? A kidnapper?"

"Yes, the same one."

"Who empowered him?"

"Surely you know that he is now the chairman of the Commission of Inquiry into the Queuing Mania. And remember that Kaniūrū, like your husband, does not act alone. There are more powerful others behind his actions."

"How can I free my husband?"

"I didn't say anything about freeing him. But if you do as I say, you will at least be able to compel them to say what they have done with him."

"What must I do?"

"My mirror tells me that a date has been set for Sikiokuu to open formally Kaniūrū's offices in Santamaria. Go home; find out the day and the hour of the ceremony. On that day, dress as you normally would for a similar occasion and be there as the ceremony begins. Show no undue interest in anything around. Tell them that all you want is to see Sikiokuu to find out where he is hiding your husband. Be firm and refuse to leave the premises until he has shown you where he buried your husband's body. If your demand is met, leave at once and, again, show no interest in whatever else is happening around."

"Is that all?"

"That is all."

"You mean I don't have to carry magic potions in my dress?"

"The most potent is the magic within you."

# 14

From the moment that Kaniũrũ was notified of the day Sikiokuu would stage the opening ceremony, he had looked high and low for women dancers to grace the occasion, but in vain. He was personally despised, and no one wished to be associated with him openly. How was he going to impress Sikiokuu and the media without women dancers? Then one evening a couple of days before the ceremony, luck knocked at his door.

He was looking through the window idly, in total despair, when there appeared outside his offices a woman dressed in a long leather skirt, a front apron, and a red-ochered top with two bunches of beads hanging from her earlobes. He rushed to open the door himself.

It was a little dark in the corridor, but on hearing what she had to say, that she was bringing a message from a group of dancers, Kaniũrũ was so elated that he started jumping up and down like a little child before swearing before the woman that if indeed she could get him a group of women dancers to perform for Sikiokuu he would personally ensure that the group got two new buses with which to start their own transport business.

He was so excited at his new luck that he did not ask many questions about the woman and her group, for he did not want to frighten his good fortune away.

So Kaniũrũ himself called the newspapers and radio and TV stations to tell them of the occasion. On the morning of the scheduled event he called again as a reminder, adding that something dramatic would be happening.

Most satisfying was the sure knowledge that, at last, his picture, he and Sikiokuu mobbed by adoring dancers, would finally appear in the press.

# 15

The dancers were among the first to arrive. In traditional garbs, they all looked much the same. But though difficult to distinguish one from the other, as a group they were impressive to an onlooker. Kaniũrũ delayed meeting them formally before the arrival of the media. But the women did not seem to mind as they settled in the yard preparing themselves for their act. The guests were mostly those who wanted to buy favor in anticipation of the abundant windfall for Marching to Heaven.

For his part, Sikiokuu had brought his own state photographers, but it was not until press reporters and cameramen arrived that Kaniũrũ and Sikiokuu stepped out into the yard and took their places, ready to be showered with praises by the dancers, now arranging themselves into a formation. As they were about to start, Vinjinia arrived.

She was startled to see the dancers in the traditional ensembles that she had taken to the Wizard of the Crow. They had cost her quite a sum, but now she was inwardly glad to see how striking the clothes had turned out to be. Mindful of the instructions at the shrine, she tried not to show any interest in them, and she made a beeline toward the front row where other guests sat. I want to speak to Minister Sikiokuu, she said loudly.

All eyes, including the dancers', now turned to the woman.

Sikiokuu leaned toward Kaniūrū and asked him who the woman was. A crazy woman, Kaniūrū replied, but because he did not want any commotion before the press, Kaniūrū tried to diffuse the situation by asking the woman loudly and in a friendly voice, Mother, what do you want? Vinjinia, just as loudly, said that she simply wanted to know where the government had buried the body of her husband, Tajirika. Sikiokuu did not react one way or another; he stared straight ahead as if he had not the slightest clue as to what Vinjinia was talking about. Kaniūrū gestured to some policemen to take the woman away. Vinjinia screamed in protest. By now the press photographers were snapping away. Sikiokuu saw that the situation might get out of hand and ordered the police officers to stop manhandling the woman. Kaniūrū was fuming with anger, for this was not exactly the kind of drama he had promised the press, but he did not know what to do. Vinjinia was shouting and demanding to know if her husband was alive, and if not the authorities should take her to his grave. In desperation Kaniūrū turned to the dancers and instructed them to start their performance.

One of the women, as if in response to Kaniūrū's appeal, raised her voice in song while the others responded with undulating hip and hand movements punctuated by rhythmic grunts.

> When I came here to sing praises to the visitor
> I did not know that it was to a house at war
> I do not sing in houses at war
> My song might become cacophony
> And my voice gets lost in my throat
> For though you see me dancing
> I have a husband and a child to look after
> I would not want the child to lose a father
> For a home is father, mother, and child

On hearing their song, Sikiokuu realized that unless he did something drastic, the situation would worsen, might become as shameful as what had happened at Eldares, and how would the Ruler react if the news was to reach him in America? He stood up and asked the women to stop singing for he had something to say to the media.

He had come here, he said, to formally open these two important offices and also make a statement. He had planned to say what he had to say at the end of the ceremony, but mindful of press deadlines he thought it better to do so now, not wanting to risk the possibility of some reporters having to leave early. Uppermost in his mind were two issues:

The first concerned Nyawīra, the outlaw. The government was aware that she was hiding among the people, and he wanted to remind them that everyone was duty bound to report her to the nearest police station. Whoever harbored the fugitive would be as guilty of treason as the criminal. He wanted to emphasize, however, that if Nyawīra herself surrendered to the authorities as her own father had asked her to do, she would not be harmed in any way. She would be tried fairly under the laws of the land. He then announced a reward of fifty thousand Burīs for anybody providing information leading to the arrest and successful criminal prosecution of the said Nyawīra for crimes against the State.

The second issue concerned Titus Tajirika. He said that Tajirika, Nyawīra's employer, was in the hands of the security forces, helping them in their search for the roots of the recent queuing mania in Eldares. He, the minister, had not known that the woman before them was Tajirika's wife. He pledged to transport Vinjinia and her children to Tajirika so that they could see for themselves that he was very much alive and well. The government appreciated the information about Nyawīra and the queuing mania that Tajirika was providing, but the minister could not go into details "for security reasons."

Sikiokuu ended his statement by asking Mrs. Vinjinia Tajirika to join the other guests of honor at the podium waiting to be entertained by the women dancers. He sat down and gestured to the official police photographer and instructed him on what to do.

The statement caught everybody by surprise. Vinjinia did not know what to do; this development had not been scripted at the shrine. Should she express indifference as the Wizard of the Crow had counseled? Should she ignore the invitation and walk away? But how could she refuse a ministerial invitation? They might even take it as rudeness and delay the promised visit to her husband. She found herself sitting at the podium next to the big ears of Silver Sikiokuu.

The women dancers now raised their voices in song, calling for peace and unity among the people of the land.

*Sikiokuu, you were given big ears so that you could hear things*
    *from afar*
*And you, Kaniūrū, a big nose so that you could smell out things*
    *from afar*
*Listen, then, to what we the people of this land say*
*We desire peace, unity, and progress*
*A good leader is the one who can bring about the three*
*I will sing what I sang for the one who was there before*
*I will sing the same song for the one who is there today*
*I will sing the same song for the one who will come after*
*When I fought against the colonialists*
*I thought that freedom would mean a cow to nourish me*
    *with milk*
*Yesterday I had nothing to eat*
*Today is the same*
*Who has ears to hear the people?*

Sikiokuu was moved by the song, presuming that the ladies were appealing to him, in coded language, eventually to become leader of the land. He clapped enthusiastically, as if suggesting that he understood their call. Kaniūrū did not like what he heard being sung, but now that Sikiokuu had calmed the situation he managed a laugh. Journalists who had been expecting a bang got only a whimper and felt disappointed at being cheated of a good story.

Vinjinia, the only one among the dignitaries who knew why everything had ended the way it did was inwardly amazed at yet another revelation of the powers of the Wizard of the Crow. He had done what lawyers, journalists, and all her friends had failed to do: make the government acknowledge that it was holding Tajirika. But who are these women dancers? She had never seen them before. Could it be that the Wizard of the Crow had transformed himself into several female selves?

What Kaniūrū, Sikiokuu, and even Vinjinia did not know was that it was Nyawīra who had been leading the women in song and dance.

# 16

When Nyawĩra had finished recounting to Kamĩtĩ the whole story of what had happened at the shrine during his visit to Kĩambugi, he shook his head in disbelief and mumbled disapprovingly: "That was dangerously reckless."

They were in their usual Chinese restaurant, Chou Chinese Gourmet, a happy medium between the high-class and the run-down restaurants, both extremes often the haunts of police intelligence.

"You are the one who once told me that the best hiding place is always out in the open, where one is least expected."

"Yes, but this was like deliberately walking into danger. Face-to-face with John Kaniũrũ, someone who knows you so well? And not once but twice?"

The waiter brought the bill together with two fortune cookies. Nyawĩra paid the bill and reached out for one of the fortune cookies. Kamĩtĩ took the other. They broke the cookies almost at the same time and pulled out the pieces of paper on which the fortunes were written.

"What does yours say?" Kamĩtĩ asked.

"No, tell me what yours says."

They started arguing playfully about who should tell first, then suddenly snatched each other's fortune and read it. Both were identical: *Expect amazing things.* They laughed.

"Okay. Finish Vinjinia's story. Amaze me more. Maybe it contains the amazing things foretold in these fortune cookies."

"Don't look so scared," Nyawĩra said, trying to calm Kamĩtĩ. "There is no way Kaniũrũ would have found me out. Our first encounter was at twilight. I wore a *kanga* on my head and a nose ring. At our next I was in traditional attire in a crowd of women similarly dressed. I felt as if I were back in college, where once on the stage, in the zone, acting a role, I could fool just about anybody, even my closest friends."

"There is no way you could fool me!" Kamĩtĩ asserted.

"Don't be so sure," Nyawīra said, and she excused herself to go to the ladies' room.

Left alone, Kamītī started turning over in his mind what they had been talking about. He was happy that they were together again, and their easy conversation had helped lift the weight he had felt since hearing about the death of Margaret Wariara and learning of the havoc that the strange virus was wreaking on his ancestral village. He had once contrasted rural tranquility and urban anxiety. Things were more complex now. His sorrow was mixed with contempt for the likes of Matthew Wangahū and Kaniūrū. Nyawīra had shown astonishing generosity and strength of character as well as self-sacrifice in her dramatic efforts on Vinjinia's behalf. He felt lucky to have her as his companion; she had bestowed on him a vision of the world. As he contemplated the assurances and possibilities of their relationship, he soon lost awareness of his surroundings and was awakened from the dreamworld only by her footsteps.

She saw his startled look and mistook it for continued anxiety over the danger she had exposed herself to in his two-week absence. She sought to reassure him:

"Listen, I would be less than candid if I didn't tell you that as I stood there face-to-face with Kaniūrū I felt like removing all my disguises to show him that I was still alive and well, or simply cutting off his nose with a knife. But I desisted from anything foolish that would jeopardize all that I stood for. Besides, I really felt for Vinjinia. I have never forgotten that she herself was once arrested instead of me. But pride also drove me to help her: I would never want it said that a person came to the shrine of the Wizard of the Crow and was sent away with needs not met. I am happy that Vinjinia can now sleep in peace knowing what she now knows."

"What?"

"The silence of the State over a person they have arrested is often a sentence of death. Tajirika was a corpse. We brought him back from the dead."

# 17

Even Tajirika thought that he would soon be a corpse. After arresting him they had blindfolded him before throwing him into a dark chamber. A tiny light above from a source he could not see was his only companion. The wardens brought him food and water in darkness and, like his captors, answered none of his questions. Day and night, amid painful silence, he was taut with anxiety. The thought that he might lose all his property was unbearable. There was nothing he would not have done to save his property, even if he had to prostrate himself before those responsible for his incarceration. But who were they?

He was struck by one suspicion after another. Had his wife, Vinjinia, lied about him while in custody in exchange for her freedom? Or had Nyawīra been arrested and implicated him in her crimes?

He was desperate to face his captors in order to counter any lies told about him and show his readiness to repent whatever omission or commission he was accused of.

Sikiokuu had assumed as much. He knew that Tajirika's present state of mind would result in all manner of unsolicited confessions. The wretched fellow was prepared to be even more at Sikiokuu's mercy. Sikiokuu could then toy with various options.

Vinjinia's intervention before the press, entirely unexpected, scuttled those plans, compelling Sikiokuu to extract as much information from Tajirika as he could before news of his arrest reached the Ruler in America. He ordered his people to start interrogations immediately.

They moved Tajirika from the dark chamber into an interrogation room and threw him into a chair. Nearly blinded by light, he blinked uncontrollably; at first he could not make out anything distinctly. Soon he understood that he was seated at a table in the middle of a room and that opposite him sat a man in a dark suit. For Tajirika this marked a big improvement on the dark chamber of his present captivity, but, pricked by humiliation, he breathed heavily with barely suppressed anger.

"Don't be afraid. I am from the police," the man said, and put his arm across the table to shake hands with Tajirika. "Call me Assistant Superintendent Njoya, Elijah Njoya."

Tajirika ignored the hand.

"Do you know who I am?" Tajirika asked angrily, having forgotten his vow to himself to plead for mercy on bended knee.

"Of course, Mr. Tajirika. Who in all Aburĩria can say he does not know of you?" Njoya said smoothly and matter-of-factly, annoying Tajirika even more by his seeming indifference at the outrage done to the chairman of Marching to Heaven. At the same time, Tajirika was flattered to hear that he was well known throughout the country.

"Why am I in police custody?" Tajirika demanded.

"In custody?" Njoya asked in a puzzled tone. *"I am sorry, but there must be a misunderstanding,"* he added in English.

"There is no *misunderstanding.* You apprehended me in *Golden Heights,* in my house, in front of my wife and servants."

"When was that?"

"Are you trying to tell me you know nothing about this?"

"I learned of your being here only last night. So I presumed you must have arrived yesterday."

"Yesterday? You should be talking of months instead of days. And I didn't 'arrive' here. I was thrown into the back of a Land Rover like a bundle of wood or a block of stone and dragged to this hellhole."

"I am so sorry, Mr. Tajirika," Njoya said, and indeed he spoke in a seemingly sincere tone, with the proper mix of fear, humility, and respect vis-à-vis someone of Tajirika's stature. "Mr. Tajirika, I am definitely going to look into this. You, as an employer, should know about *subordinates.* You might tell them to bring just one item and they bring ten instead. In fact, had it not been for your wife . . ."

"What about my wife?" Tajirika growled.

"Well, I believe she is the one who called late last night to alert the police that you were missing, and she wondered if you were here at the station."

"You mean, she let all this time pass without alerting the police? Suppose those who abducted me had been thugs? I would have been a corpse feasted upon by worms."

*"Please don't blame your wife.* Maybe she did not know where or how to start. You know how it is with rural women . . ."

"My wife is not rural. She is very highly educated. She has a school certificate."

"Excuse me. I am sorry. Whatever the case, she did a smart thing in letting those in authority know about the situation, and that is why I myself came to see you instead of sending a junior officer. By the way, as to your wife, please call her on the phone and assure her that you are in the hands of the government and that she should not worry unduly."

Like a master conjurer, the officer produced a mobile phone from his pocket and handed it over to Tajirika. Holding the thing, Tajirika felt as if a bit of the life he had known had come back to him. He punched the numbers with firm authority and leaned back as he would have in his own office. Superintendent Njoya tiptoed out of the room as if out of respect for Tajirika's privacy. Tajirika did not speak much because he was annoyed with Vinjinia for her tardiness in reaching out to the authorities. He told her, almost as if bragging, that he was in the hands of the government and she should not worry about him, that her duty was simply to look after their home and the business. He ended the call without asking her about either herself or the children and without giving her a chance to respond. Njoya now returned to the cell followed by another person who pushed a trolley with a plateful of hot chicken and rice.

Tajirika ate ravenously: it was the first tasty meal he had eaten in many a day. The aroma of good coffee capped his enjoyment, and as he belched with satisfaction he started thinking that maybe this Njoya was not such a bad person after all and that he might even turn out to be a friend of the policemen that Tajirika used to treat with Christmas gifts at the Santamaria post. Yes, he must be a friend of my friend Wonderful Tumbo. Or maybe a friend of a friend of his own friend Machokali.

"Thank you," he told Njoya sincerely.

"You are most welcome," Njoya said. "Now, Mr. Tajirika, I am sure you want to know why we asked you to come here. We just want you to help us clear up a few things, and then you will be a free man."

"So you admit that I am not *free*?"

"It is just a manner of speaking. But let me advise you *as a friend*. It's only an infant who does not understand the implications of things. You are clearly not an infant, and you do not appear to me to be a thickheaded fellow. Every person of means has enemies. You are no exception, Mr. Tajirika. There is no better way of defeating one's enemies than by unburdening oneself. Your responses and manner are very important. Let out whatever troubles you. That is my honest advice."

"Ask, for no person was ever taken to court for asking a question. I have nothing to hide or cover up. I have always sung the praises of the Ruler."

"That is the spirit. But as you well know, there are some who sing praises to the Ruler all day and plot against him all night. So tell me this. Why didn't you obey the summons to appear before the Commission of Inquiry into the Queuing Mania, as the commission was set up by the Ruler?"

That was not the kind of question Tajirika was expecting. He was about to say, You mean the commission chaired by my deputy? But he held back so as not to fall into the trap of appearing to split hairs when it came to the wisdom of the Ruler.

"I was ready, but things came up and I overlooked the day and time. Such a person as I needs to be given *enough notice* so that I may organize my affairs accordingly. We businessmen have a saying: *time is money.*"

"Like the English, eh?"

Flattered by the presumed similarity, Tajirika was about to say yes but recalled his recent illness when words had remained stuck in his throat, the source of the malady being his aching to be white. He shook his head from side to side.

"Well, please tell us about the queuing mania," Njoya continued.

"What do you want to know?"

"Everything. There is not much that could have escaped your notice."

"You have spoken."

"The queuing started at your place?"

"You have spoken."

"What?" Elijah Njoya asked, a little irritated by the "you have spoken" business.

"I don't know about all the queues, but I do know that one of the queues started outside my office the day Minister Machokali announced that I had been appointed the chairman of Marching to

Heaven. It was a short one, and the people dispersed after I had dealt with their needs, but even so I could see signs of bigger queues to come. You see, many businesspeople, on hearing about my elevation, started phoning me immediately; many came to my office to congratulate me and to introduce themselves. They so crowded in the reception area that my secretary had to ask them to form a queue to ensure more efficient service on a first come, first served basis."

"A very good principle indeed. What did they want?"

"They'd heard that the Global Bank was about to release funds for Marching to Heaven. They wanted to make my acquaintance before the construction started so that later I would recall their faces when it came to awarding contracts for the completion of the project."

"What about the workers, the job seekers, the wretched . . . whatever we may call them. What about them? Did they also hope to secure lucrative contracts?"

"I don't know much about that because on the day when my appointment as chairman of Marching to Heaven was announced, they were nowhere in sight. But just before we called it a day, my secretary came up with the idea of engaging temporary staff to deal with the volume of calls and the number of businessmen visiting in person. All that—attending to the telephone, receiving distinguished visitors, keeping meticulous records—could not be handled by one person. I thought it a good idea. So I authorized her to plant a billboard inviting applications. The new signpost would replace the old one that said *No Vacancy*."

"And who is your secretary?"

"Oh, please don't remind me of her—she is evil," Tajirika said furiously.

"What's her name?"

"Nyawīra."

"The terrorist?"

"The same."

"Was she the one calling the shots in your firm? Or did she terrorize you until your head spun and you said yes to whatever she wanted?"

"No, in those days she appeared to be a good person and quite mature in her thoughts and in the way she carried out her tasks."

"And physically? Was she also good-looking?"

"She was very beautiful, it is true."

"Outstandingly beautiful?"

"Beauty itself."

"The kind of beauty that makes all other beauties pale in comparison?"

"Oh, you should have seen her. Those cheeks. Those breasts. The way she walked. And those clothes that seemed as if the Creator Himself had outfitted her!"

"It seems that even today your mouth waters at the very thought of her."

"My mouth is watering from bitterness, not love."

"So there was a time it used to water with desire for her? Let me be direct, or shall I ask directly: was there something between you and her?"

"Our relationship never came to that," Tajirika said, slightly agitated by the tone and tenor of Njoya's line of questioning.

"You mean you never wanted to become acquainted with what was between her thighs? Why? Are you one of those 'Jesus is my personal savior' employers?"

"Me?" Tajirika asked, reacting to what he saw as a challenge to his masculinity. He even laughed. "I have shown many a woman a thing or two. But Nyawīra was a little intimidating. Not that she spoke aggressively. How can I put it? It seemed as if her eyes could see straight into a person's heart. Those eyes and the way she carried herself could make even the most lustful of males go limp. Perhaps if she had stayed longer I might . . . a real man never takes no for an answer, and when it comes to women my motto is Never Give Up."

"So you lusted after her? Were you *in love,* perhaps?"

"That's not exactly what I am trying to say, but . . ."

"I know, I know," Njoya hastened to add. "As a man I know that once a man's heart has become captive to a woman, there is nothing he would not do for her. *I understand you completely,* Mr. Tajirika."

"But I have just told you. Nyawīra was like a firebrand without a handle."

"So I understand you to be saying or trying to say that you longed for the firebrand but it had no handle."

"No, no, it is not how you are putting it. But let me tell you, if today, this very day and hour, I were to hold that woman in these arms, I would wring her neck until she was dead. *She is a traitor,*" Tajirika declared with venom.

"Okay. Let's set Nyawīra's case aside. Let's assume that she was only a secretary. You mean to tell me that your secretary comes to you, her employer, and tells you to hire more labor, and you agree and even okay her request to put up a billboard outside?"

"Yes," Tajirika said, although he still did not like the way Njoya strung words together, making them sound so sinister.

"How many tempas were you hoping to employ?"

"Say about three," Tajirika said. "Possibly five."

"And for three people, possibly five, she persuaded you to put up a billboard to announce to all Eldares that there were jobs to be had?"

"How else would we have put it?" Tajirika asked. "There was more than one job available, so we had to put it in the plural."

"You assented to her putting it in the plural, suggesting the availability of thousands of jobs?"

"I can't recall the exact wording," Tajirika said, feeling a little helpless before this professional twister of words and their meanings.

"You left it to her to arrange the words any way she wanted?"

"Look here, Mr. Officer. She was my secretary. A boss gives a good secretary a general notion of what he wants and it is up to her to respect the letter and spirit of his command."

"And so it would be correct to say that Nyawīra was in general interpreting your wishes and carrying out your orders?"

"Yes, when she was on my premises. Beyond that I made no claims on her time."

"Okay. A good interpreter of your wishes while on your premises, and a free agent outside the official orbit, right?"

"Right. You can put it that way."

"So how did the queue of the workers begin?"

"You see, for some time after the day of my extraordinary elevation, I was not able to go to the office . . ."

"Why?" Njoya interrupted.

"I succumbed to an illness."

"You were ill?"

Tajirika paused. How was he going to explain his strange illness to the inquisitor? An illness without a name?

"A heart problem."

"A broken heart?"

"No, just heart trouble."

"A heart condition? That is very serious for a man of your age and bulging flesh. I am so sorry to hear of this, Mr. Tajirika. How long were you in hospital?"

"I didn't actually go to any hospital."

"You saw a private doctor?"

"Yes . . . No . . ."

"Is it yes or is it no?"

"Both."

"What do you mean?"

"I went to see a diviner. I am not sure we can quite call his kind doctors."

"A witch doctor. So you are one of those! *Afathali Mchawi* type?"

"It is better to call him simply a diviner."

"But Mr. Tajirika, what if you had needed a *bypass* or a *transplant*? Would your witch doctor have managed?"

"Mine was not an illness of the organ itself," Tajirika tried to explain. "I meant the heart as mind. Something like that."

"You mean you were mad? Crazy?"

"Nooo! *Hapana! No, no!*" Tajirika denied the suggestion in three languages for emphasis. "I meant heart as when we say so-and-so is heartless or so-and-so is full of heart."

"*A psychiatric disorder,* something like that, is that correct?"

"I don't know much about the names of illnesses. But I think that a diviner could be called a *psychiatrist* of sorts."

"Mr. Tajirika, let's not worry about names. Whatever its name, your heart condition must have been very serious for you to boycott your office soon after becoming chairman of Marching to Heaven. Unless . . . ?"

"What?"

"It was a ploy, a 'diplomatic illness,' or what in our line of work we call an alibi. You draw the plan and you leave the execution to others. Is that not what you told me that bosses do?"

"What do you mean?" asked Tajirika, a little confused.

"Supposing, and we are just supposing, that Tajirika wants an illegal assembly of workers, the riffraff of our society, say potential rioters, to queue outside his office, might he not want to absent himself and leave everything to the trusted interpreter of his wishes? You see, should he be called before a commission of inquiry he would say 'I was not there' and produce his alibi, a hotel bill or a hospital admission slip or a doctor's letter. You know the story of the thumb and four fingers? They used to be together, all five, a kind of brotherhood of the fingers. Then one day Thumb proposes, Let's go. Where? the others ask. To Mr. Ndego's bank, says Thumb. To do what? the others ask. To rob the owner, to rob the bank, Thumb says. What if we are caught? they ask. Hey! I will not be there, Thumb says, and up to this day Thumb remains his innocent self, apart from the other four, who remain bound together by their crime."

Tajirika wanted to pick holes in the story. In the traditional, it is the little finger that comes up with the idea of theft and there is no mention of a bank. Njoya had also mixed up the story of the thumb with a very different one in which a mother, avoiding a direct answer to her child's question as to where she is going, talks vaguely about a visit to a fictional Ndego's home for a meal consisting of one bean only. But Tajirika did not. He was angry and terror-stricken at the drift of Njoya's inquiry and tone, which smoothly implied treason and death.

"I don't like what you are insinuating. I am a loyalist. To be very frank, I was taken to the shrine of the diviner without my knowledge. I was that ill. And I missed work not just one day but several days, more than a week. Why should I risk my life's work and property for the sake of starting a queue of riffraff and job seekers? A job-seeking queue is not exactly a beauty pageant."

"You claim that you were away from your workplace for days, even weeks. Did you close the office?"

"No."

"Who ran the office in your absence?"

"The secretary. I mean, she was the only one there who . . ."

"By the secretary you still mean Nyawīra?"

"Yes . . . but my wife, Vinjinia, later went there and was *in charge. Completely in charge.* What did I tell you? She is not a village woman. She is highly educated. She has . . ."

"So Nyawīra and Vinjinia were the ones present when the queuing mania started? Is that what you are saying?"

"Yes!"

"So only those two can give eyewitness testimony as to what occurred?"

"You have spoken."

"What?"

"Only those two can give a proper account because they were there. All I know is hearsay."

"When did you go back to work?"

"After the convocation at the site for Marching to Heaven."

"The one held at Eldares Park?"

"You have spoken."

"Spare me the Jesus speak. What are you implying, Mr. Tajirika? That I'm Pontius Pilate to your Jesus Christ?"

"*No, no, no.* There is no way I would even dream of such a thing. I am human. I am a sinner."

"Then confess your sins!"

"What do you want me to confess?"

"I was not there when you sinned."

"What do you want me to do?"

"Answer my questions fully and simply. The day you say you resumed work, was that the same day you got cured?"

"By that time I was already cured. A couple of weeks before, in fact. I had been resting at home, not doing much of anything."

"Mr. Tajirika, you confuse me even more. Please clear this up for me. Are you telling me that between the day you learned that you had been appointed chairman of Marching to Heaven and the day of the dedication of the site, you never once went back to your office to see for yourself how things were?"

"I did go there once, on the morning that I left the doctor's . . ."

"You mean the witch doctor's shrine?"

"Yes, the diviner's haven. To be very frank, that was also when I beheld the queues for the first time and, believe me, Officer, it was an overwhelming sight. A frightening sight. The queues were all over Santamaria. My own offices were almost under siege. I slipped in through the back door, a special entrance."

"Let me see if I am getting this right. On that day, you were not ill?"

"I have told you that I had just then come from the doctor."

"The witch doctor?"

"The diviner."

"Let's not quibble over a word. What I want to know is this. You were then completely free of your illness?"

"I assure you that I was completely cured. I never felt better in my life."

"So now, Mr. Tajirika, why did you then stop going to the office even after you were cured? Or did your heart troubles start up again at the sight of all those queues?"

"You said I should speak the truth, the whole truth, and nothing but the truth, so help me God."

"*And the truth shall make you free.* Is that not what the Bible says?"

"But you said that I was not in custody."

"It is just a way of talking. Tell the truth and shame the Devil."

"You see, after I had managed to sneak into my office, I telephoned Machokali."

"The minister?"

"There is only one Machokali in the country, and he is my friend."

"I just want to make sure. We policemen are like doctors. Modern doctors, not your witch doctors or diviners as you call them. A good modern doctor makes sure that he knows all the facts about a malady. For only then can he prescribe the correct drug. We police detectives are truth diggers, and we like to base our case on facts. So do I take it that when you mention Machokali, you are talking about Machokali, the one and only Minister for Foreign Affairs in the government of the Ruler of Aburĩria?"

"That's right. I was calling him to ask him whether he could arrange for armed forces to come and disperse the crowd."

"That's strange. Had the minister ever told you that he had powers to call on the army to do this or that?"

"I thought that as a minister he would know whom to contact."

"Tell me, Mr. Tajirika, had the minister ever told you that he knew of any person or groups of persons other than the Ruler who thought that they had the power to authorize actions by the army?"

"*Oh, no, no, no. Nothing of the sort.* But what he told me made me look at the queues in a very different light."

"What did he tell you?"

"He told me that those queues were very important."

"Important?"

"Yes, because the queues served to show that the people fully supported the Marching to Heaven project. The queues were demonstrations of support."

"*Go on*. What else?"

"As a matter of fact, it was the minister who advised me not to go back to work, that I should stay at home as if I were still ill . . ."

"Pretend that you were ill? But why?"

"So that the queuers would not disperse after their job-hunting needs were settled one way or another. As long as they waited for me, they had some hope and hope would keep the queues alive."

"So what he told you is that you should lie and say that you were still ill even though you had never felt better in your life?"

"No, not the way you are putting it. He just wanted the queues to remain in place for as long as the Global Bank mission was in the country and not disperse before the dedication of the site for Marching to Heaven."

"Okay. Let's see. You are in this grip of a false illness. You have agreed to stay home to recover. Who was looking after your business?"

"Vinjinia, my wife, became the acting manager, with the . . . the . . . you know . . . the secretary as her assistant. A helper."

"You mean Nyawīra?"

"The same."

"And because Vinjinia was not very experienced, it was really Nyawīra who was entrusted with managing your affairs, is that not so?"

"Yes, Nyawīra had more experience, but she was definitely not in charge. She was a minion."

"Demoted? You know how women are: they are jealous of one another. Some women are not satisfied unless they are the only woman in a male domain. The One Woman syndrome."

"No, she was not demoted and there was no jealousy. To make her happy and ensure continued loyal service in my absence, I had given her the quite meaningless title of assistant to the acting manager. But she was nothing but a glorified receptionist."

"Machokali . . . were he and Nyawīra acquainted?"

"No, I don't think so."

"But Machokali used to call you at your office?"

"Yes."

"And all his calls went through the receptionist."

"Sometimes. But he also called me direct. I would say most times."

"Did Machokali ever visit you in your office?"

"Yes, but not often. Only when passing through this side of Santamaria. Eldares is a big city, you know. Several towns in one, if you ask me."

"And so if Machokali and Nyawĩra had made private arrangements to meet elsewhere in this city, which, as you say, contains multitudes, you would not know, would you?"

"That is right, but I somehow don't think they ever met outside my office."

"But if they did, you would not know?"

"That's right."

"When was Machokali's last visit to Santamaria?"

Tajirika hesitated. He could not remember whether their last encounter was supposed to be a secret or not. But he decided to err on the side of truth. Besides, deep down he did not mind showing this police officer that he, Tajirika, was well connected, that Machokali was his friend.

"He came to see me just before he and the Ruler left for the USA."

"He came to the office?"

"No. We met at the Mars Café."

"So he did not come to the office to say good-bye to Nyawĩra?"

"I think that Nyawĩra had fled by then."

"But you have already admitted that if they had made secret plans to meet, you would not know?"

"I really and honestly don't think they met."

"How can you be so sure? Did you know where Nyawĩra was then hiding?"

"No."

"And you were not with the minister all the time, everywhere?"

"No."

"No to what?"

"To the suggestion that I might have been with the minister the whole day. We met at the Mars Café, and after our talk he left me there."

"So all that you can say is that you never saw them meet?"

"Yes, but that does not mean that I believe that they did," Tajirika continued assertively, sensing a trap.

"But you cannot swear in a court of law that they never met on that or any other day?"

"That I cannot swear," Tajirika hastened to say, alarmed at the mention of a law court.

"What was the purpose of his visit? Why did he want to meet with you?"

"He came to say good-bye. *We are friends.*"

"Nothing else?"

"Nothing."

"Let's go back to your illness. You say that you were taken to a witch doctor for a cure. Who took you there?"

"My wife, Vinjinia."

"How did she come to know of the witch doctor?"

"The secretary told her about him."

"Nyawīra?"

"Yes. Nyawīra."

"So in everything, be it your business or personal and family matters, this Nyawīra was somewhere in the background? A chief personal and family adviser?"

"Please spare me the name. Were I, with all that I now know, to catch that Nyawīra woman, I . . ."

". . . would wring her neck until she was dead," Elijah Njoya finished the sentence as if echoing him in mockery. "I know exactly what you would do powered with hindsight, and I commend you for it. Now, Mr. Tajirika, let's be serious. I want to assure you that you have been very helpful and that if you continue cooperating with us you will see a change in your circumstances. The only thing I would warn you against are lies. *Remember? Only the truth shall make you free.* Are you sure that you have told me everything?"

"*I have told you all the truth I know.*"

"There is nothing you are holding back, a little detail, anything?"

"Nothing."

"And by the way, what is the name of the sorcerer who cured you?"

The question caught him unawares. He was about to say the name, Wizard of the Crow, when the implications of revealing it suddenly struck him. Money. The three bags of money. What if the diviner revealed the existence of the three bags of Burī notes and, worst of all, that they were "visiting cards" from those who hoped for later gains from Marching to Heaven? The last thing Tajirika wanted anybody else to know was that he had already pocketed money from a scheme involving the Ruler. The three bags of Burī notes must remain a secret buried forever in the innermost recesses of his head.

"I don't know his name."

"Are you sure? You don't know the sorcerer's name?"

"A diviner is simply known as Diviner. I am not alone in this. Many who visit these healers don't bother to remember their names. A diviner is not exactly someone you would have over for a party or a tête-à-tête in your office."

Njoya laughed at this.

"You have a sense of humor, Tajirika."

"Thank you, Mr. Officer . . ."

"Call me Elijah. Your friend."

"Elijah, my friend," said Tajirika. "Can I go now?"

"Why not? Let me see about your *transportation. Good luck,* Mr. Tajirika."

At first Tajirika felt a sudden depression at being left alone. But as he reviewed the encounter, he felt relief and even triumph as he realized that not only had he deftly thwarted all attempts to link him to Nyawīra, the queuing mania, and Machokali's supposed plots, he had also avoided telling details of his illness, had gotten away with lying about the name of the Wizard of the Crow, and, most important, had not revealed anything about the three bags of money. Besides, he had won Njoya over and turned him into a friend and by tomorrow he would be lying in his own bed in Golden Heights.

# 18

But his new friend Njoya did not come back that night or the next or any other, for that matter, until Tajirika stopped trying to measure the passage of time. And then one day they came for him and blinded him as before, and when later they removed the blindfold he found himself seated in the lone chair in an otherwise empty room, amid a circle of light. All else was darkness. At the edges of the circle of light he saw what looked like traces of fresh and dried blood, confirming his worst fears. They were going to do to him what they had done to countless others, whose blood on the cement floor attested to their menace. He got up and wandered into the darkness in a daze. The spotlight followed him, and out of still more darkness came a voice.

"Who told you to get up?"

"Who are you?" Tajirika asked in terror, stopping dead in his tracks.

"I am Superintendent Kahiga, Peter Kahiga."

"Where is Njoya, Superintendent Njoya? He promised me . . . What happened to my transportation?"

"That all depends on your answers to my questions."

"I have already told you all that I know. What have I left unsaid?"

"Only you can tell us. And I want you to know that I am hardly as understanding as Njoya. I am not easily swayed by tears. I am as hard as a rock. If you fool around, your feet will soon be hanging from the roof."

"What do you want from me?" Tajirika asked, getting an eerie feeling as he addressed the disembodied voice.

"Back in your chair," the voice demanded.

Engulfed by light, Tajirika did as he was told.

"Answer all my questions, even the least. Why did you really go to the witch doctor?"

"You mean the diviner? I told Njoya that I had gone there because I was ill."

"How would you say you felt after he healed you?"

"At peace. Happy."

"So you were elated by the person who healed you?"

"Would you be sad after being healed?"

"I ask the questions around here, do you understand?"

"Yes."

"And, now, Tajirika, having been healed so well that you felt so good, so peaceful, so happy, were you not even mildly curious about the person who had wrought such wonders? Not curious enough at least to learn his name?"

Tajirika felt pushed into a tight corner. He had lied about not knowing the name of the man who had healed him for what he then thought were good reasons. But now he started questioning the wisdom of his lies. It seemed as if the unseen Kahiga knew something about the diviner. Had his wife, under threat of torture, told about the money? No matter what, Tajirika would stick to his story.

"I just forgot his name. Everybody forgets things sometimes."

He had not expected the blow, and so when it came, a full and forceful slap across his face, Tajirika saw a thousand stars in the darkness of his mind. His instinct, when the dizziness subsided, was to rise and fight, but how do you fight a shadow in the dark? He felt tears of rage and frustration streaming down his face.

"Why did you hit me? I have not refused to answer any of your questions!"

"I told you that my name is Peter Kahiga, not Elijah Njoya. Come clean with me. I'm not here to play word games."

"I have nothing to hide."

"And you still claim not to remember the name of your witch doctor?"

"No. Forgetfulness is not a crime."

"I will bring you friends to help jump-start your memory . . ."

Even as Kahiga was completing his sentence, Tajirika felt presences behind him, but before he could turn around two of the men grabbed him by the shoulders and the neck and pinned him against the back of the chair. The third yanked Tajirika's hand behind him while a fourth stuck a needle under the nail of his index finger. Tajirika struggled, but pointlessly.

"I beg you, stop. I'll try to remember. What do you want to know?" he asked the men in the shadows.

"How many times must I repeat myself?" the voice in the dark asked. "We want to know everything about the witch doctor, or whatever you choose to call him. I mean everything, every word he said to you, the number of times you met, even the clothes he wore."

"Then ask your men to take their hands off me," he said.

"What men?" Kahiga asked. "No one is touching you. Are you hallucinating?"

Tajirika was able to move his hands freely. He quickly turned his head around and saw no one. Am I out of my mind? Or are they playing mind tricks?

"Where are the men who were just here?" Tajirika asked.

"They have gone back whence they came, but they will surely return if you don't stop asking questions. Now about the witch doctor . . ."

"I met him only once. The clothes he wore, I cannot remember, but I think, well, I only saw his face."

"And his name?"

They were definitely on to something, he sensed: there was no point in claiming loss of memory anymore.

"The Wizard of the Crow. That is his name."

"And why didn't you say so earlier?"

"The effects of aging. As you get older, memory weakens."

"Is there anything else about the Wizard of the Crow that you want to tell me? Aside from your cure, what else did you two talk about? Did he mention Nyawīra or Machokali or anybody like that? Have you been to see him since he came back to Eldares from wherever he went?"

Tajirika did not know what they knew and didn't, especially about the three bags of money. Should he continue to hold back? How could he account for the witch doctor's possession of his money? He could see where they were headed. If he could give the witch doctor three bags of Burī notes, surely he must have hundreds of them hidden in his house or at his farm. Upon not finding the money they might kill him out of frustration anyway. So Tajirika decided to hang tough. He now knew what to say.

"To tell the truth, I have not met with this Wizard of the Crow since the day he healed me. I did not even know that he had left Eldares and come back. But there was one other thing that he and I discussed, and you can understand that the subject is a little embarrassing since it has to do with property. Just before I left the shrine I asked him to arm me with protective magic so that my property would not be blown away by the wind and my life would meet with no harm from my enemies. In short, I asked and got protective magic against harm to my life and property."

An awkward silence followed this disclosure. Despite the fact that he could not see Peter Kahiga, Tajirika felt that what he had said about magic had had some effect on his inquisitor, whose next question was not about the Wizard of the Crow.

"Now, what about Machokali? Know this: if you lie to me again, there is no magic in the world that can protect you from my wrath. *Now*, why did Machokali come to see you in Santamaria?"

"To say good-bye. Isn't that what I told Njoya?"

"Stop answering me with questions. Tell us what took place between you two, word for word. And don't take this matter lightly."

Tajirika told the story of his meeting with Machokali at the Mars Café, mentioning that the minister was curious about the kind of questions Vinjinia had been asked when she was in custody.

"Why did he want to know that?"

"I don't know. He did not say. And I did not ask him."

"What did you tell him?"

"Just what Vinjinia herself told me: that the questions were mostly about Nyawīra."

"How did he react when you mentioned Nyawīra?"

"He said that she was the biggest enemy of the State and if one is asked any questions about her one should tell all one knows."

"That's all?"

"Yes. I don't think he was particularly interested in talking about Nyawīra. He just wanted to see her in custody. I remember him consoling me and telling me that I should not worry myself to death over the fact that I had employed her. The sins of the employed cannot be visited upon the employer. Or something to that effect."

"So when he saw you show concern and remorse over the fact that you had engaged the services of a traitor, he, the minister, was telling you not to worry?"

"Not in the way you're putting it. He consoled me because he saw that I was badly shaken by the discovery of Nyawīra's true identity."

"He himself did not show any anxiety over the matter? He was quite calm even though he knew that a traitor had eluded the police?"

"No, he did not seem anxious about her."

"He did not show any anger at Nyawīra's treachery?"

"It is not as if we talked about Nyawīra all the time."

"What else did you talk about, then?"

Tajirika said, among other things, that Machokali did let him know that Kaniūrū was going to be deputy of Marching to Heaven.

"And what did you feel when you heard that?"

"I was quite happy to get a clerk to help me with my work."

"Was it Machokali who told you that Kaniũrũ was going to be a clerk?"

"I assumed as much."

"Why?"

"What is a deputy, after all? Is he not the person who keeps the seat warm for the man in charge when he is not around?"

"How many times must I tell you not to answer me with questions? I'm warning you. That you took him to be a clerk, might this be the real reason why you refused to obey the summons issued to you by the chairman of the Commission of Inquiry into the Queuing Mania? You dared to look down upon a person who had been appointed to his post by the Ruler? Or were you afraid of appearing before the commission?"

"No, I had nothing to hide."

"Didn't you say the same thing in the previous interview? And yet as it turned out to be the case today you had left out quite a lot about the Wizard of the Crow?"

"That's correct, but now I am telling the whole truth and nothing but the truth so help me God."

"How am I supposed to know that? If you were not afraid of appearing before the commission, then the only reason you did not appear was because you disrespected its chairman, the Ruler's choice!"

"No, no," Tajirika said, alarmed at this accusation. "Ask Machokali himself—he will tell you that far from feeling bad about the appointment of a deputy, I saw his help as enabling me to suggest that perhaps I should be a member of the delegation going to the USA. It was Machokali who didn't think this was a good idea."

"Why?"

"I cannot recall exactly the reasons he gave, but he did talk about my being his ears and eyes here while he was away."

"Did he actually talk about ears and eyes? Are you sure?"

"I am sure he mentioned those organs."

"What did he mean? Have you ever heard of M5?"

"Yes, His Mighty's eyes, ears, noses, legs, and hands?"

"So he wanted to form his own M5?"

"I don't think he meant it that way."

"Why? Could you read his mind?"

"No."

"Then why are you defending him?"

"I am not trying to defend him . . ."

"Are you sure that he did not leave you behind to organize a network of eyes, ears, noses, legs, and hands to rival that of the Ruler?"

"I am sure."

"Is that all you talked about?"

"That's all."

"Are you sure?"

"I am very sure."

"Where did he park his car?"

"He did not come in his car."

"What do you mean? He came on foot? Or in a bus, donkey cart, rickshaw, matatu, mbondambonda, or mkokoteni?"

"I believe he came and left by taxi."

"Tajirika, do you take the government for a fool? Do you want to tell us that the Minister for Foreign Affairs, busy as he was preparing for the American trip, still found the time to come to you just to say good-bye, to hear about the kind of questions that Vinjinia had been asked while she was in custody, and to inform you about Kaniūrū's appointment as your deputy? Is that a plausible story? About Vinjinia, he could easily have found out by simply looking at the files on her. To say good-bye and tell you about your deputy, he could easily have done so by phone. And why did he come in a taxi instead of a Mercedes-Benz? You had better confess the details of the plan to overthrow the legitimate government of the Ruler."

"Me? Talking about overthrowing the government of the Ruler? Never. At no time then or ever did Machokali and I discuss any such thing . . ."

"You will tell us everything. The mouth that told us more about the Wizard of the Crow will now tell us about the anti-government plans that you and your friend were hatching at the Mars Café."

No sooner had these words been uttered than the circle of light disappeared and Tajirika was dragged into the darkness. They tortured him day and night, with needles and whips, drowning, and electric shocks. Each act of torture was accompanied by a fusillade of questions about the impending coup d'état he and Machokali had planned, but Tajirika refused to acquiesce, screaming only what he had already told them: "That was the last I saw of Machokali. He has not once called me from America . . ."

He cried, "Please, I beg you, don't torture me for things I never said or did," and yet, deep inside, he felt good that he had not said a word about the three money bags and had resisted their attempts to make him say that Machokali had been plotting against the Ruler.

Still, it went on day and night, torture by unseen hands, until Tajirika finally collapsed, unconscious.

# 19

He woke up to find himself in bed on a soft mattress and pillow, under clean white sheets and a blanket. Daylight streamed through a window. He could not believe his eyes. He got out of bed, pain shooting through his knees, and hobbled toward the window and tried to open it. His fingers smarted and he could not get a firm grip, but eventually the window swung open inward. Looking through the wire mesh, he saw the walls of other buildings across the yard. He surveyed his new room. At one corner was a sink and next to it a shower and toilet. He felt a need to relieve himself and soon after, he felt his body lighten. No, he cannot have been dead. Next he stripped, piling his clothes on the floor, and showered with avid resolution. He was about to put on what he had been wearing when he saw in another corner a table with two chairs. On one of the chairs there was a suit, to his amazement. He tried it on. It belonged to him but, emaciated as he was from being tortured, it was now a size or so too large. What was going on? His eyes drifted to the door. Maybe it was open. Maybe he would be released secretly. Was the Ruler back? Had fear of what his friend Machokali would do to his torturers sent them packing?

As he reached the door, it opened as if by itself. Tajirika did not know whether to shout for joy or to scream in anger when Njoya entered and carefully closed it behind him.

"So you found your clothes?" Njoya said, as if responding to the perplexity on Tajirika's face. "Your wife, Vinjinia, sent them. Did you ask her to send them?"

"No," Tajirika said curtly.

"Ah, well, women and clothes! I am so sorry, Mr. Tajirika. I know I should have come back earlier—a man must keep his word, you know—but every time I asked about you they told me that you were fast asleep."

*"What do you mean?"* Tajirika asked in English. "No one told you what they have done to me? Even the donkeys of Santamaria market are treated with less cruelty."

*"Is that so, now? Take it easy.* Let's sit down and you tell me all about it. But have you had a bite this morning? Some breakfast?" Two men entered bearing eggs, bread and sausages, and a steaming teapot, placed everything on the table, and left the room. Tajirika was overcome by hunger, and Njoya noticed how Tajirika's hostility was abated by the food.

"My nails hurt. My knees are aflame from the beatings," Tajirika complained, wiping sweat from his brow with the back of his right hand. "And you claim not to know anything about it?"

"You don't always know what your subordinates are up to, even in your absence, do you? You yourself told me that you didn't know that Nyawīra . . ."

"Is Kahiga your subordinate?" Tajirika asked quickly to deflect the talk from Nyawīra.

"Superintendent Kahiga? *Oh, dear,* he is the one they sent to you? May I let you in on a secret? That officer? He is crazy. He has killed many in the course of his interrogations. And you know what? The matter ends there. Tajirika, I want to help you and get him off your back. But if I am to help you, you must level with me. I must also level with you. Let's say, we must level with each other. Let me start. Look at the far corner. What do you see?"

"Nothing unusual," Tajirika said.

"Look very carefully."

"Ah, yes."

"It's the eye of a camera, a video camera. Everything that takes place between us will be captured on film. I don't want you to leave here claiming that I too have tortured you. If there is anything you want to say off the record, let me know right away and we can go elsewhere to talk. Mr. Tajirika, should we leave the room?"

"That won't be necessary. I have nothing to hide," Tajirika said promptly, for he did not want to imply by word or gesture that he had any secrets left.

"As I said, let's first ignore Kahiga's deeds or misdeeds. They shall be investigated; I will make sure of that. I want us to revisit our first interview. Did I torture you?"

"Oh, no, no, you and I shall become friends."

"You promise?"

"Yes!"

"I just want you to clear something up for me, just one thing. It is a puzzle, and it concerns your illness. I want to paint a scenario with words, and I really want you to weigh the matter carefully, the better to appreciate the problem we have in believing your story. You are now the judge. Here are the facts of the case. Early one morning the radio announces that a Mr. Tajirika has been appointed chairman of Marching to Heaven. This is a rare honor. The same evening, Mr. Tajirika falls ill. The following morning queues start forming outside his office. After a while, call it a week or two, Tajirika is hale and hearty, the picture of perfect health. But instead of Tajirika resuming his business, he is told to resume his illness, and he does so. You will agree with me that a reasonable person would not be wrong were he to conclude that this illness was like a hat that can be put on and off at will. Now comes a time when all the queues that had formed outside Tajirika's office head toward the site of Marching to Heaven. And lo and behold, the same Tajirika is once again hale and hearty and he readily joins the flow of humanity to the ceremonies. After the ceremonies, he resumes work. An unbiased observer cannot be blamed if he were to wonder: Why did Tajirika become well only after the queues had accomplished their intended goal? And the goal? Not a soul in all Aburῑria is unaware of the shameful deeds of those women. And note an even more curious fact. Nyawῑra, who had put up a billboard precisely where the queues began, turns out to be one of those performing the acts of shame. And she is Tajirika's trusted secretary. As for your bizarre illness," Njoya said, as if addressing not a judge but a culprit, "let's say I believe that you had a heart attack or what you described as heart trouble. Mr. Tajirika, explain this to me: instead of getting yourself admitted to a private or state hospital, you chose to head straight to the shrine of a witch doctor? Even assuming that you have no faith in modern Aburῑrian medicine, you had the option, which by the way you didn't even consider, of flying to London. If the famed Harley Street surgeons can give your friend

Machokali a completely new set of eyes, enlarged and probably fitted with night vision, why were they not good enough for you? These are the facts of the case. You are the judge. What is your judgment?"

"My friend," Tajirika said, assuming, without realizing it, the tone of a jurist. "I quite see the logic of your suspicions, but I can speak only the truth, even if it clashes with logic. For just as you told me, only truth, the whole truth, and nothing else but the truth will remove all doubts from your mind and set me free. Some things are hard to talk about because, as I told you the last time we went over this, these things, even diseases, are embarrassing to the one who is talking about them. When gonorrhea and syphilis were deadly menaces, people suffering from them were often described as having fallen victim to a severe strand of flu. It is the same today with the virus of death. Every victim of the virus is said to have died of a kidney problem. My illness was not quite of the heart . . . I mean, it was really an illness without a name."

"Please, Mr. Tajirika, stop joking. In our first interview you freely told me of your heart condition."

"My illness is without a proper noun."

"An illness without a proper noun?"

"Diseases do not knock at the door and say, I'm so-and-so, please let me in; they force their way, more like a coup d'état. Look, soldiers are coming for you, and . . ."

Njoya did not wait to hear the rest but bolted and started banging the door furiously. Two wardens came in with guns raised. For a moment Njoya thought that these two were part of the coup and tried to tell them that he was on their side, but no words would come out. The wardens clamped handcuffs on Tajirika, dragged him back to the chair, and trained their rifles on him. Njoya realized his mistake and signaled the wardens to leave, muttering a lame excuse: Just testing your readiness and you have passed with flying colors.

*"What's wrong with you?"* Njoya asked as he turned toward the handcuffed Tajirika. *"This is serious business."*

"But what's the matter?" a perplexed Tajirika asked.

"I asked you a simple question and you answer me with 'coup d'état' and soldier nonsense . . ."

"You presented me with a scenario," Tajirika explained, "so I responded by drawing you a picture to show how such an attack can so overwhelm a person that he loses speech and gets stuck with a tiny word like . . ."

"So you were not thinking of a real coup d'état?"

"Me, think of a coup d'état?" Tajirika said, and felt like laughing at the absurdity.

"Stop drawing pictures and tell me about the illness."

Tajirika haltingly began to recount his sorry state preceding his visit to the wizard, still mindful of what he chose to reveal. So he explained how seekers of future contracts had come to his office soon after his elevation to lead Marching to Heaven and how each person would leave a little something in an envelope, a few coins, perhaps, to suggest that the project promised future riches. He thought no more of the coins until he went home and he too started thinking about the wealth untold to be generated by Marching to Heaven. "The coins left in the envelope were nothing much, only tokens of appreciation, but they obviously triggered something in my mind that made me start imagining ever-increasing wealth. The worst was yet to come. For I soon imagined people being envious of me, crowds of the envious coming at me from every direction. I ran and locked myself in the bathroom. And still they came, wanting to tear the skin off my face. Imagine a man without a face. Haunted as I was by my wish to be unimaginably rich, I lost my ability to express myself through words. My body truly staged a coup against me. Imagine thought without words, what a curse! In the end, all the thoughts, all my feelings and emotions, were bodied forth by the word *if*."

Tajirika stopped abruptly and looked about him as if he did not quite know where he was; then he snapped back to awareness of the cell and Njoya, his inquisitor.

"And what steps did your witch doctor take to stop you from barking the word?"

"He showed me that the *if*ness had resulted from my longing to be white. Officer, I wished to become a white man. It was a severe case of white-ache."

Njoya burst out laughing, holding his belly while pointing at Tajirika.

"You? You? A white man? A white European? With those lips, that kinky hair, and that skin? And that pouch? So, how did he bring about a cure?"

"He showed me that I would end up a poor white and somehow this did it. I believe that my white-ache is now in total remission," Tajirika hastened to add, a little offended by Njoya's derisive laughter.

"Well, it's a good thing that you've been cured," Njoya said. He coughed a bit, then cleared his throat. He was now serious, businesslike again. "Mr. Tajirika, you have really helped to clarify some things: I will do my best on your behalf on your assurance that you have told me everything. Now I must take leave of you."

And saying so, he stood up and started for the door.

"Am I now *free* to go?" Tajirika shouted the question after him.

"Not just yet," Njoya said, stopping near the door. "I will show the footage of our conversation to my superiors, and I hope they will see what I myself saw: that you did open a little window into your soul . . ."

Tajirika was a little down, but impressed by his cleverness in dealing with the issue of the money. He had given an inch for a yard. Were the Wizard of the Crow to mention the money, Njoya and company would think that he was referring only to a few inconsequential coins. And of course he had conceded nothing to the allegations of a Machokali plot and would never do so. But soon he was weighed down by grief and self-pity. Why had the interrogation been recorded? He felt his knees weaken; he held on to the bed to avoid falling. Would he survive this ordeal? he wondered anew.

# SECTION II

# 1

When you, research scientists and historians of this country, come to write about this era we hope you will not overlook the role played by the Tajirika video confession, not so much for its content but for how it was taken by Sikiokuu and Kaniũrũ. Timing can also affect the course of history and the destiny of nations, and the time of its release may have been an even more significant factor in the video's influence.

Sikiokuu, as it turned out, got his copy soon after he had already received a call from the Ruler's camp that the delegation would be returning any day now, certainly not the most welcome of news. Like a mosquito in the dark, the Ruler's unequivocal order that by the time he came back from America he should find Nyawĩra in custody, kept on z-zinging in Sikiokuu's ear. Nyawĩra's capture had always been a priority, but now, after the call, the z-zinging intensified: she must be taken into custody. While waiting for the video, and now as he was about to play it, he thought of nothing but her. Was she in the country or not, dead or alive? The undercover agents engaged to comb the entire country had not brought news that was even remotely useful, and it was with some justification that he felt that he had turned over as many stones in the land as he could. Was there a stone left unturned? he now wondered.

Yes, perhaps the *video*. Sikiokuu, who had found the results of Njoya's and Kahiga's interrogations unsatisfactory, had himself ordered the video interview and had hoped that by examining it himself he would be able to detect in Tajirika's words, tone, and body language significant leads to Nyawĩra's lair. After all, Tajirika had been her employer, and Sikiokuu did not believe his denials that he had nothing to do with her. As soon as his copy arrived he gave strict instructions that on no account must he be disturbed. He locked himself in his office and tied his long ears behind him so that their shadow would not interfere with his study of Tajirika's every gesture and facial expression.

Sikiokuu was not known for his humor. Few people had ever seen him laugh or even smile, except sarcastically, but the image of Tajirika as a white man made Sikiokuu suddenly laugh, just as Njoya before him, and he continued laughing till his ears fell loose and his ribs ached. Tajirika, a white man?

After the entire video, his laughter ceased, replaced by anger and frustration expressed in *Useless! Nothing in this about Nyawīra!* He was about to throw the cassette into the dustbin when he was struck by indecision. He leaned back in the chair, closed his eyes, and replayed it in his mind, frame by frame.

Even as he reviewed it through his mind's eye, there was much that was still unclear, but what now impressed him as odd in the narrative was not only Tajirika's claim that words had gotten stuck in his throat but his use of the word *coup* to describe his illness. Had he slipped up in some way, a Freudian slip? This suspicion triggered a host of questions, including: why did Tajirika get well only after learning that his destiny as a white man was abject poverty? Sikiokuu experienced a burst of clarity, opened his eyes, placed the cassette on the table, and started whistling and stroking his earlobes. All along, he now concluded, Tajirika's use of the word *white* had been a code for *power*. Tajirika had longed for Whiteness as Power and must have hoped to get it by force of arms, for how else in Aburīria could one attain power? But Tajirika did not look to be the type who initiated things; he was more a follower than a leader. His longing must have been set in motion by the plans either he and Machokali had hatched or that he had heard others talk about. The latter was more likely, for just as there are those who can only repeat what has been spoken by others, there are those who can only recycle the thoughts of others. That would explain why the words had gotten stuck in his throat. The thought had not originated with him, and he had either forgotten or jumbled it. And since Tajirika was as unlikely ever to hold power as he was to be white, the longing must have appeared impossible, hence the *if*s. Moreover, even the dumbest Aburīrian knew that dreaming about, wishing, or imagining the death of the leader under any circumstance was an act of treason punishable by death. That explained not only why the man's thoughts refused to express themselves through words but also why, when eventually forced to do so by whatever tricks the witch doctor had used, the actual desire for power came out coded as a desire to be white.

Sikiokuu stood and proceeded to prance about his office, and even when he stopped jumping up and down, he trembled from excitement that things were looking up for him. The capture of Nyawīra was no longer a matter of life and death. If he could simply prove that there were plans to overthrow the government, that in itself would be a great triumph. With that one stone he could kill two huge birds: take attention away from his failure to capture Nyawīra and also get at his political archrival, the big-eyed Minister for Foreign Affairs. But Sikiokuu knew that he needed more than his surmises and inferences. He needed proof, to be gotten from only one person: Tajirika. Sikiokuu had to find a way of persuading Tajirika, through words, physical coercion, or both, to join his side and testify against his friend Machokali. And he could do so only by confronting Tajirika with the reality of what he, Sikiokuu, supposed.

He took the video, kissed it, and put it in a safe place. He did not reflect further. There was no time for delay; he sent for Tajirika.

"Your life is entirely in your hands," Sikiokuu told him.

# 2

The impact of the video on Kaniūrū was different; he dwelled on Tajirika's talk of symbolic Burī coins in the envelopes as an omen of wealth to come. Kaniūrū knew from his own experience as deputy chairman that Tajirika was lying about the amount of money in the envelopes. Not a day had passed since taking up his duties as the deputy of Marching to Heaven that Kaniūrū himself had not filled up one or two bags with these envelopes of introduction. How much more must the boss have gotten prior to his own bounty?

But, like Tajirika before him, Kaniūrū would not and had never uttered a word about this to his friend and benefactor Sikiokuu. So although he knew very well that Tajirika was lying about the money, Kaniūrū also knew that he himself would never raise this aspect of Tajirika's confession to anybody, for doing so would mean revealing his own sources of sudden wealth. Kaniūrū also knew that Tajirika must know that he, Kaniūrū, was receiving money, and there was a moment when viewing the video that he panicked, fearing that Tajirika might have told on him. But when he came to the end of the video and heard nothing more about the money, Kaniūrū took self-satisfied comfort in the fact that Tajirika had lied about the matter. There was a tacit pact between them about disclosing personal gains from Marching to Heaven, and in this Kaniūrū trusted his nemesis. Anything else would have been a recipe for mutually assured destruction. In the matter of money gained from Marching to Heaven, he and Tajirika were on the same side.

The only other person who knew of Kaniūrū's wealth was Jane Kanyori. She had taken some courses in accounting at the Eldares Polytechnic, where Kaniūrū used to teach, but their acquaintance came later, at her workplace as a teller in the Aburīrian Bank of Commerce and Industry. Kaniūrū kept an eye on her as she rose in her job, not in adoration but in reference to the future. He courted her with uncharacteristic patience, taking her out to lunch or coffee and even sending her Christmas and birthday cards. Kaniūrū liked the fact that Jane Kanyori was only a secondary school graduate who showed no interest in university education and seemed completely innocent of Nyawīra's women's lib nonsense.

When he learned that she was promoted yet again to senior sales representative and could access duplicates of coded signatures and could okay checks, Kaniūrū acquainted her with his needs. Kanyori would not countenance any vulgar misuse of her access to the bank secrets, but she could help by not asking too many questions about the signatures of anybody in whose name he wanted to open an account.

Though satisfied with Kanyori's help and loyalty, he remained worried. The greater the flow of Burī notes his way, the more he became anxious about this bubble of good fortune bursting, his wealth disappearing into thin air. His anxiety made him toss and turn in bed for entire nights; he needed something more secure than bank vaults and the accounting schemes of a loyal friend.

The mention of symbolic coins made him recall that, in the pre-video interrogations by Peter Kahiga, Tajirika had also talked of bene-fiting from protective magic. He had dismissed this as one more example of Tajirika's stupidity. But now "protective magic" was as cool water to a thirsty person; he felt a touch of gratitude toward Tajirika. Why had he not thought of this before? Should he not seek a bit of protective magic for his person and property to augment Jane Kanyori's aid?

And so he thought of the Wizard of the Crow: Kaniũrũ might not have been a deep believer in magic, but cautionary measures, hardly expressions of cowardice, had to be taken, and he made his way to the wizard's shrine.

# 3

"My life is in my hands?" Tajirika asked defiantly. "Did I arrest myself, put myself in handcuffs, and drag myself to the dungeon?"

Sikiokuu's personal reception area was a veritable living room, with settees and plastic flowers in a vase placed on a low coffee table. Generous curtains and a liquor cabinet completed the décor.

The minister exuded unbridled self-confidence in the way he walked, sat, and gestured, stroking his earlobes or rolling his tiny eyes. For a moment Tajirika feared that something was up with the government. Had a coup d'état taken place? Was Sikiokuu the man in absolute charge?

Sikiokuu did not respond immediately but first poured his guest a little brandy, handing him cigarettes and a lighter as well. Tajirika grabbed everything offered as if he feared Sikiokuu might change his mind. He had not had a drink or a cigarette in a long while.

"You are quite right. You are not under self-arrest," Sikiokuu told him. "But there is a reason for your being here. I am sure that Intelligence would not have detained a person of your stature without proper cause. What did the Waswahili say? *Dark clouds herald rain*, or, more appropriately, *where there is smoke there must be fire.*"

"So where is the smoke that led them to me?"

"Nyawĩra."

"Has she been captured?"

"State secrets," Sikiokuu said vaguely.

"Hear me out, Mr. Sikiokuu. If she is under arrest, I am glad. Then I can confront her and refute anything she may allege against me. You have employed workers, I am sure. Can you honestly say that you know where and with whom they sleep every night? Or what's going on in their heads?"

"Mr. Tajirika, the M5 have relative autonomy; they reign over us. They gather information about us all, at work or play. They bring us information, but we don't know how much they have kept to themselves. Obviously, we have to make decisions on the basis of that information. *Personally, I believe you,* Mr. Tajirika. And let me confide in you *as a friend.* Nyawĩra, your former secretary, has not yet been caught, but you can be sure that sooner or later she will be. She cannot outrun the State. So the good news for you is that she has not said anything against you. Still, you are in deep trouble."

"Why? What have I done wrong?"

"Keeping bad company. Showing poor judgment in your choice of employees and even friends in government. And what is more, being unable to control the company your wife keeps."

"Mr. Minister, *please* explain. Stop talking in riddles and proverbs. What do you mean, the company my wife keeps? I can tell you that Vinjinia is a true housewife. Her routine is very simple. She goes to the fields, to the market, and to the office in my absence and to church on Sunday."

"Is that what you think? They say that a husband is always the last to know."

"What are you implying, Mr. Minister?" Tajirika said, almost jumping from his seat.

"Sit down, Titus. This has nothing to do with her seeing other men. If that was all there was to it, I would not even mention it. In Aburĩria married women have become easy lays, but to be very frank I have never heard it said that your wife has even been found in a compromising situation."

"So what are you talking about, then?"

"Pictures. I have some photos here and I would like you to look at them and tell me what you know about them."

Female Daemons

Sikiokuu went to a drawer by the wall and came back with an
envelope, which he handed over to Tajirika. Tajirika took out a picture and looked at it long and hard. Then he quickly went through
the others, shaking his head from side to side. Then he began all over
again. No, his eyes were not lying to him; yet he still could not believe
what he saw.

The photos showed Vinjinia seated somewhere in the open in
front of a group of dancing women, all dressed in traditional garb.
Sikiokuu did not disclose that he had personally ordered these photos
taken on the day Vinjinia had confronted Sikiokuu outside Kaniūrū's
offices. The pictures were taken from different angles and in such a
way that Kaniūrū and Sikiokuu and the other dignitaries who were
present on the occasion were not in any of the scenes depicted. But
Vinjinia, either alone or with the dancing women, was in every one of
the ten pictures, and it appeared as if the women were dancing solely
for their guest of honor, Vinjinia.

Tajirika felt as if his tongue had been stuck. His lips opened and
closed without the utterance of a word. His hands were trembling.
He sat down and threw the pictures on the table. His lips still quiver-
ing, he looked at Sikiokuu, and said without conviction:

"I still don't believe it."

"What don't you believe? That she is your wife? Or those are not
her photos? Or that these are not the kind of women who brought
shame to the site of Marching to Heaven?"

"I don't believe that Vinjinia would do this to me."

"Maybe you'll be kind enough to explain a thing or two. The security men tell me that all along you have denied any knowledge of the
women who did the deed. They say that not only have you denied personal knowledge but you have issued denials on behalf of your wife.
And *yet* you did admit that when you were ill, Nyawīra and your wife
ran the business, the very twosome who took you to the wizard. How
do you know that they were interested in healing you? How do you
know that their purpose was not to confuse your mind with a magic
potion? And even if you believe in their innocence and good intentions, can you say the same for the sorcerer? Can you be sure that he
did not bear you some kind of grudge, and now saw his chance,
deceiving the women? And you know how gullible women are."

"Please stop. I beg you man to man, please let me go home this
very minute and deal with this treacherous woman."

347

"Titus, you know that if it were up to me you could go home whenever you wished. But as we're dealing with matters of state security, my personal feelings count for naught when it comes to assessing the gravity of a situation. We deal simply with facts. I'm sure, Titus, that if you were in my position you'd understand. So let's look at the facts as they will be presented to the Ruler when he returns. You employed Nyawira. The queues started outside your offices and at the very spot where the night before this Nyawira had planted a billboard. Here are photos of Vinjinia, your own wife, being entertained by dancing women in traditional wear. Titus, let me be very frank with you. How do you propose to disentangle yourself from this mess? That's why I called you here, to let you know the gravity of your situation so that you and I can put our heads together and see what can be done to extricate you from the tangle."

Tajirika felt as if he were going crazy. He tried to support his head in cupped hands, then leaned back against the chair and stared at the ceiling.

One indisputable fact had clearly emerged from the conversation: there had been no change in government, the Ruler was still the leader, and that meant that his friend Markus Machokali, the Minister for Foreign Affairs, still held his powerful post. Tajirika somehow seized on this to buoy his spirits.

"Mr. Minister," Tajirika started in a contrite tone. "I know that you and I cannot be said to be the best of drinking friends. But please believe me when I say that I would never countenance sedition against the Ruler by anyone, my wife and children included. My loyalty to the Ruler and his government is absolute."

To Sikiokuu, the discernible weakening of defiance in Tajirika's voice augured well for what he wanted to extract from this encounter. Yet he was not amused by the apparent sincerity of Tajirika's denials or firmness of his attitude toward the Ruler. Convictions are far harder to smash than conscious defiance.

Sikiokuu replenished Tajirika's glass with more brandy.

"*Here. A little brandy is good for you.* As I said from the very beginning, personally I *believe you.*"

"*Then help me. Please,* help me," Tajirika pleaded between gulps of the brandy.

"I have never said no to a cry for help. But as you know, God helps those who help themselves. That's why I told you that your life is in your hands. I cannot help you unless you really want me to help you."

"I'll give you half my wealth."

"I don't need your wealth or anybody else's. What's of most concern to me is the security of the Ruler and his government."

"Then how do I help myself to get you to help me?" Tajirika asked in a teary voice.

"Let's start with the question of your illness. I believe that you described it to my men as a malady of words, words getting stuck in your throat, am I correct?"

"Yes. Something like that."

"Had you ever suffered from this illness before the queuing mania?"

"No."

"And since?"

"No."

"And the malady was triggered by your longing to be white? An unfulfilled desire to be a white European?"

"A white Englishman, that's correct."

"Now, Titus. I want you to take a deep breath, count to ten, and think about the next question. As a result of your presumptive cure, what did you learn about the real significance of whiteness?"

"What do you mean?"

"You did not suffer from an unfulfilled desire to be a poor white?"

"Okay. I longed for the power of whiteness," Tajirika agreed.

"Political power, military power, the power to rule," Sikiokuu added quickly, stressing his words as if he were a teacher enriching the understanding of his pupil. "Nay, not just to rule, but to create protectorates, colonies, empires; to make the glory of Rome, London, Paris, fade by comparison? *Titum Imperium Tajirikum Majestica?*"

"*No. No. No.* Never. I reject that," said Tajirika, jumping to his feet as if he had accidentally sat on a pin. "I have never thought or dreamt of power to rule, much less of taking it by force. I completely reject those thoughts and dreams," Tajirika insisted unequivocally. "I simply wanted something that would distinguish me from all other blacks. *But not political power—no, not me.*"

"*Titum Imperium Tajirikum Majestica* is taking it too far, perhaps," said Sikiokuu, a little taken aback by the vehemence of

Tajirika's denial. "But how did your longing for whiteness originate? If not with you, then surely with someone else who must have expressed this simple wish, perhaps even indirectly: If only I had the power of a white man. Or, If this government were in my hands, I would be as powerful as a white man. Anyway, something like that. So think, Titus, think and have the courage of your thoughts, no matter where or to whom they might lead you."

Conflicting thoughts and fears swirled in Tajirika's head as he dwelled on the compromising pictures, the image of his wife as a guest of honor at a gathering of women intruding into every train of thought. There was no doubt in his mind that the pictures he saw were authentic. He even recognized the dress she wore. But the whole thing was absurd, cruel, and jarring, and he was having trouble keeping up with Sikiokuu's twists and turns of argument. Instead of responding to Sikiokuu, Tajirika drained the last drops of brandy in his glass and put out his hand for more.

Sikiokuu was quite happy to oblige and went to the cabinet. He could see that Tajirika was weakening and a little confused. Maybe a drink or two more would ease a voluntary confession implicating his rival. The whole exchange was being recorded. A confession was a confession, even out of the mouth of a drunken captive.

"Yes, Titus?" Sikiokuu prompted him as he handed Tajirika another brandy.

"Tell me, please, Mr. Minister. When your men once put my wife in custody did you then know about her association with those traditional women, or did you discover it only after grilling her?"

"You want me to tell you the truth?"

"Nothing can surprise me more than what I have already heard and seen today."

"We started suspecting her long ago. But Titus, why do you ask about her?"

"Don't you see? If my wife, the mother of my children, the person with whom I share a bed, could so deceive me and I was unable to see through the deception, who else could have been doing the same to me without my knowing it? Mr. Sikiokuu, I am not sure about anything anymore," Tajirika said in despair.

Sikiokuu saw the opening he had been looking for.

"That's exactly what I have been trying to tell you all along. A person like you should not trust people. A certain Frenchman, I think his name is Descartes, says: Doubt yourself. Doubt your closest friends. Doubt everything. I doubt, therefore I am. That's what they call Cartesian logic."

"There, you have spoken nothing but the truth," Tajirika said, assuming Descartes to be a contemporary French version of the biblical Thomas his wife always talked about.

"Which of my truths are you referring to?" Sikiokuu asked.

"That a person should never trust another."

"That's the right way to think."

"Before this, I never had any cause to suspect my wife of any conspiracy."

"You mean it never crossed your mind that she might have been told to whisper evil thoughts in your ear at night?"

Tajirika felt weaker and weaker. Was this so? Was he the victim of thoughts submitted into his subconscious by his wife at night?

"I wonder who would want her to whisper evil thoughts to a sleeping man?" he asked weakly.

"Your buddy. The man you call your friend. Some people have weird notions of friendship."

"Who? You mean . . ."

"Anybody," said Sikiokuu quickly, retreating from mentioning Machokali, hoping Tajirika himself would bring up the name.

"And what would they want her to whisper in my ear at night?"

"Something about power. Taking power."

"Yes, but why by a whisper through Vinjinia? And at night, when I am asleep?"

"They may have been trying to soften you up to recruit you into their treasonous acts later," Sikiokuu said lamely.

Despite Tajirika's anger at his wife for not reporting his disappearance in time and now for having herself photographed with strange women, he still could not see Vinjinia having conversations on politics with anybody. An inner voice, an instinct of self-preservation, told him to be wary of the direction in which Sikiokuu was trying to push him.

"Let me tell you again," Tajirika said quickly, as if retreating from the edges of a cliff. "I have never heard any talk, by anyone at any time, awake or asleep, about overthrowing the government."

"Why do you trust people so much? Why are you so sure that an acquaintance, a close friend, a person high up in government even, has not used your wife for his own evil designs?"

"Quite frankly, Mr. Sikiokuu, I don't think Vinjinia is capable of political plotting."

"So you are defending her again? Where have all your doubts gone? Have you forgotten about the photographs so soon?"

·"Silver Minister, they pain me; I beg you again to let me go home right away and face this treacherous woman. One night will suffice for me to extract the rotten truth."

Sikiokuu grew alarmed and annoyed at the direction of Tajirika's thinking, leading not to Machokali but to his wife's possible treachery to him, the husband.

"Let's go back to the beginning. Apart from yourself, have you ever seen or heard or been near any other person who desired to be white? Take your time. The trouble with you, Tajirika, is that you are loyal to the point of being, well, innocent. Don't rule out anybody just because he may be your friend. Descartes says you doubt everything and everybody . . ."

"Even the Ruler?" Tajirika asked, genuinely puzzled. "Does he say we doubt the Ruler and his government?"

"I didn't say that," Sikiokuu answered sharply.

"Is this Descartes your friend, or adviser?" asked Tajirika.

"Mr. Tajirika!" Sikiokuu said coldly, barely hiding his anger and frustration. "I don't really have time to waste. But you obviously need more time to think about the real meaning of your own words *if, white,* and *wish*."

Sikiokuu rose from his chair.

"Please don't go," pleaded Titus Tajirika. "Don't leave me in captivity."

"Captivity in my office?" said Sikiokuu scornfully. "Tajirika, you seem to have a very high opinion of yourself. Were you seriously thinking that I was going to leave you alone in this office? Perhaps having fantasies of one day becoming a minister? Sir Titus Tajirika. You will never be anything more than *a clumsy collector of bribes*. The Waswahili say that if a Muslim must eat pork, then he might as well choose the juiciest. The same with the English. Better be hanged for a sheep than for a lamb. If you must accept bribes, at least have the imagination to ask for more than just a few symbolic coins, or else keep your nose clean like John Kaniūrū, your deputy, and now, in your absence, both deputy and acting chairman of Marching to Heaven. And if he is confirmed in the seat, well, it is all because of your ungrateful refusal to cooperate."

Sikiokuu pressed a button. Within seconds Tajirika was blindfolded and led out of the office, screaming in desperation, What do you and your Descartes want me to do?

# 4

Sikiokuu sat back in his chair and for a while tugged at his earlobes.

Then he took Vinjinia's pictures and looked at each without taking in the details. The pictures had been his own invention, and it had almost broken his man. Everything was going on well until he mentioned the Frenchman. Why did I ever mention this Descartes? What if this idiot of a businessman should one day say that I was urging him to doubt the existence of the Ruler and his government?

What most annoyed him was the fact that he knew very little about Descartes and his philosophy of doubt. He had first heard the phrases bandied around at a cocktail party he once attended at the Eldares French Cultural Center, and they sounded very learned and beautiful on the tongue. Little knowledge was danger, it had been said. In disgust at himself, Sikiokuu suddenly threw the pictures on the ground. What shall I do to contain the situation?

It did not make matters any better when the following day he got yet another e-mail from Big Ben Mambo, Minister of Information, still in America, telling him to make preparations for the greatest airport reception for the Ruler.

Sikiokuu did not know what he feared most: the return of the Ruler while Nyawĩra was still free or the Ruler's return with a loan from the Global Bank that would result in an even more powerful Machokali. A more powerful Machokali would mean a more powerful Tajirika. Was his star beginning to dim? Yet the e-mail had not specified the date of return or whether the Global Bank had approved the loan. But this was a mere postponement of the inevitable, for he had given up hope of apprehending Nyawīra in whatever time remained.

As he slowly sunk into depression, he got an urgent call from Kaniūrū with the incredible news that Kaniūrū had finally found a way to get Nyawīra, but he did not want to discuss it on the phone.

Sikiokuu felt like a drowning man who had been thrown a lifeline. He did not delay. He sent his own chauffeur to fetch Kaniūrū and bring him to the office.

# 5

Kaniūrū had gone to the shrine disguised as a worker in a dirty and creased blue uniform and a baseball cap with a fading American company logo.

He had parked his Mercedes-Benz a mile away and walked. He had not breathed a word to anybody about his intended visit, and it was only when he reached Santalucia that he allowed himself to ask for the way to the shrine. He had made sure that he got there in the evening hours just as darkness was falling. No other client was waiting. A woman received him silently and pointed the way to the waiting room. After a few minutes, the same woman came back and showed him the way to the divination room and left him there, again without a word. He felt relieved that the woman had not asked him for anything about himself and, as no one knew his name, he grew even more confident in his disguise. He would give the Wizard of the Crow a false name and invent a history of himself.

Through a tiny window in the wall, Kaniūrū saw the Wizard of the Crow holding a small mirror in his left hand. The Wizard appeared to be reading it like a book, not raising his eyes even as he talked to the supplicant.

"You live in Eldares," the Wizard of the Crow stated.

"Yes," assented John Kaniūrū.

"And you do not want anybody to know that you have been to my shrine."

"Yes. Yes."

"Even your bosses don't know that you are here."

"Yes."

"Your work, or your name, has it something to do with smell?"

That statement rattled Kaniũrũ, and it made him pause for a second. It was so close to the truth of his name that he saw no point in denying it. This mirror has a lot of power, he thought.

"Yes," he said at last.

"So you can be called the Smelling One . . . no, no . . . One-Who-Smells . . . Oh, why is the image of your name becoming blurry? . . . Oh yes, it's back. Much clearer now. Something to do with Nose or Noses, something like that."

Kaniũrũ almost jumped off his seat. The Wizard of the Crow had not yet looked up at him. His eyes were fixed on the book of the mirror the entire time. How did he know that my name is derived from *nose?* he wondered.

"Yes," Kaniũrũ agreed in a slightly tremulous voice.

"And now your job! You used to capture shadows of humans, animals, plants, brooks, the bush."

"How?" Kaniũrũ asked, pretending not to know what the Wizard of the Crow was talking about.

"On paper or in stone, the likeness of things?"

"Yes. Yes," Kaniũrũ agreed quickly.

"But now you shadow people instead of capturing their shadows."

"What?"

"You know, the Lord told the fishermen to leave their nets behind and follow him; he would make them fishers of men. You too must have heard the call of your Lord and Master to leave the images of things behind and follow him so as to become fisher of men and women."

"Yes, something like that," said Kaniũrũ lamely.

"The writing on the mirror has vanished," said the Wizard of the Crow as he raised his head and looked directly at Kaniũrũ. "I am now ready to hear your story. But wait a minute!" the Wizard of the Crow said, looking at the mirror again. "There is more writing here. It is to do with your being captive. I see a heart held prisoner. Is your heart being held captive by somebody?"

"What does the mirror mean by that?"

For a moment Kaniũrũ thought that the Wizard of the Crow was referring to Jane Kanyori. He felt like laughing at the thought, because he had used her only for sexual release and money laundering.

"You mean the woman who works at the bank?" Kaniūrū asked, as if the Wizard of the Crow already knew about her. "Jane Kanyori will never capture my heart. She is not bad, but she is not my type and class," he said, forgetting that he had gone there posing as a base workman.

"Why so? Has another of your class or type already captured your heart?"

"Yes," Kaniūrū said quickly, wondering how the Wizard of the Crow could know about both Jane Kanyori and Nyawīra. There was clearly no need to deny what the wizard already knew. "There is one who captured my heart long ago. She is special, Mr. Wizard of the Crow."

"Where is she now?" the Wizard of the Crow ventured to ask.

"I don't know. I wish I knew."

"Are you looking for her?"

"Day and night. But that is not the reason I came here today."

"The images have all disappeared. There is now only darkness in the mirror," said the Wizard of the Crow, now fixing his eyes on Kaniūrū. "Say, what ill wind blows you to my shrine?"

"Mine is not an ill wind," Kaniūrū said. "Mine is the healthy breeze of property."

"Land? Cows and goats?"

"No, more than land, goats, and cows. Money."

"Newly rich? New money that suddenly came your way?"

"Yes," Kaniūrū said. "But you know how our people are. Driven by envy."

"And you fear that they might cast evil on your new wealth? That they might make the riches disappear as quickly as they came?"

"You have read my mind, Wizard of the Crow. So I want a magic potion, a magic spell, anything that will protect my wealth forever so that I can sleep in peace."

"Does your boss know about the new wealth?"

"No."

"Does anyone?"

"Wizard of the Crow, there is a saying that he who eats alone dies alone, but there are some delicacies that a person should eat alone, even at the risk of dying alone."

"You are so young and yet so well versed in proverbs."

"Gray hairs are not necessarily a sign of wisdom," said Kaniũrũ, happy at the compliment.

The flattery made him feel that the Wizard of the Crow was a real diviner, a true seer of useful truths, and he began to like him.

"This shrine is for treating the sick—you know that?" said the Wizard of the Crow. "Here we bewitch evil. So let me ask you, has your property sickened you already?"

"Oh, no, no, I'm not at all sick of it. I mean, mine is not a real illness."

"Here I know only how to chase away real illnesses in even the deepest recesses of the body or mind. So I can be of no use to you."

"Please help me," Kaniũrũ pleaded. "Whatever you want for your services I will pay."

"What's ailing you? Your heart or mind or both?"

Kaniũrũ quickly decided that he had no alternative but to fake an illness. But what illness? Then he recalled the video and Tajirika's account of the malady of words getting stuck in his larynx. Well, nobody holds a monopoly on any illness. If he could take over Tajirika's seat as chairman of Marching to Heaven, why not also his ailment? Kaniũrũ now bent his head like one weighed down by grave matters. He raised his head and cleared his throat.

"To tell the truth, talking about my illness is a little embarrassing. The situation is like this. Sometimes, when I think too much about my new wealth, words get stuck in my throat, Wizard of the Crow, and when I try to force them out, out pops 'If.'"

"Only one word?"

"Yes, but it repeats itself many times."

"And when does this terrible thing come upon you? What triggers it? Do the words get stuck only when you think about your new wealth?"

"Sometimes, but also when I'm not thinking about anything in particular."

"So, what do you want?"

"First, I need medicine to prevent words from getting stuck in my larynx."

"When did you last have an attack?"

"Oh, this morning. I mean, late this afternoon. That's why I came here in darkness. Emergency."

"But now the malady is gone; it's in remission."

"I told you. It's an on-and-off thing. It's sudden."

"Is it even worse than usual?"

Kaniũrũ tried to recall what Tajirika had said in the video but he could not remember all the details. So he just improvised as he went along.

"It normally happens at home in the evenings, after office hours. It is worse when I look at a mirror."

"What do you see in the mirror?"

"My face."

"Are you sure?"

"Yes. My face. I know my face."

"The reflection of your face: it makes you say 'If'?"

"Yes."

"So the malady attacks you only when you look at yourself in the mirror?"

"Yes, yes. *That's true*. You got it right."

"Even in the office? I mean, when you look at yourself in the mirror in the office?"

"Everywhere, I tell you," Kaniũrũ added, and now he gave his imagination free rein as he tried to elicit maximum sympathy from the Wizard of the Crow. "It's a terrible malady, Mr. Wizard of the Crow. Wherever there is a mirror I know the malady is lurking behind it. In the toilets of the big hotels and nightclubs. In buses and taxis. It is as if my enemies inflict me with the malady every hour, wherever I may be. Mr. Wizard of the Crow, I am now scared to leave my home."

Suddenly the Wizard of the Crow did what Kaniũrũ had not expected. He handed him a mirror.

"Here! Take this. It sees everything," said the Wizard of the Crow. "Even what is most hidden."

Kaniũrũ's hands were shaking as he took the mirror. Many thoughts whirled through his mind. For a second he thought of faking a seizure and spurting a profusion of *ifs*, but he got scared. Suppose the mirror can see all my secrets? No, I am not going to look at myself in his mirror, *no way*. Kaniũrũ did not even pretend to look at it.

"I am not saying that words get completely stuck," he said, trying to dig himself out of the hole he had dug. "What I am talking about is more like a whisper, an echo; it is not a distinct sound. The word whispers itself to my brain. Oh, Mr. Wizard of the Crow, whispers in the brain are worse than actual sounds because they impede the flow of thought. I need protective medicine around my property, for this will allay my anxiety, which is obviously the cause of these whispers. I need protection from my enemies, a permanent cure. Here, take the mirror back."

The Wizard of the Crow did not take back the mirror. He looked long and hard at Kaniŭrŭ's face.

"Is that all you want?" he asked Kaniŭrŭ.

"That's all I want."

"Then don't worry yourself to death," the Wizard of the Crow told Kaniŭrŭ. "You are young. You can still turn your life around. What you need is to get rid of those things that trigger anxiety standing in the way of a new self, a different self. They are the enemy."

"Thank you, Mr. Wizard of the Crow. You have read my mind correctly. Get rid of the enemies who stand in my way or at least neutralize their power over me. I believe in you and your medicine."

"Hold the mirror before you," the Wizard of the Crow told him. "Hold it firmly. Now look directly at it and don't let your eyes wander. Concentrate all your thoughts, all your desires, all your needs, into the gaze. If you lie, you are lying to yourself. If you speak the truth, you are speaking the truth to yourself. When you feel yourself ready to receive the magic of curative and protective words, let me know."

"I am ready. I am ready for the cure and the protection," Kaniŭrŭ said quickly, fearing that the Wizard of the Crow might suddenly change his mind.

"Are you are looking at the mirror directly?"

"Yes, yes."

"Say after me: *Remove from me the enemy of life; the days of thieves and robbers are numbered.*"

"*Remove from me the enemy of life; the days of thieves and robbers are numbered.*"

"I want you to chant that seven times."

Kaniŭrŭ did as he was told and chanted the magic words seven times, his eyes and their reflection gazing at each other, his lips and their reflections mimicking each other seven times.

"Now remove all the wax in your ears and anything else that may block my words," the Wizard of the Crow pronounced with authority. "Listen to me. Every morning you must stand in front of a mirror, look at it, and say the formula seven times. Do that seven days a week for seven months."

"Is that all?" Kaniũrũ asked.

"That's all," said the Wizard of the Crow, now taking back his mirror.

"And will that cast a protective spell over my life and property?"

"Yes, if you do it right."

"What is the fee?"

"There is no charge because I did not dispense any herbs, powder, or liquid. Yours is a malady of riches and property, and the medicine for that resides in the heart. Your soul and all you have will be well if and when you arm yourself against your enemies of the soul with the right words."

"Words?"

"Yes, words. And actions born of the right words. So take good care of what you say from now on. What poisons a person goes through his mouth. I must never hear that you have repeated to the ears of another what you have seen or heard in the shrine of the Wizard of the Crow. Do you hear me?"

"I hear you."

"Say after me: And if I say what I should not say, may the words tell on me."

"And if I say what I should not say, may the words tell on me."

# 6

Kaniũrũ felt a big load off his mind. His riches were now protected. His monies were beyond the reach of his enemies, whoever and wherever they were. He was so preoccupied with his lightness of being that when the same woman who had earlier received him now gave him a piece of paper, he just took it and put it in his pocket and moved on without a thank-you, a glance, or a word. The only person to whom he felt enormous gratitude was the Wizard of the Crow. The man is a true wizard, Kaniũrũ kept saying to himself, marveling at how much the witch doctor knew about him and his condition. And that he had not asked for a fee proved his authenticity all the more. The false are always ready to take and the true to give. No less amazing was how the Wizard of the Crow had managed to lull his fears so that, except when he had lied to the wizard about his malady, Kaniũrũ had felt at peace and talked to the wizard as if they had met somewhere else and were just renewing their acquaintance. He quickly dismissed the possibility of a previous encounter and attributed the ease and familiarity of their conversation to the wizard's divining skills.

That night he hardly slept: his entire body was taut with joy, relief, hope, and self-congratulation on the success of the deception. He had even gotten the better of the Wizard of the Crow, he thought.

But the face of the Wizard of the Crow kept appearing to his mind's eye. The face danced just so in his mind as to awaken his dormant artistic instincts. At school, his artistic bent was in portraits; his mind had been a storehouse of the different faces he had encountered. He had, however, become disillusioned with art as a means of material accumulation; his memory had lost its clarity and sharpness. Now he turned the face of the Wizard of the Crow over and over again in his imagination. There were moments when he saw the face exactly as he had seen it during the divination. But there were others, particularly in the twilight of sleep and wakefulness, when he saw the face floating above the streets of Eldares, calling unto him: Come, follow me and I shall make you fishers of everything: trees, property, people, men, women. Yes, women particularly . . .

He recalled the woman who had given him the piece of paper. What was all that about and what was written on it? He felt too lazy to get out of bed and retrieve it from his pocket. But unable to sleep, he slipped out of bed, put on the lights, and read the heading: *The Seven Herbs of Grace*. This witch doctor was endlessly amazing: hmmm, talking about the care of animals and plants and even insects? *How funny!* A witch doctor who cares about life all around him? A modern witch doctor, an environmentally conscious witch doctor, he said and yawned, returning to bed.

He dreamt of the Wizard of the Crow and himself chasing each other in some forest. Sometimes it was he, Kaniũrũ, who was in pursuit of the Wizard of the Crow. At other times it was the Wizard of the Crow who was chasing him, and wherever Kaniũrũ sought to hide and take breath, a tree would be saying: Look at the mirror in your heart seven times.

He woke up in the morning and went to the mirror in the bathroom and chanted the sorcerer's incantation seven times, only to have the word *seven* echo in the corridors of his mind as if it had a life of its own and was asserting itself. The magic must be working. Seven. The Seven Herbs of Grace. The word kept playing tricks on him. Sometimes the word *seven* found itself in the middle of a sentence: The Herbs of Grace were Seven. Sometimes at the beginning: Seven were the Herbs of Grace. Seven Grace. Grace Seven. Grace Mũgwanja. Grace Mũgwanja?

Nyawĩra's other names were Grace Mũgwanja. *Was this possible?* He felt paralyzed with disbelief at the thoughts now forming in his mind. Had the Wizard of the Crow been trying to communicate something to him about Nyawĩra? That Nyawĩra could be found? Seven herbs of Grace. Grace. Seven. Grace Mũgwanja. The different faces of the Wizard of the Crow started floating in the air. He was now certain that he had seen that face before. It was the face of the person who had changed himself into a beggar outside the gates of Paradise.

Kaniũrũ was so disoriented that he had to hold on to the wall of the bathroom in order not to fall. The man was no ordinary sorcerer. He was one of those djinns reputed to wield potent magic. That explains why he knew all about me even though he had never seen me. He even knew the drama in my heart! That's why he asked me whether a woman was holding my heart captive. He was upset with himself, now recalling his response: that although it was true that he was looking for her, that had not been his mission in coming to the shrine.

The more he thought about that extraordinary exchange, the more it became clear that the Wizard of the Crow had been trying to direct his thinking toward Nyawĩra. The man was as much as saying that he knew Nyawĩra. Indeed, Kaniũrũ himself now recalled that he had once seen this man and Nyawĩra talking animatedly on the side street next to Tajirika's office. And according to Tajirika in the video, Nyawĩra herself had proposed the visit to the shrine of the Wizard of the Crow. The Wizard of the Crow was offering his help. He should have taken up the offer.

An idea struck him. The Wizard of the Crow could easily find Nyawĩra through the powers of the mirror. The more he thought about the astonishing divining power he had witnessed, the clearer it became that the wizard was the only person in Aburĩria who could effect Nyawĩra's arrest. The solution stared him in the face. The government needed to enlist the Wizard of the Crow and his mirror to find Nyawĩra's whereabouts.

Kaniũrũ would kill several birds with one stone. Nyawĩra would be captured. The Wizard of the Crow would get a reward for enabling her capture, Kaniũrũ's gift of gratitude for the Wizard of the Crow's blessings upon his life and property without charge for his services. Most important, Kaniũrũ would reap all the benefits arising from the arrest of Nyawĩra. He heard a tune forming in his head.

> *What are you waiting for?*
> *What are you waiting for?*
> *This is the moment*
> *What are you waiting for?*

It was then that Kaniũrũ went to the phone, dialed Sikiokuu, and heard a most welcome response: the minister was quick to send his chauffeur to help Kaniũrũ through the morning traffic.

# 7

*"Thank you, my brother,"* said Sikiokuu as he embraced Kaniũrũ and welcomed him into the office.

Kaniũrũ was taken aback by the sheer warmth of the embrace, implying that they were equals. Already he had felt flattered by being the sole passenger in a chauffeur-driven Mercedes-Benz flying a miniature Aburĩrian flag. Never had he dreamt that he would one day find himself sitting in the backseat of a vehicle bearing a license plate beginning with CM for cabinet minister. The wizard's magic was working in ways he had not expected, and for a moment he was lost for words.

"Take a seat, my brother," Sikiokuu said, showering him with lavish attention. Kaniũrũ was by now a prince in his own mind, thanks to the magic of the Wizard of the Crow.

But he faced a quandary. The Wizard of the Crow had explicitly warned him against disclosing what he had seen or heard at the shrine. What precisely did the witch doctor mean? That he should never speak about the Wizard of the Crow? Or discuss his medicine? What would happen if he violated his oath to the wizard? Kaniũrũ was not about to find out at the expense of his own future. No matter how brotherly Sikiokuu was being, Kaniũrũ was not about to sacrifice his life for his minister.

Besides, Kaniũrũ feared Sikiokuu's possible reactions. How was he, Kaniũrũ, going to explain his visit to the shrine without revealing that he had gone there to seek the very magical protection that Tajirika had talked about in the video? He feared that he might inadvertently disclose the sources of his new wealth, prospective contractors for Marching to Heaven. No. Sikiokuu must be kept in the dark. He might demand a share and even rights of seniority. No, the sources of his new wealth and the bank accounts would remain a secret known only to him and Jane Kanyori. But how was he going to impart information without placing himself at risk vis-à-vis the Wizard of the Crow or jeopardizing his own interests by letting Minister Sikiokuu know more than he should know?

Once again, memories of the Wizard of the Crow came to his rescue. The wizard had said, *Take good care of what you say from now on. What poisons a person goes through his mouth.* He knew that in Aburĩria the truth could get you in trouble: he must control how much of it issued from his mouth.

It was as if Kaniũrũ had rehearsed the story, so effortlessly did he now tell how he, after watching Tajirika's video, had gone to the Wizard of the Crow to verify the truth of Tajirika's whole story and had pretended to suffer from the same malady of words.

"Brilliant," exclaimed the minister in admiration of the wiles of his brother Kaniũrũ.

"You know the most amazing thing about this sorcerer?" continued Kaniũrũ. "He knew my name, my new employment, everything about me, and he read all these facts in a mirror he held in his hand. Unfortunately, he also knew straightaway that I was lying about my illness."

"He did?"

"Yes, and to tell you the truth, I was even more surprised by his reaction. He has time for only those with true illnesses, so he dismissed me from his presence and told me never to be seen there again. So I did not leave there any wiser about Tajirika's extravagant claims. In fact, I did not see or hear anything useful to repeat. What I am telling you now is, therefore, not what I heard or saw at the shrine but rather what I reasoned in retrospect. You see, once I was back at my place, I started contemplating the enormous powers of this individual, and it immediately occurred to me, like some kind of revelation, that the sorcerer might be the one to deliver Nyawĩra to us."

"This Wizard of the Crow seems to be the object of obsession of every Tom, Dick, and Harry," Sikiokuu commented, a little disappointed. "But I hardly knew that he was a detective to boot," he added sarcastically.

"Believe me, Mr. Minister, from my brief encounter with him, I can claim that he is every inch a seer. The eye of his mirror sees far and deep," Kaniũrũ waxed poetic, only to stop himself upon recalling the sorcerer's solemn warning. "I regret lying about my illness, for if I had not done so, I would have found out much more. As to what I saw and heard, I have forgotten the details and so cannot repeat them. But my exposure to him convinces me that the Wizard of the Crow is the way to go."

Sikiokuu kept quiet for a while as he turned over in his mind what Kaniũrũ had just said. Up to now Kaniũrũ was the only person who had managed to come up with information that yielded any success in the State's attempts to crack down on the Movement for the Voice of the People. He had helped to flush Nyawĩra out. He had come up with the pictures of Nyawĩra as a young unmarried woman and some as the wife of Kaniũrũ: these were the only photos of the woman that the police had. He had helped trap Tajirika and had been instrumental in securing the pictures of Vinjinia and the dancing women. How, then, could Sikiokuu dismiss outright Kaniũrũ's idea, however crazy it sounded? After all, the Ruler had told him that he must leave no stone unturned in the hunt for Nyawĩra.

"You have told me that this sorcerer deals only with sickness. How then are we to employ him in police work?" Sikiokuu asked skeptically but with a measure of curiosity.

"Money and power," said John Kaniūrū. "Nobody is averse to rubbing shoulders with money and power. Your title alone, Mr. Minister, and your deep pockets, are enough to make the sorcerer feel so elevated that he will give us Nyawīra without a murmur of protest. I told you, his mirror has more power than . . ."

"Okay," said Sikiokuu decisively. "We shall talk about that later. Right now there is a job to be done, and I want it done quickly. I want you to go back to the Wizard of the Crow immediately. Tell him you have brought him greetings from me personally. Tell him that I have authorized you to accept whatever price he names for undertaking to locate Nyawīra."

Kaniūrū was about to accept the mission when he once again remembered the warning of the Wizard of the Crow. How would the wizard interpret what Sikiokuu had instructed Kaniūrū to do? Would he take his reappearance and mission as conclusive proof that Kaniūrū had violated his oath? Kaniūrū felt further compromised by having lied about his encounter with the Wizard of the Crow, claiming he had been chased away and warned never to return. What if Sikiokuu later recalled this and started questioning Kaniūrū's truthfulness in other areas?

"I don't think it is a good idea for me to go back there. After all, he did tell me never to come back. I am a very poor liar, Mr. Minister, I really hate lying, and I would not know how to wriggle out of it. I think it would be better for you to invite him to your office and . . ."

"A sorcerer in my office? Never," said Sikiokuu, rather vehemently.

"My guess," Kaniūrū went on, "is that he will be so overwhelmed by your presence that he will not even ask for a fee."

Sikiokuu kept quiet for a while, thinking about Kaniūrū's latest proposal. He wondered whether this fellow might spark rumors that he had invited a witch doctor to his office, the Ruler's office. No, Kaniūrū must not know of the minister's further dealings with the Wizard of the Crow.

"John. You have done well, and I will certainly never forget your devotion to me. You have been very helpful, and I appreciate your not lying to me. Just leave the whole thing in my hands. I shall figure out the best way to handle it. It is dangerous to mix politics and sorcery. From now on I want you to forget that you and I have spoken about the Wizard of the Crow and any possible role he may or may not play in the hunt for Nyawīra and other dissidents of the Movement for the Voice of the People."

Kaniūrū could not have been happier with the outcome. He may have pushed the envelope a bit, but he had not broken his word to the wizard. And Sikiokuu had not dismissed his idea altogether. If things went wrong and the wizard failed to deliver, the minister could not blame Kaniūrū. And if things work out well and Nyawīra . . . who knew? When he left, he was whistling tunes to himself, savoring Sikiokuu's having treated him as an equal, almost, and even embraced him as a brother.

Back in the office, Sikiokuu was deep in conference with his trusted lieutenants Njoya and Kahiga.

"It is thanks to your video and masterful questioning. But I want you to be very careful in how you go about this. Wear civilian clothes, and at no time must you mention my name," Sikiokuu told his loyal emissaries to the court of the Wizard of the Crow.

# 8

"I am Elijah Njoya," one said.

"And I am Peter Kahiga," said the other.

"We are police."

"Would you like to see our badges?"

"That won't be necessary," he told them. "All are the same to the Wizard of the Crow."

"We are glad to hear that," they said in unison.

"What brings you to my shrine so early?"

"We have a message for you from the government," said Kahiga.

"Your powers with the mirror have reached the ears of the State," said Njoya awkwardly.

He sensed fear in their demeanor, but this did not signify much.

He had often seen a similar unease, especially among religious zealots, educated professionals, and high-ranking civil servants who on the surface pretended not to believe in the occult. A priest who used to denounce sorcery every Sunday once came to him at dawn, only to bump into one of his parishioners at the shrine. Each had proceeded to claim the wizard as a relative and offered this as the reason for their visit. Both had excused themselves and said they would come back another time.

We humans are complex, he thought as the memory of that encounter crossed his mind.

One of the policemen jolted him from his reverie.

"Listen up. We have been looking everywhere for a woman named Nyawīra," Njoya said, leaning forward and lowering his voice.

"And we have completely failed in our search," added Kahiga.

"Who might this Nyawīra be?" the wizard asked.

"Surely you have heard of her," Njoya answered. "She is a terrorist sworn to overthrow the Ruler's legitimate government."

"A terrible woman," Kahiga added. "She has twisted the minds of many."

"Especially women," added Njoya.

"Didn't you hear about the women who shamed the site of Marching to Heaven?"

"The Wizard of the Crow does not attend ceremonies of which he is not the master," said the Wizard of the Crow.

"We want her in custody," said Njoya.

"And you are the only person with the power to find her," Kahiga said.

"We are asking you to resort to your mirror," Njoya said.

The Wizard of the Crow kept his eyes fixed on their faces, but he did not detect any hints of sarcasm or mockery.

"Mine are healing powers," he told them.

"We are offering you a contract. Money is not a problem. Name your price," Njoya and Kahiga said together. "You do your part, we do ours."

"Burī notes are not the issue," he told them. "Every profession has its own concerns and expertise. You would never ask a dentist to perform a heart transplant. Your skills lie in pursuing those who break the laws of the State. My skills lie in pursuing the forces that threaten the laws of life."

"But Nyawīra is a disease. By working against the State, she threatens the lives of many," Njoya said.

"Yes, smoke her out of her lair. She is an infectious disease," Kahiga said.

"Bring her here to my shrine," said the Wizard of the Crow. "And everyone who has been infected by her."

"She has infected a multitude," they said in unison. "Crazed the minds of youth. We cannot gather all the infected. Arrest the virus to end the infection."

"Bring me the virus and I will find the cure," the Wizard of the Crow said in a tone determined to end the discussion. "Are my healing powers now supposed to be an arm of the State? What would my clients think were they to know about it? Would this build trust in me? You might as well invite me to the State House and say to the whole country: Here is Sir Wizard of the Crow. He lures clients into his shrine to help the State catch criminals," he said decisively.

Instead of getting angry, Njoya and Kahiga looked at each other as if they understood what the wizard was hinting at or what he wanted.

"We will take your message back to those who sent us," Njoya told him. "Meantime, we ask you to come up with a price for your services to the State."

"There is nothing more to think about," he told them firmly. "You are guardians of the State, and I am a guardian of life."

# 9

"Are you sure that they are not just lulling us to sleep?" Nyawīra asked after Kamītī told her what had just taken place.

Since their return to Eldares and despite the occasional policeman who came for magic, they had felt as if an invisible wall protected Nyawīra from the gaze of the enemy. But since Kaniūrū's visit, she felt as if the wall had suddenly collapsed.

"If they ever come for me," Nyawīra said, breaking their silence about those fears, "assure me that you will never give up the shrine.

Promise me that you will keep faith with the way of the Seven Herbs of Grace."

"Please stop talking like that. As long as you are hiding among the people, no enemy shall spot you."

"There is no escape from a spy camped in your courtyard," Nyawĩra said, in a resigned mood. "I don't know how long I can keep up playing different characters and changing costumes. A cautionary measure is not a measure of cowardice. I would feel more at ease if I could extract that promise from you," Nyawĩra said.

"What kind of a healer would I be were I to abandon those who seek promises of life amid the threats of death? As for the Seven Herbs of Grace, they are a way and that way belongs to us all. I will also extract a promise from you. If ever they took me away, make sure that the work of the Wizard of the Crow goes on."

"Don't say that," she said.

"Okay, let's stop talking as if we are saying farewell," Kamĩtĩ said. "You are not going anywhere, Nyawĩra. And neither am I. We are secure in our shrine."

They hugged and clung to each other even longer, as if they wanted to seal that sense of eternal security with an eternal embrace.

"It's back to work," Nyawĩra said, finally pushing him away.

"Let me appeal," said Kamĩtĩ, still clinging to her hands.

"Against going back to work?"

"The recent ban on checking each other's scars in daytime."

"Not in daytime, in the evening," she said.

They always looked forward to their mutual explorations, but now the lingering feeling that she could be captured intensified the hunger.

But in the evening, when all the clients and workers had gone and she thought the exploration would soon begin, Nyawĩra spied Kahiga and Njoya in the yard.

"Let me talk to them," Kamĩtĩ said, trying to calm her with a confidence he did not feel. "Stay hidden here, ready to flee. You know our agreed signal and the path to take."

# 10

"Listen," Njoya told the Wizard of the Crow, "the Minister of State wants to see you tonight."

"What does he want?"

"We are only messengers."

"Go back to the one who sent you and tell him that he is very welcome to visit me in my shrine," the wizard told them. "If I am to administer to his needs . . ."

"He has no need of healing," explained Kahiga.

"So why does he seek me out?"

"He is simply issuing an invitation," said Njoya.

"You will be his personal guest. A guest of honor," Kahiga added.

"Tell him that though I am honored by his invitation, he needs to propose a date and time that are good for him and me."

Njoya and Kahiga looked at each other, wondering how they were going to make the sorcerer nicely understand that he had no choice in the matter.

Njoya cleared his throat and said, "Mr. Wizard of the Crow, we know that you may not be too *familiar* with what we in government call *protocol, and, quite frankly, I don't blame you.* Oh, I am sorry for speaking to you in English. What I meant is that you may not know all the rules of good manners in dealing with the government."

*"No need to explain,"* the Wizard of the Crow replied in perfect English. "Even witch doctors are not strangers to languages. *Manze enda mtell buda na masa wenu ati sitago. Mũrogi wa Kagogo hachorewangwi na mtu. Haneed vinaa. Hello-na-zuribye,"* the Wizard of the Crow said in Sheng.

Hardly had Njoya and Kahiga recovered from their amazement at this witch doctor who spoke not only good English but also the latest lingo in town when they saw the Wizard of the Crow start walking back to the house as though his business with them was finished.

"Hey, wait a minute," they shouted in unison, and the Wizard of the Crow stopped.

"*I am very sorry,*" Njoya told him, "but we cannot leave without you."

"Is it your intention to arouse my wrath?"

"Oh, no, no, nothing of the sort," Kahiga quickly explained, made uneasy by the menace in the wizard's voice. "But you know how it is in our country. A citizen cannot refuse an invitation from the government without good reason."

Why this odd mixture of fear and authority on the part of the police officers? wondered Kamĩtĩ. Had they really come to arrest him, or was the whole thing a cruel sport, their intention all along being to pounce on Nyawĩra? Kamĩtĩ pondered his options. Play the angry Wizard of the Crow, threatening fire and brimstone? But suppose they called his bluff? Refuse to go? They could still drag him away by force. Besides, resistance might make them suspicious and lead them to probe more deeply into the affairs of the shrine. Suppose they raided the shrine and captured Nyawĩra? He would never forgive himself. Far better for them to take him away from her hiding place.

"Is that so?" the Wizard of the Crow asked innocently. "Wait just where you are; I shall be ready in no time," he told them, aware that if they had come to arrest him they would not let him out of their sight.

And sure enough one of them did make a move to follow him, but the Wizard of the Crow turned around and glared at him.

"Are you sure you want to follow me? Cross my magic lines?"

"Oh, no! No!" both police officers said in unison. "Take all the time you want, Mr. Wizard of the Crow."

He went straight to Nyawĩra and apprised her of the situation, instructing her to stay under cover until he and his newfound acquaintances left the compound.

"It is better this way," the Wizard of the Crow told her. "It takes their noses away from the shrine and you."

As the Wizard of the Crow and the police officers were about to leave, Nyawĩra suddenly emerged from the shadows and ran toward them, an open gourd in her left hand and a fly whisk in her right. The threesome stopped in their tracks. The play of light and shadow on Nyawĩra made her look otherworldly. She stood in front of them without saying a word, and for a moment Kamĩtĩ thought she had lost her mind. Where was the Nyawĩra he left cowering speechlessly? Why was she doing this? Nyawĩra then dipped the fly whisk into the gourd and shook it over their heads while chanting incantations.

"If he comes back with even one strand of his hair missing, I will hold you two accountable, accountable, accountable."

She circled them and repeated her ritual time and again and with different variations on the same warning.

At the end of the seventh round, she stopped abruptly and stood a few inches from their stupefied faces. Then, slowly and firmly, as if she did not want them to miss any of her words, she said:

"And should he become a missing person, you who took him away shall be swallowed by this earth thus!"

And, saying so, she raised high the bowl and poured the remaining water onto the earth.

"Or break into pieces like this calabash!" And she crushed the calabash to the ground.

She then ran back into the house.

Njoya and Kahiga stood motionless; when they tried to lift their feet, it was as if their legs were chained to the ground.

"Don't worry," the Wizard of the Crow told them. "She is my guardian spirit. My eye of life. As gentle as a lamb. But oh, once aroused to anger, she is possessed by a dangerous daemon. Even to me her word is law."

The spell was broken. Mobility returned to the police officers' feet and they took the Wizard of the Crow to Sikiokuu, Minister of State in the Ruler's Office.

# 11

As they drove him away, Kamĩtĩ thought about Nyawĩra and the scene outside the shrine. Since meeting Nyawĩra his life had changed in ways he could never have foreseen. He often felt as if he were walking in a field of dreams. The most fleeting images of her would make his blood rush, suffusing him with a sense of goodness, peace, hope, and great though yet unknown expectations.

What most amazed him about Nyawĩra was her humor and laughter in spite of her travails. But no matter how much he thought he knew her, every day brought new surprises. He would never have imagined that, instead of staying inside the house as agreed until he and the police had left, Nyawīra would appear with the force of a hurricane and stage so spellbinding a performance. The police had now spirited him away from her hiding place.

But soon he was awash in doubts, his knees suddenly weak. What if the police officers were already on to Nyawīra? If not, what if they suspected him of really knowing her whereabouts? What if they tortured him?

He decided not to worry about that which he could do nothing about. Even if they tortured and interrogated him about Nyawīra and the Movement for the Voice of the People, there was very little he could tell them. Of Nyawīra's hiding place, he would die rather than reveal it. And what he knew about the movement was only what Nyawīra had told him, which was not much.

He was so absorbed in these conflicting thoughts and emotions that even when the car stopped outside some buildings he did not realize that they had arrived at their destination.

During the ride, Njoya and Kahiga had talked neither to him nor to each other. The drama outside the shrine had propelled each into his own world as both tried to figure out the implications of the witch's dance for their respective lives.

When they arrived, Njoya left Kahiga and the Wizard of the Crow in the car and went to find out what the minister would have them do with his guest.

"It is night, a bit late," Sikiokuu told him, rather curtly. "I will see him tomorrow morning. I don't want him to think that he is such a big deal that I would stay up all hours of the night to receive him."

"Are we meant to take him back to his place?"

*"Of course not,"* said Sikiokuu in English, without elaborating.

"Where should we put him up?" Njoya asked, his heart sinking at these unforeseen developments. "A hotel?"

"You must be joking. As he is a guest of the State—take him to the government hotel."

"I understand that all the cells are full," Njoya said, trying to wriggle out of having to imprison the Wizard of the Crow.

"Have him share a room with the madman."

# 12

Tajirika felt humiliated at the manner of his removal from Sikiokuu's office, but he turned his anger against Machokali and Vinjinia. Why had his friend not allowed him to be part of the delegation to the USA? he asked himself time and again. Machokali had said that he would call him now and then, but since leaving for America Machokali had not done so once. The doubts Sikiokuu had planted in his mind started to fester. Yet he still could not imagine any connection between Machokali and Vinjinia. But the pictures of his Vinjinia and the dancing women had shaken his trust in her. Not that he had much to begin with. Tajirika subscribed to the saying that the word of a woman or a child should be believed only after the hearer had slept on it. Nevertheless, there had been things he would have been prepared to swear that Vinjinia was incapable of, but now he was not so sure.

The reports of his wife's misdemeanor, in having women dance for her, were what hurt most. Although he believed that a woman was inherently untrustworthy, he took it that a man's wife should be a paragon of virtue. A good man was judged by the goodness of his wife, and a good wife was known for her discretion and ability to cover for the failings of her husband. Such was the woman he had married. A woman who did not demand much from life! A woman who had long ago stopped asking him questions about where he spent the night. A woman who seemed completely satisfied with life around the kitchen and in the fields. A woman who never raised any questions about politics. That was the woman he thought he knew. Could she have feigned all that?

Maybe Sikiokuu and company were right when they hinted that Nyawīra, whom they supposed to be the mother of all hypocrites, had something to do with the new Vinjinia. Indeed, there was no disputing that everything had started going wrong the day he became ill and Vinjinia started going to the office. If he himself had succumbed to Nyawīra's slickness, why not Vinjinia? He acknowledged as much, yet he had expected her to have the wherewithal to avoid being so deceived as to end up in the company of shameless primitive dancers.

Wife beating was a privilege if not a right of male power, and now in the cell he had no opportunity to measure his manhood. Grinding his teeth in frustration, he was reduced to imagining slapping his wife around and her screams for mercy and forgiveness. This allowed him to think more soberly about other things that weighed on him.

Like the matter of Silver Sikiokuu.

It was clear that the minister was setting an elaborate trap for Machokali and needed Tajirika to pull it off. But what role was he meant to play? Sikiokuu's call for him to think about "the real meaning" of *if*, *white*, and *wish* still buzzed in his ears. Was the role hidden in those words? And what was the payback? What was the deal? Sikiokuu had been enigmatic about it. Why?

Sikiokuu was softening him up by having him put back in a cell where a bucket was his toilet. The guards emptied the pail once in three days, and sometimes they would not even keep to the schedule. So there were days when the pail overflowed with shit and urine, the stench becoming his daily and nightly companion. But Sikiokuu was underestimating his will to survive, as well as his business acumen. There was no way that Tajirika was going to accept just any deal without some kind of give-and-take.

Tajirika did not put too much store in friendship. There was nothing he would not do to save his skin provided the price was right, except take part in anything touching the Ruler's life and power. That would mean certain death. So he was not about to accept that he may have heard others talking about a plot against the Ruler.

How he wished he knew precisely the hour and the day when the Ruler and his entourage were returning! Tajirika concluded that he had no alternative but to wait for Sikiokuu to put a deal on the table or for Machokali to return from America, whichever came first.

Late one night his jailers opened the door to his cell, flung a man inside, and closed the door again. Tajirika kept absolutely still in his corner, listening intensely to the breathing of his fellow prisoner. Unable to bear the silence after a while, Tajirika asked: "Who are you?" But the man, whoever he was, did not answer him.

He is perhaps a killer brought here in secrecy at midnight to do you harm, an inner voice told Tajirika. He broke out in a cold sweat and started shaking. The tension getting the better of him, he started screaming:

"Don't kill me. I beg you, don't kill me. I have committed no crime. Have mercy on me. I have a wife and children. Please don't spill innocent blood because of money. Whatever they have given you, I promise to double it."

"Sshh!" the man responded, but Tajirika was so self-absorbed that he did not hear him.

"How much money have they given you?" Tajirika asked, and this time paused, anticipating a response.

"What for?" the man asked.

"To kill me."

"Why should I kill you? I don't know you. I have never met you."

"That's exactly what I am trying to impress upon you. I am innocent. I have never harmed a soul."

"Then you have nothing to fear. I will not kill you," the man told him.

"What did you say?"

"Keep quiet. I will not kill you."

"Thank you, my savior. How much do you want?"

"Why would I want your money?"

"For sparing my life. For sparing me."

"Who told you that I am here to do away with you?"

"Then who are you? And why have they brought you here?"

"Listen," the man said angrily. "I have no idea who you are. I'm not in the mood to chat. Go to sleep and let me do the same," the man said, and then kept quiet.

But to Tajirika, the man's ensuing silence was ominous. He is all pretense. He wants to lull me to sleep, then murder me.

"Don't think that you can fool me," Tajirika said.

"Why?" the man asked.

"I know you want me to fall asleep . . ."

"Are you nuts?"

Despite Tajirika's provocations, the man refused to respond the rest of the night, serving only to confirm Tajirika's suspicions that Sikiokuu wanted him dead. He did not close his eyes once. Dawn found him staring at the corner where the man lay.

Neither believed his own eyes.

"Titus Tajirika!"
"Wizard of the Crow!"

# 13

Tajirika was ecstatic at the apparition of someone with the power to get him out of prison. Nothing was beyond the reach of the Wizard of the Crow, who might even have come precisely to relieve Tajirika's tribulations. Tajirika did not even bother to inquire as to what the Wizard of the Crow was doing or how he came to be there.

He simply proceded to unburden himself of all that he had suffered since receiving the summons to appear before Kaniũrũ's Commission of Inquiry into the Queuing Mania. He told of his arrest, his interrogation by both Njoya and Kahiga, his encounter with Sikiokuu in the minister's office, and his return to this dark cell. The only thing he could not bring himself to tell was Vinjinia's shameful betrayal, and especially her posing for pictures with the dancing women.

"Look at what Sikiokuu has done to me! See that bucket? That is the toilet. When did they last empty it? Seven days ago. Luckily I am not shitting much. Still, as you can see, the bucket is almost full."

"All yours?"

"Yes. No one else has been in this cell since I've been here. How dare he do this to me? What should I do about it?"

"What do you think?"

"You know the saying that when two elephants fight, it is the grass that suffers? I feel like that grass in the struggle between Sikiokuu and Machokali for power behind the throne. The problem is that Sikiokuu has not been clear about what he really wants me to do."

"How much clearer does he have to be, given what you told me he asked you about Machokali?"

"He didn't even mention Machokali by name. He was circumspect, talking to me in riddles about a disciple of the doubting Thomas, a Frenchman named Descartes. Then he told me to go away and think more deeply about my lust for whiteness."

"Can't you see that he just wants you to say in your own words that somebody else infected you with white-ache? But who can you single out and say, This or that one infected me, or, That one is the host of the disease? Is there anyone among those you call your friends who does not suffer from the malady, the white-hot greed behind his self-centeredness? The man was right to ask you to think further about the meaning and implications of what you said. But what do you do after you have brooded?"

"And that is what I want to know. What should I do?"

"First, examine yourself."

"*Of course* one must examine oneself to see where one's interests lie and how to protect them."

"I mean, look to your heart; find out why you ended up here."

"I did not incarcerate myself."

"Who, then, has jailed you?"

"Let me tell you. Sikiokuu and Kaniũrũ are my enemies. They want me to die in prison. Why? Because they don't want me to continue as chairman of Marching to Heaven. They want to make sure that I am not around when Marching to Heaven begins. They want to be the only ones controlling the benefits from the entire project. But you wait. They don't know who they are dealing with, Mr. Wizard of the Crow. Help me. Please help me to break free from prison and I will never forget you."

"From which prison do you want to free yourself?"

"Mr. Wizard of the Crow, this is a serious matter. How many prisons do you see around here?"

"Two. One of the mind and one of the body."

"Then break the walls of these prisons with your mirror power."

"I did not bring a mirror with me."

"Oh!" groaned Tajirika in despair.

"What if we make our own mirror?" the Wizard of the Crow asked suddenly.

"How?"

"Our minds. Is there any mirror greater than the mirror of the mind?"

"Whatever you say," Tajirika said, happy that the Wizard of the Crow was now talking about using a mirror, any mirror, however made.

"Close your eyes . . . Paint pictures of Kaniũrũ and Sikiokuu in your mind."

He wants to help me by disabling the power of the two ruffians, Tajirika told himself as he tried with all his might to imagine Sikiokuu and Kaniũrũ. But the images would not stay still in his mind's dark mirror.

"Now I see them, now I don't," Tajirika said. "They are in and out of focus."

"It does not matter if their images are indistinct," said the Wizard of the Crow. "Now point at those who are ruining the country. Show me where they are."

That's easy, Tajirika thought, as he stretched his hand and pointed in the distance, but the finger kept on moving around like the images in his mind.

"Over there," Tajirika said, still pointing vaguely in front of him.

"Hold it right there," said the Wizard of the Crow. "Now open your eyes, and keep on pointing at the corrupt and the greedy."

Tajirika did as directed. His heart was bursting with joy at the imminent death of his enemies, greedy, corrupt robbers.

"Look at your hand carefully. One finger is pointing at your enemies, and the three others are pointing at you."

"I don't quite understand."

"What don't you understand? Do you remember the children's story about the five fingers who set out to rob someone? Pinky says: Let's go. Where? To do what? asks the finger next to it. To steal, says the middle finger. What if we are caught? asks the fourth finger. Do you know what the thumb says?"

"I am not one of you," Tajirika answered, playing the character of the thumb, ending with laughter.

"That's why the fat finger still remains apart from the other four to this day. One thief standing apart from the others and pointing at . . ."

Tajirika examined his fist again. It was obvious that the pointing finger and the three others were pointing in definite directions. Where and what was the thumb pointing at? One could not tell. And suddenly he thought he knew what the Wizard of the Crow was driving at.

"So even children's stories can teach us a thing or two about the ways of the world?" Tajirika said excitedly. "Mr. Wizard of the Crow, I now know what you have been trying to make me understand: Like these four fingers, the foolish take definite positions. Everyone knows where they stand. I have been too definite in the company I keep. I should maintain at all times the deceptive appearance of the thumb. Mr. Wizard of the Crow, thank you, thank you a thousand times."

"No wonder Jesus wept!" said the Wizard of the Crow loudly, as if talking to himself, clearly frustrated.

"Why do you say that Jesus wept?" Tajirika asked, genuinely puzzled by how the mind of the Wizard of the Crow worked. He was now into the Bible.

"Because he told them things, and even though they had ears they did not hear. He showed them things, and even though they had eyes they didn't see."

He even uses the Book for his rites. That's why his magic is so powerful, Tajirika thought to himself. If he puts his mind to it, there is nothing the Wizard of the Crow cannot do for a person like me.

"And that is why it is said that even God can only help those who help themselves," said the Wizard of the Crow.

"Mr. Wizard of the Crow, how do you want me to help myself so that you can help me?" said Tajirika encouragingly.

"Again, look into your heart. Review whatever is inside you."

"How?"

This man cares only about himself, thought the Wizard of the Crow. He hears and sees only what he wants. The Wizard of the Crow, Kamītī wa Karīmīri, grew angry, very angry.

He had not forgotten how Tajirika had humiliated him on the premises of Eldares Modern Construction and Real Estate; he was flooded by the memory at odd times. He had never imagined that a human being could behave toward another with so much evil and malice. Kamītī had long decided not to seek revenge himself, for to do so would erase the difference between him and Tajirika. *Don't argue with a fool*, the saying went, *for people might not see the difference.*

But now he decided to jog the man's memory and remind him of their first encounter to see if Tajirika would show some shame. People like these, so self-centered, needed to be told things directly, without ambiguity.

"Do you want to hear a story?" he asked Tajirika.

"Yes," Tajirika said quickly. "I will gladly do so if the stories will help you spring me from this prison."

"I am not so sure about this prison, but if you listen to the story very carefully it might help spring you from a prison bigger than this one made of stone and iron."

"I knew it. I knew that that's why you came. I knew that there is no way you would have allowed me to rot in this prison. So please tell your story, begin it right away, and I promise you that I shall not even allow a cough to interrupt you."

# 14

Have you ever heard of Mahabharata, Ramayana, or Bhagavad Gita? The three, or shall we say two since the Gita is a chapter in Mahabharata, are the key texts in the religion, culture, history, and philosophy of the Indian peoples. They were written in Sanskrit, the ancient language of India, though now, like Latin, Greek, Geez, and Sabean, it is dead.

Mahabharata tells of a war between the Kurus and the Pandavas, two branches of the same family. Arijuana, the hero of the Pandavas, is an expert archer, reputedly able to shoot an arrow at targets on the moon. But Arijuana and his teacher Drona hear of another archer, Ekalaivan, whose skills surpass those of Arijuana by far. He can shoot seven arrows into the mouth of a dog as soon as it opens its mouth, giving it no chance to bark. Ekalaivan had taught himself those skills but under the shadow of the statue of Drona, which Ekalaivan himself had erected as a source of inspiration. Still, Ekalaivan claims that Drona is his teacher. Now, the law, dharma, requires a student to give something to his teacher, as a token of gratitude. Although Drona never taught Ekalaivan, he demands his dues. Anything you ask, says Ekalaivan. Then give me your thumb. They cut off Ekalaivan's thumb. Do you see the humiliation, the cruelty? Drona refuses to teach Ekalaivan, a son of the poor, but when the same, through his own creativity, rises to excellence, Drona disables him so that sons of the rich will have no competition. Arijuana's superiority is affirmed by Ekalaivan's forced inferiority.

Do you think that this is a story of ancient India only? It is the story of our times. A rich man has come into riches through the housing business, buying and selling, developing and selling, overseeing construction and getting paid for it. To be fair, the rich man has been considerate and put up a billboard stating clearly that there are no jobs available. But you know how it is! Need, like love, is blind! A tired bird in flight, they say, will land on anything. So one evening a stranger looking for a job enters the man's office. Even though it's the end of the workday, the rich man agrees to interview the stranger. He scrutinizes the documents of the job seeker and asks him many questions. But what do you think the rich man does next? Please follow me, he tells the stranger, so that I can give you a proper interview. The rich man takes the stranger to the gate and asks him to read the billboard to test the stranger's reading skills and comprehension. Now, before I go on, let me make clear that nobody can blame an employer for not having jobs. But think hard and tell me this: how does one find humor in humiliating the already humiliated? Tell me, Tajirika, why this joy at the cry of misery? How would you feel if someone derived joy from your wandering around this prison cell?

Why did you do it, Tajirika? How did I wrong you by asking you for a job?

# 15

These revelations hit Tajirika with a force both unexpected and to him, now, seemingly inevitable. He recalled the encounter and knew, even before the Wizard of the Crow had confirmed it, that the stranger and the Wizard of the Crow were one. So that's why, during the divination and cure of his white-ache, he had felt intimations of a previous encounter? Then, he had dismissed the feeling as a hallucinatory side effect of white-ache. And now it had come to this! Tajirika had never heard of dead languages, and he assumed that the Wizard of the Crow was talking about the languages spoken by the dead. The wizard was in possession of the secrets of dead sorcerers from Africa, India, the world. Faced with the new unknown, he felt terror grip him as never before. For a few minutes he remained frozen in his corner as his mind raced swiftly, feverishly, sinister images giving way to others even more sinister. Still, incredibly, the revelations seemed to throw a light, as he imagined it, on what had been a mystery.

This wizard must be the source of all his troubles! He must have put a spell on the ground outside his office, sparking the queuing mania. The queues had started only a day or two after he had driven this job seeker from the premises of Eldares Modern Construction and Real Estate. He had tied Tajirika's tongue. He had put a spell on Vinjinia and Nyawīra and turned them against him. He had not even been looking for a job but for an occasion to practice malice born of envy and I, an innocent, fell into his trap and gave him a reason to seek vengeance. He even stole my money.

"I gave you three bags of money," Tajirika said, hoping this would mollify him and blunt the edges of his fury.

"Your kind of money smells evil. You can have it back. I buried it in the prairie," said the Wizard of the Crow, and to Tajirika's incredulous consternation, he described the burial spot.

Had he been sent now, once again, by Tajirika's enemies? Brought to his cell at the midnight hour to entrap him with stories and lie about burying money in the ground? He could think of only one enemy with the clout and opportunity.

Sikiokuu's words haunted him: *"Think very hard about . . ."* His last words, and what happens next? The Wizard of the Crow mysteriously turns up in the cell. It was the wizard who had first diagnosed his wish to be white. The wizard had now been sent by Sikiokuu to do away with him once and for all. Sikiokuu had been toying with Tajirika, had even foretold, in his shady way, what would happen. Surely the wizard would start by cutting his fingers off. He probably would have killed me last night, except for my being awake.

Death in human form was walking toward him in slow motion while he remained frozen in a corner, unable to move or do anything about it. Then and there, Tajirika decided that, come what may, he would not spend another night under the same roof with the murderous presence of this India-educated sorcerer who had already cast evil around his offices and home, making problems upon problems rain down on him like hailstones.

Though his strategy was to escape death, his tactic was to keep the Wizard of the Crow engaged in conversation while Tajirika figured a way out.

The clarity of the strategy and the tactics calmed him a little so that, despite the commotion of thoughts and images within, the words that now came out did not betray fear or anxiety.

"I did not mean any harm. I assure you, the test was *truly a little joke among men*. In fact, I had expected that you would join me in laughter. I wanted to make the weight of not getting a job more bearable."

"Don't you think you should think twice about that kind of humor? Such humor can bring about death."

Death? He has come out in his true colors. Witchcraft and state-craft have joined hands against me. What a powerful combination! This wizard has talked with the dead for a thousand years. He has read all the manuals of sorcery from ancient India and Greece to the present. Whether I am in or out of jail, there is no escaping the all-seeing eye, the all-pervasive power of the Wizard of the Crow. I am badly cornered.

His situation was hopeless. He was depressed. But then a ray of sunshine: since the Wizard of the Crow could indeed see whatever he wanted to see from wherever he was, why did Sikiokuu bother to send him to the prison? All the Wizard of the Crow needed to do was cap-ture Tajirika's shadow in his mirror, scratch the shadow, and Tajirika would be gone. Sikiokuu does not want me to die just yet, Tajirika told himself, hope rising. Sikiokuu desperately wants to land a deal with me. He wants me alive, but of course if I refuse to do what he wants or am unable to deliver . . . But why should I refuse to do what he wants when I don't even know what it is that he wants?

Tajirika thought he had indeed seen the light: it was safer for him to be in the hands of Sikiokuu than under the continuous gaze of the Wizard of the Crow. Sikiokuu was more his type; they shared a com-mon language of deceit and evasion. He, Tajirika, would bow, kneel, crawl, do anything to gain mercy from Sikiokuu. All in all, it was eas-ier to deceive Sikiokuu than the Wizard of the Crow. Tajirika would weave tales and shift the blame for the origins of the queuing mania elsewhere. Why not blame his wife? Yes, he would blame it all on scheming Vinjinia. How clever, he thought, feeling really good about himself. This way he would shoot down three birds with one arrow: exact vengeance on Vinjinia for posing with the women dancers, no doubt having a good time while he had disappeared; save himself from the doom portended by the Wizard of the Crow; and, most important, avoid loss of thumbs and death.

Soon, whatever doubts he may have had about being in danger from Sikiokuu vanished. The Wizard of the Crow posed the most immediate threat to his mind and body, and the only person who could save him was Sikiokuu. Tajirika could not afford to wait for night. He had to flee the power of witchcraft immediately and seek protection from the State. But what was he to do without provoking the ire of his wily nemesis? There was nothing he could do, he felt, and he sat there in despair, waiting for death. He regretted his inability to give Vinjinia a thorough beating, but in so doing, he remembered her churchgoing and prayers and started murmuring prayers for deliverance from death. His prayers were answered almost immediately, but in ways that even he could not have expected or imagined.

Just then, two wardens who normally came to collect the bucket of shit and urine, and who had not done so for seven days, suddenly opened the door. Tajirika acted with a reckless instinct of self-preservation. Before the wardens could get to the bucket, Tajirika had sprung from his corner and grabbed it. He threatened to pour seven days of shit and urine onto the two wardens if they even so much as moved. They stood transfixed as Tajirika wobbled and stood between them and the door.

The Wizard of the Crow, too, was taken by surprise and assumed that Tajirika had become unhinged. Indeed, during the conversations, Tajirika had seemed to make no sense at all. The weeks of isolation and torture have taken their toll, he thought. But when Tajirika began to speak and the Wizard of the Crow realized what was going on, he felt like laughing but did not, the better to remain a detached spectator of the proceedings.

"Listen to me," Tajirika was telling the prison wardens. "Get me away from this witch doctor. Take me to Silver Sikiokuu, the Minister of State in the Ruler's Office. Slap handcuffs on me. Or give them to me and I'll do it myself to show you that I am not trying to escape from lawful custody. If you fail to do what I am telling you, or if I see any sign of resistance from any of you, I am going to pour the entire contents of this bucket onto your heads. For the last three days I have been shitting and urinating blood. I am suffering from that virus of death."

At the mention of the devastating virus, the two wardens smelled their own death in the air and commenced their supplications. They assured Tajirika that they had absolutely no grudge against him, that they completely understood him and sympathized with his plight, for they, for their part, would never dream of sleeping under the same roof as a witch doctor. So you see, you and we are on the same side in this and we shall take you wherever you want to go. They threw handcuffs at him and he clapped them onto his own wrists. They asked him to let them take the bucket, but he refused. It was his own shit, his weapon, he said, to the relief of the wardens, happy to be spared contact with his death-infected shit, but also to their greater anxiety, for now they were at the mercy of this crazy prisoner. Now in their company, he told them to make sure to lock the door firmly behind them. He did not want the Wizard of the Crow to escape.

The Wizard of the Crow had looked on the madness with a mixture of pity and sadness. At the same time, he felt like laughing: his revelations had compelled Tajirika to carry his own shit, for the time being, at least.

Outside, Tajirika ordered the men to lead the way and warned them once again not to do anything foolish, following closely behind with the bucket of his own shit dangling between his legs.

The news quickly spread throughout the camp. The entire squad of the guards rose in arms. Police reinforcements arrived at the scene. But the wardens who were no more than a step from Tajirika kept on shouting: Leave him alone. He has *it*. He is in handcuffs. Don't provoke him. His shit carries death.

Thus they marched, guns cocked all around, until they reached the office of the chief of the Eldares Remand Prison. The chief, the armed guards, and the police reinforcements were all scared of the prisoner rumored to carry death. They knew that he was handcuffed so there was no pressure on them to take any action that might make the situation worse. When asked what he wanted, Tajirika remained consistent in his one demand: he must be taken to Sikiokuu.

The camp chief called Sikiokuu: There is a prisoner here who has virtually taken over the camp with a bucket of shit. He demands to see you. What should we do with him?

# 16

What? Has Tajirika lost his head completely? This was Sikiokuu's first reaction to news of the crisis. Anticipating the return of the Ruler, the last thing he needed was more aggravation to add to his stressed nerves. But the absurdity of the situation struck him: Tajirika taking over an armed camp, a bucket of shit as his only weapon? Sikiokuu cracked up, which momentarily served to lighten his manifold burdens. Yet the more he thought about it, the less amusing it became. Suppose the media found out that the chairman of Marching to Heaven had chased a detachment of the Ruler's armed forces with a bucket of shit? Suppose they carried the picture side by side with that of the Ruler returning home with buckets of dollars for Marching to Heaven, a welcoming crowd of dancers and diplomats around him? He imagined the caption: THE RULER RETURNS HOME WITH BUCKETS OF DOLLARS FOR MARCHING TO HEAVEN. THE CHAIRMAN OF MARCH-ING TO HEAVEN GIVES MARCHING ORDERS TO ARMED GUARDS WITH A BUCKET OF SHIT. Horrible! Remove his handcuffs immediately, he ordered, and ask the man to surrender the bucket. Then, not trusting the camp chief to handle the matter with the necessary discretion— he was not even supposed to know the identity of the two prisoners in the cell—Sikiokuu dispatched his henchmen, Elijah Njoya and Peter Kahiga, to the scene to lead the negotiations.

Tajirika insisted that he would hand his bucket over only after a meeting with the minister. He even had a say in the travel arrange-ments. While Kahiga sat behind the wheel and Njoya next to him, Tajirika sat in the backseat alone, a configuration that suited every-body. Tajirika would keep an eye on the officers, ready to douse them with shit if they tried to cross him. The officers were spared having to sit next to the bucket.

When they arrived at Sikiokuu's, Njoya and Kahiga shielded their captive from public view, taking him through the back door.

Sikiokuu motioned to Njoya and Kahiga to leave and join two other police guards in the outer room. Tajirika and Sikiokuu stood there sizing each other up.

# 17

What Sikiokuu saw in Tajirika was the look of a trapped, wounded animal. So dangerous was Tajirika's look that Sikiokuu searched high and low to offer him a way out. He tried humor to ease the tension.

*"Huī, sasa, story zako? Ni nini makalau wanakubringiya kinaa? Nī haarī wanakuitia?"* Sikiokuu asked in Sheng.

"I don't much care for your outdated Sheng," Tajirika snapped angrily, thinking that Sikiokuu was taking him lightly. "You and I are no longer children. I am not here to play *Fathe* and *Mathe*."

"I was just welcoming you, Mr. Tajirika," Sikiokuu responded quickly, somewhat disappointed that his Sheng had been rebuffed. "What's gone wrong between you and these policemen?" Sikiokuu asked, as if he himself had nothing to do with it.

"Nothing," Tajirika pressed on. "I want to talk man to man."

"Okay! But first let's uncuff you, and please put that bucket down. Let my men take it out. It is stinking up the whole building."

"Why should I trust you with my shit?"

"My word is my bond."

"Swear in the presence of one or two of your police officers that no matter the outcome of our talks, you will never again put me in the same cell with the Wizard of the Crow."

"Only that?" Sikiokuu asked, completely taken aback by the request.

"For now!" said Tajirika. "The rest is between you and me."

Despite his anger at the sorcerer's intransigence, Sikiokuu had not planned on keeping him in jail for more than a day. As soon as the Wizard of the Crow used his sorcery to locate Nyawīra, Sikiokuu planned to release him. In fact, Sikiokuu had thought that if he kept the two together for one night, Tajirika's scary stories of torture would terrorize the Wizard of the Crow and soften him up before their meeting the following day. A lesson in manners.

"What went wrong between you and the Wizard of the Crow?" asked Sikiokuu, relieved and curious at the same time.

"Do you know what it means to share a roof with one who learned sorcery from the dead and regularly talks with the tongues of the dead? Will you swear before a police witness or not?"

How did a lesson in manners turn out like this, with Tajirika babbling all manner of paranoic foolishness?

"Okay!" said Sikiokuu to mollify him a little, for indeed the minister had no idea what Tajirika was talking about. Maybe under torture the man had lost his mind. What was he to do with a crazed chairman of Marching to Heaven? How would he explain it all away? He decided to go along with Tajirika's nutty request, and he shouted for Njoya and Kahiga.

Thinking that their chief was shouting for help, Njoya and Kahiga rushed in followed by the two other police officers, their weapons drawn.

"Put your guns down," Sikiokuu hastened to tell them. "This gentleman and I are old friends. In fact, I needed only two of you, but it is probably better that you all are here because I want all of you to witness what I am now going to say. He must never be put under the same roof as any witch doctor of whatever name. If anyone breaks my rule he will lose his job without notice, period. Besides, this gentleman is not a prisoner. He is in protective custody because he is assisting the government in matters concerning the security of the State. Okay, my friend?" Sikiokuu asked him.

"It's okay," said Tajirika, as if a big weight had been taken off his mind, but he still looked dazed, and his voice quavered.

"Remove the handcuffs," Sikiokuu instructed Kahiga.

Tajirika stepped forward, but as he put the pail of shit on the table, the better to extend his hands for the handcuffs to be removed, he suddenly tripped over a chair and fell, splashing the contents of the bucket all over the office. Some of it found its way onto Sikiokuu's face and clothes; some on Kahiga, Njoya, and the two police officers, and some on the Ruler's portrait on the table. They thought that Tajirika was enacting what he had been threatening the whole day. Njoya and Kahiga ran back to the anteroom and hid behind the door as a shield against more filth. The two other police officers jumped up and down, screaming, *The deadly virus!*

"*Shit!*" shouted Sikiokuu, shaking his big befouled ears, and as he ran toward an inner chamber he was heard to shout: *The idiot deserves to be shot!*

Tajirika heard the words *be shot* and thought that Sikiokuu had issued an order to that effect.

On the ground, smeared with his own shit and urine, Tajirika implored: "*Don't shoot me. I beg you, don't shoot me.* I was lying. I don't have the death virus."

The two additional police officers were so relieved by his confession that they felt grateful, helped him to his feet, removed his handcuffs, and took the bucket away.

As he stood waiting for them to return, Tajirika felt as if a cloud had been lifted from his head, as if he had suddenly woken up from the delirium of a high fever. He also felt a little foolish and unsure of the next move. What should he do? Wipe his face with his soiled shirt? Followed by the two other police officers, Njoya and Kahiga came back, swearing under their breath: Let's hustle him back to the torture chamber and teach him a lesson. Emerging from the inner chamber, Sikiokuu caught Njoya and Kahiga's words and warned them to stop the nonsense. He then ordered the two police officers to get soap and water and clean up the mess under the supervision of Njoya and Kahiga.

"After you finish, go back to the other room and wait for further instructions. And you," he said, turning to Tajirika, "follow me."

But before entering the inner chamber, Sikiokuu suddenly remembered the portrait of the Ruler. He rushed to the table and grabbed it.

"There is a sink in the bathroom over there," Sikiokuu told Tajirika, pointing at a door. "Go in there and clean up a bit. I am afraid I don't have any spare clothes."

Even Sikiokuu had not changed into fresh clothes. He had certainly tried to wipe off the mess from his own shirt, but the soiled spots could still be seen. Now he started working on the portrait of the Ruler, trying to clean the spots, but every time he thought he had finished another seemed to emerge as if from inside the portrait, and in the end he gave up and covered it with a towel. Tajirika found him trying to freshen the air in the chamber with perfume, but no amount of perfume could quite remove the stink in the offices of the Ruler.

*"It's hopeless,"* Sikiokuu said, and he kept the bottle of perfume on the table and sat back in a chair. He then pointed to another chair for Tajirika to sit, and once again they faced each other as before in the outer office, but this time there was only the coffee table between them.

"Mr. Tajirika, what you did today is the same thing as taking hostages, a crime in national and international law. And I must tell you: but for the fact that you were in handcuffs, they would have shot you dead. Let me give you a piece of advice. Don't ever play with fire again, and I really hope to God that the reasons that drove you to hold the armed forces at shit-point are solid enough to withstand the wrath of the State. Tell me everything you came here to tell me. And let me warn you. I don't want more foolishness from you. No more playing around. First: what happened between you and the Wizard of the Crow? Or should I send for him to tell me his version so that you both can argue about your differences in my neutral presence?"

# 18

Sikiokuu's mention of the Wizard of the Crow and the possibility of his coming to the office revived the terror that had driven Tajirika to demand that he be brought to Sikiokuu. Would he never escape the wizard completely? Were their fates tied together? Maybe the Wizard of the Crow had already bewitched him beyond recovery with potent brews from India. Tajirika once again imagined death in the human form of the Wizard of the Crow approaching him relentlessly, like clockwork. Death could now be anywhere, even right outside. Tajirika relived the encroaching helplessness that had brought him to seek Sikiokuu's protection. He now jumped up, went around the table, knelt down, and grabbed the legs of an astonished Sikiokuu in an abject embrace.

"*Please,* I beg you. Ask the Wizard of the Crow to release me from the spell of death he put on me last night. Wasn't that why you sent him to me? His witchcraft is powerful. I knew it from the moment he cured me of my malady. But little did I then know that he gets secret recipes from the dead. If you ask the Wizard of the Crow to remove all the spells of death from me, I promise to do and say whatever it is you want me to do or say. Save me. Rescind the order to kill me. *Please.*"

As soon as he recovered from the shock of Tajirika's embrace, Sikiokuu started sorting things out. So, Tajirika thinks that the sorcerer and I are working together, that I sent the wizard into his cell to cast a deadly spell on him? How could such a thought have occurred to him? Here was a misunderstanding he was not about to clear up, for it served his purposes well. The Wizard of the Crow had become a secret ally who had brought about what torture had failed to do: make Tajirika offer to cooperate.

"Mr. Tajirika, will you please go back to your seat and tell me what is on your mind?"

"No, you must first ask him to remove the evil spell."

"What did the Wizard of the Crow tell you?"

"It is not what he said. But it was not hard for me to figure out that you sent him to my cell with orders to kill me. I recalled my conversation with you the other day and how it ended. Were the three words you told me to think about not the same as those whose meaning the Wizard of the Crow had divined when I first went to him with my malady? You followed our conversation by smuggling him into my cell at midnight. Why did you send him in the dark of night if it was not because you wanted him to harm me? Mr. Sikiokuu, I am not a fool. I know exactly what you are really after. You want him to return the malady of words into my body. Thoughts without words are like steam without an outlet. You want me to drown in my own thoughts or else explode under their pressure. And if that fails, he will chop off my thumbs. The Wizard of the Crow even confessed to me."

"Confessed to you? Confessed what?"

"That he started the queuing mania."

"He told you so?"

"Not directly. But last night he reminded me that the day I went to his shrine was not the first time he and I had met. A while back I had put up a 'no jobs' sign at the main entrance to my office building to keep away the many job seekers who swarmed it. So whenever a job seeker ignored the writing on the signboard and strayed into my office, I would routinely ask him to go back outside and read what was on the sign: *No Vacancy*. But the Wizard of the Crow made me do something I had never done before. He made me walk him to the sign and stand over him as he read it. A day later, I became afflicted with my malady; and then the queuing started at the very spot where the Wizard of the Crow had stood as he read the sign. Can all this be a coincidence?" asked Tajirika, shaking Sikiokuu's legs as if seeking an answer from them. "What more proof do I need to see that he was the origin of the queuing mania? The question is this: who sent him to my office and why? Or am I supposed to believe that a person with a good and lucrative business in sorcery would just stray into my office and ask for a job he does not need unless driven by other motives? He was clearly sent to try me with afflictions as Satan once did to Job, but unlike Job I had no chance against his wiles. To have given him a job would have been to give him ample opportunity to cast an evil spell on my business. My business would have died slowly, and with the failure of my business I would no longer have been found fit to continue as the chairman of Marching to Heaven. And if I denied him a job, as I did, he would exact vengeance, as he did, first by making me ill and then by starting the queuing mania. Two questions remain: when I met him at his shrine he never gave the slightest hint by tone or gesture of the fact that we had met before, so why did he do so now, after you had put him in my cell? Mr. Minister, if you are not the one who sent him on a mission to start the queuing mania, then who was it? Who else would have a motive for destroying me and undermining my chairmanship of Marching to Heaven?"

"Mr. Tajirika, what you say is very interesting, except that you are mixing things up a bit. For instance, your thinking that I could have started or sent somebody to start the queues verges on a delirium. Let us examine your story guided by reason. I take it, from what you have told me so far, that you think that the Wizard of the Crow was on a mission, that somebody had sent him to set off the queuing mania. Or, to put it another way, you seem to be saying that somebody deliberately started the queuing thing? Please return to your seat so that we can talk about this clearly."

"First things first. Ask him to lift the curse of death from me."

During this exchange, Sikiokuu had time and time again tried to push Tajirika away, but every time he did so the latter would tighten his grip on Sikiokuu's legs. Now he tried again, in vain, and realized that there was no way Tajirika was going to sit back down until he received reassurance of some kind. Sikiokuu decided to try a little performance. He picked up the phone, called the front room where the police were waiting, and asked for Kahiga. When Kahiga walked in and saw the scene he pulled out his pistol, but Sikiokuu winked and gestured to him to put his gun back into the holster. If Kahiga felt like laughing, he kept it to himself; he just stood there waiting for further instructions from his boss.

"I want you to go to the Wizard of the Crow and find out exactly what he told Tajirika. Tell him that I am not now as angry with Tajirika as I was when I sent the wizard to deal with him in his cell. Accordingly, I now order him to lift all curses and evil spells he may have put on Tajirika. If he does not do so forthwith, shoot the bastard. *On the spot. No discussion.*"

Sikiokuu touched his ears and shook them from side to side slightly to signal to Kahiga the farcical nature of the proceeding.

Outside, Kahiga started chuckling; this Tajirika was a riot, first with his bucket of shit and now kneeling, holding on to Sikiokuu's legs.

Tajirika relinquished Sikiokuu's legs and returned to his seat.

"Thank you, brave Minister," said Tajirika.

"*Don't mention it,* as the English say," said Sikiokuu. "But let us return to our story. Now did I hear you say that this sorcerer once came to your office pretending to be looking for work?"

"Yes."

"And Nyawĩra, was she still your secretary at the time?"

"Yes."

"And a few days later, this same Nyawĩra took you to the sorcerer's shrine?"

"Yes. Nyawĩra and my wife, Vinjinia."

"Nyawĩra and this son of a crow, did they know each other?"

"No. Nothing suggested that, neither when he came to me in search of work nor when I went to his place in search of a cure."

"But you cannot say for sure that they did not know each other?"

"That's correct."

"And you never heard Nyawīra mention his name afterward?"

"That's correct."

"And you can say with absolute certainty that it was somebody else who had sent the sorcerer to your office to look for work? And as for this somebody, his real interest was to start the queuing mania?"

"Yes, that's how it seems to me when I piece things together."

Sikiokuu paused as if pondering what Tajirika had said. He felt malicious joy within, but he did not want to show it. Sikiokuu found Tajirika precisely how he had always wanted him to be: a supplicant in search of mercy and forgiveness. There were a few dots, though, that had yet to be connected. What was the connection, if any, between Nyawīra and the Wizard of the Crow? Why would the Wizard of the Crow want to pretend that he was looking for a job? More investigations were necessary. What pleased him most was that Tajirika had agreed finally that the queues had not simply sprung up, that somebody had started them according to a plan. The mastermind had to be rooted out.

"Mr. Tajirika, listen to me. I am not going to lie to you. *You are in a lot of trouble.* But I am going to help you. Let's first agree on the facts. You don't deny that the queuing started outside your office?"

"That's correct."

"And now you have stated firmly, unequivocally, that it is your belief and even calculation that the whole thing was a plot? And that somebody was behind it?"

"Yes."

"Now, we know that the somebody is not me. It is not you. We know the somebody was not the Wizard of the Crow, because you do admit that he was only a messenger. What concerns us all is the identity of the *mastermind.* That's why the Ruler set up a Commission of Inquiry with Mr. Kaniūrū as the chairman. So you see that when you refused to obey the *summons,* whatever your reason, you were actually disobeying the Ruler. See my point?"

"Yes. Help me; please do whatever you can to make sure that this matter does not reach the ears of the Ruler."

"God helps those who help themselves, and we shall soon find out how far you are prepared to help yourself. For my part, I can make sure that the confessions you make in this office will be sent to the Commission of Inquiry to be made part of its records. It will seem as if you had indeed appeared before that august body freely and willingly, or that you had made *a written submission* to it. Either way, you will seem to have fully cooperated with the commission; your having defied a legitimate summons, broken the law, and challenged the Ruler's authority would no longer be the case. In return for that favor, you will promise that you will never mention to anybody that you were arrested or that you spent time in a cell. And all talk of Thomas and Descartes must end."

"*Thank you, Mr. Sikiokuu. Thank you,*" Tajirika said. "Do not worry about those sects. I do not belong to any."

"Okay! Let's proceed and see if we can identify the criminal mastermind. You have already said that you think that there is a connection between the wizard's search for a job and your malady of words. In both cases the Wizard of the Crow was instrumental, so we can assume that the person behind his search for employment and the one behind your affliction are one and the same. Now tell me, did you manage to solve the riddle of the three words? Did you figure out who really infected you with the virus of white-ache?"

"Any of us could have given another the affliction," Tajirika said, without realizing that he was repeating part of the conversation he had had with the Wizard of the Crow about the three words. "I'm not the only one who may have suffered from the disease."

"In short, what you are saying is that somebody else infected you with the illness?"

"Perhaps."

"Forget perhaps. Whom do you suspect? Friends? Maybe your friend Machokali?" Sikiokuu asked, a little irritated at being forced to voice the name.

"He could have. The trouble, if you followed my argument, is that even you could have done so."

"Leave my name out of this, Tajirika! What you are trying to say is that Machokali gave you the virus. Do you still doubt this?"

"How can I doubt anything? You told me to forget Thomas Descartes."

"So you have no doubt that it was Machokali who infected you with the virus?"

"I am still trying to figure out who else could have given me the germs. The way I now understand it is that the higher we climb in our circle the more vulnerable we become to the virus of white-ache as both carriers and recipients. So you see that even you, Mr. Minister . . ."

"Mr. Tajirika, I really thought you were serious about helping, but I see you are *still playing games,*" Sikiokuu said icily.

"I am sorry, Mr. Minister, but I mentioned you as an example only. I wanted to say that the only person with whom I socialized and who obviously belongs to a rank higher than mine is Machokali, and it is possible . . ."

". . . that you heard him say *'if'?*" Sikiokuu completed his thought for him.

"Yes," Tajirika said. "Or, it is possible . . ."

". . . that you heard his desire for higher office, his wishing that someday he might become, say, president?"

"Not directly. But because he is a politician, it is not impossible to imagine that he may have, once or twice, said that if this happens then that could happen, or if it had been he who was . . ."

". . . holding the highest seat of office in the land?"

"Yes. Something like that. But is there a politician who does not harbor those dreams?"

"Mr. Tajirika, do you know that what you are saying is *very serious?* That it is against the law to wish or dream of ever becoming president as long as the Ruler himself is alive? *Treason, in fact?*"

"Yes. You might say so."

"Let's be clear about this. Have you harbored those thoughts, wishes, or dreams?"

"Me, ruler of Aburīria? Oh, no, no! Even for a parliamentary seat or a ministerial post, I have no ambition. My main and only interest in life is making money. Give me a prosperous business, and you will see a very satisfied man."

"I believe you," said Sikiokuu, as if congratulating him for his lack of political ambition. "You love riches and this is borne out by the fact that it was only after you learned that your destiny as a white man was to be poor that your white-ache got cured."

"That's right. The jingle of coins in the pocket is beautiful music. As for political office, I leave it to you ministers . . ."

"Look, Tajirika, let's not be like two bulls circling each other, reluctant to engage. Here I am the only bull in the kraal. So stop skirting the issue. Get to the point. What you are trying to say is that Machokali used to say something like . . . ?"

"If he had more power. Like all politicians, yes. Isn't that what we were saying just now?"

"You mean what *you* were saying!"

"He might have expressed a wish for even higher office, like all politicians."

"But we are not talking about all politicians, are we?"

"I agree. We are talking singular, not plural."

"You are now talking good grammar. You do agree that two people cannot hold the same office at the same time?"

"That's true."

"So when a politician eyes a seat held by another he can only be saying: I wish the incumbent were swallowed by the earth! I wish he would disappear or be made to disappear."

"As you say!"

"Not as I say, as you say. Mr. Tajirika, what you are saying is vital to the security and well-being of this nation. Would you be willing to put in writing what you just said, or repeat it before the Commission of Inquiry?"

"Yes," said Tajirika, unsure of what exactly he was prepared to repeat.

"Let's now summarize and agree on what you have told me willingly, freely, without any coercion from anybody whatsoever. And when you go to write down your confession before Njoya and Kahiga, you will not deviate from the summary. This is what you have told me: At different times and occasions you heard Machokali express his longing for the highest political office in the land, often with the conditional *if the Ruler were not there . . . etc.* This shocked and caused you so much anguish that when you tried to recall his sentiments and their implications, your larynx rebelled and refused to give words to those thoughts. When you recovered from your malady of words, you tried to cover up the real reason by saying that you had simply been expressing a wish to be white. White-ache. But we know what the word *white* stands for. Besides, this was not even your own wish: you were regurgitating what had already been thought out and spoken by others cleverer and more cunning than you. You were actually covering for your special friend. Even when you recovered from the malady, Machokali told you to continue pretending that you were still afflicted, keeping those thoughts alive in your mind so that you would continue to be his surrogate."

"You forgot to add that he did not want the queuing to come to an end, for the queues were very important to the Ruler."

"What a friend you have in this man! So he claimed that it was the Ruler who needed the queues? That it was he who sparked the mania?"

"Not exactly in those words," Tajirika tried to clarify.

"You seem to be very keen on defending the actions of your friend."

"*Oh, no, no.*"

"Then you should keep the name of the Ruler out of this. What Machokali told you is that you should continue claiming to be ill so that the queuing could continue, or words to that effect?"

"That's correct."

"You see? So what you are trying to say is that in asking you to continue the charade he had two aims: to multiply the queues so that when people got tired of them they would riot, and to advance his ambition for the highest office in the land by way of your own, his surrogate's, thoughts. Let's wrap up the summary of your confession. You told me that before Machokali left for America he and you had a secret meeting at the Mars Café. It was then that you asked that you become part of the delegation to the USA because, after all, you were the chairman of Marching to Heaven, but Machokali refused even to consider it. The vehemence with which he refused surprised you at first, but soon it was clear why. For, a few minutes later, he asked you whether in his absence you would become his eyes and ears in Aburīria. In short, he wanted you to be the nucleus of alternative intelligence loyal to him. But you, as a good and loyal citizen, did not say yes or no, because you did not want such a thought to foul your mind. You knew very well that it was only the Ruler who had the right to run an intelligence network. Now you knew why he had appointed you chairman of Marching to Heaven. You were to become his surrogate or representative in the project, for he was more or less sure that in the future he himself would be in charge. As time went by, you became so concerned about this matter that you demanded to see me because of my reputation as a loyal and responsible member of the Ruler's government."

Female Daemons

Tajirika started seeing Machokali through Sikiokuu's eyes. That Marching to Heaven was intended eventually to come under the control of Machokali struck him as being especially true. So that was why Machokali had come up with the idea of the birthday gift in the first place and later pretended that it was the members of the Birthday Committee who had initiated the idea? *What a friend,* Tajirika thought, amazed, as if coming to terms with the real Machokali for the first time. Machokali had even made him think that Sikiokuu was an enemy. In his moment of greatest crisis the person he had thought a friend had not even bothered to call him from America out of courtesy, and the person he had thought an enemy was the one who had come to his aid. Sikiokuu had not only gotten the Wizard of the Crow off his back, but had also found a clever way of getting Tajirika off the hook for refusing to obey the summons, and now, more important, he had even started thinking for him. How restful it was to surrender one's mind to another person, he sighed with relief. Exhausted, broken in mind and spirit, overwhelmed by everything that had befallen him, Tajirika felt not only that the summary gave a true account, but that Sikiokuu had kindly taken onto himself the burden that had been weighing on Tajirika's mind.

"Thank you. You have straightened me out," Tajirika said.

"No need for *thanks, this or that.* I am only doing what comes naturally to me. Besides, this is a very serious matter, and the security of the land is the collective responsibility of all who love the Ruler and his works. Tajirika, I will personally let the Ruler know that he is very fortunate to have exemplary citizens like you. Now, Titus, listen very carefully. Just now you talked about my straightening you out. Whose summary is this? Does it represent exactly what you want to confess before the authorized government witnesses?"

"Of course," said Tajirika. "What is in the summary are my exact words."

"Did I induce you with threats of violence or any other form of coercion or seduction, like drinks?"

"Oh, no, although just now I wouldn't mind a drink."

"In a while, Titus. Business first. Celebration afterward. Now, I want you to remember everything in the summary. You will make two confessions. The first will deal with the question of queuing and Machokali's connection with its origin and development. If I were

401

you I would leave out the stuff about the Wizard of the Crow coming to your office and looking for work, because there is no evidence linking Machokali and the sorcerer. What you should stress mostly is Machokali's insistence on your pretending to be ill to give the queues a chance to spread. This particular confession will go to the chairman of the Commission of Inquiry into the Queuing Mania. The other confession will deal with the connection between Machokali's ambition and your malady, how in fact your malady embodied his lust for the highest office in the land, confirmed by his instructions to you to set up his own intelligence network. This confession will be *top secret, a state secret,* reserved only for the eyes of the Ruler—well, and mine, too."

Tajirika was most pleased that his confession would be a *top secret, a state secret.* His face brightened and his eyes were radiant.

"One more thing. I will not be with you when you make these confessions. I don't want you to ever say that I had somehow coerced you into making them. But know that as soon as you have made and signed your statements, you will be free to go. And I assure you that if your confessions conform to the summary, the Ruler will never forget the work you have done for the State. Your future is secure, Mr. Tajirika. He might even consider you for a ministerial post. Maybe not a full cabinet post, but a junior rank."

"Me, a minister? A good joke, but thank you from the bottom of my heart," Tajirika said with a touch of emotion in his voice.

"Don't mention it," Sikiokuu said. "The pleasure is mine. As to your confessions, my men, Njoya and Kahiga, are at your disposal. You can trust them. They are professional editors and witnesses."

# 19

A few hours later, Tajirika's extraordinary admissions were locked in a security safe in Sikiokuu's office. Sikiokuu stroked his earlobes, looking at the safe, savoring his victory over his nemesis. In there, he had more than enough dirt on Machokali.

Tajirika was brought to him and Sikiokuu escorted him back to the inner chamber. He poured scotch into two glasses.

"Titus. *A toast. To your health. Cheers."*

"*Cheers* and thanks a million, Silver," said Tajirika, his face aglow, excited at the company.

They drank like the best of social friends, chatting a thousand irrelevancies.

"Can I guess the first thing you are going to do once you get home?" Sikiokuu said. "Jump on your wife. I can only imagine how much you must have missed *it.* That's what you are thinking about. *Admit it,* Titus."

"You are right. I am thinking of jumping on her, but not in the way you are imagining."

"Titus, are there that many ways of jumping on a woman?" said Sikiokuu, laughing. "Maybe I am too conservative. I have three wives, not to mention several *mistresses,* and believe me, I have never departed from the MP."

"MP?" Tajirika asked, wondering what being a member of Parliament had to do with wives and mistresses.

"Missionary position," Sikiokuu said, laughing.

"Oh, I did not even have that in mind. I was thinking of lashes on her body."

"Why would you want to do that on the very first hour of your homecoming?"

"Because of her involvement with the women," he said.

"Women? Is your wife that kind? I thought you said . . ."

"If it was just a matter of tumbling into bed with another woman," Tajirika said, "I would call it a private act, her own business. But sitting there in public while those women danced for her? That's a different matter. Had you not been so kind as to bring me those pictures, I might never have known the truth."

Lost in his victories, Sikiokuu had forgotten all about the pictures. But now he recalled them with alarm. If Tajirika beat Vinjinia or even quarreled with her about them, the truth might come out before the confessions had played their assigned role.

"By the way, Titus, I am glad that you have mentioned those pictures, because you have reminded me of something I was going to tell you before you leave for home, but I might as well tell you now. When you get home, don't say a word about those pictures or even about the women dancers. I want you to listen to Vinjinia's story, or rather to her lies. But you must not touch her before we have investigated every aspect of this affair."

"Are you trying to tell me that I cannot beat my wife without your permission?" Tajirika asked defiantly.

"I am not asking you to retire from wife beating. How can I ask you to give up what defines modern Aburīrian manhood?"

"Okay, a temporary truce, but . . ." said Tajirika.

"I will tell you what. Let's establish a hotline. Anytime you feel the urge to beat your wife, please call me and I will tell you if the time is ripe."

"Okay!" said Tajirika, pleased with the idea of a hotline.

# 20

Early in the evening of the same day, Sikiokuu sent Njoya and Kahiga for the Wizard of the Crow. He had just had one success—why not go for a second? Strike while the iron is hot, he said to himself, whistling a tune of satisfaction and expectation.

What hit the Wizard of the Crow, on entering Sikiokuu's office, was a strong odor of decomposing flesh. He was reminded of Tajirika and his bucket of shit. Tajirika must have been here, he thought, and hence the scent of prison all around the chamber. He felt a little dizzy as he tried to fight the stench and steady himself by looking around the room, resting his glance, for a moment, on the photographic portrait of the Ruler on the table. Why a towel on the picture, he wondered idly. Then he saw some spots on the eyes, ears, nose, and mouth of the image, and for a few seconds he had a strange sensation of seeing, or thinking that he saw, a thick darkish liquid oozing out of them. Sikiokuu saw what he was looking at.

"A little intimidating, isn't it," Sikiokuu said as he casually picked up the portrait, glanced at it ever so briefly, then dusted it fondly, almost tenderly, with the towel before placing it on top of a drawer at the corner. "Even when he goes away, he leaves a bit of his power behind, and you can feel it even in his pictures. A kind of stigmata," he added with a smile that took in the Wizard of the Crow and the two escorts, Njoya and Kahiga, who stood by the door. "Please leave us alone," he said to his two loyal lieutenants. "I want to have a private conversation with, *well,* my guest," he added, gesturing for the Wizard of the Crow to sit down.

An awkward silence followed the departure of Njoya and Kahiga. The two men sized each other up. Sikiokuu then leaned forward, lowered his voice a little, and tried to strike a note of intimacy.

"I am sorry to have kept you waiting, but I had an emergency on my hands. Ah! The burden we ministers have to carry! Your fame has reached the ears of the government. Or, more accurately, me. But let me confess. When I heard of the Wizard of the Crow, I thought of an old man, of seventy years or more, supporting himself with a walking stick, a fly whisk in hand, a tobacco pouch hanging from his neck. And now, behold! A young man in a designer suit. *A modern sorcerer, eh? Or is it postmodern?*"

*"Postcolonial,"* the Wizard of the Crow added.

"A *postcolonial* witch doctor?" Sikiokuu added, laughing out loud. "A sorcerer with a sense of humor, too? They tell me that there is no manual for sorcery you have not devoured. By the way, do you know what most attracted me about you? Your caution. When I heard that you did not want your clients and neighbors to know that you might be involved in a criminal investigation and you wanted to approach our cooperation with the utmost secrecy, I sat back and said to myself: Now here is a man who knows what is what in this world, and the moment word gets around that he is helping us catch criminals, he would cease to be of much use to us because possible suspects would shy away from him and his shrine. That's why, to bring you here, I sent my lieutenants in civilian clothes and in a Mercedes-Benz. Have you ever heard of any other sorcerer treated with this kind of consideration by a cabinet minister? Nothing but respect for you. I wanted us to do business last night but, alas, I was caught up in some important matters of State. Believe me when I say that a beggar in the streets has more peace of mind than a cabinet minister . . ."

"Uneasy lies the head that wears the crown?"

"Precisely," said Sikiokuu. "Sometimes we don't even sleep. But do not let me burden you with our problems. Let me tell you what I am thinking about our agenda for the night, eh? As soon as you finish what you are here to do, we will whisk you back to your shrine under the cover of darkness. None of your neighbors will be the wiser; it will be as if you had never left—you have my word that the matter will remain within my trusted circle of us three. This does not mean that the State will ever forget you. Oh, no. The government has many ways of showing its gratitude to people like you. The most important thing is for you to do your work well and help us apprehend the criminal, Nyawĩra."

"I don't quite get what you are asking me to do," the Wizard of the Crow admitted.

"We have looked high and low for Nyawĩra, all over the country, and have not come up with the tiniest trace of her shadow. We want you to use your power of divination, of prophecy, whatever, all your powers of sorcery to tell us two things. Is Nyawĩra alive or dead? If she is dead, where is she buried? If she is alive, where is her lair?"

"Excuse me," the Wizard of the Crow said. "It seems as if your men failed to understand what I told them. I thought I'd been clear, but I was wrong. I told your people that my task is to capture dae-mons that afflict the mind or body; theirs is to capture felons."

"Don't take the police for fools. They know when one is serious and when one is not. They know that words have surface and deeper meanings. The habit of taking bribes has taught them the language of parables. When a policeman wants a bribe he does not say, Give me a bribe; he says, It is very cold today, even if it is as hot as hell. And you are supposed to say, Why don't you take this Burĩ note for tea? So, although you did not say yes directly, the police knew that your *no* was a kind of *yes*. You see, they recognized that you knew what they know: that even walls can have ears. *You are a very cautious person, Mr. Witch Doctor,* a wise man. Haste is the mother of failure. But while caution is good, too much of it can court danger. Believe me, my friend, whatever you tell me, it will stay within these walls. Nobody will ever know that you or any witch doctor helped us cap-ture Nyawĩra."

"Mr. Minister," cried out the Wizard of the Crow. "Let us try this again: my powers are for protecting the laws that govern the body and the soul, and yours are to protect the laws that govern society. I look not for those that break the law of society but those that destroy the law of life. I fight illnesses; you fight criminals."

Sikiokuu felt his hope fall and his anger mount and, with a tremendous effort of will, prevented himself from screaming abuses at the audacious fellow.

"Mr. Wizard of the Crow, you may be the greatest sorcerer in the world, but you are not above the law. The law says that every citizen, be he a sorcerer or a priest or whatever, must help the State in apprehending criminals. If one sees a person committing a crime and one does not report the person to the authorities, then one is also committing the crime."

"What I'm telling you is the truth. I don't have the power that you are ascribing to me," the Wizard of the Crow said, his raised voice hinting at defiance.

Sikiokuu stood up abruptly and walked about, occasionally pulling and pinching his ears nervously, as if he could not believe that he, a senior cabinet minister in the government of the Ruler, now in charge of the country, could be sitting in his office at night arguing with a sorcerer about the use of witchcraft. He calmed himself and sat down, intent again on achieving what he had set out to get.

"Okay, let's accept that there was indeed a *misunderstanding*. So what? Let's forget the past. What's done is done. No sense crying over spilled milk. Isn't that the saying? I need to ask you a question or two just to clarify the situation. You are not refusing to help the government, are you?"

"No."

"Okay, just as I thought. You are a power to reckon with, but you also know how to reckon with power. Now look into your mirror and tell me what you see in there."

"I did not bring my mirror," said the Wizard of the Crow.

"Why the hell did you come here?" exploded Sikiokuu, no longer trying to cover up his chagrin. "To waste my time, or what? My instructions that you bring your mirror were loud and clear."

The Wizard of the Crow was about to remind the minister that his presence here had been forced, but he thought the better of it. Nyawīra's life, after all, hung in the balance. If the minister were to keep sending his men to the shrine every other day, Nyawīra would continually be in danger. So instead of open defiance, he employed a different tactic.

"It is not their fault," the Wizard of the Crow said. "They told me to bring my mirror, but I assured them that I could use any mirror ready at hand. In most cases it is actually better, more effective, to use the mirror of the person afflicted, for such mirrors have the added advantage of having already captured the shadows of their owners."

"That's good," Sikiokuu said, somewhat mollified. "In my apartment are many rooms, and each has a mirror. When we work late and we are too tired to go home, we spend the night here. Our apartments are really extensions of our offices. Which reminds me, oh, please forgive me for being such a bad host. Would you like a drink? Beer? Whiskey? Wine? Whatever you like!"

"No, thank you. I don't drink. Alcohol is not my personal savior."

Sikiokuu went into some other room, laughing. Even when he came back carrying a mirror he was still laughing.

"Alcohol is not your personal savior?" Sikiokuu asked, handing over the mirror. Then, all about the business at hand, he became deadly serious. "I want you to look at this mirror. Look all over it until you see Nyawĩra. If you find her, I shall make sure that whatever you want is yours: money, shares in a company, a farm in an area formerly for whites only, a building plot or two in Eldares—the choice is yours. Okay? And remember that if I ever rise to a higher office I will make sure that you become *chief government witch doctor*. Count on it. I shall reciprocate your good deed today."

He talked as if words came out first and thought followed, although just now it was more like thought had become tired of following words and got stuck in only one desire: the way to Nyawĩra's lair. Strange that the tone of one man's voice could carry such a mixture of prayer, bribe, threat, fear, and ambition.

It was clear to the wizard that Sikiokuu was desperate, capable of anything, so he resolved not to antagonize him. He must do whatever was necessary to deflect Sikiokuu and his henchmen from any thoughts of going back to the shrine.

"Give me the mirror," he said. "But I must advise you: I have never done anything like this before. So don't be surprised by the unexpected."

"Just try and see what you can see through the mirror. Trying over and over again is the gateway to success."

Even with the mirror in his hands, the Wizard of the Crow was no clearer about the details of his performance except that he had to protect Nyawĩra. He stood up and started walking about in the office, deep in thought. Sikiokuu remained seated but his eyes followed the wizard's every movement. Now the wizard sat down again and cleared his throat.

"I want you to dim all the lights save one by which to see the mirror," said the Wizard of the Crow. Even before he had finished his command, Sikiokuu had jumped to his feet and started turning lights off, except the one dramatically illuminating the table.

"Sit on the other side of the table, facing me," said the Wizard of the Crow.

The Wizard of the Crow held the mirror just above the table.

"Listen very carefully. It's my turn to ask you a few questions."

"Ask whatever you like. No one was ever convicted for asking questions."

Sikiokuu saw the mirror begin to shake in the hands of the Wizard of the Crow.

"What's wrong?" he asked.

"Can't you see?"

"What?"

"I don't really know. But let's find out. What did you say when I told you that I had some questions for you?"

"I said that no one is ever convicted for asking questions."

The mirror shook violently, even as the Wizard of the Crow tried, with both hands, to rest it on the table.

"When you say that no one is ever convicted for asking questions, what do you mean?"

"Even a little child would know what I am talking about," Sikiokuu said, resenting the wizard for seemingly belittling his intelligence.

"The mirror is not a little child. And it wants to know."

"Okay. Okay. I am saying that one is never prosecuted in a court of law for asking questions. You don't put a person in prison for asking questions."

The mirror responded by shaking so uncontrollably that it was with much difficulty that the Wizard of the Crow prevented it from flying toward Sikiokuu.

"Why is it shaking so? What have I said to upset it so?" asked a frightened Sikiokuu.

"Mr. Minister. You have to look into your heart. Are you very sure that one is never prosecuted and convicted for asking questions? Even in Aburīria?"

Sikiokuu thought about the question. He was beginning to grow a little concerned about the wizard and the mirror.

"Well, sometimes we do actually imprison people for asking questions, but only those that question established truths or that undermine the rule of law or how this country is governed."

The mirror became still. "The mirror has stopped shaking," said the Wizard of the Crow as he wiped sweat from his brow. "I told you to listen to my questions carefully. You must answer truthfully, for you have seen that a mirror is not something to be trifled with. Does this mirror belong to you?"

"Yes."

"Are you the only one who uses it?"

"Why?"

"What did I tell you? A mirror is so ordinary, and yet it is a most incredible instrument. A mirror captures shadows of ourselves. Shadows that pass through the mirror don't go away. Traces remain, reflections of ourselves, our hearts, the effects of our actions on ourselves. The only problem is that shadows can intermingle, preventing now one, now another, from being seen clearly. This could very well be the case with this mirror if others have touched it. In addition, Mr. Minister, there might be some shadows you don't want seen by eyes other than your own. That's why I am asking whether others besides you have used this mirror. But if you don't mind my seeing their faces, it is all the same to me. I am very discreet."

Sikiokuu recalled the faces of the women, especially other people's wives, to whom he had made love in his bedroom. One of them had turned out to have been a regular bed-maker for the Ruler. The Ruler was very protective of his bed-makers. He did not want to know of any other person having touched them before or after. How many husbands had he exiled abroad, giving them jobs far away, that he might have unfettered access to the woman? One person, a prominent businessman, had lost his head for dating, and boasting about it, a lady known to be one of the Ruler's favorite bed-makers. Without further ado, Sikiokuu launched to grab the mirror.

"I will get you another one," he said.

Again Sikiokuu dashed into another room, looking for a mirror that only he had used, and brought it to the Wizard of the Crow.

"And you are now absolutely sure that you are the only one who has used this mirror?"

"I am not one hundred percent sure. But let's try it."

"And you know that traces of your own shadow have been retained in the mirror?"

"Where am I going to get a mirror that I have not used before? Divine with the mirror you now have and let me deal with the consequences."

"You know that if you lie or don't answer questions honestly you may interfere with the search for the object of your pursuit?"

"I will answer all your questions, but remember that I am not here to take a *lie detector test*. And if I may remind you, you are here to look for Nyawīra, not me."

"I just wanted you to know how the mirror works so that you can make an informed decision whether we should go forward with the search or not. It's all up to you."

"Let's get on with it," Sikiokuu replied, a trifle impatiently.

"Kneel down, close your eyes, put your hands together as if you were praying, a supplicant at an imaginary shrine. Focus on the image of Nyawīra in your head. On no account must you take your mind's eye away from the image or let thoughts of another intrude."

Sikiokuu tried to do as he was told but his mind kept wandering from subject to subject. He was glad that he had asked his two lieutenants to stay in the waiting room. What would they say if they were to come in and find him kneeling before a sorcerer, the lights dimmed? He jumped up and hurried to lock the doors to the other rooms from the inside. He even took the telephone off the hook to ensure that no calls, not even from the Ruler, would interrupt the proceedings. He resumed the posture of a supplicant. Even now no clear image of the woman would form in his mind, only vague intermittent silhouettes, but he kept trying. Sometimes he would peek at the Wizard of the Crow, and he felt better about what was transpiring when he saw the sorcerer's eyes fixed on the mirror. The voice of the Wizard of the Crow now pierced the silence of the room, as if responding to what appeared in the mirror. Sikiokuu would have liked to look at the mirror himself but did not dare, awed as he was by the solemnity of the occasion.

"Here comes a shadow. There. It stopped. It walks. It walks. Now it's gone; it's back. It is the shape of a woman, not very clear, but, oh, yes, it is a woman. A young woman. She is running like an antelope in the woods. Her shadow merges with the trees. There, there, she's crossing a river. She enters a hole as in *Alice in Wonderland*. Darkness. Light. She is coming out of the hole. I see her in the woods again—no, no, among people. She is lost in the crowd . . ."

"Stop her. Please stop her," cried Sikiokuu. "Or follow her. Follow her and find out where she is going or who she will be meeting or talking to, anything, but don't let her out of your sight . . ."

"Ssshh. Another shadow has appeared, superimposing itself on the scene. It is huge, blurry. Good. It's clear again. It is the shadow of a man of power and confidence. He looks like a minister, a government minister. He is dressed in clothes that look like those of . . . Let me stop there. I don't want to see more," said the Wizard of the Crow, taking his eyes away from the mirror.

"Why did you take your eyes off the mirror?" Sikiokuu asked, also opening his own.

"Are you sure that you want me to go on?"

"What did you see? Whose shadow was it? Was it Machokali? Was he following the female? Did they talk, greet each other, look at each other? Tell me. Tell me everything that you just saw . . ."

"It was yours."

"Leave my shadow out of this," Sikiokuu said in frustration. "Go back to the mirror and see if you can bring back the shadow of that woman. Try hard. Concentrate on her."

No matter how many times or how hard he tried, the Wizard of the Crow reported the same scene: the shadow of the woman would always appear running in the woods, crossing a river, only to disappear in a crowd, and precisely at that point, Sikiokuu's shadow would cover up the crowd.

"Wow! Your shadow has a lot of power . . ." said the wizard, as if complimenting Sikiokuu.

"Power? Did you say *power*?" asked Sikiokuu, his interest in his own shadow now aroused.

"Yes. It's as if all the other shadows fear it."

"Fear? Forget Nyawīra for a moment and find out more about my shadow. What does it look like? How is it dressed?"

"It's your spitting image. It is dressed like the Ruler . . . and it walks with a similar gait . . ."

"Wait a minute. Stop. Look for, no, no, let me think clearly . . . let me think this through . . ." said Sikiokuu, panic in his voice.

Sikiokuu was trembling. What was the meaning of all this? Had something bad happened to His Mighty . . . Or was this simply a sign of things to come? Was it Sikiokuu's destiny to become . . . ?

He was dying to know. But how to ask the Wizard of the Crow to look into that particular aspect of his future without compromising himself by uttering a word of what was in his mind? He closed his eyes and tried to imagine a different future, but no matter how hard he tried his thoughts always went back to the image of himself in a suit that looked like that of His Mighty Excellency. The same gait? He saw himself walking, inspecting the military standing at attention in salute . . . The Wizard of the Crow had said the mirror could capture . . . Suddenly things came to a standstill. Had this mirror captured one of his most secret performances of power?

These days, with the Ruler in America, Sikiokuu would lock himself inside his office or apartment, dress exactly like the Ruler and even sit in an elevated seat very much like that of the Mighty Excellency. As his role playing was known only to himself, how had the Wizard of the Crow managed to uncover it?

Even to his skeptical and cynical mind, this served only to confirm that the Wizard of the Crow had preternatural powers. His desire to know the destiny of his own shadow became an irresistible hunger for more signs. But he could not or would not clothe his thoughts in words. Suddenly he said, "If." Every time he tried to say something, he would simply mutter, "If." Soon he was barking a series of *if*s, the Wizard of the Crow looking on in astonishment. Sikiokuu fell to the floor and started crawling, his ears drooping on either side, his snout and eyes raised toward the Wizard of the Crow as if seeking help. It was then that the Wizard of the Crow gave him the mirror and told him to look hard at himself and focus his mind on one and only one concern.

"Listen. I can help you to express your thoughts with words. But, again, you must answer all my questions truthfully; otherwise the mirror will simply reveal your lies."

"If, if, if," Sikiokuu barked as if saying yes, yes, yes, nodding his head for emphasis.

"Give me back the mirror. Let's start. Do you ever dream of occupying the seat now occupied by the Ruler?" he asked, looking at the mirror, glancing now and then at the face of the minister.

Sikiokuu could hear very clearly what he was being asked but found it difficult to answer. Finally he nodded his head.

"No, tell me in words," the Wizard of the Crow insisted. "Do you ever dream of occupying the highest office in the land?"

"Yes. I have," he said through clenched teeth.

And with that Sikiokuu gathered steam and started talking, words all of a sudden flooding from his mouth like a rushing river.

"There is no minister who does not dream of one day becoming the Ruler. We lust for power, and what power is greater than that of a supreme ruler? You raise a fly whisk or a club and men kneel before you. You sneeze and you silence a multitude. You hold the key to all the wealth in the land. One word, just one word, and the doors of the Central Bank are open to you. And if the national chest is empty, no problem. One word from you and thousands more notes are made. Oh, imagine it: when you say, Wipe your noses, a million handkerchiefs are raised to a million noses. You say to your ministers, Put a comma, and they do it. Put a full stop, and they do it, without question. Imagine your ministers and ambitious members of Parliament feeling honored that you have taken an interest in their wives, ecstatic when they know you have made love to them? Power. I dream of that power every hour of the day, whether awake or asleep. And why not? The fact is that today I am the de facto head of the State, the power behind the throne, so to speak, and were the Ruler to fall ill and die today . . ."

Before he had finished the thought he remembered that to mention, imagine, dream, think, or talk about the death of the Ruler was high treason, punishable by death. His face twitched at the horror of what he had just said and its implications for his future.

The Wizard of the Crow noted all that and pretended to be in a trance, completely unaware of what had been spoken. Sikiokuu stole a glance at the Wizard of the Crow to see if he had heard his last words, and he was not sure what to think when he found the wizard still bent over the mirror. He waited for the sorcerer himself to say a word or turn his head, but the wizard remained in his trance, transfixed by the mirror. Now Sikiokuu got off his knees and sat back in his chair.

"Mr. Wizard of the Crow! Mr. Wizard of the Crow!" Sikiokuu called out, as if trying to wake up somebody who was deep in slumber.

The Wizard of the Crow woke up with a start.

"Sshh. Don't talk. The shadow of the woman came back, and I am trying to follow it. There she is. In a marketplace. In a church. In a mosque. In a temple. Stop there. Woman, stop," he shouted, holding the mirror firmly in both hands. "Ah, the shadow has disappeared, once again covered by your own. I am sorry," he said, taking his eyes from the mirror and looking straight at Sikiokuu. "Now, what were you saying? I asked you a question and I am still waiting for an answer, or don't you want to answer me?"

"You mean you didn't hear what I said?"

"What?"

"No, no," Sikiokuu said as if he had been talking to himself, unable to believe what had just happened to him.

"Wait a minute," said the Wizard of the Crow, staring at Sikiokuu. "Why do you look so glum? Congratulations, Mr. Minister."

"Why?"

"Have you forgotten so soon? You are now free to say what's on your mind. Your malady of words has been cured."

Sikiokuu felt a big weight off his mind, but still he was troubled. "What did I say when my words started to flow freely?" he asked the Wizard of the Crow. He thereby would know exactly what the wizard had heard and, should the wizard repeat his treason, Sikiokuu was prepared to accuse him of the unspeakable. But the Wizard of the Crow saw the trap and avoided it.

"I was distracted by the sudden appearance of the image of that woman. I thought she would stop so that I could study her properly, you know, find out her contacts and coordinates. But now it does not matter what you may or may not have said in response to my questions. What is important is that you're cured. But what am I to do now that we've arrived at this impasse: your all-obstructing shadow?"

"No, there must be more to this than meets the eye," Sikiokuu said as if thinking aloud.

"Is that so?"

Sikiokuu stood up and again walked about the office, deep in thought. How was he to know for certain that this sorcerer had not heard what he said so indiscreetly? How could he be certain that the mirror had not retained traces of his treason? He wanted to ask the Wizard of the Crow directly whether he had heard the specific words. But Sikiokuu would have to repeat them and thus commit the treasonable offense twice. And suppose the Wizard of the Crow had not heard the words? Would he not then be putting him in the know? An idea took shape, and he stopped walking about.

He turned the lights in the room back on, returned to his seat, and looked directly at the Wizard of the Crow.

"My dear wizard," Sikiokuu said in an even tone, "I know you have done your best. You did cure me, after all, and I thank you for it . . ."

The Wizard of the Crow was elated. He would soon be rejoining Nyawīra. He had so much to tell her.

"Can I please have the mirror?" Sikiokuu continued.

The Wizard of the Crow gladly gave him the mirror. Sikiokuu immediately threw it to the floor and started stomping it, his ears flapping rhythmically. By the time he finished, the mirror shattered into tiny bits, he was panting like a hippo, his nose sweating like a dog's. Relieved that he had rendered it impossible for even the cleverest of sorcerers to access his treacherous musings that may have been captured by the mirror, Sikiokuu relaxed in his chair and looked at the still perplexed Wizard of the Crow. He now spoke as if he were recounting the most ordinary of things to an intimate.

"Now that that's done and the mirror is no more, let's turn to you. Mr. Wizard of the Crow, I have seen for myself that your fame is not based in fiction. You have power, in fact more power than even you realize, and it should be put in the service of the nation. Imagine your power in the service of the State, with the police able to locate the hideouts of criminals, and defense forces, the enemy's positions, merely by looking at a mirror! You and I must work together and make sure Nyawīra, the criminal, is apprehended. Understand, I will not let you go until then. Nyawīra must be in our hands before the return of the Ruler."

The Wizard of the Crow felt his spirits sink but tried not to allow panic into his voice or demeanor. He would neither antagonize the minister nor beg for freedom. He even started to see his predicament in a positive light. The longer he stayed in prison, the longer Sikiokuu would stay away from the shrine, Nyawīra's hiding place. Sikiokuu may break a thousand mirrors, but whatever mirror he would bring would tell a story that ended in the same truth: Nyawīra among the people. It was only right that she should disappear among those over whom lay Sikiokuu's shadow.

Sikiokuu's shadow? An idea suddenly formed in his mind.

"We reap what we sow," said the Wizard of the Crow. "You broke the mirror to deny the vision of yourself. Bring me a mirror your shadow has not contaminated."

# 21

What are we to do? Njoya and Kahiga asked themselves after they had locked up the Wizard of the Crow. They were upset. They had failed to keep their promise to return him to the witch the night before. How would they explain the new turn of events to her? A woman's witchcraft was more potent and deadly than a man's, they believed.

They decided to arrange for the Wizard of the Crow to talk to her on the phone. This might mollify her. It would show that Njoya and Kahiga were not in agreement with Sikiokuu. By secretly listening to the conversation, they might decipher what the woman intended to do with them.

So early the next day, they gave the wizard a mobile phone and told him that they were doing him a favor by allowing him to explain to his mate what had happened. They even offered to leave the room to give them some privacy.

Hardly taken in by their kindness, the wizard sensed a trap, but he decided that any contact with Nyawīra was better than none. At the very least it would let her know that he was still alive.

"The ones who came for me are the ones who, on their own authority, have made this call possible, and they are so considerate

WIZARD OF THE CROW

as to leave me alone to talk to you and tell you I am well," the Wizard of the Crow started. He and Nyawĩra were used to speaking circumspectly, and her response let the Wizard of the Crow know that she had the gist of everything he told her.

"I am glad that you are helping the government, but I am not happy that they have kept you for yet another night. Those who took you from here must return you here. Should they bring you back with even a single hair missing, they will suffer the full extent of my wrath. My anger is hotter than the hottest zone in hell. Aburĩria will tremble with troubles as yet unseen. Let them not forget the broken pieces of calabash."

Soon after this some cleaners appeared in the cell. At first the wizard did not pay much attention to them, but soon he could not ignore the bizarreness of their undertaking: they were closely inspecting the floor, picking up barely visible debris, and putting it in a tiny plastic bag.

"What are you up to?" he ventured to ask.

"Who are you? We have been ordered to collect all strands of hair that may have fallen from your head for safekeeping."

The Wizard of the Crow felt like laughing but didn't even try.

# 22

Sikiokuu did not take the challenge to come up with a mirror uncontaminated by his shadow lightly, so desperate was he to catch Nyawĩra before the Ruler's return. At first he thought it an easy matter, just order a fresh mirror from an Aburĩrian factory. But a native mirror was likely to be contaminated by other local intrusive shadows. Only from abroad could he get a pure mirror.

Not wanting to put all his eggs in one basket, Sikiokuu ordered mirrors from Japan, Italy, Sweden, France, Germany, Britain, and the USA.

But no sooner had he solved this problem than Njoya and Kahiga walked into his office to complicate his life.

# 23

As faithful servants of the State and loyal lieutenants to Sikiokuu, Njoya and Kahiga felt duty bound to acquaint him with the intelligence they had gathered on the phone without disclosing how the information had come to them. They mostly wanted to convey the seriousness of what Sikiokuu had done.

"It is our duty to let you know of any threats to the security of the State," Kahiga started, "and we now fear that Aburĩria is facing anger untold."

"Aburĩria may come to tremble with troubles as yet unknown," Njoya added.

"What kind of troubles?"

"Unimaginable," Kahiga said.

"Brought about by what or whom?" Sikiokuu asked, recalling his own indiscretions of the night.

"The Wizard of the Crow," Njoya added.

"The result of jailing him," said Kahiga.

"He might lose some of his hair," warned Njoya.

"Or some of his nails," Kahiga added.

"Or fall and sprain his ankles," Njoya said.

"He might suffer a bellyache from the food we feed prisoners," Kahiga said.

"He might be scarred by beatings."

"His bones might ache from the prison bed that's as hard as rock," Kahiga said.

"He might disappear the way the enemies of the State disappear in Aburĩria," said Njoya.

"Then those of us who have had anything to do with his disappearance will vanish from the face of the earth."

"Like dinosaurs," stressed Njoya.

"Or implode, break into pieces like a broken mirror . . ."

"Shut up!" Sikiokuu shouted at his lieutenants. "Go away, misery. Do you think that the Wizard of the Crow is God's twin brother?"

# 24

Njoya and Kahiga were Sikiokuu's most faithful lieutenants in the power struggles, and their dissension over this matter affected him like an ache from one's bodily organs. He recalled the mirror he had shattered. The two men were not in the room when he stomped the mirror, so how did they come to dangle before him the image of broken pieces? Had the wizard transmitted to them, through his sorcery, the words they were saying? Was this the beginning of the breaking up of his social and bodily organs? He was overcome with fear.

Tossing and turning at midnight, Sikiokuu would hear a voice saying, almost mockingly, *The Wizard of the Crow will break you into pieces,* and, shaken, he would sit up instantly and wipe the sweat from his brow. He could not go on like this. He must get a hold of himself. Then he came to a resolution. The sorcerer's life was in his hands. There was no way the sorcerer could strike vengeance from Hell. Yes, it had come to this: it was the wizard or him. He had to rid himself of this sorcerer, but not before forcing him to assist in capturing his prize: Nyawīra. The irony tickled his more malicious side: that in enabling Nyawīra's capture the Wizard of the Crow would be ensuring his own ticket to Hell. Sikiokuu felt a kind of peace as he contemplated a secure future without threats from the Wizard of the Crow.

With the resolution, he had achieved clarity of mind, he thought, and early the next morning he went to the office, expecting important news about the Ruler's arrival date. There was a time when he did not look forward to the return of the delegation, for it meant Machokali's triumph. But now, sure of Tajirika's confessions and the certainty of the wizard's inevitable descent into Hell, he felt no unease. He was even looking forward to it. He found no faxes so he opened the computer. But before he had cleared his e-mail, the telephone rang.

It was Tajirika. Why was he calling so early? A good omen? As they exchanged greetings and the reasons for the early call, Sikiokuu opened an e-mail message and started reading it silently. *What?*

*What's the meaning of this?* he said loudly and put the receiver down, completely unaware of Tajirika on the other end of the line. The message was disturbingly clear. All preparations to receive the Ruler were to be kept on hold. The Ruler was not feeling well.

The sender was Machokali. Sikiokuu was sick to his stomach. Was the Ruler dying? What if the Ruler were to anoint Machokali as his legitimate successor? The thought was too horrible to contemplate, and in his own mind Sikiokuu started planning to seize power.

He thought he had better read the full text of the message carefully to see what might be hidden between the lines. He was dumbstruck. For there, in the main body of the e-mail, was the name Wizard of the Crow. He could not believe what his eyes were reading.

Sikiokuu was to send for the Wizard of the Crow, issue him a diplomatic passport, help him secure a visa, and put him on the next available plane to New York.

He felt paralyzed. His lieutenants, Kahiga and Njoya, had forewarned him of troubles unimaginable. He recalled his resolution. He sat back in his chair, stared at the ceiling, and tugged at his earlobes meditatively.

# SECTION III

## 1

After going home, Tajirika acted like a person cured of one malady only to become victim of another even deadlier one. He had an irresistible yearning to beat his wife. Every night he dreamed of it, woke up in the morning with the thought of it, and spent the whole day nursing every little hurt into a provocation that would justify it. Still, nothing in Vinjinia's words and actions warranted a beating.

Tajirika was surprised to find that Vinjinia had run all his businesses efficiently. She had kept good records. If anything, under her stewardship, the businesses had actually grown and had attracted new clients and orders. All in all, she had come through as if she had been a businesswoman all her life. Instead of making Tajirika happy, this faultless performance served to increase the doubts he already had about her. Where had this new Vinjinia been hiding before this? To catch her in a lie, he tried every ruse, springing questions on her at random, but she would answer them all simply and clearly.

"Okay, you can now resume your place in the kitchen," he told her without a word of thanks.

She had run the home as efficiently. And in her accounts of her social ins and outs he saw no inconsistencies. Left alone to his thoughts, Tajirika concluded that all was a show; Vinjinia's supposed competence and wifely rectitude were nothing but hypocrisy. Was this not the picture she had always presented to him before his abduction? The face of a person without too many questions about this or that? The face of loyal silence? But a woman who, while presenting him with the wifely ideal, had still found time and energy to consort with shameful dancers? And yet not once during all the years of wedded bliss and procreation had she once mentioned them. If anything, she had expressed only contempt toward tradition and ritual performance. How, then, had she come to know these women to the extent of being photographed together in public? When did she start keeping their company? Where and when did she find the time to meet with them? At what time of day or night?

Tajirika's doubts and questions only added to that irresistible urge to rain blows on Vinjinia's back, and all that restrained him was Sikiokuu's temporary ban on wife beating. Lacking the means to quench his thirst for blood, Tajirika became increasingly frustrated, sullen and silent most of the time. He did not want to talk about his experience in prison for fear of fueling his anger toward his wife, leading to forbidden consequences. He sought safety in muteness.

His brutal, unrelenting silence was hurtful to Vinjinia, denied as she was an opportunity to share with him her trials, tribulations, and partial triumph over the twin evils of Kaniũrũ and Sikiokuu. She longed to tell him how she had looked for him everywhere, in police precincts, hospitals, mortuaries, and how she had received help from the Wizard of the Crow and some mysterious women dancers whom she had met neither before nor after. The complete breakdown in communication frustrated her even more than the anger she still felt at discovering his readiness to denounce her, in an unfinished press statement that she came across after her release from prison.

When Vinjinia received the call from the police that Tajirika had been released, she had felt unalloyed joy, not because her anger had subsided but because she saw his return home as an opportunity for them to repair their lives. She had expected him to be pleased with her success in running his business despite her lack of experience. She had thought that, at least, money would talk. But even a sizable bank account was unable to unlock the man's heart. She went all out to please him but found it impossible to unburden his soul. Why? Why this silence?

One morning she made him a special breakfast of pancakes, eggs, and sausages. Without looking at her, Tajirika stretched his hands to take the tray but failed, and the tray fell to the ground, creating an unsightly mess. Vinjinia could no longer keep her mouth shut.

"How have I wronged you, Titus? What have I done to you to make you so bloated with anger? And when you open your mouth it is only to ask questions that have no legs or arms. What did they do to you in prison? How did they manage to turn you into a dumb creature?"

If Tajirika had so much as spoken a word he would have beaten Vinjinia mercilessly, but recalling his contract with Sikiokuu, he summoned all his inner strength not to strike her. He ran out of the house to the garage, got into his car, and drove to the office. He was aflame with anger. He had never heard Vinjinia speak to him so brazenly. Her outburst, however, did finally reveal her hidden self. This Vinjinia was the one who had met secretly with the women dancers. Oh, yes, at last! He felt that if he did not beat her today, his body would break into pieces. He had to speak to Sikiokuu. He reached for the telephone.

"Why are you calling me so early, Titus?" Sikiokuu asked jovially.

"I want permission. Now."

"For what?"

"I'm not in the mood to play games!"

"What are you talking about?"

"I need to beat my wife. Otherwise anger will choke me to death."

"Why? Did you find another man topping her?"

"No. It is not that. Please allow me."

"Titus! *What are you talking about?*"

"You told me not to beat my wife without first consulting you."

"*Oh, yes, of course,*" Sikiokuu said vaguely. Then he recalled the famous photographs and their role in the confessions. "Did you quarrel about those photos?" Sikiokuu asked, now alarmed.

"No, *but* . . ."

"Then don't you think about it, Titus. Leave her alone. Or better, fuck her instead of fucking up matters of state security. You are to uncover her connections to the subversives; patience, my brother. Don't rush into anything you'll regret. Better wait for the return of the Ruler and that arrogant enemy of the State, Machokali. Fortunately, you don't have long to wait . . ."

"When are they coming back?"

"Anytime now. I am waiting for word from America. That's why I'm here so early; I had just turned on my computer when you called. Oh, yes, there is something on the screen . . . wait a minute . . . *What? What's the meaning of this?*"

425

Those were the last words Tajirika heard. He continued holding the receiver to his ear, saying, Hello? Hello, wondering who had disconnected them. Or had the minister decided to end their conversation abruptly? He hung up and redialed time and again, but the line remained busy. Tajirika did not know what to do.

He decided to go to Mars Café for a cup of coffee to calm down and achieve some clarity. Just outside the door, he bought the *Eldares Times*. He sat in a corner waiting for his order of coffee, eggs, and bacon, and glanced at the newspaper. Bitter reflections came between him and the front page. How dare Sikiokuu end our conversation without first hearing all I have to say? How dare he cut me off so rudely without hearing my pain? The humiliation was so intense that he felt dizzy; his eyes clouded with tears.

Have I fallen so low? How did I come to this: letting another man dictate to me what I can or cannot do in my own house? Beg another man to give me permission to discipline my wife? He need not refer to her connection to the dancers, for that indeed might interfere with state security investigations, but beating her was his male prerogative and he was not about to cede that right to another bull in the kraal. Why had he not thought about it in these terms before?

He did not wait for his breakfast. He drove back home like one crazed. As he entered the house his fists were already clenched.

People say that women all over Aburĩria, Nyawĩra among them, could hear Vinjinia's screaming.

## 2

Just before they put him on the plane for America, Kahiga and Njoya brought the Wizard of the Crow back to the shrine to change into fresh clothes and to say good-bye to his companion. They took care to impress upon her that the wizard's impending visit to America had prompted their first appearance but they could not then have disclosed this because they had been sworn to secrecy. He was needed in New York, they told her, to use his magic to strengthen the hand of the Aburĩrian negotiators while softening the hearts of the directors of the Global Bank to make them release the funds for Marching to Heaven. But Nyawĩra was not fooled by their exaggerated claims, and she genuinely feared for Kamĩtĩ. Stories of people abducted by the police in broad daylight, tortured, and left in the wild as food for hyenas, were many. Even when Kahiga and Njoya phoned her to tell her that all had gone well, she hardly felt reassured, and she reminded them that she would hold them accountable for whatever happened to the Wizard of the Crow.

Several days later, Kahiga and Njoya came to see her at the shrine and presented her with a small jewelry box. They stood around her with self-satisfied smiles as she opened it. She almost collapsed but retained her composure.

"Why have you brought me hair in a box?" she asked, fearing the worst.

"It belongs to the Wizard of the Crow," Kahiga explained.

Nyawĩra suddenly recalled her threat and felt like laughing. But this was not a laughing matter. Why did they bring his hair to her now, and in a box? What did it really mean? Was it a casual joke? Was Kamĩtĩ dead after all?

She felt better only after she received a call from Kamĩtĩ to say that he had arrived in New York safely. He sounded rushed but he promised to call again, and when she did not hear from him soon, she began to worry. Their forced separation gave her the time to reflect. She and Kamĩtĩ did not always see eye to eye, particularly in matters of ideology and practical politics. Kamĩtĩ's suspicions of organization and the discipline involved was opposite of her belief that organization was the only way by which people could effect meaningful changes. Agonize less; organize more! But despite the fact that she belonged to an organization and Kamĩtĩ did not, they were united by a shared belief in the humanity of people and service to community, and they differed only in the means of getting there. All in all, theirs was the firmest of bonds.

She missed him and their conversation terribly. Playing her guitar was often her refuge in such moments, but these days she could not even pluck the strings. What else to do? Long ago in school and later at college Nyawĩra had kept a diary off and on. She resumed it. Writing made her feel better, almost as if she had talked to the spirit of her absent love. One night she tried to account for what she called her political catechism.

"I believe that black has been oppressed by white; female by male; peasant by landlord; and worker by lord of capital. It follows from this that the black female worker and peasant is most oppressed. She is oppressed on account of her color like all black people in the world; she is oppressed on account of her gender like all women in the world; and she is exploited and oppressed on account of her class like all workers and peasants in the world. Three burdens she has to carry. Those who want to fight for the people in the nation and in the world must struggle for the unity and rights of the working class in their own country; fight against all discriminations based on race, ethnicity, color, and belief systems; they must struggle against all gender-based inequalities and therefore fight for the rights of women in the home, the family, the nation, and the world . . ."

No, those were not the words in the catechism she had in mind. For whom am I writing this, anyway? she asked, and tore it to pieces.

The more she missed Kamĩtĩ and feared for his safety, the more she applied herself to organizing and healing. Involvement in other people's suffering turned out to be the best way of coping with her personal woes, for she was able to see that these woes were not peculiar to her situation but were shared by many others.

Early one morning a woman came to see her. The woman wore a veil. A Muslim, Nyawĩra thought as she received her in the chamber they had come to call the confessional. She tried to read the woman's face, but how does one read a veiled face? Even so, she could see that the woman's eyes were flush with sadness.

"Mother, what brings you to the shrine of the Wizard of the Crow?" Nyawĩra asked her.

When she tried to answer the woman broke down and sobbed, tears flowing down her cheeks. Nyawĩra waited patiently to give the woman time to recover her composure. Then the woman removed the shawl that covered her head and face. Vinjinia? Nyawĩra almost forgot her own guise as the Wizard of the Crow and stopped just short of shouting the name. The face behind the veil was so swollen that the eyes were almost shut. In shock, Nyawĩra did not press for a reason for the visit. She attempted no small talk, and neither did she remind her of her last visit to the shrine to seek help in finding her missing husband. She would allow Vinjinia the right to reveal as much as she wished. Nyawīra knew of visitors to the shrine who came repeatedly, each time pretending that it was their first visit. But Vinjinia seemed too overwhelmed with sorrow to speak.

"What is the matter, woman? Did a beast attack you, or what?" Nyawīra finally asked to break the long silence.

"The beast has a name. It is called a husband. Night and day. Quarrels without reason. Fights without a truce. Marriage is a prison. Prison for life, more so when a couple has children. Even our religions sanction the prison for life for a woman."

"The times we now live in are different from the ones gone," Nyawīra said. "Today one can walk freely out of this prison if one so wants. Even in the past women could always go back to their parents or choose to live on their own. There were women who married other women, even."

"Why should I walk out and leave a home we have built together?" Vinjinia asked.

"I am not asking you to wreck your home."

"There is no home left to wreck. He has already done that by his actions!"

"What did he do?" Nyawīra asked. "What was he demanding from you? Sex?"

Vinjinia paused as if she was not quite sure where or how to begin. Should she leave out the more shameful details?

"If you want my help, you must tell me everything," Nyawīra said, as if she had read the mind of her client. "Even if he tried to rape you. Rape is rape, even when done by a friend or a husband."

Vinjinia felt relieved of the burden of editing her story. She went so far as to reveal her name and reminded the wizard that she had been to the shrine on two previous occasions. Her needs had been met, and that's why she had come back yet a third time. She was unstinting in recalling all that had happened in her home since Tajirika's return.

"I still don't know why he is so angry with me or what he wants from me."

"Woman," Nyawīra called out gently, "you have a husband who assumes that he has a natural right to beat and discipline his wife. Unfortunately, he is not alone. Violence against women bedevils many a home—rich, poor, white, black, religious. In the world today, a husband measures his maleness by mauling his wife. A wife swal-

lows insults in surly silence instead of resisting the violation of her
sacred self. A sacred self soon becomes a scared slave, leading a
scarred life. You have told me your story and I have listened. Now
what brings you to the shrine? To tell me the story or to gather herbs
for your wounds?"

"The wounding of my heart will never heal as long as the man I
call my husband is alive."

"What do you want?"

"I want him dead. Dead and buried. Give me poison for his food.
Give me poison to send him to Hell. Or, better still, capture his
shadow in your mirror and scratch it out."

Her vehemence startled Nyawīra. She would never have thought
that Vinjinia's heart could harbor so much venom.

"I only poison evil in pursuit of the good."

"What can be more evil than what he has done to me with his
fists?"

"Do you want to end his life or his violence?"

"His violence can end only in death: his or mine."

"What about making him first see the evil in his ways?"

"Tajirika is incapable of seeing the error of his ways. He can spot
the mote in a woman's eye but not the dust in his own."

"Even if a delegation of the wise were to reason with him?"

"That would only inflame him and make him more violent after
they left."

"What about taking him to court?"

"Aburīrian courts? How many women judges and magistrates have
you seen on the benches of justice? In any case, in Aburīria justice
ends up in the pockets of the highest bidder. Do you think I can out-
bid my husband? No, I am not able to massage justice with bribes."

"Massage justice with bribes?" Nyawīra repeated the phrase
loudly, but inwardly she wondered what to do about Vinjinia's plight
without giving her any poisonous herbs, which she would never do,
and without killing hope, the basis of all healing arts. Unable to settle
on a course of action or words, Nyawīra's mind drifted and she
started thinking more about the woman in front of her. In some ways
this woman continually amazed Nyawīra, and if the situation had not
been one of pain and pity, Nyawīra might have been tempted to
laugh, at least inwardly, at Vinjinia's metamorphosis.

Is this not the same woman who used to be so prudish in reference to the body and matters of sex? Is this not the same one who used to play dumb about Aburīrian politics? Nyawīra asked herself, recalling all the arguments and disagreements they had during the days they spent together in the offices of Eldares Modern Construction and Real Estate. To Vinjinia, nothing was wrong with Aburīria. And yet, had she not just made one of the most insightful comments about justice in the Ruler's Aburīria? Or about violence and gender inequality in the home? She had even rolled out a critical insight into religion and its tendency to gloss over domestic violence against women. Awareness of being wronged was the first step in political self-education, Nyawīra concluded.

It was while idly turning over these thoughts in her mind that she had an idea. It was not a new idea—she had thought about it before and had even considered taking it to the leadership of their movement for discussion and possible adoption as policy, but she had not yet done so. But why not try it out with Vinjinia?

"Go home now," she told Vinjinia gently. "Leave the matter in the hands of the Wizard of the Crow. He will have to deal with a delegation of elders, wise elders of reasoned justice, wearing magic robes. As for you, take these words home with you. Know that the most potent magic emanates from the heart. Women must dig deep within themselves to decide that they will no longer allow themselves to be beaten by their husbands and boyfriends. When that happens, wife bashing will be no more. Homes shall be run on the maxim that conversation is the gateway to love and understanding. Thoughts locked up inside never solve anything. The silence of women in the face of male violence is the nursemaid of more violence. If he continues to rain fists on your body after the delegation has called on him, come back to me. But let me ask you a question I should have asked you at the start. Have you made up your mind never to be beaten again?"

"Yes."

"Then go home. The elders of justice are on their way."

"I hope they will not let my husband know that I was here."

"That should not worry you. There is no healer worth his weight in herbs who would hurl to the wind what is gathered in the peace and silence of the shrine."

# 3

The silence engulfing Tajirika's home was deeper than that in the thickest bush in the darkest night. Gacīgua and Gacirū, their young ones, were in boarding school. Domestic workers were there during the day; husband and wife were left to their own devices at night. Tajirika often did not feel like going home early after work and would stop at a bar.

One evening he felt fed up with hard liquor, which did not always numb his loneliness, and decided to go to the Mars Café for a cup of coffee instead.

Since beating his wife, Tajirika felt better, but whenever the images of the dancing women came to his mind and he imagined the lifestyle in which Vinjinia had indulged during his incarceration, he would still feel a sudden resurgence of anger. Ironically, this resurgence and the intense focus on Vinjinia's misdeeds served to deflect his mind from dwelling on what had happened to him during police custody. How could he dwell on the picture of himself with a bucket of shit dangling between his legs? It was not a pretty sight, even to himself, and dwelling on Vinjinia's dirt made him feel purer.

The only memory that gave him enormous satisfaction was that of the Wizard of the Crow in police hands, for he took it that he was now safe from the sorcerer.

Tajirika knew nothing about the latest twist in the saga of the Wizard of the Crow, and he would not have believed it anyway were he told that the wizard was now in America at the behest of the Ruler. All he cared to know was that Sikiokuu had ordered the sorcerer to remove the magic spell he had cast on Tajirika and nullify all short- and long-term side effects.

He looked forward to the Ruler's imminent return. Sikiokuu had assured him of getting back the chairmanship of Marching to Heaven with all powers, including those that Kaniūrū had taken illegally. He truly had a new friend in Sikiokuu, and whenever memories of his old friendship with Machokali forced themselves on his mind, he would dismiss them very quickly. But sometimes they would not go away and he would actually pause to reflect on the situation and ask, What shall I do when Machokali returns?

Not that this was a question that would have made him lie sleepless at night. Tajirika prided himself on being flexible in everything to ensure his own survival. He moved with the world and not against the world. His relationship to his former friend and benefactor would depend on the relative strength of Machokali and Sikiokuu in the game of power. If Machokali should prove the stronger, then Tajirika would tell him everything he knew about what Sikiokuu had been cooking in Machokali's absence. But if Sikiokuu proved himself the stronger, then Tajirika would continue on his side and forget the past. As he now crossed the street toward the Mars Café, the thoughts of how he would maneuver between the two giant rivals for the power behind the throne preoccupied his mind and he forgot the prospects of another lonely night at home.

He felt people pressing against him on one side but quickly dismissed this as one of the inconveniences of walking on crowded streets. Eldares is attracting too much riffraff from the rural areas, he said to himself, slightly irritated. But when he tried to push forward and he still felt the pressure, he looked about him only to see people in head masks with two menacing slits for the eyes. Even then he did not immediately associate this with himself. He had always read and heard about victims of *kupigwa ngete*. Was he about to become an eyewitness to that kind of daylight robbery?

But before he could figure out what was happening, he felt rather than saw himself being lifted and pushed inside the back of a waiting van, which then took off immediately. The whole thing occurred so quickly that none of the passersby noticed the activities around the van as anything unusual. Inside the dark van, Tajirika found himself firmly held by his left and right arms and seated between two of the captors. He tried to extricate himself from their grip but he could not even move his hips, so tightly did they hold him. His first reaction was that these were thieves.

"I don't have much money on me. Where are you taking me?" he asked, but received no response.

He thought it best to keep quiet and wait for their arrival at wherever they were taking him, and once outside the van he would try to escape. But as soon as the van stopped, his captors blindfolded him, took him into a house, and pushed him into a chair. When now they removed the cloth and Tajirika found himself surrounded by masked persons, beads of sweat appeared on his forehead. Who are you? he asked again, his voice trembling.

They removed the masks. What! Women? He was shocked, deflated, and ashamed, all at the same time. He, a man, to be kidnapped by women? Then came contempt and defiance. There was no way nine women could hold him against his will, he thought and quickly dashed toward the door. It was locked.

"Go back to the chair and wait for the ceremony," one of the women told him, but Tajirika did not heed her.

"Open this door or I will teach you to know a man when you see one," he told them, kicking the door with his shoes.

Tajirika did not even know who touched him first or from what direction, but the next second he found himself lying flat on the floor with three women sitting on his back; one at the neck, another at the waist, and the other one at the feet.

"What is your name?" the one on his feet asked him.

Fury blocked his throat. How could he, a man, be wrestled to the ground by a bunch of women?

"You are being asked. What is your name?" the one who sat on his neck asked.

"Tajirika," he said, from the side of his mouth, breathing heavily under the combined weight of the three women.

"And other names?" the one in the middle asked.

"Titus."

"Just wanted to make sure that we did not pick up the wrong man."

"Get off my back," he hissed. "What do you want from me? A ransom?" he said as he tried to shake them off, to no avail.

"Let's introduce ourselves. We are not killers. We are not robbers. We want you to count all the money in your possession because we do not want to ever hear you claim that anybody here has taken even a penny from you."

"No need for that. I have one thousand Burĩs, and you can have them all."

"We don't need your Burĩs," one of the women standing told him; the others laughed.

434

"What, then, do you want? Surely women don't rape men?"

"See how his mind works?" one of them said. "Rape is entering another person's body by force. It is violence, and if that's what you want we can certainly . . ."

"No, no, I mean if it is sex you want, we can make a deal. Work out a routine, a time, and the order . . ."

"He does fancy himself a man," another one said. "Nine women all to himself?"

"Who are you?"

"A new order of justice created by today's modern woman. You are now appearing before a people's court."

"I refuse to recognize your authority," Tajirika replied with a little bit more defiance.

"Don't worry yourself. By dawn you will."

"Get off my back," he said again, annoyed with himself for sounding as if he was pleading.

"Not so fast. We want you to feel the full force of our weight."

"What is this all about?"

"Justice. We are hawkeyed justice. We float in the air, our ears wide open to the cries of women. Now it has come to our ears that you beat your wife night and day."

Tajirika felt himself choking with anger. How dare these hussies interfere with his business?

"Listen to me. There is no power on earth that can tell me how to run my home."

"That might very well be so, but man, woman, and child compose a home, and if one pillar is weak, the family is weak, and if the family is weak, the nation is weak. So what happens in a home is the business of the nation and the other way around."

"I don't need to be lectured. My wife is not our wife; she is mine."

"You said, 'my wife,' but I did not hear you say, 'my slave.'"

"Listen. Tradition is on my side; it is the man who wears the pants in the house."

"You talk of tradition. Remember that in the past husbands who ill treated their wives faced trials before a council of women."

"Even the Bible says that woman is man's rib," Tajirika said.

"Why don't we pluck out one of his ribs so that he can show us how a rib turned out to be a woman?" another one added.

Now a big woman wielding a shiny machete emerged from

another room. "Why do you let this man give you so much trouble? Let me show you how it's done. Take his pants off. Let us cut off his penis."

The woman looked and sounded so serious that Tajirika felt he was about to piss on himself as he let out a single involuntary groan. Suppose these women were actually crazy? Possessed of female daemons intent on destroying man? It was much safer for him to go along with their so-called court proceeding. He would keep them busy while figuring out how to escape.

"Please get off my back; let us talk. There is no court of law that decides cases solely on the basis of a plaintiff's story, and especially one who is not even present."

"Let's give him a chance to defend himself."

They allowed him to take his seat again but warned him not to show contempt, or else . . .

"Listen to me," he said in a disingenuous respectful tone. "I don't know who you are. And I don't even know who has accused me of wife beating. Vinjinia and I are *one of the happiest couples in the world*. I don't believe in domestic violence. Ours is a Christian home, and we belong to the middle class. Wife beating is for the poor pagans, you know, people without any understanding of what it means to be modern. I suspect that all this talk of my wife beating and whatnot may have come about when some neighbors saw my wife with a swollen face and a few scratches sustained when she slipped and fell on the cement floor. You are women, and you know how clumsy your kind can be sometimes. I really despise neighbors who have nothing better to do than poke their noses into other people's affairs."

"There are only two people who know what happened. You and your wife. You say she is clumsy and she fell on the cement floor. So we are now asking you: do you want us to summon her here?"

Tajirika was taken aback. This was the last thing he expected, the summons of his wife. But he believed that Vinjinia would never say anything untoward about their domestic affairs to perfect strangers. The Vinjinia he knew was the key to his freedom, and he was sure that she would stand by her man.

"Yes, call her," he said with braggadocio.

"Give us directions and describe her to us," one of the women said, to indicate that they were not in league with Vinjinia. "We know only about you."

After an hour or so Vinjinia was in the room. The women seated her opposite her husband. One of the women chaired the council. The others were the jury. Vinjinia had covered her head with a shawl. Her eyes showed fear, and she did not look at her husband directly. Tajirika gave her a stern look, which he tried to hide with a false smile.

"Tell them the truth that I did not touch you," Tajirika hastened to say before the chairperson could utter a word. "Is it not a fact that your swollen face resulted from your falling on the cement floor?"

The judge told her to speak her truth as she knew it. The silence in the room was riveting. Vinjinia glanced at Tajirika, at the women, and then looked away.

"I fell on the cement floor," she said, in a barely audible voice.

The women looked stunned. Tajirika made no attempt to hide his triumph.

"You have heard for yourselves," he crowed, openly arrogant.

"There is nothing more to say about this sad affair," the judge said.

Tajirika wished he had the means to wreak instant vengeance on these women. At the door he put his arms around his wife and whispered: "You did well. Anything else and the last beating would have paled in comparison with the one I would have given you tonight."

Vinjinia trembled. He simply had gone too far. If he could threaten her just outside the hearing of these women, what was he not capable of at home? If she was going to die, at least let there be witnesses. She quickly disengaged herself from him and turned around.

"I am sorry," she said, directing her remarks to the judge. "I have lied to you, and lied to myself while lying for my husband. This man rains fists on me whenever it suits his temper. If he has a disagreement with others in his workplace or in a bar, he takes it out on me. The heart of my husband is as hard as a concrete floor."

Tajirika lost it before the woman who had just betrayed his manhood. He jumped on her and was going to beat her yet again, but the women were too quick for him. They restrained him before he landed a blow. But even as they dragged him away from his wife, Tajirika continued wagging his finger at her.

"You wait till I get you home! Just you wait!" he shouted at her, throwing caution to the wind.

"But who told you that you are going home?" the machete-wielding woman said as she rushed toward him, waving the machete in the air menacingly. Tajirika jumped back a step, convinced that these women were prepared to kill him if he gave them the slightest cause.

The judge told them to sit down, which they all did, including Tajirika, who was inwardly grateful to the judge for keeping the machete woman at bay.

"You," the judge said, pointing at Tajirika. "Your own actions before our very eyes confirm what we've heard. But this court will not condemn you without giving you a chance to defend yourself. Why did you beat your wife?"

"Don't call her my wife," Tajirika said, panting with frustration at his inability to teach his wife a lesson. "This woman is a hypocrite. When the police detained me recently, she seized the opportunity to hire dancing prostitutes and gangsters to entertain her."

Vinjinia, who had not the slightest clue what Tajirika was talking about, shook her head in disbelief. But the mention of dancing women made her recall the women who had forced the government to admit that it was holding Tajirika.

"Who lied to you that I did nothing about your arrest? That I was partying with women dancers? Some people are truly incapable of gratitude. When the police arrested me a while ago, this man did nothing. I even came across a press statement in which he was going to denounce me. But when he was arrested and held in secrecy, there was no police precinct, hospital, or newspaper office I did not set foot in to find out what his so-called friends had done to him. But when he came out of his tomb, instead of asking me how it was at home when he was away, he went about sniffing for gossip, and whatever his drunken friends told him he took as the gospel truth and sound basis for killing blows."

"The woman has asked you a question," the judge said, turning to Tajirika. "Who made allegations against her? Tell us so that we may fetch him and bring him here to testify."

Tajirika remembered that Sikiokuu had forbidden him to talk about the photographs or the dancing women because of ongoing security investigations. He did not respond.

"Do you have anything else that you want to tell this council?" the judge asked Vinjinia.

"I just want to say before you all that I will not accept blows on my body anymore."

"Stop lying, woman. I have never touched you with these hands the way a real man should," Tajirika shouted, standing up and clenching his fists.

The women pushed him back to his seat.

"Your actions before our very eyes testify against you," the judge told Tajirika. "We have enough evidence for the jury to issue a just verdict. Vinjinia will be taken back to her place," the judge said with a tone of finality.

As he saw Vinjinia being escorted out of the room, Tajirika felt like crying out to Vinjinia: Please don't leave me here with these crazy women! But he did not. How could he, a man, call on his wife, a woman, to save him from other women?

The judge fixed her eyes on Tajirika.

"You are sentenced to receive as many blows as you rained on your wife."

"But if you ever appear before us again, you will not leave here with your penis dangling between your legs," said the woman with the machete as she did a little war jig while brandishing her weapon. Even as the women pummeled him, his eyes were focused on the machete. His pain was dull; his stare was blank.

# 4

When Tajirika finally found himself outside the gates of his residence, he simply could not believe it. Had they let him go? Was he really safe at Golden Heights? His initial impulse was to enter the house and immediately set upon Vinjinia and break her legs and arms. But the last words he remembered hearing were unambiguous: "Remember: resume your wife beating and you will surely feel the full force of female daemons." So he had been right, after all, about who the women really were. As he imagined them suddenly emerging from the surrounding cornfields for retribution, he started trembling, overcome by a mixture of relief, shame, anger, and helplessness.

Instead of opening the door, Tajirika leaned against it and started to sob. Tears raced down his cheeks and fell onto the veranda. They increasingly became bigger and faster, soon turning into torrents that gushed down as from a broken dam, making two tunnels on the earth just outside the veranda. But he was not aware of the tunnels as he eventually opened the door and quickly locked it from the inside.

# 5

The drama of the female daemons was not something Tajirika was overly eager to shout from the rooftops. He could imagine the nasty derisive comments of passersby: There goes the man beaten by women. So he confined himself within the walls of his house and ran his business over the phone.

Vinjinia was also keen to avoid questions about her bruised face, and, like him, she stayed indoors.

Thus they found themselves spending their nights and days inside the house, avoiding each other. They even tried to hide their bruised faces from each other, Tajirika by donning a wide-brimmed hat and Vinjinia with a cloth over her head.

Vinjinia had been so sure that Tajirika would exact vengeance that she became more worried when after a few days no violence had surfaced. But, under the cover of silence and calculated indifference, was he planning something more sinister? After a few days of this, Vinjinia started wondering: What did those women do to him? Did they cut his manhood off?

She resorted to stalking him, casting surreptitious glances in his direction, hoping to catch him naked as he emerged from the bathroom or the toilet. Once or twice she opened the door to his bedroom at a time she thought he might be changing into his nightclothes but, finding him fully clothed, she closed the door quickly, as if she had made a mistake through force of habit.

Tajirika had also started feeling restless and perplexed by several questions for which he had no satisfactory answer.

Some of them were prompted by his ego: to be captured, sat upon, put on trial, and beaten by women defied all that he knew about the world. At such moments he wished he had the means to annihilate them, but weren't they creatures from the netherworld? Anyway, who had told them about him and Vinjinia? Wife beating in Aburīria, after all, was so common as not to be noticed. What made for a peaceful home was not the absence of such blows but the ability of a couple to keep the knowledge of the violence within the confines of the walls of their house.

What fascinated and irritated him at the same time was the knowledge that there was not a single falsehood in the women's allegations, forcing him to brood on his conduct of this affair. Why had he not checked Sikiokuu's story with Vinjinia?

He also could not deny the truth of Vinjinia's claim that he had not done much for her when she herself was arrested, and now he felt ashamed for not having been man enough to stand by his woman.

And what to make of her claims that she had left no stone unturned in search of him? Was this true? He wanted to know more, but how could he break the silence without demeaning himself? He, too, started stalking her, casting surreptitious glances at her to see if he could detect a sign of any softening in her.

The two started circling each other, often finding themselves in the same part of the house, both looking for an opening to satisfy their respective curiosities about one another. One afternoon they encountered each other on the veranda and were struck by the same surprise: starting from just outside the veranda wall were two tunnels. What rains have done this? they loudly asked in unison. Yet they were not aware of any rains recently. With each walking along one of the tunnels, they followed them through the cornfields, all the way down the valley. And then? The second surprise.

On the boggy, marshy valley floor, a pool had formed. They stared at each other. They each dipped a finger into the pool and tasted the liquid. It was salty, like tears. Neither of them could believe the evidence of their tongues. Needing confirmation, they returned their fingers to the pool and now placed a finger on each other's tongue. The water was still salty. They giggled a little, in unison. They quickly put their fingers back in the pool, each hoping to be the first to place more salty water in the other's mouth. But it was as if they had read each other's intentions. Vinjinia dashed into the cornfields, with Tajirika following her in a playful chase.

They at once succumbed to the fatigue of it all and suddenly felt the kind of warmth they used to arouse in each other in the days of their youth: for a moment they stood looking at each other, mesmerized by what was happening to them. They knew rather than talked about it. But there in the open fields, under the corn leaves, it felt good, very good, and for a few minutes the pain of the bruises on their faces and in their hearts seemed soothed away by the sweetness that whistled tunes ending in a rapturous crescendo.

# 6

Neither Tajirika nor Vinjinia could have dreamt that out of the tears of sorrow could come such intense screams of joy. But the scream that next issued from Vinjinia's mouth was not joy or sorrow, and for a few seconds she could not utter a word. Tajirika looked to see what she was pointing at. The sight made him tense up also: a flock of birds was frozen in flight above the lake. Some yards into the pool, a dog, barking at the birds, suddenly froze before their very eyes.

Tajirika and Vinjinia took to their heels and did not once look back until they reached the house. The valley floor used to shake as if hollow below. What had brought the waters to the surface? What of the arrested motion of beings?

They came back the following day, hoping the whole thing had vanished. It had not, and now, in addition to the birds, were bees and butterflies also in frozen flight. On the surface, ducks and chickens, including a cock trying to mount a hen, were all frozen in motion. So also two antelopes, one in the air and the other about to jump.

They gave up trying to unravel the mystery. When Gacirū and Gacīgua came for holidays, Tajirika and Vinjinia forbid them to go anywhere near the valley or talk about it, reinforcing the ban with stories of daemons that lured children into a pool in the valley and swallowed them. But Gacirū and Gacĩgua whispered the stories to their friends, and eventually the stories reached the ears of parents, who sternly warned their children to avoid the area.

Parents added their bits to the scary lore: The pool became a lake that turned any living thing that touched its surface or flew over it into stone. Even looking in its direction or looking at it, others added, could turn somebody into stone, which made people walk with their eyes facing away from its supposed location. Silence about the lake ensued.

But Tajirika and Vinjinia were attracted to the lake like a moth to the light. They found a spot from where they could see it, especially in the evenings, because when light fell on the motionless objects the things would change colors dramatically, depending on the intensity and angle of the sun.

Tajirika and Vinjinia named the scene Museum of Arrested Motion.

# 7

It was while seated in their usual place facing the Museum of Arrested Motion that Tajirika, out of nowhere, asked Vinjinia how she had come to be the guest of honor at a women's ceremonial dance, warning her not to lie because he had seen, with his own eyes, photographs of the occasion. She assumed he meant press photos, although she had not seen any. Without mentioning her visit to the Wizard of the Crow, she described her fruitless search for Tajirika and finally her decision to confront Sikiokuu at the official opening of Kaniũrũ's office, where some women dancers whom she had never met forced his hand. But it did not really matter that she had never met them, and all he should know was that but for those dancers he would never have been found alive.

It was Tajirika's turn, and he too omitted any reference to his encounter with the Wizard of the Crow in prison, his commanding a whole camp with only a bucket of shit, and his bargaining his way to freedom by betraying his friend and benefactor Machokali. Instead, Tajirika described how he defied those who had arrested him and threatened to report their criminal mistreatment of him to the Ruler. It was then that the officials told him that the involvement of his wife with subversive female elements was the real reason they had arrested him, and, to prove it, they showed him photographs of Vinjinia seated in front of the dancers.

The shock on Vinjinia's face made Tajirika believe that she knew nothing about the pictures. She did not deny that there were people with cameras there, but she had assumed that they were from the newspapers. And why would newspaper people take the pictures of her and the dancers and erase the images of Sikiokuu and Kaniūrū from the scene, since they were the chief dignitaries at the ceremony?

"There is more to these pictures than meets the eye," said Vinjinia, shaking her head from side to side.

Her words stung Tajirika into silence. So that was why Sikiokuu did not want him to talk to Vinjinia about the pictures? So that's why he had forbidden him to beat her? Now he recalled how Sikiokuu had recently put the phone down while Tajirika was about to seek permission to beat Vinjinia. His anger drove the matter of his abduction into the background.

"Let me get ahold of Minister Sikiokuu, and I will teach him never to toy with me again," he said at last.

He could not figure out the form the vengeance would take. He even thought of hiring professional assassins to finish off Sikiokuu, but he had no clue as to where to find them. Besides, that was risky and would take time to arrange; he wanted instant vengeance. Tajirika's failure to settle on a course of action made Sikiokuu's lies burn even more. Why had he lied to him? To make him cooperate against . . .

Suddenly Tajirika knew what he would do: he would refuse to conspire against Machokali.

He went to the office to call Sikiokuu.

# 8

Sikiokuu could tell by the way that Tajirika was breathing on the other end of the line that something had gone terribly wrong. "What's the matter?" he asked.

"What's the matter?" Sikiokuu repeated.

Tajirika was about to declare that he would no longer cooperate in the matter of Machokali when he remembered that he had already put his signature on a false confession. Sikiokuu clearly held him by the balls and was prepared to squeeze hard to make him comply. Was there no way out of this nightmare?

"And you did not even have the guts to say that you and Kaniũrũ were the stars of the show?" he said, trying to inject as much bitterness and scorn as he could into his tone.

At first Sikiokuu did not know what Tajirika was talking about.

"Did you beat your wife?" Sikiokuu asked straight out, ignoring the taunts.

Tajirika hesitated, wondering how Sikiokuu knew about what had transpired at home. Had Sikiokuu set up surveillance around his home? Or was Sikiokuu in league with Vinjinia and the women who had humiliated him? That might even explain why they were so concerned with Vinjinia's safety. And come to think of it, Sikiokuu and those women were the only ones who had ever asked him not to beat his wife.

"Be a man and fight me in the open instead of sending women to do your bidding. I have thrown down the gauntlet. Pick it up, Mr. Minister of lies and cowardice."

"Women? What women?" Sikiokuu asked.

"But of course you know nothing about them. Of course you didn't send them to abduct me. Sikiokuu, you are truly amazing. I have caught you red-handed, and all you can do is deny and deny?"

*"Please hold yourself together,"* Sikiokuu said in English, completely perplexed, for in truth he did not know what Tajirika was talking about. "You listen to me. I have no clue as to what you're talking

about. This is the gospel truth. You and I are now working together, remember? I have specifically ordered the police not to harass you. So if anyone has bothered you at your home or your workplace, he is disobeying my orders and will be dealt with accordingly. *You are a very important person to this government,* Mr. Tajirika. So tell me in short or just take your time: what happened to make you doubt my word?"

Sikiokuu managed to soothe Tajirika somewhat. He now told Sikiokuu an edited version of what had happened. He diminished his relentless and brutal wife beating to a single blow to the face. And the number of his female assailants changed from ten to twenty-five. The single machete became nine guns.

Sikiokuu felt like laughing but started wondering who these women were. And they even had the nerve to set themselves up as a people's court? And armed, too?

"Mr. Tajirika, I don't need to remind you that I had expressly forbidden you to beat your wife. Now you see the consequences. An entirely new situation has arisen, but we shall do our best to handle it. I am now asking you to please proceed with life as if nothing unusual has happened. The government will secretly investigate the matter, and we shall not rest until we get to the bottom of it. I promise you that the investigation will be conducted by a very select few. What kind of a world would this be if men lost the right to discipline their wives? I will make another request of you. Please don't let on to Vinjinia that you have talked to me about this business. And don't tell anyone else about what you have had to endure at the hands of women. We don't want this type of thing to spread through the entire country. I still advise you to declare a moratorium on wife beating until things are back to normal."

"Thank you, Mr. Sikiokuu," Tajirika said, surprised to hear himself mouthing gratitude instead of curses and threats. "It has been said truly that the nature of women is incomprehensible. They are very emotional. Even my wife, I don't think I will ever be able to trust her again. From now on I will be like your friend the Frenchman Descartes. To tell you the truth, I am beginning to doubt whether I have really seen the things that I have seen with my eyes. Reality and illusion are getting mixed up."

"Please, Mr. Tajirika." Sikiokuu lamented that he had ever mentioned the Frenchman to this idiot of a businessman. "You must really forget about the Frenchman. I told you he died many years ago, and that is a fact."

Tajirika appreciated Sikiokuu's concern for discretion. He also liked Sikiokuu's promise that the investigation would be conducted by a select few.

So after their telephone conversation, Tajirika felt much better, and he now walked as sprightly as he did before the women and Sikiokuu and Kaniūrū had stripped him of his dignity. Good times were around the corner again, Tajirika felt like singing.

# 9

Kaniūrū did not like Tajirika's release from jail, much less its being effected without his being consulted in his capacity as the chairman of the Commission of Inquiry. He was not amused by Tajirika's alliance with Sikiokuu, as it denied him the minister's undivided support in his bid to fully assume the chairmanship of Marching to Heaven. The key to his uninterrupted flow of personal wealth without personal sweat was the occupancy of the chair. If businessmen nowadays were ready to give him big money based on faith and hope, untold fortune would be his when the Ruler returned with loans galore leading to actual construction. Tajirika's release from jail was the fly in his ointment. Otherwise his affairs were running smoothly and Kaniūrū believed himself to be secure in life and property.

Even Nyawīra would come back to him someday, he thought, because of protective magic and the persuasive power of money. Like most of the other Ruler's disciples, Kaniūrū believed that money could buy just about anything and anybody, and certainly Nyawīra would be neither the first nor the last to change her political views for cash.

The only person who showed no interest in money was Jane Kanyori. She helped him in all his banking and yet asked for nothing more than the occasional lunch of collard greens and roasted goat meat. In money matters, she was a poster girl for innocence. This used to puzzle Kaniũrũ at first, but then he worked it out. Surrounded as she was by heaps of money all the time, she had become indifferent to its value, the way a cook loses appetite for a dish he has been sniffing all day. Kaniũrũ of course liked it that way.

So between the free services of Jane Kanyori and the free protective magic of the Wizard of the Crow, Kaniũrũ felt safe as he contemplated his maneuvers in the precarious politics of Aburĩria.

He did not know how far Sikiokuu had pursued his suggestions about securing the services of the Wizard of the Crow, whether Sikiokuu had sent for the sorcerer or had gone to the shrine in disguise at night. Not that it mattered to Kaniũrũ. He had done his part. The rest was for Sikiokuu to do and he, Kaniũrũ, was content not to be too closely involved in all this sorcery and witchcraft. For though it was all right to be close to a sorcerer long enough to secure protective magic, it was not all right to remain too close to him, for one could never know when he might turn against one.

The major task remaining for Kaniũrũ before the Ruler's return was to complete the work of the Commission of Inquiry into the Queuing Mania and write down its findings. Tajirika's confessions provided the basis of the report, and, because it had to conform to Sikiokuu's plans, he did not lose sleep over the task.

But Tajirika's release kept gnawing at him. Tajirika might resume the chairmanship with all its powers. So even as he received his stuffed envelopes and banked them safely and wisely with the help of the loyal Jane Kanyori, his mind was always busy trying to figure out how he could trick Tajirika into some foolishness that would compromise him.

He was in the midst of entertaining various scenarios when the telephone rang. It was Sikiokuu, but why was he calling so early?

"Women? What women? They beat up Tajirika?" Kaniũrũ asked, collapsing in laughter, unable for a minute to utter a coherent phrase. "They sat on him? What were they up to?"

Kaniũrũ's peals of laughter turned into a cry of sheer delight when Sikiokuu told him to investigate the gang of women.

# 10

The rumors that Aburĩrian women were up in arms against their husbands, which later spread to all corners of the country, had origins in Kaniũrũ's investigations. Despite the fact that he had been instructed to do it secretly, Kaniũrũ decided that this scandal was precisely what he needed to strip Tajirika of all dignity and manhood. He started by hinting to one or two people that some women had attacked Tajirika, made him lower his trousers, and then lashed his buttocks thoroughly. Rumor took over from there, but to Kaniũrũ's disappointment Tajirika's name did not figure much—any man's name would do among the many scary stories that were now told of women's replacing wife beating with husband bashing.

Kaniũrũ almost became a victim of the success of his own malicious initiative, for he later received urgent instructions to press ahead with the investigation to stem the tide of these rumors. A national gender war posed a serious threat to established family values.

Who are these women? What was the connection between the women of the people's court, the women dancers, and the Movement for the Voice of the People? For a moment he dwelled on the women dancers who came to grace the opening ceremony of his office.

After the ceremony he had expected them to come back to hold him to his promise to buy them a fleet of buses, but they never did. He was a little disappointed, for he would have liked to tell them a few things. He recalled the women dancers' intervention on Vinjinia's behalf. What had they been up to? What was the nature of Vinjinia's involvement?

Should he summon her to his office or not? But whether he called her to his office or went to see her, Vinjinia was sure to tell the same story she had told her husband. Should he summon Tajirika again? He would no doubt repeat what Vinjinia had recounted. And why would they cooperate with him anyway? Besides, Sikiokuu had told him very clearly that he must take care not to disturb the Tajirikas unduly. After all, Sikiokuu had chosen Kaniũrũ to conduct the investigation instead of the police because he wanted it done quietly, and he wanted Kaniũrũ's report to reach him first before it became an official document. Not that this was anything new. Sikiokuu was always self-serving. But, still, convinced as he was that she was essential to his investigation, Kaniũrũ had to get at Vinjinia.

He focused on the details of the gang of women who had abused Tajirika. They had ambushed him as he was walking to the Mars Café. They had thrown him into a waiting van, blindfolded him, and taken him to an unknown location, all in broad daylight. And immediately Kaniũrũ was struck by something. He whistled a tune of satisfaction. He would follow in the women's footsteps, even if it meant not following every one of Sikiokuu's orders not to importune the Tajirikas.

# 11

From the day of the rapprochement between husband and wife, Vinjinia had prayed and hoped for a new beginning to their lives. Not that she believed that their relationship would be back to where it should be, but talking was the first step on the road to healing.

She did not ask too much of life. A God-fearing, churchgoing family; a husband uninvolved in politics and civic matters; college-educated kids with secure jobs; a house, a farm, and two cars. This had been their dream when Tajirika and she were teachers in primary school.

As a certified teacher, Vinjinia had been the more secure of the two. Tajirika had been mainly a substitute teacher, his employment depending on women teachers going on maternity leave. They had married and had thought of naming their first child, a girl, Nyawĩra, but then they decided against it because Nyawĩra meant "work" and they did not want to condemn their child, even symbolically, to the life of a laborer. Instead they called her Ng'endo to symbolize their hopes for a life journey better than theirs as teachers earning a miserable income.

That was in the colonial days, and their life did not change until independence, when racial barriers to bank loans were relaxed and more business opportunities became available to Aburīrian blacks. Tajirika started a new career selling furniture and household goods. He was not a carpenter, but he had the gift of a smooth tongue. He first got orders for various items, then he would engage carpenters, and soon he was the proud owner of quite a big store, with a workshop and salaried carpenters. When they later bought a farm, Vinjinia gave up teaching to become the full-time manager of home and farm. She often looked back to those days when they would rejoice at every good turn in their fortune: the fulfillment of the prophecy implied in the name Titus Tajirika. Yet the wealthier they became, the greater their dispiritedness as they entered into discords that intensified into domestic violence.

If only the closeness at their recent wonder could be reproduced in their other dealings at home, Vinjinia sighed, but the possibility made her break into one of her favorite lyrics:

> *After darkness came light*
> *That shone on all things*
> *My heart waits patiently*
> *For love to rule my life*

She was in the fields outside her house, picking green corn for dinner, and she now continued in song all the way to the gates of her yard.

It was evening after sunset and everything felt peaceful, when she was suddenly grabbed by people she had not seen approach and was dragged into a vehicle that drove off immediately. The whole thing happened so swiftly that she did not have the time to scream. She did not even realize that she had dropped the sisal bag in which she had gathered the green corn.

# 12

She found herself seated between two men stinking of alcohol. It was dark in the back of the vehicle, and she could not tell how many people were in it. Like Tajirika, at first she thought that these were ordinary criminals who had kidnapped her in the expectation of a ransom. But suppose her husband refused to pay the ransom? Or had plotted all this as vengeance?

There were many stories of spousal murder in Aburĩria: husbands arranging their wives' deaths and then shedding crocodile tears while claiming to be hunting down the killer; wives incinerating their husbands at home while making sure that they themselves sustained superficial burns as proof that they had narrowly escaped the fire. Had Tajirika gotten into his head to hire thugs to silence her forever? Maybe this whole thing was a dream, a nightmare, and when she woke up everything would be back to normal? But it was not a dream, and Vinjinia was now horrified at the thought that she was about to be raped. Where are you taking me? she asked in a tremulous voice.

"Mrs. Tajirika," Kaniũrũ replied from the passenger seat next to the chauffeur. "My name is John Kaniũrũ. I don't think that this is the first time that you and I have met. But in case you have forgotten, let me remind you. I am your husband's deputy for Marching to Heaven. You graced the opening of our office with your presence. I am also the chairman of the Commission of Inquiry into the Queuing Mania, appointed to that position by the Ruler himself. But more to the point, I am also the leader of the Mighty's youthwings in these parts. I am telling you all this to make sure that you know and understand that your life is in my hands depending on whether you tell me the truth. Only you can decide whether you want to go back home to cook for your children or to the Red River as food for crocodiles."

"Young man, why are you doing this to me? How have I wronged you? Or has my husband proven himself too strong for you and you have decided to take it out on me? You should be ashamed of yourself."

"Your husband? He should not rejoice too soon. I am not through with him yet. But today, or rather tonight, we are not after your husband. In fact, you could say that he and I are on the same side. We want you to tell us about the women you have been consorting with, the women who have embarked on this campaign of terrorizing men. These dancers and jurors: how do you know them?"

"I don't," Vinjinia said without hesitation, though she felt pained at Kaniũrũ's suggestion that he and Tajirika were working together.

How could her husband close ranks with his own enemy simply to destroy her?

"Okay. You have sealed your fate. Not a single soul in all Aburīria knows where you are tonight. Driver, drive on. You have heard for yourself. This woman has elected to feed the crocodiles of the Red River."

The car accelerated. After an hour or so it stopped, and three men forcefully removed her from the back of the vehicle. They were in the bush and despite the moonlight it was a little dark. The men dragged her across some empty space toward the river, Kaniūrū and the driver following. There at the bank of the river now under the clear light of the moon she saw some crocodiles rear their ugly heads among the reeds. She who had been so stoic, she who had not so much as raised her voice, now screamed so hard and loud that she thought her head would split. But to her horror all she heard in response was her own echo. "Nobody can hear," Kaniūrū, one or two steps behind, now said. "You know this river? It is called the Red River because these crocodiles have come to love the blood of any person who entertains any foolishness against the Ruler. Has your husband been foolish enough to promise to make you Mama Aburīria? Tajirika to overthrow a government? He is deceiving you. He is not capable of even throwing a stone across a river if he knows it has crocodiles. Like these you see here. These are very hungry because, to tell you the truth, since the Ruler went to America, they have not had their normal ration of human meat."

She could not tell whether it was because of the words, the tone of their delivery, or a combination of both, but Vinjinia had never been so sure of anything: Kaniūrū was not simply trying to scare her; he meant what he said; he might even be looking forward to throwing her to the crocodiles. How would she extricate herself from this madness? The fear that gripped her whole being with the certainty of death clarified her predicament. If she was going to save herself from these cutthroats, she had better think very fast and come up with something, anything, to buy herself some time. She stopped screaming. She said a quick prayer, asking God to help her calm her nerves. And she decided that the Wizard of the Crow would rescue her.

"I am a bit confused. You asked me about two groups of women, dancers and jurors."

"Yes, that's correct."

"The truth is that I have no idea who the dancers were. I had come to the opening ceremony to see Minister Sikiokuu. I found them in the compound outside your offices. I assumed they were there for the ceremony."

"Yes, I invited them," Kaniũrũ said as if he did not want to dwell on how they had betrayed him. "What about the women who beat up your husband?"

"What is it about them that you want to know?" Vinjinia asked, calmly as if she was ready to cooperate.

"Who are they? Where do they live? And what is your connection with them?"

"I don't know them."

"You must be joking."

"They are not real," she said bluntly.

"What do you mean they are not real?"

"They are just shadows. Virtual. They exist only inside the mirror of the Wizard of the Crow."

# 13

Tajirika did not understand how his wife could decide to stay out so late, especially now, when they were trying to put their lives back together. The workers at home told him that they had seen her go out to the cornfields but they never saw her return. The fact that her car was still in the garage confirmed that she may not have gone far. But when midnight came and she still was missing, Tajirika wondered: Might she have gotten stuck in the Lake of Tears and become part of the Museum of Arrested Motion? He jumped out of bed and went in search of her.

He stood a few yards from the lake. The moonlight fell on the surface, making it glisten with the color of silver. His eyes fell on the birds, the cat, the dog, the antelopes, the butterflies, all suspended in motion, but he was relieved to find no sign of any human figure. He decided to go back into the house. At the gates to the yard he stopped. His heart was pounding. A sisal bag full of green corn lay on the ground, with a few cobs scattered on the grass.

Why should she have gone to pick corn only to dump it here? Had she been attacked and dragged away by an animal? But there were no signs of struggle. Or maybe she was simply the victim of a crime? These days criminals had become so bold that they raided people's homes with impunity, and despite electric fences, high stone walls topped with broken glass, security guards with attack dogs, and even the latest devices for electronic surveillance, no house was really safe.

Then he recalled his most recent conversation with Minister Sikiokuu. Maybe Sikiokuu's men had struck again? But had Sikiokuu not solemnly promised him that any investigation into the case of the women would be done quietly and secretly? They had not spoken about the possibility of questioning Vinjinia, let alone detaining her in any way, and even if they had, this time he would have said, Hands off my wife.

Since they had started talking again, Tajirika's feelings for Vinjinia had returned. He actually felt grateful to her for her efforts in forcing the government to admit that he was in their custody. But his was gratitude tinged with fear, fear of the women of the people's court, the shining machete pointed at his penis.

He was up and about early, and he reached for the phone to call his new friend Sikiokuu but there was no answer. Then he looked at his watch and realized that it was not even seven o'clock and the minister might not be in. Tajirika decided to go to his own office to make the call from there, hoping that by the time he got there it would be nearer to eight o'clock and Sikiokuu would be at work. At the gate, the sisal bag stared at him and he wondered, How will I explain Vinjinia's disappearance to the women?

No sooner had he thought this than he saw Vinjinia walking toward him. One look at her and he could tell she had had a rough and perilous night.

"What happened to you?" he asked with concern. Vinjinia could instinctively tell that there was no hypocrisy in his tone.

She collapsed on the spot as if weighed down by all the fatigue in the world. Tajirika lifted her up, took her inside, and put her on the bed. Vinjinia sat on the edge of the bed without saying a word. Tajirika thought that she was angry with him, and he started to explain himself.

"I don't know where you have been, much less what happened to you. But whatever the case is, I am very happy to see you back and alive. I have hardly slept. You just caught me as I was going to the office to work out how to look for you, where to begin. I had already tried to get Minister Sikiokuu, but no one picked up the telephone."

"Leave Sikiokuu out of it," Vinjinia said. "This was all Kaniũrũ's work."

"John Kaniũrũ?" Tajirika asked, feeling like hacking him into pieces. Kaniũrũ had gone too far, intruding in his affairs. Not only had he taken over his job, but he had had him arrested and tortured for not obeying his summons. Now this same Kaniũrũ had dared touch his wife. "This has to stop. Both of us cannot be tethered in the same kraal," he said bitterly, tears in his eyes.

"Don't waste your time on the likes of him. Let him be. He did not beat or rape me. I managed to untie the noose around me."

Vinjinia told him everything, from being kidnapped at the gate to almost becoming fodder for the crocodiles of the Red River.

When Tajirika heard the nature of Kaniũrũ's interrogation, he knew immediately that Kaniũrũ was acting at the behest of Sikiokuu. He felt ashamed that he himself had been party to the inquiry into the women who had beaten him, for now he felt indirectly responsible for the kidnapping. He held his tongue and said nothing that might reveal his own complicity. He was glad that he had not said a word about his telephone conversation with Sikiokuu. Still, it was hard to keep anger and frustration at bay. Why did Sikiokuu entrust Kaniũrũ with a task that clearly belonged to the police?

"How did you manage to get away?" he asked.

"The Wizard of the Crow! I remembered him in my hour of need," Vinjinia said, but she did not tell him that she had disclosed to Kaniũrũ that she had been to the shrine to ask for help. She still did not want Tajirika to know about her earlier face-to-face involvement with the Wizard of the Crow.

By the time she finished relating her story, Tajirika was beside himself with laughter. He laughed until his sides hurt.

"You told them with a straight face that those women did not exist, that they were figments of the imagination, mere shadows? And they believed you? Kaniũrũ's brains must be mush!" Tajirika said, recalling how the women had sat on him; how heavy they had been; how they had swaggered, one even brandishing a machete; how, finally, they beat him up. He broke into hilarious laughter again.

"Why do you laugh so? A wounded bird will land on anything."

"Oh, I can't wait for them to go to the shrine in search of the wizard to question him," Tajirika tried to explain amid his laughter. "They will not find him there."

"Not find him?" Vinjinia asked quickly, guiltily, because she feared that the story she had told Kaniũrũ might mean trouble for the Wizard of the Crow.

"The Wizard of the Crow is in prison under heavy police guard."

"In prison? How do you know?"

"Because I saw him there with my own eyes. I was with him in the same cell. And I left him there, under Sikiokuu's care."

Vinjinia did not say another word.

Tajirika's jollity persisted. Had Kaniũrũ, his archenemy, been outwitted by Vinjinia, a woman? He was full of admiration for his wife, and, on his way to the office, he savored Kaniũrũ's injured manhood.

As for Vinjinia, she was stunned: How had the Wizard of the Crow managed to be in two places at the same time? How could he be in jail and at the shrine, promising to send a delegation of wise elders to restrain Tajirika? The Wizard of the Crow had indeed fulfilled his part of the bargain. Now it was time for her to fulfill hers. She changed into the traditional leather skirt and ochered top.

# 14

"What?" Sikiokuu lashed out the following day when Kaniũrũ called to report the goings-on at the banks of the Red River.

"Just what I told you. They are not real women. They are shadows out of a mirror—mere reflections. That's why, now you see them, now you don't. Like the women dancers at the ceremonial opening of my office. I have never seen or heard of them again."

"Is that what Vinjinia told you? Those shadows—who creates them?"

"The Wizard of the Crow. Through his mirror. Something like a hologram. What they now call *virtual reality*."

"Wait a minute. The women who beat men, alias the women of the people's court . . . Are you saying the Wizard of the Crow sent them as holograms or virtual reality to actually beat up Tajirika?" Sikiokuu asked with a touch of sarcasm. "Is that what she told you?"

"Yes."

"You know, don't you, that Tajirika's wife beating took place after, not before, his release from police custody?"

"Yes."

"And you know that it was only after he beat his wife that he himself was beaten?"

"Yes, by those women, certainly. With clenched fists, lashes, and open-handed blows," Kaniŭrŭ added, laughing, as if giving an eyewitness account. "Powerful magic indeed."

"This is no laughing matter."

"I know, and that's why I need a squad of plainclothes policemen to attack the shrine and arrest the Wizard of the Crow together with all those who work for him or who go there for healing. The police will then burn the place down. Witchcraft hates fire like nobody's business. We need to act quickly, unexpectedly, before his magic can react."

"Hold it. Not so fast. One thing at a time."

"*Yes, Minister.*"

"Vinjinia: did she tell you that she herself went to the shrine?"

"Yes. And that's why I believed her. Her tone betrayed no lie. She freely admitted that she had gone there in person to ask for help. Her admission is significant because, although many people of our class, like you and me, will go to see a sorcerer at night, they would never admit it, not even if you tortured them day and night."

There was a pause, as if each was pondering what had just been said, while both considered their respective encounters with the Wizard of the Crow. Kaniŭrŭ himself had lied about his own visit to the wizard. And Sikiokuu was wondering, Does this Kaniŭrŭ know anything about my meeting with this Wizard of the Crow in my office? Who would have told him?

"Listen. We are not talking about the poor or the rich, this or that class. We are not communists. What I want to know is this: did Vinjinia tell you that she and the Wizard of the Crow met face-to-face?"

"Yes."

"You are very sure—*I mean,* that she said she had seen him with her own eyes?"

"Yes."

"John, you are very highly educated, went to university?"

Kaniũrũ did not detect irony in the question. He took it as a compliment.

"Yes. And was later a lecturer," Kaniũrũ said proudly, trying to embellish his educational achievements.

"And so you know the proverb that a woman's word should be believed only after one has slept over it?"

"Yes, and that's precisely why I didn't bother to tell you about it right away. I wanted to review her claims to see if there were any holes in her story. I did not find any. I believe that I did tell you about my hunch that this Wizard of the Crow is the one mostly behind much of the strange things happening in this country. And if I may speak the truth and shame the Devil, that man has peculiar gifts. I don't even understand why you did not arrest and detain him for questioning when I first told you about him. If you had done so we would have known quite a lot by now. Mr. Minister, give me the force I need and I will show them how to turn the Wizard of the Crow into a lamb."

"And what if I told you that Vinjinia's story is an impossibility, that the Wizard of the Crow could not have been involved, that he's not even around?"

Kaniũrũ felt belittled, humiliated by this revelation. Sikiokuu had been toying with him. He was angry but directed his anger at the absent Vinjinia.

"When I catch that woman . . ."

"Don't touch her," Sikiokuu told him. "I asked you to look into the identity of the women who beat up Tajirika. Instead you kidnapped his wife. Kaniũrũ, I don't need to remind you that this is the second time that we have detained this woman, and all because of your mistakes. Tajirika has been calling me and is understandably furious about the treatment of his wife; even I felt embarrassed by my lame

excuses. I don't want to aggravate Tajirika further. I need his cooperation in other matters."

Kaniũrũ was not exactly amused to hear that Tajirika now occupied a significant place in Sikiokuu's scheme of things. Why is this
minister changing like a chameleon? Was he about to dump him
despite his loyal service? He fumed: he had no way of voicing how
angry he was with Sikiokuu, Tajirika, and especially Vinjinia.

For a few seconds he recalled Vinjinia's voice in the moonlight by
the banks of the Red River, swearing by all that was most sacred to
her that she was telling the truth when she told him that she had met
with the Wizard of the Crow. He remembered testing her by asking
her to describe the shrine, and she was able to tell him details of the
place that he himself already knew.

"The Wizard of the Crow: where is he?" Kaniũrũ asked. "Is he
dead, or . . ."

"You ask too many questions," Sikiokuu snapped back. He was not
very pleased with Kaniũrũ's critical tone about his own dealings with
the wizard. "Take my advice and give up the habit. And while you're at
it, please give up your belief in mirrors and fantasy. I want the women
themselves, not their shadows," Sikiokuu said, and hung up.

# 15

Sikiokuu hung up because he was on the verge of hysterics and
thought better of laughing on the phone. He admitted to himself
that the Wizard of the Crow had extraordinary powers. But the claim
that the sorcerer had created living shadows that abducted people,
put them on trial, slapped them around, punched them, bruised
them—that was a little hard to swallow. Had the wizard created his
shadows in America and sent them across the Atlantic to Aburĩria?
How had it been possible for him to be with the Ruler in New York
and with Vinjinia in Eldares at the same time? And to think that
Kaniũrũ had fallen for this? He stopped laughing when it suddenly
crossed his mind that the Wizard of the Crow might not have boarded
the plane for America. But he dismissed the thought as quickly as it

had come, for he remembered that Kahiga and Njoya had taken him to the airport, escorted him onto the Aburīrian plane, and waited until its ascent.

Then it occurred to him that he had never received confirmation of the sorcerer's arrival in America. Sikiokuu decided to call America to dispel any doubts raised by Vinjinia's allegations.

Sikiokuu hoped to also find out more about the Ruler's condition. Who could predict what would happen in Aburīria were the illness to worsen? Would this ignite a coup d'état? He felt uneasy thinking about illness, death, and succession. It was treason to even imagine these thoughts, and this revived his earlier fears that the Wizard of the Crow might have divined Sikiokuu's secret wish for life at the top. Would the sorcerer whisper something about Sikiokuu's treacherous desires in the Ruler's ear? Success in treating the Ruler might result in the sorcerer's being made a special physician to the leader. The sorcerer posed a threat. It was better to be informed and therefore to know the exact situation now rather than later.

He made the call to New York, and although he hated the very sound of his archrival's voice, Sikiokuu had no choice but to ask to speak with Machokali, because it was he who had sent the e-mail in which the Ruler requested the Wizard of the Crow.

He could not believe what he was hearing. Was Machokali playing games? Lying to him, perhaps? This could not be. Machokali spoke with a mixture of sadness, anger, and even fatigue, unless of course he was pretending. He confirmed that the Wizard of the Crow had indeed arrived in America and had met with His Mighty Excellency once. But then he disappeared. He was nowhere to be found, yet nobody had seen him leave. His absence had been discovered only the day before, and no one could say for sure when he had vanished or even whether he was still in America.

The news of the sorcerer's mysterious disappearance haunted Sikiokuu. Was the Wizard of the Crow back in the country? Perhaps even for a while? Was Vinjinia speaking the truth when she said that she had met with him, talked to him face-to-face? What were the implications of his ability to create living shadows? What if he created an army of shadows and took over the country now that he knew the extent of the Ruler's illness? Oh, he'd forgotten to ask about the Ruler's illness! Was the invisible wizard playing tricks with his mind?

He was shocked, yes, but was quick to realize the need to do something about the situation. He remembered that even before the Wizard of the Crow left for America, he, Sikiokuu, had hatched plans to eliminate him. The Ruler's sudden and unexpected summons of the wizard had interfered with the maturation of his plot. But now, with the confusion concerning the sorcerer's whereabouts . . .

And suddenly Sikiokuu felt elated. God loves me, this I know, he murmured to himself. Now is the time to send the Wizard of the Crow to Hell, together with all of his sorcerer's paraphernalia, including mirrors that might have captured or could capture images of Sikiokuu's ambition. If he acted now, nobody would know exactly where, when, and how the Wizard of the Crow had met his fate, because apart from Vinjinia there was no other credible person who knew that the Wizard of the Crow was back in his shrine.

Or should he forge an alliance with the wizard? An army of shadows loyal to Sikiokuu? No, that would mean giving too much power to an unreliable sorcerer. No, Sikiokuu would instead have him secretly captured and brought to his office, where he would induce him, by guile and threats, to produce Nyawīra. Then he would have him fed to the hungry crocodiles of the Red River. Instead of using his loyal lieutenants Kahiga and Njoya to do the dirty work, these two being afraid of the Wizard of the Crow, Sikiokuu would use irregulars, and Kaniūrū's youthwingers fit the bill perfectly.

He was back on the phone to Kaniūrū, and he made it seem as if he were simply calling to continue a previously interrupted conversation.

"Our line was cut off before I finished what I had to say," Sikiokuu started. "You know what our phone system is like. I hope a day will come when our telephones work as smoothly and efficiently as those in Japan and America. What was I saying before the connection was cut? That the Wizard of the Crow was not there then or now. But I have chewed over what you said, and here now is my thinking. Let us assume for the sake of argument that Vinjinia is speaking the truth, that she did indeed see and talk to the Wizard of the Crow. Gather a gang of trusted and reliable youth. Get me the Wizard of the Crow. Bring him to me alive. But take everybody else at the shrine, clients or workers, to the Red River. The crocodiles are sick with hunger."

Kaniūrū did not like the idea of leading a squad of thugs on a raid of the shrine. That's why he had earlier asked for a police squad to whom he could give orders while remaining in the background or, better yet, away from the scene altogether, in order to avoid the sorcerer's curses.

"Why can't . . . the police . . . Why don't you give me a police squad armed with big hunting rifles—you know, the kind that can blow an elephant to smithereens."

"Don't you understand? We don't want to announce what we are doing to the whole world; the government had nothing to do with it. It's all off the record. So get your youth squad ready. I believe some of them are armed. But remember one thing: I want the Wizard of the Crow alive."

Sikiokuu wanted many things from this final encounter with the Wizard of the Crow: the location of Nyawira's whereabouts, a full report on the Ruler's illness, and a possible alliance. But there were lingering questions: When and how did the Wizard of the Crow escape from America? And why? Or had he been killed in New York and was now the object of a cover-up?

# 16

Not a day went by that Nyawira did not miss Kamĩtĩ, but that morning she woke up aching for him so terribly that to assuage her sense of loss she put on the traditional clothes that she had worn on the night they returned to Eldares after their sojourn in the mountains. She dwelled obsessively on their return, her way of trying to find some peace. She took her guitar and played a little. A combination of the traditional wear and guitar as a modern instrument piqued her imagination, and she put it back on the wall, feeling better.

Later that morning, Nyawira saw a woman, also dressed traditionally, coming through the gate. What a coincidence, she thought. Why did so many people feel that they had to dress in traditional wear on their visits to the shrine?

Nyawira recognized Vinjinia! What brings her here? she wondered. Has her husband not given up beating her? And why is she dressed that way? On previous occasions she had worn a simple dress with a *kanga* head and shoulder wrap.

"What do you want to tell the Wizard of the Crow today?" Nyawīra asked.

"Listen to me," Vinjinia said. "Let's go out and talk in the open, where we can see ourselves and what surrounds us."

"Don't be afraid! The Wizard of the Crow has many eyes."

"Do you remember me from the other day?"

"Many come here and go. But I shall look at the mirror," Nyawīra said.

She did not know what Vinjinia wanted. She had never seen her like this: speaking at once anxiously and assertively. Was her husband in pursuit of her? Vinjinia's eyes were fixed on Nyawīra's face, as if she were debating whether to trust it and say what had brought her to the shrine.

"Don't trouble yourself. I am the same person who was here the other day to put an end to my husband's violence."

"Has he not stopped?"

"He has, at least for now."

"So he heeded the elders I sent his way?"

"That's why I have come to see you."

"Don't be afraid. Say whatever ails your heart."

"The matter is a little urgent. I don't want to talk behind closed doors in case *they* are already on *their* way here."

"Who?"

Vinjinia glanced over her shoulder, then leaned forward.

"Kaniūrū and his gang," Vinjinia said in a tone that seemed to say: There, I have said it, come what may.

Fear struck Nyawīra, but she did not panic in case this was a trap.

"Kaniūrū? Who is he?" Nyawīra asked, as if she were indifferent to the name. "But let us go outside if that will free your tongue."

Nyawīra went inside to alert her fellow workers to be on the lookout. She then joined Vinjinia in the yard, both women dressed identically. They walked in silence toward the gate, as if one were seeing the other off. Suddenly Vinjinia stopped and looked at Nyawīra straight in the eye. Nyawīra was completely taken aback.

"Nyawīra," Vinjinia called her by her name. "Let's not play games. I did not want to say your real name inside the shrine."

"When did you find out?" Nyawīra asked in her normal voice.

"Every time I have come here I would go home with a feeling that I knew you. But when this very morning my husband told me that he left the Wizard of the Crow in jail and that he is still in Sikiokuu's hands, it dawned on me that it was you playing the role of the Wizard of the Crow. I felt I had to come and tell you about the danger you face. I wanted you to come out into the open for, as they say, even walls have ears. But I also wanted to confirm my suspicions by watching your gait, how you carried yourself."

And as they resumed their walk, Vinjinia told Nyawīra the whole story of her second abduction by Kaniūrū and his thugs. Without hesitation, she told her how she had saved herself.

Nyawīra felt both elated and depressed. What, she asked herself bitterly, had once attracted her to Kaniūrū?

"I just came to tell you of the danger I have put you in, because even if your companion is still in jail, Kaniūrū and his men may still want to come here to find out exactly who the other wizard is with whom I've been consulting. I can't presume to tell you what you ought to do; you must decide for yourself. I must go now. But before I do, I want you to know that I am very grateful for all that you have done for me, going so far as to risk your life. All the same, I don't believe in your kind of politics. But if there is anything I can do for you . . ."

Nyawīra stood silently, holding back tears with difficulty. She was struck by Vinjinia's generosity of spirit: she had fought the fatigue of a sleepless night of torture in order to come and warn her of danger. She had walked from the dark into the light: Nyawīra had just witnessed the coming into life of the new, more assertive Vinjinia.

Vinjinia said farewell and started to walk away. As in previous visits, she had left her car on the side of the road quite a distance from the shrine. Nyawīra caught up with her and said: "Please, don't think that I was silent because I am angry with you. I am grateful for what you have done: endangering yourself to warn me. I am moved to know that you have never disclosed your suspicions about me to anyone. Don't worry too much about what took place at Red River last night. I know how to take care of myself, but I will keep in mind your offer to help. Let's agree on a code."

They discussed various names they might use should communication between them become necessary, with Vinjinia, no longer a passive recipient of other people's ideas, fully participating.

"Let's use the name Dove," suggested Vinjinia finally.

"That's good," Nyawīra agreed. "Dove is the messenger of peace and salvation."

"I must ask you a question," Vinjinia felt emboldened to say. "I won't mind if you don't want to answer."

"Go on."

"The other Wizard of the Crow. Is he still in jail?"

"No. He was when Tajirika was in prison. He is now in America."

Vinjinia gaped with wonder and disbelief.

"In America?"

"The Ruler is ill. He sent for the Wizard of the Crow."

# 17

It was the unbelieving look that Vinjinia gave her that brought back a suspicion she always harbored: was the illness a ruse to get the Wizard of the Crow? As Nyawīra stood at the gate irresolutely, watching her friend disappear in the distance, a song she once heard sung by the girls of the village popped into her mind, a silent lullaby to herself. She went inside the shrine and took out her guitar again. She sat on the veranda and, now, almost miraculously, the strings responded to the touch of her fingers. She played and hummed the melody softly, her eyes now set on a distance far away.

> You vowed never to go away
> Now you have gone
> Leaving me here alone
> Pleading with you to stay
> Stay one more night

She thought of him, the Wizard of the Crow, in America, in the care of the dictator, no longer sure that she would ever see him again.

# BOOK FOUR

# Male Daemons

# SECTION I

# 1

A record of the Ruler's illness exists in a paper by the distinguished Harvard professor Din Furyk. The professor had hoped to read it at the annual conference of the Euro-American Medical Association and duly sent them an abstract, but the description of the illness sounded so unbelievable that he was not allowed to present it. The professor did not give up. He sent the paper to a famous journal in England, *Nature & Nurture,* and on reading it the editors who earlier had shown interest in it changed their minds. They said that since the illness in question involved the head of state of a friendly country, the publication of the paper would almost certainly strain the relations between Britain and Aburīria to the detriment of cooperation between the two countries in matters of science and technology. Another journal returned the paper to the author, recommending instead a disreputable publisher of science fiction!

A copy of the professor's diary in which he describes how he came to write the paper fell my way, and I will draw on it freely to supplement my other sources.

# 2

It seems that the Ruler's body had started puffing up like a balloon, his whole body becoming more and more inflated, without losing the proportion of parts.

Dr. Wilfred Kaboca, the first to examine him, immediately called for Machokali as a witness to his dealings with the sick man. Machokali in turn called in all the other ministers, including security personnel, who stood around flabbergasted at the uncanny sight. Not only did the Ruler seem on the verge of bursting, but he had also lost the power to speak.

The ministers retreated to a meeting to plan how to deal with the Ruler's illness and the multitude of problems it generated. Where would they put him?

# 3

He would sit and sleep on the floor, it was decided. What would he wear? As his hypertrophy proceeded, his clothes were ripping at their seams; the Ruler appeared to be dressed in rags. They covered him in bedsheets. But what to do about the Ruler's unrelenting inflation? How to stop it, how to slow it down?

Dr. Wilfred Kaboca had tried everything within his knowledge and experience to contain the process but had now reached the end of his tether.

Should they take him to a hospital? they debated time and again. But how to prevent the news from spreading? They authorized Dr. Kaboca to seek the help of a specialist willing to apply himself only in the Ruler's suite. Dr. Wilfred Kaboca contacted Dr. Clement C. Clarkwell, a New York specialist in obesity and the like, but when Clarkwell saw the body visibly expanding before his very eyes, he dialed Professor Din Furyk for help.

# 4

"I came to know about the illness," writes Din Furyk of the Harvard Medical School in his diary, "because Dr. Clarkwell was a former student and whenever he came across difficult cases he would often call me for advice. His description of this particular case so aroused my curiosity that I dropped everything and went to New York. I was taken past security right to the Ruler's suite, the top three floors of the Fifth Avenue VIP Hotel, where I quickly consulted with Dr. Clarkwell and Dr. Kaboca, and the gravity of the situation was accentuated by the shaking of their heads from side to side in disbelief saying that, according to the preliminary exam, everything about the Ruler, except for his swelling up, seemed normal. I entered the Ruler's room. I would ask other questions only after I had seen the patient.

"The patient was seated on the floor, his back to the wall. I felt his forehead, took his temperature, listened to his heartbeat. All was normal, though he seemed to be panting a bit from fatigue. But his eyes, those eyes, I have never encountered a look like that in an adult. They looked scared and helpless, like the eyes of a child stricken with fear at the unexpected and the unknown.

"The Ruler, as his followers invariably called him, seemed to have lost the power of speech. Fortunately he could still read what was put in front of him and he would then nod for *yes* or shake his head for *no*. But even these gestured *yeses* and *nos* were rare and rather abrupt."

Din Furyk tells of how he asked for blood samples to be taken to find out whether the patient exhibited symptoms of hyperthyroidism, nephrotic syndrome, polycystic kidney disease, or some form of Cushing's syndrome brought about by cortisal hormones in the blood, or any disorders associated with obesity known to science. He was also concerned about the possibility of steroid-induced obesity, despite Dr. Wilfred Kaboca's assurances that the Ruler had never taken any steroids, that Viagra was the only drug for which he had shown an insatiable appetite.

Furyk then describes his attempts to get a sense of the Ruler's medical history from his entourage of ministers and security folk. "No one was able to shed any light on the matter. When I asked them a question, such as 'When did the illness strike?' or 'When did you first notice signs of the illness?' they would look in the direction of the Ruler, then at one another, and would say that they did not know. Africans, or shall I say black people, in general, are strange."

At this point the professor digresses to discuss the African character. The diary is full of phrases like "faces that cannot be easily read," "a face like a mask," and "the ministers could not look me in the eye; they had a shiftiness suggesting mendacity." The Ruler's own personal physician is also questioned, and he is described as being no different from the ministers, volunteering bits of information grudgingly and only when he was outside the hearing of others.

The only person praised in the diary is the Minister for Foreign Affairs, Mr. Machokali, who spoke without an accent and was direct in his manner. He was presumed to have been educated in the West. "A rare mind, this, quite exceptional. Could easily have been a product of Harvard or another Ivy League school."

"Because they were all hopeless," Professor Furyk writes, "I thought it better simply to wait for the results from the lab.

"Imagine my shock when they showed that everything about him was functioning normally! How was this possible? Why this continued self-induced expansion of the body? His belly was as taut as a drum, and whenever I tapped it a sound issued from the mouth. *Crr,* or was it *coral* or *crawl* or *cruel*? I took Dr. Clarkwell and Dr. Kaboca outside for a conference. What could the Ruler be signifying by *coral* or *crawl* or *cruel*? Dr. Kaboca's response was strange: he was a physician of the body, not a decipherer of words; it was better to ask the ministers because they were politicians and politicians are known for their words.

"I confronted the ministers. All turned their eyes to Machokali."

# 5

Machokali himself flinched inwardly. It was bad enough to have this case, of a body spluttering meaningless words, on his hands. Now he had to deal with accusatory looks: You arranged this visit; get us out of this predicament. How did he, a highly educated individual with a BS in economics from the University of Aburĩria, an MA in political science from Michigan University, and a PhD in the psychology of power from Uppsala University in Sweden, find himself in this mess?

He needed to buy time. So he said at the meeting that he needed to go back to the Ruler to elicit more words that might help him to interpret the three words. As soon as he got new information, he would convene another meeting.

So with a boldness he did not feel, Machokali marched into the Ruler's room and said only, "How are you!" The Ruler stared blankly past him as if he had not seen him or heard his greetings. So Machokali backtracked, and as soon as he was outside the room he darted to his own room, locked himself inside, and knelt down to pray for divine intervention.

Suddenly he heard a knock at the door. He jumped up and hesitated before opening the door. It was one of the Ruler's security men. Had the Ruler's condition worsened? Or . . . Or . . . worse than that?

"I wanted to see you alone," said Arigaigai Gathere, alias A.G.

"What's the matter?" Machokali asked him after he had gestured for his visitor to take a seat.

"I really don't know where or how to start, but I want to begin by begging you not to take lightly what an underling like me . . . Do you know the story of Elephant and the thorn?"

"Please spare me the wisdom of folktales," Machokali said, forcing himself to laugh as if he had been joking, but in his heart he was burning with anxiety, for another thought had crept into his mind: had Sikiokuu seized power?

"Let me tell you the story all the same. Elephant felt something sharp in his foot, and when he removed it and saw that it was a tiny thorn, he was very angry. How can such a tiny thing prevent a big animal like me from walking? He pushed the thorn back into his foot and walked on, stamping the ground with defiance. The infection that later developed in the foot killed Elephant. Hence the saying 'Never look down upon the small.' True! *Haki ya Mungu!* I, too, ask you, Don't despise the messenger, however lowly, or take lightly the message, however strange."

"Say whatever you have come to say," Machokali said.

"I know of a man who can handle this illness."

"A doctor more qualified than Professor Furyk?"

"Well, he is not a doctor in the ordinary sense. He's a sorcerer."

"A sorcerer?"

"Well, a diviner."

"A diviner? A sorcerer? In New York?"

"In Aburĩria. His name is the Wizard of the Crow."

# 6

"True! *Haki ya Mungu,*" A.G. would say when he later narrated what happened during that fateful visit to the USA. "Right from the time it first struck, I knew that it was no ordinary illness. I also knew that there was only one person who could wrestle it to the ground. But I did not want to volunteer my knowledge. Who would believe my claims that the Wizard of the Crow could succeed where the masters of science from the West had failed? So I held back the information to give the ministers time to see what their Western doctors could do. The ministers had more education than I, but you all know, don't you, that too much education can make men blind to what's around them.

"But when I heard that the Ruler had started to hallucinate, uttering words that nobody could tell the meaning of, I said to myself, That's it. I will speak out or forever hold my peace. It was clear to me that whites were at the root of this illness. Do you know how white people hate it when a black man comes up with an original idea? And what could be more original than our Ruler's vision of Marching to Heaven? These whites! Wherever they are, whoever they are, they all stink of racism. I had made up my mind, and the only thing remaining for me to figure out was how I would speak to these ministers in a manner that would bring them around to my view of the problem.

"There were three ways of going about it: tell my idea to all the ministers at once; speak to Machokali alone, for he had emerged as their leader; or write a note to the Ruler and deliver it to him in secrecy. True! *Haki ya Mungu!* I was prepared to talk to the Ruler and remind him that I was the same man who once confronted djinns outside the gates of Paradise and chased them across the Eldares prairie in the dark of midnight without fear.

"Well, I didn't think it a good idea to tell them as a group, because, being in the presence of these white doctors, the ministers would almost certainly dismiss it as superstition and pretend that they did not believe in such things. And I didn't know how I could find myself in only the Ruler's company. So I decided to confide in Machokali, though I was hesitant. You might say that my decision became final only when I heard him tell us that he was going to try to talk to the Ruler. I followed him and waited for him outside the Ruler's room.

"His face told me that he had not met with success, and this emboldened me to follow him. When I uttered the words 'the Wizard of the Crow,' I saw doubts and faith struggle inside the man. How do you know that he has the power to heal? he asked. I told him the story of the night of the beggars at Paradise, but of course I did not tell him all the details. I did not tell him that the protective magic of the Wizard of the Crow had effected my promotion from an ordinary constable to an honored place in the Ruler's office and now as a member of the delegation to America. Soon I saw his desire to believe quell doubt, but he told me that he could not make a decision on this by himself, that he had to mention this to the Ruler and, if that failed, then discuss the matter with the other ministers.

"I thought that Machokali would get up immediately and go to the Ruler, but he seemed distracted. Imagine my surprise when the minister asked me to accompany him. True! *Haki ya Mungu!* This request was entirely unexpected, but I took it as an honor. Imagine the most senior minister in the government asking me to accompany him to the Ruler! When we got there, I saluted the Ruler and the minister bowed. But instead of his doing the talking or the writing, Machokali simply pointed at me, clearly not wanting to be a messenger for sorcery. Well, I took out my pen and wrote down my name on a piece of paper just to remind the Ruler that it was me, A.G., or, as he once called me playfully, the Conqueror of Djinns. Then I wrote down what I had already told the minister: that I knew of a sorcerer who could heal him. I saw from the sudden light in his eyes that the Ruler was not averse to my suggestion; he looked at the minister and nodded his head as if to say that he was in total agreement with the idea.

"Machokali's face brightened, and outside the room he put his arm around my shoulder as if we were the closest of mates. This matter of sorcery is entirely between us, he told me, for if the New York media were to know that the Ruler was sending for sorcerers from Aburĩria, they would flock here and camp out at the hotel. Even Professor Din Furyk and Dr. Clement C. Clarkwell were not to know anything about this new development. As for the other ministers, he would tell them only after the sorcerer had arrived.

"I was with him when he e-mailed Sikiokuu to say that the Ruler wanted the minister to send the Wizard of the Crow to New York, USA. When Sikiokuu replied with the wizard's travel plans, Machokali told me that he and I would go meet the sorcerer at the international airport.

"Now, I had thought that, with so prompt a response from Aburĩria, Machokali would be all over himself with joy in anticipation of the wizard's arrival. But he did not look happy. Something still worried him.

"'What I most fear,' he told me candidly, 'is that the sorcerer will arrive at the airport dressed in a garb of uncured leather, a necklace of sharp animal bones around his neck, a gourd of stinking oil and green leaves in his hand, amulets on his wrists, and bangles around the ankles of his bare feet. These people here are very sensitive to the importation of agricultural products for fear of dangerous viruses. What if customs officials stop him? What if Immigration mistakes his powders for drugs, and the sorcerer then discloses that he is here at the Ruler's request? The Ruler could meet the fate of that Latin American head of state imprisoned for life in an American jail for drug offenses!' Worried that a scandal might erupt around the sorcerer's visit, he now wished that he had specified that the wizard be dressed decently and his paraphernalia be shipped in a diplomatic bag!

"Well, I could not help laughing at the minister's words and worries.

"'The Wizard of the Crow is a modern sorcerer,' I told him. 'He dresses in suits. Besides, he uses only a mirror for his divinations.'

"True! *Haki ya Mungu!* Minister Machokali's jaw fell and his eyes almost popped out at my description of the Wizard of the Crow and his divine mirror."

# 7

Machokali did not much believe in witchcraft and divination. But a bird exhausted in flight lands on the nearest anything, and for him the Wizard of the Crow was now that anything. If the Ruler's health was to improve, it would not matter what he, Machokali, believed or did not. What now most preoccupied him were the measures to take to prevent news of the sorcerer's presence from leaking beyond the inner council of ministers and the security officers. As Minister for Foreign Affairs, Machokali was responsible for projecting a favorable image of his country, and he would not now want to make the Ruler and Aburĩria laughing stocks in the eyes of the world, particularly in the corridors of the United Nations. He could imagine the snickering that would greet him wherever he went: How are your Ruler and his sorcerer getting along?

Machokali was relieved at the airport when he saw the Wizard of the Crow in a dark suit, a briefcase in hand, looking every inch a businessman like any other in New York.

They did not speak much on the way to the hotel, where Machokali whisked him straight up to the Ruler's floors without registering the newly arrived guest. There was to be no record of the sorcerer's visit.

"Do you need anything?" Machokali asked him as soon as he had been shown his room. "Take a bath, change, and then let's go to the Ruler. Or how about a bite of something first?"

Instead of answering, the Wizard of the Crow looked now at the minister, and then at A.G., as if puzzled as to who was whom.

"Is either of you in a position to tell me what the Ruler wants to see me about?"

"Excuse me, my sirs," said A.G. in Kiswahili quickly, sensing the tension, somehow trying to address them both as equals. "We did not do what the English call *an introduction,* or, in Kiswahili, making people know one another. This here is the Minister for Foreign Affairs, Mr. and Dr. Machokali."

The words, *my sirs,* irritated Machokali, and he cast a fierce glance at A.G., as if to warn him that he, the minister, was the only sir here.

"Didn't Minister Sikiokuu tell you what this is about?" Machokali asked.

"Only that the Ruler had sent for me."

Machokali did not go into details about the Ruler's illness but told the wizard that he was to use all the powers he was reputed to possess to heal the chief. He was to return to Aburĩria the following morning. It was that simple.

"I am a little jet-lagged," the Wizard of the Crow told Machokali firmly. "Let me get some rest so that my head can work clearly."

Jet-lagged? What would a sorcerer know about jet lag? Machokali did not voice his curiosity but stressed the need for speed.

A.G. again sensed tension between the two sirs, and he hastened to whisper in Machokali's ear. Let's do what he wants. We don't want to make him angry.

Machokali was not happy with the sorcerer's attitude. He was equally unhappy with A.G.'s fear and humility. Yet he felt he had no choice but to accede to the sorcerer's request. In the event of the sorcerer's failure, he did not want it said that he was somehow responsible.

"Let us meet tomorrow, then," Machokali said.

# 8

That very evening, Machokali called all the ministers to his room. Dr. Luminous Karamu-Mbu, the official biographer, or TOB, as he was known sometimes, wanted to attend but he was barred because he was not a member of the cabinet. A special exception had been made for Dr. Wilfred Kaboca and the security men only because of their expertise in matters under review.

Karamu-Mbu was not the most popular of fellows. He was a man of few words and even fewer friends. The size of his pen was intimidating, and nobody was quite sure what it was that he wrote in the equally huge notebook. Everybody was a little scared of his nearness to the throne and avoided him as much as possible. Normally TOB was too busy recording the tiniest details of the Ruler's existence to miss company. But since the Ruler had fallen ill, TOB had written the same thing over and over. *Today the Ruler remained ill and speechless. Today the Ruler remained bedridden and speechless. Today ditto.* TOB did not know what to do with all the time on his hands, so his exclusion from the meeting was especially disconcerting. He retired to his room to arrange in proper and readable order the notes he had taken since the delegation arrived in America.

Machokali did not know quite how to break his news but decided that plunging into the matter was the best policy. Still, he wanted to go about it gingerly so as not to offend the ministers' egos. He began not with the sorcerer's arrival but with a brief account of how it came to be that this sorcerer was in New York and how the Ruler himself had nodded in agreement. He stopped to assess the impact of his words. There was no snickering, to Machokali's surprise; a few even admitted that they had heard of the Wizard of the Crow, had been thinking along the same lines, and had kept their views to themselves only because they had wanted to give science a chance. Even Dr. Wilfred Kaboca did not express any doubts.

"So when will he come to New York?" they all wanted to know.

Machokali broke the news. They looked at one another, stupefied. But soon they recovered from the shock and curiosity took over. What did he look like? Was he young or old? How was he dressed? They agreed, after much discussion, that they should not show too much eagerness to meet the wizard, that they should simply cast quick glances in his direction in order not to give him the notion that he was in the same ranks with ministers. They also resolved not to tell the wizard about the white doctors and not to tell Drs. Furyk and Clarkwell about the wizard. Were the Ruler's health to improve, what did it matter if Harvard science took the credit?

# 9

Early the next day Machokali called on the Wizard of the Crow. The sorcerer, who was fiddling with his tie in front of a mirror, gestured to Machokali to sit and continued fumbling. But the minister just stood and looked on.

"You slept well?" Machokali began in an attempt at small talk.

The more Machokali encountered the Wizard of the Crow, the more he had his doubts. How did such a youth become so adept at healing?

"I am told that you diagnose and heal by means of a mirror?"

"It depends on the illness and the mirror. Mirrors can be thick or thin, convex or concave: every illness calls for a mirror appropriate to the challenge it poses. It takes time for me to interpret the images in the mirror. I must also speak to everyone who has had any contact with a patient. You and all the ministers, for example . . ."

What if Sikiokuu had hired this man to implicate Machokali or the other ministers in a conspiracy to harm the Ruler?

"You know, don't you, that this matter should not spread beyond these walls? That it should be confined to the small circle of those who are here?"

"Mr. Minister, my motto is Get It by the Roots, and the Illness Shall Be No More. If I am to root the illness out, I must talk to whomever I deem necessary."

"Okay. You may see all the ministers, the security men, and his doctor."

"How many doctors does he have?"

"Just one. Dr. Wilfred Kaboca. *His personal physician*. He never leaves his side."

"Is he the only doctor who has seen him? No other doctor?"

"Yes."

"Fine with me."

"That's wise. There is no point wasting time talking to too many people. Time is of the essence. Consult your mirror and . . ."

"Take the next flight home," the Wizard of the Crow completed

Machokali's thought. "Believe me, Mr. Minister, I am not keen on staying in America a minute longer than necessary. I prefer the bush and its healing properties. My procedure will be quick or slow depending on whether or not those who have had dealings with the patient are telling all they know."

"Would a government minister lie to you?" Machokali said, offended.

"Are you now telling me the truth?" the Wizard of the Crow asked him offhandedly, continuing to fumble with his tie.

"*Don't play with me, Sorcerer Kagogo,*" Machokali said angrily in Kiswahili. "Why would I lie to you? I don't want anything from you. I am not the patient here."

"Excuse me, but please come over here," the Wizard of the Crow said, beckoning him with a finger.

Machokali was not happy with the sorcerer giving him orders, but to speed up matters he toned down his own antagonism and did as asked.

"Please look in the mirror," the Wizard of the Crow requested, stepping aside to give him ample room.

Machokali did so as the Wizard of the Crow looked at the palm of his own right hand.

"What do you see?" the wizard asked Machokali.

"My reflection," Machokali said. "And yours standing there staring into your hand."

"Focus on your own reflection. Look at it carefully."

"So?"

"If you look hard at yourself you will see what I am seeing. I will ask you again. Is Kaboca the Ruler's only doctor?"

"And I will answer you again: why would I lie to you?"

"Keep looking at the mirror," said the Wizard of the Crow. "What do you see? Do you see something white, like the whiteness of white people? Two white figures?"

No matter how hard he tried, Machokali could not see any face other than his own. Where were the white figures the wizard was talking about?

"No. *This is a charade,*" he said, and looked away.

But the Wizard of the Crow continued to look intensely at his palm as if it were a handheld mirror.

"There, there they are," the wizard said excitedly.

Machokali quickly turned his eyes to the mirror and stared feverishly. He saw nothing.

"There are two wearing stethoscopes. One walks like he comes
from New York. Very confident in the streets. And the other? Where is
he from?" he said, fixing his eyes on Machokali.

Machokali's lips trembled. How did he know about Furyk and
Clarkwell, and that they were from different places? Machokali had
forgotten that last night he had left the Wizard of the Crow in A.G.'s
company. He looked at the wizard and for a few seconds they sized
each other up.

"Oh, those two," Machokali said, not wanting to be caught in
more lies. "It is strange, but really I never thought of them as doctors.
I thought that you would not want to see Professor Din Furyk and
Clement C. Clarkwell. I have heard it said that white science and
black sorcery do not mix, that they are like night and day. Are you sure
that you want to talk to them as well?"

The Wizard of the Crow indicated with a gesture that the two of
them should now sit down for an additional chat.

"Mr. Minister. When I said that I wanted to talk to everyone
who has had some contact with the patient, I meant what I said,"
explained the Wizard of the Crow.

"How do you want me to introduce you?"

"Tell them the truth."

"That you are a sorcerer?"

"That I am a healer. An African healer. That I trap the bad to save
the good."

"Okay. Leave that to me," Machokali said. "Whom would you like
to talk to first?"

"You!"

"What do you want to know?"

"How it all began."

# 10

If Machokali's affairs had begun to take the wrong turn when he failed to secure a state visit for the Ruler, they had worsened after the delegation's arrival in America. He tried to ameliorate the failure by appealing to his American friends to influence the president to receive the Ruler of Aburīria, even for fifteen minutes. But apparently the American president was fully booked.

As for the vice president, the secretary of state, senators, and right down to congressmen, the results were similar. Finally, through much furious lobbying, a prayer breakfast with the president was secured.

The Ruler was very glad to hear that he and the American president were going to have a prayer breakfast, his only regret being that he had forgotten to include a cleric in his delegation to put in a word of prayer for Aburīria. The Ruler chartered a plane to Washington, where he and his entourage were met by the Aburīrian ambassador and his deputy, Yunice Immaculate Mgenzi, who addressed the Ruler as if she were the real ambassador. From there, in a fleet of limos, they headed toward the place of prayer.

Machokali was beginning to feel his spirits rise when, as luck would have it, they arrived at the venue only to confront demonstrators carrying placards and chanting slogans all denouncing the Aburīrian dictator and his plans for Marching to Heaven. Who are these crazy fellows who dared to call themselves Friends of Democracy and Human Rights in Aburīria? Machokali wondered bitterly. He peeked through the window of the limo and recognized one of the demonstrators, perhaps even its mastermind, Materu, former professor of history at the University of Aburīria, who earlier had been released after serving ten of ten and half years of hard labor in the country's maximum-security prison for writing about the independence of Aburīria and failing to mention that the Ruler had been a freedom fighter. And this professor had yet to thank the Ruler for giving him back six whole months of his life. Machokali's anger deepened as he watched the arrogant bearded professor strutting about in a foreign land, betraying his country and Ruler and spoiling the good feelings about the coming breakfast.

He was relieved that the Ruler did not ask him about the demonstration. But bad luck continued to stalk him; as soon as they entered the reception area and the Ruler realized that he was only one among thousands who had paid thousands of dollars a plate, he looked menacingly at Machokali as if to ask, What's all this about? Will I not be able to shake hands with the president and sit next to him?

Machokali had assumed that the Ruler had all along understood that the occasion was to raise money for the American president's charities. It was obvious that a misunderstanding had occurred; the prayer breakfast had turned into a disaster, a further blow to Machokali's prestige in the eyes of the Ruler.

He did not give up; he made strenuous efforts to mollify his wounded pride by trying to get the Ruler on such television shows as *Global Luminaries & Visionaries* and *Meet the Global Mighty*, which were then very popular among foreign politicians because they gave them a chance to make their cases directly to the American people while addressing a global audience. But the producers had shown no interest in the Ruler.

So the only opening was an address before the General Assembly of the United Nations. But a mutually convenient date had proved problematic because the Ruler wanted to address the august body only after he had secured the loan for Marching to Heaven.

Those were troubling days for Machokali; nothing he did seemed to lift the cloud developing between him and the Ruler. Nothing seemed to work in his favor.

And then one day the Ruler invited the entire delegation to a luncheon in his special dining room. They had not eaten together with him for quite a while, and they were all struck by the celebratory atmosphere. There were flowers and champagne on the tables. What's going on? Machokali asked himself; all the other ministers were asking the same question. But when they saw how the Ruler talked to them jovially, they concluded that something good had happened.

This was confirmed when the Ruler turned toward the protocol officer and asked him where he thought the chairman of the Board of

Directors of the Global Bank should sit. But, of course, since he is coming here in his capacity as the Bank's messenger, maybe he should simply stand at the door or else kneel down or even crawl, or what do you think? They all laughed. Since the drama of the women at Eldares, they had not seen the Ruler so fancy-free. Everybody could see that the chair between him and Machokali was empty, confirming that the Ruler had not the slightest doubt that the chairman of the Global Bank was really coming, and there was no way such a dignitary would come in person unless he was bringing good news about the long-awaited loan for Marching to Heaven.

Just then the police guard announced that there was a messenger from the Global Bank at the door. Let him in, the Ruler himself said. When they turned their eyes to the entrance, they saw a man holding an envelope in his hands. Before he uttered a word, they all concluded that whatever else he was, he was not the chief of the Bank. Or maybe it was all a mistake. For though the reception desk and the hotel security had been instructed to let through anybody from the Global Bank, they may have let in the wrong person. But the man did not keep them in doubt for long. He was from the Global Courier Service, Manhattan, and the letter he brought was from the Global Bank. Would somebody sign for it, please?

The Ruler nodded toward Machokali. Machokali handed the letter to the Ruler, who was about to take the envelope when he realized that his hand was trembling in anticipation. To avoid exposing this to everybody, he asked Machokali to open it and read its contents aloud for all at the table to hear. What was important, after all, was the message and not the messenger.

"So you understand that even then the Ruler and all of us were expecting good news," Minister Machokali told the Wizard of the Crow. "But on glancing at the letter, I felt something cold in my belly."

The letter was about ten lines. After reviewing the entire project, the Global Bank did not see any economic benefits to Marching to Heaven. To argue that the project would create jobs, as the Aburīrian government had claimed, was a case of outdated Keynesian economics. Neither old-fashioned nor neo-Keynesianism had any place in the modern global economy. The Global Bank cannot release funds *on the basis of the current representation*. If Aburīria wanted to pursue the matter further, it would have to make a better case. Money was not the problem. But the Global Bank cannot pour money into a project in which the sky was literally the limit. Aburĩria was given seven days to come up with better facts and arguments for the Global Bank to reconsider funding Marching to Heaven.

Everyone in the room was stunned. They did not know where to look—down, up, away, sideways, or what! All they knew was that they did not want to look at the face of the Ruler.

It was worse for Machokali, and even now, as he told the Wizard of the Crow the story of that day, the minister could feel the chill in the room after he had read the letter. His lips trembled. He felt paralyzed. Should he hand the letter over to the Ruler? Should he opine that at least the Global Bank had not closed the door? The sepulchral silence seemed to intensify by the second. The Ruler stretched out his hand as if to see the letter for himself. Machokali handed it to him and quickly sat down.

The Ruler rose to make a speech, completely unaware that the letter in his hand was now shaking. They sat glued to their seats, anticipating his every word. But when the Ruler opened his mouth, no word came out. The Ruler stood there, trying pointlessly to speak. What? The Ruler, lost for words? Terror struck them all: here was the Ruler, his mouth open, attempting to say something but producing only hot air and bronchial wheezing. The true horror was only a few seconds away.

Suddenly his cheeks and stomach began to expand. No, not just the cheeks and the tummy but the whole body. They looked at one another in dismay. They had never seen anything like this. The Ruler gestured with his hands that he wanted pen and paper, but he could not even hold the pen properly, his fingers fattening by the second. The official biographer tried to give him his thick pen, but the Ruler waved him away. Then the Ruler indicated that the gathering was over.

Even now as Machokali narrated the events of that day, his heart was beating wildly, as if the whole scene was unfolding afresh before his very eyes.

"Let me sum up what you just told me," the Wizard of the Crow said. "The Global Bank denies a loan for Marching to Heaven. The Ruler's body begins to swell. He loses the power of speech."

"Something like that, although it was more complex than you are making it seem," Machokali said.

"I am trying to understand. Was the Ruler's food checked for poison?" the Wizard of the Crow asked.

"We entertained similar thoughts," Machokali replied, "but no food had yet been ordered. We left the tables with the champagne unopened. And since then . . . well, you know the rest."

"How long has this been going on?"

"We have lost count of the days. Perhaps weeks, but it is only a guess. Maybe I can ask his biographer, who records all his deeds and sayings."

"That won't be necessary. At least not now. And you say that he has not spoken a word since?"

"Furyk claims he heard him try to say *coral,* or *crawl,* or *cruel.* You had better ask Din Furyk, though I think he was hallucinating. But if in the light of my narrative you have now decided that it is not necessary to see Din Furyk or Clement Clarkwell, I can ask them myself. Or get Dr. Wilfred Kaboca to meet them and try to get the exact words and even tape their answers for you."

"This is what I need from you," the Wizard of the Crow said, ignoring Machokali's hints and offers. "Two things. Get me a big wall mirror that two or three people can look into at the same time without crowding one another. The mirror should be put against the wall facing the bedroom or the seat of the patient."

"There is a mirror on the wall."

"Then ask Din Furyk to come in."

# 11

"Who? A doctor?" asked an astonished Furyk after Machokali had summoned him. Machokali allowed that the man was some kind of specialist or spiritualist; only after many probing questions did he admit that he was talking about a witch doctor.

"What? A sorcerer in New York?" an astounded Furyk asked.

"I looked at Machokali to reassure myself of my sanity," he wrote in his diary, "and I found his big eyes begging me not to reject the summons. So instead of giving a resounding no as I had intended, I found myself telling him not to worry. He is a doctor of the mind and I of the body, so between us we should be a dream team. I was simply trying to calm him down even as I grew curious. I looked forward to meeting the man who seemed to have a hold on this Western-educated high-ranking government minister. As I was about to enter the man's room, I wondered how we would communicate. With hand gestures?

"Imagine my surprise when I encountered a witch doctor who spoke English as if he had been educated at Harvard! I said to him: You speak excellent English. Where did you learn the language so well? He said: At the University of Treetops. I had never heard of that university or seen it cited anywhere. He asked me: What about you? You speak excellent English. Where did you go to school? I was a little irritated by both the question and the tone, for could he not see that I was white? What else did he expect me to speak? Harvard, of course, I said curtly, and I asked him: So in your country they teach sorcery and witchcraft at the university level? He replied: Oh, yes, the art and science of witchcraft are the core of the university system of Treetops. We have both teaching and research departments that specialize in magic. Don't you? Of course not, I said. We have departments of medicine and psychiatry and pharmacology.

"I quickly changed the subject and told him how glad I was to meet him to discuss the strange illness that had befallen their leader, a strange malignity, this self-induced expansion. Rare. Never ever heard of it before.

"Yes, that was it, and I suddenly realized that I had given a name to the oddity. SIE: self-induced expansion.

"He listened attentively to my story without interruptions. But when I talked about pressing the patient's belly only to hear the word *coral, crawl,* or *cruel* issuing from his mouth, the so-called Wizard of the Crow raised his head.

"He asked me: Did he say *coral, crawl, cruel,* or *corwar*? At first I could not tell the difference in the sounds. He repeated the words, pronouncing each slowly and distinctly, until eventually I heard the differences; I had to admit that his own word sounded nearest to that emitted by the Ruler. So I told him, Yes, yes, that's the word. But why should the man be obsessed with the cold war, now a thing of the past?

"He asked again: And this word or sound came out only when you tapped his tummy? Yes, I said. Are you sure? he asked, and I answered yes. He wrote that down in his notebook. What about when the other doctors tapped the Ruler's tummy? I told him that I was the only person who had done so. I asked him: Any other questions? At first he did not answer me; it was as if he had not even heard me. I was about to leave when I heard him call out to me. He came nearer. Up to then he had said or done nothing to suggest that he was a witch doctor. His way of doing things and asking questions was not much different from that of any modern doctor. I saw no signs of voodoo or juju paraphernalia.

"But when he now explained in a low voice what he wanted me to do, I could not tell whether he was playing tricks with me or not. Then I felt like laughing. He wanted me to walk past a mirror on a wall."

# 12

The Wizard of the Crow had never met the Ruler face-to-face, and his image of him—tall, big-bodied but not fat—had been formed from watching television and reading newspapers. The Ruler cared about his appearance, but he was not one of those leaders who wears colubus monkey skins, dashikis, or collarless shirts. He was always in Western-style suits decorated with patches from the skins of the big cats that were exclusively his. Of course there was the famous leopard-skin hat shaped like a crown, the symbol of his exalted office and power. That was more or less what was in the wizard's mind when he entered the sick chamber. He had expected a difference, especially in one now so afflicted, but never this that appeared before his eyes.

He was struck by a stench such as he had often detected in the streets of Eldares, except that now it seemed to be oozing out of the Ruler's body.

The Ruler's eyes were full of fear, and the Wizard of the Crow could not tell whether it was fear of the illness itself or of him, an unknown presence. The first thing, resolved the wizard, was to still any doubts in the patient's mind, because confidence in the healer is paramount in the healing process.

"Listen very carefully," he told the Ruler. "First things first. If you hear what I am saying please nod your head twice."

The Ruler nodded twice.

"Good. If you can hear, you will certainly be able to talk. Don't worry. There is a strange illness in the land. It is a malady of words; thoughts get stuck inside a person. You have seen stutterers, haven't you? Their stammer is a result of a sudden surge of thoughts, or calculations, or worry. Now I ask you: who has more worries than a head of state? Who said that uneasy lies the head that wears the crown? What I want you to do is very simple. Look at the mirror on the wall. The people who have had close contact with you—the ministers, the security men, the doctors—will all pass in front of the mirror. Your task is simply to look at their reflections. Let your mind wander freely, forming its own impressions. But don't worry about putting your thoughts into words. What is important now is for the mind and the heart to think and feel. Let your images, feelings, and thoughts float freely. I will trace the path of your thinking to see where you are obstructed; I want you to help me. I will give voice to your thoughts and feelings. I want to help you break your own silence to yourself. I am only a catalyst conveying your very own thoughts."

The Ruler nodded in agreement.

# 13

Machokali was first to pass by the mirror. The Ruler narrowed his eyes and the skin on his forehead broke into discernible folds as he followed Machokali's move across the room before leaving it. He shook his head from side to side so slightly that had the Wizard of the Crow not been concentrating on the Ruler's image in the mirror he would have missed the motion. In the folds of the skin on the

Ruler's forehead and the light in his squinty eyes, the Wizard of the Crow detected intense anger.

The other ministers took turns before the mirror, but none triggered the look that the Ruler had given the Minister for Foreign Affairs. When it came to the security men and his personal physician, the Ruler averted his eyes as if he would prefer them not to see him in these circumstances.

Din Furyk and Clement Clarkwell were last. Suddenly, the Ruler made efforts to stand up but to no avail, still managing to blurt out: IF!

When Din Furyk heard this he forgot that he was supposed to walk past the mirror and leave without saying a word. He turned to the Wizard of the Crow and shouted, That's the word! That's the word he was saying.* As if responding to Furyk's fury, the Ruler kept on repeating the *if* word, vainly trying to use the wall as support in his attempt to get on his feet. The Wizard of the Crow signaled for Furyk and Clarkwell to leave the room.

The Ruler was panting: trying to stand up while uttering the *if* word had left him exhausted. He rested his eyes on the wizard as if demanding to know: What is it? The Wizard of the Crow answered him, No, you are not lost for words; it is just that the thought of the indignity heaped on you before your ministers and underlings was so overwhelming that initially no words would come out. Now when you saw those two whites walking nonchalantly before the mirror as if they were not aware of your presence or what their kind have done to you, you wanted to give them a piece of your mind, but you got stuck. Stutterers are sometimes unable to get past the first word. Just like you. You got stuck at the word *if. IF I had been white, would they have done what they did to me? Or, IF I had been white would they have treated me the way they just did in the presence of my ministers?*

"That's right," said the Ruler, loud and clear. "That's what I was trying to tell them. Go and tell my ministers that I want them all here to hear for themselves what I was trying to tell those whites."

Now it was the Wizard of the Crow who was at a loss for words. He was so taken aback by the Ruler's quick recovery of voice that he did not know how to respond to the order. He was about to tell him

---

* The sound he had been hearing was *korwo*, which means *if*.

that his diagnosis had barely begun when the Ruler repeated his command.

"Be quick. Get them here without delay," he said, as if talking not to a healer but a messenger.

The Wizard of the Crow left the room and passed the message on to Machokali, who hastened to gather the others. As the Wizard of the Crow returned to his room he ran into Furyk and Clarkwell. They wanted to know what had happened. Had he met with success?

"I managed only to release his tongue, nothing more. At least he is now talking," replied the Wizard of the Crow, looking directly into the eyes of Din Furyk. "He's still monstrously obese, though his rate of increase is slightly less than it was."

Furyk's reaction was entirely unexpected.

"You are a fraud," he said, wagging a finger at the Wizard of the Crow. "You are claiming success based on my work. I discovered the illness and even gave it a name. I challenge you in the name of science to a race for the cure for self-induced expansion. But I warn you. The patient is mine and I will patent the patient, the name of the illness, and any cure."

# 14

"I don't know what drove me to challenge him that way," Furyk wrote in his diary, "but I suppose I did not want him to think that his methods, whatever they were, could outdo science. Admittedly, in its way, what he did was quite *extraordinary*. In a matter of hours he had untied a knot that tested our skills to the limit. Had I not been present to see and hear for myself, I would never have believed it. Still, I was convinced that whatever he had done to avert the hypertrophy of the body and make the Ruler talk was somehow a development of the work that Clarkwell and I had already done. It would have been good to have conferred with him privately to find out the details of his treatment, but he, like those gifted in the arts of conjuring, was not as voluble off the stage as we would have hoped. But he had yet to find a definitive cure for SIE, and I resolved to do whatever I could to solve its mystery before he did.

"The first priority was to register the patent on the patient himself, and on our discovery of the unique phenomena to which we had given the name of self-induced expansion (SIE). That way anything the sorcerer might come up with, if anything, would fall within the intellectual property rights of our new company, which we named Clem & Din. Although we encountered a hitch in patenting the patient, or even his body, because the name Ruler was too general and it would have meant that we had patent rights on all the bodies of all the rulers of the globe, we were satisfied with rights to the discovery of SIE.

"I would now use all the latest gains in the human genome, cloning, and stem cell research to come up with a cure. Science versus sorcery. The battle between me and the Wizard of the Crow was shaping up as one between darkness and light; I felt connected to a long line of Christian soldiers all the way back to the Holy Crusades."

# 15

The Wizard of the Crow did not immediately respond to the challenge. What he now wanted was a little rest and to give the Ruler time to confer with his ministers before resuming what he knew was going to be a difficult case. He really needed the sleep. Coming from isolation in the prison cell in Eldares to an audience with the Ruler in a New York hotel had been a jolt, and his mind and body needed to adjust. A nap would release whatever tension he carried within, and this would enable him to cope with additional pressure.

He lay on his back and while staring at the ceiling felt weightless, ready to succumb to sleep. But questions persisted. This affliction that had visited the body of the Ruler had defied his divining skills. How was he to prescribe a cure without first divining the cause of the malady? He felt as if the illness was mocking him, which reminded him of Furyk's challenge. What nerve this Furyk has to think that he can know everything about an African after only the most minimal of contact? I will take up the challenge, he heard himself saying, addressing both the illness and Din Furyk. Where do I begin the race?

And then, to his amazement, he heard a voice. Nyawīra's? The voice became more distinct: Go back in time. Arise and go to all the crossroads, all the marketplaces and temple sites, all the dwelling places of black people the world over, and find out the sources of their power. There you will find the cure for SIE.

He wanted to obey, but he could hardly move his legs or any other part of the body. The spirit is willing, all right, he sighed in resignation, but the body is in the way. The voice would not let him go, and it was now singing to him.

> *Wake up, brother spirit*
> *Wake up, sister spirit*
> *If you let sleep rule over you*
> *Blessings will pass you by*

The song sounded more like a lullaby than an appeal, and he would have sunk to slumber except that this time the voice had a Nyawīra shape, and she stretched out her hands to him from above. He felt his whole self lighten and he saw himself rise, rise and float, reaching beyond the grasp for Nyawīra. He had left his body behind, and now a bird, he was flying freely in the open sky . . .

He woke up in flight, laughing, recalling his travels from the pyramids of Egypt to the plains of the Serengeti and Great Zimbabwe; Benin to Bahia and on through the Caribbean to the skyscrapers of New York, alighting everywhere to glean wisdom. The form in which he had traveled had been so real that he automatically touched his mouth: to his relief, his lips were not a beak, and his arms not feathery wings, and the clothes on him were the same as he had on when he first lay on the bed to rest.

How long have I slept? he wondered. Just then a familiar smell hit his nostrils, the stench wafting from the sick chamber, prompting him to return to the task that had brought him to America. He would go back to the sick chamber to see if the Ruler had voided all the words from within. He would see him alone and ask him a few questions. He felt rested; the sooner he found a cure or a safe way of extricating himself from the whole mess, the sooner he would return to Aburĩria and to Nyawĩra.

He met three men, white, brown, and black, with identical briefcases, coming out of the sick chamber. The white was cursing: *Oh, damn, we are already late!* Late? The Wizard of the Crow asked himself. Had the Ruler of Aburĩria died?

# 16

It is said that when his ministers and the entire entourage entered the Ruler's sick chamber, he did not greet them with the usual preliminaries: how are you, where have you been, thanks for coming, or thank God I am now feeling better. He simply started talking as if resuming the interrupted luncheon. Even the letter delivered by the messenger of the Global Courier Services, Manhattan, was in his hands, exactly the way he held it the day Machokali handed it to him, and he kept on waving it as a prop, evidence and talisman.

"Yes, if my skin was white, would the directors of the Global Bank have insulted me as they have in this letter?" he asked the ministers, who roared back a resounding NOOO!

To say that the ministers were astounded is to understate their various expressions of relief and disbelief. The Ruler was panting as if he had not gotten used to the burden of speech, though his body showed not the slightest sign of deflating. But at least it no longer seemed on the verge of bursting. So his words, whatever their sense, were most welcome to their ears.

"I have thought a great deal about the letter, and I have decided that we have to take up the challenge and come up with arguments that can and will make the governors of the Global Bank change their minds."

Even though they had many unanswered questions, they all gave him a thunderous ovation. This time, he told them, he would not write a paper; he would press the case in person, through oral arguments. He asked Machokali to draft a quick note inviting the governors of the Global Bank to a meeting in the hotel the following day, to hear additional facts and arguments in support of the funding for Marching to Heaven. Give the note to the same messenger who was here a few minutes ago, the Ruler told him, confusing the Wizard of the Crow with the messenger from the Global Courier Services.

Machokali went out and came back in the room to report that though he found the messenger already gone, he had personally faxed the note and followed it up with a telephone conversation, and he was now proud to announce that the wishes of the Ruler had borne fruit, that though the directors regretted that they would not be able to make it the next day or the following, they had assured Machokali that representatives would be sent within seven days for a hearing. Machokali waved the faxed confirmation in celebration of the concession won from the bankers.

The Ruler signaled satisfaction. Now before his ministers, he planned to rehearse his oral arguments, to their great delight and unabashed admiration. They clapped in appreciation for the privilege of a preview.

"Listen carefully, for I may use the same speech in my address to the United Nations General Assembly. Assume that you are now the directors of the Global Bank," he told the ministers, "and even the United Nations General Assembly . . ."

The man's unfathomable and indefatigable mind always intrigued them; they were now willing captives to what promised to be an incredible performance.

# 17

Rumor has it that the Ruler talked nonstop for seven nights and days, seven hours, seven minutes, and seven seconds. By then the ministers had clapped so hard, they felt numb and drowsy. Some did not realize that they themselves had become hoarse and were now producing barely audible whispers of *more, give us more, couldn't agree with the Mighty One more*. Some could barely complete a sentence, then a word, then a syllable.

When they became too tired to stand, they started kneeling down before the Ruler, until the whole scene looked like an assembly in prayer before the eyes of the Lord. But soon they found that even holding their bodies erect while on their knees was equally tiring, and some assumed the cross-legged posture of a Buddhist. Others opted for the crouching posture of a Muslim at prayer, touching the floor with their foreheads and taking their time to lift their heads. A few, unable to lift their heads, pretended to be in continuous obeisance, with heads and hands on the floor and their buttocks in the air. In the end, each person tried any posture that gave his legs, neck, arms, and even lips some rest. The biographer lay flat on the floor, trying to write down everything the Ruler said; eventually he rested his head on one side of the book and somehow managed to continue scrawling notes for the book of life. By the seventh hour of the seventh day, the security men, who used a wall to prop themselves up, were some of the very few who remained on their feet. Among civilians, Machokali held out longest, but he, too, felt his knees about to buckle. Ever careful not to offend, he tried to approach the Ruler for permission to sit down, but found himself kneeling, groggily, moaning, yes my lord, amen, anything, as if engaged in a call-and-response ritual with the Ruler.

# 18

That, it is said, was the scene that confronted three messengers— white, brown, and black—from the Global Bank when they arrived at the chamber at one o'clock on the seventh day. They did not show undue surprise, not when they saw the hideousness that was now the Ruler seated on the carpet, leaning against the wall, the ministers in the various praying postures, and, no, not even when they looked at the men and saw the agony of their haggard faces, because the visitors took this to be a native religious ritual.

They were Bank diplomats who had been trained to understand that money knew no religion, race, skin color, or gender; that money was the root of all money, the only constant law of the new global order. Still, they had been trained to be sensitive to the diversity of cultures, and so their only fear was intrusion, lest they hurt any nerves by intruding into a live religious rite. One of the diplomats looked around to see if there was anyone to whom he could offer apologies.

Fortunately for the visitors, they had entered the chamber at precisely the moment the Ruler had paused, as if the words stuck within him for weeks had all been used up and he was awaiting a fresh infusion. He saw them, and without making any effort to stand up he shouted, *Welcome, welcome*. On hearing the word *welcome*, the ministers forced themselves out of their different postures and dragged their bodies to get chairs for the visitors and for themselves, inwardly grateful to the Bank officials for interrupting seven days of fatigue, thirst, hunger, and lack of sleep.

The Ruler wasted no time; he asked his Minister of Finance and the Guardian of the National Treasury to summarize their deliberations on the role of Marching to Heaven in the economies of Aburīria, Africa, and the world at large, addressing all questions raised in the rejection letter from the Global Bank. But before the Minister of Finance could clear his tired throat and offer his précis, the Ruler had taken over and was riding high on a new wave of words.

The Bank diplomats grew restless and kept looking at their watches, but, as they still felt guilty for having interfered in a religious rite, out of politeness they waited for an opportune moment to say a word. After one hour, the messengers from the Bank looked at one another and at the ministers to see if there was anyone who could tell the Ruler to give them a chance to say what had actually brought them there. But no minister seemed ready to assume the responsibility.

The most senior of the three Bank officials now took it upon himself to get down to business. Excuse me, sir, he said, to no avail. He made a few more attempts, trying with difficulty to keep his voice level and his tone polite, but in the end he was forced to raise his voice considerably: Mr. President, sir! Mr. President, we bear an urgent message for you and are pressed for time because of other engagements.

The phrase *urgent message* did the trick, and the Ruler switched off. He beheld the briefcases in the hands of the three officials. These must contain the contract between the Global Bank and Aburĩria. The sight of the briefcases also stirred life in the ministers. Hope was alive. The persuasive arguments of the Ruler must have moved these officials. So they all clapped in what looked like slow motion, and there was no way of telling if they were clapping out of relief that the flow of words had stopped or in anticipation of the good news in those briefcases.

"We have been sent to you because you had intimated that there was new information you wanted the Bank to take into consideration. But before we come to that, we have in our hands two reports concerning the present state of your country, and the Bank has a few questions regarding them.

"The first concerns your women. We have heard that Aburĩrian women have started beating up men. In our view, this is taking women's liberation too literally and too far. Female violence to counter male violence is not the answer to domestic violence, and it poses a serious threat to family values, which, as we know them today, are the very foundation of a stable social environment.

"The second concerns this business of queuing. You told us, I believe, that you had put a stop to mass queuing. But we hear that there are people on motorcycles going around saying that you want the queues to resume, and that in some areas people are taking this call seriously. What, Mr. President, do you have to say on these two points?"

"What are you talking about?" the Ruler asked, puzzled, having forgotten all about the motorcycle riders, in fact slightly annoyed that they seemed to be more informed about his country than he was. "I am sure that the queuing nonsense is the work of a terrorist dissident movement. But what I don't understand is your claim that men, true men, are allowing themselves to be beaten by women. Do these women want to become husbands, turning men into wives?" he said, trying to make light of the matter.

"*That's the point, Mr. President. Everything is upside down in your country.* Your women are challenging the natural order of things, even setting up what they call people's courts; and the queues challenge the social order. We don't need to remind you of the obvious: if the masses take the law into their own hands, you will have nothing but chaos on yours. Extreme democracy. Direct democracy. The Greeks of old, in the city-state of Athens, I believe, tried it, and what happened? It brought down Greek civilization. Mr. President, go back to Aburīria. Put your house in order. Then send us a memorandum addressing anything new you wish us to consider. The Bank will review it thoroughly . . . *but please excuse us. We have another appointment,*" the Bank official said, glancing at his watch and, followed by the other two, also clutching their shiny briefcases, he went out, muttering under his breath, "*Oh, damn, we are already late . . .*"

The Ruler was aghast that the Bank's officials would walk out without having heard his economic theories and philosophy and especially his architectural vision for Marching to Heaven.

His jaw fell. His neck became limp and he inclined his head to one side against the wall. His was a silent scream.

"Oh, no, not again," Machokali said under his breath; déjà vu all over again. He remembered the Wizard of the Crow. He anxiously looked for him all around the chamber but did not spot him among those present. He went to the door, where A.G. was standing.

"The malady of words has struck a second time," he whispered. "Where is the Wizard of the Crow?"

# 19

These must be the representatives from the Global Bank, the Wizard of the Crow thought as he was about to enter the Ruler's infirmary. They must have just finished listening to fresh arguments for the loan from the Ruler. But had Machokali not said that they would be here in seven days? Had he been sleeping all that time? I must have been very tired. He turned around and looked hard at the men walking away. There was something familiar about them, yet he could have sworn that he had never met them before. What was it in their looks, their dress, their gait, that made him feel so? And now he could not believe what dawned on him. Their general deportment was exactly like that of some of the people he had encountered in his flight as a bird: was he still dreaming?

He had heard and even read stories of people who walked in their sleep, who could even go to market and buy goods while still asleep, return home, and go back to bed; when they awoke they would wonder how the goods had appeared in their rooms. He had read about the case of a man who had killed his wife and in court claimed that he had sleepwalked through all of it. Was he, the Wizard of the Crow, sleepwalking?

He decided to find out. Instead of entering the Ruler's room, he went back to his and grabbed his briefcase; in it were pen, paper, all his wordly possessions. He took a lift to the ground floor.

He looked from side to side to spot the three men from the Global Bank. He noticed two beggars, a man and woman, their hands outstretched toward every passerby: I am a veteran, the man said. I am hungry. Have you some change to spare? Where could the threesome have disappeared so quickly? He should not have gone for his briefcase.

Now he saw the three enter a cream-colored limousine. He tried to stop yellow cabs but the drivers sped away from him, one stopping to pick up a white couple farther down the road. Fortunately, a black cab driver came to his rescue. Follow that limousine, the Wizard of the Crow told him.

# 20

"True! *Haki ya Mungu,*" A.G. would say later whenever a listener expressed doubts and tried to dismiss the tale as balderdash. "I am a teller of tales and not a monger of rumors," A.G. would add, and then, as evidence, he would remind his listeners that he himself had been there. "I was tired, very tired, but Machokali's question startled me back to life. Where indeed was the Wizard of the Crow? When had I last seen him?

"I now remembered that during those days when all of us were captives of our Ruler's theories of a world governed by the economy of happiness and sorrow, I never once saw the Wizard of the Crow. It says something of the mesmerizing power of the voice of the Ruler that I never even thought about the Wizard of the Crow. Like everybody else, I had forgotten that it was he who had set free the mouth of the Ruler.

"I left the sick chamber and went to look for him in his room. He was not there. I went down to the reception desk. They had not seen the person I described. I went back to his room. There was nothing that spoke of his presence. Where had he gone? What had happened to him? I went back to Machokali.

"Everything was as I had left it. The Ruler's mouth still open as if frozen in the act of speaking. The ministers, their faces haggard with fatigue and lack of sleep, heads drooping to one side, were still in their seats, looking for all the world like corpses. Machokali was the only one among them who answered to his name, Ferocious Eyes: he seemed alert to what was taking place, although with him it was not always easy to tell, because his huge eyes were always the same size and never closed, even when he slept. We, the police, were trained to endure hardship, and I was not surprised that most of us were awake and mindful of our calling, guardians of the Ruler and our nation.

"Machokali gestured to me with a slight wave of the hand, and I understood that he wanted us to meet outside. I told him that the Wizard of the Crow had disappeared without a trace. He kept quiet, very quiet, staring ahead, slowly pulling his hair above the right ear, as if his mind had wandered, leaving his body behind. Questions crossed my mind: Had the Ruler succumbed to a heart attack, accounting for Machokali's state? Where was the Wizard of the Crow, who could raise the dead?"

# 21

The Wizard of the Crow settled in the backseat, relieved that the smell from the sick chamber had not followed him into the cab. This was also a good opportunity for him to see the real New York, for since his arrival he had not had the time to stroll outside the hotel.

He thought about the Fifth Avenue VIP Hotel, and soon he was engrossed in comparing the little he had seen of it with others he had seen in Aburīria, and this took his mind away from meditations on reality and illusion.

At a traffic light, the driver noticed that the limousine had stopped a block or so away. Your people have stopped, the driver said, waking him from his introspection. The three men got out and ran across the street as their limo sped away. He asked the taxi driver to pull over, paid him, and then got out of the cab quickly. The men entered an imposing skyscraper. He crossed Global Avenue as if he, too, was bound for the same address. He was mesmerized by the power encased in all that glass and concrete. All the laws and regulations governing the economic and monetary policies of the nations of the earth issued from this building: whatever the tune the Bank sang, the leaders of the earth danced to it; whenever it sneezed, the whole world complained of migraines. What should he do? Enter and confront the three men? Pretend that he was coming for their literature on their role in the development of the new global community? As he approached, still undecided, he passed a side street marked DEAD END.

He was a little dizzy, unable to believe his eyes. This was a scene he had seen while in his bird form. Was this sign an omen? He pondered its possible implications, smiled to himself, and decided to return to the hotel. He was now more focused on the Ruler's condition than he had ever been.

At the Fifth Avenue hotel, the Wizard of the Crow walked past reception toward an elevator. No matter how hard he pressed the buttons, the elevator would not ascend beyond the third floor. It was the receptionist who cleared the matter. The floors above were private and could be accessed only with a special pass, which he did not have.

The receptionist asked for his last name to look him up in her register. He was about to babble Kamītī wa Karīmīri when he remembered that his passport had a different name, Abdi Mganga, for Sikiokuu's security reasons, and he had no recollection of having been checked in. The receptionist offered to call the suite, but nobody picked up the phone. There was nothing she could now do for him, she told him, but he was welcome to wait in the reception area; perhaps someone in his party might call or wander down.

He sat; he waited. Why were matters becoming so complicated?

# 22

The Wizard of the Crow hung around reception, not knowing what to do with himself. He bought a newspaper but he could not follow the stories. He scrutinized everyone, hoping to catch a glimpse of one of the delegates. A visibly pregnant woman exited a cab and entered the hotel; his eyes followed her until she disappeared. Out of nowhere, he started thinking of Nyawĩra as an expectant mother. He had always longed for a family founded on love and respect among husband, wife, and children.

His need to see Nyawĩra was by now bottomless; he had been away far too long. He recalled that even Machokali had told him that he was needed only for a day and would be returned home the very first day after he had administered his cure. Maybe the Ruler had recovered, become well; maybe he was still talking. Whatever the case, it was clear that his services were no longer needed. He had to go back to Aburĩria. Luckily he still had his passport and plane ticket.

But he did not want to leave just like that, without telling anybody. So he walked to the reception desk and asked for a piece of paper. He would leave a note for Machokali. But as he bent down to write, a succession of images blurred his vision. First, a bloated Mighty Excellency. The image transformed itself into that of the pregnant woman, and then into the three men from the Global Bank. Now he saw Furyk and the delegates proceeding before the big mirror in the sick chamber. Again the Wizard of the Crow recalled how the Ruler had glared at Machokali, a glare vivid for its ferocity. His body tingled with anxiety, and he felt immense pity for Machokali. The Wizard of the Crow was quite clear as to what that look and the Ruler's shake of his head from side to side signified; but he also knew that nobody, not even Machokali, would believe him were he to put it down on paper. Still, as he bore no person any ill will, he felt it his duty to warn Machokali, without being explicit, of the danger that faced the minister.

He wrote: *I have no pass. Take care of yourself. The country is pregnant. What it will give birth to, nobody knows.*

He looked over the note, folded it, addressed it to Machokali, and handed it to the receptionist.

Then he hailed a yellow cab and headed for the airport to catch a flight, any flight, to Aburĩria, anticipating a reunion with Nyawĩra.

# 23

At that very moment, Machokali was still in his room, depressed, weighed down by fatigue, defeat, and indecision. What was he to do about the Ruler's relapse? The Wizard of the Crow had mysteriously disappeared without a trace. How dare he defy authority?

The word *authority* led him to recall what the Bank officials had said: there are people going about the country calling for a resumption of queuing. He recalled that just before the women did the shameful deed at Eldares, the Ruler and the cabinet had authorized the five riders. They never called them off. What was going on?

The phone rang and he picked it up. *Just trying my luck. For seven days nobody has been picking up the phone,* said the receptionist. Machokali was about to tell her to mind her own business but changed his mind. Even anger feeds on energy, and his was now in short supply. Minister Sikiokuu was calling from Aburĩria! There were no preliminaries. Sikiokuu simply wanted to know if the Wizard of the Crow had arrived in America. Machokali told him yes, he had arrived, but just now they did not know his whereabouts. I just wanted to confirm, Sikiokuu said quickly, and put down the receiver without explaining his own need to check on the wizard.

Why this belated concern with the arrival of the Wizard of the Crow? Why now, when the man had disappeared? The telephone conversation removed any doubts Machokali may have had about the connection between Sikiokuu and the mysterious disappearance of the Wizard of the Crow. He noted that Sikiokuu did not ask about anything else—the status of the loan, the day of their return, or even the Ruler's condition. No, there was something dangerous afoot, and he was not about to keep his suspicions to himself.

He left his room, not noticing that A.G. stood outside the door. He went back to the sick chamber and found the others as he had left them: in various and desperate positions of prostrations, completely exhausted by the torrential seven days' verbiage. Machokali dragged himself to where the Ruler sat, his mouth wide open and his head slumped to one side, a lifeless deity. Machokali felt it his duty to tell the Ruler his suspicions about what was happening in Aburīria, whether he understood or not. He put his mouth close to the left ear of the Ruler and whispered. Many governments in Africa, Asia, and South America had been overthrown while the Ruler was out of the country. The renewed call for queues was a plot for a coup d'état in the making.

The words had an immediate effect on the Ruler: he straightened up. And what are you all doing lying about on the ground instead of packing? We have to go, he said, turning to Machokali as if assigning him the responsibility for ensuring that everybody and everything was ready for their departure to Aburīria to counter threats posed by the queuing and husband bashing.

# 24

"It was sad, very sad, because it looked as if they had all forgotten about the Wizard of the Crow," A.G. was later to say in his narration of the visit. "But not me—oh, no, not me. True! *Haki ya Mungu.* I tried every which way I could to see the Ruler to tell him about the mysterious disappearance of the Wizard of the Crow, but it was difficult to get a private audience with him because most of the time he was surrounded by sycophants, each wanting to show that he alone knew how to take care of the needs of the Ruler.

"Once I did manage to steal a moment with him alone, but when I broached the subject of the Wizard of the Crow I saw that the Ruler did not seem to know what I was talking about. He took it that I was talking about witchcraft, bewitchment, and news from home. He told me, There you have spoken some truth, because those fellows who are queuing and the women who are beating men must be under the influence of cunning wizards. But these queuers and man beaters don't know who they are dealing with; I will teach them a lesson they will never forget. He tried to scratch his stomach as if to remove an itch, but his hand could not reach it. Then he turned to me and told me to forget witchcraft for the time being, to go and do like everybody else: get ready to leave America. Wonders as yet unseen awaited, he said, twisting his lips into an enigmatic smile; to me it was as if he was holding something back, trying, with difficulty, to prevent himself from laughing in triumph at what he contemplated. It was a smile of suppressed anger, and, to be honest, I could not tell what had made him angrier: his bodily self-inflation, the Global Bank, the reported return of the queuing mania, or this business of women beating up men. True! *Haki ya Mungu!* I did not like that twisted smile one bit. And what were these wonders as yet unseen that he claimed awaited us? But I was soon caught up in the complexities of our imminent departure."

# 25

How would they move the Ruler from his hotel room? How would they get him through the doors? And what about getting him to the airport? Piles of money from the Aburīrian treasury, paid to a company, the hotel, and the airline, facilitated solutions and confidentiality about the operation they code-named Hotexit.

A relieved Machokali stopped at the reception desk to make sure that everything was fine. The receptionist handed him a neatly folded piece of paper. "This has been lying in your box for more than seven days," the receptionist told him. Machokali was about to ask him how he knew this, but then he decided against it. He was feeling good at the success of Hotexit, and why should he let the chatter of a nosy receptionist get under his skin? This is old news, he told himself, and he was about to throw the piece of paper into a garbage can without opening it when he changed his mind and put it inside the inner pocket of his jacket as he rushed to the waiting limo and on to the airport.

Arrangements were made for two planes: a jumbo jet with seats reconfigured for the Ruler, his security team, personal physician, biographer, and one or two ministers, and a smaller one for the rest of the delegation.

"The loading of the Ruler onto the plane indeed proved to be a wonder yet unseen. The pushing and squeezing, the huffing and puffing! True! *Haki ya Mungu!*" A.G. was later to say. "When I saw how we were struggling and worrying ourselves to death, I asked myself, If the Wizard of the Crow were here, would we find ourselves in this mess? I am sure he would have found an easier way of getting the body onto the plane. To be honest, I had not given up hope. So during the ordeal I kept looking back behind me in the expectation that I would see him running across the tarmac to help us.

"Just before we boarded the plane, I tried to talk to Machokali about the unknown fate of the Wizard of the Crow. I showed him a newspaper I had bought, in which every other story seemed to involve the arrest or the shooting or the imprisonment of a black male. And hostility to immigrants was not unknown. Didn't he think we should consult with American authorities about the wizard? Machokali was unmoved. Let him rot in an American jail, Machokali grunted back, and added that he would have nothing more to do with sorcerers and their disappearing acts. But for my part, I never stopped worrying and thinking about him. True! *Haki ya Mungu!*"

# 26

Machokali felt tight as he got into the same plane with the Ruler, Dr. Wilfred Kaboca, Dr. Luminous Karamu-Mbu, and A.G. and the security men, and it was only when they were aloft that he regained his composure. He took off his jacket, folded it twice, and placed it on the empty seat beside him. Now he would have the time to ponder things in their proper perspective. In all his years as Minister for Foreign Affairs, he had never been on a mission plagued with so many twists and turns, and he did not know what had complicated matters more: the Ruler's special condition or the Global Bank's dragging its foot.

The Ruler's illness had made it impossible for him to take initiatives to enhance his and the Ruler's advantages, including the United Nations General Assembly address. But that was just as well, he now thought, as Marching to Heaven was on hold until the money from the Global Bank was forthcoming. Machokali saw a ray of hope in the fact that the door to further negotiations had not been slammed shut. The return to Aburīria would buy time to enliven the scheme without his having to worry constantly that the Ruler might explode into bits in a foreign land.

During the Ruler's marathon talk to his ministers at the hotel, Machokali had been able to discern, in the thicket of the verbiage, further arguments for Marching to Heaven. Upon his return to Eldares, he would convene a group of leading economic experts from the business world and academia to embellish the Ruler's case, the better to impress the Global Bank. He might even hire additional experts from America and Europe to bolster the Aburīrian team. As he dwelled on the matter, he reached for a handkerchief in his jacket pocket and felt the folded piece of paper handed to him at the reception desk. He was feeling good inside and he did not want to bother with this triviality, so he crushed it in his palm. He was about to throw it away but thought: Who was this who had left a handwritten message for me? Could it be Mgenzi? Yunice Immaculate Mgenzi, the Deputy Ambassador of Aburīria in Washington?

Machokali never ceased to marvel at the Ruler's way with women, especially this woman, who stopped being an ardent follower of Mao Tse-Tung to become a faithful lapdog of the Ruler!

When they first arrived in America, Yunice Mgenzi had a few private sessions with the Ruler in his chamber, some lasting a whole night. But since the onset of the Ruler's malady, the two had not seen each other. Machokali and the other ministers had decided that it was not a good idea to allow any woman to see the Ruler in his present condition. Yunice Immaculate Mgenzi had kept on phoning and asking to speak to the Ruler, compelling Machokali to concoct all sorts of stories about how the Ruler was totally immersed in delicate matters of international diplomacy. In the end he told her that the Ruler had said that he himself would call her back, and even then she threatened to come in person. What if the Ruler and Mgenzi later found out that he had not passed on her note to the Ruler?

Machokali quickly unfolded it: information was power.

The four lines did not make sense. He turned the note over to see if there was more. Nothing, so he read it again. *I have no pass. Take care of yourself. The country is pregnant. What it will give birth to, nobody knows.* It was initialed WOC. The Wizard of the Crow, of course. *No pass!* So he had gone out and found himself unable to get back to the Ruler's suite! Machokali admitted to himself that he, the minister, was to blame for the wizard's disappearance. As he scrutinized the wizard's enigmatic note, he wondered whether it was addressed to him personally or to him in his capacity as a senior cabinet minister who was to bring it to the attention of the Ruler. He wished that the other ministers were on his plane, for he would have sought their views. What if he suppressed the contents of the note only to have the Wizard of the Crow suddenly reappear to claim that he had left him a formula for the cure? This might even be a trap laid by his political enemy, Sikiokuu, using the sorcerer to carry out his evil designs. He had to cleverly unburden himself to the Ruler. He would gauge his mood and might even broach the subject of the return of the queuing mania, and again voice his fears about the possibilities of a coup. The Ruler would thereby be forced to focus not on the disastrous visit to America but on Sikiokuu's treachery.

He went to the section reserved for the Ruler. The engineers had been unable to devise a chair or a bed large enough to contain him, so the floor was all he had.

"And what do you propose to do about your Marching to Heaven?" the Ruler asked, without giving Machokali a chance to say what had brought him before his august presence.

"The Global Bank did not slam the door completely," Machokali responded. "What we need is a moment to arrange everything you told us into a manageable memorandum. I was thinking that as soon as we get back to Aburĩria, and with your blessings and guidance, I shall put together a task force from the business community, the University of Eldares, and a few universities abroad, with the sole duty of putting your views and vision into written form. Then we shall send the memorandum to the Global Bank. *Memorandum Addendum.*"

"Memorandum Addendum," the Ruler repeated, clearly pleased with the way the phrase rolled off his tongue. Machokali felt as if he had been congratulated.

"*The last word,* we shall tell them," Machokali said in a triumphant voice.

*"Our last stand,"* added the Ruler. "Do it as soon as we get home."

"Your word is law unto me," Machokali said humbly.

"Say, Do or Die!" added the Ruler.

"Do or Die!" Machokali chimed in. "That's your real name."

"But these directors of the Global Bank are acting as if they have never heard of that name," said the Ruler.

Machokali now saw an opening to bring up the wizard's note. With a casual "by the way," he asked the Ruler if he still remembered the man who helped unlock his voice. But neither by word nor by look did the Ruler show any sign of remembrance of what Machokali was talking about, a time when words got stuck in his throat, let alone any awareness of anybody having treated him. It was as if his entire ordeal of speechlessness had never occurred. Machokali had to ask again, and this time he made sure he mentioned the name Wizard of the Crow.

"A sorcerer?" the Ruler interrupted him. "Why do you people keep on pestering me with questions of sorcerers, even in America? The other day a policeman came to talk to me about sorcery. And now you. Is it because you think that sorcery is responsible for the queuing and husband beating back home? Not to worry. Just wait and see! We are going to take care of business."

Afterward, when things around him had begun to crumble, Machokali would ask himself time and again why he had not obeyed his inner voice telling him to leave the matter of that note alone and go back to his seat once he saw that the Ruler did not remember a thing about the Wizard of the Crow. But too much fear fuels misery, and the thought that his political enemies might be plotting against him made him ignore his better instincts as he handed the note to the Ruler. The Ruler read the four lines and turned the page over, as Machokali had done. Finally he raised his eyes.

"Who wrote this?" the Ruler asked in a cold and even tone.

"The Wizard of the Crow," Machokali said.

The Ruler leaned back and closed his eyes as if trying to recall a dream forgotten or a distant memory.

"I don't know if I am dreaming or not, but when I close my eyes I seem to see or hear a person answering to that name. It is as if he and I are talking, or, rather, he is talking to me. But no. How is that possible?"

"Your Mighty Excellency, you are not dreaming," Machokali hastened to say, hoping to channel the Ruler's suppressed anger toward the Wizard of the Crow. "There was indeed somebody like the one you now think you saw."

Machokali reminded the Ruler how his words had gotten stuck in his larynx, and how even Professor Din Furyk and Dr. Clement C. Clarkwell had failed to come up with a satisfactory cure, and how the Wizard of the Crow had managed to restore the power of speech to him.

"He was sent to us to deal with this, eh, this, I mean, this problem of your expansion, but now . . ."

"Where is he?" the Ruler interrupted.

"I don't know. Maybe he returned to those who sent him," said Machokali, trying to distance himself from the Wizard of the Crow.

"Who sent him?" the Ruler asked, his eyes still closed.

"Sikiokuu."

"Sikiokuu? Did he not have his hands full with my assignments in Aburĩria? How did he know to send me a sorcerer? How did he know of my malady?"

Machokali hesitated. The Ruler opened his eyes and fixed them on Machokali.

"Why do I have a vague recollection of you yourself asking me about the Wizard of the Crow? Asking me if he could come to America?"

"It was not really my idea. Anything to do with sorcery and divination, I try to keep a . . ."

"Whose idea was it?" the Ruler snapped.

"A.G. Arigaigai Gathere."

"Gathere who?"

"The one who once wrestled with djinns until the break of day."

"I thought he only pursued the djinns, not wrestled with them?"

"Yes, he pursued them across the prairie. There is something odd and strange about that policeman."

"And since when did you appoint A.G. your assistant minister?"

"Your Mighty Excellency, you know very well that I would not and could not even dare to dream of taking it upon myself to . . . !"

"Is that why he came to tell me about the sorcerer of the crow when all the others were busy packing their things?"

"Your Excellency, I did not even know that A.G. had come to see you. What did I tell you? That policeman . . ." Machokali was hoping that the subject of A.G. and his strange ways would supersede the note, but his hope was quickly dashed.

"Read this note very carefully," the Ruler told him, handing him back the piece of paper.

Was the Ruler being sarcastic, Machokali wondered, or was he merely luring him into the range of the club? He could not very well say no and walk away. Machokali took two steps forward, reached for the note, and instinctively stepped back, acting as if he were looking for better lighting to read.

No matter how hard he looked at it, how often he turned it over, Machokali did not see anything beyond what he knew to be there. When Machokali lifted his eyes, he was startled to see in the eyes of the Ruler a light so intense that for a moment Machokali feared the worst.

"Your Mighty Excellency, I must confess that before coming to see you I had already read these words to see if they implied any hidden messages. But I failed to see what the Wizard of the Crow was trying to say, and that is why I brought you the note."

"Read it again and tell me what you think is *not* so very clear about the meaning of those words."

Machokali pretended to reread it silently, but in truth by now he knew each and every word by heart.

"I did not ask you to read it silently to yourself," the Ruler said. "Read it aloud and firmly like a man. Substitute the word *Ruler* for *the country*, as I am the Country."

Machokali cleared his throat. He started reading the note. "*I have no pass. Take care of yourself. The Ruler is . . .*" Machokali stopped abruptly, like a person who finds himself on the edge of a precipice.

"Go on. Read it," the Ruler told him impatiently. "Finish and tell me what's so unclear about the meaning."

"*The Ruler is pregnant. What he will give birth to, nobody knows.*"

"What's not clear? Tell me!" His Mighty Excellency said with mounting anger.

"Oh, no," Machokali said when the full meaning and implications of the words struck him. "I swear that if ever . . . that man . . ."

"Machokali," the Ruler again interrupted him, as if he did not much care to hear what Machokali was swearing to. Machokali was now unnerved by what he detected as a slight change in the voice of the Ruler. It sounded broken, more teary than icy. "You are a very highly educated man—is that not so, Markus?"

"Yes, Your Holy and Mighty Excellency."

"You know the history of the world."

"I would not make such a claim, but, yes, I would not say that I am totally ignorant."

"In all the books that you have read, have you ever come across the case of a pregnant ruler?"

"A pregnant ruler? No! Unless he is a woman . . . Definitely not."

"Can't you see what he is saying? That this self-induced expansion is a pregnancy of sorts?"

The Ruler started laughing, and Machokali wondered whether he should join in to show that he too got the joke, whatever it may have been. There are times when silence is golden but this was not one of them, for Machokali took the occasion to ingratiate himself with the Ruler and prolong the laughter by boldly saying:

"Congratulations! You are making history. It is a good thing that I arranged for the Wizard of the Crow to come to America. I even personally went to meet him at the airport. I think we should call a press conference and announce this to the world."

The ensuing silence dampened his enthusiasm and made Machokali realize immediately that he had just made a profound blunder. He started searching for words to extricate himself even as he slowly retreated, step by step.

"You? You! Even you?" said the Ruler, wagging a finger at him, blind with rage. "So you were in cahoots with the sorcerer? You took it upon yourselves to insult me, in my face, just because I am hobbled? You call me a woman?"

He tried to raise himself to jump all over Machokali but could not. He tried to grab his ceremonial club to hurl it at the big eyes of Machokali, but he could not reach it. Machokali stopped walking backward when he saw that the Ruler could not reach him with his club, but he kept eyeing it on the floor. Shielding oneself against a blow was prudence, not cowardice. He chose to do so with words.

"I was extending congratulations solely on account of your quickness in seeing *through* the chicanery of this fellow who calls himself the Wizard of the Crow. I said that I did a good thing to make arrangements for his coming to America because had he not come for you to see *through* him, he might have lived to a ripe old age, deceiving millions with his slanderous lies about your being pregnant."

"So you enjoy saying it over and over again, you smelly cunt of a man. You piece of dirt. A poor excuse for manhood. Away from my sight," said the Ruler, waving him away. Even before the Ruler had finished calling him names, Machokali was in full flight back to his seat.

"Wait!" the Ruler shouted at him. "Come back here. Give me back that note! Or are you planning to share it with the others?"

Machokali had forgotten that he was still holding it. He returned and gingerly handed it to the Ruler. As Machokali backtracked, he was agog: the Ruler had grabbed the piece of paper, put it in his mouth, chewed it, and swallowed it, all while staring at Machokali.

"I must never hear this matter out of anybody's mouth."

# SECTION II

# 1

It was the sound of the plane landing that announced the return of the Ruler from his famous visit to America, for it was louder than thunder. People said that only His Mightiness could produce thunder without lightning and rain, but there was something wrong with it, people added, because the Ruler came back home under the cover of darkness, like a thief. The procession of diplomats, ministers, and dancers that always greeted him at the airport whenever he returned from visits abroad was nowhere in sight. And when he did not appear on television, people confidently asserted that, yes, something had to be wrong; the Ruler always appeared on live television whenever he returned from abroad. When after many days there were still no photographs or television footage of his return, people started whispering: had his corpse been shipped back from America?

Even when Big Ben Mambo, the Minister of Information, issued a statement that the Ruler was in retreat in the State House to think about the future of the country, the rumors did not abate. If anything, the statement only added fuel to their fire.

Many of the ministers were also in the dark as to why the Ruler had become inaccessible in the State House, and even fewer knew that he was sobbing like a child, though no tears fell from his eyes. Unbeknown to them, his desire for vengeance against the Wizard of the Crow was all-consuming. But unlike that other time when his tears filled several drums, this time no tear would actually fall, which increased his frustration and made him sob all the more. Unshed tears of an unrequited desire for vengeance are exhausting and require privacy.

The only people allowed into his presence were the leaders of the armed forces, because he wanted to hear their reports before he met with Sikiokuu and other ministers. When they finished he asked them to command from the State House, really to keep an eye on them because he feared the possibility of a military coup. But although the Ruler was cordoned off and protected by the military, the words in the wizard's note still found a way of creeping into his mind—*the Ruler is Pregnant*—and, hearing them, he would start as if somebody were actually whispering the words in his ear. Rumors say that there was a time when he grabbed one of the army leaders who happened to be nearby and asked him, Did you dare to say "the Ruler is pregnant"? And the military man cried out, Oh, no, no, I have not spoken a word. When the Ruler realized his mistake, he claimed that it was a joke: I wanted to test that you are alert at all times. But still he warned the man never to repeat the incident to anyone, even himself. The officer said, What are you talking about? I don't remember a thing, and the reply, apparently sincere, made the Ruler become even more anxious, because if the man could so easily forget what had just transpired, how could the Ruler be sure that the man would not as easily forget that he had just been warned never to repeat the incident to himself or anybody else? But he did not want to ask him what it was that he was not remembering, because he did not want the army officer to repeat the words *the Ruler is pregnant*. His mind was abuzz, and, not knowing what to do, at such times he would sob tearlessly, with even greater frustration and bitterness, his shoulders heaving and his body shaking, as did not only the building but the entire country, some people mistaking this effect for an earthquake or volcanic eruption somewhere.

How dare this bastard of a Wizard of the Crow call me a woman? he would ask himself over and over again. Is he implying that my power is waning? Is that why the leaders of the West did not receive me? Maybe they had looked down on him because recently there had been no blood as in the early days of his rule, when he had unflinchingly killed Aburĩrian communists galore. How can I show them that I am still the man I was? he wondered. But he was still mindful of his self-imposed moratorium on shedding blood in order to impress the Global Bank, and his sense of helplessness deepened his frustration. He felt abandoned by his friends in the West and despised by his own people, to the extent that a sorcerer dared call him a woman to his face. And not only the sorcerer. Even women themselves . . .

He did not complete the thought, for it suddenly made him recall the women of the drama of shame at Eldares, and the memory of the deed, in the presence of diplomats from all corners of the globe, made his brain heat up with renewed fury. The drama of shame was the origin of the current lack of fear and respect. Nyawĩra came to mind. Has she been apprehended? he wondered. He remembered the recent spate of husband beating. Did I not give Sikiokuu the task of investigating the whole question of women and their role in dissident politics? He decided to summon Sikiokuu, thus breaking his self-imposed isolation, at least from his ministers. Sikiokuu, Minister of State in the Ruler's Office, felt a surge of pride at being the first cabinet member invited for an audience with the Ruler since his return from America.

The Ruler did not waste time with preliminaries, going straight to the heart of the matter. Before I set out for America I gave you several tasks: to arrest Nyawĩra, break the backbone of the Movement for the Voice of the People, and investigate the queuing mania. Reports reached me in America that women are the ones now ruling Aburĩrian homes and have become so bold as to establish people's courts and beat up men in broad daylight. What have you to say to this?

# 2

If Sikiokuu was taken aback by the new size and shape of the Ruler, he did not show it by look or gesture. Sikiokuu had a few informants among the security folk, as well as allies among ministers. Even when the chief told him to cut out his prologue of praise and get to the point, he did not seem unduly perturbed.

He did not know where or how to begin, Sikiokuu said, for he had much to report, and although he had not yet broken the back of the Movement for the Voice of the People completely, he had planted undercover agents in virtually every sector of society and had managed to harass the illegal movement into inactivity. Most important, he had been able to unearth and identify the brains behind all the evil in the land. He paused to see the effect of his revelations. The Ruler raised his eyebrows and asked: Who? Sikiokuu's face tightened and his cheeks became puffed up with barely suppressed anger.

"How can I say when I hate the very thought of my tongue having to repeat his name?"

"Who is he?" the Ruler asked, raising his voice with impatience, which is exactly what Sikiokuu had wanted, to seem as if he were simply acceding to the Ruler's command.

"The Minister for Foreign Affairs," he said, lowering his voice in sadness at this obvious betrayal of trust.

"Machokali?"

"He of the very name you have just mentioned," Sikiokuu said, once again showing the greatest reluctance to say the name.

"Machokali?" the Ruler asked again.

"Yes."

Silence. Sikiokuu stole a quick glance to see what the Ruler was thinking, but the only thing he noticed on the otherwise immobile face was a twitch, one of those involuntary reactions to fear of pain, and that twitch, together with the next question, *How do you know?* prompted Sikiokuu not to respond with words but to open his briefcase and take out two voluminous typescripts, "The Kaniũrũ Report on the Origins of the Queuing Mania and Its Possible Connection with Anti-government Activities" and "A Secret Report on Acts of Treason." He dramatically placed them on the table, his cheeks still puffed with anger at the presumed traitor.

"Everything is in there," he said, pointing at the two volumes, "and it might be a good idea for me to go away and let you read them for yourself," he added, knowing that the Ruler had not much patience with lengthy written reports and would no doubt ask him for a summary. Sikiokuu was therefore surprised when the Ruler stretched out an arm to receive the two volumes, and the minister nearly tripped over himself as he rushed to hand them over. The Ruler took one, leafed through it, put it down, and did the same with the other.

"Are you sure that all your allegations are true?" said the Ruler.

"I swear before you, the Almighty on Earth, and to the One in

Heaven that the people who compiled these two reports are absolutely
loyal and trustworthy," said Sikiokuu, pulling his right earlobe in confirmation before adding, "Even a bank could entrust them its keys."

"Who are they?"

"John Kaniūrū, deputy chairman of Marching to Heaven and
chairman of the Ruler's Commission of Inquiry into the Queuing
Mania. The second volume is by Elijah Njoya and Peter Kahiga, both
first-rate intelligence officers."

"Would you repeat these charges in the presence of the accused?"
asked the Ruler, fixing his eyes on Sikiokuu.

"I am not afraid of traitors," Sikiokuu said, this time pulling both
earlobes.

The Ruler sent for Machokali.

"And do you understand that I don't want Machokali to know of
the existence of these reports?"

"I understand, Your Mighty Excellency. Top secret. They're
between you and me."

"Give me a brief summary of the main findings of the reports
before the traitor arrives."

Sikiokuu would have preferred not to have a personal confronta-
tion with Machokali but eagerly took advantage of the invitation to
fill the Ruler's ears with poison to ensure that the Ruler viewed everything through Sikiokuu's eyes.

*"The bug that bites one's back is carried in what one wears,"* the
Ruler said, greeting Machokali with barely hidden sarcasm. "Have
you ever heard of that proverb?"

"Oh, yes. It is a well-known Swahili proverb. *Kikulacho kimo
nguoni mwako.*"

"And do you know why the Waswahili coined it?"

*"Well . . ."* Machokali said and paused, not quite knowing where
the Ruler was going with the question.

"Sit on that chair and face your mate," the Ruler told him. "That
way you will soon learn the proverb's true meaning. And you,
Sikiokuu, say what you have to say about Machokali to his face, just
to teach you all that I don't rely solely on what is spoken behind a person's back."

Sikiokuu now told the story of treason as culled from Tajirika's
confession, but without once mentioning the source, and accused his

rival of being behind the recent queuing mania and planning to create an intelligence network reporting to him directly.

"This plot was hatched at a secret meeting at the Mars Café just before Machokali accompanied you to America," he finished.

At first Machokali hoped that the Ruler would see through the patent fabrication and dismiss it as mere nonsense, but when his eyes met those of the Ruler, awash in bitterness, he simply fell on his knees and began swearing to God in Heaven that he had no connection whatsoever to the queuing mania. He had never dreamt of taking power by any means. The allegation of a rival intelligence network issued from Sikiokuu's envy and hatred.

"Tajirika is my witness!" Machokali said in desperation but confident that Tajirika, owner and CEO of Eldares Modern Construction and Real Estate and chairman of Marching to Heaven, and his dear friend, would fully back him up.

"Let's call him," Sikiokuu said with alacrity, and this readiness made Machokali uneasy, though he was still confident that his friend Tajirika would not let him down.

"I will certainly send for him," said the Ruler. "It is now late. My men will make sure that Tajirika is here the first thing tomorrow morning. But as I don't want any of you to interfere with the witness, both of you will spend the night here. You don't mind sharing a bedroom in the State House, do you?"

# 3

Sikiokuu and Machokali were locked in a room with displays of the bones and skeletons of past enemies of the Ruler adorning the walls. After a while lights were turned off and they found themselves in total darkness. The room was cold and miserable; they were paralyzed by terror, as they could not tell whether or not they had already been condemned to death, with their skeletons slated to become part of the grisly décor. They did not speak a word to each other, each huddling in his own corner, at the mercy of his own thoughts and imaginings that the spirits of the dead were present. Machokali was first to sense a silhouette in the dark, and as he thrust his hand in the air, he pinched what he was sure was a spirit. Sikiokuu felt the pinch and he too assumed that it was one of the spirits, and as he thrust out his hands to ward off another pinch he pinched something himself, and this confirmed his worst fears. In the morning, each one was relieved that he was still alive and well. Now Machokali and Sikiokuu prayed that Tajirika had been found, for, apart from the fact that each expected support from his testimony, they did not want to spend another night in the company of emissaries from the underworld.

# 4

The police whisked Tajirika from his Golden Heights residence to the State House early that morning and ushered him into a room with white drawn curtains. They did not tell him why he had been summoned, and, though he had all sorts of conjectures in his head, the last thing he expected was to see Machokali and Sikiokuu enter the room barely minutes after his arrival. He did not know how to react or whom he should greet first, so he just said good morning without addressing anybody in particular.

Neither answered back, both avoided eye contact with him. He quickly figured that his confession was at stake here. He tried to work out what he would say if asked about it, only to come to a mental cul-de-sac, for quite apart from the fact that he could not possibly recall each and every word, he had no idea which of the two ministers was in favor with the Ruler. He decided to be as vague as he could when answering the first few questions put to him, the better to find out.

The curtains parted and Tajirika saw before his very eyes a human monstrosity emerge. Tajirika was about to bolt but when he saw that Machokali and Sikiokuu took this apparition in stride, he took courage and sat still. The Ruler must have eaten a lot of steaks in America, Tajirika thought to himself, recognizing a semblance of the Almighty Ruler in the figure that now sat in judgment.

In the dock were Machokali and Sikiokuu, who sat opposite each other; an observer could not tell the difference between the prosecutor and the accused, because their faces were equally solemn. Tajirika sat in the middle, facing the judge directly. Inwardly, the three waited for Tajirika's words as if he were an oracle.

Machokali was fairly confident that the words would help clear him of all the false allegations against him. Sikiokuu was equally sure that the words would confirm the charges.

The Ruler was the only one not worried whether the words supported the charges or not, for he had a different and more immediate agenda.

He had read the two volumes that Sikiokuu had given him, and what captured his attention, to the point of its becoming an obsession, was the fact that Tajirika had already collected money from the Marching to Heaven scheme. The unexpected discovery that some people had already profited from the project hit him hard: so people had already started making money from Marching to Heaven and no one had said a word about it? So here I am, roaming the world, my hat in hand, enduring insults from the Global Bank, and these people are amassing fortunes behind my back? How much money had they collected? Who else was involved in the scheme? Those were the questions to which he now hoped to get answers, but he knew that he had to tread carefully in order not to frighten Tajirika and make him retreat into his shell before disclosing the names of his fellow schemers.

So Tajirika was not only at the center of charges and countercharges between Machokali and Sikiokuu, but also at the source of suspicions and resentments in the mind of the Ruler. He sensed the tension but assumed it had something to do with his confession, and, like Machokali and Sikiokuu, he expected to be asked about it. But even the two ministers, familiar as they were with the unexpected ways of the Ruler, were taken aback by the first question from the judge.

"What have you brought us?" the Ruler asked Tajirika almost gently.

"Your Mighty Excellency, they came for me in the morning and I did not have the time to, uh, to . . ." Tajirika stammered and then stopped.

The Ruler realized what had made Tajirika pause and hastened to put him at ease.

"Don't worry about coming here with empty hands. Send your gifts later. What I am now asking you is this: what do you want to tell me in the presence of these counselors?"

"About what?" Tajirika asked, puzzled, for he felt that he was being treated as if he was the one who had asked for the audience.

"Whatever weighs on your conscience. Anything that troubles you," said the Ruler, trying to make it easier for Tajirika to confess about the money. "Do you have a weight in your heart that you want to lay before me?"

The question threw Tajirika into turmoil. He had always dreamt of an opportunity for precisely such an audience with the Ruler, and now he was at a loss for words. Maybe he was caught off-guard by the Ruler's solicitous tone, which had reminded him of a pronouncement he had heard long ago: *Come unto me all ye that are heavy laden, and I will give you rest.* Or was this a trap? Will I reveal my innermost thoughts and in the process land myself in more trouble? *Come unto me all ye that are heavy laden, and I will give you rest.* How alluring the words! Relief was being tendered! Where would he start? He went over recent events in his mind—from the humiliation of having his chairmanship of Marching to Heaven weakened to being beaten by women—to see which burden he would first lay at the feet of the Lord. He recalled lying on a cold cement floor under the weight of three big strong women, and he felt the pain of being beaten with renewed force. He thought of Vinjinia, his own wife, being dragged to a dark forest by none other than Kaniūrū, his usurper who had him arrested simply for refusing to obey a summons to appear before him. How could Kaniūrū dare lay his dirty hands on his wife? This seemed a bigger blow to his manhood than anything else. He remembered that Kaniūrū had been acting on behalf of Sikiokuu, and the bitterness of the humiliations from the man who now sat before him almost choked him. He now unconsciously opened his mouth to unburden himself.

"What I don't understand, even now," Tajirika said, as if continuing a soliloquy already begun, "is the connection between Sikiokuu and the women of the people's court."

"People's court?" asked His Mighty Excellency, glancing in the direction of Silver Sikiokuu.

"Your Mighty Excellency," Sikiokuu said defensively, "I have not had the opportunity to brief you fully on everything. I think Tajirika is referring to the women alleged to be beating up men."

"And they started with me," Tajirika said in self-pity. "I ask myself: why me?"

While Sikiokuu was baffled and worried by the direction of things, Machokali for his part felt a bit more buoyant, for the conversation was drifting away from the charges of treason. He even felt like laughing at the thought of his friend being beaten by women, but he controlled himself.

"This is not a laughing matter," said the Ruler, as if he had sensed Machokali's thoughts. "It is very serious," he added for emphasis, recalling the drama of shame at Eldares, especially the women's call to set Rachael free. Somehow these reflections made the Ruler feel closer to Tajirika as a fellow sufferer of shame at the hands of women. "Go on, Titus," he told him.

Tajirika sensed pity in the Ruler's voice, giving him the courage and strength he needed to tell the story of his misadventures. He told how the women kidnapped him and then later charged him with domestic violence before sentencing him to several strokes of the cane, and as he now came to the end of his ballad of woes, Tajirika felt overwhelmed by a sense of joy and gratitude at having shared his misery with a sympathetic audience. May His Holy Excellency live for ever and ever, he sang to himself.

"And how does Sikiokuu come into this?" asked the Ruler.

*"No connection. Absolutely no connection!"* said Sikiokuu, flapping his ears from side to side.

"I am not asking you," the Ruler told Sikiokuu.

"What I don't understand is this: why did Sikiokuu stop me from beating my wife? Or let me put it this way. Sikiokuu orders me not to beat my wife. But I, desiring to assert my male prerogative, lay my hands on her. A week hardly passes before these women come for me. And after they punish me, they warn me not to beat my wife, the very same words that I had first heard uttered by Sikiokuu. *What a coincidence!*" he added in English.

"Those were not real women," shouted Sikiokuu in desperation, unable to restrain himself. "They were shadows created by the Wizard of the Crow."

Tajirika looked to the door as if he feared that the wizard might be standing there. Machokali and the Ruler did the same, but the latter pretended not to have heard properly and now fixed his eyes on Sikiokuu. For a few seconds there was nothing but silence.

"Mine were real women," asserted Tajirika, breaking the silence.

"When did the women beat you up?" Machokali asked Tajirika sympathetically.

"When the Ruler was in America," said Tajirika, trying to nail the date down.

"But that was when the Wizard of the Crow was in America," said Machokali, forgetting that Tajirika did not know this.

The Ruler, Sikiokuu, and Tajirika looked at Machokali at the same time but for different reasons: the Ruler because Machokali's mention of the Wizard of the Crow revived the pain inflicted by the sorcerer's letter; Sikiokuu because he knew well that Machokali was trying to keep alive a story that was against his interests; and Tajirika because he was hearing about the Wizard of the Crow being in America for the first time. What games were the two ministers trying to play, with Sikiokuu claiming that the women who beat him up were mere shadows and Machokali claiming that the Wizard of the Crow had somehow escaped prison and gone to America? Tajirika thought.

"I know nothing about the Wizard of the Crow being or not being in America. All I know is that I left him in prison," said Tajirika.

"You were in prison?" asked the Ruler. In the reports that he read the night before, there was no mention of this. "Why were you in prison?"

"Your Mighty Excellency, I was intending to brief you on this and other matters," Sikiokuu said. "Tajirika wasn't actually arrested—it was just *protective custody*. Or, what do you say, Titus?" Sikiokuu asked, hoping that Tajirika would confirm this.

"No, no," protested Tajirika. "I was being detained for real. I was imprisoned in a real cell. But Your Mighty Excellency, being put in a prison cell was not the worst . . ." Tajirika paused as if overcome by the recollection of past wrongs.

"Go on, Tajirika," the Ruler said encouragingly. "You have the floor. What is this that you say was worse than prison? A conscience troubled for not disclosing some wrongdoing?" the Ruler added, hoping to direct Tajirika's revelations to the question of money.

"No, not even that."

"What could be worse than withholding vital information or keeping bad deeds locked up inside oneself?"

"Being thrown into the same cell with that sorcerer. The Wizard of the Crow."

"What is all this about?" the Ruler asked Sikiokuu.

"I will explain everything when I report about Nyawīra," Sikiokuu said, looking at the Ruler with eyes desperately pleading for mercy and understanding.

"Tell me something, Sikiokuu: when you put the Wizard of the Crow in prison, was that before he left for America or after?" asked Machokali innocently, but still trying to stoke the fire of tension. "The Wizard of the Crow cannot have been in two places at once. If he was in America when Tajirika was being beaten, when did he manufacture and unleash these shadows?"

"You should know," Sikiokuu shouted at Machokali. "Stop pretending. You were the one who requested that the Wizard of the Crow be sent to America. I have kept all your faxes and e-mails on the matter. The Ruler is ill, you alleged in one of them."

"I did not call you all here to hear you crow about the wizard," the Ruler said, wagging his finger at Machokali and Sikiokuu. "Why can't you two talk plainly like my chairman of Marching to Heaven?" he added, nodding toward Tajirika approvingly.

Tajirika felt joy continue springing within. If things continue this way, he might emerge from this ordeal free from the power of these two ministers.

"Thank you," he told the Ruler.

"Titus," the Ruler called him by name, still trying to soften him up with regard to the money, *"you see now the kind of ministers I have?"*

"Well, you will have to do with what you have. What gives birth in the wilderness suckles in the wilderness," Tajirika said.

"What did you say?" the Ruler shouted at Tajirika. "What did you say about giving birth?"

Only Machokali knew why the Ruler had become so touchy. Still, he did not show by look or gesture that he understood. He and Sikiokuu turned to Tajirika as if adding oil to the fire with the unspoken *Yes, why did you say that?*

"It is just a proverb," Tajirika said quickly, wondering why the Ruler had so suddenly turned against him. "I'm sorry."

"You're sorry?"

"Forgive me."

"Forgive you for what? Just answer my questions plainly. Riddles and proverbs are for evening entertainment at one's own home."

"Yes, Sir Holiness."

"Listen to me. I have it on good authority that the queues started outside your office," the Ruler said, to change the subject from pregnancy and sorcery to queues and money matters.

Tajirika had no clue that the Ruler was so sensitive on this subject, and in his eagerness to undo the error he had made with his proverb he now hastened to expound his theory that it was the Wizard of the Crow who had started the whole queuing mania. At that, Sikiokuu cast him an evil eye, for he had expressly told Tajirika not to make the Wizard of the Crow the originator of the queuing mania, for that explanation would tend to exonerate Machokali. Machokali, for his part, cast him a glance of gratitude. Tajirika saw the evil look from Sikiokuu, but he knew that the eyes of a frog in a brook do not prevent cows from drinking water. Instead of halting his narrative, Tajirika now sat up and recounted how the Wizard of the Crow came to his office disguised as a job seeker . . .

"Why are you so obsessed with this sorcerer?" the Ruler interrupted him. "Cut out the business of who started the queues and go straight to the question of envelopes of self-introduction."

In a second it dawned on Tajirika what the Ruler had been driving at all along. Was that really why he had been summoned to the State House? To answer questions about money that he had not used or even banked? The money was cursed, and it had now come to haunt him even inside the State House.

"The envelopes? I was coming to that. You see, there is a connection between the queues and those envelopes," he said without hesitation.

He told how he had learned of his appointment to the chairmanship of Marching to Heaven and how soon after that a queue of seekers of future contracts had formed outside his offices, how they handed him envelopes of self-introduction, and how by the end of the day he had filled up three big sacks, each at least five feet by two, with money.

"Three sacks full of money? And each bag more than five feet by two? In one day?" asked the Ruler.

He could not tell where or how it came to him—it may have been triggered by the eagerness for knowledge in the Ruler's eyes—but the idea of vengeance against Kaniūrū suddenly formed in his mind and Tajirika found himself exaggerating the story of the money and enjoying it.

"It was not even a whole day," he now said. "Just a matter of a few hours in the afternoon."

"One afternoon? A few hours?" pressed the Ruler.

"Yes, a couple hours."

"And three big sacks, each more than five feet by two, full of money?"

"Not just full. I had to push the notes down with my hands and even with my feet until each bag was tight and as heavy as a sack of grain. But, alas, just when I thought that I had finally crossed the valley of poverty into permanent wealth, I became ill."

The idea of vengeance, initially vague, was growing, and now it formed itself into a definite plan. So far he had talked only about money in general, and his listeners understood it to be in the form of Burī notes. Now in the plan the Burīs became dollars. All he had to do was find a way of dropping the name of the currency to ensure maximum impact on his listeners. Tajirika paused and bent his head slightly in a dejected manner, and this reflected in his voice as he now said:

"But after getting well I never once received another envelope stashed with dollars, all in hundred-dollar bills."

"Dollars? They bribed you in American dollars?" the Ruler kept asking.

"Well, they were out to impress me. Some said openly that they knew that the Aburīrian Burī was nothing, that it changed its value every other day the way chameleons change color. *Burī ni bure,* some would say in Kiswahili, and, because they wanted our friendship to be firm, they thought that it could be made so only by money that was global, firm and permanent in value, and the American dollar fits the bill."

"They said Burīs were valueless?" the Ruler repeated. He was about to explode with expletives, but he changed his mind. "Why no more dollars afterward?" he asked.

"Your Mighty Excellency, when I recovered from my illness, I found that all the powers of my office had been assumed by my deputy, John Kaniūrū."

"And your deputy, did he also receive envelopes of self-introduction?" he asked.

"I don't know for sure. I think the person who can best answer that question is Minister Silver Sikiokuu. Kaniūrū works for him. They are very close friends."

"I swear, I know nothing about this," said Sikiokuu, alarmed and shaken by the implications.

"Go on, Mr. Tajirika," the Ruler said, ignoring Sikiokuu's interjection. "Please continue."

"Even though I don't know much about it," said Tajirika, "I have heard that the queues moved to his place and that up to now Kaniūrū continues to receive an endless stream of seekers of contracts. I have heard it said that there are some who have been to visit him twice or three times, with newer and fatter envelopes of continuous self-reintroduction. Dollars to help keep hope alive," Tajirika added.

"Three big bags of dollars a day," repeated the Ruler slowly.

"At least twice or thrice a day," said Tajirika.

"That makes it at least six or nine bags of dollars every day. Sikiokuu, how many months have gone by since your Kaniūrū took over as deputy chairman for Marching to Heaven?"

Instead of answering, Sikiokuu rose to deny once again that he had any connection with the envelopes. He swore time and again, pulling his earlobes for emphasis, that this was the very first time he was hearing about the scheme.

"But I will conduct an investigation. I will get to the bottom of this matter. I will set up an investigating team tomorrow," said Sikiokuu, the veins of his neck popping.

"No, not tomorrow," said the Ruler. "I must have some accounting for this. I am sending for that Kaniūrū now."

"Yes, yes," said Sikiokuu enthusiastically. "Let him come here to expose the naked lies of some people and their cunning friends," Sikiokuu added, obviously referring to Tajirika and Machokali.

The Ruler phoned instructions for Kaniūrū to be brought immediately to him, wherever he might be, even if it meant sending a helicopter to fly him to the State House.

Sikiokuu was happy at this turn of events. If there was anybody whose loyalty Sikiokuu was sure of, it was John Kaniūrū. He had done many favors for the youthwinger, raising him up from a simple lecturer at a polytechnic to a powerful presence in the land. There was no way Kaniūrū would have collected such an amount of money without telling him and clearing it with him. Tajirika's lies will be exposed, he mused, and to whom will this betrayer of friendship turn for help? And just as he was laughing inwardly in triumph at the image of Tajirika beating a hasty retreat, his tail between his legs, Sikiokuu heard Tajirika say:

"This is the same Kaniūrū who is the leader of the gang of thugs that kidnapped and beat my wife."

"Why? Is there something going on between them?" asked the Ruler.

"No! No!" Tajirika protested, and started to tell his story.

As he told how Vinjinia had been humiliated, his voice broke with the memory of the shame, and for a few seconds after he had concluded his story, there was an awkward silence in the room. They all could not help but be touched by the sincerity in his voice. The Ruler broke the silence by looking askance at Sikiokuu.

"I am the one who asked Kaniūrū to investigate those women of the people's court," Sikiokuu said. "But Kaniūrū went too far. I was only trying to help Tajirika. He and I had spoken, and he had agreed to the investigation. If anything, it was Tajirika who urged me to take strong measures to uncover the women who had beaten him."

"Is that so, Tajirika?" asked the Ruler.

"Yes, the part about my agreeing to an investigation is correct."

*"Thank you, Titus,"* Sikiokuu said in English. *"You are a good man surrounded by false friends."*

"Stop it, Sikiokuu," the Ruler said. "I did not ask you for an *assessment* of anybody's character."

Machokali did not like that Kaniūrū would give a report on the investigations into the queuing mania and was all too happy to see and even contribute to the undermining of his credibility.

"And is John Kaniūrū, this friend of Sikiokuu's, not the same who had earlier made false allegations about Vinjinia, resulting in her arrest and illegal detention?" asked Machokali with feigned innocence.

Sikiokuu could no longer restrain himself at the antics of his rival.

"Kaniūrū is my friend," Sikiokuu said. "But you, too, Machokali, have lots of strange friends in Santamaria. If not so, to whom did you go to say farewell in Santamaria just before you left for America? Or will you deny that you made a secret trip to Santamaria?"

Caught unaware, Machokali, not sure how much his archenemy knew about this visit, decided to come clean but tinker with the truth here and there.

"Yes, I did visit Santamaria, as I do many other parts of Eldares. I did not know that it was prohibited to visit certain parts of Eldares."

"Yes, but why then did you go there incognito?"

"Look. I went there to meet with my friend Tajirika. We met openly at the Mars Café. Is that what you call incognito?"

"Why did you take a taxi instead of your chauffer-driven Mercedes-Benz?" Sikiokuu challenged him.

"Surely everybody knows how difficult it is to drive through Eldares during rush hour. It might even be quicker to take a *mko-koteni* pushcart."

"Was the taxi going by some other route?"

"Taxi drivers know side streets better than anyone."

"Was it not during the meeting at the Mars Café that you asked Tajirika to be your eyes and ears in Aburīria while you were away?"

"Don't twist my words," Machokali said heatedly. "I told Tajirika that, in my absence, he should be my ears and eyes as far as Marching to Heaven was concerned. In other words, I had gone to see him not only as my friend but also in his capacity as the Ruler-appointed chairperson of Marching to Heaven. *Strictly speaking, as the chairman he should have been a member of the official delegation to the USA,* and I was there to explain to him why his name had been left off the list. But I did not know then that some people would scheme behind my back to prevent him from effectively carrying out his duties. I did not know that his designated deputy, your friend Kaniūrū, would take away from Tajirika what the Ruler had given him," he finished, pointing a finger at Sikiokuu before turning toward Tajirika. "Is that not so, Titus?" he asked in a solicitous voice.

"You have spoken some truth," Tajirika said, without too much enthusiasm, for he still resented not having been included in the delegation.

The Ruler was always happiest when his ministers, especially these two, were at each other's throats, for it was during these heated exchanges that he was able to learn a thing or two that may have been hidden from him. But now he did not want their bickering to take the focus away from the bags of money, knowing that dollars, not Burīs, were at stake. Three, six, nine bags of dollars a day? Probably more?

"Mr. Sikiokuu, I asked you how many months have gone by since Kaniũrũ assumed his position as the deputy chairman of Marching to Heaven. You have yet to answer me," the Ruler said to Sikiokuu.

Before Sikiokuu could respond, it was announced that Kaniũrũ had arrived and was now waiting at the door.

"We can now hear from the horse's own mouth," the Ruler said.

# 5

Kaniũrũ strode into the room confidently, holding a briefcase in his right hand. For him to be summoned to the State House in his own right for whatever reason, bad or good, was a great honor. One look at Sikiokuu, though, and he knew that all was not well. Then he saw the Ruler pointing at him. The size of the hand and of the Ruler came as a surprise to Kaniũrũ, but he did not let it show or unsettle him.

"We want to hear a full report from the deputy chairman of Marching to Heaven," the Ruler told him, waving him to a seat next to Sikiokuu.

He also told Tajirika to move and sit next to Machokali, the two pairs facing each other. The arrangement made it possible for the Ruler to keep everyone within his gaze at all times.

"Your Mighty Excellency, I have a lot to tell, only I don't know where or how to begin," Kaniũrũ said as he opened his briefcase and ostentatiously pulled out file after file and put them down at his own feet on the floor.

"Why don't you start with the visitors who bring you money?" the Ruler commanded.

Kaniũrũ did not look perturbed. The question and the hostile tone simply confirmed his own observation that Sikiokuu was in a tight corner and that, in the event of a crisis, his friend would not be able to help him. Now it was every man for himself.

He took his time arranging his files and receipts in proper order. He then sat up to explain himself.

It was indeed true, he quickly admitted, that when the Aburĩrian business community learned that he had been accorded the unique honor of serving his Ruler and country as the deputy chairman of Marching to Heaven, they started visiting him, giving him what they called their visiting cards, which of course amounted to envelopes stashed with paper money. At first he did not know what to do with these envelopes, but after discussing the matter with his friend and benefactor, Minister Silver Sikiokuu, it was agreed that, of the money received, he would keep twenty-five percent, and the rest, seventy-five percent, he would put into Sikiokuu's various accounts.

Sikiokuu could not believe his ears.

*"What? Are you crazy?"* he said in English, jumping up without knowing exactly what he would do. So he just stood there, pulling his earlobes in fury while appealing to the Ruler. "Your Excellency, *can't you see?* My enemies have conspired with this man to discredit my name and character. I swear that I have had nothing whatsoever to do with these visiting envelopes. Kaniũrũ, so it is true what the Waswahili say, that a donkey shows gratitude through its kicks? Yes, *asante ya punda ni mateke.*"

"My friend," Kaniũrũ said affably, "I have one life like you and everybody else in Aburĩria. The difference between my life and the lives of others is that mine is completely dedicated to the Ruler and there is no way I would ever tell a lie before him. Believe me, my very body would denounce me."

"This man is lying through his teeth," cried Sikiokuu in sheer frustration.

"Young man," said the Ruler, "do you know that what you are saying is very serious? Do you have any evidence to back up your claims?"

"Your Mighty Excellency, I don't understand why Sikiokuu is denying any knowledge of the envelopes and their contents. I can assure you that it is neither Sikiokuu nor I who solicited the gifts from these businessmen. *This has absolutely nothing to do with bribery or corruption,*" he emphasized in English.

"Yes, but I have had nothing to do with it," said Sikiokuu.

"That's true," agreed Kaniũrũ, "but it is because I handled everything."

"Where is the evidence?" the Ruler intervened. "I want evidence, not endless arguments."

*"May I approach?"* Kaniũrũ asked the Ruler as if he, Kaniũrũ, were a lawyer asking permission to go near a judge's bench.

Without waiting for an answer Kaniũrũ took a bundle of canceled checks and handed them over to the Ruler, showing that, every day for several months, Kaniũrũ had written checks payable to Silver Sikiokuu. All had a seemingly valid bank stamp showing that they had been cashed or deposited in Sikiokuu's accounts.

What Kaniũrũ did not disclose was that his friend at the bank, Jane Kanyori, had set up a bogus account in Sikiokuu's name to facilitate Kaniũrũ's supposed deposits. Neither did he disclose that Jane Kanyori had given him a bank card in the name of Sikiokuu, enabling Kaniũrũ to withdraw the money he had deposited in Sikiokuu's account and redeposit the money in his own at other banks. Everything according to the book. Kaniũrũ was an artist, and his calligraphic skills became useful in forging Sikiokuu's signature.

"If my share of twenty-five percent is ever needed for any of our Lord's self-help programs, I will part with it anytime," Kaniũrũ declared, and returned to his chair next to Sikiokuu.

For once in his life Sikiokuu was at a complete loss for words. His mouth remained open, unable to deny, protest, or affirm his innocence. But his head was busy trying to figure out, without success, how and when he had wronged Kaniũrũ. Instead, what came to the fore were his own generous deeds on his friend's behalf.

"Your Mighty Excellency, there is more to this than meets all of our eyes," Sikiokuu finally said in a teary voice. "Please, I beg you to let me look into the whole matter and bring to light what is hidden in the dark."

"There is a shorter and easier way of verifying this," said the Ruler. "I will demand your bank statements."

He gave the order and in a few minutes had the information he sought from the National Bank of Commerce and Industry. The records supported everything that Kaniũrũ had claimed.

In abject frustration, completely helpless, unable to expose Kaniũrũ's lies, Sikiokuu, close to tears, just stared ahead.

The Ruler seethed inside. So much money made from Marching to Heaven, his own project, and not one cent had come his way? Sikiokuu and even Kaniũrũ, a mere youthwinger, had already banked millions.

But suddenly he remembered something Tajirika had said earlier.

Substance was in the details. He quickly picked up the canceled checks and bank records and scrutinized them again.

Sikiokuu prayed with all his heart that the Ruler would find a discrepancy, something, however tiny, that would undo the harm done by Kaniũrũ.

"Let me ask you," the Ruler said, waving some of the checks toward Kaniũrũ. "Here I see only records of Aburĩrian money."

"Yes, my Lord," Kaniũrũ said. "It's all Burĩs."

"Where are the dollars?" the Ruler asked.

"Dollars?" asked Kaniũrũ, puzzled.

"Yes, dollars. American hundred-dollar bills. Three sacks each five feet by two in one afternoon. Like Tajirika before you. Or did your visitors not look down upon the value of the Burĩ? They didn't say, *Burĩ ni bure?*"

*"Got you, sucker!"* Sikiokuu said to himself, rejoicing. "The cunning fellow has been caught red-handed."

Tajirika also rejoiced, sure that his wiliness had placed Kaniũrũ in a situation from which he could not extricate himself.

And suddenly it all dawned on Kaniũrũ: Those businessmen had been paying Tajirika in dollars all along? Why had they not done so with him? Tajirika had not been the fool he had taken him to be. Still, Kaniũrũ thought quickly on his feet. Without seeming flustered in any way, he replied to the Ruler:

"There were some who wanted to pay in dollars. But Sikiokuu and I refused their offer. By accepting foreign currency we would have broken all the rules and regulations of the Central Bank concerning foreign exchange for nothing but self-gratification, and I am not very good with that kind of thing. Personally, I wanted something on the record that I could defend, even if I was found to have done wrong. I want to be judged on my record. I myself grew angry when I heard some of them talk as if they looked down on the Burĩ; one even said, *Burĩ ni bure.* I am not the kind of person who can stand idly by while people say nasty things about our national currency. My friend and benefactor, Sikiokuu, was even more furious with them for their lack of patriotism. In short, we refused to be bribed in dollars."

"Your Excellency," interjected Sikiokuu, "I pray you to please believe me when I say that no such conversation about Burĩs and dollars ever took place between me and this scoundrel."

The Ruler registered very little of what Sikiokuu had said. His mind was still preoccupied with the three sacks of dollars, for, to him, a bag of dollars was more valuable than all the Burīs in Aburīria. He, too, thought the national currency worthless, its value always changing like a chameleon. He now saw Tajirika in a new light: here was a bright mind that knew how to make a dollar out of thin air. Kaniūrū and Sikiokuu seemed to him foolish for insisting on being paid in Burīs.

"Mr. Tajirika," he said, turning toward Tajirika, "Kaniūrū has told us what he did with his Burīs. What did you do with your three bags of dollars?"

All eyes turned to Tajirika.

# 6

"I am talking to you, Tajirika," the Ruler repeated. "Are you hard of hearing? What did you do with the three sacks of dollars? With whom did you share the money?" he added, glancing at Machokali.

The tables are turning against me, Tajirika thought to himself. Why did I lie about having dollars?

It was too late to change his story. He would have to live with the untruth, no matter its consequences. From now on, he swore to himself, he would stick to what he knew best: bending the truth as opposed to telling downright lies.

"I left the three bags of dollars with the Wizard of the Crow," Tajirika said.

The Ruler broke into mirthless laughter. Sikiokuu felt life returning. Kaniūrū's nose twitched. Machokali looked at his friend with pity. Couldn't he come up with a better explanation?

"What?" asked the Ruler.

"I left the whole lot with the Wizard of the Crow."

"I don't understand. Did you owe him money?"

"It was his fee for curing me." Tajirika told of his own malady of words. "I was so happy to regain my voice that I did not worry about the fee. At that moment, my giving away the money was no big deal: there was more to be had where that first lot had come from."

"What did the wizard do with the money?" the Ruler, Machokali, and Sikiokuu asked in unison.

"Three big bags of dollars! Wow!" Kaniūrū added, not to be left out.

"When we were locked up in the same prison cell, he told me that he had buried it," Tajirika said.

They all laughed, as if in agreement that now Tajirika had gone too far with his lies.

"No doubt he failed to tell you where he planted it?" Sikiokuu said sarcastically.

"As a matter of fact," said Tajirika to the astonishment of all, "he did."

They quickly looked at one another before turning to Tajirika with the one unspoken question.

"He buried the money in the prairie behind Santalucia."

"And of course you never went to look for it," said Kaniūrū.

"No," said Tajirika promptly, "because I assumed the sorcerer was lying to me. And honestly, I did not want to have anything to do with it, and I never will—it's cursed. Let it remain buried—that is, if he was telling me the truth. And if it does not exist, again, let it be. The Wizard of the Crow is the only one who can enlighten us about the fate of the dollars."

The Ruler seemed oblivious to Tajirika's plea. He was obsessed with only one thing: these men had been caught with their own hands deep in the till. Bank records showed that Sikiokuu had pocketed millions, but here he was, busy denying it in the face of a preponderance of evidence. And here was Tajirika with his childish lies. Tajirika was protecting his accomplices, Machokali, perhaps, among others. The only one who had been fairly honest and straightforward was Kaniūrū. What do the others believe? That I am a fool? I will show them that this Ruler has still got a trick or two up his sleeve.

"We are not going to decide just yet who is telling the truth and who is not," the Ruler told them, looking from Sikiokuu to Machokali. "I want you two to give me three of your most trusted police officers or even youthwingers from among those who have had some contact with this Wizard of the Crow and have been courageous in facing him."

"Peter Kahiga and Elijah Njoya," said Sikiokuu immediately. "They don't lie like some people I know, and, most important, they know how to keep their mouths shut."

"I recommend A.G.," said Machokali.

"Yes, and A.G.," Sikiokuu agreed.

"Tajirika. I want you to know that I hate lies being told to me more than anything else. It is better to speak the truth to me, like Kaniũrũ here, and plead for mercy after than to resort to lies. But I will give you one more chance to redeem yourself. A second chance. A last chance. You have already said that you want nothing to do with the buried treasure. So show Kahiga, Njoya, and A.G. where it is—they will do the unearthing. You are to supervise the digging to keep the police officers honest. But let me warn you! If the dollars are not found, make sure to jump into the hole and beg to be buried in it. Do you understand? I am not to be trifled with."

Bitterly regretting the moment he had lied about dollars and weak in the knees, Tajirika stood up and staggered toward the door, a broken soul, sure that the task he had been given amounted to a death sentence.

# 7

Even Machokali, Sikiokuu, and Kaniũrũ felt they had just witnessed a death sentence. Tajirika would never be seen alive again, and this made them feel grateful that their own lives had been spared. Kaniũrũ congratulated himself on his art of lying, which he attributed to his clever head so unlike Tajirika's. That man was a numskull whose lies screamed to be seen as lies.

Machokali and Sikiokuu thought the same. Both knew that Kaniũrũ had also lied, but he at least had managed a reasonable cover-up.

Yet their joy was tempered by the fear that they might find themselves strung up by the end of the day. In the silence following Tajirika's departure under the escort of armed policemen, each was busy figuring out how to save his own skin at the expense of the other two.

The Ruler again broke the silence.

"Mr. Sikiokuu," he called out, "you know, don't you, that a good shepherd knows a hyena when he sees one, even if it is in sheep's clothing?"

"Yes, Your Mighty Excellency," Sikiokuu answered quickly, even as he assumed that the Ruler was about to expose Kaniũrũ. "May the Ruler be praised for his great inborn wisdom," added Sikiokuu.

"It comes directly from God," Kaniũrũ opined.

"But it also springs from his own efforts," Sikiokuu said, resenting Kaniũrũ's attempt to join his song of praise. "He has mastered all the book learning."

"He is the true dispenser of knowledge," said Kaniũrũ, "the teacher of teachers, the number one teacher. The Ruler is the source of all the knowledge in the world."

"That's enough," the Ruler said, pretending to be angry with their excess. "It is not good to praise a person in his presence; it might embarrass him."

"I, too, share that sentiment, Your Mighty Excellency," said Sikiokuu. "Oh, you should hear me when I am not in your presence, for that's when I feel most free to sing your gifts."

"I, too, praise you all the time, wherever I am," Machokali said, not to be outdone.

"Deep in my heart," Kaniũrũ said, "I know no calling higher than that of singing your praises at all times because of what you have done and continue to do for us. One day I overheard my own heart saying, *If God and the Ruler were standing together side by side and their hats were blown off their heads at the same time, I would pick up the one that belongs to the Ruler first,* and without realizing it I had said loudly: *Alleluia, may my Lord and Master be praised for ever and ever, Amen.*"

"I am going to ban this business of people putting me on a pedestal with God," said the Ruler, with disingenuous firmness.

"You would turn every person into a lawbreaker, because that is one law that people cannot possibly obey," said Sikiokuu.

"And I am glad that you have come to the point, Mr. Sikiokuu," said the Ruler, "for, as you know, some people have decided to break my laws, and I am determined to crush them. You are a good shepherd, Mr. Sikiokuu, and as we wait for Tajirika to come back with a report on his fieldwork, why don't you tell us what you have done to bring that woman Nyawĩra to justice?"

Sikiokuu had hoped that by now the Ruler was distracted from the case of Nyawīra, so shocking were the detailed reports on the origins of the queuing mania and treason.

"Oh, that woman?" he asked, clearing his throat. "She will soon be in our hands. I am waiting for some things before I pounce on her."

"What things?"

"Mirrors and their handler."

"Their handler?"

"Yes, their handler. Call him their interpreter. I ordered mirrors from Japan, Italy, Sweden, France, Germany, Britain, and the USA," Sikiokuu said with enthusiasm, as if the Ruler knew all about his scheme. "The best mirrors for the matter at hand, as they are not contaminated with my own shadows."

"*Sikiokuu, are you okay?*" asked the Ruler in English. "I mean, in the head?"

"I am fine. I feel great. The handler is the link between the mirror and Nyawīra."

"And who is he, this handler?"

"The Wizard of the Crow."

"The Wizard of the Crow?" he asked.

"The man can look into a mirror and see many things beyond the ken of common eyes."

These revelations made the Ruler wince, like a person who starts walking confidently along a path he believes to be clear of all obstacles only to suddenly step on a thorn. Sikiokuu's passionate avowal of the wizard's abilities rattled him. But he tried his best not to show it, leaning back and closing his eyes. For a second or so he found himself back in a New York hotel room where, as in a dream, he seemed to see a human shadow asking him to look closely at a mirror on the wall.

Sikiokuu had no idea that his words had hit the Ruler hard. He had hoped that the process of tracking down Nyawīra would distract the Ruler from the failure to arrest her. So he continued to chatter enthusiastically about the wizard's powers.

"I believe the man has the gift of second sight and can see into the hearts of men," Sikiokuu added.

"Where did you find this sorcerer?" the Ruler asked, his eyes still closed.

"Right here. In Eldares, Aburĩria."

"When?" the Ruler asked, straightening up, opening his eyes and fixing them on Sikiokuu.

"Before he went to America," said Sikiokuu. "I first heard of the sorcerer's gifts from people who claimed that he could read mirrors like books."

"Let me remind you that actually I am the one who apprised you of the matter," Kaniũrũ said to take credit, but Sikiokuu ignored him.

"All my preparations to capture the woman were going smoothly until news of your illness in America reached us. When I was told that the Wizard of the Crow was needed there, I said that the apprehension of Nyawĩra would have to wait until the return of the Wizard of the Crow. Now here is my problem: the mirrors will arrive shortly, but their interpreter is nowhere to be found."

The story prompted the Ruler to worry that if the sorcerer could really read what was hidden from the common eye, what did he know about the country, no, the Ruler being pregnant? And why had he chosen to impart his wisdom to Machokali instead of . . . he did not even want to complete the thought, for he suddenly felt horrified yet again at being compared to a woman. This sorcerer must be silenced.

"Where is he? Where is the Wizard of the Crow?" the Ruler asked angrily.

"I don't know where he is. Since he went to America . . . perhaps Machokali might care to . . ." Sikiokuu said, trying to shift the burden of the sorcerer's disappearance on Machokali.

"He is not in America," said Machokali curtly, signaling that he did not want to get involved in this issue.

"He is not in Aburĩria. And he is not in America. Where is the sorcerer?" the Ruler demanded. "Surely he must be somewhere on this earth?"

The Ruler suddenly was exhausted by the topic, as it was taking his mind away from more momentous matters. He was now staring straight ahead, entirely preoccupied with what Tajirika might bring him and what he would do to him if he came back empty-handed.

Machokali, who all along had surmised that there was a connection between Sikiokuu and the Wizard of the Crow, now felt malicious joy at the fact that the Ruler had sent a police squad to unearth the dollars. The angrier the Ruler became with the Wizard of the

Crow, the angrier he would be with Sikiokuu once the plot between the minister and the sorcerer was exposed.

"As to where the sorcerer is," said Machokali, "it does not really matter. For what you have done, Your Mighty Excellency, in sending the three policemen to unearth the buried treasure, is an act of unfathomable wisdom and foresight, for even if no dollars are found, the act will serve to expose the lies of this man and his associates," Machokali said.

"Which man? Which lies? The lies told by your friend Tajirika, or the Wizard of the Crow's?" Kaniũrũ asked mischievously.

"Since when did you become a champion of truth?" asked Sikiokuu.

Childish one-upmanship ensued, each trying to have the last word. It is said that they continued thus for seven days and nights and by then they had lost their voices and spoke in whispers so low that they did not hear one another at all. They made out what the others were speaking only through the motion of the veins on their necks and foreheads and the automatic opening and closing of the lips.

The Ruler, however, remained as he was, oblivious to their duel with words, his head resting in his right hand, even as he looked now and then at his watch, waiting for a voice from the prairie to tell him the outcome of the hunt for the buried dollars.

# 8

"True, *Haki ya Mungu,* we also longed for a voice from the prairie," A.G. would tell his listeners, trying anything to win them over so that they could tell him what he then sought among them.

Encouraged by their surrender to his words, A.G. would tell how the foursome of he, Kahiga, Njoya, and Tajirika drove to the Santamaria police station, where they took an unmarked vehicle. They told the police chief, Wonderful Tumbo, that they were going to the prairie to trap Nyawĩra, and that if reports reached the station that there were strangers wandering in the wilderness, Tumbo and his men were to ignore them.

A.G. was excited by the prospect of the adventure as one of the Ruler's messengers, but he thought that his companions were a bit fearful. Tajirika especially: his face was crestfallen, and he did not speak much to Njoya and Kahiga. In fact the three talked through A.G., and he suspected that this was not the first time that the three had met.

They drove some distance into the prairie, stopped the car by an acacia bush, and walked toward the interior, Tajirika leading the way and the others following in a file carrying hoes, spades, and pickaxes.

"We looked like a procession of gold prospectors," A.G. would whisper to his ardent listeners as if imparting a great secret, "with Tajirika as the leader of the party."

Although they were going to dig for dollars, their thoughts were mostly on the Wizard of the Crow, who never ceased to amaze A.G. How many people in Aburĩria would bury money gained from the practice of one's profession, and then disclose the fact and its location to another? A.G., however, was a trifle concerned about the whereabouts of the Wizard of the Crow. Was he in America or Aburĩria?

Njoya and Kahiga were troubled by the whole business and would rather have had nothing to do with it. Since learning that the Wizard of the Crow had not returned from America, they brooded on the threats made by his other; she would no doubt hold them accountable for his disappearance. Not a day went by without their worrying about retribution. Was the mission a setup on her part?

Tajirika saw a trap. Why would anybody bury money anyway? What if someone had already unearthed and taken it away? What if the whole thing was a sorcerer's joke? How could he go back to the Ruler empty-handed? It was clear to him, no matter how he looked at it, that the Wizard of the Crow had put him in a terrible fix.

He had no particular destination. What they were looking for, according to Tajirika, was a bush among countless bushes. The Wizard of the Crow had not described the particulars; he had just talked about a bush in the prairie not too far from Santalucia. Where exactly should their search begin?

"True, *Haki ya Mungu,* we stayed in the prairie for I don't know how long, digging holes in the ground like ants," A.G. said. "Nobody from Santalucia or anywhere came to question or trouble us in any way. We were fatigued by the routine, searching and digging day and night, endlessly. I took it upon myself to tell the others, Listen to me: even God when he created Heaven and Earth rested on the seventh day, but we have already worked for more than seven days. What are we trying to prove? Only Tajirika demurred; we accused him of opposing rest because he did no work except move from bush to bush, and hearing this he took a pickax and started digging furiously to show us how a man should apply himself. We stood by and watched him dig nonstop like a crazy person, till he collapsed in one hole and we had to drag him out, and I tell you, by then we were so exhausted that we too collapsed beside the body of our leader, falling asleep."

They slept for several days. What met their eyes when eventually they woke up were endless anthills, like mounds of earth, scattered all over the prairie. Kahiga and Njoya suggested that Tajirika should call the State House to let the Ruler know that they had been unable to find the bags of dollars. Tajirika fiercely objected and adamantly insisted: "We must continue with digging until we find the money." Njoya and Kahiga were just as adamant that the digging of holes should be left to archaeologists, prospectors, and miners of precious metals. All visible terrain had been dug up to no avail. They would sooner rob a bank than lift another pickax.

Tajirika begged them to persist one more day, but really they were weak and had lost all hope. A.G., who had not taken sides in the dispute, now intervened and told them all that he was tired of their endless wrangling, that while he would abide by whatever decision they arrived at, for now he simply wanted some space to himself: he stood up and started walking deeper into the bush.

Kahiga and Njoya followed him so as not to break the law that bound them to keep an eye on one another. Tajirika ran after them, imploring them not to shun their duty or leave him in the prairie alone. Not that he himself had much energy left.

When he came to this point in his narrative, A.G. would pause and ask his audience dramatically: Why do you think I am stressing exhaustion? But before anybody could respond, A.G. would answer his own question.

"I don't know what it was—maybe the bush made me think about the night I chased the Wizard of the Crow in his guise as a beggar or two all the way from Paradise to Santalucia. Just as on that night I felt driven by a force so powerful that I could not stop even if I tried, so too on this night, true, *Haki ya Mungu,* I felt myself propelled by a power unknown to me. At one point I almost tripped over a ridge. I stopped. Before me was a rock ridge cleft into two, the space between them covered by grass and wild growth.

"All of a sudden I had a funny feeling in my belly for, true, *Haki ya Mungu,* when I looked all around, I remembered being in the same bush the night I ran after the Wizard of the Crow, and that this was the same ridge over which I had tripped and fallen, losing him, or both of them, or whatever. Later, I would come to learn that my fall had not been accidental, that it had been the work of the wizard. *But what is the meaning of the coincidence now?* I asked myself. Had the Wizard of the Crow buried the treasure here, guarded by the powers of the netherworld?

"I sat down on the rock and Kahiga, Njoya, and Tajirika followed suit in silence, for, to be very honest, speech had become unbearable, a burden. We were absorbed in our own thoughts, yes, but I heard myself saying to my companions, The Wizard of the Crow is capable of many tricks. I once chased him across the prairie, and I believe that he led me through a place like this . . . I thought that they would take up the subject, but none seemed interested in what I was saying. In our own isolation, we all were wrestling with the daemons that so possess a person exhausted in mind, body, and spirit that they make him begin to imagine seeing bright stars in daylight . . ."

Tajirika thought he was seeing things. The leaves of the three bushes in front of him were no ordinary leaves, but, no, he could not believe his eyes, and he tried to cry out to the others. He could not find words to tell them what he was seeing so he just pointed, whispering hoarsely, Look, please look, and tell me if this is not more trickery by the Wizard of the Crow. Tell me if those are not American dollars growing on those bushes?

"None of us could believe what we were hearing. We looked at one another with the same thought: Money growing on trees? Tajirika had gone mad. On closer inspection, we had to agree that those leaves did look like American dollars. Yet we harbored doubts, which disappeared when Tajirika took money from his pocket and, with hands shaking, approached the bushes to compare what he had in his hands with what was there. True, *Haki ya Mungu,* from where we sat, nobody could tell the difference between the two; if anything, those that grew on the bushes seemed smoother and greener, a little less wrinkled, than the bills from Tajirika's pocket. Some of the leaves had tiny holes in them and others were frayed at the edges, but Tajirika, our leader, explained that this was the work of worms and other insects who did not understand the value of a dollar."

Tajirika fell on his knees before the bushes and started sobbing with joy like a death-row inmate whose sentence had been commuted when execution seemed inevitable and imminent.

We are saved! he cried, and the others said Amen in unison.

# 9

Kaniũrũ, Machokali, and Sikiokuu sat as if frozen in time, bickering. The Ruler continued to check his watch now and then, oblivious of them. It is said that, in the light of the weirdness of the scene, heads of the police and army eventually came into the hall to see if something was the matter. But, ascertaining that the Ruler was wide awake, they retreated, muttering to themselves, Politicians do love talking, don't they, marveling at their ability to confer even in silence. Not like us, men of action, they said to themselves, resolving not to disturb them again. Let them talk till the end of time if they so desire.

The telephone rang, and the Ruler picked up the receiver.

"What? What did you say?" the Ruler was asking. His face darkened and his hands shook, sending a tremor through his whole body. The entire State House, the whole country, and the people, feeling the earthquake, recalled the seismatic disturbance during the Ruler's return from America. On the telephone, unaware of the effect of his shock, the Ruler continued:

"How can that be? . . . *Are you pulling my leg?*" he asked in English "Three of them? . . . Okay, okay, wait a minute . . ."

He tried to cover the mouthpiece with one hand but, failing, rested it on his prodigious belly and turned to Machokali, Sikiokuu, and Kaniũrũ, looking at them as if he were seeing them for the first time and asking himself, What are these intruders doing here? Then he remembered that it was their arguments and bickering that had kept him awake:

"Go," he told them. "I will settle your case another day."

As they stood up to leave, he commanded them to stop exactly where they stood and to listen to him very carefully. Because he did not ever want to hear that any of them had so much as whispered what they had seen or heard during their stay at the State House, he would require them to sign a pledge: *I will never reveal whatever I have seard or seen in the State House.* He would match the degree of forgiveness to the quantity of signed pledges. He then asked some police to lock them up in their different locations within the State House.

They had hardly left the room when the Ruler resumed his telephone conversation: "Are you still there? . . . Good, now tell me, are you sure about all this? The four of you? . . ."

# 10

He gave orders to the army chief to send three armored cars to the prairie as fast as possible to retrieve the dollar trees and the precious soil in which they grew. And they were to return as slowly as a tortoise so as to risk nothing. Emotions welled up inside: he smarted at the recent humiliations he had suffered at its hands; now he was freed of the need for the Global Bank. How happy he would be to look the Global Bank directors in the eye, with all the contempt he could muster, and tell them to shove it. No more memoranda to those impertinent fools. He would simply relish his newfound wealth. May these money-producing trees live forever! Impatient though he was for the arrival of his men from the prairie, he was still glad that he had cautioned against the armored cars rushing back to prevent the possibility of any of the soil falling by the wayside.

When they saw the convoy, armed with all manner of firepower, slowly making its way into Eldares, citizens, fearing a coup d'état, hid behind closed doors. How happy the Ruler was when, after seven days of anxious waiting, he heard the roll of the convoy on the grounds of the State House! Given his present condition, he could not, of course, go out to meet it but instead ordered the police and army chiefs to see to the immediate delivery of the bounty without the usual security checks.

# 11

It is difficult, even today, to make sense of what happened afterward. Even A.G., despite his gift of words, was taciturn, but people claimed that this was because he, Tajirika, Njoya, and Kahiga had been sworn to secrecy under the penalty of their tongues being cut out for blabbering. But when they would close in on him and beg him to explain with ardent pleas enriched by generous offers of drink, A.G. would tell them to gather around so he could whisper a thing or two. And indeed, true to his word, A.G. would tell this part of the story in a whisper so low that it was hard for some listeners to make out all that he was saying, but they would refrain from interrupting him lest he change his mind and leave the story untold. He spoke loudly only when he paused to swear "True, *Haki ya Mungu,*" his way of punctuating what might otherwise have seemed too incredible a narrative of magic and greed.

"We were each told to stand behind each present, wrapped in sisal, and, in turns, untie them under the Ruler's watchful eyes. Kahiga was first to unwrap his. It took him a while because his hands were shaking uncontrollably. This was not chiefly from fear or fatigue. Kahiga was certain, as was I, that as soon as the Ruler beheld what we had brought him, he would, out of gratitude, raise our salaries or ranks or both."

At this point A.G. would whisper even lower, and some frustrated listeners, believing that he had really lost his voice, would get up to leave, allowing that rumors of what he would say would overtake them anyway.

"People, how shall I put what happened next? If I had not been there and seen it with my own eyes, I myself would not believe it," A.G. would whisper and then shout, "True, *Haki ya Mungu!*" so suddenly and unexpectedly that he would startle his listeners, stopping even those about to leave dead in their tracks, now convinced that it was better to hear the story from the horse's own mouth than secondhand.

"So what happened?" they would ask him, and A.G. would take his time, shaking his head as if still incredulous at what he had seen and heard.

"You mean after Kahiga unwrapped his parcel?" he would ask to make sure that he understood the question precisely.

"Yes, yes," his listeners would say in unison.

"Kahiga's jaw fell," he would say, and then pause to let the image etch itself properly in their memories.

"Why? Why?"

"The pestilence. They had the body of a white termite and the head and mandibles of a red ant. How can I describe them? They were as big as locusts. I don't even know if they were termites, but I may be wrong. There are more than two thousand species, and these could have been one of them or a mutant breed. I'll just call them pests, white pests."

"What are you talking about?" they would ask, wondering if the storyteller had had one beer too many. "All the leaves and all the roots of the bush had been eaten by the pests, leaving nothing but bare twigs."

Kahiga and Njoya cried out in unison, *What is this?*

Kahiga rushed and turned over the soil, as he recounted, to see if the leaves were buried there, only to find more termites fattened to the size of big worms or caterpillars after feasting on leaves of money for more than seven days. He, like the others, could not say what was more amazing, the size of the termitelike creatures or the fact that the pests had eaten all the money.

The Ruler did not utter a word but pointed to the next parcel and its guardian.

It was Njoya's turn. Here, too, the termites had eaten all the leaves as well as the bark, leaving the plant completely denuded.

And now came A.G.'s turn.

"The termites had not been as thorough with mine; they were still devouring the few remaining leaves before our very eyes. I quickly brushed the pests away; they fell to the floor, leaving shreds of money dangling as if to mock me. Now I can say that the protective magic of the Wizard of the Crow had served me well, for, judging by the look in the Ruler's eyes, none of us would be breathing today but for those remnants of leaves. True! *Haki ya Mungu,* I believe they saved us from his wrath, for they had enough green left on them to show that there may have been a time when they had the fuller greenness of a natural dollar."

Tajirika, heretofore dumbstruck and immobile, now ran to try to put the shreds together and back on the bush, provoking the first word from the Ruler.

Stop! he yelled.

The Ruler stared at the scene, brooding on the fate of we mortal sinners. Frozen with anger, he pondered how best to express his wrath.

Tajirika felt all of his joints drained of strength, as did Njoya and Kahiga, who concluded that the retribution promised by the deputy wizard they had encountered was about to be visited on them.

Kahiga decided to deflect the blame.

"We two had suggested that we pick the leaves right away," he told the Ruler and, pointing at Tajirika, continued, "But this man over-ruled us and insisted that we pull out the bushes by the roots together with the soil. Your Mighty Excellency, it is a well-known fact that these pests build their termitaries in the prairie."

"And so this fiasco would have been avoided," said Njoya, "if we had picked the money and left the stems and the roots in the prairie."

"Beware of this man, O Mighty Excellency. He is very bad, and his head is full of dangerous trickery," Kahiga added with a hint of passion.

"He once held a whole police camp hostage with a bucket of shit and urine," added Njoya in agreement.

"Is that true?" the Ruler asked Tajirika.

Tajirika did not answer immediately, unsure as he was whether the Ruler was asking him about the bucket of shit or the manner in which the treasure had been uprooted.

"I don't know what these two are accusing me of. I was simply carrying out your orders," Tajirika said.

"My orders? To hold hostage an armed police camp with only shit and urine?"

"Oh, no, not that," Tajirika said, now aware where things were headed. "Your Mighty Excellency, some things are difficult to explain."

"I did not ask you to explain anything. I asked you whether these allegations concerning the police camp are true. Was it the first act of a coup attempt?"

"A coup against you? Never. I would kill myself first. Go back to my ancestors."

"I will turn you into an ancestor. A spirit, if you don't explain."

These two policemen must really hate me, Tajirika said to himself. I'm sure I shall not leave this place alive. But instead of despairing, he bolstered his sagging spirits by recalling the saying that even an animal about to be slaughtered tries to kick those leading it to the slaughterhouse.

"Your Mighty Excellency, as I told you the other day, it was all Sikiokuu's fault. He had me arrested for nothing whatsoever. He then tried to convert me to a religious sect that believes in St. Thomas and Descartes, one of his French disciples. When I refused, he locked me up and put the Wizard of the Crow in the same cell at midnight, the witching hour. What could I do, Your Mighty Excellency, but seize the only means left to fashion my escape? Believe me, Your Lordship, this Wizard of the Crow is no pushover—he is capable of anything. He has been the bane of my life, always after me. He started the queuing mania. He made me contract that strange malady of words, and why? So that I would go to him for a cure. And he, like Satan of old, first lured my wife. He deceived my gullible woman into handing over the bags of money under the pretext that he would set things right. But what does he do with the bags? He plants them in the prairie, then comes to my cell under the cover of darkness to tell me where to find them. Now, after seeing what these pests have done, I wonder whether they were termites after all. I wish we had hearkened to the words of A.G. when he tried to tell us about the night he chased the Wizard of the Crow across the same prairie. If we had, we might have figured out that the Wizard of the Crow had already bewitched the place. We would have known that all was not well even when it looked well."

"There, Tajirika has said well," A.G. interrupted, happy at the implicit praise and Tajirika's acknowledgment of his thwarted attempt to narrate the story of the famous chase.

A.G. loved telling the story of the night he chased two beggars who, on jumping over a cleft rock in the prairie, turned out to be one person. He knew that the Ruler knew about his chasing the djinns of the prairie, but not from the horse's own mouth. How blessed he would be if the Ruler were now his audience? Here was his opportunity. He cleared his throat, ready to tell the story.

"True, *Haki ya Mungu*," A.G. began, "a force I cannot explain from whence it came was propelling me, but when we reached the ridge, the force subsided and suddenly stopped. It was then that I recalled the night that the Wizard of the Crow had split himself into two powerful djinns. Your Mighty Highness, I am not a Muslim, but, True! *Haki ya Mungu,* if you read the Holy Quran, you can see that djinns are . . ."

"Yes, there is no doubt that the Wizard of the Crow belongs to a family of djinns," interrupted Kahiga, a little envious that A.G. had taken center stage.

"A dangerous spirit. And that's why we had warned Sikiokuu not to lock up the sorcerer," Njoya added.

"But instead of heeding our warning, he ordered us to put him in the same cell with Tajirika," Kahiga continued.

"So you two have seen the sorcerer with your own eyes?" the Ruler asked, as if he had forgotten that the police officers had been selected to be part of the expedition because of their previous connection with the wizard. But to Kahiga, it seemed as if they had succeeded in distracting the Ruler from the issue of the money trees and the termites, and, really, Kahiga did not mind that at all.

"Actually, my partner here and I were the ones who went to get him from his shrine," said Kahiga.

"But it was Sikiokuu who sent us," added Njoya.

"So that the sorcerer would help us ferret out Nyawĩra."

"The mistake he made was locking him up for no good reason instead of being simply persuasive," Njoya said.

"And mark you, we had told him quite strongly that such action against the wizard could bring harm to the country," added Kahiga.

"But he responded by saying that the Wizard of the Crow was not a deity," Njoya said accusingly.

"And he dismissed us from his presence, saying that when he needed our advice on matters of sorcery, he would call us," added Njoya.

"So when we heard about your illness . . ."

"We knew right away that the Wizard of the Crow . . ."

"Had something to do with it . . ."

"We were happy to take him to the airport for the flight to America . . ."

"But we became very apprehensive when we heard that he had returned to Aburīria without anybody seeing him . . ."

"It is now clear, Your Mighty Excellency," Tajirika jumped into the conversation, not to be left out, "that it is the Wizard of the Crow who produced these white termites. Yes, the Wizard of the Crow is the one who sent these pests. Have you ever seen termites this size, Your Mighty Excellency?"

"Did you say *sent* them?" A.G. asked rhetorically. "He is capable of turning himself into a termite and multiplying. For, as I was saying before Kahiga interrupted me, the night I chased the Wizard of the Crow from Paradise across the prairie . . . Shall I start from the beginning, Your Mighty Excellency?"

He stopped abruptly and looked to see what had caught the attention of the Ruler. It was not only the Ruler. All eyes had turned to the floor. Some termites were crawling all over the carpet; others were climbing up the walls; yet others slid through thresholds leading to the other rooms.

Where had all these termites sprung from? The Ruler frowned, but Tajirika, Kahiga, Njoya, and A.G. could not tell what his frown portended, and they glanced at one another with the same fear. Would he jail them? Would he simply dismiss them from their jobs on the police force? Or would he exact his vengeance only on Tajirika? They assumed the worst as they waited for him to rage.

But none anticipated anything remotely resembling the Ruler's reaction. It was the tone of his voice that first caught them unaware. He spoke like an elder talking to his children about matters he himself had experienced. He was soothing as he told them not to worry about what had happened and actually commended them for doing their best, considering the treacherous, cunning mind they had been up against. They should have no fear, he told them, for the cunning fellow would never outsmart the Ruler. He told them to remain seated and be patient, that he wanted a couple of ministers to join them as he, their Ruler, announced what was to be done about the dangerous mind.

But he enjoined them not to so much as whisper about the money trees or the termites. This was now a state secret.

"Do you hear me?" he asked, now looking at A.G., Kahiga, and Njoya in turn. "You must never even dream about plants that produce natural dollars or any other currency, or I will turn your dream into a nightmare."

What's going on? they wondered, baffled by the unexpected reaction.

"I will now send for the ministers . . ." the Ruler said, and he was about to instruct his minions when he suddenly remembered that Machokali, Sikiokuu, and Kaniũrũ were still sequestered in separate rooms to write down their pledges. He had forgotten all about them during the period of waiting for the treasure from the prairie.

Now he sent the three police officers to fetch them. The Ruler and Tajirika were left alone.

# 12

"I have reviewed many things in my mind," the Ruler started as soon as Machokali, Kaniũrũ, and Sikiokuu were brought before him, "and I now know the identity of the real enemy of the country. But in order for me to wage an effective fight against this enemy, there are a few things I want to straighten out. Sikiokuu?"

"Your Mighty Excellency?"

"When I summoned you here, what did I tell you? That when I was in America I was informed that there are people going around the country preaching the virtues of queuing in my name. I was also told about women beating up their menfolk in accordance with the judgment of some sort of people's court. So far you have said nothing about these matters. You told me that you stationed M5s all over the country. So are there other men, apart from Tajirika, who have been tried and beaten up by this female people's court?"

Sikiokuu did not know if the Ruler knew something that he did not know. So he was not sure what was most prudent to say: yes or no. He tried to evade the question.

"Your Mighty Excellency, if you have read the two reports that—"

"They say nothing about the matters at hand," the Ruler said curtly.

"Our Mighty Excellency, there are many security issues that require only your ears and mine," said Sikiokuu, tugging at his earlobes. "There are some among us here who cannot be trusted with any secrets," he added, his eyes darting at Kaniũrũ.

"Like whom?"

"Let me speak frankly. Like Kaniũrũ."

"But you trusted him enough to recommend him to me as chairman of the Commission of Inquiry into the Origins of the Queuing Mania?"

"Yes, Your Mighty Excellency, but—"

"And you trusted him well enough to order him to look into the people's court?"

"Yes, Your Mighty Excellency, but—"

"And you trust his report sufficiently to ask me whether I had read it?"

"Yes, no, but—"

"But what?" scoffed the Ruler as he turned his eyes to the others. "I want to expand the Directorate of Security Services, DSS, currently led by the Minister of State in the Office of the Ruler, Silver Sikiokuu, and create within it a subdepartment, or a special unit, in charge of Youth and Women Affairs. Many a government in the world has been brought to ruin because it had been lax and allowed students, youth, and women to say and do whatever without proper guidance and supervision. The sole responsibility of the unit I am now creating is to oversee the activities of these segments of the population. John Kaniũrũ, stand up. You have proven that you can be trusted to organize youth and be tough with women, even the wives of the rich and the powerful. Effective today, you are Head of Research Regarding Youth and Women's Conformity with National Ideals. Your main task is to continue to investigate and combat any manifestations of the queuing mania and to investigate and put an end to this domestic violence against men. ASS Kahiga will assist you in organizing an effective system of surveillance."

Kaniũrũ pranced about in joy and disbelief. Kahiga did not know whether to follow Kaniũrũ's example and jump up and down, elated, or risk seeming ungrateful by remaining seated. For a second or two Peter Kahiga was unable to figure out what he had actually heard. He had been referred to as ASS, whereas before today he had only one S. Now two and an A to boot. Should he ask the Ruler to clarify his honorific? His uncertainty disappeared with the Ruler's next words.

"I want the leaders of rebellious youth and women to be crushed like ants, and I don't think this should pose a problem to Assistant Senior Superintendent Peter Kahiga."

Kahiga felt his heart skip a beat. The other wizard had yet to seek retribution. For now he was safe and felt joy in his heart. He now rose and ran a lap of victory around the room. The Ruler gestured for Kaniũrũ and Kahiga to resume their positions, and he told them that the State House was not an athletic field, that they should remember that they were in Aburĩria, that if they wanted to be runners they should emigrate to Kenya or Ethiopia.

"May I say a word," Sikiokuu said, stung by the promotion of this traitor. "You asked me about queues and the queuing mania. Since you banned the mania, queues have not come back. I am confident when I say that the queues are practically gone. In addition, I have already lined up people to report to me should there be a resurgence of the mania anywhere in Aburĩria," he added, hoping that further inquiry into the queuing mania would be denied as a mandate to the proposed unit.

"So if I hear that the queuing mania has resurfaced, I will have heard lies?" asked the Ruler.

"Well, not lies, but misinformation," said Sikiokuu. "I can say that whoever were to tell you this would not be in possession of all the facts, and he should have checked with me. Some people will say anything to get promoted," he added, glancing at Kaniũrũ, who he assumed had lied yet again.

As the Ruler still resented the way the Global Bankers had condescended to him as if they knew more about his own country than he did, he did not mind hearing Sikiokuu's reassurance, though his suspicions about the motives of the Global Bank in urging him to return home increased.

"You have done well to contain the queuing mania," said the Ruler, "but this does not mean that we should become any less vigilant. What do the English say? The price of internal vigilance is freedom."

"Thank you, Your Mighty Excellency, for your faith in my abilities," said Sikiokuu, though he was sure that the Ruler had jumbled the words of the English proverb.

"Yes, Sikiokuu, and here is one more test for you," said the Ruler. "I want you to come up with a repayment plan for the money you have made so far on Marching to Heaven," he said curtly. "And another thing: before I went to the USA, I instructed you to comb the land, leaving no stone unturned, to find that woman Nyawīra. I have been back for several weeks, and no one has come to tell me she is in custody. If you thought that I was going to relieve you of this duty, think again. Put aside your envy of other people's abilities and deliver her to me. I will make it easier for you. ASS Njoya will assist you. *Here is the deal.* If you bring me the woman, I may even forgive the money you owe me."

The Ruler is truly gifted with the carrot and the stick, Sikiokuu said to himself, grateful that he had not been fired from his ministry and had retained one of his loyalists, Njoya. But still, he smarted at the thought that Kaniūrū had been promoted and given a subdivision to head. Sikiokuu foresaw nothing but conflict.

"Your Mighty Excellency, I would like a clarification of the chain of command. To whom will Kaniūrū be reporting?"

"Kaniūrū's unit is part of your ministry, so he will be reporting to you most of the time and me, sometimes, as I see fit. *Is that clear enough?*"

"Yes, sir," Sikiokuu said, although he could see that his hands were now tied.

"What did I tell you?" the Ruler asked them before answering his own question. "I know who the real enemy of the country is." He paused and stared at each of their faces, finally resting his eyes on Machokali. "And I will tell him this," he said, wagging a finger at Machokali as if to identify the culprit, "wherever he is, he might think he is very cunning, but . . ."

Anger silenced the Ruler for a few seconds, as if all the pain he felt, all the troubles he had been through, all the humiliations he had endured, were flooding his brain.

It was not clear to Machokali where the Ruler was headed. At first he was happy about Kaniũrũ's rise because it meant Sikiokuu's demotion. But now with that wagging finger directed at him . . . ?

"Any questions?" the Ruler asked, to buy time to compose himself.

Kaniũrũ stood up. He cast an eye of triumph first at Sikiokuu, then at Machokali, and finally at Tajirika, and he was even more joyous to see Tajirika cowering with fear of the unknown that awaited him. Kaniũrũ seized this moment to ask to be made full chairman of Marching to Heaven.

"Speaking on my own behalf and on behalf of all the others . . ."

"Speak for yourself . . ." Sikiokuu and Machokali struck back in unison.

"Okay. Speaking on my own behalf, and on behalf of everybody who knows the meaning of patriotism, I will repeat what I said the other day. Your Mighty Excellency, you will recall that I said that if a hurricane were to blow God's hat and yours off your heads at the same time, I would pick yours up first. I know you have warned us against comparing you to God, but my Lord and Master I cannot help it. *Asante sana,* my Lord. I have a tiny request. May I?"

"Ask and it shall be given."

"What about the deputy chair of Marching to Heaven?"

"He will still be reporting to the chairman."

"And who is he?" Kaniũrũ asked, almost certain that he would be asked to take on the full chairmanship.

"Thank you for asking," said the Ruler. "I was about to forget. Allow me to introduce the Governor of the Central Bank to you."

They turned their eyes to the door to see the new governor. But they saw nobody come through.

"Titus Tajirika, my new Governor of the Central Bank and Permanent Chairman of Marching to Heaven, please stand up and be properly acknowledged."

They could hardly believe their ears. Even Tajirika first looked over his shoulder as if there was another person with the same name. But when he understood that the reference was to himself, Tajirika fell to his knees in humility and gratitude, even as the others were terrified by the potential consequences of his elevation.

"Our Holy and Mighty Excellency," he said. "I don't know how to thank you. You are a deity who dispenses fair justice to us mortals, giving hope where there is despair, even resurrecting dead souls. How can I repay your tender mercies? I renew my pledge: Now and forever, your enemy is my enemy."

Kaniũrũ saw an opportunity for him to show that he appreciated his elevation better than had Tajirika his. He got to his feet and jumped into the arena.

"Down with the enemies of the Ruler!" he shouted.

"Down with all the enemies of the Mighty Ruler!" Sikiokuu shouted, not to be outdone by Kaniũrũ.

"Down with every enemy of the Mightiest Ruler!" joined in Machokali, not to be left out of the circle of praise singers.

These people may have been tired after seven days and nights of writing the pledge over and over again, but now their rivalry gave them a new lease of energy as they, now on their feet, tried to outdo one another in barking out their hatred of the Ruler's enemies. They would have gone on, out of the fear of losing the right of the last word to the others, but the Ruler himself shouted at them, Down with all of you, in response to which they now suddenly shut up and retreated to their seats.

But Kaniũrũ, Sikiokuu, and Machokali did not even take one step forward. They stopped and stood there, frozen to the ground with fear, each gazing with wide-open eyes at the scene before him. Tajirika, A.G., Kahiga, and Njoya turned around to see what it was that had made them freeze.

"True! *Haki ya Mungu!*" A.G. would later tell his listeners. "Even the Ruler seemed shaken. Wouldn't you if you saw termites building anthills on the floor and walls before your very eyes? The Ruler knew as I knew that this was the work of the Wizard of the Crow . . ."

With white termites multiplying ad nauseam in the room, the Ruler could no longer afford to ignore the powers of the Wizard of the Crow, a threat to his perceived omnipotence. This sorcerer had insulted him by calling him a woman, even claiming he was pregnant, had sparked the queuing mania, had inspired wives to rise against their husbands, and now this: an infinitude of white termites making mounds of earth inside his palace! This man could not be left free to roam the country. Neither could he be left with a power that the Ruler did not possess! He would have him apprehended and soften him with flattery and promises till he revealed the secrets of his knowledge: how to cultivate money trees and divine through mirrors. Having incorporated the powers of the wizard into himself, the Ruler would have him thrown into a dungeon, fry the pig in his own fat, for the Ruler now intended nothing short of becoming sorcerer number one.

Heaving with rage and expectation, the Ruler ordered Kaniũrũ, Sikiokuu, and Machokali to stand up.

"Whoever has wax in his ears, dig it out so that you can hear clearly what I have to say. Machokali. Bring the Wizard of the Crow to me. With the assistance of SS Arigaigai Gathere, bring him to me not dead in a shroud but alive in chains. And to you three: From today on I want to see results. I want to see which of you will be first to complete his task!"

The competition to see who would come out on top in the three-way rivalry among Kaniũrũ, Sikiokuu, and Machokali would start in earnest, paling in intensity and expected outcome, next to their writing down of the pledge, about which the Ruler had said nothing. The prize for success, each thought, would be exhilarating, the cost of failure fatal.

He dismissed all except his newly appointed governor of the Central Bank. He felt good about the decisions made; he had finally started to take full control of events since the Global Bank mission and his own calamitous visit to America, returning empty-handed.

"And now, Governor Titus . . ." He smiled, welcoming Tajirika to the inner counsel.

# 13

One day a man on a motorcycle arrived at the police headquarters in Eldares, demanding to see the police chief urgently. His hair was down to his shoulders; his beard reached his knees. His clothes were more like rags and the paint on his beaten up motorcycle was long gone, though on closer scrutiny one might have imagined the color red. Had he not shown his badge of office, nobody would have believed that he was a policeman: the police chief would not have wasted so much as a minute on him. Responding to puzzlement, he claimed that he was one of five police riders dispatched to all corners of the country to tell people about the virtues of queuing. When was this? he was asked, and he could not remember how long ago or how long he had been gone; all he knew was that he had been ordered by his superiors not to return without accomplishing his mission. When the bearded rider was asked about his four fellow riders, he said he did not know their fate, and that if they had not yet returned, he clearly had won the race. What race? the police chief asked. The race to prolong the queuing, of course. The bearded rider seemed irritated by what seemed pointless questions when he had more important news to deliver: that in the central region, school kids, following in the footsteps of the university students, were forming queues, not for food in the cafeteria but to demand additional books and teachers and an education that would teach them about their own country and its relation to the world. Were these old or new queues? To tell the truth, he said, there was no discernible difference between the old and the new, for all had neither beginning nor end. The police chief rushed the report to Sikiokuu, who rushed it to the Ruler, who at first reacted with an angry frown, as if to say, What is this nonsense you bring to me? But, recalling what the Global Bank in New York had told him, that there were people going around his country preaching the virtues of queuing, and considering that this had ended his visit abruptly and might even have cost him the loan for Marching to Heaven, and now, realizing that the agents for this sedition were members of his security team, he ordered the rider to face a firing squad and the Minister of Information, Big Ben Mambo, to announce this on the airwaves, as a warning to any other miscreants in his armed forces.

The rider would have been executed except for his pleas that they should not kill the Ruler's messenger without reading a note he had sewn inside his jacket to ensure its safety. And, sure enough, the piece of paper was discovered, and when the police unfolded it, they saw its heading, *Messengers of the Ruler,* and a line below, *To My Messenger to the Central Region,* followed by a directive to the rider to tour the region spreading the gospel of queuing. It said that the Ruler would be pleased with those who had heeded the call, and, most important, it ended with the Ruler's clearly legible signature. The police chief referred the matter to Sikiokuu, who remembered writing such words and who took the piece of paper to the Ruler, who, when he saw that the signature was his, rescinded the earlier order and said that the rider should be told that the Ruler had felt mercy. The rider was to go away, shave, and cut his hair short, then take an indefinite leave without pay. The rider pleaded, pointing out that he had faithfully executed the spirit and letter of the Ruler's command, setting in motion another round of consultations, after which he was assured that he could return to duty after several months of needed rest; he would be put under Kaniũrũ's command as a road specialist in case it became necessary to track the students of the central region.

# 14

Kaniũrũ could not believe his luck. He had not known where or how he would start the search, but now? He hated university students with a passion, for their radicalism had deprived him of a good wife. If Nyawĩra had not entered student politics, she might very well still be living under his protective wings. He dwelled on the news brought by the crazy rider. These students had been behind the snake incident at the aborted birthday ceremony. They were definitely behind the recent queuing mania. Kaniũrũ recalled that even the Ruler had said that students and youth caused the downfall of many a government. And all at once he saw the solution, simple but effective. Crush the university students, and all forms of queuing would come to an end. But how would he go about it? The students had been poisonously indoctrinated. Empty their heads of all foolishness and fill them with good and correct ideas supportive of the State. But how would the government go about this?

Kaniũrũ recalled that, according to the recent reports, the students were demanding to be taught about their own country first. Was the Ruler not the Country? Kaniũrũ immediately got pen and paper and started drafting a memorandum for a new national education program. Everybody in Aburĩria knew that the Ruler was the supreme educator. Teacher number one. So all institutions of learning, from primary schools to university colleges, would be required to teach only those ideas that came from the supreme educator. They would be required to offer the Ruler's mathematics, the Ruler's science (biology, physics, and chemistry), the Ruler's philosophy, and the Ruler's history; and this would definitely take care of their demands to know their country first. But the students also wanted to be taught how their country was related to other regions of the world. That was also quite simple. They would be taught the geography and demographics of all the countries the Ruler had visited or intended to visit. As for the books to read, this too was simple. In recognition of the fact that the Ruler was the number one writer, all books published in the country would carry the name of the Ruler as the original author. Anybody who aspired to write and publish could do so only under the name of the Ruler, who would allow his name only on those books carefully examined and permitted by the subdepartment of Youth Conformity. All new editions of the Bible, the Quran, the Torah, and even Buddha's Book of Light, or any other religious texts read in schools, would have prefaces and introductions by the Ruler. Such an education system was bound to produce students with a uniform knowledge streaming from the same source: the Ruler or those imbued with his thought.

Kaniũrũ formed an advisory board consisting of university professors from history, literature, political science, law, philosophy, and the sciences. They were all members of the Mighty Youth and under his command. He gave them the memorandum and asked them to look at it critically and make comments and necessary corrections, but they all came back full of praise: the document was well written and it contained the best educational program they had ever seen. They sat down to work out the best way of effecting this educational initiative, and they were all of the view that the best way was to sell the idea to university and secondary school students. Once the students had accepted it, and the advisory board did not see a problem in this, since the memorandum had met all the student demands, Kaniũrũ would present it to the Ruler for it to become the official government policy on education. They gave the memorandum a weighty but memorable title: *The Kaniūrū Memorandum on New Educational Initiatives for Youth and Women to Make Their Minds Conform to National Ideals and the Ruler's Philosophy.*

One of the professors, a specialist in all aspects of parrotology, came up with the idea of regional seminars to educate students and the public about the new educational program. The first seminar was to be held in Eldares, and Kaniūrū was charged, at his own suggestion, with seeing whether the Ruler himself would open the proceedings.

Kaniūrū simmered in joy. He knew that the Ruler could not make it to the seminar. But he did not mind his name being mentioned in the same breath as the Ruler's. But a message, a word or two of greetings from the Ruler, would suffice.

# 15

There is nobody quicker to anger than a thief who has been robbed. This adage was no less true in the case of Silver Sikiokuu, Minister of State in the Ruler's Office, for though over the years he had extorted bribes in the millions and did not see anything wrong with that, he now felt hurt and aggrieved that the Ruler had ordered him to repay money of which he had not seen a cent. He had been clueless about Kaniūrū's exploitation scheme in connection with Marching to Heaven. What pissed him off even more was that he had groomed the youthwinger into prominence. Why are people so untrustworthy? he asked himself time and again. How could Kaniūrū be so ungrateful to his benefactor? He thought of avenging himself against Kaniūrū, but he could not figure out how to land a stinging blow. The only light in his dark night was the Ruler's promise to relieve him of his debt should Nyawīra be captured. But so far she had proved depressingly elusive.

One day, in the throes of his agony, Sikiokuu received a notice about a parcel awaiting him at customs. He dispatched a courier to fetch it. It was one of the mirrors he had ordered from London, and it was soon followed by many more from Tokyo, Rome, Stockholm, Paris, Berlin, and Washington.

Sikiokuu shook his ears for joy at the goodness of the omen. He started imagining how he would capture Nyawīra, drag her before the Ruler, and dramatically announce: Here is your enemy—what do you want me to do with her? What would the Ruler say? You have done well, you faithful and loyal minister, and I forgive the money you owe me; from now on you may do whatever you want to those who have wronged you and especially those who have falsely accused you of corrupting the bidding process of Marching to Heaven. However, the clarity of his daydreams was muddled by a concern: the mirrors are here, but where is their handler and interpreter? Where is the Wizard of the Crow?

Sikiokuu was not happy that the Ruler had assigned the task of capturing the Wizard of the Crow to Machokali, because he still harbored fears that the wizard might disclose to his archenemy what he had gleaned about Sikiokuu's ambitions. He would have wanted the task for himself, though he was ambivalent as to what to do with the wizard. On the one hand, Sikiokuu wanted him dead; yet the wizard was his only hope for finding Nyawīra. But what was Machokali up to? What had he set in motion to effect the capture of the Wizard of the Crow? He knew that Machokali would not disclose anything to him, that far from enlightening him he would more likely mislead him. Sikiokuu decided that he had to get to the Wizard of the Crow first. So the race was on.

He set up a surveillance team to spy and report on the activities and movements of Machokali and Kahiga with a view to exploiting whatever intelligence they had come upon. He asked Njoya to hire an artist to sketch the Wizard of the Crow for a Wanted poster specifying a reward and the number to call. Given the secrecy required, the artist could rely only on Sikiokuu himself and his assistant, Njoya, for a description of the wizard. But Sikiokuu did not want it known that he received sorcerers in his office at night. So he asked Njoya to leave him out of it.

For his part, Njoya also wanted nothing to do with describing the face of the wizard, for he feared retaliation from the other wizard. So he described instead the minister, and the artist was surprised to see, emerging out of the sketchbook, a face that bore an uncanny resemblance to that of Sikiokuu. To disguise the resemblance, the artist gave the sketch long hair and a beard, resulting, to Sikiokuu's consternation, in a black, long-haired Jesus Christ with the face of the minister. Njoya advanced another idea. The poster would offer a prize to the Wizard of the Crow, who was required to present himself in order to receive it. The heading read THE WIZARD OF THE CROW: WANTED FOR A PRIZE, and at the foot a telephone number, but one that only Njoya and Sikiokuu could answer. Thus, when people saw the posters, they would assume that the picture was of the giver of the prize and that the Wizard of the Crow needed only show up and receive it.

But Sikiokuu did not want simply to sit back and wait for the Wizard of the Crow to hand over Nyawīra. Why put all his eggs in a sorcerer's basket? He had to find other ways of getting to her. Besides, he wanted to hide from his rivals that he too was secretly pursuing the wizard. He would pull the wool over their eyes by pretending to be entirely preoccupied with the hunt for Nyawīra. And what better way to do this than to post new photographs of her all over Aburīria? Yet another problem presented itself: what had he done with the photos of Nyawīra that Kaniūrū had shown him when he started working for him?

Nothing is going right, he thought in despair as he sat back in his chair. He recalled Kaniūrū's lies about him and Tajirika's refusal to go along with the confessions. He leaned forward and banged his desk with his right fist as his anger and frustration mounted. He stopped, folded his arms on the desk, and rested his forehead on them. Where was this woman? Every time he thought he had found a way to get to her, something would make him lose sight of her. How could he have lost her pictures? But bemoaning his bad luck was pointless, he told himself, attempting composure. He had better start looking for the photographs. And then, as if his eyes felt pity for him, he spotted a file under the piles of paper on his desk and pulled it out.

He leapt with joy. It was the file with the pictures of Nyawīra that Kaniūrū had given him. He looked at each carefully to ascertain which was best suited for a poster. The only hitch was that Kaniūrū himself was in many of them. He and Nyawīra had, after all, been husband and wife, and the pictures had been taken during their season of wooing and marriage.

Then Sikiokuu chuckled. He selected a photograph showing

Nyawĩra and Kaniũrũ embracing in a studio. Sikiokuu ordered the picture enlarged and reproduced a thousand copies.

Even as he searched for Nyawĩra, he had found a way to compromise the traitorous Kaniũrũ.

# 16

Machokali, who had been officially entrusted with the capture of the wizard, was keen to achieve this before his rivals had completed their assigned tasks. Since the disastrous visit to America he had felt his power on the wane, and he thought he would recover his standing only through the release of monies for Marching to Heaven. But there were no signs that the Global Bank would release the funds anytime soon. To regain some measure of influence in the heart of power, the capture of the wizard was paramount. But he could not figure out where or how to embark on the search for the Wizard of the Crow. It was not even clear that the sorcerer had returned to Aburĩria. He, too, considered a Wanted poster, but A.G. talked him out of it.

"True! *Haki ya Mungu,*" A.G. was later to claim, "I told him that no human hands could draw the likeness of the Wizard of the Crow. Ask yourselves: Who was the Wizard of the Crow? Was he a man or a woman? Personally I knew that he possessed the ability to change himself into a man or a woman or into anything else. He is a whirlwind. He is lightning. He is a thunderstorm. He is the sun and the rain. He is the moon and the stars. How can you draw the likeness of air, breath, soul? The Wizard of the Crow is the being that animated everything, and how can you draw a picture of that? I told him: Give me the time, give me a free hand, and I will track him down."

Machokali agreed and entrusted A.G. with the search for the Wizard of the Crow. He released him from his ordinary duties. But wherever he went, A.G. was to report regularly.

Just before they parted, the minister gave him a mobile phone and a red motorbike.

# 17

A.G. rejected the way of force and opted for that of words. He would use his tongue to find his way around and unloosen the tongues of his listeners. He went on foot, mostly, but he also rode in *mkokoteni*, donkey carts, bicycles, *matatus, mbondambondas*, buses, or trains to get to wherever people gathered. He stopped at market centers, bars, churches, mosques, and in all these places he would tell them: I am looking for the being that animates all things, including speech.

His cryptic words would ignite a debate among his listeners. Yes, what is the being?

And gradually the debates and heated arguments would give way to stories, anecdotes, and remembrances of what the being was. A.G. would come into his own, and soon people would forget the heat of the previous arguments as they listened to this traveling bard telling the amazing story of the Wizard of the Crow. In his tongue the real and the marvelous flowed out of each other. He would even talk about the Ruler. He would hint about plants that bore money. They listened to his stories and later improvised on them in the retelling. Soon the stream of stories became common lore. The ceaseless transformation of the stories soon resulted in rumors throughout Aburīria that the Ruler was pregnant and had a secret garden with dollar-producing plants. Was that why he had remained out of sight since returning from America? Was that why the Ruler always donated money to self-help schemes, claiming the amount came from him and his friends?

While traveling on foot, one day A.G. saw pasted on an electric post a poster bearing what seemed to be a picture of the Wizard of the Crow. It was the name more than the picture that took him aback. It was not a photograph. It was more like a police sketch. He recalled his talks with Machokali and his warning to the minister that no human hand could draw the likeness of the Wizard of the Crow because he was many things: a man, a woman, a child, a cap on somebody's head, a bird, lightning, a whirlwind! This sketch looked like a cross between Jesus and Sikiokuu, and it offered a prize to the Wizard of the Crow.

Was this the work of Machokali? A.G. asked himself angrily. Machokali, who had entrusted him with the task of finding the Wizard of the Crow? Is he of so little faith that no sooner do I turn my back than he has these drawings of the Wizard of the Crow posted all over the country?

He called Machokali. The minister denied that he had authorized any such thing and wondered who could have done it.

"Find out who is doing this," Machokali said, "but in so doing, don't stray from the main business, capturing the Wizard of the Crow. One more thing. Stories abound that the Ruler is pregnant. Get to the source of those slanderous rumors."

A.G. did not know that he himself had somehow been the source. I will look into the matter, he assured Machokali, and he resumed his travels, having taken note of the telephone number on the poster. A.G. had many friends throughout the police and intelligence network. There were some who owed him a debt of gratitude for letting them know about the Wizard of the Crow early on, long before he and his magic had achieved fame. So it did not take long for him to get to the bottom of the source of the poster. But he was not overly concerned. All this is mere foolishness, he said to himself. The Wizard of the Crow would not be bribed or tricked into submission.

He decided not to be drawn into the power struggle between Sikiokuu and Machokali. He would leave Sikiokuu to his own schemes. He simply would continue in his search for the being that animates all things.

"True! *Haki ya Mungu*, I was armed with faith and hope that if I persisted, I would hear somehow, somewhere, a voice saying: The man *is* here."

# 18

Kaniũrũ had always wanted to see his picture in a newspaper. He felt frustrated and angry with the press, because even after he had been promoted to a senior youthwinger and then to the deputy chair of Marching to Heaven, not a single newspaper had evinced an interest in him, and none had carried his picture. So when he saw two reporters packing cameras at his first seminar, he was very pleased.

The one-day seminar on *The Kaniũrũ Memorandum on New Educational Initiatives for Youth and Women to Make Their Minds Conform to National Ideals and the Ruler's Philosophy* was going to be the first of several in different parts of the country, so a lot was riding on its success. It was being held at the Ruler's Hall, Eldares, and it was supposed to start at ten in the morning. Attendance was abysmal. Even the members of his youthwing had not bothered to turn up, because they assumed that the seminar was intended for those who had not yet accepted parrotry as a norm. By eleven o'clock, the main speakers—a professor of the history of parrotology, a professor of the philosophy and psychology of parrotology, a professor of the politics of parrotology, a professor of literary parrotology, a professor of the science of parrotology, and finally the chairman of the seminar, Kaniũrũ—were the only people present. They sat at the podium, waiting for the people to turn up, but the two reporters were the only ones in the audience. "We seem to be on African Time," Kaniũrũ tried to joke with the reporters.

But when the expected students had not arrived by two o'clock, the reporters became restive and asked Kaniũrũ, When is the Ruler going to arrive? Oh, is that why they came so early? Kaniũrũ thought. He had hinted to the newspapers that the Ruler might open the seminar, but Kaniũrũ, knowing the present state of the Ruler, had not even bothered to broach the subject with him. Kaniũrũ told them that he would not come but had sent a message. They asked if he could please give them a copy of the message so that they could leave. This made Kaniũrũ decide to begin the seminar even without an audience, for, as he put it, quoting a proverb, the sun never waits for anybody, not even a king, and he was not yet a king. He advised the restive reporters to focus their cameras on the podium and not the empty seats. And he offered himself for an interview, but after the meeting.

Kaniũrũ opened the seminar by saying that toward its close he would convey the message of goodwill from the Head of State to the seminar. Meantime, he had a few words to say. The queuing mania in the country had been started and fueled largely by university students, and their bad example was unfortunately followed by many people till—

But before he had said another word, he saw a long line of young people approaching the hall. Elated, he hastened to amend his remarks.

"It does not of course mean that all queues are wrong and immoral in all places at all times," Kaniũrũ said, gesturing the newspaper people to train their cameras on the arrivals. "When you get orderly queues made by intelligent people who know why they are falling in line and where their queues are headed, like these good youth who are about to enter the hall . . . let me welcome them at the door."

Kaniũrũ, eager for a photo op, was so excited that he almost tripped over himself as he left the podium and headed for the door to welcome the youth.

Suddenly, Kaniũrũ found himself surrounded by the youth, who were brandishing Wanted posters showing him arm in arm with Nyawĩra, shouting: He is here! He is here! The professors were confused by the turmoil, but when they saw the posters they jumped through the windows, yelling that they had been misled into attending a seminar organized by a terrorist. The reporters were busy clicking away, recording this extraordinary scene of students tying Kaniũrũ's hands together and dragging him along, others pushing him from behind, still others prancing about on the sides, waving their posters in the air. They took him to the nearest police station.

When Kaniũrũ told the police who he was, they did not believe him. Stop lying, they said, pointing at his picture on the Wanted poster, adding in Kiswahili: Is this not you holding hands with that woman terrorist Nyawĩra? Kaniũrũ agreed that the picture was indeed of him, but he was angry when they refused to hear any qualification, interrupting him with laughter, especially when he told them to call the State House to find out the truth of his identity. What made the police even more suspicious was that when they finally offered to call the Minister of State, Sikiokuu, the prisoner looked terror stricken, beseeching them to contact the Ruler instead.

When the police called the Minister of State to ask what they should do with the criminal, they failed to reach Sikiokuu or any other person in charge who could dispose of the matter. So Kaniũrũ was held at the police station overnight.

Kaniũrũ's picture, his hands roped together, appeared on the front page of the two main newspapers, next to an image of the Wanted poster; the caption in both instances was STUDENTS APPREHEND NYAWĨRA'S ASSOCIATE.

Ironically, the picture and the story saved him from having to spend more time in prison, for when ASS Kahiga saw the newspaper, he called the State House to ask why his boss had been arrested and what he should do about it. The Ruler ordered Kaniũrũ's immediate release.

When Sikiokuu was asked about the poster, he claimed he did not mean to harm Kaniũrũ, his only interest was to capture Nyawĩra, but unfortunately the only picture of her that he had showed her holding hands with Kaniũrũ. Now the Ruler was hearing of Kaniũrũ's connection to Nyawĩra for the first time. As he put it, There is more to this than meets the eye, and I will get to the bottom of it! Still, he decreed that Kaniũrũ's image be removed from the poster.

Kaniũrũ, who used to claim that he was brought up by a blind grandmother, his parents having died when he was only a baby, the truth being that it was his grandmother who had died then, was dealt further denigrations when a few days later the newspapers carried pictures of his aged parents from a rural village looking for him in the streets of Eldares after they had seen images of him being dragged along the road.

So despite his release, Kaniũrũ remained bitter that his first-ever picture in a newspaper had been a humiliating fiasco.

# 19

After the ordeal, Kaniũrũ viewed Sikiokuu, the students, and newspapers as a grand alliance against him, and this intensified his determination to seek vengeance. First he unleashed his thugs to beat students wherever they were to be found. This caused a scandal throughout the country, but it did not deter him. Against Sikiokuu he decided to try to capture Nyawĩra himself, thwarting Sikiokuu's chances of winning the race. He would effect this through his own capture of the Wizard of the Crow, convinced as he had always been that there was a link between the two. Kaniũrũ would also get from him information on the women of the people's court.

Kaniũrũ designed his Wanted poster featuring a hazy illustration based on his recollection of his various encounters with the wizard. At the bottom he asked the sorcerer to make himself known through a telephone number to answer a few questions about the husband bashing that was now epidemic.

He ordered Kahiga to keep a close watch on Sikiokuu and Machokali to steal their respective plans for the capture of Nyawĩra and the wizard. He also charged Kahiga with overseeing the demolition of all Sikiokuu's posters, replacing them with Kaniũrũ's, and gave him a black motorcycle to make him flexible in the choice of highways and country paths. For his part, Kahiga decided to simplify the tasks heaped upon him by following A.G. secretly to put to his own use whatever A.G. discovered.

Sikiokuu retaliated by having Kaniũrũ's posters pulled down and replaced with his, which is what turned their struggle into a poster war. He gave Njoya a golden-colored motorcycle to supervise the poster war, and Njoya decided that the most effective way of carrying out his new duties was to follow Kahiga secretly.

# 20

Having had a feast of students' bones broken, and confident that he would win the poster war and the race, Kaniũrũ now turned his attention to the media. But he had yet to find a way to punish the journalists.

The opportunity he sought suddenly knocked at his door when *matatus* and buses went on strike to protest a new decree that banned any queuing of passengers before entering public transport. Passengers, it seemed, had been ignoring the ban on the queues of more than five people and making long lines. The new decree required that people get on buses and *matatus* by pushing and shoving. The strike almost paralyzed the country, particularly the major towns, until the owners of factories and business enterprises complained that they were being ruined. This forced the government to modify the decree, allowing for both queuing and rushing. Here passengers formed queues; there they climbed all over one another as they rushed to enter *matatus*, buses, or trains. But, above all, the government wanted chaos, so it restricted the licensing of new passenger vehicles. Plans to add to the railway system built by the colonial regime were scuttled. Disorder reigned supreme, for any attempt on the part of the people to organize themselves was deemed by the Ruler's government as a challenge to its authority.

At the height of the strike, when people who could afford it took taxis for transport, word reached Kaniũrũ that at ground transportation in the airport there was a long queue of journalists with cameras and the like and of course their pens and notebooks. Kaniũrũ did not even bother to find out who they were or what they were doing at the airport. He dispatched his thugs, his patriotic citizens, to set upon the journalists, who, caught unaware by the thugs' relentless fury, fled in every direction.

Kaniũrũ felt joy erupt as he savored every aspect of his victory over the journalists and the media.

# 21

The media had come from many parts of the world to cover the widely circulating rumors that the Ruler was pregnant. They now filed stories that claimed that organized thugs were attacking people who had come to verify the rumors. But, far from keeping curiosity at bay, the stories and TV images of bone fide journalists on the run at the Ruler's Airport served only to attract yet more media: The rumors must be true, it was thought. The Ruler, after all, had disappeared from public view. Big Ben Mambo, Minister of Information, condemned the allegations, leading to even greater circulation of the rumors. Journalists continued to pour into the country, and when all hotels were full they started pitching tents in the prairie among mounds of earth. These mounds were so many and so big that some discerning observers began to wonder what kind of ants had built them, and proceeded to report on the strange landscape of Aburīria. The stories attracted tourists. So now, in addition to sex beaches and fauna and flora, monstrous anthills and an unnatural pregnancy had become tourist attractions. Despite his contribution to the dramatic rise in tourism, the Ruler was furious: in America they had managed to keep a lid on his condition, but in Aburīria, where his word was law, his condition was the talk of the whole world. It was a terrible blow to his manhood, and of course he blamed his travails on the note written by the wizard to Machokali.

Amid his fury, he got a call from the American ambassador, Gabriel Gemstone, asking him to receive a special envoy of the American president. Things were looking up. Maybe the special envoy was coming on behalf of the superpower to apologize for how the Ruler had been treated in America. He considered refusing to see the envoy to register his unhappiness with how things had gone in the States but thought the better of it. This was nothing to sneeze at. The apology would be too sweet.

# 22

The special envoy was accompanied by Ambassador Gabriel Gemstone. His Mighty received them at the State House, Eldares, together with his ministers, including Machokali; Sikiokuu; the new governor of the Central Bank, Titus Tajirika; and the official biographer, Luminous Karamu-Mbu. There were two photographers selected from the Ruler's special unit, and they were instructed to take pictures of the visitors as they entered and left the State House. All the other pictures, of the Ruler receiving the visitors for instance, were to be taken with cameras without film.

The visitors did not show any surprise at the bodily expansion of the Ruler. The envoy, in fact, went straight to the point. He had been sent by Washington and by the capitals of the leading industrial democracies to convey their concern about what was happening in the State of Aburĩria, especially the unprovoked attacks on members of the international press. They were also concerned about the on and off queuing in the country, especially the skirmishes between opponents and supporters of queuing. They were alarmed at the possibility of a complete breakdown of the rule of law, and there was nothing worse for a people than their country falling into the hands of thugs, evildoers, and warlords and becoming a terrorist haven.

When he heard the word *queuing* issue from the mouth of the special envoy, the Ruler felt upbraided, criticized for being unable to control his own people, so he cut the man short with ironic laughter. He then said that the government had already apologized for the inconveniences the foreign press had suffered. He had issued a stern warning to his citizens that Western journalists must never again be made to suffer even the slightest inconvenience. But a quid pro quo was in order. Queuing, as an expression of order, organization, and discipline, was a very Western idea, and they should be mindful that they were now in Aburĩria, Africa, where people are guided more by emotion than by reason, and therefore to scramble for things is "what comes easily" to Aburĩrians. "Your ambassador," the Ruler said, "should have told you that we are a people of hearts big with warmth and not of heads swollen with ideas, and that is why we love dancing and opening our houses to guests. But a guest observes the rules of hospitality laid down by the host. So when in Aburīria, do as the Aburīrians do."

He went on to reassure them that as far as unauthorized queues were concerned, they should not worry or doubt his ability to bring them to a halt. He paused and sent for the heads of the military and the police. He wanted them to outline to his visitors the measures that he had asked them to carry out in order to teach unauthorized processions, particularly of women, lessons they would never forget. But the Ruler did not give them a chance to speak—he just continued. He reminded the ambassador and the special envoy of what he did when he assumed the presidency of the country. America seems to have forgotten how, in the early days of the cold war, he had crushed the Communist insurgency in Aburīria.

"You heard me laugh, and you may have wondered why," he went on. "I was bemused by the short memory of a superpower."

The Ruler was proud of having eliminated seven thousand and seven hundred citizens in just seven days for posing a threat to the stability through protests in the major cities demanding social change. He would take this opportunity, he said, to renew old friendships and earn their trust by showing that he had not forgotten how to use strong-arm tactics against dissidents.

*"What I did before against Communists, I can do again against terrorists!"* he said slowly and deliberately, and then turned to the heads of the army and the police.

"Yes," the head of the military said, "we are waiting for this ragtag army, first reported to us by a motorcycle rider, to reach the capital. Then we shall encircle it with the armored cars and the latest guns you sold to us some time ago—old, but against unarmed civilians, still lethal—"

*"A national massacre. To be televised. Live,"* added the head of the police with unmistakable pride.

"You have heard from the horses' own mouths," the Ruler said, turning toward the special envoy and Ambassador Gemstone. "Everything is under control," he added. "Have no fear of those who threaten your interests and ours, for gunfire awaits them."

The envoy cleared his throat and said: "You have actually touched on one of the issues that our president wanted me to discuss with you. The West and the civilized world are eternally grateful to you for your role in our victory over the evil empire. We are now embarking on a new mission of forging a global order. That is why I am now visiting all our friends to tell them to move in step with the world. To everything its season, says the preacher. There was a time when slavery was good. It did its work, and when it finished creating capital, it withered and died a natural death. Colonialism was good. It spread industrial culture of shared resources and markets. But to revive colonialism would now be an error. There was a time when the cold war dictated our every calculation in domestic and international relations. It is over. We are in the post–cold war era, and our calculations are affected by the laws and needs of globalization. The history of capital can be summed up in one phrase: *in search of freedom*. Freedom to expand, and now it has a chance at the entire globe for its theater. It needs a democratic space to move as its own logic demands. So I have been sent to urge you to start thinking about turning your country into a democracy. Who knows? Maybe with your blessings, some of your ministers might even want to form opposition parties."

"No, no," the ministers hastened to say, almost in unison. "We in Aburīria know only One Truth, One Party, One Country, One Leader, One God."

"Your views and ours are not too far apart," the envoy explained. "Let me make our position clear. We cannot build a global economy under the old politics of the cold war. What we are saying is this: many parties, one aim—a free and stable world where our money can move across borders without barriers erected by the misguided nationalism of the outmoded nation-state. The goal is to free up the resources and energies of the globe. All your countries and peoples will benefit."

The Ruler was angry at being lectured in front of his ministers. He had invited them so that they could hear for themselves a special envoy delivering an apology, and instead of *I am sorry* they were hearing him being reprimanded and ordered about. He tried to control his anger, genuinely puzzled at how his relationship with Washington, London, Berlin, and Paris had so soured as to compel them to dispatch a special envoy to chastise him in front of his cabinet. In the days of the cold war, they used to shower him with praises for dispatching thousands of his own people to eternal silence. And now, even after he had assured them that he was ready to repeat what he had done for them, they were lecturing him about restraint and the new global order! He now stood on injured dignity. He had to show his ministers that he was not afraid of the special envoy, even if he was an emissary of the West.

"Mr. Special Envoy, I want you to know that our country is independent, and we cannot allow ourselves to take orders from the West all the time. We have said good-bye to colonialism and left it on the dunghills of twentieth-century history. I want to remind you that we are in Africa, and we, too, have our *African forms of governance.* The democracy that is suitable for America and Europe is not necessarily suitable for Africa. In our country we have a saying that one does not build his home according to the needs of his neighbor. We don't try to *keep up with the Joneses,* as you Americans would say."

"We are your friends," the envoy replied, "and friends deepen their friendship by speaking openly to one another."

*"Then let's agree to disagree,"* the Ruler said, and then he asked, with a touch of impatience, if that was all that had brought him to Aburīria.

The special envoy said that he indeed had another message but he was afraid that it was only for the Ruler's ears, as he glanced nervously at the ministers.

The Ruler would have preferred that the apology be delivered in front of his ministers. The imminent apology would ameliorate the humiliation he had suffered in America before them. But still his face lit up because the ministers would now see that his relationship with America was still close enough to warrant a message that could only be delivered to him privately by a special emissary of the most powerful presidency in the world.

The ministers left the room. The envoy did not waste time with polite preliminaries.

"As I said a few minutes ago, friends are friends because they can speak to one another freely. And that is why my president sent me, because he and other leaders of the West are concerned about reports concerning your health and condition—you know, uh, some thoughts are difficult to put into words. Your Excellency, I am sure you know what I am talking about: the rumor that has prompted international media to descend on your country. We have also heard that you are thinking of building or growing a money-making plant to produce dollars and other Western currencies. I am sure you know that any unauthorized printing and circulation of dollars is not only a crime in international law but would destabilize ours and the global economy, and the West would not tolerate that. We do not believe any of it, of course, and I shall not dignify the rumors by asking you if they are true. But there are a few other things not in doubt. There is your publicly stated intention to put up a kind of latter-day Tower of Babel, what you call Marching to Heaven. So your friends in the West are asking you this: Have you, Your Mighty Excellency, ever thought of taking it easy? I mean, like taking a rest—a vacation or something? I think it was your ancestors who said that age needs to pass on the torch of wisdom to youth. You have youthful ministers who love you and share your vision. They said as much in front of us. We are wondering, and I was told to stress that this is only a suggestion from friends, why you don't take things easy and cede the presidency to one of these young men so they can relieve you of the daily stress? Your ancestors said something about a stone of ages and wisdom. You could become an elder statesman dispensing advice born of long experience."

If the envoy had been a citizen of Aburĩria, he would have faced a firing squad on the spot. The Ruler understood only too well what they were telling him: that he was senile and no longer fit to govern. Their position puzzled him because it was riddled with obvious contradictions. Here they were cautioning him against the use of force only to tell him minutes afterward that he is unable to exercise power! How can they tell him not to unleash the army on his own people and then accuse him of being too senile to do it? He felt like throwing them out of his presence but fought to keep his composure, wondering which of his ministers they had in mind as a successor.

The envoy thought that the Ruler was softening and was giving his proposal serious consideration, so he hastened to make it more attractive.

"Thank you for even considering what I have said. You are very wise, Your Excellency, and the West will make sure that you retire with all your wealth and that of your family and friends completely intact. We can even help it to multiply. And also, we can make sure that your successor passes a law to ensure that you are never brought to court on charges involving any of your actions during your tenure as the head of the state. And of course if you feel that you have to move to another country, that, too, can be arranged."

"I should say thank you," the Ruler sighed, "for you have spoken the truth. We rulers are vain, and we never realize when age has knocked at the door and lodged snugly within us," he continued in a weary voice. "But believe me, I have often thought of getting rid of this burden of leadership so I can have time to enjoy my grandchildren. The problem is in really knowing which of the young men around me I should trust to steer the nation in the right direction."

The special envoy was pleased with the response, and he casually mentioned the name of Machokali as an example.

"He made quite an impression during your last visit to Washington. He is young and seems quick on his feet. He is devoted to your philosophy. He reasons more than he emotes, and we in the West can certainly do business with him. But this is just the opinion of your friends—of course it is entirely up to you to pick and groom your successor."

The Ruler remained calm on the surface, for within he felt like hurling his club at them. Could these people have had a hand in his malady, his bodily expansion? Maybe they had put something in his food, probably during that prayer breakfast in Washington, so as to undermine his standing with the allegation of male pregnancy?

"Friends Tell Each Other the Truth is my motto," said the Ruler, chuckling. "But I am sure you don't expect an answer on the spot. I will certainly think about the matter. Please, convey my best wishes and gratitude to your president, and assure him that I am hale and hearty."

The special envoy and Ambassador Gemstone left feeling that they had done a good job in conveying the warnings, threats, and wishes with candor, and they appreciated the way the Ruler had reacted, with even a touch of humor.

But the Ruler thought otherwise. For a moment he missed the cold war, when he could play one side against the other. But now? There was only one superpower and it knew only how to be wooed, not how to woo. Or could he have misread the envoy's intent?

That night he went over the entire conversation and certain coincidences began to strike him as odd, especially the envoy's reference to pregnancy and age, though he had peppered it with African sayings. A coincidence? The Americans, Machokali, and the Wizard of the Crow in league together? He broke into mirthless laughter. This is Aburĩria, not America, and *I will have the last laugh*, he said in English. He knew that in Aburĩria there was only one ruler, and his name was the Ruler of Aburĩria. America might have helped install him in power, but this was no longer the twentieth century; now he was his own man and he would not let America tell him when to retire.

With that clarity of vision, he calmed down.

He would demand that his Western-anointed successor, Machokali, bring him the Wizard of the Crow alive forthwith. The need to appropriate his sorcerous powers had never been greater.

# SECTION III

## 1

Nobody knew whether he had returned to Aburīria or not, and nothing generated so much controversy as the subject of his escape from America. But had the Wizard of the Crow escaped or just disappeared? Even A.G. was at a loss, for when he reached the point in the narrative at which he told how they had gone to the New York airport and he had had no clue as to the whereabouts of the Wizard of the Crow, he would pause and relive the pain and grief he felt at the time. His grief was infectious, and his listeners would get quiet and look at one another as if asking, What can we do to revive his spirits? And they would buy him a beer or two, *just to wet your throat, man,* and urge him on, *tell us more.* Those who heard him would later go home and pass the evening telling the stories about a drunk who claimed to have been in America when the Wizard of the Crow disappeared, as a prelude to their own legends of the wizard. Every listener would thus become a teller of tales, insisting on his own authority. Some swore by whatever was most sacred to them that they knew for sure that the Wizard of the Crow had been detained by American immigration authorities for not possessing a valid visa. They had put him on a plane that had taken him to Peru by mistake, and the Peruvian authorities had refused to allow him to enter their country because of course he did not have a visa, and they in turn had put him on another plane that took him to New Zealand, where he met the same hard luck, and so on, hither and thither, from plane back to plane, and that is how he became so worldly, because though not allowed to set foot anywhere he ended up visiting everywhere, from Mozambique to Mongolia, Kazakhstan to Cameroon, Tanzania to Tasmania, Hawaii to

Hong Kong, India to Iceland, Kenya to Korea; a person without a home, a citizen of the world. Others said no; there was no truth to this story of his moving from country to country, and they claimed that American immigration authorities had simply jailed him because he had no papers to say who he was or where he came from, and he remains imprisoned there to this very day as a terrorist suspect or else killed in the streets of New York by the Mafia for refusing to tell them the secret of growing money on trees.

Yes, it is true that he is still in America, others would say, but not in jail, unless you consider schools and colleges to be prisons. The man had simply enrolled in a school of sorcery, and he was working his way to a PhD in comparative sorcery, ancient and modern, and, really, what is there to entice him back here? Aburĩria of crooked roads, robberies, runaway viruses of death, hospitals without medicine, rampant unemployment without relief, daily insecurity, epidemic alcoholism? Yes, an Aburĩria whose leaders had murdered hope? He should stay in America and acquire the sorcery that invented the fax and the Internet and e-mail and night vision and labs that grow human organs and even clone whole animals and humans, the magic of objects that propel themselves to war and other worlds, the sorcery by which the dollar rules the world! Amen, some would say, and even this would sometimes generate more arguments among them: Why do you say amen? Amen to what?

The different versions of the Wizard of the Crow in America would vie with one another for dominance, but all were united in their common attempt to explain why, despite the posters of the Wizard of the Crow all over the country, he could not be found. Where in Aburĩria, they asked, could the man have hidden himself so as to elude the Ruler's ubiquitous eyes, ears, noses, legs, and hands?

Okay, okay, a few would scream, let's not have too many cooks dipping their spoons in the broth. Let's hear the stories, one after the other, but we urge the tellers to know that too much salt makes food difficult to swallow.

The problem in deciding if there was any truth to any of the rumors lay in the fact that the original source of most of them was A.G. himself. And even when the stories differed, A.G. would swear that all of them were true, arguing that just as an ocean feeds on different rivers with sources in diverse hills and mountains, allowing one to talk of streams, rivers, seas, and oceans though in each case one is talking about water, it was the same with narratives.

This would revive all their interest and quest for certainty: What happened? people would ask, all eyes on A.G.

# 2

When Kamītī, the Wizard of the Crow, came back to Aburīria from America, he wanted to go straight home and be with Nyawīra. He was homesick and felt as if he had been away for years. Still, he could not help recalling the nightmare that had become his life even before he had left for America. He had been arrested, forced to share a prison cell with Tajirika, released from prison, and put on a plane for the USA, where he had been unable to rejoin the Ruler's entourage. And in New York he had seen and experienced things that he had never dreamed. Now that I am back, he asked himself, will I be able to resume my life and not be drawn into the mess of the Ruler and his ilk? Will the Sikiokuus and the Machokalis leave me alone? He just wanted to be with Nyawīra and continue to heal those in need. That was the vision that Kamītī had in mind as he rode a bus from the airport to the center of Eldares, where he took a *matatu* to Santalucia.

Some passengers were talking about the visit of the Ruler to America and how well it was going. How would they react, he wondered, were he to tell them that the Ruler was suffering from some kind of self-induced expansion? What if I were to tell them that I have just come back from America, that I have just left the Ruler and his entourage at the VIP Hotel between Fifth and Sixth avenues in Manhattan, near Washington Square and New York University?

It was early in the morning when he got to Santalucia. The bliss of a future with Nyawīra possessed him, and now, at the nearness of their reunion, he wondered how he would react on seeing her and how things had gone at the shrine. Should he run and embrace her, or should he hide behind the hedge and then walk stealthily behind her and put his hands over her eyes?

About two hundred yards away, he suddenly stopped and rubbed his eyes. Was he not seeing properly? He looked again. Did I take the wrong turn? But surely even if he were blind he would still know the way home. He hurried along. But the closer he got to the site, the more he felt strength draining from his legs and arms. He now stood dead in his tracks.

The site where once stood the house that he and Nyawĩra had built together, his home, his shrine, was a mass of burnt black debris.

# 3

A cat stood some yards away, staring at him with green eyes as he walked about listlessly, picking up one thing and another and then letting them drop. Where do I begin the search for her? he asked himself as he sat down again to work out what he would do next. And what if the fire had not been an accident?

He would ask his neighbors what had happened, but the nearest were some distance away. He had to approach them circumspectly so as not to raise suspicions about who he was and his interest in the matter.

The reactions of the neighbors he approached were all disconcerting. He would start with greetings, which were met with friendly responses, but the moment he mentioned the shrine of the Wizard of the Crow, their faces and demeanors would change—friendly eyes would assume the look of fear. I don't know what you are talking about, they would say as they scampered away or reverted to their chores or shut the door in his face. He stopped knocking at people's doors and took to the streets.

He met an old man carrying a parcel dangling from one end of a stick over his shoulder. Kamĩtĩ dispensed with politeness and asked him about the burned-down shrine. The old man took to his heels, shouting as if he wanted the whole world to know that he was running: My heels are smoking; witness my heels smoking from the swiftness of my running! In happier times, Kamĩtĩ would have burst out laughing.

He sat down on a mound of earth and covered his face with his hands as if to hold back tears. He felt defeated. He had called her from America but had found the line dead, not unusual for telephones in Aburīria. He had thought nothing of it. Now he wished he and Nyawīra had taken advantage of mobile phones.

Suddenly he became aware of a presence near him. He opened his eyes and was startled to see the old man standing there; he had heard no footsteps.

"Why did you ask me about that house?" the old man asked.

"I just wanted to know what happened," Kamītī answered.

"Why? Can't you see that the house is burnt down?"

"Who burned it?"

"Do you believe in God?" the old man asked.

Kamītī was about to say something rude, but he restrained himself.

"Yes, I do."

"And you believe that he is the Lord, Ruler of Heaven and Earth?"

"I am not into religions, but that's correct."

"Praise the Lord," the old man said, raising his voice as if he wanted passersby to hear him.

"Was it an accident or arson?" Kamītī asked irritably.

"Accident? Praise the Lord," the old man repeated.

"Were there any casualties?" Kamītī asked, thinking that the man was crazed.

But instead of answering him the old man bent forward a little, looked Kamītī in the eye, and spoke in whispers.

"Didn't you just now say that you believe in God, the Lord above?"

"Why? How many Gods are there?" Kamītī asked impatiently.

"That's the question. There is only one God. But there are many Lords. Have you ever thought about that?"

"Please don't speak to me in riddles. Say directly what you are trying to tell me."

"I just wanted to assure you that the God above is just and wise."

"And therefore?"

"He works in mysterious ways."

"So what?" Kamītī asked desperately.

"Praise the Lord and thank the Almighty that dwells high above us," he mumbled, and started walking away, shouting, "Praise the Lord!" He soon disappeared.

# 4

What was the man trying to tell him? The Lord could be heavenly or earthly. The people who had burned the shrine down had some connection to the Ruler. Praise the Lord. There had been no casualties: so Praise the Lord. This interpretation was a relief. Nyawīra was very much alive. But where was she? Was she hurt or not? Was she in the hospital, or had she been captured? How would he find out? Where would he begin his search? But if Nyawīra had been captured, the story would have been in the newspapers. He combed through the archives of the *Eldares Times* in vain: no recent references to Nyawīra, the Movement for the Voice of the People, or arson. He went to the police headquarters under the guise of a reporter from the *Eldares Times* to learn of recent arrests or accidents in the different regions of the country, but again he came up empty. He visited hospitals only to learn nothing.

As the days and weeks of his search went by, he grew thin and began to look a far different person from the one who had come back home from America. Because his search had yielded no bad news, there were times when he was certain that Nyawīra was alive and free. At other times, he wondered whether she was in the custody of the secret police controlled by Minister Sikiokuu. When he had divined for Sikiokuu he always saw Nyawīra as ending up in a crowd, and so he started looking for her wherever people gathered to do good.

He visited Catholic, Protestant, and Orthodox churches; Muslim mosques; and Hindu, Sikh, Jain, and Jewish temples throughout the country: there were no signs of Nyawīra in these places of worship.

It was then that he came across some queues, slow, inexorable processions, and he did not know if they were new or a continuation of the old ones. But whether old or new, it did not matter to him: he saw only a gathering of people where the spirit of Nyawīra might dwell and so started looking for her among them. He himself did not fall in line. He ran beside each queue, his face turned to the right or

# Male Daemons

left depending on which side of the line he ran along. Since every day and everywhere the queues were multiplying, this severely strained his neck.

Once he bumped into a procession that seemed better organized than any he had come across so far, its clear sense of purpose expressed in a song:

> *The people have spoken*
> *The people have spoken*
> *Give me back my voice*
> *The people have spoken*
> *Give me back the voice you took from me*

The scene changed daily; increasingly he met more people singing about the people's voice and heading for Eldares. Still, he persisted in his search, tagging along most of them but, like the motorcycle riders, finding that they had no beginning or end.

It came out of nowhere: What if Nyawĩra had left him and taken up with another, maybe one of her young comrades? He recalled how Margaret Wariara, later a victim of the deadly virus, had left him. Was there something about him that drove the people he most loved away from him? But try as he might, he could not imagine Nyawĩra leaving him without saying good-bye. But then again, had he ever imagined that Wariara, a homely woman, would prostitute herself among tourists in big hotels?

This image of Wariara jolted him into looking for Nyawĩra in the bars mushrooming all over the country. They sold all brands of beer and liquor, and fights often erupted as drinkers made claims and counterclaims about the superiority of their brand. He felt awkward just standing around or sitting in a corner without a drink, at least a soda.

He started having a little taste now and then to blend with the drinking crowd. At first he confined himself to one glass a day. But with every passing day, the amount of alcohol he consumed grew. The beer was now his temple. On waking up from a drunken stupor, his reality threatening to engulf him, he would rush back to the temple for salvation. Alcohol never disappointed, always keeping his worries at bay.

His resources were depleted, and he now spent his days looking for cheaper but more potent brew instead of Nyawīra. He would come to think of Nyawīra and even the Wizard of the Crow as characters in a dream in another country far away and long ago. He now had new friends, drunkards like him, and when he had no money he would beg them for a shot or two.

There was much storytelling and ribald joking among the drinking crowd. One day in a bar he found a man reading to a crowded bar from a book he called *Devil on the Cross*. Whenever he emptied his glass, he would stop and announce that his beak needed wetting. He would resume only after his glass had been replenished by those around him. Inspired by the man's success in procuring free drinks, Kamītī himself became a talemonger. He told how once he had left his body in a garbage dump and flown high above it as a bird before returning to it just as garbage collectors were about to bury it. The crowd was not impressed with Kamītī's tales, except for a drunk who always sat by himself in a corner as if in hiding. He who hardly ever said anything now suddenly raised his voice: What did you say?

The other drunks were surprised to hear the man's voice, and they asked one another: Has Baalam's donkey found his voice at last? Thinking that he was finally beginning to attract an interested audience, Kamītī repeated his story. The drunk, known as Mr. Walking Stick—he sported one with a cross-shaped handle—walked over and gazed at him with something like terror in his eyes, shook his head, and walked back, mumbling, No, it cannot be, he does not carry a bag on his back like the other one. And he has no horns. Nevertheless, the drunk, who had been a permanent fixture in that bar, changed location and thereafter moved from bar to bar, saying to inquisitive tongues, Too long a stay in one seat tires the buttocks.

On another occasion Kamītī told the same drinking crowd how he became a bird and visited all of Africa and the Caribbean Islands, and this was too much for his listeners, who told him to take his naked lies to gullible fools elsewhere. Somehow his stories or the manner of their telling lacked the power that carried people to worlds they had never visited, that showed them wonders they had never seen, that made them forget, for a time, the familiar milieu of endless misery, and so they did not bring many replenishments of drinks. He gave up storytelling, though grudgingly. With not much flowing into his glass,

Male Daemons

he sometimes left the bars early for what had now become his home, his razed shrine, where he would wake up to find a cat snuggling against him, the same cat that he saw when he first came to the charred ruins. As on that day the cat would mew once and walk away, leaving him wondering if he should follow it but without once bringing himself to do so.

One night, as he was walking out of his favorite bar, he noticed a poster on the wall and something about it made him stop in his tracks. It bore a vague resemblance to him, at least to how he looked before alcohol had taken over his mind and body. No, it was not his face, then or now, because he had never grown his hair long, and the beard made him look like some kind of black Jesus. As he went nearer and touched the poster, the face depicted now slightly suggested Sikiokuu. The writing declared THE WIZARD OF THE CROW. WANTED FOR A PRIZE. He rubbed his eyes and looked at it again. There was a number to call. Why a prize? For what? Was the prize for him, or for whomever turned him in? He was completely at a loss to know what to do, especially when in the days that followed he found other posters with conflicting messages.

One afternoon he went to his bar, Sell-Me-Death, and although he was already totally drunk he still hoped for one more glass. He saw a riderless red motorcycle against the wall where one of the posters of the beard of Jesus Christ on Sikiokuu's face hung, but this did not bother him; in fact, the war of posters no longer worried him.

What made him envious, even in his drunken state, was the sight of people crowded around a storyteller whose tales and manner of telling them captured the imagination of the audience so much so that some of them had even forgotten that they had come here to drink. The climax came when the storyteller lowered his voice and made hints about knowing something about the pregnancy of a president. People whistled. Then silence, waiting for more. A pregnant president?

"It's true! *Haki ya Mungu!*" said the storyteller in a raised voice.

# 5

Kamītī could not see the face of the storyteller clearly. But the phrase *True, Haki ya Mungu* jolted him out of a slumberous languor. When and where did he last hear that phrase?

"Even the white doctors were baffled by the strange happening," the storyteller continued. "But the Wizard of the Crow? Oh, no, not him. I was in the plane when the letter was read and I heard everything. Mr. President, the letter said, you are pregnant and nobody knows what you will bear."

Who is this man who is mouthing my words? thought Kamītī. And why is he distorting them? Why is he turning them into lies? He felt that he could not let the storymonger go on twisting the meaning of his words. He felt like a writer whose work has been lifted by another only to skew its form and content. Despite being drunk, he felt a need to insist on his writing integrity.

"*Hapana!* That was not how it went!" he heard himself speaking out, to the consternation of the audience.

They turned toward Kamītī. Those who knew him from this or other bars simply dismissed him as the same drunk who was always trying to spoil a good story. The storyteller was both intrigued and bemused by the intervention. Who was this who had questioned his story in a way that no other listener had done in all the places he had told his tale? "*Hapana!* It is not how it was. Machokali is my witness. I left him a note there, at the reception, yes, of the, I mean at the reception of the hotel—uh, what did they call it? VIP. New York, yes, Very Important People Hotel, New York, with so many yellow taxis and black garbage bags. Why yellow? Why black? Don't ask me. Now, what was I saying? My note was addressed to one person and one person only, Machokali, the Minister for Foreigners, I mean, Affairs. And I just wanted to tell him one thing only. One thing. *Take care of yourself.* Why? I will say it again. This country is pregnant, and what it will bear, nobody knows. That was all. I cannot take this war on my words anymore. I am leaving . . ."

Kamītī staggered toward the door. But even before he reached it, a few listeners had blurted, This drunk has spoken the truth. There is something not right about this country. Then they suddenly ceased to speak, so mesmerized were they by what was unfolding before them. The storyteller, shaking with terror, was running, trying to catch up to the drunk.

"Wizard of the Crow," the storyteller called out. "Don't you remember me? I am Arigaigai Gathere, alias A.G."

Still more wonders were to come. A man who had just arrived at the bar called out: "Wizard of the Crow! I am Elijah Njoya, the one who took you to the airport, remember?"

Kamĩtĩ showed no sign of recognition.

The roar of a motorcycle outside was heard, and within seconds its rider was standing at the door, panting. "Wizard of the Crow," he said, "I am Peter Kahiga. You remember me, don't you?"

Kamĩtĩ did not so much as open his mouth.

The three men, A.G., Kahiga, and Njoya, now said in unison: You are wanted at the State House!

But Kamĩtĩ wa Karĩmĩri, alias the Wizard of the Crow, did not seem to hear the trio but continued staggering toward the door, followed by the three police, who were in turn followed by the bar crowd. He went outside, stumbled a bit along the road, stopped, and threw up on the grass by the roadside. He fell and lay in the vomit; almost immediately he started snoring.

A.G., Njoya, and Kahiga, who had trooped behind the Wizard of the Crow, now fell into sharp disagreement, each claiming to have been first to apprehend the wizard and that it was his right to take the sorcerer back to the boss who had ordered their mission. Those who watched from a safe distance say that the bickering among the three got so bad that they took out their guns and would have shot one another had they not reached a compromise. They would bypass Sikiokuu, Machokali, and Kaniũrũ and take the Wizard of the Crow directly to the Ruler at the State House, and they agreed that on account of A.G.'s seniority—he was SS while they were ASSes—A.G. should call the State House to alert the Ruler of his prized trophy. When they reached the State House, they would call their respective bosses on mobile phones and inform them of the *fait* that was about to become *accompli*. That way none of the three bosses would have the advantage of prior knowledge over the others and the three officers themselves would get all the credit for handing over the wizard.

For his part, the Wizard of the Crow heard none of this. He showed no sign of consciousness, not even when tied to the backseat of A.G.'s motorcycle. With Njoya in front and Kahiga at the rear, the three motorcyclists zoomed triumphantly toward the State House.

# 6

Those left behind at the bar fell into a heated dispute as to what had just happened, each trying to impose his version on others, all except one, who hid behind the door, clutching a cross-shaped walking stick as if to defend himself, his mind absorbed by the drama outside. He was Mr. Walking Stick, a wanderer from bar to bar after he had heard Kamītī tell how he had once floated in the sky while his body reposed on a dumpsite. Now the very apparition he had tried to avoid had found him. Stricken with terror, as soon as he saw the motorcycles vanish in the distance, he quietly left the bar, clutching his walking stick, not quite believing his own luck. Once on the road he started running in the opposite direction.

He ran for seven days and nights without resting until he reached his destination, the Santalucia headquarters of the Soldiers of Christ. Exhausted, he collapsed at the feet of the Christian soldiers, and it took them a while to decipher what he was trying to tell them.

"I am one of the three garbage collectors that Satan once ambushed at a dumpsite in the prairie a couple of years ago. You remember me? Much has happened since. We three took different measures to protect ourselves from the Evil One. One joined your group, armed as you always are with the Bible and the cross and the word of the Lord on high. Another, the driver, sought protection from the Mighty's Youth, with their guns and whips and the mandate from the Ruler. But I did a foolish thing. I tried to hide wherever people gather to drink. With my walking stick I would defend myself against any sudden Satanic mischief, I thought. What can I say? I first saw and heard him boasting where I used to drink regularly, and I said, You will never see me again, for from now on I shall be on the move all the time, never drinking at the same place twice. Well, I was wrong, because, lost to alcohol, I did not know that Satan would follow me from bar to bar; no matter where I hid, he would find me. He finally caught up with me. Well, let me tell you. I had a narrow escape. Had it not been for this cross-shaped walking stick, he would have seen me and I would not now be here to bear witness that I have seen with my own eyes the very Satan who appeared before us at the dumpsite in the prairie. I am here to say that I have converted. All these years past, I have foolishly sought solace in booze. Now I need the support of Jesus. I want to become a Soldier of Christ."

As they were not so sure about this man, they sent for Sweeper-of-Souls, who was overjoyed at seeing his former workmate. They embraced, and this touching scene confirmed to the others what had already been revealed to them: that the newcomer was a messenger from Christ sent to lead them to Satan's hiding place. They received him as one of them and baptized him Soul's Walking Stick.

"Where is he?" the Soldiers of Christ asked him after the baptism. "Where did he go? Where can we find him?"

"You will never believe this," said Soul's Walking Stick. "Three hell riders on red, black, and golden motorbikes took him to the Ruler at the State House."

"Does he think he can hide in there?" one of them asked.

They would keep watch on all the roads to the State House with a view to capturing him as he came out, no doubt having led the Ruler astray like that time when Satan had forced the Ruler to go to the All Saints Cathedral riding a donkey in imitation of Christ. But they must take care not to draw hostile curiosity that could abort their plans. They were as adamant as ever: arrest Satan, drag him through the streets of Eldares, and then put him on trial.

# 7

A.G. tells a slightly different version of what happened at the bar they called Sell-Me-Death. According to him, the Wizard of the Crow was not drunk with alcohol; he was simply overwhelmed by a vision of all the evils he saw before the land; his throwing up on the grass by the roadside was his way of saying that the land needed cleansing. Otherwise, in his narrative A.G. is short on details about the episode, and there are things he is not able to explain. When pressed by some spoilsports who do not know a good story when they hear one—what was the Wizard of the Crow doing in a cheap bar that served poison? they wanted to know—he would answer rather cryptically: Remember Jesus? Muhammed? They dwelled among the poor.

What he tells with more clarity and authority was how the three motorcyclists, of whom he had been one, stopped at the graveyard of All Saints Cathedral before reaching the State House to call their respective bosses on their mobile phones, simultaneously informing them that the wizard was in tow.

At the agreed-upon time, A.G. had quickly dialed Machokali's number to tell him the news. A.G. emphasizes how happy the minister sounded, that A.G. had never heard him exude such joy.

"True! *Haki ya Mungu.* I knew the minister quite well, nearly all his moods. He and I were in America together, remember? He and I used to share meals, and it was he and I who went to receive the Wizard of the Crow at the AIA, the American International Airport. So when I tell you that he was unusually happy on hearing that I had successfully completed the task assigned to me, you'd better believe me. Imagine that even when I told him that Njoya and Kahiga had unfairly claimed a share of the credit, harvesting where they never planted, Machokali did not seem upset that his rivals, Sikiokuu and Kaniũrũ, would partake of the glory."

According to A.G., Machokali cared most about the fact that the Ruler's wishes had been met. I have fulfilled my duty to my Lord, he told A.G., and then revealed that the Ruler had already summoned him. He assured A.G. that he would never forget the diligence and commitment displayed by SS Arigaigai Gathere.

A.G. then goes on to tell how, upon reaching the State House, they were shown a room where they put the Wizard of the Crow who, still passed out, continued snoring. After securing their captive, they were taken to the Ruler.

They found Machokali, Sikiokuu, Kaniũrũ, and Tajirika already there, as on the day the two ministers and Kaniũrũ were charged with their missions. The reception of the three police heroes, A.G. noted with amusement, was tense with rivalry. Each boss greeted his own policeman as if he alone had captured the Wizard of the Crow, lauding him with congratulations for his heroism. Each shook hands with the other two policemen, thanking them particularly for their assistance.

The Ruler was in a jolly mood, and he immediately promoted Kahiga and Njoya to Senior Superintendents of Police. A.G. was made Assistant Commissioner of Police. The Ruler then told them to go home for a much-needed rest, but that they should report for duty at the State House the following morning and that henceforth they would be reporting directly to him. The three police heroes were in a world all their own as they headed toward the door.

"I don't know why, but when I reached the door I turned my head and looked back and I saw Machokali wave at me slowly, a kind of personal farewell to me. True! *Haki ya Mungu*, and I must say that his big eyes lit up as I had never seen them before, but I did not then try to make too much of it because I, too, was very happy, and doubly so for knowing that my work, despite my travels and endless storytelling, had brought a little happiness to everybody, and of course I was also happy with my new rank, and, as if to add a little of what the English call *icing on the cake*, I would now be reporting for duty at the State House and be answerable to only the Ruler."

# 8

When Kamĩtĩ woke up the following morning he thought that he was in a hotel, so luxurious the room seemed to be. He thought he was dreaming and when this dream ended he would find himself atop the charred remains of the shrine, the cat again snuggling by his side. But his splitting headache convinced him that he was fully awake. He sat on the edge of the bed and rested his chin in cupped hands. How had he gotten here?

He vaguely remembered a person telling twisted stories about the note he had written to Machokali; he even recalled walking toward the man in order to correct him, but what was it about the incident that made Kamĩtĩ so angry? Again the phrase "True! *Haki ya Mungu*" reminded him vaguely of a policeman whose presence in the bar he could not account for. He also recalled motorcycles and faces resembling Njoya and Kahiga. What was their relationship to the policeman, and what had brought all three to the same bar?

He stood up to open the windows and peer outside to see if he could tell where he was; they were small and too high up the wall for him to reach, reminding him of a prison cell. He grew despondent, full of disgust with himself for having lost the trace of his goal—to find Nyawĩra—by succumbing to alcohol.

Two soldiers entered the room, threw some rags and soap at him, and told him to wash up and get ready, but for what? He had hardly finished washing the caked vomit from his face when they ordered him to accompany them as if he were a free man. He should not be foolish and try to create a scene or escape. They went through corridors and hallways past other police and soldiers.

How surprised he was when he was ushered into a room and found himself face-to-face with the Ruler and Tajirika! He noted that the Ruler was still suffering from self-induced bodily expansion: Was this why he had been abducted, to attempt over more time to effect a cure? Was this the reason for the Wanted posters? But what was Tajirika doing here? In his state of alcoholic grace, Kamĩtĩ had hardly ever read newspapers or listened to the radio, so he did not know that Tajirika was now the governor of the Central Bank. Tajirika, he thought, was truly baffling: What connection was there among the many Tajirika faces he had encountered? Tajirika who was Nyawĩra's employer, Tajirika who insulted him with a mock literacy test outside Eldares Modern Construction and Real Estate, Tajirika who had visited him in search of a cure for his malady of words, Tajirika and his bucket of shit, and Tajirika now seated in the august presence of the Ruler?

Suddenly terror seized him. Had Nyawĩra been captured? And could this explain why Tajirika was here?

He was offered a chair, and the soldiers were dismissed. The Ruler started the conversation. He introduced Kamĩtĩ to Tajirika, and Tajirika smiled as if encountering an old friend. Their jovialness convinced Kamĩtĩ that they were playing a cat and mouse game with him regarding Nyawĩra.

"I believe that you and I last met in New York City," said the Ruler affably.

"And I before you left for America," added Tajirika, still smiling.

"There are a few things you can help us with," continued the Ruler in the same friendly tone. "But let me first correct myself. When I introduced Titus to you, I forgot to mention his new title. I trust you know that Tajirika is now my new governor of the Central Bank. So let's start our get-together with money matters, but I should let the Lord of Money explain."

"You remember the money I paid you for healing me, three big bags?" Tajirika was about to mention the word *dollars* but he held back in the nick of time. He had not paid him in dollars and he did not want the Wizard of the Crow to start by disputing the currency in which he had been paid. "And you remember you told me that you buried the bags somewhere in the prairie?" Tajirika added. "Tell us this: why did you really bury the bags in the ground?"

"You know, like a farmer planting seeds in the ground?" added the Ruler encouragingly.

"Please tell us: were you hoping that the money would grow?" Tajirika asked circumspectly.

"You know, like money breeding money or whatever?" the Ruler added suggestively.

Who has ever heard of money being buried in the earth, like a grain of wheat, in order to multiply? Had the Ruler and Tajirika lost their minds? This suspicion was deepened by the fact that they would not let him get in a word in response. It was as if their need to know whatever it was that they needed to know had trumped up their capacity to listen. As if the Ruler had been reading Kamĩtĩ's thoughts, he hastened to add:

"Before we start getting into the details, let's first get to know one another better, because even though you and I were together in New York, my minister, the late, I mean, the honorable Machokali, never allowed us to properly bond. I seem to remember that you had nice, smart clothes. What happened to them? Or do you prefer crumpled ones, in keeping with your trade? Let me be clear on this: if you explain everything that you know thoroughly, you will not leave our presence empty-handed. But wait a minute. Let's first make sure that we are talking to the right person, and so I shall now ask you, as they do in a court of law, to say your name. Are you the Wizard of the Crow?"

If only he knew what they were up to! If only he could remember how he ended up here! If only he knew Nyawīra's fate! Was she alive, in custody, or free? If only . . . Without certainty, anything said might compromise both him and her.

"Didn't you hear the Ruler's question?" asked Tajirika, feigning anger. "The Ruler is asking you: are you the Wizard of the Crow?"

Kamītī opened his mouth as if he wanted to say something and started to wheeze as if he were suffering an asthmatic attack. Then out popped one distinct word: *If!* Whatever they asked, he responded in the same way: he would attempt to speak, would hiss some sounds, and then out would come *If!*

The Ruler and Tajirika looked at each other in dismay, sharing the same thought. Each recalled his bout with the illness that had defied every doctor except the Wizard of the Crow. Now, it seemed, the healer needed healing at a time they needed him most to share vital knowledge. Frustrated, they did not know what to do. They tried a few more questions, and his response was always the same.

"His words are stuck," the Ruler said.

"What shall we do?" Tajirika asked. "How shall we free the trapped words from his mouth?"

"Oh! Not to worry," the Ruler said menacingly. "I might just have to pry his mouth open and pull his voice box out with my own hands."

The Ruler summoned the soldiers who had brought the Wizard of the Crow before him and asked them to take the man away.

# 9

The next morning Kahiga, Njoya, and A.G. reported for duty at the State House and were led in to the presence of the Mighty One. Njoya and Kahiga were surprised to find the Ruler without his usual counselors, Sikiokuu and Machokali. Tajirika seemed to have taken their place at the right side of the Ruler. But how had Tajirika risen so quickly? Through magic, or potent concoctions? This Wizard of the Crow is playing havoc with people's lives, they both thought; his magic lifts some people a few steps up the ladder of power while bringing others down a rung or two. Not that they were thrilled by Tajirika's ascendancy. They had, after all, tortured him in the past: would he exact vengeance? There was nothing they could now do about it, so they resigned themselves to what may come.

Their task was to guard the Wizard of the Crow at all times, night and day. There must always be two guards inside the chamber with him and one outside. They were to be the Ruler's ears. All the sorcerer's utterances, while awake or asleep, were to be conveyed only to the Ruler, not to be discussed among themselves much less with others, on pain of losing one's tongue. Njoya and Kahiga were to start their duty inside while A.G. remained outside the door.

The Ruler did not of course disclose to them that the Wizard of the Crow had been in the same room earlier that morning, or that he was suffering from the malady of words, so the policemen did not anticipate any problems.

In fact Kahiga and Njoya were happy when they learned of their assignment because they wanted to speak with the Wizard of the Crow to make amends and reassure him that they had no personal ill will toward him. They were simply messengers not privy to the contents of the message, and they had to do their duty. If he met with trouble, he should not turn his anger against them. But if he should come across good times, he should not forget that they had always been on his side.

No sooner were they inside the chamber than they started chatting him up. They asked: Do you remember us? The word *if* and the force with which it was uttered almost made them run away; they stayed put only because they knew that fleeing would cost them their jobs if not their lives, and, besides, they had already encountered this *if* from Tajirika's confessions. But despite their previous acquaintance with it, the word and its implications instilled fear in them. Had the Wizard of the Crow fallen ill after they had brought him in last night? they now wondered. They kept on trying to engage him in talk, only to have to deal with *if*. They waited and hoped for a more fulsome utterance, but when it became clear that none would be forthcoming, they decided that Kahiga should take the *if* to the Ruler.

A.G., who had been stationed outside, now entered the chamber and joined Njoya and the Wizard of the Crow.

Kahiga was a little puzzled to see that the Ruler did not show any surprise at the news. He told Kahiga that as long as the wizard's only utterance was *if,* they should not bother to report it. When Kahiga returned, he positioned himself outside the chamber, so he did not immediately pass on the Ruler's message to the other two. So when A.G. tried to speak to the Wizard of the Crow and he croaked the word *if,* he just rushed out, gestured for Kahiga to take his place inside, and sped to the Ruler. I just told one of you that if *that* is the only utterance, you should not bother me with it, growled the Ruler. A.G. returned to his former place outside the chamber. Njoya was the only one who did not fly out to report the word, because Kahiga passed on the message from the boss.

So all three waited day and night, Kahiga and Njoya inside with the Wizard of the Crow, and A.G. outside the door. Food was brought to them, newspapers, too. The *Eldares Times* connected them to the world outside. They spent the whole day perusing it while they waited for the wizard to go beyond *if.*

It was the *Eldares Times* that broke the news about Machokali.

# 10

Njoya and Kahiga looked at each other, big-eyed, their bodies aflame with anxiety. This must be the work of the Wizard of the Crow, they thought simultaneously, and both stared at him to see if they could read anything in his face. The wizard was in another world, as always, gazing ahead. The police officers winked at each other, and Kahiga casually turned the newspaper so that the page with the news of Machokali was now facing the Wizard of the Crow while Njoya kept a surreptitious eye on him to see if and how his face would change on reading the headline: MACHOKALI MISSING.

But the Wizard of the Crow seemed completely unaware of his environment, and his face registered nothing.

They resumed their examination of the newspaper article. What day was he reported missing? Again they stared at the Wizard of the Crow. Their supposition of his involvement in the drama of the missing minister was confirmed when they realized that the minister had vanished on the same day they brought the Wizard of the Crow to the State House. It was easy to see the connection. Had Machokali not been entrusted with apprehending the wizard? They felt better knowing that it was not they who had tracked down the Wizard of the Crow; that honor fell squarely on the shoulders of A.G., Machokali's assistant. All unpleasantness, all the vengeance, would bypass them and fall on A.G. Njoya in particular felt proud of himself, recalling that he had refused to describe the face of the Wizard of the Crow to the artist charged with the Wanted poster and had instead described the face of Sikiokuu. He was particularly confident that he would not face harm from the sorcerer. Machokali was the wizard's first victim; A.G. would be next.

In all Aburĩria, people were asking themselves: How can a cabinet minister disappear, like a goat or a child, without a trace? A Minister for Foreign Affairs, who had so ably represented the Ruler in the courts of the great all over the world—how could he just vanish like that? A minister surrounded by bodyguards day and night—how could there be no witnesses?

Njoya and Kahiga continually whispered their imaginings to each other, but there were times when they forgot that the Wizard of the Crow was present and would raise their voices. This did not unduly worry them, for they assumed that, as he was unable to speak, he was also unable to hear and understand. Day and night they traded stories and speculations about Machokali. They gleaned bits of information and rumors from the papers and those who brought them food.

But nothing they heard or read could make them change or even shake their strongly held belief that the arrest of the Wizard of the Crow had something to do with Machokali's disappearance.

# 11

All over the country, people were buffeted by the winds of rumor, disinformation, and even some facts as they tried to make sense of what had happened.

Machokali's chauffeur and his bodyguard said that they had left the minister behind at the State House at his own request; that he had sent them a message with one of the guards excusing them for the night because he and the Ruler had many matters to settle and that on finishing state business he would find his way home. But they could not give the name of the guard who had brought the message. People would ask, How did they know that the message had really come from the minister himself?

Machokali's wife said that her husband had not come home that night or the following night and she had not heard from him, and this was unusual because he always kept in touch by phone. He had not gone to work on the morning of his disappearance and had not called his secretary.

It was only after seven days of rumors and counterrumors that the government had issued a statement acknowledging that Machokali, the Minister for Foreign Affairs, was missing. If anybody had information about the minister's whereabouts or the mystery of his disappearance, he or she should report it to the nearest police station. Some people claimed that the government issued the statement only after many world leaders had voiced concern over the disappearance of the minister.

After another week, the government issued a terse statement saying that according to an ongoing government inquiry, A Secret Report on Acts of Treason, Machokali was implicated in a plot to overthrow the legal government of the Republic of Aburĩria. The statement strongly hinted that the minister might have fled to a foreign country to hide his shame or might even have committed suicide once he got wind of the inquiry. The statement called on any state considering giving the minister political asylum to let the Aburĩrian government know so that it could start extradition proceedings. The government had a few questions it hoped the minister could shed some light on. The statement was signed by Big Ben Mambo, Minister of Information, heretofore known as a supporter of Machokali. There were a few, even then, who whispered that the missing minister was somewhere within the walls of the State House, that his bones were fortifying the walls of the famous temple of the spirits, that there were times when the Ruler was heard laughing triumphantly, saying, So you thought you were more cunning than me, just because of your degrees and the support of London and Washington . . . A cunning robber may well meet his match in a stealthy thief . . . Go tell your friends that I am not to be trifled with.

# 12

"True! *Haki ya Mungu!* Sitting there, outside the chamber, alone, without anybody with whom I could share my feelings, I posed similar questions to myself, but it was hard. Imagine what it means for a person to wrestle with his own thoughts without a soul to help him deal with the numerous whys and hows in his mind or help him sort out fact from fiction? Imagine brooding like this day in, day out, in light and darkness!"

What A.G. kept on reviewing in his mind was the two-line letter that the Wizard of the Crow had written to Machokali. He grew obsessed with one phrase: *Take care*. A.G. recalled what the Wizard of the Crow had spluttered in a drunken haze that day at the bar: *My note was addressed to one person and one person only, Machokali, the Minister for Foreigners, I mean, Affairs. And I just wanted to tell him . . . Take care of yourself.*

"True! *Haki ya Mungu*, the Wizard of the Crow had foreseen all this!" A.G. would shout when later he told the story of those times.

But what exactly had the wizard foreseen? The more he turned the matter over in his head, the more A.G. became inclined to dismiss the thought that the Wizard of the Crow was the author of the minister's disappearance. The unthinkable began to force itself on him, tentatively implicating the Ruler. Before the disappearance, A.G. did not see the contradiction between his belief in the Ruler, God, and the Wizard of the Crow, seeing the three entities as embodying ideals somehow beneficial to humans. But now for the first time he had serious doubts. So although he would have liked to have company, he stopped wishing for any, for how could he share these thoughts? I would rather struggle with my doubts, he said to himself, and keep any answers to myself. Perhaps, after all, this was the work of Machokali's archrival, Sikiokuu, the Minister of State.

"The strange thing was that while my brain was muddled with numerous questions, I always recalled with clarity Machokali's raising his hand and waving to me as if to say good-bye. Who would be disappeared next? Only the Wizard of the Crow knew for sure, and he was saying nothing but the word *if*."

A.G.'s hope of finding out lay in the restoration of the voice of the Wizard of the Crow.

# 13

Sikiokuu, who did not know that the sorcerer had been stricken with the malady of words, anxiously awaited what he would say. Instead of joy at the disappearance of his nemesis, Sikiokuu was shaken when he learned that the minister was missing. He recalled their last time together at the State House. After the three policemen had departed, Sikiokuu was first to leave; the Ruler, Machokali, Tajirika, and Kaniũrũ staying behind. What happened after he left? he now wondered. Were Tajirika and Kaniũrũ connected somehow to the disappearance of the minister?

However much he wanted to inquire of them, he thought the better of it. If Machokali was murdered, had Tajirika or Kaniũrũ been entrusted with the deed? Sikiokuu started worrying about himself. What if the Wizard of the Crow had told the Ruler of Sikiokuu's ambition, which he had divined? The more Sikiokuu thought about it, the more he too appeared to be in danger. Should he flee to another country? Or walk into a Western embassy in Eldares and apply for political asylum? But how would he explain the danger facing him?

And so he grew desperate to know what the Wizard of the Crow had said. He tried to consult with his former subordinates, Njoya and Kahiga, to buy information from them, but they were always in the State House.

He was wallowing in these anxieties when he received a summons to the State House, his first invitation since the reported disappearance. Expecting the worst, he was relieved to learn that he was only being asked to abridge the original *Report on Acts of Treason* and amend it to link Machokali with forming queues, part of his alleged plan to overthrow the legitimate government of the Ruler.

When later his summary became the basis of the government statement implicating Machokali in plans for a coup d'état, Sikiokuu said to himself: So it was the report on treason that had led Machokali into trouble? He felt a little guilty because he knew that a lot of the evidence and citations in the report were pure fabrications extracted from Tajirika through torture. But the relief and guilt gave way to outrage when he realized that the report might have contributed not only to Tajirika's governorship of the Central Bank but also to his even more enviable position of always being next to the ears of the Ruler. Tajirika could say anything he wanted to the Ruler. What was to prevent him from whispering words against Sikiokuu, who had tortured him? If Kaniūrū, his ex-protégé, could turn against him, why not Tajirika, his ex-prisoner? Best to brace himself for the wrath to come! If the Ruler could do what he did to Rachael, his own wife, confine her to a golden prison for years and years without mercy, no amount of loyal service would restrain him.

So in those days Sikiokuu went through emotional highs and lows, but mostly lows because of the closeness of the Wizard of the Crow, Tajirika, and Kaniūrū to the Ruler. Of the three, the one who terrified him most was the wizard, for he alone knew of Sikiokuu's secret ambition.

# 14

Kaniūrū, too, waited on the Wizard of the Crow. As he looked back to the night the sorcerer was brought to the State House, he found many things unclear. What a coincidence that Machokali should vanish on the very day the Wizard of the Crow was found? What, if any, was the connection between the two events? He recalled being excused to leave after Sikiokuu, which he did reluctantly, for it meant Machokali and Tajirika remaining behind to bask in the glory of greatness. What happened after his departure? he now wondered. Did Tajirika have a hand in Machokali's disappearance? Had the new governor been tasked with dispatching the minister? At the thought Kaniūrū felt a mixture of fear and envy. If Tajirika had been so entrusted, he was very close indeed to the Ruler, which meant that he would have even greater clout in the future. Kaniūrū feared retaliation for the misery he had caused Tajirika and his family; he was angry with himself for not having foreseen that the chairperson of Marching to Heaven might well turn out to be a trusted keeper of the gate.

He tried to figure out how to make amends with Tajirika, but in vain. What consoled him in the weeks that followed was to know that the findings of his commission on the queuing mania were being used by the government to explain away the minister's disappearance. But when he thought that the false confessions attributed to Tajirika may have contributed to the man's rise to the top of those controlling the circulation of money in Aburīria, Kaniūrū's heart sank. He could outsmart Tajirika and seize more power for himself only by crushing all the queues old and new by apprehending Nyawīra before his other rival Sikiokuu did. The Ruler had already congratulated Kaniūrū for teaching those racist, meddlesome foreign journalists a lesson or two, but this had been done privately. Were he to bring in Nyawīra, the Ruler would no doubt congratulate him in public to greater acclaim.

But only the Wizard of the Crow could lead him to Nyawīra, and that is why he was eager to hear what the wizard had proclaimed. For him, information had literally been power. That was why he was restless for not having the slightest clue as to what had transpired in the State House. He tried to make contact with his erstwhile assistant, Kahiga, but pointlessly. Kahiga was always at the State House, and there was no way of getting in without an invitation or a permit.

And then one day, while bathing, he jumped out of the bath and ran around the room, naked, shouting Eureka! at the top of his voice. He would crush a certain number of queues every week and then request to visit the State House to report his weekly progress. He would have a weekly audience with the Ruler and while there would try to see Kahiga and buy from him the information he so desperately needed. He was certain that he would find out what the Wizard of the Crow had disclosed about Nyawira. Eureka! he shouted again.

# 15

The Ruler was growing anxious, too. Regarding the captive in the State House, he felt torn by numerous and often conflicting desires. He wanted him dead and alive at the same time. He wanted him alive so the man could disclose the secret of how money grows and dead so that he could never reveal it to another soul or reveal that he had revealed it to the Ruler. He wanted him alive so that he could help in the capture of Nyawira and the leaders of the Movement for the Voice of the People, and dead for having heretofore kept privileged information to himself. He wanted him alive to cure him, the Ruler, of his bodily expansion, but dead for claiming that he was pregnant, attracting, to the Ruler's chagrin, the pest known as world media. But what chagrined him even more was that on weighing the two desires he found the one for the body alive outweighing the one for the body as corpse. The captive carried much knowledge that, harnessed properly, could benefit the Ruler enormously, but this thought made him angry, because with it he was admitting that the Wizard of the Crow had powers that he, the Almighty, lacked, and this would not do in a country where he had come to believe the claims of his praise singers that he was the number one in everything. How to unlock the words of knowledge trapped in the larynx of the Wizard of the Crow? The

Ruler agonized over this, and that is why he kept Tajirika by his side at all times. It was not a matter he wanted to discuss with any of his ministers, for he did not want any of them to acquire the knowledge of how money grows on trees. Tajirika was different.

The Ruler had not always been so enamored of Tajirika. He had appointed him chairman of Marching to Heaven initially as an interim measure, pending the release of funds by the Global Bank. But he had started to think well of Tajirika the moment he realized that the man was a crook, better at the art than any of his counselors. It was Tajirika's disclosure that as chairman of Marching to Heaven he used to demand payment in dollars from potential contractors that first impressed the Ruler and made him decide that he could certainly do business with this man. A person who could make others beg to pay in fresh dollars for services yet to come was way ahead of the game. Kaniũrũ and Sikiokuu suffered by comparison. These two had asked for kickbacks in Aburĩrian Burĩs: what a different approach to wealth and well-being! This showed that Tajirika could be entrusted with any task that required bending or breaking the law under the guise of legality.

Even more, the Ruler was impressed with Tajirika's discreetness. The contrast with Kaniũrũ was telling. Kaniũrũ had rushed to share his plan of crooked gains with Sikiokuu, but Tajirika never so much as whispered a word to Machokali. Not even under torture did he let the secret out. The Ruler needed such a person of unalloyed loyalty by his side.

Events took on a logic of their own, making the unlocking of the wizard's words of knowledge even more urgent. The queues, which had seemed random and pointless, took on greater organization. The students and the youth, mostly unemployed, were beginning to gather outside Parliament buildings, courts of law, and radio and television stations, media outlets serving as the Ruler's mouthpiece. Skirmishes with the police occured with greater frequency, and not only in Eldares! Reports suggested that queues were spreading in all urban centers of the country with an intensity not seen before.

Coincidentally, questions about the missing minister from all corners of the globe gathered momentum, especially those from London and Washington. Even after the government issued its statement implicating Machokali in a coup plot, the barrage of questions was unrelenting. These trends could not be allowed to continue: his alleged pregnancy made him a laughing stock, insurgents were wreaking havoc all over the place, and pressure from abroad was building. His absence from public view only intensified the pressure and the questions.

He tried to silence the tongues of those wondering why he was not seen in public by recalling the deputy ambassador in Washington to become, effective immediately, the official national hostess at receptions and other functions that required his ceremonial presence. She accepted and signed her e-mail of acceptance as Dr. Yunique Immaculate McKenzie, PhD, NOH, thus changing her name yet again to fit the new rung in her rise to power.

The appointment and acceptance, announced on the radio and carried in all the other media, only fueled the rumors of a debilitating pregnancy as the cause of his absence from the public. The Wizard of the Crow was the only person who, in addition to providing knowledge of money growing on trees, a knowledge that would lessen the Ruler's dependence on the Global Bank, could squelch all these rumors of pregnancy immediately. The Ruler would force the wizard to confess in public that it was his letter to Machokali, which had generated tales of pregnancy as part of the minister's coup plot. The only hitch to these solutions was again the tiny word, *if,* that blocked the wizard's speech. A wizard to cure the wizard had to be found.

The Ruler pointed a finger at Tajirika and said to him solemnly, "You are a resourceful man, Governor. You were once stricken with the malady of words and you found a cure. A person who can take over a whole armed camp with a bucket of shit and piss as his only weapon can surely find the sorcerer I need. Governor, over to you!"

# 16

Weeks after his elevation, Tajirika could still not believe that he was now governor of the Central Bank of Aburĩria. He could not be blamed for being a little cautious about accepting his new status, for his fortunes had swung from one end of the pendulum to the other, time and again, since the Wizard of the Crow came into his life on that fateful evening at Eldares Modern Construction and Real Estate to look for a job he clearly did not need.

Many were the times he had found himself saluting his reflection in a mirror—Hello, Governor, are you really he? The sound of the word *governor* thrilled him, recalling as it did the long line of colonial governors of territorial Aburīria. What had started as a playful act of self-affirmation now became a need, and more and more he found himself conversing with his reflection, especially on matters he could never talk about with anybody else. Hello, Governor, what shall we do today? he would say to the image in the mirror as he brushed his teeth or tied his tie. And just before departing from the house: Bye-bye, Governor. And in the evening: I am back, Governor. How was your day at the office? And any of these lines could trigger a dialogue with himself in the mirror.

So when the Ruler gave Tajirika the task of finding a sorcerer to exorcise the evil blocking the voice of the Wizard of the Crow, he was back at the mirror, speaking to his reflection.

"Where shall I start? Should I go along the streets, stopping people and saying, Excuse me, I am the new governor of the Central Bank. Can you please tell me where I can find a sorcerer? A bit embarrassing, wouldn't you say, for the governor of the Central Bank to go about the streets of Eldares asking for a witch doctor?"

Many Aburīrians did not believe that people, except the aged, died of natural causes. They believed that all untimely deaths were caused by witchcraft. Were Tajirika to openly look for witch doctors, might he himself not be deemed an agent of death and held responsible for harm suffered by others, Machokali, for instance? And suddenly he had a vision of being blamed for all deaths in Aburīria, and he shuddered at his foolishness. He stared helplessly at the mirror, not realizing that he was shouting: "Governor, what shall I do? What shall we do to get the Wizard of the Crow a cure without putting ourselves in danger?"

"What danger?" Vinjinia, who had just come into the bathroom, asked him. "Why are you talking to the mirror? Have you forgotten the past?"

# 17

Since Tajirika's capture by the women and Vinjinia's by Kaniũrũ and his youth, the two had improved their relationship. Their social life had also changed, and not a week went by without invitations to cocktails and dinner parties at seven-star hotels. The glittering socials and the closeness to power were attractive to her, and the political talk and gossip did not repulse her the way they used to do. The only thing in her previous lifestyle to which she clung with the same intensity was her churchgoing. She went to the same church, All Saints, but since her husband's promotion she noticed significant changes in how she was now received. She and her children had a special pew reserved for them at the front near the altar, and the number of men and women who now and then stopped to say a word, shake hands, or simply ask a question and get advice even on spiritual matters had risen dramatically.

Just when she thought that her affairs were running smoothly and that she could sit back and enjoy life, she grew alarmed at seeing her husband talking once again to a mirror. She recalled that other time when Tajirika was stricken by his malady of words and how it all began. Was he about to have another seizure? The earlier one had come after his appointment to the chair of Marching to Heaven. Would his ascendancy to governorship be followed by another loss of words? The only difference this time was that he was not clawing at his face. Tajirika's name and his last meeting with Machokali at the Mars Café were mentioned in the government statement compromising Machokali. Was this haunting her husband? She was not sure, and in her prayers she begged God to exorcise whatever daemons might be bedeviling her husband. Vinjinia started surreptitiously stalking him in the house. There would be no more surprises, she told herself.

One morning she heard him clearly mention the name the Wizard of the Crow, and he was so absorbed in whatever had made him cry out that he did not even notice her presence. She decided to confront him: What danger? What about the Wizard of the Crow?

It was a Sunday morning. At first Tajirika was rattled by the sound of Vinjinia's voice. He managed a smile but did not succeed in hiding his anxiety. He now seemed relieved to see her. Even though they were variously occupied during the day and did not see as much of each other as they would have liked, Tajirika was always happy to brag about himself to Vinjinia, especially about how the Ruler trusted him or how his enemies like Kaniūrū and Sikiokuu were now desperate to appease him. I am now the man, he would tell her, and he loved it when she cautioned him not to be drunk with power like some people she knew. This would make them laugh, because they knew that by "like some people I know" she meant Kaniūrū. But even so, he did not tell her everything that happened in the State House. Nothing about the money trees, or the night that Machokali went missing, or even the capture of the Wizard of the Crow. This business of advising the Ruler is not easy, Vinjinia, and I am burdened by state secrets, he would sigh. But he would quickly beam with pleasure when he heard Vinjinia say: Don't worry, *you can't have your cake and eat it.* This all comes with the territory.

Now her questions suddenly reminded him that it was she who had introduced him to the Wizard of the Crow when he was stricken by white-ache. He was sure she could come up with another sorcerer. Women had a sixth sense.

"I need some sorcerers and witch doctors," Tajirika said to his wife without any preliminaries.

"What!" Vinjinia exclaimed, taken unaware. Was he joking, or had he gone feeble in his head?

"I want you to get me the most powerful sorcerers and witch doctors available," Tajirika repeated.

"Sorcerers?"

"Even one will do," Tajirika said. "But many are better than one, for I can choose the best among them."

"What are you talking about? What do you all of a sudden want with sorcerers?" Vinjinia asked when she saw that he was serious. "Whom do you intend to bewitch?"

He sat her down and told her about the capture of the Wizard of the Crow and of his affliction. Still the Ruler wanted to ask him a few questions that only he, the Wizard of the Crow, could answer. The task of getting a healer to heal the healer had been thrust upon him, he explained.

"What on earth do I know about sorcerers or where to find them?" Vinjinia asked, shrugging it off.

"You are a very resourceful woman, Vinjinia," Tajirika pleaded. "I am dead sure that you can find me a sorcerer as you did before."

Vinjinia was about to remind him that it was Nyawīra who led her to the Wizard of the Crow, but thought the better of it.

As the wife of a governor and a successful businesswoman in her own right, she wanted no part of Nyawīra, the Wizard of the Crow, or the razed shrine.

It is true, though, that when news of the arson first reached her, Vinjinia felt despair, worsened by her not knowing whether or not Nyawīra had perished in the shrine. Vinjinia felt responsible; she was burdened by guilt and could talk to no one without revealing what she knew about the identity of one of the faces of the Wizard of the Crow. She was haunted by images of the charred remains of Nyawīra, but in time she had managed to suppress them.

Now Vinjinia recalled the many times that Nyawīra had come to her aid and was surprised to find herself feeling as when she first heard that the shrine had been burnt down. How could she tell Tajirika that Nyawīra, who had led her to the Wizard of the Crow and was the only one who could show them the way, had been reduced to ashes? How could she tell him that she knew nothing about sorcerers, witches, diviners, and healers? She did not want to break his heart, so she tried to be diplomatic.

"Well, I will keep my ears open," she said, sounding sympathetic.

"Please try—I believe that even among your fellow churchgoers there are many who go to sorcerers at night," Tajirika pleaded. "Pray to God to show you the way."

Vinjinia tried hard not to laugh, as she realized that Tajirika was serious about her seeking God's guidance in finding his sorcerer. Alone in the car on her way to All Saints Cathedral, Vinjinia laughed openly, so ludicrous had been her husband. She was, after all, a middle-class Christian woman. A respected churchgoer, the wife of the governor of the Central Bank and chairman of Marching to Heaven, and now a full managing director of all Tajirika Enterprises, including the well-known Eldares Modern Construction and Real Estate, how could she go to church on a Sunday and ask her fellow worshippers: Can you tell me where I might come across a diviner? Or, Our Sister in Christ, please tell me about your personal witch doctor? No. Let Tajirika and the Ruler conduct their own witch doctor hunt.

A few yards from the church door, she bumped into Maritha and Mariko, who told her that they had been waiting for her, but she assumed that this was the usual case of people wanting to shake hands with her and to make themselves known to her. But what would Maritha and Mariko want from her? They always looked completely at peace with themselves, as if they dwelled in a world of their own.

"We just wanted to catch you before you went in," Maritha said quickly.

"Yes, because after the service, it is very difficult to get close to you. There is always a crowd around you," added Mariko.

"And you important people are always so busy," said Maritha, "that . . ."

"After church, you might simply drive away," said Mariko.

"Is it something that can wait until after the service?" Vinjinia asked impatiently, time being of the essence, for she wanted to be present at the beginning of the service. Vinjinia was one of those who felt lost if she arrived after the beginning of a service or any performance.

"It is only a message," said Maritha.

"But it can wait until after the service," added Mariko.

"From whom is the message?" she asked, curious.

"A dove," Maritha and Mariko said together.

"A dove?" Vinjinia asked, frowning.

But instead of replying directly, Maritha and Mariko started to sing and dance around, like two children at a party.

> Dove sent me on a mission, mmh
> It needs a bigger beak, mmh
> To enable it to swallow seeds, mmh
> When now it tries to swallow them, mmh
> They get stuck in the throat, mmh

Maritha and Mariko were well known in the church community for their comic ways in going about things. But now they had gone too far. Prancing about, only a few yards from the entrance to the church? Vinjinia quickly looked around in sheer embarrassment, fearing the disapproval of potential onlookers.

"Let us meet after the service," Vinjinia said very quickly. "Let us meet over there, where I have parked my car," she added, pointing to her Mercedes-Benz by the road. "If you get there before I do, please wait for me," she added, hurrying into the church.

# 18

It was during the service that Vinjinia recalled who Dove was and started shaking so much that she could hardly follow what Bishop Kanogori was saying at the altar. Thank you, Lord, thank you, Jesus, she heard herself say in silent prayer. Nyawīra was still alive! Her guilt was assuaged, and she realized that she had been deceiving herself in imagining that she had successfully repressed all thoughts of Nyawīra. But where was she? And how did Maritha, Mariko, and Nyawīra come to know one another so well that she could trust them with such a message to Vinjinia?

She recalled the many rumors provoked by the couple's declaration of victory over Satan. Some gossipers had claimed that Maritha and Mariko may have visited the shrine of the Wizard of the Crow, where they got a magic potion that rekindled their love to a level that rivaled that of their youth. But soon anxiety replaced Vinjinia's initial relief and curiosity. What was the content of Dove's message? What did Nyawīra want from her?

Did she want to give herself up? The recently appointed national hostess—what's her name, Yunique Immaculate McKenzie—was she not at one time an advocate of bad politics? When she gave herself up, the Ruler forgave her and even gave her a job. Maybe Nyawīra had read about McKenzie's appointment and had seen the light and was now willing to kneel at the feet of the Ruler. Maybe she wants me to take her to him.

But what would the consequences be of her being associated with Nyawīra? Should she, the wife of the governor of the Central Bank, be encouraging contact with an enemy of the State? After the service she could simply avoid the usual crowd of well-wishers and favor seekers and go straight to her car and drive away. That would send a clear message to Nyawīra that Vinjinia did not want to renew their relationship. But she decided that she should first hear the content of the message before settling on a course of action. After all, she could be wrong about the dove's identity and intent.

As soon as the service was over, Vinjinia got out and hurried to her car. Maritha and Mariko were already there. She asked them to get in the car, drove some distance away, and stopped. Caution was of utmost importance. Maritha went straight to the point. She had been sent to tell Vinjinia this story.

Once upon a time, there was a person who used to give Dove a nest and some castor seeds to eat, and now Dove heard that the person was in a place where no eyes of an ordinary citizen could reach him. Dove was hungry and wanted Vinjinia to find out everything she could about the person, where he was, how he was, things like that. Vinjinia should try to tell the person that Dove's nest had caught fire but Dove was fine and was now breathing the same air as all other citizen birds. Maritha ended by telling Vinjinia that if she had any castor oil seeds that she wanted delivered to Dove, she should bring them to All Saints Cathedral on any Sunday and Maritha would make sure that Dove got them.

When she finished the story and without waiting for a reply, Maritha tugged Mariko's sleeve and they got out of the car. They danced away, singing loudly:

> *Dove sent me on a mission, mmh*
> *It needs a bigger beak, mmh . . .*

As she drove away, Vinjinia thought about Dove's message. Nyawīra wanted to know about the Wizard of the Crow.

For a week or so, Vinjinia thought of nothing else but Nyawīra and her message. What a time for Nyawīra to intrude, just when her life with Tajirika was beginning to be good! Nyawīra wanted her to glean information from her husband, but how could she engage in such underhandedness? Tajirika was now an esteemed player in the government. Nyawīra was a reviled enemy of the State. How could she collude with an enemy of her husband?

She felt pulled in two different directions. She recalled her last meeting with Nyawīra and how her heart had so welled up with gratitude that she told Nyawīra that if she was ever in need she should call on her. A promise was a contract of sorts, and she should not break it. But then, she would argue, nobody was obliged to keep a promise destructive to herself and those around her.

She went so far as to consider finding Nyawīra's whereabouts and turning her in, to her husband's advantage. But opportunity knocked. Her husband had asked her to look for a sorcerer to heal the Wizard of the Crow. Who could do that better than the other Wizard of the Crow? She would help Nyawīra, and Nyawīra would help her. Then she would betray her, or rather let Tajirika do it, and that way Tajirika would rise in the government and might even succeed the Ruler. Her husband would be bound to her in eternal gratitude.

The following morning Tajirika rushed to the State House to confer with the Ruler. And on the next Sunday Vinjinia rushed to All Saints to see Maritha and Mariko.

# 19

The news came from the State House through Big Ben Mambo, Minister of Information, and it was broadcast by all the media. The Ruler had devised a philosophy that would cure the people of the stresses of modernity. The government printer even issued a booklet: *Magnus Africanus: Prolegomenon to Future Happiness, by the Ruler.* The book said, among other things, that during his retreat and meditation it had been revealed to the Ruler that the real threat to Aburīria's future lay in people's abandoning their traditions in pursuit of a stressful modernity.

And so, according to the teachings of *Magnus Africanus,* children and youth, even those at the university, must seek out and follow the advice of adults, and when they fail to do so they must be caned on their bare buttocks. Women must get circumcised and show submission by always walking a few steps behind their men. Polygamous households should not form queues. Instead of screaming when they are beaten, women should sing songs of praise to those who beat them and even organize festivals to celebrate wife beating in honor of manhood. Most important, all Aburīrians should remember at all times that the Ruler was husband number one, and so he was duty bound to set an example by doing in the country what individual men were to do in their households. The government would distribute the booklet free through churches, mosques, temples, and schools. Television and radio stations would be required to feature an excerpt daily, as a thought of the day. Teachers would be strongly encouraged to impart to schoolchildren the virtues of the past, of unquestioning obedience. Instead of using the word *past,* they would talk about African modernity through the ages, and they should talk of the leading figures in Africa's march backward to the roots of an authentic unchanging past as the great sages of African modernity.

On the very day of the publication of *Magnus Africanus,* the Ruler issued a special decree that traditional African healers would no longer be called sorcerers, diviners, or witch doctors. Henceforth they would be called specialists in African psychiatry, in short, afrochiatrists, and they would be allowed to call themselves *Doctor.* The Ruler was making plans to set up the Ruler's Academy of Authentic Afrochiatrists.

But the most dramatic in a week of dramatic statements was to follow soon, and it instantly became the subject of gossip, rumor, and speculation in every home in every village in every corner of Aburīria. The Ruler announced that all those who wanted to become the founding doctors of the new academy must present themselves at the State House for a national test. The very best among the founding doctors of the academy would comprise the Ruler's advisory council to advise the Ruler on how best to ensure that people's heads were on straight—behind the Ruler's thought. The test would be given on the basis of first come, first tested.

# 20

Nothing like this had ever been seen or heard of in Aburĩria: experts in sorcery and witchcraft, with their paraphernalia, winding their way to the State House to take the first-ever national achievement test in their trade. The sheer number who came forward was astounding. Some were among the most regular attendants at mosques and churches; nobody would ever have suspected these zealots of ever practicing sorcery and witchcraft on the side. There were a few others who knew nothing about sorcery and witchcraft but nevertheless came forward, hoping somehow to pass the test and earn a place in the Ruler's advisory council as a base for personal advancement. Some had traveled at night, and by the early hours of the appointed day there was already a queue visible by even those at some distance from the gates of the State House.

Ever vigilant of opportunities to capture Satan, the Soldiers of Christ stood watching, but they were puzzled by the momentous proceedings. They were not alone in being puzzled by this gathering, for there were only two people, the Ruler and Tajirika, who knew the purpose of the national achievement test in sorcery and witchcraft.

# 21

An assistant for protocol fetched sorcerer or witch doctor in front of the queue and led him or her to a waiting room, from where Njoya, Kahiga, or A.G., depending on who happened to be guarding the door, escorted him or her to the testing site.

The test itself was simple. Each competitor would try to cure a man afflicted with a malady of words causing words to become stuck in his larynx. None was told the name or other details about the sick man; none knew that the patient was the Wizard of the Crow.

# 22

Kamĩtĩ had heard Njoya and Kahiga whisper about the impending arrival of a delegation of afrochiatrists to the State House. He gleaned that these were leading African specialists in mental disorders. But he did not know that they were coming up to see him.

Many of the sorcerers went through identical preliminaries: they would do some acrobatics, some even blowing horns or whistles to unsettle the evil spirits that possessed the patient, and then would venture a question to which Kamĩtĩ always responded by spitting out the word: *if*. They all left the room defeated, muttering to themselves that they had never encountered a case of so complete a possession by bad spirits. Some tried to cover their failure by saying that they were going for stronger medicines, that they would surely come back, but there was very little enthusiasm and conviction in their voices.

Kamĩtĩ began to feel good about his own performance. It was difficult even for the most astute of doctors to diagnose an illness in which the patient was silent about symptoms. But after dismissing one after the other, he came across one afrochiatrist who terrified him to the core.

This master surgeon started by elaborating on his experience, as if offering his credentials to the two examiners in the room.

"I tell you, it is not just one or two on whom I have operated and removed bits of iron buried deep in their bellies or their joints—their knees, for instance," he said, confiding in Njoya and Kahiga. "I have operated on many, and seven out of every ten have come out of it alive and well. Not bad, eh? And I do it swiftly," he added, reaching for the surgical tools in his bag and carefully spreading them on the floor.

Kamĩtĩ counted hammers, tweezers, miniature saws, razor blades, needles, knives, scissors, and nails of different sizes and shapes. He did not know what was more terrifying, the array of surgical tools or the master surgeon's matter-of-fact tone in talking about his past successes.

Kamĩtĩ decided to take matters into his own hands. He stood up, walked toward the surgeon, barking, *IF! IF!* and spraying saliva in the direction of his nemesis, who was counting the tools. The master surgeon imagined that Kamītī intended to infect him and his tools with evil, and started collecting his paraphernalia and putting them back into the bag. It was too late. His gadgets were slimy with spit. A glob attached itself to his face; the surgeon did not wait for more. He let out an involuntary scream, threw the last of his gadgets into the bag, dashed out of the room, and ran as fast as his jingled legs could carry him toward the gates of the State House, moaning loudly for all the world to hear that his things had been bewitched with saliva. Me, too, he added, moaning, "I have just been cursed." In his frenzy, he felt death knocking at his door. "I am going to die" soon changed into "I am dying," and by the time the master surgeon had reached the queue outside, the cry had become "I am dead." When asked by the others what was the matter, he blabbered about his bewitchment and certain death.

When they understood the implications of what he was saying, the remaining candidates took to their heels, initially following him, shouting questions, before dispersing in different directions.

The news of the flight of the sorcerers immediately reached the ears of the Ruler, and it made him very furious. He ordered his security men to chase the candidates and bring them back to be flogged and then complete their tests. How dare these cowardly fellows disgrace afrochiatry?

But it was as if all the sorcerers and witch doctors had vanished into thin air, except one who was unable to run because his left leg was shorter than his right and he could only limp, shouting to the others: Oh, my brothers and sisters in sorcery, don't leave me behind! Please don't leave me behind—we are all equal in matters of sorcery!

Oh, we are not leaving you behind, said the security men as they pounced on the crippled sorcerer, and it was only their fear of sorcery that prevented them from raining blows of vengeance on his body.

# 23

The Ruler ordered that the cripple take the test or be whipped with a *sjambok* until he revealed where all his brothers and sisters in sorcery had gone. When told that the sorcerer was a woman, he said it did not matter, but if she passed the test she would be spared the *sjambok*.

The Limping Witch, as they now called the crippled witch, had a repulsive face. One of her eyes oozed, and when not talking her lips twitched; when talking to her, people felt compelled to look away. But she also cut a laughable figure. She had no divining charms, only a walking stick and an ungainly wrap. Her hair was so matted that it became the subject of spirited conversation among her captors, who thought she had taken the idea of dreadlocks too literally.

Kamĩtĩ was still in shock from his narrow escape from the master surgeon; he was now grimly on guard for whoever came next. So when the Limping Witch was ushered in, Kamĩtĩ jumped up and retreated even farther into his corner, ready to let flow his lethal saliva. I will not turn my back on this one, Kamĩtĩ swore to himself: he was highly suspicious of the stick she carried. He and the Limping Witch defiantly glared at each other for a few seconds as if to see who would blink first.

In spite of his alertness, Kamĩtĩ did not anticipate the witch's next move, or see it, for that matter. All of a sudden, her stick was touching his Adam's apple. Kamĩtĩ attempted a few *if*s, but they were smothered in terror. Every time he tried to move his neck away, she would press his Adam's apple a bit more firmly as if to warn him, Don't play tricks with me, and in the end he desisted. I must be careful about what I do, he thought to himself, or I am a dead man.

"My walking stick never lies. The Devil is hiding there, just where my stick is touching. The foolish and the wise—who is it that cannot see? Speech is the beginning of knowledge. And lack of speech? The beginning of foolishness. But how did the Devil get here? This place reeks of alcohol."

Njoya and Kahiga exchanged frantic glances. "Tell me," she loudly insisted, "where did you collect this man?" Once again they looked at each other, unsure as to whether they should admit that they had found the man in a bar. They were not even sure if they were allowed to answer any questions posed by the sorcerers beyond those relating to the requirements. They conferred in hushed tones and decided that Njoya must go and ask what they should do about the question. As soon as Njoya left, A.G., in accordance with the two-man rule, entered the room. But this brought about a few complications for Njoya, who when he returned realized that the same rule forbade him to enter. He simply took A.G.'s place outside.

"What did I ask you?" the Limping Witch intoned ferociously at Kahiga. In desperation, Kahiga opened the door, quickly dragged Njoya inside without a word, and replaced him outside. With permission granted to answer her question, Njoya now admitted that he and others had picked up the man in a beer hall; he had been drunk, but since then the man had not taken a drop or even set eyes on alcohol. Having just entered the room, A.G. did not know what was going on. He was peeved at what appeared to be Njoya's attempt to take credit for the man's apprehension. He had to set the record straight. And without consulting his partner, A.G. plunged into the conversation.

"True! *Haki ya Mungu!* I am the one who discovered him in the beer hall, and so if you have any questions about him and alcohol ask me, and if you want to confirm the truth of what I am saying, True! *Haki ya Mungu*, ask . . . I mean . . . if the Wizard . . ."

He was about to reveal the identity of the man when he realized his faux pas, and tried to cover it with exaggerated coughing, until the witch angrily intervened.

"Stop or else you will contract his illness. One victim of the evil is enough for a day. My walking stick has divined its source and will tell me all . . ."

A.G. stopped coughing, only too glad to obey, as the Limping Witch now turned her attention to the patient.

"You, listen to me with both your ears," she said, jabbing the man's throat with her stick. "I want to speak to the Devil hiding in your voice box." Kamītī forced himself to look intently at the eyes of the witch, and he thought he saw or imagined he saw her wink. But the runny eyes and the twitching lips repulsed him. Still, he listened to her intonation.

*The body is the temple of the soul*
*Watch ye what you eat and drink*
*Greed maketh death greedy for life*
*Cigarettes arrest life; alcohol holds mind prisoner*
*The good comes from balance . . .*

She went on through the entire catechism, with him now almost suspended in wonder and disbelief.

"Now I have ordered the Devil in you to speak to me through you," said the Limping Witch. "Speak, Devil!"

"IF!" Kamĩtĩ barked tentatively, as if challenging her to clear his doubts.

"It is you . . ." the Limping Witch responded, as if accepting the challenge.

"And I . . ." he said, and stopped.

"Who were . . ." said the Limping Witch.

"In the prairie . . ." Kamĩtĩ said, then paused.

"Dancing . . ." the witch replied.

"Naked . . ." said Kamĩtĩ, to shock her.

"Under the moonlight, the way witches do . . ." she said, as if to imply that he had failed to shock her.

"Then lead me out of this prison of IF . . . OH . . . IF . . . IF ONLY . . ." Kamĩtĩ said, the Devil inside him begging for release, seduced as he now was by the allure of the Limping Witch.

She turned her eyes to A.G. and Njoya, who were mesmerized by the miracle they had just witnessed. This Limping Witch had done what no other sorcerer, despite their spears, knives, needles, razor blades, and threats, had been able to do: extract a word other than *if* from the patient. She had managed to put the fear of the Lord in the mean Devil lodged in his voice box. They now eagerly waited to hear what the Limping Witch had to say. "If I am to get more out of him, you must bring him to my shrine, from which my medicines derive their potency. Do so whenever it suits you."

Njoya and A.G. conferred in a corner. A.G. then left the room. Kahiga now entered. When A.G. returned, he did not stay outside but came right in.

"We have been told to go to your shrine right now," A.G. told the Limping Witch. "You must fully cure him without delay. Then we shall bring you and him back here."

Kamĩtĩ could not believe his ears. All his doubts about the witch had vanished. Nyawĩra has effected a miracle, he said to himself, and it was with difficulty that he held back tears of joy, gratitude, and admiration.

# 24

The Limping Witch refused to travel by Land Rover.

"Oh, so we are not going far?" asked the three policemen in unison.

"Not very far," she said. "Over there," she added, pointing to the horizon.

"Yonder where the earth meets the sky?" asked Njoya.

"Yes," said the Limping Witch.

"But that is a long way from here," said Kahiga.

"It is never a long way to a person's home," she said. "My power comes from my contact with this soil," she added, prodding the ground with her walking stick. "I never allow anything to come between me and Mother Earth. Why don't you go ahead? If you get there before I do, just wait for me."

"Oh, no," the police trio said in unison.

"Our orders are that our eyes must not at any time stray away from you," added A.G.

"When not on foot, what carries you from here to there?" Njoya asked.

"A *mkokoteni*. A donkey cart. Anything pulled by a living being with feet touching the earth."

"You want us to travel on human- and donkey-pulled carriages?" asked the police trio in unison.

"Donkey carts and *mkokoteni* are difficult to find at this time of the day," added Njoya.

For a response she simply pointed at the writing on her garments: *shauri yako*. My problem? Njoya seemed to ask himself but ignored the insolence.

A.G. guarded the Limping Witch and the "prisoner" while Kahiga and Njoya went in the Land Rover to look for the carriages.

They had not gone very far when they saw a donkey cart and a human-pushed *mkokoteni*, both full of goods, but they decided to hire the carriages.

The Limping Witch now demanded that she and Kamĩtĩ ride in the *mkokoteni* while Njoya, Kahiga, and A.G. rode in the donkey cart with the Land Rover following in the rear, gas fumes being very bad for the spirits of magic. The convoy of *mkokoteni*, donkey cart, and Land Rover crept along, slowing down traffic, as the drivers of other vehicles honked with impatience and frustration at its snail's pace. Above, in the sky, helicopters monitoring the procession of protesting youth pouring into the grounds of the Parliament buildings made for noise and commotion.

Just then a Mercedes-Benz rushed toward them from the opposite direction, the driver ordering the donkey to stop, which halted the entire convoy. It was Kaniũrũ. Thereafter, nothing but chaos ensued. The Limping Witch immediately ordered the two *mkokoteni* drivers to take off, which they did as if possessed of wings. In pursuit of the *mkokoteni*, the donkey cart threw off Kahiga, Njoya, and A.G. The Land Rover picked up Kahiga. Njoya commandeered a bicycle and A.G. followed on foot, running, calling on Njoya to let him get on the bike.

The *mkokoteni* had the advantage of being able to weave in and out of traffic; the Mercedes-Benz had trouble pursuing it down the narrow two-lane road. The donkey cart blocked the Land Rover. Pedestrians on the sidewalks wondered why a Mercedes-Benz was pursuing and honking at a pushcart, a donkey braying at a Mercedes-Benz while defecating, a Land Rover honking at the donkey cart, a cyclist ringing bells at the Land Rover, and a policeman running and shouting, *Simama!* They could not figure out whether he was saying stop or calling out to somebody by that name. A.G. was the first casualty of the chase. He stepped in donkey dung, slipped, and fell, passersby describing it as a mighty fall.

The speeding *mkokoteni* went past the railway, crossing just in time before the red barrier came down and blocked the Mercedes-Benz. "Run for it to Maritha and Mariko's place," the Limping Witch told the Wizard of the Crow. "Don't ask any questions. We'll talk later."

The Wizard of the Crow got out and ran, even as the *mkokoteni* sped off. When the Mercedes-Benz finally crossed the rails, Kaniŭrŭ just spotted the *mkokoteni* in the distance.

Go get it, he told the chauffeur.

# 25

It was later said that a donkey had stood in the middle of the road, impeding traffic until the Limping Witch and the Wizard of the Crow had safely fled. But other rumors said no, all the donkeys of Santamaria had lined up and down the road, defecating and urinating, making it so slippery that vehicles could hardly move, and when the police tried to pursue the two they slid all over the place and eventually resorted to commandeering whatever bicycles were to be had.

"Was that true?" Vinjinia asked her husband, Tajirika, the evening of the following day.

"Leave rumors to rumormongers," Tajirika said irritably, for he was not happy about the news that the Limping Witch and the Wizard of the Crow had escaped. His evolving monetary policy involved the production of foreign currency, naturally grown dollars, and it all depended on the Wizard of the Crow doing the will of the Ruler. He feared that the wizard's flight might put his governorship of the Central Bank at risk.

Vinjinia was a little crestfallen: so the news of the escape of the Wizard of the Crow was just rumor?

"The bit about his escape is true," Tajirika said. "But he was helped by the Limping Witch, not asses, whether one or many."

"A limping what?"

"One of the sorcerers. The sorcerer's left leg was shorter than the right, and so the nickname," Tajirika explained, and then paused. "Vinjinia, your suggestion that we openly advertise for witches and sorcerers to come for a national achievement test at the State House was brilliant. It would have almost certainly borne fruit but for the Limping Witch."

"A man?"

"No! A woman, and she and the wizard have vanished!"

"How is that possible? I mean, their escape?"

"I can only tell you what I heard Kaniũrũ tell the Ruler when accusing the guards of negligence, asserting their unfitness to wear the uniform of loyal officers. But you know that the nosy one is a liar and with him it is difficult to tell fact from fiction."

"How does Kaniũrũ come into this?" Vinjinia asked, genuinely puzzled.

Even though he was tired, Tajirika managed to recap the story.

That the Limping Witch had escaped made Vinjinia happy, for she was most likely one of the women who had helped her in her time of need. She was also pleased with herself for having rejected the temptation to betray Nyawĩra. But what made her even happier was knowing that she was in solidarity with people she had once thought evil, people who, despite her disagreement with their politics, she now saw as humane and generous at heart. She certainly preferred them to the beastly and mean-spirited Kaniũrũs of Aburĩria. Now she was elated at having worked out, all her own idea, how best to thank Nyawĩra.

She went over what she had done. She had gleaned all the information about the condition and whereabouts of the Wizard of the Crow from Tajirika during shared meals and pillow talk, and had imparted it to Maritha.

It was Vinjinia who told Maritha that the Wizard of the Crow was captured in a bar and that he had contracted the malady of words after being hauled to the State House. It seemed to her, she told Maritha, that it was only the males of the species who were susceptible to the disease. She told her about the national sorcery achievement test and that its object was to cure the wizard. Vinjinia did not once hint to Maritha what she was to do with the information, for she of course knew that Maritha would relay every bit of it to Nyawĩra. Yet she had not foreseen the escape. She had simply intended to put Nyawĩra in touch with the Wizard of the Crow. Her machinations, it seemed, had succeeded beyond her wildest dreams.

Still, she was irked that Kaniũrũ had somehow managed to insert himself into the events, and in this she and her husband were in complete agreement.

"Can you believe that despite his interference in matters that did not concern him and his failure to capture the runaway *mkokoteni*, Kaniũrũ has been entrusted by the Ruler to bring in the fugitives?"

"That man! I don't know what it will take to stop him from benefiting from his evil ways," Vinjinia said. "What about the three policemen? How did they explain their behavior?"

"A.G., Kahiga, and Njoya have joined the ranks of the jobless," Tajirika said.

The news gnawed at her. "How could the Ruler dismiss the three who had served him so loyally?"

"The Ruler is never wrong," Tajirika hastened to say. "I am sure he would not have dismissed the officers without good reason."

# 26

"True, *Haki ya Mungu*, when we went back to the State House we found that Kaniũrũ had already poisoned the atmosphere with lies. He even claimed that he found us surrounded by tourists with cameras clicking away at the sight of policemen riding a donkey cart, a scene that gave the impression that the Ruler was so broke he could only afford carts for his police force!

"They dismissed us from our jobs and told us to get out of government housing immediately. Stray dogs, even when they have snatched something, are treated more kindly by passersby than we were treated by those we had faithfully served all our lives.

"I don't know about the other two, but I had no land or house or any property that I could call my own. In discussing the options before us, we realized, too late, that we had no skills other than those of arresting, torturing, and taking people to court. The only jobs that offered possibilities were the private security firms that were mushrooming throughout the country. With the much-flaunted IMF-brokered prosperity confined to a few, the houses of the rich had become luxurious prisons. But imagine the shame of two ex-superintendents and one ex–assistant police commissioner reduced to guarding people's houses with a terrier's leash in one hand and a knock-berry club in the other! Or simply armed with bows and arrows?

"We sat down by the roadside near the same railway crossing, wondering why fate had dealt us such a blow. Where are we to go? Why has good fortune abandoned us when we most need it? Who was this Limping Witch?" Kahiga moaned.

The Limping Witch and the Wizard of the Crow are one and the same, a worn-down A.G. told Njoya and Kahiga solemnly. A disagreement erupted among them, Kahiga and Njoya maintaining that the Limping Witch and the Wizard of the Crow were different and distinct entities. A.G. tried to explain that there were times when the wizard appeared as female and other times as male. The Limping Witch is the other face of the wizard, and the captive was simply his shadow. He told them of the night he had chased two human-shaped apparitions in the prairie but that when they jumped over the rock cleft as two—"You remember the rock and the bush where we saw the plants with the dollar-shaped leaves?"—they became one person . . .

No sooner were the dollar-shaped leaves mentioned than Kahiga snapped to attention. "I say, let us go and look for the Wizard of the Crow, be he the Limping Witch or not, a woman or not, a shadow or not," he said excitedly.

"What? After what the Ruler has done to us?" asked A.G., surprised by his own critical tone.

"Yes, a donkey expresses gratitude by its kicks," Njoya observed.

"There, you have said it," Kahiga said. "Remember the holes we dug night and day in the prairie? Did we ever get anything for our effort? We don't even know what they did with the plants. And now this? Dismissals based on brazen lies! No. We are going to look for the Wizard of the Crow, all right, but this time for ourselves. See? We tell him about our jobless misery. We will pray to him to tell us the secret of growing money on trees. We don't need to know about the dollar-producing type. For us a Burī-producing plant will do," Kahiga noted as the other two nodded in agreement.

Before parting they entered a pact of mutual cooperation. They would go their separate ways but whoever came across information about the whereabouts of the Wizard of the Crow would share it with the others immediately. All three had to be present when the Wizard of the Crow disclosed how to grow money on trees.

"True! *Haki ya Mungu!*" A.G. would later tell his listeners. "From that day we clothed in civilian clothes and joined the ranks of thousands of others, from the foot soldier to members of the elite air force, who had been fired. From being fishers of men to sustain the State, we three were now fishers of the Wizard of the Crow to sustain ourselves. But for me—True! *Haki ya Mungu!*—it was not the lure of the money-producing plants that attracted me to the search but the desire to know the secret of the being of all things.

"One day I heard that the Wizard of the Crow had been seen in the vicinity of All Saints Cathedral, and I searched out Njoya and Kahiga to share with them this bit of information. They, it seemed, had beaten me to the cathedral. Had they forgotten our pact? Well, I, too, headed there, and imagine my surprise when I found that the entire cathedral . . . but surely you, too, must have been there that day?"

# BOOK FIVE

# Rebel Daemons

# SECTION I

# 1

Given all that was happening in the country, that the Limping Witch and the Wizard of the Crow were on the loose made the Ruler feel like a cornered, toothless animal. At the State House, where he monitored everything, he received hourly reports from different sources, chaotic reports reflecting the chaos of events taking place. Queues, which had formed in the different regions of the country for different reasons, were amassing by the Parliament buildings and law courts. As the crowd grew, the Ruler felt restricted in the choices before him.

Since Kaniũrũ's patriotic gang had beat up foreign journalists at the airport, provoking protests from the Western embassies, the Ruler had ordered the police, the paramilitary units, and even Kaniũrũ's boys to be careful, very careful, before foreign cameras. If they really felt like cracking a few skulls, they should do so in rural areas and small towns. Not that he was angry with those who had ignored his call for self-restraint and had broken a few bones of those inciting others to go to the so-called People's Assembly. But he did not want them to do anything that might suggest that he was afraid of a peaceful gathering on the grounds of Parliament and the courts. So even though he seethed with murderous rage, he refused to succumb to instinct and unleash his killers against the dissidents. His hope was that people would eventually tire of all speechifying and go home thirsty and hungry.

But that was not to be. Many had packed food. The owners of small restaurants and kiosks provided snacks, and some *matatus* brought in food from the rural folk. So the assembly continued to grow in strength, confidence, and courage. When early on the police tried to remove a loudspeaker from a makeshift platform, people had roared in protest, threatening chaos and forcing the police to leave it.

Soon a pattern began to emerge at the proceedings. Religious leaders would lead the assembly in prayer, a common theme being that God vanquishes Satan so that peace and prosperity could reign in Aburĩria. Hymns followed the prayers, then sermons from the clerics, adhering strictly to the holy books. And then anybody who wanted to speak could do so. The Ruler was of course not amused by any of this. Only the prospect of Global Bank money restrained him.

For a few days, the mystery of Machokali's disappearance became the unifying theme. If even the Minister for Foreign Affairs, moreover one known all over the world, could vanish without anybody being held accountable, who could claim to be safe anywhere in the Republic of Aburĩria? We want the truth! We want the truth! became a recurring cry. Some even said that if the truth about the missing minister was not forthcoming they would march to the State House to look for him there. Let them talk themselves hoarse, said the Ruler, grinding his teeth, but woe to them that dare to come here. He considered sending Kaniũrũ's goons to provoke a march on the State House but thought the better of it, as he did not think that images of such a march would play well on television screens around the world. And so, with both sides waiting for the other's next move, there was an impasse, both camps eyeing each other warily, testing each other only with words.

It was then that the American and French ambassadors paid a second visit to the State House. As usual Ambassador Gemstone was all business and to the point; he did not mind letting the Ruler know that his position was shared by the major Western democracies and that was why he was accompanied by Monsieur Jean Pierre Sartre, not to be confused with the existential philosopher of the same name, he joked, as M. Sartre nodded. The West had invested a lot in the future of Aburĩria and was quite naturally anxious about developments that might jeopardize its interests. The Ruler had to come up with peaceful measures to end the unrest in the country.

The Ruler raised his voice in anger. He was tired of the arrogance of the West. He was tired of these lectures about what to do in his own home. He never would presume to tell the American president what to do with those wild demonstrations he himself saw when he was last in Washington for a prayer breakfast. He was tired of being pushed around. They had told him to come up with measures to end the so-called crisis, and yet when he threatened to use the only language his own people understood, they had told him not to. It is your people who say that you cannot have your cake and eat it, he told Ambassador Gemstone. When in the past he had used force and silenced a few thousand forever with the West's full knowledge and blessing, did the West babble about using peaceful means? Why now?

"That is precisely the point, Your Excellency," replied Ambassador Gemstone. "Circumstances have changed, and we believe that alternative measures exist. Give your people something to make them happy. Don't you have a proverb that says that if you throw peanuts to a monkey you will distract it long enough to be able to snatch its baby?"

"What kind of peanuts do you suggest I throw at these monkeys?" the Ruler asked sarcastically.

"For one, go talk to them . . ."

"And tell them what?"

"Address the issue of the missing minister, Machokali. Their speeches have all been about him."

"And say what about him? That I know where he is?"

"That is up to you. But I can tell you that intelligence services all over the world are telling us that your minister is not seeking asylum anywhere, as your statement seemed to indicate."

The French ambassador nodded in agreement.

"Why are you so interested in the fate of a minister charged with plotting to overthrow my government?"

"Your Excellency, we have no evidence suggesting as much."

"So you don't believe the official report released by my government?"

"Your Excellency, why should we believe it when it was put together by his political rival Sikiokuu?"

"How do you know that it is he who wrote the report?"

"Your Excellency, we have ways of knowing things," Gemstone said.

The Ruler had not forgotten the humiliation he felt in New York when Global Bank emissaries had told him of rumors of new and better-organized queues in his country long before his own intelligence service had been able to piece together what was happening. And now here comes this ambassador boasting of how well informed he is, even about other people's state secrets!

"So you spy on your friends?" the Ruler asked icily.

It is said that their conversation ended abruptly, with the Ruler telling Gemstone that the next time he had something to say to him it would be better to pick up the telephone, write him a letter, or send the French ambassador. Is that all you have to say? asked Gemstone. He stood up and, with the French ambassador in tow, walked out without waiting for an answer.

*The arrogance of white power,* muttered the Ruler under his breath. Why are they so keen for me to expose myself in my condition before the crowd?

For some reason the silence of the French ambassador began to bother him. During the cold war, France used to front for the West in military interference in African affairs and often assured him that she would help him with troops should there be an uprising against him. Did she have a candidate in mind now that the American and British minion was missing? Who?

He recalled Gemstone hastening to say that M. Sartre had no connection with philosophy. Where had the Ruler recently heard something about France, philosophy, and the Aburīrian State, he asked himself, and, remembering the occasion, summoned Governor Tajirika.

"Tell me, which philosopher did you mention to me in this very room some time ago?"

"Philosopher? Me?" asked Tajirika, a little taken aback because he had thought that he was being summoned to be questioned about the dramatic escape of the Limping Witch and the Wizard of the Crow, or about the crowds occupying the grounds around Parliament and the law courts.

"A Frenchman?" said the Ruler to jog his memory.

"Oh, it is not me, I swear," said Tajirika as if defending himself against an accusation. "It was Sikiokuu who was trying to tell me about him. But I told him clearly that I did not want to have anything to do with the crazy fanatic of doubts."

"That's what I am trying to find out. Who is he? What is his name?"

"Oh, Des Cartes or Descartes."

"And you are sure, very sure, that his name is not Sartre? Jean Pierre Sartre?"

"I am very sure. The name is definitely Descartes. Perhaps there is a Thomas in it—I don't know. Apparently the French people love the deity and talk about him a lot. Sikiokuu told me that he had first heard about the deity and its religion of doubt at a special dinner party in his honor at the house of the French ambassador."

"In his honor? Why honor him?"

"Because long before he became a minister he had already shown his faith in French technology by choosing Paris rather than London for the elongation of his ears."

For a while the Ruler was silent, as if contemplating a dawning thought.

"Does he go there alone, secretly perhaps?"

"I don't know."

"Thank you, Titus," he said, almost affectionately. "You can now go back to your work."

Soon the Ruler started getting reports that some army officers had received invitations for cocktails and dinners at Western embassies. Coming on the heels of his encounter with the diplomats, he decided that enough was enough; he must find a way to remind these Westerners that in Aburīria he was still the man, regardless of the loans for Marching to Heaven, and there was nothing these arrogant bastards could do about his slaughter of his own people.

He issued an ultimatum followed by an order for the armored division to clear the People's Assembly.

The sight of armored cars on television, their long guns poised to murder, relentlessly moving down the streets of Eldares made him feel manlier. The media swarming around the columns excited him. Let them see blood, the Ruler whispered to himself, pointing at the television screen. Let them see that I am still in charge.

Suddenly his finger became limp and his hand fell to his side. For the first time since his ascension, he was terrified. For instead of tanks running over the dissidents, there, on the television screen, were army boys and young civilians greeting one another with high fives for the entire world to see, to his embarrassment. Here was the sunset of his reign. But who had choreographed it?

The Ruler was anything but naive and foolish when it came to matters of his own survival. He recalled the visit of Ambassador Gemstone and their heated exchange.

He went over Gemstone's words very carefully, and what now stood out in his mind was the ambassador's call on him to give the insurgents something to hold on to, and he decided to do just that. Given his condition, he would relay a few words to them through the Minister of Information.

Big Ben Mambo, who had always fancied himself a military man, saw an excellent chance to enact his fantasies. Instead of speaking from the platform, Big Ben elected to stand atop one of the armored vehicles, prefacing his official message with a statement that he was speaking on behalf of the commander in chief of the armed forces of the Aburĩrian State.

There would be a commission of inquiry into the facts and circumstances surrounding the disappearance of Machokali, our beloved Minister for Foreign Affairs, he now pronounced, hinting that the Ruler was even thinking of asking for help from Scotland Yard, London, and the FBI of Washington to show that he and his government had nothing to hide concerning the late minister. As soon as he said the word *late* Big Ben Mambo realized his faux pas, but he decided not to correct himself so as not to draw further attention to it. He proceeded.

People could not believe their ears: how could the Ruler suspend a minister who for many years had been his right-hand man? They whistled in disbelief when they heard that the police had raided the offices of the Minister of State and collected all his files for further investigation, and that Minister Sikiokuu himself had been arrested and was now being held to account for the disappearance of Machokali. Mambo alluded to the long-standing rivalry between Machokali and Sikiokuu, going all the way back to the days when Machokali chose London for the surgical enlargement of his eyes and Sikiokuu, Paris for the surgical enlargement of his ears. Speaking off the cuff, Mambo said that these two were fighting proxy wars for the British and the French. It was a well-known fact that these two nations, England and France, had always fought for the dominance of Europe, dating all the way back to the days of Napoleon and Nelson. That was why he, Mambo, had refused to follow in their misguided footsteps and gone to Germany for an adjustment of his tongue, which he was now putting to good use as the voice of the commander in chief. Mambo now returned to his prepared text, insinuating that Sikiokuu was involved in a dangerous cabal spreading doubts about the government. But why? Actions spoke louder than words.

Among the items seized from the minister's offices was a suit that was more or less a replica of those worn only by the Ruler, complete with lion-skin patches, reserved by law for only the Ruler. Sikiokuu had even copied the seat on which the Ruler sat when chairing cabinet sessions. Big Ben Mambo, however, urged the people not to draw any conclusions before the commission of inquiry had completed its work.

But this did not mean that people would have to keep their mouths shut, and anybody who had any information about the disappearance of the beloved son of the soil or about Sikiokuu's religious sect would be given a chance to present oral or written evidence to the government commission.

And now, speaking in the name of the commander in chief of the Aburīrian Armed Forces, he was ordering all the armored cars off the streets. He was also asking the crowd to disperse peacefully now that the government had responded to their main concerns.

But even as the armored cars retreated to side streets, people did not scatter; they intensified their singing and prayers, now and then shouting: We want our voice back.

# 2

The two main pillars on which his rule depended, the armed forces and the West, had loosened considerably. The Ruler had to find a way of shoring them up, and he would do so by showing both that his hold on power was not entirely dependent on them. And what better way of showing this than dispersing the defiant crowd without the aid of a reluctant military? But what other than the military and the police could he use to effect it?

The Ruler knew that he could no longer rely on any of his cabinet ministers. He had received reports that some ministers, like military officers, perhaps taking their lead from the disgraced Sikiokuu, had recently been seen cozying up to Western embassies. Gemstone's remarks that he knew fairly well what was going on in the cabinet made him suspect that some of his ministers were paid informants. To frustrate these informants, he had decided not to hold cabinet meetings. Now that Machokali and Sikiokuu were no longer around, the Ruler realized how much he had depended on them in times of crisis. Not that he missed them, for he had replaced them with Tajirika and Kaniũrũ, who could be trusted to say what he wanted to hear. He played them time and again against each other. The Ruler would often meet with each separately. There were things that he wanted to remain between Kaniũrũ and himself, and others that he wished to share only with Tajirika. He also knew that they were crooks. Although they hated each other, he knew that he had to forestall the possibility of a conspiracy between them against him. My special advisers, he fondly called them, and it was to them that he now turned for help in finding the most appropriate means of dispersing the crowd. First up was Kaniũrũ.

Kaniũrũ came up with two proposals. If for some reason the Ruler did not want to deploy the armed forces, then he should play deaf to all pleas of restraint from foreign countries and give Kaniũrũ's boys the license to trash the arrogant gathering as a lesson. Alternatively, efforts should be intensified to recapture the Wizard of the Crow, who should be compelled under threats of torture and death to use his powers to cure the maddening crowd of its queuing mania and cleanse it of all impure thoughts. He, Kaniũrũ, had already set snares for the wizard, and although they had yet to catch the quarry, he was positive that the Wizard of the Crow and the Limping Witch would not evade Kaniũrũ's nose for long, he added, and laughed.

Tajirika, too, advised enlisting the services of the Wizard of the Crow but stressed the unlimited manufacture of Burĩ money, which would be divided into two piles.

The first lot would go to buying foreign currencies to be stashed in Swiss banks, adding to what was already there. The Ruler could also use the money to buy properties in tax havens abroad. As governor of the Central Bank, Tajirika would of course ensure that the new money got into circulation without a hitch; even so, he argued for the creation of new banks, Mwathirika Ltd.

The other pile would be used to disperse the crowd in the most effective, public, and peaceful manner possible. The Ruler would simply announce a day when money would fall on the waiting crowd like manna from Heaven. At an appointed time, four helicopters would drop Burī notes starting in the center of the crowd and fanning to the east, west, north, and south. The scramble would scatter the dissidents to the four winds.

The setting up of money-laundering banks sounded like a stroke of genius, and the Ruler could not help thinking that if the Wizard of the Crow were forced to reveal the secret of dollars growing on trees, this windfall income could also be put into national and international circulation easily, along the paths already tested with the Burī. The idea of Mwathirika banks was so appealing that the Ruler insisted that Vinjinia, Tajirika's wife, become its nominal founder and managing director and the Ruler's sons, its board of directors. Tajirika's other suggestion was equally brilliant, achieving the desired result without recourse to bloodshed.

A crook after my own heart, the Ruler muttered to himself, mesmerized by the simple beauty of Tajirika's plan, and he was glad that he had appointed him governor.

"And Titus," said the Ruler suddenly, as if rewarding him for the clarity of his plan. "There is a chair and some clothes that I understand were taken from Sikiokuu's offices. You now see the kind of ministers with whom I had surrounded myself? Appointing themselves heirs to my seat? I don't trust—I mean, keep this evidence of treachery under lock and key for me until I decide what to do with Sikiokuu and his coconspirators."

Tajirika sensed in this the Ruler's discomfiture with the armed forces and, emboldened by the new trust the Ruler had placed in him, he deigned to offer more general advice.

"Thank you for the trust you have invested in me, and I swear never to betray you. And if I might say so, you may need fresh eyes and ears in the State House to uncover what some people might be up to, eyes that can also quietly oversee the leaders of the armed forces, a kind of super-eye on the military."

"I don't think that your experience in military affairs goes beyond your taking over an armed camp with shit and urine," the Ruler said coldly, resenting Tajirika's intimations of his unease with the military. "Stick to money matters."

That was a misstep, Tajirika thought, and in an effort to recover he hastened to ask, "When may I start putting my fiscal plan in motion?"

"I will think about it," said the Ruler.

Tajirika's plan was appealing to the Ruler's philosophy that greed and self-interest ruled the world. But Kaniũrũ's plans had the ascendancy.

And then other events occurred that suddenly moved the Tajirika plan from the realm of aesthetics to that of the practical and immediate.

# 3

Tajirika had gone to the Central Bank early to get some work done before calls started coming in. This late to bed and early to work was one of the changes in his lifestyle since becoming the governor. He would read the local, then foreign papers, mainly the business pages, and then check the Internet for the latest international stock market results and exchange rates; that way he would start his day with a proper overview of the money market of the world.

But before he had even settled into his chair, the telephone rang. Shall I take it or not? Tajirika wondered. But what if I don't take it and later it turns out to have come from the State House? The Ruler had the habit of calling his advisers at any time of day or night. Tajirika took the phone; it was someone from the *Eldares Times*.

"We tried the State House and we could not get through," the reporter told him. "So we thought of calling you instead."

Even though he was not a minister, Tajirika did not mind people thinking or even knowing that the Ruler trusted him more than he did the ministers. And if he played his cards right, perhaps . . . who knows? he would sometimes tell Vinjinia.

"You have not strayed too far from the path," Tajirika said, a touch of pride in his voice.

"We are actually calling you in your capacity as chairperson of Marching to Heaven," the man said.

Tajirika felt his whole body tingle with excitement. Had the loans come through? In Marching to Heaven lay the biggest and most endless source of money, moreover money that did not require secret plantations and laundering facilities.

"You are talking to the right person," Tajirika hastened to say. "What can I do for you?"

"A few words about today's headline."

"Today's paper?" Tajirika asked.

"Yes," the man said. "Your reaction to the news."

"I have not yet read it. Can you call back in five minutes? Or, better still, why don't you just read it to me?"

"Global Bank Refuses to Lend Money for Marching to Heaven."

"Excuse me," Tajirika muttered.

"The Global Bank does not think that Marching to Heaven is a viable project. It is a case of free enterprise going too far."

Tajirika's hands shook. He did not wait for the reporter to stop reading.

"No comment. Please try the State House again," said Tajirika in a tremulous voice.

He put the receiver down and reached for the *Eldares Times*. It was not just the loans for Marching to Heaven. The Global Bank and its policy-making body, the Global Ministry of Finance, had put on hold even those funds previously agreed upon. Worse still, the funds would remain frozen until the Aburīrian government had instituted economic and political reforms and took concrete steps to end inflation and corruption.

Tajirika did not know whether to cry for loss of these loans or laugh for joy: his proposed monetary policy was now more pertinent than ever.

The phone rang again.

Tajirika headed straight for the State House.

# 4

The floor of the Ruler's sanctuary was littered with newspapers, the Ruler not apparently present. Tajirika looked up at the ceiling and his jaw fell; he took a step back for a clearer view. He could not believe his eyes. The Ruler's legs hung in the air, his head touching the ceiling and his whole body gently swaying.

"Don't just stand there with your mouth open—get me down," the Ruler told him.

Tajirika felt weak in the knees and tried hard not to faint.

"Should I call the guards for help?"

"*Of course not, you fool.* Get me down."

Tajirika could not reach the dangling feet, even on tiptoes. The Ruler's body, now more passive than ever, seemed impossibly light; only the ceiling prevented it from floating away. Tajirika stood on a chair and grasped at the Ruler's feet, but no matter how often he did, the Ruler would again rise like a balloon.

"What shall we do now?" asked Tajirika.

"That's why I had you summoned," replied the Ruler, looking down from the ceiling.

Tajirika thought that the Ruler was talking about his floating body.

"Yes, this matter is truly amazing," Tajirika said, vaguely, sympathetically.

"There must be forces working against me at the Global Bank," the Ruler said.

No, the Ruler is talking about the news, and I was about to suggest I chain him to the ground, Tajirika said to himself. He now sat on a chair with his head leaning back, the better to hear and see.

The Global Bank news had hit the Ruler hard, especially because the Bank had not seen fit to grant him the courtesy of first informing him through diplomatic channels or a special envoy but had released their communication to the media in New York.

"Look around you. Look at those papers. Look at all the headlines. Is there a soul in the whole wide world who is not reading this?

Where have diplomatic niceties gone? Imagine how my enemies must be rejoicing, believing that their agitation was responsible for halting our plans for Marching to Heaven!"

"*Racists,*" said Tajirika, putting as much hatred as he could into his voice.

"*Exactly* what I myself said," the Ruler said. "But we shall show the Bank that we were not born yesterday. What do you say, Titus?"

"You have spoken the truth, Your Mighty Excellency. We will *fight back,*" Tajirika said, noting that the Ruler had called him Titus as if they were the closest of friends.

"That's why I made you the governor of money. *Yes, fight back.* Good words. You know that Gemstone is behind all this. He is the source of this undiluted hatred of me."

"*Racist,*" Tajirika said again.

"You have spoken the truth, as always," the Ruler said again, before he started complaining of a stomachache and demanding that his personal doctor be called.

Tajirika went to the telephone, feeling relieved that someone else would soon be joining him to help him cope with the astonishment he was witnessing.

# 5

In response to Dr. Kaboca's "How are you?" a seated Tajirika simply pointed at the ceiling. The doctor did not understand the meaning of Tajirika's gesture, and for a moment he thought that maybe Tajirika was mentally unbalanced and that it was because of him that he had been summoned to the State House. Where is the Ruler? Dr. Kaboca asked. "*Can't you see that the Ruler has conquered gravity!*" Tajirika said impatiently.

Dr. Kaboca looked up, and soon Tajirika found himself bent over the doctor's prostrate body, fanning him with a handkerchief, trying to revive him.

"It looks as if the doctor himself is in need of a doctor!" came a voice from the ceiling.

"It is the heat," Dr. Kaboca said after he had regained consciousness. "Now, Mr. Tajirika, please leave the room."

"No," said the Ruler. "Tajirika is my special adviser. In all matters. Feel free to treat me in his presence."

The Ruler was quite candid with the doctor. He explained that when he read the news from the Global Bank, he had become so angry that his body started to expand even more. He had called his special adviser to have somebody to talk to in the hope that this would ease the anger within. While waiting for Tajirika, he had read some more newspapers, only to feel his anger mount until it almost choked him, and that was when he felt himself lifted uncontrollably. He could not tell exactly when it started, but it was definitely when he was already in the air that his tummy began to ache. At first the pain was manageable, but now it had become unbearable.

With the help of some carpenters who rigged a platform of sorts, Dr. Kaboca and Tajirika were able to pull the Ruler down and secure him with straps for a medical exam.

They did such a good job that it now looked as if the Ruler was actually seated on a high chair of authority, his voice reaching those seated below his feet as if it were God's voice from above. The men were made permanent state carpenters and they would leave the State House only when the Ruler willed it.

Dr. Kaboca climbed onto the platform, examined the Ruler's tonsils, and took his temperature and blood pressure. Nothing seemed amiss. He felt the Ruler's stomach and, recalling prevalent rumors in the country that he might be in a certain way, thought it best to prescribe the need for a team of medical doctors. He reminded the Ruler that when they left America it had been decided that Dr. Clarkwell and Professor Furyk would be invited to Aburĩria to look further into his condition. Now was the time, he suggested, to confer with them on this new complication of symptoms: further bodily expansion, lightness of the body, and bellyache.

# 6

"What? His legs dangling in the air?" Vinjinia asked Tajirika.

The image of a Ruler suspended in the air with only the soles of his shoes visible from the floor made her laugh until her ribs ached.

It was the same day, late at night. Tajirika did not always tell Vinjinia about the goings-on in the State House, but this story he could not keep to himself. Yet he took the precaution of swearing Vinjinia to secrecy.

"Do you think this is the work of the Wizard of the Crow? Or the Limping Witch?" Vinjinia whispered.

"With the wizard you cannot rule out anything."

"What if the house did not have a ceiling and a roof?" she wondered loudly.

"He would have reached Heaven before Marching to Heaven," Tajirika responded, but Vinjinia was the one who saw the fun in the quip and laughed again.

When Vinjinia next met with Maritha and Mariko she took Maritha aside, made her also swear not to tell anybody, and whispered the Ruler's story. But of course Maritha told Mariko, and he did not see any harm in telling Dove, and Dove did not see any harm . . .

And so on, until the story reached the People's Assembly, which meant that soon all of Aburĩria was talking about it.

# 7

"His SIE has hypertrophied beyond our wildest imagination," Dr. Wilfred Kaboca wrote to Clarkwell and Furyk, urging them to come to Aburĩria at once, all costs, of course, to be picked up by the Aburĩrian State. Uppermost in Kaboca's mind was the note the Wizard of the Crow had once written and the rumors of the Ruler's pregnancy circulating in the country. A sonogram was definitely in order, he added.

In his diary, Furyk records his astonishment at the content of the letter, especially the reference to contractions and sonograms. But he also saw opportunities. Research into this phenomenon might throw scientific light on age-old theological disputes about virgin births. He also saw a commercial side to it and formed Clem&Din Productions Company, which sought and got the Ruler's guarantee that, subject to some royalties to the Ruler, the company would have the sole global production and distribution rights of all the films and videos on all aspects of SIE.

Din Furyk and Clement Clarkwell became the only beacons of hope for Kaboca and the Ruler. If only they could stop his body from conspiring against him!

# 8

Kaniũrũ had just gotten news about the Wizard of the Crow and was preparing to break it to the Ruler in person when he learned that His Mightiness had suffered another bout of bodily expansion and was now floating in the air. The Wizard of the Crow must be behind this, he thought, and, fearing that he might be the next target, decided to keep the news to himself until he learned more about the situation. And, to be on the safe side, he retreated to Kanyori's place. The ever-faithful Kanyori did not raise any questions, not even when Kaniũrũ asked her to chain one of his legs to the bedpost and lock the door from the outside. She left a plate of food and a jar of water next to him. Kaniũrũ stayed inside the apartment the whole day. Whenever the wind shook the windows, Kaniũrũ would hold the bedposts with both hands. But in asking to be chained he had forgotten to seek support for other needs, and so when in the evening Kanyori unchained him he dashed past her without a word and stayed in the toilet for a long time. He feared that the noises he had emitted had reached Kanyori in the living room, and, embarrassed, Kaniũrũ returned to his own place to work out better preventive measures against any attempts by the Wizard of the Crow to take him by surprise.

For a few days, he drove everywhere, even the shortest of distances, to make it impossible for the Wizard of the Crow to use the wind to blow him into the sky. For short walks, he got himself boots with soles reinforced with iron, but dragging the boots became cumbersome and after a while he settled for the much simpler idea of weights in his jacket. After a couple of days without anything stranger than constipation happening to him, he felt his courage come back. The news he had was too important to keep to himself, and he would not let slip an opportunity to endear himself to the Ruler.

As his Mercedes-Benz sped through the streets toward the State House, Kaniũrũ reviewed things, and it dawned on him clearly that he was the only person who had crossed swords with the Wizard of the Crow and come out of the encounter with only minor bruises, a thought that further deepened his confidence.

Though Kaniũrũ believed the claims that the Ruler was floating in the air, he retreated two or three steps in fright when he heard the Ruler's voice come from above. But on raising his head and seeing the Ruler on a platform in a chair with a back that seemed to touch the ceiling, he thought of the final judgment, fell to his knees, and clasped both hands to his chest as if humbling himself before an angel of the Lord. He started moaning, *Oh God, oh my God.* Then he burst into a hymn of prayer: *Nearer My God to thee . . . Nearer to thee . . .*

"Kaniũrũ, did I not command you and the others to stop comparing me to God?" the Ruler rebuked him from above.

"What is the difference?" Kaniũrũ asked, with apparent sincerity that amused the Ruler.

"What do you want from the Lord?" the Ruler said, smiling, and his slightly bantering tone was so calming to Kaniũrũ that his heart was no longer aflutter.

"I know where the Wizard of the Crow is hiding out," he exclaimed, unburdening his soul before the Lord.

The Ruler kept silent as if he had not properly heard. Kaniũrũ thought the Ruler awaited more details and started arranging a narrative in his head, but this turned out to be unnecessary. For when the Ruler came to terms with what Kaniũrũ was saying it was he who now felt as if an angel of the Lord had come to him in his time of greatest need. A servant in need is truly a servant indeed.

"What?" the Ruler asked.

Kaniũrũ told him how, since the escape of the two wretched sorcerers, he had put all his cunning into their capture, but even he had to admit that he had gotten help from the gang he had deployed all over Santamaria and Santalucia.

"As soon as I got the news, I said to myself, Kaniũrũ, you cannot keep this matter to yourself, not even for a second, and that is why I am here," he said, still kneeling down.

"You have done well," said the Ruler, his right hand raised in a gesture of blessing. "Go home and continue in your righteousness, for I now know that I can call upon you at any time. But from now on, leave everything to do with this Wizard of the Crow to me. I will never forget your devotion."

Kaniũrũ hastened to his car, looking to neither the left nor the right. He was light as a feather despite the weights in his jacket. He could not even tell how and when he got into his car or even his residency.

That night at home he left all the lights on. He hardly slept. The image that kept on playing in his head was that of the Ruler talking in a voice that sounded as if it came from Heaven. What besmirched the image was the ceiling that looked earthly, the walls that looked even more earthly, and of course the expanded Ruler, whose body, despite the straps, kept swaying slightly from side to side like a balloon in a light breeze. The fact that the straps and the platform were visible ruined the illusion of a deity in the sky.

And suddenly Kaniũrũ felt as if he had sprouted wings and was about to rise and float in the air like the Ruler. He, an art student, had seen, for the first time in his life, a definite role for art in human life, or at least in his life, in ways more useful than what had been wrought by his forgeries of Sikiokuu's signatures and drawings of the Wizard of the Crow on a poster for a wanted fugitive.

He would place his chosen God in a tangible heaven, and it was then that he thought he knew the full meaning of the words of his namesake, John the Baptist, when he said: *And behold I saw a new heaven and a new earth. Amen.*

For his part, no sooner had Kaniũrũ left his presence than the

Ruler had phoned Wonderful Tumbo, the officer in charge of the Santamaria police, to give him instructions: The time of the Wizard of the Crow is up. I want him here. Right away! Alive!

# 9

When Kamĩtĩ got off the *mkokoteni* he went to Maritha and Mariko, just as Nyawĩra had instructed him. The sun was setting. His long shadow fell on Mariko out in the yard. Impassively, Mariko shouted to Maritha that it looked as though some rough wind had blown a stranger into their yard. And Maritha shouted back, What is the matter? Why don't you bring him inside? Mariko did not say a word to Kamĩtĩ but simply went inside, Kamĩtĩ following. Maritha pointed to a chair, but still neither she nor her husband addressed the visitor directly. One does not converse with hunger, Maritha and Mariko agreed, and after a few minutes tea and bread were set before the visitor.

Kamĩtĩ did not know what to say to them because he did not know how much Nyawĩra had told them about him and his present condition. His two hosts continued being oblivious of him; they just kept talking as if he were absent, even about matters that clearly concerned him.

A cat with a white mark on its forehead appeared at the door, took in his surroundings, and went straight to the visitor, snuggling against him and purring all the while. Kamĩtĩ felt a strange sensation in his belly. This was the cat that he had seen at the charred remains of his shrine. He was about to acknowledge their previous acquaintance but thought the better of it and covered the awkwardness by stroking the cat.

"Our wandering hero has returned," said Mariko.

"And he does not make friends easily," said Maritha.

"Yet he takes to the guest . . ." added Mariko.

"As if they were old friends," said Maritha.

They went on talking to each other, hopping from one thing to another. Kamĩtĩ continued to stroke the cat while trying to glean what he could from their conversation.

They talked of their volunteer services at All Saints.

"If we can feed doves, surely we can do the same for a homeless beggar such as this one?" Maritha said to Mariko.

"Yes, the basement is cozy, and the homeless know that they are on holy ground, where they must share and learn to live in peace."

This strange talk, he realized, was directed at him; they would take care of him.

And that was how he became a dweller in the basement of All Saints. For the first few days his only company was the cat, which came at night to snuggle against him after being gone all day. Morning and evening, Maritha and Mariko would bring him food and make sure that all was well. On the rare occasion when Maritha or Mariko came alone, he or she would impart information by talking loudly and seemingly distractedly.

"There is a lot to do in this church. I will wipe the pews this morning, but still I must return in the evening. And my birds? They have a language of their own. And to think people don't believe me when I say that a dove has sent me a message that humans should take courage; that no night is so long as not to end in dawn!"

On another occasion: "Oh, I don't know how this drama outside the grounds of Parliament and the courts will end. Thousands of people descending on the place from all over the country! Why do they keep on pestering the Ruler about his pregnancy? Don't they know that though men can plant, they can't produce?"

At times he had to restrain himself from laughing at their antics. Mostly he thought about the Limping Witch, her unique elegance of mind and body, and whenever he recalled how she had also fooled him with her limping legs and twisted face, he felt his spirits rise even more in joyful appreciation of her resourceful daring. He was aflame with the desire to touch Nyawĩra, hear her talk, see her laugh, or just be in her presence. Yet, his euphoria aside, he would often brood on the dangers to which she was now exposed, which made him become fearful, sad, and anxious.

And then one night two other homeless came to the basement. It was good to have company besides the cat, hitherto his sole companion. But when in the morning he woke up to find the newcomers stealing glances at him, he felt a coldness in his tummy. It was Njoya and Kahiga. The officers had successfully tracked him down to this place, and now there was no escaping them. Kamĩtĩ decided that his best defense and offense lay in silence.

"Don't worry," Njoya hastened to tell him. "We know that you are the Wizard of the Crow, but we shall not let this out to anybody, not even to this man and woman. Let them continue their taking you for a homeless. We two are now the real homeless, but we shall continue to pretend that you are one of us."

He learned of their dismissal and indeed from their ceaseless chatter he gleaned enough to help him fill up the empty spaces of his knowledge of what had been going on in the country.

But what do they really want? wondered the Wizard of the Crow again, but he did not have long to wait. What they wanted to tell him was for his ears alone, and even as they said so they had already started approaching.

The cat meowed and left the basement, and its departure seemed like a signal for the next act. With Kahiga crouching over his left ear and Njoya his right, they intensified their whispering.

The Wizard of the Crow was puzzled, for though they spoke in earnest, what they said did not make sense. Did he hear right that the money he had buried in the prairie had given birth to three dollar-producing plants, later eaten by an army of strange-looking termites, allegedly sent by him to the State House?

"You did a good thing to send the termites," they told him. "The Ruler has not a grain of gratitude in him."

They became a nuisance. If he moved a step back, they moved with him, and if he turned they did the same, each clinging to his chosen ear.

It was a Sunday morning, and with the cathedral seething with worshippers, the hymns and prayers above incongruously interacted with the ceaseless whispering around his ears.

And then suddenly came an even more jarring note: the sound of a bullhorn.

"We know the sound of that bullhorn," added Kahiga. "Please, tell us the secret," he pleaded urgently.

"You can surely save our families with just a few words," added Njoya.

"Please tell us the secret of growing money," they urged him in unison.

At long last it was out. So all of them, the Ruler, Tajirika, and these two, were after the secret of money growing on trees? But that thought was now superceded by the more immediate worry of what they said about the bullhorn.

Just then the cat meowed again, twice. It had come back to him. And then he saw Maritha and Mariko at the far end of the basement beckoning him to follow.

All at once he made a decision. In the past he had escaped from many a tight situation because of words. His words. But now he had trapped himself inside a wordless silence. Who was he, without a voice?

"Leave me alone," the Wizard of the Crow suddenly said, just to get Njoya and Kahiga away from his ears and also prevent them from following him farther.

The startled pair moved back a step but when it suddenly dawned on them that the Wizard of the Crow had actually spoken, they rushed back to his side and set their ears close to his mouth. He did not disappoint them.

"It is unnatural for money to give birth to money," he said irritably. "Banks alone know the secret of money producing money. They hide the secret in ledger books and computer screens. I am now going for the word of God," he said in a tone of finality, and began to move.

Njoya and Kahiga brimmed over with joy. Was that why Tajirika had started Mwathirika Ltd.?

"Here!" shouted Njoya as he and Kahiga ran after him.

"We promised your assistant, remember?" said Kahiga, pulling a small plastic bag out of his pocket. "In our joy, we almost forgot."

"Your fallen hair," said Njoya, as he and Kahiga headed for the exit.

# 10

In those days church and mosque attendance had gone up considerably, mainly because many religious centers preached and prayed for the banishment of Satan, who had come to stand for all that was wrong with the country. Some religious leaders had strongly defended the right of free assembly and had become heroes of the new democratic surge.

No religious center attracted more people of so many persuasions as All Saints Cathedral. Orthodox and non-Orthodox, Christian and non-Christian, all made their way to the place. Debates about the origins of the cathedral's popularity still rage to this day.

Some said it stemmed from when Maritha and Mariko told weekly stories of their strange desires and their battles with Satan, pointing out that many of those who first came to the cathedral to hear of the couple's temptations had joined the church even after the pair had stopped baring their hearts.

Others asserted that the church's rise started long before the confessions of Maritha and Mariko, tracing its beginnings to the Sunday when Bishop Kanogori chased away the daemons that the Ruler, riding a donkey in imitation of Christ, had brought into the building.

Yet others insisted that one did not have to go beyond the personality of Bishop Kanogori himself. His reputation for voicing in the light of day the many concerns whispered at night had spread so wide and far that some even believed that he spoke with God. Many went there just to hear his interpretations of the Bible. One of his most popular was his rendering of the Sermon on the Mount, and when he declaimed, in a slightly tremulous voice, that the poor shall inherit the Earth, sighs of agreement could clearly be heard all over the place.

It is said that the Ruler did not like his outspokenness, and so when some thugs raided his house one evening and roughed him up, everybody in Aburĩria assumed the State House was responsible. The thugs had warned him to keep his mouth shut or else.

But Bishop Kanogori did not; instead, he begged his congregation to pray for his attackers so that they might emerge from darkness into light. His church would always be open to receive them. This declaration was met with disbelief and uncertainty. It was one thing to forgive those who have sinned against us; another to welcome them into the building.

The cathedral had also started attracting crowds from the People's Assembly outside Parliament and the law courts, as well as the media. Kanogori's sermons, albeit in truncated form, started appearing in the papers.

One Sunday, when the bishop was in the middle of prayer, a bullhorn outside was heard making a strange demand. At first the worshippers ignored the bullhorn's interruption; they remained on their knees, their eyes shut in prayer. But when the demand was repeated, people opened their eyes as the bishop rushed to conclude what he was saying. Those packed near the windows and outside the door were first to scream. The cathedral was surrounded by armed police. Marksmen had climbed the trees, their guns trained on the compound. The operations officer, Wonderful Tumbo himself, stood atop an armored car; through his bullhorn he ordered everyone to go inside; any who tried to escape would be shot on sight. The entire congregation was to remain inside until Bishop Kanogori delivered the fugitive: the Wizard of the Crow.

Bishop Kanogori asked his followers to be orderly and peaceful. He was sure there had been a misunderstanding and it would all be cleared up once he spoke to the officer in charge. He had no idea what the police were talking about. Who was this Wizard of the Crow? Why would he be in the cathedral? Wonderful Tumbo told Bishop Kanogori that he was not in the mood for evasiveness. The church had to surrender the sorcerer or face the consequences.

The Bishop went back to the altar and asked the congregation if there was a sorcerer among them. Their solemnity broke; they laughed. He called upon all the sorcerers who might be in the congregation to see the error of their ways and repent. Anybody who genuinely repented would no longer be a sorcerer; if they were sorcerers before setting foot inside the church, they no longer were, having been born again in Christ.

And that is what he told Wonderful Tumbo: that the church was God's abode. Outside was subject to earthly powers. Neither Bishop

Kanogori nor Officer Tumbo would give an inch, and people feared that the standoff would end in bloodshed. The officer had been on the phone with the Ruler. So when he proclaimed his ultimatum, everyone knew that it had the backing of the State House. All Saints had one hour to give up the sorcerer, and after that the police would storm the holy abode.

Then Maritha and Mariko stood up, and there was silence all around. They asked if they could speak to the bishop alone. People thought that Maritha and Mariko were intent on recounting a new episode in their battle with Satan. I thought their battle with the Tempter was over, some whispered among themselves. Even the bishop told them to please hold back their testimony until after the crisis was over. In the meantime, would everybody please close their eyes so that we can ask the good Lord for a peaceful end to the situation?

In the midst of their prayers they heard a cat meow. Upon opening their eyes, they saw a man followed by a cat emerge from a door near the altar at the far back of the cathedral. The man and the cat stopped by the altar where the bishop stood. Maritha and Mariko looked at each other: Why did he come out when we asked him to wait in the back room? Why did he not leave everything to us?

"I am the one they call the Wizard of the Crow, and I don't want anybody hurt on account of me. I, like other homeless, have sought shelter in the refuge of your basement. I thank you all for that. I brought myself here in peace and I will take myself from here in peace."

All watched as the man, followed by the cat, walked down the aisle and out of the church. Officer Tumbo himself put handcuffs on him.

# 11

Sweeper-of-Souls and Soul's Walking Stick were among the hundreds who had not found a seat inside and so had remained outside, from where they had witnessed the entire drama. The two, now veterans in the war against Satan, knew this to be the same figure that once appeared before them at the city dumpsite and later followed Soul's Walking Stick from bar to bar. The Devil had once again eluded them. But they would not lose heart, and, with fellow Soldiers of Christ, they broke into their song of defiance, renewing their vows to crush Satan, stepping on the ground in unison so hard that the earth beneath their feet shook, increasing their joy as if they could see their enemy squirming and writhing beneath their united onslaught.

Just then Soul's Walking Stick saw two green eyes watching from behind the hedge that enclosed the church grounds, and he immediately remembered that the cat that followed closely behind Satan down the aisle had disappeared mysteriously the moment the police had put handcuffs on the body of Satan. It was a revelation. Satan had allowed the police to capture his human shadow while all along he was hidden inside the body of the cat. He added new lyrics to the melody, alerting the others to the eyes that watched them.

When the others understood the import of his gestures, they formed two flanks to encircle Satan, but it was as if the cat read their intentions. It jumped out of its hiding place and ran away, with the ever-determined Soldiers of Christ in pursuit, shouting, Catch him! Catch the coward!

# 12

"True! *Haki ya Mungu!*" A.G. would later say, talking of the Sunday, shaking his head in remembrance of what had happened. "I had just gotten to the grounds of All Saints. Wonderful Tumbo seemed delighted with his success, but I was saying to myself, You fool, you think you have arrested the Wizard of the Crow? His other self is free.

"But when they threw him in the back of the Land Rover and drove off, I became angry. A faithful servant of the State, I had lost my job and had no way of knowing where they were taking him. I cannot explain the depth of my resentment at no longer being an insider.

Only weeks before I had stood in the State House, a daily witness to the workings of power; now I stood outside the walls of All Saints, powerless.

"I watched the Christians sing with gusto and I wondered why they were so obsessed with Satan when they had just narrowly escaped a bloody Sunday. Where was the outrage at what had just happened? My perplexity turned to amazement when I saw the dancing youth darting after a cat. The crowd watching the songfest seemed equally astonished and started to disperse.

"It was then that I saw my ex-workmates, Njoya and Kahiga, moving away. Apparently they had been part of the crowd of onlookers. I was happy to see them and I hastened toward them. I told them that as soon as I got a tip that the Wizard of the Crow was in the environs of the cathedral, I had gone to look for them, just as we had agreed to do on the day we parted, only to be told that they had already left for the church. I saw them cast quick glances at each other; then they told me that they had actually talked to the wizard in the homeless shelter but he had revealed nothing. What were they now going to do? I asked them, hoping, I must admit, that they would ask me to join them to discuss the extraordinary happenings of the day. They muttered something about everything being *iffy* and quickly excused themselves, citing other commitments. Their behavior struck me as a little odd, as if they were withholding information from me, and I thought that maybe . . . had they betrayed the Wizard of the Crow by revealing his whereabouts to his enemies?

"For a few days I wandered from place to place to see if I could somehow catch a glimpse of the Limping Witch, the wizard's other incarnation. Why? I don't really know; it wasn't only about the secret of growing money. Something else drove me. I thought that if I bumped into the Wizard of the Crow in his other form, he might tell me something that would enable me to hear clearly this thing that I felt forming in my heart . . ."

# 13

Nyawīra was engrossed in the activities of the People's Assembly, the brainchild of their movement, when news reached her that the Wizard of the Crow had surrendered to the agents of the regime outside All Saints. She felt as if she had been hit on the head with a club. Since their escape she had not found a safe moment for them to meet, but she had thought that as long as he was in the church basement under the care of Maritha and Mariko, that moment would come. But now this? Had he given up hope, or what? She felt worse when later she got news from Maritha that not even Vinjinia knew where they had taken him. Have they disappeared him the way they did Machokali?

She and the other cadres of the movement put their heads together for an appropriate response, but they could not immediately think of anything to thwart the Ruler's triumph. Helpless, she sought, as usual, solace in work, burying herself even more deeply in the day-to-day details of the People's Assembly. But to what end, all these activities? The movement had not started the queues; it had simply inserted its ideas into what were, initially, spontaneous demonstrations and given them a united purpose in a march to Parliament, rallying around the call for the return of their collective voice. Would they be able to sustain the assembly without a clear, attainable goal? What if the recapture of the wizard signaled the beginnings of a more heightened and determined assault on the assembly?

They came up with a short-term solution, which was also a response to the recapture of the wizard.

Their activities would climax in a day of self-renewal during which the people would call for the dictator to move or be moved and renew their vows to step up efforts to steer the country along a different path. They settled on a date and named it the Day of National Rebirth or Self-Renewal, announcing it by word of mouth and in thousands of leaflets. They also called for a one-day general strike and festivities throughout the country to mark and celebrate the day. A joyous revolution, they hoped.

# 14

Even the police who ushered the Wizard of the Crow to the Ruler's chamber in the State House knelt down and automatically crossed themselves before retreating to the door. The captive did not follow suit, but nothing in his last encounter with the Ruler could have prepared him for the scene.

The ceiling, painted white, blue, and gray, gave an impression of a sky with sun, moon, and stars. The walls and the canvas covering the Ruler's tummy and extending outward to the walls and down to the carpet were painted green, yellow, and orange, a realistic rendering of an undulating earth. A staircase spiraled from the carpet and disappeared in a mist that also enveloped the head of the seated figure. The lamps that lit the stairs and the mist generated by a hidden smoking machine had turned the Ruler into a righteous deity looking down from the sky in judgment over a sinful earth.

The Ruler was pleased with the impact of the illusion on those who came to see him. Kaniũrũ's wiles had not only helped him nab the wizard but also changed a thing of shame and weakness into one of power and glory. Here was a good example of committed art. He rewarded the artist by allowing him to stay with him as he questioned the captive. I need your counsel, he had told Kaniũrũ, who, seemingly believing in his own illusion, now stood by the bottom rung, a big key in his left hand and a pitchfork in the other, guardian at the gates of Heaven and Hell. The deity explained, in a conciliatory tone, that the wizard, now that his voice had come back, would go before the assembly at the grounds of Parliament and the courts and confess to putting the daemons of queuing into the people. The Ruler even cited as evidence the fact that the Wizard of the Crow had gone to Tajirika's place disguised as a job seeker only for queues to have sprung up the day after. He must also tell the public that he had gone to America at the behest of the late Machokali to strike the Ruler dead. When the sorcery failed, the wizard and the late minister came up with the baseless rumor that the Ruler was pregnant. He must remove the daemons of queuing, cleanse the crowd of defiance against the State, and then fill their minds with wholesome ideas. If people dispersed peacefully, the Ruler would let him live, a fully licensed sorcerer, the Ruler's Permanent Personal Afrochiatrist, and his adviser on the mind of the nation, the capture of fugitives like Nyawīra, and a couple of other things about which he would speak to him in private. "I will let you think it over for one night," the Ruler offered graciously.

When confronted for an answer the following day, the Wizard of the Crow said that his powers did not lie.

It was not a question of what he wanted or not, the Ruler now said in a menacing voice. He would have to do whatever was expected of him.

Kaniūrū intervened: "That is what the English call an *ultimatum.*"

"Yes, an ultimatum," the Ruler echoed.

Dictators thrive on fear, reflected the Wizard of the Crow. They loved to see their subjects quake and make desperate pleas for mercy and forgiveness. If the dictator intended to kill him, he would do it anyway, no matter what the Wizard of the Crow said. Even an animal taken to the slaughterhouse offers resistance, the wizard said to himself.

The standoff—the same question, the same answer—went on for some time, with Kaniūrū adding to the tension with sarcasm geared to deepen the wizard's frustration while fueling the Ruler's anger.

The dictator gave the wizard one last chance to come up with an acceptable answer, underlining his determination to extract compliance by having the Wizard of the Crow thrown into the temple of human bones.

By the dawn of the third day, the wizard had made a decision. It was better to die in the public view of the living than to die out of sight in the temple of human bones.

"When do I appear before the People's Assembly?" the Wizard of the Crow asked.

# 15

Nyawīra and the other cadres of the movement kept their ears glued to the national radio to hear the latest and gauge the State's response to their call for a general strike and the day for the rebirth of the nation. The radio was the dictator's mouthpiece, but listening to it was not always in vain. Through a scrutiny of the regime's own sources, they had, in the past, learned many things and acted on them, at times leading the dictator to believe that the movement had informants inside the State House.

But this time they felt completely baffled by the thinking and the plans of the dictator. They strained their ears the better to make out what the radio was saying. The radio first talked about the Ruler's birthday and reminded people that this was the real occasion for national celebrations. It also reminded the nation that the Ruler himself had yet to choose the most appropriate date. They should stay tuned. They did not have long to wait.

What? they asked, turning to one another in disbelief at what the radio had just said, almost as if they had not quite heard the words. The official celebrations fell on the day that the Movement for the Voice of the People had selected and advertised as the Day of National Self-Renewal. The date and the day of the climax of the People's Assembly had been turned into this year's official celebration of the Ruler's birthday, reminiscent of those others that had given rise to Marching to Heaven. Their call for a one-day general strike to mark the day lost the power of threat with the government's declaring the day a public holiday. What should the movement now do to scuttle the regime's plans and rescue the Day of National Self-Renewal?

They had hardly started to recover from the blow when they suffered yet another shock. The radio announced that the Wizard of the Crow would make a public confession to the People's Assembly on that day.

They debated moving the Day of National Self-Renewal to another date. But they had already announced the day. If they chose another date, would this not signify a victory for the dictator and embolden him to strike more psychological and even physical blows against the assembly? No, they resolved after much passion, they would keep the date and outperform the dictator's own performance. But what were they going to do about the Wizard of the Crow?

# 16

"When I heard the radio say that the Wizard of the Crow would be addressing the People's Assembly," A.G. was to recount, "my head spun, amazed once more by the Wizard of the Crow. Only the other day he was being dragged in handcuffs. And now this! Even more baffling was the government's invitation to all citizens to join the People's Assembly. But wasn't it just yesterday that the police were violently breaking up queues? Was it not only the other day that the Ruler himself had threatened to mow down the People's Assembly with armored cars? Now he was ordering his police to arrest anyone who interfered with the great assembly. I was a little bit concerned, especially with so many conflicting stories floating in the air . . ."

Those of you who were there in those days can remember how the war of rumors intensified day by day. Was the assembly a government-engineered show or a genuine People's Assembly? The principal vehicles for the claims and counterclaims were the state radio, nicknamed the Dictator's Mouthpiece, and the people's word of mouth, nicknamed the Bush Telegraph. When the Mouthpiece talked about the dictator's birthday, the Telegraph talked about the dictator's day of giving birth. When the Mouthpiece claimed that the man who had manufactured the lies about male pregnancy had agreed to make a confession before the People's Assembly, the Telegraph countered with the claim that the Ruler had agreed to confess his pregnancy before the entire assembly.

By then, even those who may have been hesitant about going to the assembly had changed their minds. They had to be there to see, hear, and find out for themselves where lay the truth between the conflicting claims of the Mouthpiece and the Telegraph. Then the

Mouthpiece came up with startling news that on the assembly day the Wizard of the Crow was going to reveal Nyawĩra's whereabouts by using a mirror.

"Well, true! *Haki ya Mungu!* I also found myself walking to, well, where else? The People's Assembly."

# 17

News of the prospective use of the divining mirror by the Wizard of the Crow reached Sikiokuu in his place of house arrest; he sought an audience with the Ruler urgently and was brought to him by night.

In his days as minister, Sikiokuu used to kneel before the Ruler, but it was more a sycophantic gesture than an act that came from the heart. But now, faced with a scene he could never have imagined, a moon- and starlit sky in the chamber, he fell on his knees, tears flowing down his cheeks for all his sins. The Ruler spoke to him gently: Sikiokuu, rise up and unburden yourself to me.

But he remained on his knees as he reminded His Holiness about the mirrors he, Sikiokuu, had once ordered from abroad. These had not been contaminated by anyone domiciled in Aburĩria. They were pure mirrors. The Ruler should have the sorcerer use these mirrors for the best results, certainly for the location of Nyawĩra. The Ruler looked a bit puzzled but was impressed by Sikiokuu's knowledge of the origins of the imported mirrors, with names like Asakusa in Japan and Venini in Italy sounding genuinely foreign and hence authenticating the claims of the kneeling supplicant.

"Thank you, Sikiokuu, for showing that even under house arrest you are still mindful of your duty to your Lord. I will never forget your devotion. Is there anything else that you wish to tell me?"

"Nothing much. You have already granted me that which I most wanted, your audience. Were I to die today, I would go to my grave in peace, knowing that you know that I had faithfully taken the necessary steps to secure Nyawĩra in handcuffs as you had ordered me to do. Your Holy Excellency, I am a sinner . . ."

"I know," said the Ruler, as if trying to silence him.

But he was not. The Ruler, like many other opponents of the Wizard of the Crow, had always wanted to secure for himself all the sorcerer's knowledge and powers, without the sorcerer's irritating, embarrassing, and even threatening presence. An idea on how to achieve this had just possessed him. He would have the Wizard of the Crow kidnapped immediately after the confessions and brought to the State House in secrecy. Whether he disappeared him after securing a cure and the secret of growing dollars or after appropriating all his powers; or retained him under lock and key in the State House, using him as the need arose, only the Ruler would be in the know. Whichever, he would have a permanent spirit in the house as his adviser on matters. And who was better placed to carry out the kidnap mission than a sinner who was deeply desirous of forgiveness? Somebody like . . . like . . . Sikiokuu? *Why not?*

"Everyone is a sinner," the Ruler now told the ex-minister. "But the sinner must show by his deeds that he is ripe for salvation. Sikiokuu, do you want to be saved?"

Sikiokuu was too overwhelmed to speak. He just nodded and tugged at his earlobes.

"I didn't hear you," the Ruler said.

"Yes, my Lord and Master. Just use my mirrors and you have a slave to your needs for life."

The Ruler assured him about the mirrors, but Sikiokuu would still have to prove himself with a task. The task was simple; the test lay in how well it was carried out.

"Have you ever kidnapped a person?" the Ruler asked him.

"Not me, personally. But using my men . . ."

"I am not asking you to use your hands. Your mind. A mastermind!"

A helicopter spewing Burīs above the crowd would be the signal. Timing was important. Sikiokuu's team was to act on the wizard the second the crowd started scrambling for the falling bills. But only Sikiokuu alone was to bring the prize to him by night.

In keeping with his new policy of taking matters into his hands, the Ruler was going to direct the entire drama of the birthday celebration from his haven at the State House, with only he alone knowing the entire script, the actors their allotted lines only. So he did not tell Sikiokuu that the money was newly manufactured for the purpose of confusing the crowd or that he had asked Kaniūrū to provide an undercover escort for the wizard. Tajirika knew about the bills—it was part of his fiscal plan—but not about the details of other plans. And definitely, he was not going to tell Kaniũrũ about the kidnap plans or the helicopters dropping money from the sky.

Sikiokuu went back to life under house arrest, elated at being entrusted with the secret mission. He would soon be back in favor. But he could not help the thought that the Ruler had somehow stolen ideas that he himself used to entertain.

# 18

Furyk, Clarkwell, two cameramen, an electrician, a sound engineer, and the production manager of Clem&Din arrived in Eldares that very morning. Since his childhood, the electrician had heard so much about darkest Africa that, despite the images of new cities of steel and concrete he had seen on television, he still assumed that the continent was dark night and day and had bought goggles with night vision. Dr. Wilfred Kaboca, who met them at the airport in a chauffeur-driven vehicle, did not take them to their hotel but straight to the State House. He is getting worse by the hour, Kaboca explained.

The team set about their work as if people floating in the air was a common sight. And what they did not understand, like the simulation of Heaven in the Ruler's chamber, they assumed to be an oddity peculiar to African rulers. They did, however, ask that the smoke machine be switched off.

Aided by Clarkwell and Kaboca, Furyk went about the usual preliminaries with the same results: nothing amiss. What was noticeably different between now and that other time in New York was not the expansion, although this had increased tenfold, but the lightness of the body. A puzzled Furyk said that he would later place some calls to Harvard to talk about this phenomenon with some physicists. Or e-mail them, suggested Clarkwell, who had brought his handheld computer. This prompted Kaboca to take Furyk aside and ask him if they had brought a sonograph machine. Ooops! Furyk said, he did not remember to bring it, but that did not much matter, because a simple blood test was enough to help determine if the expansion had mutated into a pregnancy.

The cameramen and the electrician were busy checking the outlets and the source, quantity, and quality of the light to see what they could add to create the necessary ambience. Furyk reminded them that this was not a feature but a documentation of a scientific procedure and they had to ensure adequate light only on the patient.

With the patient touching the ceiling, they had a few problems in eye-level camera placement, but the permanent state carpenters constructed ladders with small platforms. They set up one camera in a fixed position to take continuous uninterrupted pictures of the patient for the doctors to use when later they reviewed the collected data. The second cameraman took establishing shots of the State House, then the chamber; otherwise his main task was close-ups of the Ruler and the operation, were that to become necessary.

With the preliminary steps completed, they sat back, observing the patient, an amazing sight, for despite his condition he followed on television what was unfolding outside and directed government responses.

Sensing Furyk's curiosity, and with the Ruler's approval, Kaboca had an extra television set up for the visitors.

# 19

Different groups and individuals positioned themselves to secure the best space and view for their needs.

The Soldiers of Christ had split into three groups, each with its own allotted task. The first group, led by Soul's Walking Stick, continued to look for the cat, which had not been sighted anywhere since its escape outside All Saints.

The second group, led by Sweeper-of-Souls, kept vigil on all the roads leading into and out of the State House, because the two times that Satan had escaped them he had gone to the State House. In both cases they did not know of his coming out.

The third group came to the assembly singing defiantly, their plan being to creep behind the Devil and capture him before he could enter the body of any other being.

The three groups were now coordinating their efforts through pagers and mobile phones to ensure that however and wherever Satan might choose to escape, the Soldiers of Christ would all be there to block him.

The media people, expecting a revolution, had already set their cameras in the streets where they expected riots to erupt, with people being stoned and houses burnt down. The poor areas of Eldares had never seen so many television cameras so interested in their fate.

The Ruler was in a self-congratulatory mood for successfully turning the day of the so-called National Self-Renewal into a national celebration of his birthday. By declaring the day a public holiday, he had taken the sting out of the call for a general strike. Even one newspaper not known for its excessive enthusiasm for the dictatorship wrote that the Ruler was a *consummate politician*.

Tajirika, who had already ensured that Burī bills were well stacked in four helicopters marked NORTH, SOUTH, EAST, and WEST, had gone to the grounds early to observe everything in case his views were ever sought, but after greeting the leaders of the various armed forces, conveying his good wishes for their welfare, he retreated and stood way back at the fringes of the crowd. He knew that the stampede set in motion by the Burī manna from Heaven posed danger, and he had even told Vinjinia and his children not to attend.

Sikiokuu had parked the getaway car just outside the assembly. With sunglasses on and a hat to cover his ears, he sat at the driver's seat, holding a mobile phone, with which he communicated with both the State House and his hired armed thugs now seated in a strategic place near the platform. Their task was one only: to snatch the Wizard of the Crow at the signal and take him to Sikiokuu's waiting car, from where Sikiokuu would take over. Though he remained inside the car, Sikiokuu kept peering outside at the sky for fear that he might miss the blessed signal of Burī bills from above.

Kaniūrū, who had interpreted the Ruler's call on him to organize an escort for the wizard as a hidden mandate to dispatch the sorcerer to Hell after the confession—for why else would the Ruler be explicit about the journey to the assembly but silent about the return?—had already organized the group that would cover the Wizard of the Crow on either side as he walked to the platform. The official plan was for an unmarked police vehicle to drop the Wizard of the Crow a few yards from where the crowds began and for him to walk the rest of the way through the throng, apparently without coercion, but he would be made aware, of course, that he was surrounded by possible assassins to discourage thoughts of escape. Kaniũrũ kept to himself his intention to eliminate the Wizard of the Crow at last. His youth knew only that after the confessions they were to escort the Wizard of the Crow and force him into Kaniũrũ's Mercedes-Benz, and then Kaniũrũ would tell them what to do next. He himself crept forward to a spot close enough to the platform to see and hear everything. For his own comfort he kept patting the gun in his pocket as if it were a protective talisman against any sorcerous tricks of his adversary.

Nyawĩra and her people were also close to the platform, ready to act on any of their different options, depending on how the scene unfolded.

And then there were the official forces of law and order, the army, which surrounded the entire field, most of them entirely unaware of any of the plots against the Wizard of the Crow. Armed to the teeth, they waited for word from their commanding officers but were careful not to provoke the crowd.

Religious leaders said prayers and called on God to bless the day that all might end well; that the day should mark the beginning of a new life of tolerance and openness in the country and that all may glorify and praise God in various voices without fear. *E pluribus unum,* one of them kept saying.

The university youth ran the proceedings, and speaker after speaker kept reminding people why the assembly had become necessary. It was a coalition of interests all united by the one desire to recover their voice in running the affairs of the land. As part of this commitment, nobody, even those with contrary views, would be prevented from airing their views. It was a day for national self-renewal and the recovery of their individual and collective voice.

> *Look in my eyes and see*
> *I don't fear death*
> *As I demand the voice*
> *You took from me*

They had sung the song for weeks, A.G. would later tell his listeners, but on that day they rendered it with special intensity.

"True! *Haki ya Mungu*," A.G. would swear to emphasize the truth of his assertions, adding, "Everything was uncertain. The very name of the day was in contention: was it the Day of the Ruler's Birthday, the Day of National Self-Renewal, or the day the Ruler would give birth? One thing was certain: everybody wanted to hear the Wizard of the Crow on the mystery of male pregnancy."

# 20

The Wizard of the Crow reached the assembly grounds early in the afternoon, led by Big Ben Mambo. To his left and right were armed policemen, followed by others who carried five parcels. All around them were the media folk, jostling for a better view of the sorcerer. People whispered: The Wizard of the Crow. Then the silence of curiosity.

"True! *Haki ya Mungu!* There was nobody, even among the children, who so much as sniggered or dared to cough" was how A.G. would later describe the moment. "I had gotten there quite early to see if I could catch his attention, even for a fleeting second, and ask him about the thing, the being of all things, for I had reached a point in my life when I came to view words differently. A closer look at language could reveal the secret of life. Many questions intrigued me: What gave the wizard so much power and insight? His magic potions, or something beyond the senses? Was it a knowledge that could be passed on to another? True! *Haki ya Mungu!* I felt that if I could talk to him my life might acquire meaning. But when he came to the grounds and I saw how he was guarded and pursued by the media, I realized that I would not be able to get near him. But I would still keep my ears open so as to catch every word that fell from his lips. I recalled his words at the bar: *No, hapana! No! That is not how it happened.* So how did it? I asked myself.

"I saw Big Ben Mambo, the Minister of Information, climb up to the dais, nudging the Wizard of the Crow forward as if guiding him to a seat. Big Ben Mambo cut a funny figure; even now he walked erect as if leading an army parade. This one should have been a member of the armed forces, I found myself musing. The police and the media sat in front of the crowd, all facing the dais. I also crept toward the dais and went as far as those seated in front of me would allow. Really, I did not want to miss a single word or act . . ."

The students who had taken on the role of masters of ceremony gave the minister time to speak and, to dissenting whistling from some sections, they explained that this was a People's Assembly and the minister, like every other citizen, had a right to speak and air his views. Big Ben Mambo was unhappy that mere students were giving him permission to speak, but he reckoned that this was not the time or place to start an argument or be defiant. Big Ben Mambo began by saying that he was there as a messenger from above, and so he was speaking in the name of the Ruler, Father of the Nation and Commander in Chief of the Armed Forces. He then thanked the Ruler for allowing the assembly to take place on the hallowed grounds of Parliament and the courts. He especially thanked him, on behalf of all those now assembled here, for accepting, in advance, the love and adoration that they all had come here to express on His Mighty's birthday . . .

"You mean his delivery date?" some people shouted, and started chanting: "Who is responsible for the pregnancy?"

"Please allow me to finish my speech," Big Ben insisted. "Now, about the pregnancy: you will get to hear all about it from the mouth of the Wizard of the Crow. He will also expose all enemies of the State."

"The enemies of this State are friends of the people," others shot back.

"I did not come here to harangue or be harangued," Big Ben Mambo screamed. "I came here to deliver the Ruler's greetings and best wishes and to ask you to give the Wizard of the Crow a chance to confess fully and to say everything that he has to say without your interrupting him or shouting him down or stoning him just because he is a sorcerer. The days when sorcerers were put in beehives and rolled down a mountain to their deaths in the valley are gone." Sensing the mounting hostility, Big Ben Mambo fled the microphone and beckoned the Wizard of the Crow to the lectern.

Slowly and deliberately, the Wizard of the Crow rose, asked the leaders of the ceremony if he could speak, and, with their assent, went to the lectern and stood before the microphone.

# 21

Kamĩtĩ did not know how to begin or what to tell the gathering. Again he wished he had had a chance to speak with Nyawĩra. But, as that was not meant to be, he was now on his own. A loner by nature, he disliked public speaking, and here was a multitude in rapt attention! He had taken on the identity of the Wizard of the Crow as a cover, a joke, and now he was expected to be true to that identity. He was hardly here of his own volition, and now he had to speak as if he had come willingly! He hated lies and lying, even for private gain, and now he was expected to lie publicly for another's gain. He had wanted to root his life in truth—even as a diviner he had tried his best to avoid falsehood—and here he was, his life hanging on a false confession!

He took courage in the conviction that he would rather die before the crowd than be disappeared like Machokali.

"You all saw that I walked here surrounded by armed guards to ensure that I don't stray from the path. So I want to start by saying how much I appreciate my guides and guards."

There was laughter, which put him more at ease.

"I have been asked to speak about the Ruler's pregnancy, Nyawĩra's hiding place, Machokali's disappearance, and the queues. I must speak only the truth. Thereafter, as I have been instructed, I must drive away the daemons possessing you, compelling you to queue and organize. I must cleanse your souls of defiance."

Again some people laughed. Others were uneasy. But when he started to confess, the ensuing silence was complete.

He felt his tongue loosen up.

# 22

The Ruler, who was following everything on television, held his breath in gleeful anticipation of an abject and contrite confession. He was so pleased with himself that he could not help chuckling a little.

Watching their own television screen, Furyk, Clarkwell, and Kaboca now and then kept an eye on their patient, jotting down observations for later review, while the first camera captured the Ruler's every gesture and bodily motion. The second camera was also busy with medium shots, close-ups, and even a few cutaways, including a few shoulder shots of the Ruler looking at the screen at the Wizard of the Crow before the assembly.

Suddenly they heard the Ruler let out a sharp, anguished cry, his airborne body writhing in pain. The Ruler groaned. Furyk and Clarkwell quickly climbed the ladder of Heaven to see what was happening. Had the hour of another mystery birth come upon them?

# 23

"I will first confess my role in the origin of the rumors that the Ruler is pregnant," the Wizard of the Crow said. "But why talk as if pregnancy is a malignancy? To be pregnant is to carry a seed of a becoming. Is it of life or death? That's the question. However, I was not sent here to sing the ethics and philosophy of pregnancy but to explain how I misled you into mistaken beliefs.

"It is all due to a parable that came to me as I waited in a lobby of a New York hotel, trying to figure out the meaning of the wonders I had seen in a flight I had made around Africa and all the lands where dwell black folk, in the form of a bird."

He told the story of his travels in time and space in search of the sources of black power and a rather long parable of how humans surrendered control of their own lives to a blind deity with a double-barreled name of M&M, or money and market, and how Africa's independence mutated to dependence. He paused to gauge the effect. Not a sound.

"Why did Africa let Europe cart away millions of Africa's souls from the continent to the four corners of the wind? How could Europe lord it over a continent ten times its size? Why does needy Africa continue to let its wealth meet the needs of those outside its borders and then follow behind with hands outstretched for a loan of the very wealth it let go? How did we arrive at this, that the best leader is the one who knows how to beg for a share of what he has already given away at the price of a broken tool? Where is the future of Africa? I cried.

"I saw this: Around the seventeenth century, Europe impregnated some in Africa with its evil. These pregnancies gave birth to the slave driver of the slave plantation, who mutated into the colonial driver of the colonial plantation, who years later mutated into the neocolonial pilots of the postcolonial plantation. Is he now mutating into a modern driver and pilot of a global plantation? But Africa impregnated its own breed, which made our people sing, Even if you kill our heroes, we women are pregnant with hope of a new lot. Therefore, don't cry despair at those who sold the heritage; smile also with pride at the achievements of those that struggle to rescue our heritage.

"So I said to myself: Just as today is born of the womb of yesterday, today is pregnant with tomorrow.

"What kind of tomorrow was Aburĩria pregnant with? Of unity or murderous divisions? Of cries or laughter? Our tomorrow is determined by what we do today. Our fate is in our hands.

"This thought must have been with me when, in a message to Machokali, I wrote: *Take care. The country is pregnant. What it will bear, nobody knows.* I left the note for Machokali because he was then the eyes of our country outside the country.

"But I had forgotten that in Aburĩria the nation and the Ruler are one. And that is why I have come here with my armed friends to tell you the truth about my role in the origins of the rumor that the Ruler is pregnant."

No sooner had the import of what he was saying dawned on the assembly than women started ululating as men whistled and cried out: "Tell us more! When will he give birth?"

# 24

The Ruler's pain subsided and he returned to watching television just in time to catch the cheering. He had not been able to follow the confessions of the wizard, but the sight of people laughing and calling out for more did not particularly lift his spirits. He was a director helplessly watching his actors straying from the script.

He called Big Ben Mambo and told him to tell the Wizard of the Crow to stop talking about this pregnancy nonsense and get on with the task of locating Nyawĩra. The pain erupted once again, forcing him to cut off further conversation with the minister. His contractions were violent, excruciating, but whenever they allowed he would greedily take in what was being shown on television.

Big Ben Mambo told the assembly that they should stop spreading slander about male pregnancies now that they had heard the confessions of a lying scamp, this man who claims to travel in bird form and to see, in mirrors, what is hidden from the eyes of the ordinary mortal.

"My people, we shall give him a chance to demonstrate his skills before this august assembly of free citizens. Let him exploit his mirrors to expose the enemies of the State. Wizard of the Crow, where is Nyawĩra? Over there are mirrors. Show us where Nyawĩra is! Once you have done that, you must then cleanse this crowd of the daemons of queuing, and the women of the daemons of violence against men. After that, you are free to go. The price of failure? A firing squad in front of all these people."

It took a few seconds for the meaning of Big Ben Mambo's words to sink in. Some in the crowd stood up defiantly. How dare you accuse us of being possessed by daemons? Did you say that we need to be cleansed! others shouted menacingly. Why don't we chase the daemons of arrogance from the minister with a few blows to his buttocks? others suggested, surging forward to execute their threats.

The situation would have turned ugly, but the master of ceremony intervened and asked people to stop any foolishness because Big Ben Mambo might well be provoking them to give the armed forces an excuse to break up the assembly. Let us listen to the Wizard of the Crow, because if he is truly a sorcerer, then there must be a method to his witchcraft.

Even the Ruler, who had caught bits of Big Ben Mambo's comments, was angered by the minister's presumptuousness. His arrogance and exaggerations were about to thwart the Ruler's intended outcome. So despite his stomachaches the Ruler called the minister and told him to stop straying from the script. He was to rescind his comments about the Wizard of the Crow having to earn his freedom. Had the minister forgotten that the sorcerer was supposed to have come there of his own volition? What on earth had made him threaten the wizard with a firing squad? He had better recant his threat, immediately.

Big Ben Mambo had no problem in reversing himself.

"I want to remind you all that the Wizard of the Crow is here of his own volition. He volunteered to use his facility with mirrors to locate Nyawīra's whereabouts," he said, and then added, "I want to apologize to him. I was only being mischievous when I talked about a firing squad. It was a figure of speech. *Pambo la lugha kama alivyosema Shabaan Roberts.* Wizard of the Crow: In the name of the Commander in Chief of the Armed Forces of the Free Republic of Aburīria, I now call upon you to do your thing with mirrors and give us Nyawīra, public enemy number one of the Aburīrian State."

# 25

While this was going on, Kaniūrū pondered his next move. He had felt a little betrayed when he saw the Wizard of the Crow enter the field under police escort. Had the Ruler not entrusted him and his youth with the task of escorting the Wizard of the Crow to the platform? But when thinking about it he realized that this did not in any way change the real responsibility he felt the Ruler had bestowed on him. The crocodiles of the Red River awaited the Wizard of the Crow.

As he reveled, he heard Minister Big Ben Mambo call on the Wizard of the Crow to disclose Nyawīra's hiding place. Kaniūrū felt a knot in his belly whenever her name cropped up in conversation or in print. He could no longer deny it. He was jealous of the sorcerer. He had once seen this man talking to Nyawīra at the roadside near Tajirika's offices. He also recalled Tajirika saying, in his confessions, that when words had gotten stuck in his throat, Nyawīra had led him to the wizard. There had to be an intimacy between her and this man. He crept closer to the platform. He now wanted to catch each and every word that came from the mouth of the Wizard of the Crow. If he revealed her whereabouts, Kaniūrū would leave the execution of the Wizard of the Crow to his gang and get to Nyawīra himself. His vision of a reunion with Nyawīra on his own terms never varied. He still entertained the madness: he would capture her and appeal to the Ruler to pardon her sins. Grateful and chastened, she would now sing praises to her husband. *Glory, glory to Kaniūrū,* he sang quietly to himself. He was glowing with optimism when one of his most fearless youths crouched behind him trembling.

"That man is not a man," he told Kaniūrū in a whisper. "Listen to me. I used to be a garbage collector. We were three. I was the driver. That man was once dead. We buried him. He rose from the dead before our very eyes and he chased us across the open field. We were saved by a group of Soldiers of Christ. One of us joined the sect right away. The other one went to hide in bars. I joined the youth. That man is Satan in human form."

Even though Kaniūrū was unnerved, the words echoed his own when he had seen the man vanish without a trace from the public toilets not far from Paradise. He realized that if this youth were to ramble on like this to the others, he would instill terror in them and all of his own well-laid plans would come to naught.

"Have you told the others about this?" Kaniūrū asked.

"No," the man said.

"Don't go back! Stay here with me," Kaniūrū told him. "And stop shaking," he added, pointing to the pistol he carried in his pocket.

# 26

When Sikiokuu, who kept watchful eyes on the sky for any signs of a helicopter, heard Big Ben Mambo ask the police to bring some packages to the platform, he leaned against his car and focused his binoculars on the packages. He recognized the paper wrappings and knew at once that these were the mirrors he had ordered from abroad. His heart leapt in joy: so the Ruler had really hearkened to his plea? All the energy he had put into locating the best glass manufacturers would not go to waste. He would have liked to have been the one officiating instead of Big Ben Mambo, but that was nothing compared to the benefits he would reap from the role his mirrors were about to play in Nyawīra's capture. History had its ironies, he thought, seeing that the recovery of his life was now dependent on a successful mirror performance by a sorcerer he was planning to kidnap! Sikiokuu was so anxious about the outcome that he forgot that he was supposed to lie low, and he now climbed onto the roof of the car to get a better view of the performance.

As the police unwrapped each parcel and showed its contents to the crowd, with Mambo announcing the country each mirror came from before the police put it at the feet of the Wizard of the Crow, the ex-minister's joy knew no bounds.

And then he suddenly realized that as they were shown to the crowd the mirrors were capturing the shadows of Aburīrians. Minister Mambo had totally missed the point behind the importation of mirrors from abroad and even why they were so carefully wrapped. He went back to the driver's seat and called the State House, but nobody picked up the phone.

Resting his head on folded arms on the steering wheel, Sikiokuu, the Ex-Minister of State in the Ruler's Office, began to weep. His heaving made the car shake, and he came back to himself only when the car started honking and he realized that he had pressed the horn in error.

# 27

The Ruler continued groaning and, remarkably, still sneaked glances at the television screen. Many things crucial to the drama outside, like the signal for the helicopters to start dropping money from on high, were dependent on him. But the contractions were clearly affecting his concentration.

Then suddenly came a strange sound. Furyk quickly climbed up the staircase to Heaven, from where he beckoned Clarkwell and Kaboca. The cloth on which Kaniũrũ had painted the colors of the earth was splitting, and the belts that secured the body to the chair were breaking.

A little scared, the three doctors descended the staircase and went into conference.

"The body is rising again," said Furyk, in obvious dismay. "What is the meaning of this?"

"It beats all scientific logic," said Clarkwell.

"The question is, what can we do to contain the expansion before it fills up the whole room?" Furyk asked, looking at Kaboca.

"What did the sorcerer do to contain the expansion in New York?" asked Clarkwell.

"The Wizard of the Crow? I don't know what he did or how he did it," admitted Kaboca.

"He should be called from the assembly," Furyk suggested.

"An order to recall the Wizard of the Crow can come only from the Ruler's lips," said Kaboca, and they all knew that the Ruler was not in a position to issue any order.

# 28

The Wizard of the Crow had calmly watched the drama of the unwrapping of the mirrors and their placement in a pile before him. But inside he was all turmoil. Time was running out, and he still had not worked out how to extricate himself from this mess. How would he play with the mirrors convincingly in front of this crowd? He was almost certainly performing his own death, but he was equally convinced that the Ruler would not do anything drastic against him on the spot in front of the local and foreign media. The reprieve would delay his death by a few hours only. What would Nyawīra do if she were in a similar position? But she had been! As the Limping Witch, she had daringly gone right into the belly of the Aburīrian beast!

He felt courage suffuse him. Why see the warts of the land only when reflected in Western eyes? No, he was not going to play the game of foreign mirrors. The truth he carried within and the eyes of the people were the only mirrors he would now use. "I have been asked to use mirrors imported from abroad to smoke out enemies of the State," the Wizard of the Crow started.

He asked a policeman to lend him a club. Then he took the first mirror, read aloud the country of its origins, and then set about breaking it. He took the second and third. Systematically he broke all the imported mirrors, and at this act of defiance people started clapping in rhythm.

"Since true divination is about revealing the hidden," he said, "I want to share with you the secrets of my heart. I know Nyawīra. I love her and will never betray her, even if I must go to the land of no return. Nyawīra, I know, will be there with me, for she found me in pieces and made me whole. What she did before, making pieces whole, she will do again." He paused as if to catch his breath.

Clever fellow, a few skeptics muttered. Trying to flush her out of her hiding place, eh? But even they were touched by his tone as he now called out softly, as if addressing someone very near:

"Nyawīra, I embrace you with all my heart and soul, with the people as my witness that truth never dies, its glory never fades. Holiness lies in wholeness."

The Wizard of the Crow felt a gentle breeze wafting the scent of flowers into his nostrils, a scent he knew so well but had not smelled for a long while. He felt a new surge of power, power rooted in his sure knowledge that his words had struck a responsive chord in the hearts of those assembled and reached Nyawīra, wherever she was among the people. He felt good because the words came from the depths of his being and he was ready to die for them.

"Nyawīra is you. Nyawīra is you and me and others," the Wizard of the Crow continued, without fear. "If you know that you are Nyawīra, please rise so that those who have been looking for you, calling you an enemy of the State, may see you. Nyawīra, show us the way."

A woman stood up; I am Nyawīra, she said. Hardly had the eyes of the people turned to her than a man stood up and said, I am Nyawīra; he was followed by every other woman and man until the entire assembly proclaimed itself Nyawīra.

Big Ben Mambo, the Minister of Information, and his official escort remained seated. The police and army officers who were already standing found themselves in an awkward position: they did not know whether or not to sit so as not to be counted as Nyawīra. They remained standing anyway, and for a few minutes it looked as if the army and the police were one with the people.

Cameramen did not know on whom to focus. And to the government agents, Nyawīra was everywhere. One woman started shouting: How many tribes are there? Others replied two, producers and parasites.

Voices rose in song:

> Come, come, the weak and the strong
> Let's build a beautiful land
> Bring your knowledge and your heart

The whole assembly was dancing now, one group working its way to the platform. And before Big Ben Mambo had time to react or figure out what was going on, a protective wall around the Wizard of the Crow had been formed.

He felt a dancing presence beside him and knew it was Nyawīra.

Their eyes met. They held hands and for a minute or so they danced to the song, a twosome indistinguishable from all the other dancers. Even so, the Wizard of the Crow and the Limping Witch felt as if they were in a world all their own, but one guarded and protected by the unity of the Aburīrian people.

When at the State House the Ruler, his body still grossly expanding, saw what was happening on television, he brooded: How dare they sing and dance for joy when I am in infernal pain? It is time to scatter them with money. He gathered whatever strength he still had to make one more effort at teledirecting. He had hardly finished instructing one of the pilots to start dropping money from on high when a new wave of agony swept through him. He dropped the mobile phone; it clattered on the floor, as by now his body was taking up the whole chamber, pushing his doctors and cameramen up against the walls.

Nyawīra heard the whine of a helicopter in the sky, looked up, and saw it dropping leaves as people shouted. The pieces of paper floated gently as if suspended. Before she could push to the microphone to tell the people that it was counterfeit, the dictator's trickery to corrupt their souls and scatter them through temptation, she had a premonition. She looked behind her. Her eyes saw Kaniūrū. She had never seen hate and jealousy burn so intensely as she now saw in his eyes.

He was pressing hard against the crowd, heading straight to the platform. Nyawīra quickly glanced around for an escape route. She saw two formations from two different directions pressing against the crowd, all converging toward the Wizard of the Crow.

Kaniūrū held a gun. At first she thought he was pointing it at her. But no! He was pointing it at the Wizard of the Crow, and before she could cry out a warning Kaniūrū had fired a shot. She was unable to scream; she threw herself on the fallen body of the Wizard of the Crow as if to shield him from further harm. She saw Kaniūrū now pointing the gun at where she lay. We are finished, she muttered to herself.

Somebody jumped on Kaniūrū and wrestled him to the ground. The gun went off in the air. People nearby screamed in horror. Kaniūrū and his adversary were rolling around on the ground, the man trying to get the gun, Kaniūrū fiercely resisting. She had seen the man's face somewhere before, Nyawĩra thought. But she had no time to dwell on the thought.

Suddenly, thunder split the sky. People felt the earth tremble. Kaniũrũ and his adversary stopped struggling momentarily. Fearing for his life, Kaniũrũ dropped his gun and simply took off. He had been preceded by his famously courageous youth, some of them crying out in despair, Oh dear, we have been caught red-handed, as they bumped against others also scampering.

Finding himself without a protector, the ex–garbage driver also fled, moaning to himself, It is Satan, not once looking back until, fortunately, he fell in with a group of Soldiers of Christ at the incinerated remains of a building and he immediately submitted himself to Christ, assuming a new name, Pilot-of-Souls.

At the People's Assembly, Kaniũrũ's adversary ran after him and shot him in the leg. Kaniũrũ fell, but despite the pain of his wound managed to limp away.

And then another crack of thunder, followed by six more, each louder than the previous one. It is raining bombs in the land! some people shouted, the entire place now a chaos of anguished cries and running feet.

Caught unaware, the armed forces at the assembly assumed that a coup was taking place at the State House. Soldiers and police waited for word from their superiors, who waited in turn for word from theirs, who waited for word from their commander in chief. Word never came. The chain of command seemed to have broken somewhere. Uncertainty and panic led to random shootings. Terrified people were running to and fro, pointing to the sky and saying, It is doomsday.

The mushroom clouds forming near the State House after the seven cracks of thunder astonished everyone.

Upon seeing the helicopter in the sky, Sikiokuu had given his thugs the go-ahead to carry out the kidnapping of the wizard. Now he was looking for paper to attest to his support of the revolution. Up with the revolution, he wrote and posted his broadside on the windshield. He stared in wonder at the all-consuming smoke, swallowing even the helicopter. Though now a supporter of the revolution, he did not want to be caught in the crossfire between the revolutionaries and defenders of the current regime. In a coup d'état, it was everybody for himself.

Everyone with a car was trying to flee the capital for the countryside. The congestion was frightening. Impatient horns blared. Visibility was impaired by the thick, foul smoke bedeviling those fleeing in cars and on foot. Covering the body of the Wizard of the Crow with her own, Nyawĩra felt warm blood oozing. Please, Kamĩtĩ, please, don't die on me, she begged.

# 29

Furyk and company ran down State House Road, with Kaboca at the rear shouting directions and urging them not to give up hope for, as he put it, they were only minutes away from the American haven.

Ambassador Gemstone had already given orders that any white person escaping the violence of the revolution should be let in without questions. Those in front entered the haven without any restraint. Wilfred Kaboca was the last to arrive, only to see the gates close before his eyes. Thinking that the guards did not understand, he banged the gate, shouting, We were together! They are my colleagues, you know! But they did not.

A bullet from inside the embassy felled Dr. Wilfred Kaboca. Too shocked to even moan, he somehow raised himself, his right hand on the left side of his chest trying to hold back blood, and amid the foul darkness he went to the highway to seek help to the hospital. No driver would stop. Dr. Kaboca, personal physician to the dictator of Aburĩria, bled to death on the side of the Ruler's Highway.

# 30

The following day people took courage and went to the grounds of the Parliament buildings and law courts, the site of the People's Assembly. Bloated corpses were strewn here and there. It was hard to tell whether the vile stench was from this decomposition or from the dark mist of the day before, issuing from the State House. The mist had spread across the sky, shutting out the sun, the moon, and the stars, plunging the whole country into darkness, and even later, when the sun, the moon, and the stars were able to penetrate the darkness, the whole country seemed enveloped in a sickening pollution.

# SECTION II

## 1

When official word about the thunder, smog, and carnage was not forthcoming, people started saying that maybe the Ruler was dead and the military had taken over the government, the truth of this seemingly borne out by the only visible face of the government: armored vehicles now and then patrolling the streets of the capital and major cities. A six-p.m. curfew had been put in place, but it was not strictly enforced and nobody was arrested for ignoring it.

But why was the military not being forthright about assuming power? Some argued for a failed coup led by noncommissioned officers displeased with their wages like everybody else. Though the coup had failed, a bullet had struck the Ruler, who was now in hiding, giving his wound time to heal. Others said, No, he is merely playing mind games. Have you forgotten that other time, not so long ago, when he let out rumors that he was suffering from throat cancer, only to emerge from his seclusion to heap scorn on all who had prematurely celebrated his death? Did he not also do this and that? Every story was dissected, reinvented, reinterpreted, many times over, because people had no hard facts on which to base a true account of what had happened at the State House. Some claimed, without disclosing their sources, that after the first or second explosion, seven or eight white men were seen running from the State House, a black man giving chase, followed at some distance by black youth, and when the white men reached the American embassy, the gates were opened and the white men entered but the black man was left outside, wagging his finger at them, accusing them of having bombed the State House. The black man was shot and the youth who had been following fled the scene. The black man was never seen again, and neither, for that matter, were the seven or eight whites.

The more the unbearable stench of the foul smog suggested environmental disaster, the more frustration, anger, and fear grew. In every village in every region all over the country, people began to demand that the government tell the truth; there was even talk of resuming demonstrations. Religious leaders called for a day of prayer, and workers for a general strike. Multiparty democracy now became the new clarion call. Soon word was out: the Ruler would not come out in the open because he was scared of Mr. Multiparty.

The Global Bank released a statement that the current absence of leadership and the recent mysterious happenings were putting serious doubts in the minds of investors about the political stability in the country.

It was Big Ben Mambo, Minister of Information, who broke the news: the Ruler had set a date when he would address Parliament and the nation, to be carried live on radio and television. Newspapers were told to plan for special editions, because the Ruler would be announcing a special gift from himself to the nation.

Big Ben Mambo's statement served only to stir the pot: what about the Ruler's rumored illness? Since coming back from America, the Ruler had not appeared in public: why now? What had prompted this unlikely promise of generosity? And the unthinkable: was he about to abdicate?

2

Parliament was packed. The cabinet, members of Parliament, and even some foreign diplomats had arrived hours before the appointed time. The media, in full fever, hoped to glean anything that might make sense of the great Aburīrian mystery: the seven cracks of thunder and the unimaginable smog. American television, which had refused to grant the Ruler an interview when he was in America, now begged for an exclusive with the Ruler. Anyone with a radio or television was glued to his set, crowded by those without.

The speaker of the house struck the table with a mallet. The eagerly awaited session was about to begin.

"True, *Haki ya Mungu*, I kept wondering how he would come to the Parliament," said A.G. "What carriage was he going to ride in? How would he enter the building, for I had not heard anything about the doors being enlarged. Would he be pushed through the entrance the way he was once squeezed into the jumbo jet? What would he talk about? Would he mention the fate of the Wizard of the Crow? And what would he say about the rumors of his pregnancy? Questions upon questions . . ."

Some workers had taken the afternoon off, a few unofficially, for nobody wanted the news to pass him by. A.G. knew of a tea shop, *Wīra-no-nda*, with a television, and he got there early only to find that others had gotten there before him, but he positioned himself where he could see the screen clearly. All crowded around the television set the way bees swarm around a hive, buzzing. When they saw the Ruler appear, they fell silent.

# 3

The Ruler entered Parliament and walked down the aisle on a red carpet. To his right was a woman dressed magnificently, wearing a diamond tiara. Was Rachael, the Ruler's wife, being trotted out for a public viewing?

A.G. could hardly believe his eyes. This Excellency on television was hardly the Excellency he had last seen at the State House. This Excellency was tall and thin. He was dressed in a dark suit, with a boutonniere, a white handkerchief in the breast pocket. In his left hand he held a club and a fly whisk. The usual patches of leopard skins were there. His head was the size of a fist, but his eyes bulged, resembling the late Machokali's.

A.G. did not hear himself as he shouted, No, no, that is not him! over and over again, the others looking at him as at a crazy person, some of them barking impatiently, Shut up! How do you know? without allowing him to explain, to which he responded, What happened to his inflated body? And at this the people laughed, but when he tried to say, Look at his tongue, look at that tongue, they silenced him with poisonous looks. Yet some also noticed that when the Ruler was not talking he would sometimes flick his tongue in and out involuntarily, but most saw nothing strange in this, attributing it to his not having used his tongue in public for a long time. When A.G. now further insisted that the tongue was forked, people around started saying: The smog—see what it has done to this man's head! And maybe he is not the only one?

The Ruler started by saying that he wanted to take the opportunity to introduce the person seated next to him, because when he gave her the job she now holds he had been in seclusion and so in no position to anoint her in person before the eyes of the nation, but there was a time for everything and he was now glad to tell the nation that this was Dr. Yunique Immaculate McKenzie, Official National Hostess.

By the time the audience recovered from the shock, for in truth since her appointment she had never been seen in public, the Ruler was already in full speaking gear. He asked people, wherever they were, in Parliament, their homes, their workplaces, or on the roads, to stand up and observe one minute of silence in memory of those who died recently on the grounds of the Parliament buildings and the law courts. He said that the deaths were the result of the activities of some bad elements in the country who had hoped to bring about confusion as a first stage in a vast conspiracy to overthrow the government. I have only one question for them: Don't they know that we defeated communism in the twentieth century? *Communism is now as dead as a dodo.* The so-called Movement for the Voice of the People had urged and agitated the mob to queue not because the movement genuinely cared for the real needs and grievances of the people but because it wanted to use the populace as instruments of its own evil designs. It had even hired sorcerers to confuse the minds of the innocents with very bad magic. The movement was exploiting genuine grievances, and he would be the first to admit that the country faced a few economic problems. But the whole world faced similar problems because these had to do with *global economic forces* and *a global economic recession* due to the oil crisis brought about by the selfish policies of OPEC.

Let me now turn to recent matters, the thunder and smog about which we are all concerned, he told an attentive Parliament and a curious nation.

It was the same self-styled Movement for the Voice of the People, in collusion with *fundamentalists* from the Middle East, who dropped bombs on the State House, but luckily the Ruler, aided by his experts, had managed to detonate them before calamitous harm could be done to the nation. When the evildoers realized this, they fired tear gas in the air to frighten the population and ignite a revolution. The point of the queues and agitation and the timing of the bombing was clear, but he would not say more about this for *security reasons*, because the matter was still under investigation.

He paused, in fact he had no choice, because members of Parliament were giving him a standing ovation with no end in sight because no MP or minister wanted to be the first to stop.

To the bemusement and then the discomfort of the foreign diplomats who sat through it all, the Ruler let the ovation go on for one hour and seven minutes before gesturing to the MPs to sit down, for he had a lot more to share with them. As for these misguided followers of the Movement for the Voice of the People, he continued, yes, those who had killed innocent citizens whose only crime was to celebrate their Ruler's birthday, he had only one message for them: his security forces would hunt them down and bring them to justice.

The Ruler allowed that there were a few wrongs he wanted to set right so that the Movement for the Voice of the People would never again find grounds for deceiving the nation. He told Parliament that Marching to Heaven had been conceived by Machokali, a *scheme so absurd as to boggle the mind*. There was devilish cunning in it, and he, the Ruler, had gone along with the scheme only for the purpose of finding out the man's real intentions. Well, unfortunately Machokali was not around to explain what he had in mind, so we shall never know what he was up to, and there is no point in speculation. The Ruler now lowered his voice and said that he was sad to say that the government had not yet been able to find out how or where the late Markus had met his fate, or even the nature of that fate. However, the private detectives he had hired from abroad had reported to him that this was a case of SID, self-induced disappearance. Let the scheme, like its author, go the way of SID.

Next, the Ruler said, he would respond to rumors that he was pregnant.

# 4

The Ruler thanked all those who had come to the grounds of Parliament and the law courts to celebrate his birthday, renaming it the Day of National Self-Renewal because according to an age-old African custom, cycles of birth and rebirth are celebrated through well-known rites of passage. He was also aware that there were those who were talking about his birthday, the Day of National Self-Renewal, as the day he would give birth.

"Well, they were not mistaken. The fact is, my people, I was pregnant. Yes, I was pregnant," the Ruler emphasized to an astonished Parliament. "Every Aburĩrian child knows that I am the Country and the Country is Me, which means that *this* Excellency, *this* Country, and *this* Nation are like the mystery of Three in One and One in Three creating the Perfect One." That was why when the Ruler spoke, the nation spoke, and when he sneezed, the nation sneezed. Because the country and the head are one and the same, it follows that his birthday is the nation's birthday and his day of giving birth is as that of the nation giving birth. "You want to see the pictures of the baby?"

On cue, Kaniũrũ, using crutches, hobbled into Parliament followed by four people carrying a huge board wrapped up in a white cloth and set it up in front of the Ruler.

And now, said the Ruler, I ask the official hostess to step forward and reveal what I have brought into the world. Dr. Yunique Immaculate McKenzie walked to the board and lifted the cloth, revealing a drawing of the Ruler holding a baby vaguely resembling Aburĩria in his fatherly arms. At the foot was the inscription in large Aburĩrian national colors: BABY D. Behold Baby Democracy, he called.

The Ruler then grandly proclaimed the advent of multiparty democracy in Aburĩria, to everyone's shock. But he added that the new Aburĩrian system was only making explicit what was latent in all modern democracies, in which parties were basically variations of each other. He would be the nominal head of all political parties. This meant that in the next general elections, all the parties would, of course, be choosing him as their candidate for the presidency. His victory would be a victory of all the parties, and more important for Aburīrians, a victory for wise and tested leadership.

As a sign of the new times, he decreed that the Ruler's Party would now simply be called the Ruling Party.

"And in case *our dear friends* are worried that we might be going too far in *our liberal measures*," he said, glancing in the direction of the row of Western ambassadors, he wanted to stress that whichever party from among the hundreds under his leadership came to power, Aburīria would remain a friend and trustworthy partner of the Western alliance. I worked hand in hand with you in fighting world communism, he said, and now we shall stand shoulder to shoulder in building the new global system of guided freedom and openness. That was why his new system would do away with secret ballots and introduce the queuing by which one openly stood behind the candidate of one's choice. Direct democracy. Open democracy. Baby D is born.

For the first time all the envoys gave him warm applause; this spurred him on.

"If at this time there is anybody from the public gallery who would like to ask a question or make some comments, they can go ahead."

This had never happened in the brief history of Aburīrian Parliament: the gallery being allowed to intervene. Most people took it for a rhetorical gesture, except for one wizened old man who stood up and spoke in a thin, tremulous voice but one loud enough to be heard by all.

"Thank you, My Lord of Infinite Mercy and Kindness. I say thank you because once a long time ago I attempted to speak to you and the minister in charge of the ceremonies ordered the police to deny me the microphone and remove me from the platform. I went away screaming for you to hear me. You heard my cry. I know that is why you removed him. And that is why I thank you, *Mkundu Wangu Mpya Rahisi*, for hearing my cry then and now giving me a chance to redeem my name so dishonored by the late Machokali. I say with you, Down with state secrets."

The phrase *My New Cheap Arsehole* had made A.G. suddenly

recall the same old man trying to speak at the ceremony where the plan for Marching to Heaven was first revealed publicly. How was the leader going to handle this? But at that point the official hostess, Dr. McKenzie, whispered in the ear of the Ruler, who now asked the security to take the old man to the State House, where both would later meet for an exchange of views in endless leisure. The Ruler was a genius of double talk, A.G. said to himself, because he knew exactly what the security had been told to do with the old man. Every opinion counts, said the Ruler. The reign of Baby D has begun.

Now, in response to the call on him to divulge state secrets, he had a few to share with the nation. He was giving amnesty to all political inmates, including those under house arrest. He was doing this because some had already confessed and repented their sins. Sikiokuu, for instance, had confessed in writing that, wearing robes of a religion of doubt, he had contacted fanatical followers of the Frenchman by the name of Descartes with evil intentions against the government. The only ones that the Ruler would never set free were those convicted of crimes of thought, mostly followers of the Movement for the Voice of the People. They were unrepentant. He challenged Parliament to come up with a comprehensive anticorruption bill, as in his view there was no corruption worse than that of the mind.

The MPs were about to give him another standing ovation but he waved them off, for he was about to reveal corruption in high places. The new Aburĩria could not afford to sweep its own dirt under the rug. It must show itself and the world that it was ready to bring to the light of day all the bones in its closet. He would also address economic chaos and sabotage. A helicopter had crashed in the hills near Eldares after a relentless chase by "our well-trained airborne police." The helicopter was full of counterfeit money. The pilot had not yet been found. He could not say much more about the matter, as it was still under investigation.

The police were trying to ascertain the connection between the helicopter, counterfeit money, and a recent spate of bank robberies themselves strange because the robbers seemed less interested in paper money than in papers about money. They often broke safes where bank papers were kept or into computers, and left safes containing money and jewelry untouched. Well, two of these odd robbers were caught in a Mwathirika bank, putting counterfeit money into the safe. From these captives the police learned that the mastermind had intended economic chaos through the unregulated supply of money and bribes to abort the birth of Baby D. The Ruler wanted to say loud and clear that in his government, and in his country, there was no hiding place for the corrupt, be they the top officers of his security forces or the highest-ranked ministers in his government. Bring out the saboteurs, he bellowed.

Two men, shackled, each with a sackful of freshly minted notes, were dragged into the chamber.

A.G. felt as if his eyes would pop out. Kahiga and Njoya were being put on display.

"These are the sinners," the Ruler hissed, pointing at them with his club as they trembled, their chains clanking. "And, even worse, these were two of my top security men! They were recently dismissed from their jobs for letting themselves be guided by witchcraft in their work. And what do they do next? Turn to bank robbery. Economic sabotage. Let me say this to all the corrupt in the land: come forward, confess, and repent before it is too late. These two will now be put under lock and key, and, believe me, by the time I finish with them, they will have told me all I need to know about those with ill intent against the newborn Baby D."

# 5

A.G., who had not waited for the end of the ceremony, caught up with the rest of the Ruler's address in the newspapers the following day. New ministers to nurture Baby D were announced. Two women were appointed to Parliament and made Assistant Ministers for Women's and Children's Affairs. The Ruler promised to rely on his two pillars of wisdom in his furtherance of the needs of Baby D. One of them was Tajirika, erstwhile governor of the Central Bank, who was now back as a member of Parliament and Minister of Finance. The other was John Kaniūrū, the ex–youth leader, now the

Minister for Defense, Youth, and Culture. The Ruler was quoted as praising a paper Kaniũrũ had once written, the result of a highly successful series of youth seminars in which he had argued that the youth must be deployed to fight the enemies within to complement the work of the security forces, and that culture should be used to cleanse the minds of the young of all rebelliousness. The Ruler, when he first read the paper, had been very impressed by Kaniũrũ's originality, and the phrase *originality of thought* was what he now used in announcing the appointment of Kaniũrũ to his new position, with a mandate to oversee the integration of youth, culture, and the military.

Among the heroes honored to mark the new birth was the Late Dr. Wilfred Kaboca, shot dead in defense of the health of the nation, now posthumously inducted into the company of the Golden Order of Loyal Devotion (GOLD).

The paper carried a smaller heading: BIG BEN BECOMES CAESAR: MINISTER COMBINES THE GLORY OF IMPERIAL LONDON AND ANCIENT ROME. The courage he displayed during the so-called People's Assembly had earned him honorary membership in the armed forces, backdated to months before the assembly. *My dream has come true,* Minister Big Ben Mambo was quoted as screaming unabashedly. In order that he may always remember the day, he added a new name, becoming Julius Caesar Big Ben Mambo, Minister of Information and Honorary Officer of the Armed Forces of the Free Republic of Aburĩria.

A boxed item under the heading ARTIST MASTERS THE ART OF WAR showed a picture of Kaniũrũ. It was thanks to him that Aburĩria was finally rid of the menace of Nyawĩra, alias the Limping Witch, and her cohort the Wizard of the Crow. Although not yet identified, their bodies were believed to be decomposing somewhere. Kaniũrũ had sustained a bullet wound to his left leg while battling these forces of evil and through his bravery had saved the country much turmoil. He became a decorated war hero. Asked where he learned strategy and tactics, Kaniũrũ told reporters that it was instinct but that he had thoroughly studied Carl Von Clausewitz's *On War* and Sun-Tzu's *The Art of War.*

A.G. felt strength leave him: so the Wizard of the Crow was dead?

# 6

The Ruler was both surprised and pleased at how smoothly everything had worked out, and he wondered why he had ever been afraid of the words *multiparty democracy*. It was the bad advice from Machokali and Sikiokuu, he decided, for it was only after he had rid himself of both that his relations to the world, Aburĩria, and himself began to prosper. But the Ruler's *Political Theory*, actually written by the late Machokali but now bearing the Ruler's name with a preface that the whole theory was written in the period when he was absent from public view, had provided the vision. According to this theory, what was important in any given country was not the quantity of political parties but the character of the person who personified the head, heart, arms, and legs of the state. There are no moral limits to the means that a ruler can use, from lies to lives, bribes to blows, in order to ensure that his state is stable and his power secure. But if he could keep the state stable through sacrificing truth rather than lives, bending rather than breaking the law, sealing the lips of the outspoken with endless trickeries rather than tearing them with barbed-wire and hot wax, if he could buy peace through a grand deception rather than a vast display of armored vehicles in the streets, which often gave his enemies material for propaganda, it would be the sweetest of victories. The theory also called on a ruler to do the unexpected, whether good or bad, in order to catch friend and foe unaware. The third tenet was what he called the principle of giving without giving. Take away ten, make a firm stand on not giving any back, then, under pressure, relent and give back one, and the result is all-around applause, of victory from foe and congratulations from friend. So far he had closely followed the tenets of the theory, with amazing results.

The most pleasing was the favorable reception of his performance in the West, including countries that had previously denied him state visits. He was congratulated for his bold and courageous steps, some editorial writers going so far as to call him a democratic visionary whose balance of pragmatism and ideology had caught his foes with their pants down.

Only Ambassador Gabriel Gemstone had seemed a bit frosty in his communication to his government. The Aburīrian leader had taken a step in the right direction, he said, but it was only just that: a step. Though a forward stride when perceived through African eyes, the step had serious hazards, and he could not in good conscience advise the West to embrace the reforms until the Ruler clarified this business of being the head of all the political parties.

No longer underestimating Gemstone, the Ruler quickly responded, without of course referring to the ambassador directly. In an official clarification of his remarks when introducing Baby D, he said that he would not intrude in the day-to-day operations of the parties; he would leave that to their chosen leaders. He would assume leadership of only the party that won general elections. The de facto leader of the winning party would automatically become vice president, solving the problem of succession in the event of the unexpected. With this clarification, the Ruler's reforms received cautious acceptance from Gabriel Gemstone, which opened many doors.

The Global Ministry of Finance and the Global Bank issued a joint statement congratulating the Ruler for abandoning—actually, the word they used was *jettisoning*—useless schemes like Marching to Heaven; accepting in advance each and every condition the two institutions would attach to their loans; and bringing technocrats, war heroes, and proven businessmen into his cabinet. But most significant was their agreement to enter into negotiations with the new government to release frozen loans and aid packages. Kaniūrū and Tajirika were invited to Washington to discuss the defense and economic policy needs of a democratic Aburīria.

All was going as well as the Ruler could have imagined. Though he had his decision and theories to thank for this goodness, he also appreciated Kaniūrū's role.

## 7

Several days after the Ruler's birthday, Kaniūrū had come to see him with a puzzling request. He wanted forgiveness. For what? Kaniūrū confessed to having killed the Limping Witch and the scheming wizard, adding that the Limping Witch was none other than Nyawīra. The Ruler was so moved by his devotion that he embraced him. Thereafter, for several weeks Kaniūrū could do no wrong, and when the Ruler decided to announce the birth of multiparty democracy, Kaniūrū was his closest confidant. It was Kaniūrū who had come up with the brilliant idea for the graphics of Baby D and the performance of its unveiling.

When the Ruler pondered the implications of Kaniūrū's act of valor, he was even more elated than at first. Nyawīra was more useful dead than alive in more ways than just the removal of a threat. He would trumpet her fate as an example to presumptuous women who dare assume male prerogatives.

His initial feelings about the elimination of the Wizard of the Crow were more ambiguous. The sorcerer had turned out to be useful after all. The claims of the Ruler's pregnancy that he had started had allowed the Ruler to turn the tables on his detractors. But still, the ordeal!

# 8

Even now, in his residence, at the table, in bed, the Ruler shuddered on recalling the day and hour of the explosions. His intention had been to direct the open-air performance outside the grounds of the Parliament buildings and law courts so as to thwart the efforts of the so-called People's Assembly. He was eager to win what was shaping up as a battle of wills between him and the Wizard of the Crow, and, despite the pain he was suffering, he had sensed victory. One way or another, the Wizard of the Crow would yield, and the Ruler had decided to dispatch him to the next world only after the wizard had conferred on him his occult powers. But then he felt the ballooning of his body and the contractions intensifying: he had managed to authorize only one helicopter to take to the sky and disburse Burī bills before the mobile phone had fallen from his hands. He was possessed by unbearable pain and about to explode. Before his descent into blankness, he felt as if his being was on the verge of bursting through the orifices of his body. When he later emerged from unconsciousness, he found himself mired in the darkness of his filth, still slowly escaping through the roof, blasted by the force of his corruption.

His only casualty was a forked tongue. Otherwise, and despite being exhausted, he felt tall and powerful as he lay there overwhelmed by his contribution to universal darkness.

He remained in a hypnotic state for twenty-eight hours, until his generals emerged from their hiding places, insisting that they had been busy investigating the source of the bombing. He knew they were lying but it did not matter: their explanations later became the unified story of the heroics of the Ruler and his generals as they battled terrorist bombs.

But he never forgot their reaction, and when later he had a meeting with Tajirika, one of his most trusted counselors, he reminded him of the advice the counselor had once tried to give about having a super-eye over the military.

"What did you mean?" he now asked.

"An eye to keep an eye on all the other eyes," answered Tajirika, as if he had thought the whole thing through. "And on the chiefs of the armed forces," he added. "Somebody who, while keeping a friendly contact with the military, would actually be checking on their contacts, conducts, and movements."

"Do you have somebody in mind?"

Tajirika had always wanted an ally in the inner circles of power, and he suggested his friend Wonderful Tumbo.

"The officer who trained that other officer who fought with djinns?"

"Yes, A.G., who unfortunately later succumbed to sorcery and lost his job," Tajirika said. "But Wonderful Tumbo had done wonders with him!"

It resulted in Tumbo's immediate promotion from a chief of a police post to an officer installed in the State House as the Ruler's General Liaison Officer.

They talked about the disappearance of Nyawīra and the Wizard of the Crow. Tajirika looked at his thumbs and realized almost suddenly that the sorcerer who had dogged his life since he had first come to his offices at Eldares Modern Construction and Real Estate, pretending to look for a job, would no longer shadow his life. His powers to ever do Tajirika harm, even a simple harm like withdrawing the protective magic he had once given him, had gone forever.

"You have conquered the Wizard of the Crow. You have triumphed over our enemies," Tajirika told the Ruler, tears of personal gratitude threatening to spill.

For seven nights and days the Ruler thought about Tajirika's words, for they echoed vague thoughts in his mind, and then it dawned on him ever so clearly why everything had been going so smoothly.

On the day of the autoexplosion he had not only conquered the bodily form of the Wizard of the Crow but had also incorporated his occult powers into himself. With the wizard and the Limping Witch out of the way, he was the sorcerer supreme, able to manipulate Aburĩria, the West, the Global Ministry of Finance, the Global Bank, democracy, the living and the dead—the whole lot. He was now the number one sorcerer in all of Aburĩria.

# 9

But he had nothing else to conquer, he moaned. No more adversaries to overcome. After sending his two beloved ministers, Kaniũrũ and Tajirika, to America for talks with the Global Ministry of Finance, the Global Bank, and the American government, the Ruler retreated to his private chambers at the State House, where he wept freely, agonizing over his dilemma. Even when the official hostess tried to calm him down the Ruler could not be consoled; he fumed for want of challenges from worthy adversaries.

One night his grief reminded him of tears he had hoped to see but had not seen. His wife, Rachael, had resisted his attempts to break her and had yet to beg for mercy and forgiveness. His grief at the lack of challenge now became a rage at the thought of a woman defying him and getting away with it. He called the guard permanently stationed at the entrance to Rachael's seven-acre plantation and engaged him in idle conversation. He learned, what had been the subject of rumors for months, that late at night when people should be snoring in their beds, Rachael could be seen roaming about the yard or the house, bearing a light, a lantern, perhaps, like a ghost. To the plantation we go, he called out to his loyal biographer late one night. He wanted this moment recorded to become a centerpiece of the official biography.

What happened when the Ruler, accompanied by Luminous Karamu-Mbu, went to visit Rachael that night is much disputed. The guard with the key to the gate at the entrance to the compound was nowhere to be seen. There are those who say that the Ruler squeezed through a narrow opening between the wall and the gate and, given his new slim body, this posed no problem. He crawled on his belly the rest of the way to catch Rachael unaware before she could wipe her tears away. When finally he reached the house, he peered through a window, and it was then that Rachael, still wearing the dress she wore the night they had quarreled over his predilections for young girls, and thinking that she had seen a long-necked something with a tiny head and a forked tongue, threw the lantern at the thing. The paraffin poured out, the house caught fire, and, seeing this, the Ruler and Luminous Karamu-Mbu ran back the way they came.

Other accounts say no, it was not quite like that, the guard had been disappeared, and when the Ruler went to the house Rachael had come to the door and told him, I know it is you, and instead of crying she laughed in his face, and because she had not laughed for a long time her ribs shook with the laughter and collapsed from within, and Rachael disintegrated into a heap of dry bones. The lantern fell on the heap of bones, caught fire, and the flames from the fire of her immolation ignited the rest of the house, spreading to the plantation. A ball of fire detached itself from the rest and pursued the fleeing Ruler and his faithful biographer all the way back to the gates of the State House.

The memory of the ball of fire in relentless pursuit gave him insomnia, and to induce sleep the Ruler had his loyal biographer, Luminous Karamu-Mbu, read him a chapter from the book he was writing. The biography was not complete, a work in progress, the biographer would say, but the Ruler told him to read from the copious notes he had taken. Every night a chapter was read, and this made the Ruler revisit the scenes of his past challenges, battles, and triumphs, a strange sensation, almost as if he were living his life twice or thrice over again. There were sections that the Ruler wanted read over and over again, often telling him what to take out and what to add. One night he told Luminous Karamu-Mbu to read the section that dealt with his most recent triumph, and the biographer faithfully read how blasts of thunder like stealthy missiles had fired from each of his seven orifices and then exploded in turns; he had described in detail how the second blast of thunder had launched the foreign doctors sky high and how he, Luminous Karamu-Mbu, bravely hung on till he, too, was launched, a human missile, into the sky, by the fifth or sixth blast of thunder, and so had no details of the seventh but . . . The Ruler did not listen to the end, for his mind was occupied with the sudden realization that the loyal biographer knew too much, that if he could write and record what happened so openly, so vividly, and so graphically, an account that completely contradicted the official version of the Ruler's and his generals' heroics as they struggled with bombs exploding, what could he inadvertently say about the story of Rachael and the plantation fire? This man had no imagination to sugarcoat reality and make it more palatable. How did I engage such a fool?

Whatever the case, Luminous Karamu-Mbu, the ex-Communist born again as a loyal biographer, was never seen again, with rumors later claiming that the man had been crushed under the weight of his huge pen and notebook.

There are some who say that the seeds of the biographer's SID came from the official hostess, because, even though the two had abandoned communism, the war they waged against each other during their revolutionary days had left incurable scars. After the smog disaster, Yunique McKenzie was asked to move her office to the State House, and she said she would never do so as long as Luminous Karamu-Mbu was a regular at the palace. It was noted that it was soon after the biographer's disappearance that Dr. Yunique Immaculate McKenzie, PhD, ONH, moved her offices to the State House and the Ruler engaged the services of one Morton Stanley, a white royalist from London, to write an unexpurgated, independent, and objective biography of the Ruler through the Ruler's eyes, with material generously provided by the Ruler and his handlers.

The eradication of Rachael may not have met his quest for challenges worthy of his new powers, but still he counted it as successful, especially after he saw that it was not followed by remonstration from his children or angry demonstrations from women.

The crowning moment of his undiluted successes came when his ministers Tajirika and Kaniũrũ returned from America with tangible results:

The Minister of Defense and war hero John Kaniũrũ signed an agreement for loans to enable Aburĩria to buy arms from the West, and the Minister of Finance and business hero Titus Tajirika signed agreements with several oil companies to explore oil and natural gas at the coast and mining companies to prospect for gold, diamonds, and other precious metals in northern Aburĩria.

But the most salient part of this success story was that the Global Ministry of Finance and the Global Bank had agreed to release the previously frozen funds now that the plans for Marching to Heaven had been abandoned, replaced by Baby D.

"You have done well," the Ruler told the two ministers.

"The power is yours, my Lord," Tajirika exclaimed.

"And the glory," said Kaniũrũ.

"Long Live Baby D," they said in unison but accidentally, for each had hoped to have the last word in sycophancy.

# 10

One evening Kaniũrũ was watching a porno video when he got a call from security about a guest at the gate. Who is that calling at this inopportune moment?

It was Jane Kanyori. He quickly glanced at the video. A woman was now on top of the hero, guiding his hands over her nipples, and Kaniũrũ realized that much time had passed since he last relieved himself on real flesh and blood. Kanyori never needed too much coaxing. Not that he was overexcited about her. These times were different from those of Marching to Heaven and money laundering, and after their romp in bed tonight he would call off their relationship.

A glance at the huge suitcase she dragged behind her and he assumed that she was bringing him gifts, but, really, did she have to do this? Denying herself to give him all? Her generosity would make parting difficult, but it would not deter him from letting her know that this was going to be their last night together.

She dragged the suitcase all the way to the bedroom, but when he heard her say that he was to send a chauffeur in the morning to bring home the remaining luggage, Kaniũrũ smelled something not right.

"What is the meaning of this?" he said, standing at the entrance to his bedroom.

"In the living room," said Kanyori. "We should talk about it as two good businesspeople. I hate the word *businessman* for it assumes that women do not do business."

"What do you want?" Kaniũrũ asked her after they sat down on the settee in the living room.

"I have come to realize that you are not the churchy type, with their ostentatious wedding ceremonies."

"Did somebody tell you that I was planning a wedding ceremony?"

"John, I know you are shy, the type of male who finds it hard to say truly what is in his heart. So I made it easy for you. Oh, John, do you know what I did? Shall I marry him? I asked myself, responding to the question locked up inside of you. I wrote down YES and NO on two separate pieces of paper, put them in a bowl, shook it, shut my eyes, then picked one. YES! What about the day? I did the same with the days of the week, each one on a separate piece of paper. I could not argue against the hand of fate. I thought it best to move in right away so that early tomorrow morning, as decreed by fate, we can go for a civil ceremony at the district commissioner's."

"Are you crazy? *Ondoka.* GET OUT!" he yelled, threatening to call the police.

"Hold it! Have you forgotten all the work you and I have done together? A husband-and-wife team?"

"What are you talking about?" he said, moving away from her.

"John, dear," Kanyori said in a softer voice, moving toward him. "You disappoint me. Has the defense portfolio turned you into *a male chauvinist black pig*? And here I thought that you were a liberated Aburĩrian male? Let me tell you the truth. My heart flew to you the day you trusted me with your secrets and all that money. That's why I never asked you for a penny for all the work I did for you. Being your confidante was its own reward."

"How much do you want to settle this?"

"Money? *What an insult to your wife!*"

"*My wife? Over my dead body,*" he said at once, and he stood up. "Or over yours?" he added, wagging a finger at her.

"*You, a wife beater?*" Kanyori asked with feigned terror in her eyes. "I have vowed that if any male so much as touches me even with his smallest finger, I would scream so loud that all the secrets that I have locked in my heart would reach all the way to the State House."

"Are you threatening me? Don't you know that I can finish you off right here and nobody will ever know or care what happened to you?"

"Oh, dear, and then those I left waiting by the road not too far from this residence will say that I contracted the same illness that finished off Machokali? Luminous Karamu-Mbu? Rachael? What do you people call it? Oh yes, SID. Tell me the truth: were you also involved in Machokali's SID? I remember you telling me that he once tried to thwart your rise to the top by refusing to say that you sketched the first images of Marching to Heaven. By the way, I checked that story and discovered that Machokali had asked your students to draw the images."

"*Shut up, woman!*"

"Oh, so you think that silence is the name of a woman? It is not my name. But I don't talk much. For instance, it is only my lawyer and a few other people who know that I came home. What will you tell them tomorrow? She appears; she disappears."

"*You have no proof,*" Kaniūrū said, a sinking feeling in his belly.

"God gave me a foolish attachment to paper, documents, anything with handwriting on it—even those pieces of paper on which you used to practice the signatures of . . . let us not mention their names. I still have them safe in a bank."

He weakened at the joints and slumped back onto the sofa. In his brief tenure as Minister Kaniūrū had seen the extent of the Ruler's greed. There was no defense contract, even the tiniest, from which the Ruler did not expect a cut. Not that Kaniūrū was judgmental. He had found out in the same period that all the big merchants of death had bribe money built into the costs of securing lucrative contracts for their companies and their governments. So the Ruler was part of a chain of global corruption in the arms trade. And Kaniũrũ, a quick learner, had no problem with that.

Still, this did not make the Ruler any more tolerant with being double-crossed. But what scared Kaniũrũ the most was not her reference to the loot from Marching to Heaven but her mention of the signatures. In addition to Sikiokuu's, Kaniũrũ had tried his hand at the Ruler's signature in an attempt to impress Kanyori with his penmanship. She had him by the balls. He thought he was toying with her, and it now turned out that it was she who had been toying with him!

"And by the way, dear Jane, does anybody else know about those papers?" he said, trying to change tack.

"There are two birds who know that if anything were ever to happen to me, SID, for instance, they are to look for the reason in the safe."

"Jane, my dear Jane, you are so secretive. And those birds . . . who are they?"

"Their names? Please allow your wife to keep those secrets to herself."

"How much money do you really want for those papers?" Kaniũrũ asked, seeing that the tack had failed.

"This is the eve of our wedding. We should be talking 'Dirty Diana,' as Michael Jackson used to sing, and not dirty money. The fact is, there is nothing you have touched with your hands that I have not kept safely away. Sometimes I feel like laughing at my foolishness, because even the irons with which I once chained you to my bed are still with me. How do you put a money value on love mementos?"

"When do you want us to marry?" Kaniũrũ said abruptly, resigned.

"To be honest with you, I married you a long time ago. What remains is for us to exchange rings and sign papers at the district commissioner's first thing tomorrow. Or shall we invite a priest here?"

"It's not necessary to call a priest," Kaniũrũ hastened to say. "But let me ask you this. Once we marry, I mean, once we sign those papers at the district commissioner's, will you tell me everything, the names of all those who know about those documents, the bank in which they are deposited, and how we can retrieve them so that we can keep them safe in our own home?"

"What is there to hide between husband and wife? I am sure you will also tell me all about your property and we'll divide it in half, or we'll go for *joint ownership of everything.*"

"*You will never get away with this,*" Kaniūrū burst out in English.

"*With what?*" Kanyori asked, seemingly perplexed. "Marrying you?"

"Listen carefully and understand my words. You are not my wife. My heart belongs to another."

"You see another woman behind my back?" Kanyori said with feigned anger. "We shall marry and file for divorce at the same time. But remember that divorce comes with a property settlement. A minister's wife must be kept in the lifestyle she has become accustomed to. I will cite Nyawīra as the other woman. You will, of course, explain why you lied about her death. *Oh, my war hero.* And you were given and actually accepted a medal for killing a defenseless woman? Your first love? Oh, I know. You killed her with words. Just as you did your parents. Remember how you used to tell me that you were an orphan brought up by a grandmother? What of the man and woman who were once in a newspaper looking for you after the students had dragged you into a police station? I could not believe it, and later I visited your village just to make sure that my in-laws were alive and well. They know me as simply Jane! They will be very disappointed if they hear that their beloved son was divorcing a woman who has been looking after them—oh yes, I have been looking after them—in favor of a woman who opposed the government."

"Leave my parents out of this," Kaniūrū said, breathing fire.

"Well, I can understand why you killed them with words. But tell me: why did you kill Nyawīra with words? So that you could see each other safely, without suspicions?"

"I am not saying that I am in contact with those terrorists," Kaniūrū hastened to say, terror-stricken by the implications of her comments.

How would he explain that a Minister of Defense was having secret meetings with terrorists? Were he to be told to produce Nyawīra, where on earth would he find her? And if dead? Retrieve her body from an unknown grave? And suddenly, unable to know what to do, Kaniūrū felt like crying. He, John Kaniūrū, a man who had conned everybody, including the Ruler, is to be out-conned by a female con artist? No matter how hard he tried, he could not find an exit formula that would leave him safe and sound.

"Willow weep for me," Kaniũrũ said, without really knowing what he was saying.

"Louis Armstrong," Kanyori said. "So you love jazz? You even love that voice that croaks like a frog? I love the blues, but you don't want to sing with Ruth Brown, 'That train don't stop here anymore.' I want your heart and mine to be stations forever where our trains will always stop."

Jesus! And this was the woman I used to think dumb? He, Kaniũrũ, could not even remember where, how, or when he got the lines from Armstrong.

"Listen to me. Why don't you go home and we'll talk about all this tomorrow, after a good night's rest?"

"But I am home. Or do you want us to go to bed and resume this talk early in the morning, after a night of relaxation?" she asked mischievously as she leaned toward Kaniũrũ and pinched his nose playfully. "Singing 'Dirty Diana' in my ear all night, oh, my dashing soldier!"

Kaniũrũ and Kanyori were married the following day at the district commissioner's, almost a repeat of his wedding with Nyawĩra.

# 11

When Tajirika learned that Kaniũrũ had married without fanfare, he suspected that there was more to this than met the eye. Modesty was not Kaniũrũ's style. Tajirika's suspicions deepened when later he learned that Jane Kanyori worked in a bank. Weren't all banks now under his ministry?

He decided to investigate.

The investigation turned out to be quite easy, especially after Tajirika got copies of the bank records and saw that the signatures that approved all the transactions involving Sikiokuu and Kaniũrũ were all Jane Kanyori's. Thereafter it was a matter of common sense and simple calculation, and now, armed with his new knowledge and the bank records, Tajirika went straight to the Ruler, confident that once the Ruler realized that Kaniũrũ was the only person who had made money out of Marching to Heaven he would strip him of his defense portfolio. Now nothing would save Kaniũrũ from the Ruler's wrath.

The Ruler took the documents, examined them very carefully, then shook his head from side to side in apparent disbelief that such a fellow could so successfully trick them all. Then, to Tajirika's surprise, he suddenly started laughing.

"What a crook!"

"Yes, a first-rate crook," quickly agreed Tajirika.

"And what is such a crook doing as my Minister of Defense?"

"Very dangerous, Your Excellency," Tajirika agreed.

The Ruler sent for Kaniũrũ.

A glance at Tajirika, the Ruler, and then at the papers on the table and Kaniũrũ knew he had been cornered, but instead of panicking Kaniũrũ saw this as his opportunity to avenge himself against Kanyori, or at least paint her character with so much dirt that were she ever to reveal his forgery of the Ruler's signature, the Ruler would not believe her. So when confronted with the accusations of making money out of Marching to Heaven and laying the blame on others, he seemed to relish gushing out all the details. He did not know what had come over him to make him take the word of a woman seriously. "Having been bitten once by the woman who later turned out to be an enemy of the State, I should have learned my lesson, but I was caught again in Kanyori's web of lies." But he was not going to blame himself too much, because even Samson, a war hero, was once lulled to sleep by Delilah.

"Your Ever Mighty Excellency, my Delilah is actually my second wife, Jane Kanyori," said Kaniũrũ, claiming that the conception of the grand deception and its execution was all Kanyori's.

"And why did you marry her knowing all this about her?" asked Tajirika, fearing that the Ruler was being taken in.

"Do you want to know the truth?" asked Kaniũrũ rhetorically. "She threatened to expose the whole thing and blame it on me. *Pure whitemail*."

"You mean, she is a bigger crook than you?" asked the Ruler, smiling a little.

The art of his tongue and the strategy of blaming everything on Kanyori was working, Kaniũrũ thought, so he invented a few more details.

"Even though she is my wife, I cannot tell lies before Your Mighty Excellency: My wife Kanyori is *dangerous*. She can lie with numbers like nobody's business. She can deceive the Devil himself."

The Ruler put on a serious face as the others anxiously looked on. "Kaniūrū, you are in the wrong ministry. The Defense Ministry needs somebody trustworthy, not a crook, at least not a crook that would lead his commander in chief astray. It needs somebody I can trust completely, somebody who can make enemy forces surrender with scare tactics but who is scared enough not to try anything against his Lord and Master, somebody who can lie for me but not to me, somebody who has shown that he would rather dig his own grave in the prairie than cross me, somebody like Tajirika, and in the era of the Baby D, I need such a man at the head of my armed forces. Tajirika, you are my new Defense Minister."

Today I will open a bottle of champagne, Tajirika said to himself, and even Vinjinia, who does not drink, will have to have a glass.

"And now I come back to you," he said, looking at Kaniūrū and barely holding back his laughter at the thought of a male being outdone in crookedness by a female. "I want fifty percent of all the money you stole from Marching to Heaven, and the interest, to go to the Ruler's Smog Disaster Fund. But I will give you another chance. Your kind of cunning is best for youth and money matters. You are my new Minister of Finance and Youth. As for your wife, Jane Kanyori, I want her transferred immediately from the National Bank of Commerce and Industry and placed in a strategic position in the Central Bank. I want her as the new comptroller of the Central Bank. But let me warn you. I am giving you and Mrs. Kaniūrū a long rope with which to hang yourselves. No more lies! Otherwise let me have crooks about me," said the Ruler, as if expressing satisfaction at his reshuffle and the appointment of a new female technocrat to a position of monetary authority. "Real crooks are guided by realism."

The lines were straight out of the Ruler's *Political Theory*, wherein Machokali had written that crooks are often more realistic in their assessment of a situation than moral idealists.

The two ministers looked at each other as if neither knew exactly who had gained more than the other from this first cabinet reshuffle in the era of Baby D. But they knew that the struggle between them, like the one between Machokali and Sikiokuu in the previous era, had only just begun.

# 12

The reshuffle was overshadowed by the news that Julius Caesar Big Ben Mambo, Minister of Information and Honorary Officer of the Armed Forces, had been arrayed before a court-martial to answer charges of plotting against the State.

Rumors claimed that the minister had been asked to plant some elderly men and women in key positions in the public gallery for the Ruler's address to Parliament so that when the Ruler asked the public to offer their opinions on the speech the groomed few would stand up to bless Baby D, but the first on his feet was actually the old man who talked about cheap presidential arseholes. This angered Dr. Yunique Immaculate McKenzie so much that she spontaneously whispered to the Ruler regrets over an affair she once had with Mambo when she worked in the Ministry of Information soon after her return to political grace from exile. This stung the Ruler, and Mambo's unusual induction into the military as an honorary officer was the Ruler's ploy for vengeance.

But what was cited in the trial was the history of Mambo's relationship with the late Machokali: Machokali once rescued Mambo from a permanent physical disability by sending him to Germany for surgical correction of his protruding tongue. Big Ben Mambo always sided with Machokali. So what a coincidence that the old man whom the late Machokali once prearranged to ridicule the Ruler during the original unfurling of plans for Marching to Heaven had somehow reappeared in the public gallery during the Ruler's speech rejecting the madness of Marching to Heaven?

Even the name of Julius Caesar became an issue. Who does not know that Julius Caesar was a renowned military general in the days of the Roman Empire who undermined the republic with his ambitions to become emperor? But even long before the Roman chapter of his life, Minister Mambo was calling himself Big Ben, the famous clock that in the days when the sun never set on the British Empire regulated time in the entire empire. The issue of the newspaper that had described Mambo as combining the glory of imperial London and ancient Rome was introduced in court as a crucial exhibit of the man's inordinate thirst for power. It had been found framed and hanging on the wall of his office. When addressing the people during the so-called People's Assembly, Big Ben Mambo boasted that his voice was that of the commander in chief of the armed forces, and, most telling, he preferred talking from the top of armored vehicles.

He had also blunted the powers of the imported mirrors by having them shown to the public first and thus ensuring that they captured the interfering shadows that made the discovery of Nyawïra's whereabouts impossible. In fact, according to Sikiokuu's testimony, that was obviously a prearranged signal between Mambo and the Wizard of the Crow, because it was soon after that the sorcerer broke the mirrors into pieces. Add to this that there was a time when the Wizard of the Crow corresponded extensively with the late Machokali and the whole plot was now self-evident. What more evidence would the presiding judge really need? the military prosecutor asked the court-martial; it was not necessary to prove the obvious.

Julius Caesar Big Ben Mambo was so totally taken aback by the whole thing that his tongue lengthened and he could not speak to the court in his own defense. The only two words that came out were *if* and *soldiers*, but spoken with great force and with a gap between them, as if there was no connection. It is said that when the judge first heard the word *soldiers* come out of Mambo's mouth, he thought Julius Caesar was commanding his forces to act, and the judge actually stood up to flee, but realizing his mistake stood still to make it seem as if he were taking the unusual step of standing up to deliver judgment because of the gravity of the facts and, more severely, what the accused was trying to do: threaten the court with his *if*s!

Julius Caesar Big Ben Mambo, an officer in the armed forces, was found guilty of plotting with civilians to overturn the properly constituted authority. Unfortunately, his fellow plotters, Machokali, the Wizard of the Crow, and the Limping Witch, were dead and beyond his jurisdiction because they were not soldiers.

A special civilian court was set up later the same day to meet the challenge the presiding judge had posed, with the proceedings of the trial of Big Ben Mambo as the only evidence in the charges against Machokali, the Limping Witch, and the Wizard of the Crow. In the entire history of the Aburīrian judiciary, it had never been heard of people already dead being tried and sentenced to death.

It is said that as he faced the firing squad the blindfolded Julius Caesar Big Ben Mambo found his tongue at the very last minute, *Crow . . . protective . . . if . . .* but the first bullet did not let him complete the sentence.

# 13

At the advice of Tajirika the Ruler declared a day when the effigies of the cursed four, Mambo, Machokali, Nyawīra, and the Wizard of the Crow, were to be burned to ensure that their spirits would never come back to haunt the ruling. With television crews following them, ministers, members of Parliament, and convoys of loyal youth outdid one another in burning the biggest possible effigy of their chosen traitor, with some even throwing the flaming figure into the sea. What showed on the screen later that day were scenes of jubilation and triumph. But rumors and eyewitness accounts told of strange happenings!

"True! *Haki ya Mungu!*" A.G. would tell his listeners years later. "The effigies of Nyawīra and the Wizard of the Crow would not burn—instead they spat balls of fire that chased those who had tried to burn them . . ."

# SECTION III

# 1

News of the posthumous sentence and state celebrations of their death eventually reached them in their forest hiding place, where Kamĩtĩ was recovering from his gunshot wound and coma.

"We died twice," Kamĩtĩ said.

"At least they have honored us with a state burial," Nyawĩra said, laughing a little.

"A state funeral pyre," said Kamĩtĩ. "Their imitation of fire in Hell."

His tone spoke of recovery, and she was grateful. The weeks had been harrowing, with Kamĩtĩ barely clinging to life. She remembered how they had rushed him to a safe house, where a doctor friend of the movement stopped the blood flow and then moved him to the mountains. The bullet had missed his heart by inches, but its successful removal and a mixture of modern and herbal medicines brought him back from the brink of death. She nursed him through it all, often supporting him when he walked, but not these last days. He was now on his feet, and they often walked in the woods.

She often told him of the details of the day they escaped death, because the trauma, the loss of consciousness, and the coma had left many gaps in his memory. When Kamĩtĩ fell, she felt as if her own soul had collapsed with him, and, in covering his body with hers, it was as if she, too, had bid farewell to life. I will die staring him down, she had resolved when she saw Kaniũrũ pointing a gun at her. I will not give him the satisfaction of showing fear. No sooner had she thought this than she saw somebody grabbing the gun from him; Kaniũrũ and his attacker, "our savior," were rolling around on the ground, struggling. She was often frustrated that she could not recall the face of their savior, and Kamĩtĩ kept reassuring her that the face and name would come when she stopped thinking about it, but it was always on her mind.

"Linking us with Mambo and Machokali was a big leap in imagination," Kamĩtĩ said.

"Or a case of Baby D blues," added Nyawĩra.

# 2

They walked along the banks of the Eldares till they came to a waterfall, and Kamĩtĩ was pleasantly surprised to recognize the very place where he once led Nyawĩra, only now it was she who led the way. In fact, the difference between their previous sojourn and now was most noticeable in her. Then she was the pupil and he the teacher. Now they were both pupil and teacher.

"When did you learn all this?" Kamĩtĩ asked her on another day, sitting under the same tree near the falls. The wound was healing well and fast, and he had even removed the bandages; he could swing the left hand more freely, and altogether he felt fitter, stronger, and more cheerful.

"You should be heaping me with praises for being an apt pupil. Do you think I was not paying attention? And remember that until the arson I was the other Wizard of the Crow," Nyawĩra explained.

"And then you became the Limping Witch?"

"What are you implying? That a Limping Witch is less powerful than a Wizard of the Crow? I challenge you to a power contest."

"How?"

"Do you see that bird on the tree over there? Make it land on the ground with the power of your sorcery. Go on, sorcerer."

Kamĩtĩ tried whistling different tunes, with varying pitch and rhythm, alternating the whistling with calling out, *chirp chirp chirp.* The bird seemed to glance toward him and then flew off and landed on a tree nearer to where they sat. This encouraged Kamĩtĩ and he tried more of the same, but this time the bird remained impervious to his call.

"You have failed," she said.

"No, no," protested Kamĩtĩ. "It came nearer."

"But you failed to make it land on the ground."

"Okay! Your turn," Kamĩtĩ said.

Nyawĩra dug in her bag, took a piece of bread from their lunch packet, and, mumbling some incantations, crumbled it and threw the pieces on the ground. I command you to come down, she called out. The bird, followed by others, landed on the ground, looking for the crumbs in the grass.

Nyawĩra laughed triumphantly.

"Are you saying the magic I taught you was just a bag of tricks?" Kamĩtĩ asked.

"It means that the pupil has surpassed the teacher and he should accept defeat with grace."

"But you know that a successful pupil owes a token of gratitude to his teacher," Kamĩtĩ said.

"What do you want for a token?"

"Your thumb."

"What do you mean?"

He told her the story of Drona and Ekalaivan.

"You mean depriving the poor, even of the least they have, has a long history?" she asked.

"No politics. I want my thumb," Kamĩtĩ said, and he tried to push her to the ground with his right hand.

Nyawĩra released herself from his weak grip and took off. Kamĩtĩ could not run, so he walked, looking for her under shrubs and bushes and even up in treetops. After a while he saw her clothes on the ground. He called out her name and, getting no response, became a little frightened.

He heard some whistling farther down the river. The sight of her made his heart palpitate. She was bathing in the river. Beautiful. Radiant. Graceful. Glorious. He juggled the words in his mind but none quite described what his eyes saw, seeing her among the reeds.

"Come for your thumb. Or do my powers scare you?"

In a minute he had removed his clothes and joined her. They did not really swim. They splashed water. They scrubbed each other's backs—no, not really scrubbing but stroking. In the end they found themselves lying down by the riverside on green grass under the shade of another shrub.

Mindful of Kamĩtĩ's scar, they had to be careful. So they went about it gently, groping, searching, but when eventually they felt their bodies soar, they forgot about the scar and let themselves float on a river across a beautiful plateau. The river flowed slowly, smoothly, almost soundlessly, except for the gentle lapping and foaming of the waters against the banks. And after it, Kamĩtĩ felt as if all the rot that had stuck to his body and soul since they last parted had now been washed away by a new beginning. He became aware of the fragrance of fresh flowers. He looked at her with gratitude in his eyes, but it was she who came up with the words.

"Thank you," she said softly.

# 3

Afterward, as they lay on their backs on the same riverbank, fully clothed, Kamĩtĩ turned to his right, faced Nyawĩra, and, without any preparatory words, brought up the subject of his return to Aburĩria from America.

"Why bring up painful memories so soon after our own landing from the clouds?"

"The sweetness reminded me of loss. You see, when looking for you I often felt tears over the many things I should have asked you but did not. The regret deepened as it increasingly appeared that I would never see you again. It is not often in life that one can say, I got a second chance. Now I don't want this moment to pass me by."

"Ask and see if it shall be given," Nyawĩra said.

"Don't you think it is time we built a new home?"

"Rebuild the shrine?"

"I am not talking about a building. I am talking about tying the knot."

Nyawĩra turned over the proposal in her mind, but not for long, since this was not the first time that she had given the question some thought.

"Do you know that in all the time that Kaniũrũ and I were friends and even lived together, I never once dreamed of having his children? But with you I dream about it every day, often trying to imagine how our children would look or whether they would have more of your features or mine. The dreams are still with me, even now as we sit here. In a way we are already married. Is there a knot more complete than the free union of souls? The rest is ceremony to bless the union, and we can do that whenever time and circumstances allow. Right now there is work to do to clear the rot and pollution that fell over the land, and clean the atmosphere."

There was such finality in the tone that Kamĩtĩ did not press the issue further. She thought she had been a little harsh and now softened her tone.

"Nothing is for free, though. A task for you. Each time you have failed to make me out in my disguise, you always vow that you would not fail the next time?"

"I must say that I would never have recognized you as the Limping Witch," he said in admiration. "But next time it will be different. I honestly don't see how you can top that performance."

"You want to bet?"

"It depends on the wager."

"If you succeed in seeing through me, I will buy the wedding ring; and if you fail, you buy it."

"I accept. Although it does not answer the question of when. Tell me more about the Movement for the Voice of the People," he asked.

Caught by surprise, Nyawĩra turned to her left and faced him.

"You know," she said after a pause, "you don't have to take a political stance just to please me. Even if we continue the way we now live, God willing, we shall have that home of our dreams."

"I know, but hear me out. During our stay here I have been able to review the many issues that you and I have talked about since we first met. I now agree with you that the task of healing the land cannot be done by one person or by any number of people when each is acting on his own."

"What do you want know? Where we stand on issues? Our view of the world is not much different from the vision you outlined at the People's Assembly. In Aburĩria there are those who reap where they never planted and those who plant but hardly ever reap what they planted. The first camp, even with its allies abroad, is small, and yet it is able to lord over the second because it divides it along ethnic and sometimes gender and religious lines. Our movement wants to reverse that. We do not ask people what their tribe is but where they stand in the conflicting interests of the two camps. You have not a say in the ethnicity into which you are born, but you have all the say in the choice of associates. Biology is fate. Politics is choice. No, the life of even the least among us should be sacred, and it will not do for any region or community to keep silent when the people of another region and community are being slaughtered. The wealth of science, technology, and arts should enrich peoples' lives, not enable their slaughter. We oppose the tendency to make women carry the weight of customs that have outlived the contexts that may have made them necessary or even useful earlier. The context is gone but the practice goes on," she said.

"I am really asking, how does one become one of you?"

"Ask or be asked. You were invited once. Your silence was taken as meaning that you were not ready or did not want to. With us, nobody is forced into the movement through trickery, oaths, terror, or bribes. Now you would have to ask to join."

"I understand. You see, even though I don't know the inner workings of your movement, its leaders, or its program, I have seen the results. How the movement gave purpose and direction to spontaneous queues showed courage and dedication. Most politicians want to master people. But your people want to master themselves before they can master others. I want to work with you. I am now asking: can I join hands with the others?" Kamĩtĩ said decisively.

"I will forward your request to the leadership."

"And now that I have healed, what shall we do?" he asked.

"Go back to Eldares," she said. "People are our best protection."

"Yes, and since the State has declared us dead twice over," Kamĩtĩ added pensively, "they will not be looking for us. Should they, by chance, see us, they will think we are ghosts and run away."

"Or kill us on the spot and bury us," Nyawĩra said somberly. "But we have to go back. We cannot leave the fate of the nation to the man-eaters."

# BOOK SIX

# Bearded Daemons

# 1

A week after their return, Nyawīra visited Maritha and Mariko. She found them grieving for their cat, crucified by the Soldiers of Christ.

"What does the cat have to do with religion?" Kamītī asked, pained.

Kamītī and Nyawīra had rented a place in the run-down but most populous area of Santalucia. There was no question about resuming their business in herbs—they would have to find other means of survival.

Nyawīra recounted what Maritha and Mariko had told her: the soldiers wanted Satan to feel the pain Christ had felt.

"These sects are turning their followers into fools. Adults, supposed grown-ups, killing a cat?"

"Actually it did not die," Nyawīra said. "When the soldiers went back after three days, they found the nails still in the tree but not the cat. Maritha and Mariko were telling me that somehow the cat had survived and was once again in their keeping. And apparently the soldiers had realized that the cat they had crucified was the same one that used to follow Maritha and Mariko wherever they went. But instead of saying they were sorry for what they had done, they went straight to All Saints Cathedral and publicly accused the couple of being servants of Satan, declaring that even the victory that the couple had earlier claimed was no victory but defeat, and thus the two had lied to God. They demanded that Bishop Tireless Kanogori expel Mariko and Maritha because they were in league with Satan. When Bishop Tireless refused, they accused him of going to bed with the Devil. Citing occasions when the bishop had let Satan escape, once through the window and secondly through the door, they demanded his resignation. The congregation, led by Vinjinia, however, stood behind their bishop. The warriors, led by three holy men, Sweeper-of-Souls, Soul's Walking Stick, and Pilot-of-Souls, broke away and formed the Church of Christian Soldiers."

"How did they come to accept the three as holy?"

"Numeral three was the sign. The sweepers, to whom Satan first appeared, were three. One of them has a walking stick with three small twigs at the handle. Into this mix bring in the Holy Trinity. Three then becomes a holy number. The Church even earned international visibility when the three holy men were invited to a Global Christian Right gathering in America. The holy men were to testify about their struggles against Satan that had paved the way for democracy in Aburĩria. But the invitation was withdrawn because the Church of Christian Soldiers did not last a week before it split into three separate entities each claiming to be the true Church of Christian Soldiers."

"Why?"

"They got into a theological dispute about the nature of Satan. Apparently, on the day of the smog, the three groups had different encounters with the vision of Satan. One group, led by Sweeper-of-Souls, claimed that Satan was a seven-bodied white American and that on the day of the smog, as they kept vigil on all the paths in and out of the State House, they saw him leave the palace in a hurry, after he had set explosions. A black man was chasing the hydra-bodied Satan. They joined in the chase at a distance. Afterward they swore in the name of Christ that they did see the hydra-bodied white creature enter the American embassy, from where, soon after, came the sound of a gunshot, and they saw the black man fall. Luckily for them, Jesus told them to run away. The second group, led by Pilot-of-Souls, said that Satan was definitely black. Pilot-of-Souls saw him on the platform during the Devil-sponsored People's Assembly and heard him boast how he freely assumed human and animal forms and traveled inside time itself. The third group, led by Soul's Walking Stick, rejects the claims of the first two and emphasizes the catlike quality of Satan, citing the incident at the cathedral when Satan entered a cat's body and then lured the police to handcuff a shadow that later addressed the People's Assembly while Satan himself was snoring within the cat at the ruins. They disagreed about everything except that once at a city dumpsite Satan did appear to them, with Soul's

Walking Stick further claiming that when he was lost to alcohol, the same Satan had pursued him from bar to bar. He was at the Sell-Me-Death bar when he saw three hell-riders carry Satan away and so . . . what is the matter?"

"It brings back memories," Kamĩtĩ said somberly. He told her about his dealings with the cat after first encountering it at the burned-down shrine, how it kept him company when he spent the night there as a homeless drunk and it did the same thing recently, at the church basement. Whenever the cat was around, he felt less lonely. "But it is not only that," he continued. "It's true there were times when I felt pursued by unseen eyes and people were running away from me. Did you ever hear rumors of a man who came back from the dead after burial at a dumpsite?"

"Yes, there was a time when rumors of souls of the homeless being taken away were rampant, but I never took them seriously. I thought it was the folks' way of explaining the fact that people were dying of hunger and disease."

"Well, that person was me. The holy men are referring to that incident. It was the same day that you and I met at Tajirika's."

"But was it true? Did you fly out of yourself?"

"Yes, and it was not the last time. Sometimes when alone, I feel out of myself—I mean, out of my body—and I float in the sky in the form of a bird. That's exactly the experience I once had. I never told you this—I thought you might think me out of my mind."

He briefly narrated his flight over Africa, the Caribbean, and South America and back to Manhattan, New York.

"Most of what I was trying to tell the People's Assembly was a slice of what formed within me during my global journey in search of the source of black power."

They fell silent, with Nyawĩra wondering how to undertake the whole thing and Kamĩtĩ how she was taking it.

"And the source? Did you find it?"

"Yes, in the unity of our blackness."

"Unity between us, the Ruler, and Tajirika? They are black; we are all black."

"Stop the sarcasm. You cannot keep on detecting classes and class struggles in everything. Race also matters."

"I don't mean to be sarcastic," Nyawĩra hastened to say. "I don't discount the fact of blackness when used to forge a sense of community across nations, territories, and continents in the quest for equality, social justice, and the fullness of life for all. But too often the appeal to blackness glosses over the valley between opposing positions. Even the extreme black rightists with anti–working people's agendas are now claiming their share of victimology. As you so clearly said in the assembly, it is from our midst that there arises those who sow discord, the seeds of our defeat."

"Yes, I saw them, half beast and half human . . ." said Kamĩtĩ.

"As a figure of speech?" Nyawĩra asked.

"They were real," Kamĩtĩ said emphatically. "The ones I saw when in my bird form were real."

Unable to take his wanderings as a bird with a straight face, Nyawĩra interrupted: "When Maritha and Mariko were telling me about the Soldiers of Christ believing in a Devil who resides in a cat, I felt like laughing but did not. Do you know why? The Soldiers of Christ remind me of my maternal great-grandmother. She was among the first or second generation of those who ran away from what they saw as savagery and sought refuge in the new Christian mission centers, though in her case she was also running away from a marriage forced on her. Do you know that my great-grandmother, to her dying day, when she was more than ninety years old, believed in the physical reality of devils and angels? That they often walked the earth? God was also real, and she described him as an old man with a white beard and long silvery hair reaching down to his feet. That was her explanation for why nobody could tell the gender and color of God. But what am I supposed to think when the one I love, whose judgment and insights I trust, tells me that he has been a bird and seems to believe it? If the soldiers remind me of my great-grandmother, you remind me of Gacirũ and Gacĩgua—you know, Vinjinia's kids. When Tajirika was stricken with white-ache and Vinjinia came to work in the office for the first time in her life, she often brought her children with her and I told them stories. They loved the Marimũ stories about the two-mouthed ogres, with one mouth at the back of the head and the other in front . . ."

"That is it," Kamĩtĩ interrupted. "You have said it. Ogres."

Nyawĩra was startled by his reaction, and she stared at him, once again struck by how seriously he seemed to take the whole thing. Kamĩtĩ noticed her disbelief.

"Nyawīra, don't ask me to explain, but do me a favor," he said, trying to reassure her of his sanity. "Go back to Maritha and Mariko tomorrow and ask Vinjinia to find out if Tajirika has grown long hair or has started wearing a cap, or covering his head at night or doing anything unusual, however small, that he was not doing before. Ask them to give her this message. At night when Tajirika is asleep, she should inspect his face well, and particularly the back of his head."

"What?" Nyawīra asked, mystified.

"I want to know if Tajirika has grown a second mouth."

Nyawīra could not help it. She laughed till she felt as if her ribs were cracking. But Kamītī did not join her laughter.

"You cannot be serious. I should not have brought you news of the cat's crucifixion."

"It is not just Tajirika," Kamītī said, ignoring her. "I suspect the same of Kaniūrū and the other followers of the Ruler."

She felt like laughing again but held back. What was going to be an uneventful return to Eldares had turned out to be a drama of sorts, Nyawīra thought. A cat, a bird, and now an ogre? Maybe she had underestimated what Kamītī had gone through. Maybe the shooting and the coma had affected his mind.

She was up early the next day and went to buy the *Eldares Times*; by the time she came back Kamītī had already cooked. They sat down to a breakfast of bread, eggs, and lettuce. As she ate she kept glancing at the headlines.

"Oh, look at this," she said to Kamītī, and pushed the newspaper across the table toward him.

On the front page was a picture of Sikiokuu. The caption said that the ex-minister had taken a delegation of the members of his Loyal Democratic Party to pledge loyalty and affirm that his party was ready to work with the Ruling Party to nurture the healthy growth of Baby D, and he called upon all the other loyal parties to follow his example. The same page had pictures of Kaniūrū and Tajirika in their new roles as Ministers of Finance and Defense, respectively.

"Did you look at the pictures carefully? Did you see how they are dressed?" Kamītī asked Nyawīra, and pushed the newspaper back to her.

"I don't see anything odd about it," she said.

"They are wearing baseball caps turned backward."

"So what?" Nyawĩra asked, puzzled.

"Fear not the caps they are wearing but the mouths the caps might be covering."

Nyawĩra raised her head from the newspaper and looked at Kamĩtĩ, her doubts about his sanity deepening.

*"Curiouser and curiouser,"* she said in English, smiling at him, humoring him. "Okay, I will ask Maritha and Mariko to visit Vinjinia."

# 2

Several weeks later, Nyawĩra got an urgent summons from Maritha and Mariko. She went to their place. Had they succeeded in their mission? What had Vinjinia reported? Nyawĩra was pleased with the way she and Vinjinia had worked together in the past. In her hour of greatest need, Vinjinia had acted as her eyes and ears at the State House. She knew that Vinjinia was doing so mainly as a thank-you to the women who had come to her rescue, but still her acts of solidarity, no matter the motivation, showed that her heart was not made of stone. Her position as the managing director of the Mwathirika banks, with the Ruler's sons on its board of governors, as well as the position of her husband, first as Minister of Finance and now as Minister of Defense, would make her invaluable to the movement. They had not communicated since Nyawĩra's presumed death, and so this message from Vinjinia was going to be a measure of where their relationship stood.

"Matters are not that good," said Maritha.

"Property and power can change hearts," Mariko said.

"Tell me the news," Nyawĩra said.

"We went to her place in Golden Heights," Maritha said.

"Because she does not come to the cathedral as regularly as she used to," Mariko explained.

"And we knew that this matter was important to you," said Maritha.

"In the front yard was Tajirika's Mercedes-Benz, with its ministerial flag waving in the wind," Mariko said.

"When Vinjinia saw that it was us, she came outside and quickly led us back to the gates."

"There was no *please come in* or anything like that."

"No welcome with a cup of tea or water."

"Not like old times."

"It was as if she was now tired of us."

"Not that we are complaining."

"Oh, no. If anything, we are still grateful for the way she came to our defense against those soldiers. Oh, what has come over young people that they would turn on their mothers and fathers?" Maritha said.

"We pray for them daily."

"That they may see the light and glory of the Lord."

"Amen," the two said in unison.

"So what happened?" asked Nyawĩra, thinking that they were straying into irrelevance.

"We talked outside, at the gates," Mariko said.

"And from the way she received us we knew that all was not well," said Maritha.

"Yes, we sensed this long before she opened her mouth."

"I asked her: How are the children?"

"She said: Gacirũ and Gacĩgua! You call them children? These days they cease to be children the moment they go to secondary school. They are young adults. Anyway, they are at home on holidays. But what wind has blown you toward these parts?"

"So we told her," started Maritha.

"That we have a message from the dead . . ." added Mariko.

"She did not even let us finish. She said that she did not want any messages from the dead. Things have changed. Aburĩria is no longer what it used to be. To us is now born a savior, Baby D. The people who used to give a bad name to the Ruler, like the late Machokali and the ex-minister Sikiokuu, with their endless fights for power, are no longer. The Ruler has a plan to improve the lot of women and give them jobs previously for men only. And he has already started to implement his plan; there are women assistant ministers and managing directors of the banks. The Ruler has called on all citizens to keep in step with Baby D . . ." Maritha paused and then stopped, as if she did not really want to come to the next part of the message.

"And then she said that the dead or her ghost should be told that

Vinjinia was very angry with her for suggesting that her husband was growing a second mouth at the back of his head," Mariko said bluntly.

"That her husband is not a two-mouthed ogre or any other type of ogre."

"The cap that Tajirika wears was a special gift from the Global Bank, and in any case it is now a fashion in the West. Even she, Vinjinia, was now regularly wearing a scarf on her head as demanded of women by the apostle Paul in his first letter to the Corinthians and the apostle Peter in his first letter to the world."

"Yes, people should give Baby D a chance to grow."

"The times of rumors and sorcery are gone, gone forever."

"And then we heard the car in the yard rev up."

"And the Mercedes we had seen in the yard came past the gate and hooted *piii-piii*."

"It was Tajirika saying *bye-bye* to Vinjinia."

"He had come for a change of clothes, Vinjinia told us."

"Very busy with the business of the nation, she added."

"And she was about to slam the gates shut before our very eyes . . ."

"Saying that she had another meeting . . ."

"When Gacīgua suddenly came running and screaming . . ."

"That his sister Gacirū was stuck in the Lake of Tears."

"Vinjinia screamed with terror and started running down the garden that sloped from the yard, with Gacīgua following behind."

"We, too, followed."

"I have never seen the likes of what I saw down in the valley below," Mariko said.

"A group of duikers were suspended in the air in the act of leaping so that from a distance they looked alive and at different stages of the act," Maritha explained, pointing a finger in the air as if even now, inside her house, she could still see them.

"And the birds, too . . . frozen in one spot in the sky as if suspended by the setting sun," Mariko added, also pointing a finger at a scene visible only to themselves.

"Yes, because the setting sun sent orange rays to where the animals hung suspended in the sky."

"On the surface of the lake were many more creatures also trapped at a standstill."

"A hen and its young ones. And a cock running after another hen."

"And just as it stretches its wings to mount . . ."

"Wonders will never cease. Ducks, too . . ."

"See that cat about to jump on that mouse . . ."

"What about that dog with its mouth open, barking silence at the birds in the air?"

"And those two goats and the cow with its young following behind, and in the middle stands Gacirũ, their daughter," said Maritha.

"Frozen in the act of running."

"A shadow."

"A human silhouette."

"Like Lot's wife."

"Except that Gacirũ had not yet turned to stone."

"Or to a pillar of salt."

"We found Vinjinia by the lake."

"And their boy . . . Gacĩgua."

"Both crying for Gacirũ . . . calling out endearingly, Cirũ, oh, our Cirũ."

"And Cirũ does not hear, does not turn."

"They are both afraid to touch the lake."

"We said . . ."

"Let's pray," they now said in unison, and Maritha and Mariko knelt in their house and started singing the prayer they had sung in the valley.

> *In times of sorrow, O Lord*
> *Don't turn away*
> *Don't hide your face*
> *At a time of tears*
>
> *Lord of all our souls*
> *Hearken to the cry*
> *Of parents and children*
> *Of boys and girls*

"It was then that I heard something make a movement in my belly," Maritha said, still on her knees. "A strange thought came to my mind, and I started laughing."

"Why is she laughing at a time of tears? I asked . . . but when I saw how she was laughing I also started laughing," said Mariko.

And now, as both recalled their laughter, they started laughing in earnest all over again. They were back on their feet, still laughing, then sat down, still laughing, and it was with difficulty that they were able to stop themselves.

"A glance at each other and we would resume laughing," Maritha said.

"We went on laughing walking down toward the lake, but in truth . . ." added Mariko.

"Not of our own will; we were under some unknown influence."

"When we reached the bank of the river we dipped our feet into the murky quagmire," they said in unison.

"And there we stopped . . ."

"See that cat . . ."

"See that dog . . ."

"See that cock . . ."

"See the cow . . ."

"And more laughter till tears started flowing down my cheeks," said Maritha.

"And me, too . . . tears of laughter," added Mariko.

"And all this time Vinjinia and Gacīgua are looking at us, amazed . . ."

"And we were wondering why they, too, were not laughing . . ."

"And then we saw Vinjinia faint . . ."

"And Gacīgua bent down to attend her . . ."

"And our tears of laughter continued to flow . . ."

"Down into the lake . . ."

"Now it was our turn to be amazed," they said in unison.

"When our tears of joy and laughter touched the still waters . . ." Mariko continued.

"Everything that had stood frozen began to move," Maritha said.

"The duikers completed their leaps to the other side and disappeared."

"The bird flew away."

"The cat and the mouse resumed the chase."

"The dog barked noisily at the birds."

"And the calf followed its mother, mooing for milk. And the goats . . ."

"Come, come, little mother, don't be afraid."

"Gacirū turned around."

"And she started walking to where we were," Maritha said.

"She walked on the water, did not sink . . ."

"As if on dry land . . ."

"Don't leave me, don't leave me here, she said."

"She sounded confused."

"Take me to Nyawīra . . ."

"For she knows everything about ogres . . ."

"There was a time you used to tell her stories about ogres."

"And she was sobbing."

"Keep still, you are now out of danger."

"She tried to talk through her sobs . . ."

"I don't know, she said, for since Mother and Father became big in government they have become strangers to the home and to us children . . . and so when I saw him . . . and she stopped and there was fear in her eyes."

"Especially when she saw Vinjinia approach."

"Vinjinia was shaking all over."

"Now Vinjinia embraced Gacirū, who was still clinging to me, and Gacīgua was trying to embrace both mother and sister as if gathering his family."

"And Vinjinia was telling her, Don't worry, *it's all right, it's all right,* I am still your loving mummy . . ."

"Don't take me to Father. I saw what he now looks like. I hid in the house until he left and then ran out . . ."

"Sssshhhh! Vinjinia said, trying to quiet her. We are going to talk . . ."

"We assured the girl that we would take her request to the storyteller."

"And that we would keep an eye on her."

"And on Sundays she should come to church."

"God lives. God rules."

"And He would look after her day and night."

"We left them there, clinging to one another."

"We went away singing."

"Because laughter had conquered tears."

Maritha and Mariko started singing about the amazing quality of the cross, where joy followed sorrow, as if they were alone in the house, and it appeared that they had forgotten that Nyawĩra was there. She stood up to leave, for she did not know how to take all of this. Were they speaking in parables?

"What? Are you leaving without hearing the rest?" Maritha asked.

Nyawĩra sat down again.

"We were long past the gate when a car stopped beside us," Maritha started.

"It was Vinjinia," said Mariko.

"Get in. I should at least take you to the bus stop, she told us."

"Well, God works in mysterious ways."

"His wonders to perform."

"Because we had just been wondering how we would get home," they said in unison.

"As she drove she said thank you and then added: I am asking you a favor," Maritha explained.

"What you have seen is not for public confession in church or anywhere," Mariko continued.

"I told her, We confess only our own sins, not other people's."

"And to share joy and laughter is not a sin."

"She gave us another thank-you, and then . . ."

"She told us to go and tell the one who had sent us . . ."

"That she harbored no ill will in her heart, but . . . And she did not go beyond this, or rather, she did not finish what she wanted to say. She seemed about to break into tears."

"Like somebody who has lost her way and knows that she has lost it but does not know how to find it again."

"At the bus stop, she found her voice again."

"Tell her who sent you that she is not to send more messages. Oh, there was a time in my life when I thought I understood, however vaguely, the language of the dove, and I even thought that I could see as in a mirror darkly but see all the same. Today I no longer understand the language of doves. I no longer see my face in the mirror. Yes, tell her we are not ogres. It is a case of white-ache with a cure that has gone wrong, and the Wizard of the Crow is dead. Does she not read the papers? It is better for her and everybody if she remains with the dead."

# 3

It was in his hotel in New York during his first visit as the Minister of Finance that Tajirika had happened to read an issue of the *Billionaire*, a magazine about the richest men and corporations in the world; almost all the men white Americans, and almost all the corporations based in America. He started musing about the fate of nations. America, a former colony, was still rising, while Britain, its colonizer, was rolling downward toward Third World misery. And suddenly, out of nowhere, the answer to a problem that had always bothered him about his white-ache came to him. The cure the Wizard of the Crow had prescribed had been in response to Tajirika's desire to become a white Englishman, moreover an ex-colonial type. The white *American* male was the desirable ideal. Yes. He should have aspired to be a white American male. But alas, it was now too late to do anything about it. The Wizard of the Crow had been shot dead by Kaniūrū and his effigy buried; and as far as Tajirika was concerned that was the end of the matter. No more *if*s and *if*ness for him, especially now with his dramatic rise from jailbird to gold digger to governor to minister and who knows what else awaited him?

And then one day at a New York street corner somebody handed him a leaflet, and when he later looked at it he saw that it was an advertisement for a clinic specializing in genetic engineering, cloning, transplants, and plastic surgery. The ad claimed that the company, Genetica Inc., grew all the body parts in its own laboratory and that its very highly trained staff could change anybody into any identity of their desire, quickly and efficiently, without any side effects.

He read the ad over and over and started to tremble. His white-ache, which had been in remission, came back with a force that almost swept him off the ground.

This time around, Tajirika did not hide his secret desire and what he intended to do about it from Vinjinia. Vinjinia agreed that Tajirika could become an American white if he so wanted, but she, Vinjinia, would stay black and settle for a mixed marriage. But she insisted on a quid pro quo, a face- and breast-lift for herself, to which he readily agreed. So while Kaniũrũ, the then Minister of Defense, was secretly buying pornographic videos on Forty-second Street, Tajirika and Vinjinia were secretly visiting the Genetica clinic. By the time Tajirika went home with the rest of the delegation, he was the recipient of a white right arm as the first stage in his transformation, obliging him to wear a glove, but that was okay.

Tajirika and Vinjinia were soon back in New York, and after one week Vinjinia was the happy recipient of a more youthful face and firmer breasts and Tajirika had added a white left leg to his one-white-armed body. Half white, half black, he always wore pants and long-sleeved shirts, and of course a glove on the right hand. When people commented on the glove he explained that it was his way of commemorating the first time his minister's hand had shaken the Ruler's.

Then tragedy struck. Tajirika was making preparations to return to America for the other body parts to complete his transformation when he read in a newspaper that the clinic had been closed because it was not licensed. He also read, to his dismay, that the company, Genetica Inc., was bankrupt and under police investigation. The feds were considering releasing the names and records of clients, the better to uncover the criminal elements and foreign spies involved in the disreputable company. So despite his incomplete state and loss of money to boot, Tajirika dared not complain, remaining a man in transition, with a white left leg and a white right arm. Luckily for him Vinjinia was privy to his predicament, and together they resolved to keep this between husband and wife until such time as they could find a licensed lab with the appropriate genetic technology to complete the transformation. He never swam in public, and even at home he had to be careful in case the workers and unexpected guests caught him with his legs and arms uncovered.

They of course did not tell the children about what they had done. Though the children noticed their mother's youthful looks and firm breasts and maybe even thought them a little strange, there was nothing completely out of the ordinary about Vinjinia. But when Gacirũ saw her father naked as she was going to the bathroom to change, she thought that she was seeing an ogre and suddenly her mother's transformation acquired a different meaning. She could hardly run to her for protection. Perhaps these ogres had taken over the bodies of their parents as ogres almost certainly did in stories, except that this was not a story, and her solution was to run away, beckoning her brother to follow, no questions asked. That was when she got stuck in the Lake of Tears.

In church one day, Gacirū had whispered to Maritha and Mariko the reason she had tried to run away, and they in turn had whispered it to Nyawīra, who whispered it to Kamītī.

"A permanent clown," observed Nyawīra.

"A man in a permanent state of transition," commented Kamītī.

# 4

Baby D's Aburīria was full of ironies resulting in daily wonders of tears and laughter. There was a year when people were told that the official celebrations of the Ruler's birthday involved their going to the nearest bookshop in the morning to pick up yet another special gift from the Ruler and then repairing in the afternoon to the Ruler's stadium to commemorate some sort of anniversary of Baby D. But why? Everyone knew how much the Ruler loathed books and writers who would not sing his praises.

Curiosity drove Kamītī and Nyawīra to the shops, where they found stacks upon stacks of a newly minted book, *The Birth of Baby D: The Ruler and the Evolution of an African Statesman: An Objective Biography*, written by Henry Morton Stanley, A White Englishman.

In the book, whatever ills had befallen Aburīria during his reign, like Rachael's disappearance and the attempted coups by the likes of Markus Machokali and Big Ben Mambo, were blamed on the late Wizard of the Crow and the Limping Witch, and that was why the State had sentenced the already dead sorcerers to a second death and burned their effigies to make sure that even in Hell they would suffer more than the other inmates.

"Our deaths are confirmed in a book," commented Nyawīra. "If you ever hear the name Wizard of the Crow mentioned, you must not respond by look or gesture."

"This applies to the Limping Witch also," Kamĩtĩ said. "Maybe that is what Vinjinia was telling us. That we let those names die."

They looked at each other, feeling sad that the characters Wizard of the Crow and the Limping Witch would have to be no more.

# 5

It was soon after this that leaflets bearing the symbol of a viper and a two-mouthed ogre with the slogan Let Them Not Kill Our Future were scattered in every village and town. It was the first open and mass challenge to Baby D. Every upheaval during the regime of the Ruler, like the drama of shame, had been preceded by leaflets.

The Ruler summoned his most trusted counselor, the Minister of Defense. Tajirika had just returned from yet another trip to Washington, where he had concluded an agreement on joint military exercises in Aburĩria. The discussion touched on a whole range of other matters, for instance, the leasing of land at the coast for permanent American military bases, and he came out feeling that he was being appreciated not only as the Ruler's Defense Minister but as a leader in his own right. He had even had a private dinner with the retired ambassador Gemstone, attended by leaders of the business community, including defense contractors. The dinner was so secret that even his own bodyguards did not know about it. In his talks, Tajirika had it be known how close he had been to the late Machokali, his friend—in fact, Tajirika had been his protégé, which seemed to go well with Washington and emboldened him to repeat the same claims in London.

"What do you make of all this?" asked the Ruler.

"It is the curse of the Wizard of the Crow."

"Even as he lies in a grave?"

"Yes—revenge of the daemons."

"But we burned their effigies."

"Nyawĩra's daemon must have merged with his," Tajirika, who never liked Kaniũrũ's getting full credit for dispatching the sorcerer, further asserted.

"Male and female daemons working together, eh?" the Ruler asked. "Giving birth to a new wave of pointless resistance?" he added.

"Female daemons are unpredictable."

Tajirika paused, remembering that that very morning Vinjinia had told him she wanted to be relieved of managing the Mwathirika banks to concentrate on running their farms and Eldares Modern Construction and Real Estate. He told the Ruler of Vinjinia's decision, fearfully expecting the Ruler's anger at such crass ingratitude.

"It is all right, let her retire," the Ruler said rather quickly. "Jane Kanyori shall move from the Central Bank to the Mwathirika banks."

Tajirika knew that Dr. Yunique Immaculate McKenzie, who had now combined the roles of official hostess and comptroller of the State House, had been complaining about Kanyori's frequent visits to the State House to report on the goings-on at the Central Bank and yet was not the governor. With Vinjinia's retirement the Ruler had found a smooth resolution of the conflict.

"Yes, Kanyori can handle it," Tajirika said quickly, not to seem as if he was second-guessing the Ruler's decision.

"But we cannot lie down and just wait for the curse of the Wizard of the Crow to thwart us," said the Ruler, returning to the subject of the leaflets. "Or let female daemons walk all over us, in silence, without retaliation," he added, recalling Tajirika's cowardice in letting himself be thrashed by women. "There must never be another People's Assembly on Aburīrian soil. We are okay with the military chiefs. Wonderful Tumbo has been superb in alerting me of any signs of anti–Baby D feelings in all branches of the armed forces. Most conscientious. And he does it while maintaining the friendliest of terms with the forces. I appreciate your advice on his appointment."

"Thank you for trusting my judgment."

"But where do we stand in the eyes of the Global Bank, the Global Ministry of Finance, and the West as a whole?"

Tajirika cited the coming joint military exercises as one more piece of evidence of the Ruler's return to favor. He had found similar positive dispositions in his contacts with European capitals, London included.

"Our friendship is back on track thanks to the birth of Baby D. Even Gemstone has good things to say about you in his recently published memoirs, *Marching to Heaven: My Life in an African Dictatorship*."

Knowing the icy relationship between Gemstone and the Ruler, Tajirika did not mention his private dinner with Gemstone attended by key leaders of the corporate community including defense contractors.

"And he has no shame in stealing my ideas?" said the Ruler, aghast at the ambassador's impertinence and irreverence.

"We should have registered the name Marching to Heaven and reserved the copyright," said Tajirika. "Still, you should rejoice that the West is embracing your ideas. However, it is said that a good reader is the one who casts his eyes ahead to see where lies a comma, a question mark, an exclamation point, or even a full stop. We should do the same. The Global Bank and the Global Ministry of Finance are clearly looking to privatize countries, nations, and states. They argue that the modern world was created by private capital. The subcontinent of India, for instance, was owned by the British East India Company, Indonesia by the Dutch East India Company, our neighbors by the British East Africa Company, and the Congo Free State by a one-man corporation. Corporate capital was aided by missionary societies. What private capital did then it can do again: own and reshape the Third World in the image of the West without the slightest blot, blemish, or blotch. NGOs will do what the missionary charities did in the past. The world will no longer be composed of the outmoded twentieth-century divisions of East, West, and a directionless Third. The world will become one corporate globe divided into the incorporating and the incorporated. We should volunteer Aburīria to be the first to be wholly managed by private capital, to become the first voluntary corporate colony, a corporony, the first in the new global order. With the privatization of Aburīria, and with the NGOs relieving us of social services, the country becomes your real estate. You will be collecting land rent in addition to the commission fee for managing the corporonial army and police force. The corporonial powers will reward you as a modern visionary. You will enjoy the irony that just as Gabriel Gemstone has stolen your intellectual property you will have appropriated the intellectual property of the corporate West."

"A tit for a tat. They steal ours and we steal theirs," said the Ruler, laughing. "That's why I have always maintained that you are a crook," said the Ruler, now laughing as if he had just complimented Tajirika. "A loyal crook," he added.

Indeed, the Ruler was comfortable with Tajirika as counselor. The Minister of Defense had the common sense and realism of a crook so his counsel was nearly always to the point, but he was a cowardly crook who was once beaten by women and never retaliated and so was safe. Were it not for the cowardly strain in his character, he would be very dangerous, the Ruler thought in passing.

"About this business of corporonialism, why can't I incorporate instead of being incorporated?" the Ruler continued. "I don't want to be a company employee," he added, and laughed aloud at his own joke. "I hope that you did not make any promises to Washington."

"Oh, no, no!" an alarmed Tajirika hastened to deny.

"I am their only sun here, and they will have to deal with the sun as is."

"And the West does not want to set with its sun," Tajirika said, and both laughed at Tajirika's wit.

"But for now you and I have some work to do," said the Ruler. "We have to neutralize the impact of these leaflets and threats of queues before they become another menace."

"Yes, we take the fight to the underworld. Scare and scatter the ghosts of Nyawīra and the Wizard of the Crow," said Tajirika.

# 6

A few days before yet another double celebration of the Ruler's birthday and the anniversary of Baby D, four apparitions covered from head to foot with long silver hair and beards converged at the headquarters of the Eldares police from four different directions and collapsed at the entrance. The startled police dragged the presumed corpses inside, but before they had decided what to do they heard whispering from the four creatures. All police could make out was the word *north* from one, *south* from the other, *east* from the third, and *west* from the fourth, but this effort seemed too strenuous for the apparitions, and they fell back, unconscious.

When they finally came to, they identified themselves as the four riders who had been sent to the four directions of the compass to tell people the blessedness of queuing and the joy the queues gave the Ruler. Yes, they had been preaching the gospel of queuing, the beatitude being: "Blessed are they that queue, for they shall receive countless rewards from a grateful Ruler."

"Riders without motorbikes?" said one skeptical officer.

"Our bikes are long gone."

"You, policemen with hair and beard all over you? Defying the long-standing law of the beard?"

"We had no wherewithal to buy razor blades and shaving cream."

"And why not cover them?"

"Our clothes are long gone," the apparitions whispered.

But each rider had retained his shoulder flap with police identification numbers, and each was clutching the license plate of his motorcycle. When the interrogating officers looked into the records they were able to confirm that indeed such men had once existed, but their files had been closed and marked MISSING AND PRESUMED DEAD.

The riders did not seem to know one another. They had never met since setting out on their mission, but their narratives were almost identical. They told harrowing stories of people from even the remotest corners of the globe forming queues and demanding change. Now, despite years of lonely toil, they were glad to report that people in Aburĩria were catching up with the rest of the world; and that from north, south, east, and west, nay, from the remotest rural villages and urban centers, queues were forming and slowly marching toward the capital, singing an end to the causes of all the cries of the dispossessed. They want a clean atmosphere so that people can have clean air to breathe, clean water to drink, and clean spaces to live and enjoy. They reject the rule of the viper and the ogre. Their songs end up in chorus with the other parts of the globe: Don't let them kill our future.

"These incorrigible liars must be charged with desertion and treason for stirring up the populace to queue and march toward the capital," the police chief said, angry at the bad name that these four had given the Aburĩrian police in the world.

But when they showed him letters carefully sewn inside the shoulder flaps, letters with the Ruler's message and signature, he recalled an earlier saga way back involving a rider in the central region and said to himself, This matter calls for a decision from above, and sent an urgent report to the State House. The Ruler said, Oh, no, these deserters are doing this because they had heard that I forgave the rider from the central region. That was the wrong message to send, and now I must show to all and sundry the fate of those who defy my decree that civil servants must never wear long hair and beards. The riders should be charged with treason before a special court, and when it came to hanging instead of a noose woven from sisal one fashioned from their hair and beards should be used.

What do you think? said the Ruler, turning to his Minister of Defense and trusted counselor, Titus Tajirika.

The counselor was struck dumb by the whole saga. The wonder of the supreme deity having covered the apparitions with natural wear from head to foot had left an indelible mark on his imagination: a sudden incandescence illuminating nameless possibilities. Was that how prophets and seers arrived at new thoughts? How the Wizard of the Crow used to get the visions of the hidden?

He felt a surge of power within, rendering him fearless of the Ruler, at least concerning the spirit riders. He did not even know how the words came to him.

"Masks of deity," murmured Tajirika at last. "Truly, God works in mysterious ways."

"What are you talking about?" asked the Ruler, startled out of his own thoughts.

"The riders. Their appearance, hair from head to foot. Natural masks. Messengers from the supreme deity. Bearded spirits."

"Did you say 'bearded spirits'?"

"It is obvious, my Lord, that these are no ordinary beings!"

"Have them executed immediately," screamed the Ruler, strangely agitated.

"Before they are executed, put them on national television exactly as they are to tell the nation that they are spirits sent by the Lord to tell the citizenry not to fall for lies by the new generation of daydreamers clamoring for a new tomorrow. After you, there is no tomorrow."

What brilliance of insight, thought the Ruler, feeling calmer having suddenly seen the way to outwit oracles and end all threats to the immortality of his rule! Aburīrians were deeply religious. Even street sweepers were forming their own sects and gaining followers! So once they hear the riders from the Lord, people will take whatever they say as a direct command from above. And if they don't heed the ban from Heaven, then the anger of the Lord will visit them with merciless vengeance.

The words that after him there was no tomorrow kept buzzing in his head. He was Aburīria, so how could there be any future after him? He recalled what he used to tell Rachael before he sent her stubborn eyes toward Hell. Yes, I used to tell her that I could bring her future to a standstill, freeze it in the moment, he said to himself, gazing at Tajirika with increasing awe and amazement. The Ruler had not been mistaken when he had seen and realized that a man who could take over an armed camp with only a bucket of shit was unusually gifted, and now he had shown him the way to outwit oracles and spirits, affirming the Ruler's belief that he himself was the supreme sorcerer.

At this moment of absolute belief in his counselor, he sensed in Tajirika's offer of advice and his confident tone the danger he posed. Yes, this man of uncanny insights might one day feel emboldened to challenge his authority. He would strike first. Confront danger before it was too late. This guiding principle in dealing with political adversaries and friends had served him well.

He had a sudden moment of inspiration. Just as the Lord of Heaven will one day call the world to account, he, too, would call Aburīria to account. What he once told Rachael he would tell to Aburīria. And what he did to Rachael he would do to Aburīria, thus enacting what had never been done by any ruler before him: freeze or even abolish the future of a country. His instrument would be none other than Tajirika. He would send Tajirika on one more mission.

His plan was simplicity itself. He would send his devoted minister, his very trusted counselor, on a last mission, to order the army for a massacre. Blood would flow. And after the massacre he would set up a commission of inquiry supervised by a couple of observers from America and the European Union, if necessary, which would end up blaming his Minister of Defense. He would then have him executed publicly.

Thought, Word, and Deed!

He told Tajirika to put the riders on television, as he had so magnificently proposed. They should say that all queuing and agitation for tomorrow must cease immediately and that if the people failed to heed the call from their ancestors, then the spirits would urge the Ruler to halt the progress of time; the whole country would be bewitched in one endless moment by sorcery, for there was no tomorrow beyond the Ruler. He then asked Tajirika, in his capacity as the Defense Minister, to order the armed forces to mow down any resistance twenty-four hours after the ultimatum.

Tajirika was hearing the last details of his mission with his thoughts wandering. The talk of a frozen future triggered Tajirika's memories of the Museum of Suspended Motion. Had that been a sign of things to come? That he would one day become the chosen instrument to freeze the future of . . . who?

He looked up and saw the intensity of light in the Ruler's eyes, and he did not like what he read in it. He acted on instinct rather than cool reason using whatever was at hand, in this case, words.

"My Lord, I am only your Minister of Defense. Everybody knows that you are the commander in chief, and for chiefs of staff and commanding officers to believe me when I ask them to act I need your written and signed authority, as much for that as to have the masked riders, awaiting execution for treason, released for their appearance on television. I need the seal of your office, my Lord, to bolster my authority. As for the four riders, I think I should first bring them to you so that when speaking on national television they will be animated by the warmth of recent contact with you. You know that your handshake means a lot," he added, glancing at his gloved hand.

This is the problem when dealing with cowards, the Ruler thought to himself. They have no backbone. It was easier to deal with and break the likes of Machokali and Sikiokuu than this dithering crook. He gave him the necessary authority, a rope long enough for the cowardly but gifted counselor to hang himself.

# 7

Tajirika acted with his usual unerring instinct of self-preservation. With the new authority ceded to him in writing, he sent Wonderful Tumbo to fetch the masked riders from death row and bring them straight to him at the Ministry of Defense. Fortunately, Wonderful Tumbo got to them and found their hair and beards still intact, for no warden dared trim the masks of spirits. A few wardens even knelt before the spirits, begging them to intercede with their ancestors on their behalf.

Once inside Tajirika's office, it was the spirits who fell to their knees, confronted by a figure different from the picture of Tajirika they carried in their heads. Ditto Wonderful Tumbo, a longtime friend and confidant of Tajirika's. Had it not been for his years of police training and experience, he would have fainted.

Tajirika sat on a raised chair, the one that Sikiokuu had made in imitation of the Ruler's at cabinet meetings. He wore a T-shirt and shorts made of lion skin. He was draped in a cape of a colobus monkey skin that reached to his feet. Tajirika had discarded the glove used to cover his right hand. To the wonderment of his guests, his right arm and left leg were white, his left arm and right leg black. The riders assumed him a deity. Wonderful Tumbo said loudly, with absolute conviction: He is the chosen one, a man set apart by the gods.

The four spirits abandoned themselves to newfound joy and gratitude for life restored, and there was nothing they would not do for their savior. They listened with all their power to every word of what was expected of them. They would conceal weapons under their hair when they went to meet with the Ruler at the State House.

# 8

Aburĩria heard the news on radio and television. The newspapers also brought out special issues. All carried the pictures of the hirsute creatures. THE SPIRIT MEDIATORS OF POWER, one paper called them. A TELEVISION COUP, another proclaimed. No newspaper had the courage to print what had been said on television, for they all feared the Ruler known for wicked wiles.

The four spirits calmly said that they had been sent by the dead, the living, and the unborn to tell the nation that the Ruler and the official hostess, Yunique Immaculate McKenzie, had been recalled by the ancestors that very morning. The people should not heed any rumors of a coup d'état. Aburĩria was different from other countries of Africa and the Third World. This was not a coup d'état. It was premeditated SID.

In fact, the Ruler must have known that his time to go had come, because a few weeks before, he had ceded all his powers to the new ruler of Aburĩria, Emperor Titus Flavius Vespasianus Whitehead.

# 9

For Tajirika, things had gone more smoothly than when he had taken over an armed camp with a bucket of shit and urine. He had taken over the country with a few bullets for the Ruler. Wonderful Tumbo had been effective in ensuring the loyalty of the heads of all the branches of the armed forces. The work he did earned him a promotion to chief of all the eyes, ears, and noses of the Imperial State. Tumbo could not help but thankfully recall the day a policeman he had trained had fought with djinns and got promoted to the State House.

To emphasize continuity, the Emperor retained for a while the Ruler's cabinet, except for minor changes. Kaniūrū was axed and was dealt further humiliation by seeing Kanyori elevated to full governorship of the Central Bank. Sikiokuu was recalled to become Minister for Toilets and Cleanliness in Public Places. Njoya and Kahiga were now the Emperor's official executioners.

The loyal opposition parties were caught with their pants down. Their leaders first went into hiding, only to crawl out of their holes when they learned the armed forces were firmly behind the Emperor. They tried to devise strategies for gain and survival under the new imperial regime. They listened to and scrutinized every pronouncement from the Imperial Palace, as the former State House was now called. Except for a few odd things, like his decree banning all classics in dead languages and all literature by Descartes, his pronouncements did not ruffle too many feathers.

Even the four sons of the former Ruler, Runyenje, Moya, Soi, and Kucera, in exchange for the Imperial State's dropping drug and money-laundering charges, agreed, in a written and signed statement by all four, that they knew that their father had succumbed to SID.

They were retired with honor from military service, but alas the ungrateful four escaped to Europe, where they claimed to be the legitimate heirs to the Aburīrian throne and formed a government in exile, with one of them as royal president, the second royal vice president, the third a royal prime minister, and the fourth royal deputy prime minister, although they had public disagreements as to whether all four posts carried executive powers.

Internationally, recognition from Washington was quickly followed by others. It was only at the domestic front where all was not well. Vinjinia refused to become Empress Beatrice, claiming that she was too old for such royal games. She would be content to look after their house and their properties. If Tajirika wanted to appoint an official hostess, she would not raise any objection unless the hostess crossed the line and violated the marriage bed.

The climax of Tajirika's ascension to power came when he addressed the nation and pronounced the end of Baby D. A new era of imperial democracy had dawned, he said, and ordered the construction of a modern coliseum on the site once earmarked for Marching to Heaven.

# 10

And then the Wizard of the Crow reared his head again and dulled the celebratory mood. Who would have thought that a dead man could raise his head in the very heart of the Imperial Palace?

It happened that as some security men were cleaning up a room rarely used, they came across a tiny bundle of hair carefully tied in a small plastic bag. The room was last occupied by the captive Wizard of the Crow just before his address to the assembly, but the men did not know. It was Njoya and Kahiga, the newly installed imperial executioners, who recognized the plastic bag they had given the Wizard of the Crow at the basement of the All Saints Cathedral and which contained all the hair they had collected before their unceremonious dismissal from their jobs. But how had it ended up in the Imperial Palace?

This question was very troubling to Emperor Titus Flavius Vespasianus Whitehead until he consulted with the bearded spirits, who came up with the answer in the crocodiles of the Red River. No charms, even those from the dead, could escape from the belly of the monsters. But how were the monsters to swallow human hair without the human person?

One night Kaniũrũ was invited to the Imperial Palace for dinner as a revered artist, and was conned into swallowing meatballs inside which were some of the remains of the hair of the Wizard of the Crow. Later the same night, Njoya and Kahiga, happy in their anticipation of sweet revenge, took Kaniũrũ to the Red River. What they did not know was that they, too, had eaten bread with some of the sorcerer's hair in it and that the four masked spirits were waiting for them at the same riverside. They joined the Ruler in the belly of the crocodiles of the Red River, afterward renamed the Imperial River, and the scaly lizards Imperial Crocs, in honor of their having swallowed up all threats from the dead Wizard of the Crow.

# 11

Nothing could have prepared Kamĩtĩ and Nyawĩra and the entire Movement for the Voice of the People for what had happened in Aburĩria, the Ruler's SID particularly. He had survived the absurdities of self-induced expansion, self-induced pregnancy, and certainly all the other previous attempts on his life, only to fall to masked spirits. That Nyawĩra's former boss and Kamĩtĩ's tormentor had successfully carried out a palace coup was stunning, to say the least, and Kamĩtĩ could not help but recall that other time when Tajirika escaped from prison with a bucket of shit between his legs.

"But shit is still shit, even by another name," commented Nyawĩra. "The battle lines may be murky, but they have not changed."

# 12

One evening Nyawĩra told Kamĩtĩ that two men would come for him on the following day and take him to meet the Central Committee of the Movement for the Voice of the People so that he could say in his own words and from his own lips that he wanted to become a member. Kamĩtĩ was expecting them and yet was shocked a little. It was the first time since their last return from the mountains that he had seen another person enter their place, and he realized how much of a sheltered life he had been leading with Nyawĩra, newspapers, and the radio his only windows to the world. The two escorts looked his age and there was a lot about which they could have chatted, but there was not much talk between them and Kamĩtĩ was left to his own thoughts. He reviewed his life since that fateful day when he flew out of his body at the city dumpsite, setting in motion subsequent happenings like his flight in time and space in bird form, that added to the miracle his life had become, making him wonder about the thinness of the line that divided the real and the unreal in human lives.

"We are already there," said one of his guides, jolting Kamĩtĩ from his reverie.

His two escorts ushered him into a room, showed him a seat, and went into another room. Alone, Kamĩtĩ let his eyes pan the walls, over posters and drawings of some heroes and heroines of Aburĩrian and African anticolonial resistance who were never mentioned in official documents. Then his eyes rested on a big map of the world with Africa at the center. On the map were red paper arrows pointing at cities circled with a black marker. He was contemplating these circles when he saw, at the Nile Delta, a neon-lit arrow. The arrow began to move down the map, and when it reached a town it would stop and flicker as if asking him to note the spot well. This was too unreal, and he stood up and went near the map to make sure. Yes, the arrow was moving along the trail he had followed and it flickered only at those towns he had visited in the body of a bird. What was the meaning of this?

"We are just trying to learn our history," Kamĩtĩ heard a voice say, and he quickly turned around to face six men and four women. One of them was speaking to him as the others listened. "We try to locate our origins and know all the places to which black people have been scattered, from India, where dwell the Siddis, to Fiji in the Pacific, where the people claim Tanganyika as the site of their origins."

"And what about this flickering arrow?"

"Which arrow?" the man asked, wondering what Kamĩtĩ was talking about.

Kamĩtĩ looked back at the map and was surprised to find that the neon arrow was not there.

"Oh, I was thinking about these red arrows," Kamĩtĩ said, as if the matter was not of consequence.

"Those arrows are pointing at the centers of ancient black civilization," the man said. "They are the sources of black power."

They sat down in a semicircle. Again, Kamĩtĩ could not believe his eyes. Were these not the ones who used to work at the shrine? However, he now kept his thoughts to himself in case his mind was deceiving him again. The man said that they were still waiting for the chairperson, but even before the man had finished—was Kamĩtĩ dreaming or not?—Nyawĩra entered.

"The chairperson of the Central Committee of the Movement for the Voice of the People and commander in chief of Aburīrian People's Resistance . . ."

# 13

The comrades took him on a tour, a journey imbued with magic more potent than that in Maritha's story of suspended motion and suffused with wonders more amazing than those in the healing laughter of Maritha and Mariko. Here, in the new venture, the extraordinary, the magical, the wonderful, and even the strange came out of the ordinary and the familiar. His guides were those he had always known as workers in the shrine. But they now looked different. Nyawīra looked different. He was seeing the Eldares Mountains anew through other people's eyes.

They took him to their farms where they grew foods, millet, sorghum, yams, and arrowroots, as well as varieties of Aburīrian berries. Elsewhere Aburīrian soil was dying from being doused with pollutants, imported fertilizer. Here they were working with nature, not against it. The forest was a school to which they often came to hear what it had to tell them: You take, you give, for if you only take without giving back, you will leave the giver exhausted unto death. The gardens were nurseries for healing plants with seeds that could be planted on farms elsewhere; the healing of the land had to start somewhere.

They took him to a cave on the other side of the falls, perhaps even one he had once shown Nyawīra. It had been turned into a living space. Three men and two women, guns slung on their shoulders, received them. We do a few drills here, Nyawīra explained, as if reading Kamītī's mind. One of the men there took up the narrative.

The so-called national army is a colonial institution. It was trained to hate its own people. The soldiers hate even themselves, shorn as they are of national pride. Those trained-to-kill nationalists fighting for freedom, how can they feel for the nation whose emergence they fought? They pass these attitudes to new recruits, the young. In time, these traditions of self-hate rooted in colonial times become the everyday. Our motto, a girl said, is simple: a New Army for a New Aburĩria, not with the gun guiding politics but a politics of unity guiding the gun, to protect laws for social justice. These weapons are to protect our right to political struggle and not a substitute for political struggle.

Another man took up the thread: You see, despite our insurgency so far, we have not been able to hold the agents of the regime accountable for murdering our people. Nyawĩra added: There will surely come a day when we shall make it impossible for these armed ogres to go about their work of terror without suffering consequences. We shall then fight on our terrain, which is the people who must know and believe that we aim only to defend them and protect their right to a better life.

They took him through underground passages to yet another cave, a large room full of books. The Ruler and now the Emperor hated books and ideas that came from within, they explained.

"We believe that all knowledge is our inheritance, but we also have a duty to add to the common store. The right to receive, the duty to give."

Yes, words that he and Nyawĩra had used, but now confronting him with all the power of their estrangement. Maybe knowledge was nothing more than the art of looking at what we already know with different eyes, and asking different questions. Knowledge is the discovery of the magic of the ordinary. Like words put into song. He was so absorbed in these thoughts about what was being said that he did not realize that he had been led to another spacious complex: a hospital, a replica of the shrine.

"We transported everything to this place," Nyawĩra said, reading his mind again. "This is where we first brought you on the night they shot you. This is where you were operated on and the bullet extracted. We want you to take charge of the facilities and develop it as a nursery of health and clean living in accordance with the Seven Herbs of Grace. We are trying to imagine a different future for Aburĩria after people united take power from these ogres . . . Dr. Patel who did the surgery is not here today but . . ."

"What? Some Aburo-Asians?"

"Yes, for it does not mean that all the Asians in Aburīria support the current program of ogres. Like black Aburīrians, some work with the forces of repression, while others toil on the side of the people. This was also true in our anticolonial struggles, but the regime tries to suppress this knowledge. Anything pointing to people being able to unite across race and ethnic lines is suppressed so that people may not realize the sources of their strength and power."

They took him to another room. He felt tears press against his eyelids. All his carvings of African deities were here.

"We brought them here long before you came back from America. For us they stand for a dream. We were hoping that you can complete them and even add the gods of all the other black and related peoples."

A global conversation of the deities, he said to himself, remembering his thoughts as a bird in the sky.

# 14

They walked the streets of Eldares one afternoon as crowds pushed past them in all directions.

"Every day, the same story," commented Nyawīra. "People continue to pour into the capital for jobs they know are hard to come by."

"It reminds me of those days when I walked these streets expecting that my academic degrees would land me a job," said Kamītī. "Then conditions looked really bad, and I could not see how much worse they could become. But they are so now, and I find myself with the same thought: can conditions become worse than this?"

"What is to prevent them from worsening? When the farmer and the manufacturer grow and make things within, the neoimperial class imports en masse the cheapest from abroad and undermines the efforts within. We live in a corporate globe under imperial corporonialism, as proudly claimed by the new ogres."

The streets they passed told the same old story. The potholes had multiplied; there was garbage everywhere for want of collection.

"The bright side of people in the streets is that we are hiding among them," Kamĩtĩ observed.

"Why don't we go for coffee somewhere and enjoy this bright side while seated?" Nyawĩra suggested. She was trying to find a place where she could address a tension that seemed to have grown between her and Kamĩtĩ. "Let's try the Mars Café?"

"Gautama, the owner, might he not recognize us?"

"No, not Gautama, his mind is always on Mars or some other planet," Nyawĩra said trying a light touch. "Mercury, Venus, Jupiter, Saturn, Uranus, Pluto? Which of those do you think he would like to make a home?"

"Actually it is not only Gautama," said Kamĩtĩ, not picking up the lighthearted tone. "There is also Kaniũrũ."

"Don't you remember the statement from his wife, Jane Kanyori, that he has disappeared? SID?"

"And the new Emperor? He still has his business. Modern construction. Your old workplace?"

It became a walk down memory lane, back to the bad and the good that had happened to them in Santamaria. Nyawĩra winced as she recalled the day she narrowly escaped arrest with the inadvertent help from A.G., thanks to his belief that she was the other manifestation of the Wizard of the Crow. They sat down almost at the same roadside spot where they sat on the day they first met.

"Whatever drew me to you on that day was blessed."

"And who would have thought that the place where you took the test would later become the starting point of the queuing mania? Or Tajirika's imperial journey?"

"Well, let's say that even then he was an emperor of wood and construction. I wonder if they restored the original board with NO VACANCY . . ." Kamĩtĩ started.

"*For Jobs Come Tomorrow,*" they said in unison, and they laughed together.

Their laughter and this reunion with their beginnings considerably reduced the tensions that lingered between them.

"Okay, let's go and get our coffee before it gets cold," Kamĩtĩ said.

"Did you make an order through an invisible phone?"

They rejoined the human traffic, but after a few blocks they realized that they had gone past the place and so they turned and went back the way they came. Again they missed the place a second time and they went back, looking at each and every building carefully.

"No, it is not that we are going past it," said Nyawīra. "Look."

The building that used to house the Mars Café had been demolished. The site was fenced off with a wall of corrugated iron sheets. By the side was a big billboard: UNDER CONSTRUCTION: GLOBE INSURANCE CORPORATION: THE TALLEST BUILDING IN AFRICA; A REAL MARCHING TO HEAVEN.

"What happened to Gautama, I wonder," Kamītī said. "Did he go to one of the planets you just recited?"

"Most likely he moved his business elsewhere in the city," said Nyawīra. "Let's leave Gautama and his Mars Café alone and look for another place."

"What about Chou's Chinese Gourmet?" Kamītī suggested.

"It is a restaurant, not a coffeehouse," Nyawīra said.

At the Santamaria market they bought the day's issue of the *Eldares Times* and went inside another coffeehouse and found a corner to themselves. They took separate sections of the newspaper and bent down to read as they waited for their order.

Nyawīra's eyes caught another reference to joint military exercises, and she commented, "I don't know why they would want to mount these Euro-American-Aburīrian exercises when the cold war ended long ago."

"And what are you going to do about your caves?" asked Kamītī.

"It does not mean that these exercises will involve looking for our hideouts in the mountains. But even if they were, remember that in Aburīria there are many hills and mountains, and where would they begin and end their search unless they decided to put permanent military camps in all the hills and mountains?"

"I don't mean they would mount such exercises merely to look for possible hideouts for possible rebels, but they could stumble upon them," argued Kamītī.

"Even if they did, remember, the people provide the best hideouts. To their joint military exercises we respond with joint political exercises with our people."

"All the same, your people should be careful," said Kamītī.

"Why do you talk as if you are outside it all?"

Kamītī did not answer immediately.

"What is the matter, Kamĩtĩ?" she asked. "These last few days, you have not been the Kamĩtĩ I know."

"I've been thinking about why the love of my life hid so much from me."

"But you were not then a member of the movement; how could I have entrusted you with its secrets? Would you respect me for that? What if everybody were to do likewise, be indiscreet with their spouses or lovers?"

"Well, I thought you were all too close to one another . . ."

"Yes, we are close—so?" Nyawĩra asked, a little defiantly.

"I felt as if you had put me aside," Kamĩtĩ said.

Nyawĩra laughed. "Are you jealous?"

"A little, yes."

"Only a little? I'm disappointed."

"More than a little!"

"Take your mind away from those thoughts. It is true that we are very close. We have gone through a lot together. That is a bond of politics and it is as it should be. Yours and mine is a bond of love. And it is also as it should be. But today our relationship is much stronger because to the bond of love we have now added that of politics. Mind you, I would be lying if I said I was not happy to see you wriggle with a little jealousy. Thank you. But jealousy beyond acceptable limits is bad for love, for it means that whenever you see me talking or laughing with a guy or coming home late you will be stricken with grief and pointless suspicions. A little jealousy warms love. But too much of it harms love."

"Well, let mine then remain the right amount to warm our love. You know I have always been behind you and I never sought to know more than was necessary. Imagine how I would have felt if, when I was in their hands, I knew that I was also carrying all these secrets of the movement? Fortunately I knew nothing, so even if they had threatened to kill me I would have given nothing. For there was nothing to give away."

"But you carried one big secret," Nyawĩra said. "You knew about me and you never betrayed me."

"Well, that is true, but I also didn't know everything about you. Up until the moment you entered the room and were introduced as the leader, I had no idea about your position in the movement. You always talked about the movement or the leadership out there. Even on that day, I could not have suspected because you never let on, by hint or gesture, that you would be coming to the meeting."

"That is because, as I told you the other time, we did not want you to make a political decision based solely on your feelings for me."

"The deception, if I might call it so, was complete."

"You admit that you were taken in?"

"Yes, and for a moment as you sat there and chaired the meeting, I thought that maybe I was looking at another person."

"Then I win," said Nyawīra triumphantly.

"Win what?"

"The bet. You remember our little bet? You swore that you would not be taken in a third time?"

"Oh, that," Kamĩtĩ said. "This time it is different because you were not in disguise, like the Limping Witch at the State House. But I am more than glad to lose the bet. When the time comes I will buy the wedding ring."

"I love you," she said softly.

"I love you, very much," he said.

They wandered through the market before deciding to avoid the throng and walk along the former Ruler's Highway, now the Imperial Highway. Soon they came to the former site of Marching to Heaven, now the site of the Imperial Coliseum.

"See the person sitting under the tree?" Nyawīra said. "What is he doing there all alone with legs crossed Buddha fashion?"

"Gautama," said Kamĩtĩ at once.

Yes, it was indeed Gautama seated at the base of the tree, legs crossed Buddha-style, his back upright against the trunk. Hanging from the tree were newspaper and magazine cuttings, in the middle of which stood out a piece on which was scribbled MARS.

"Probably the only material he was able to rescue from Mars Café," Kamĩtĩ murmured, recalling the last time he and Gautama talked about Mahabharata, Ramayana, Gita, stars, and space.

Kamĩtĩ told Nyawīra that they should just continue with their walk, but then came a breeze that seemed to push him toward the lone person. He changed his mind. They should at least express some kind of solidarity.

"*Namaste! Gurudeva!*" Kamĩtĩ called out.

Bearded Daemons

Gautama thought that he had gotten some followers, and without responding to the greeting directly or changing his posture he started telling them the good news:

I am not alone, see? This tree and the stray animals who come to visit me are all my friends. Even the sun, the wind, and the rain are my friends. Do you recall Hanuman's parting words to Rama in Ramayana? Beautiful words that speak to the oneness of creation, he said, and, picking up a book beside him, read aloud: Dear Rama, we are indeed your old friends from long ago, and your companions of ancient days come to help you. We are your forefathers. We are your ancestors, the animals, and you are our child man. As for our friendship, we have known you a long time, Rama, and the number of those days is lost in silence.

Ah, the silence of being, said Gautama as now he took his eyes off the book, sighing. Human dreams have no end. Oh, if we would stop hate and wars we would inherit not just the earth but the universe. Listening to what the universe is telling us is the only way for the nations of this our earth to come together and find union with life. Light comes from the sun. Let there be universal light. Space is our refuge. Let's oppose all intents to take death to space . . .

They went away wondering if what they just saw and heard was not coming from a man who had lost his head over the loss of the Mars Café. Clouds were darkening; rain seemed imminent. They decided to go back to Santalucia, which involved walking back through the city center to catch a bus. They passed near Paradise, then crossed the Imperial Avenue, the Imperial Road, the Imperial Street, and past the Imperial Conference Center before arriving at the Imperial City Square. Construction workers were indeed busy changing landmark names to the Ruling Emperor's this or that.

The Imperial City Square was a wide-open space, one of the few remaining, and it was here that the unemployed mostly came to rest and pass the time between hunting for work. Some even spent nights there when the police were not around. It was, as usual, crowded this afternoon, and entertainment was provided by impromptu street acts, including prophets of doom preaching fire and brimstone to the unrepentant.

Nyawĩra and Kamĩtĩ drifted from group to group till they came to a crowd around a storyteller with a single-stringed violin.

"It's A.G.," Kamītī whispered. "You remember, the policeman?"

At that very moment, A.G. shouted, "True! *Haki ya Mungu*, that is exactly what the Wizard of the Crow did."

The people listened as he sang the story of his search for the Wizard of the Crow, hoping for a blessing from him: the thing of life. "Let nobody lie to you—the Wizard of the Crow will never die. True! *Haki ya Mungu!*"

A.G. appeared crazed, and Nyawīra thought that he feigned that to be able to say the things he was saying without interference.

It began to rain: people clapped, some saying that maybe the rain would wash away some of the filth on the streets of Eldares.

It was then that A.G.'s eyes met those of Nyawīra and Kamītī. He stopped singing, frowned, and shook his head as if he thought his mind was deceiving him. He resumed his ballad of the famous Wizard of the Crow, who could change himself into anything.

"It's him," Nyawīra whispered as they walked away.

"Who?"

"The man who wrestled the gun from Kaniūrū."

"A.G., who once chased us from the gates of Paradise?"

"And also snatched us from the gates of Hell!"

Kamītī and Nyawīra went homeward holding hands, a mixture of teardrops and raindrops running down Nyawīra's face, the sound of the one-string violin and the man's voice following them as if the player was telling them that he, too, remembered the night he chased the couple from the gates of Paradise, mistaking them for beggars. To the sound of the violin Nyawīra added her own from her guitar, and the two blended inside her. She let the fusion linger in her mind, knowing that they might never meet him face-to-face to say, "Thank you, A.G. . . . Thank you for the gift of life."

# NGATHO—ACKNOWLEDGMENTS

Thanks to my editor, Erroll McDonald, for his tremendous input into this translation; my literary agent, Gloria Loomis, for her faith and encouragement; and my assistant, Barbara Caldwell, for proofreading and editing; Njenga and Njeri Gĩkang'a, Gatuawa Mbũgwa, Cege Gĩthiora and Wambũi Gĩthiora, for detailed comments on the early drafts; Elizabeth Alexander for the maps of Chennai and Susan Prethroe for the safekeeping of earlier drafts; my ICWT colleagues Colette Atkinson and Chris Aschan for providing a creative work environment; the commemorative circle for the late Dr. Judy Wambu that met every Thanksgiving at Wambu's in Riverside Drive, New York, to whom I read portions of the novel; my brothers and sisters, Wallace Mwangi, Charity Wanjiku, Wambui Njinju, Njoki, Wanjiru Gitakaya; the Limahouse crowd (residents and members of the Kenya Council for Cultural Revival); my comrades in the struggle in Kenya, Africa, and the world (Kamoji Wachira and Wanjiru Kihoro, you deserve more recognition) for their inspiring presence. Special thanks to John la Rose and Sarah White for their active role in the Kenyan struggle. And always in my heart, my children, Thiong'o Senior, Kĩmunya, Ndũcũ, Mũkoma, Wanjikũ, Njoki, Bjorn, Mũmbi, and Thiong'o K., niece Ngina and my grandson, Ngũgĩ.

Thank you Jancita Wabera Rebo for giving Thiong'o and Mũmbi a home environment to learn Gĩkũyũ, and Henry and Rosalind Chakava and your children Sharon, Laura, and Yolanda, for giving us a home when we most needed it. Thanks to Pat Hilden, Tim Reiss, Sonia Sanchez, Susie Tharu, Peter and Mary Nazareth, Bhahadur and Yasmine Tejani, Manthia Diawara, Kassahun Checole, Kofi

Anyidoho, Haunani-Kay Trask, Gayatri Spivak, Meena Alexander, Susan Wheeler, Eva Lanno, and Ngũgĩ wa Mĩriĩ for always being there. There are many more of you not mentioned here by name, but your spirit is part of this narrative.

But I simply have to mention my compatriots in the London-based Committee for the Release of Political Prisoners in Kenya (1982–1987), which organized a worldwide campaign against the Moi dictatorship in Kenya and for democracy. They allied with other London-based groups struggling against the Marcos dictatorship in the Phillipines, the Pinochet dictatorship in Chile, and the apartheid dictatorship in South Africa. Thank you Abdulatif Abdalla, Yusuf Hassan, Shiraz Durrani, Wanjirũ and Wanyĩrĩ Kĩhoro, Nish Mũthoni, and Wangũi wa Goro. The images of dictatorship in this narrative date back to that period of our struggle.